12/00

1.00

Received W F Ford
1/20/01

*A Falling Star*

# A FALLING STAR

Pamela Belle

St. Martin's Press
New York

Library of Congress Cataloging-in-Publication Data

Belle, Pamela.
    A falling star / Pamela Belle.
      p.  cm.
    ISBN 0-312-05084-4
    1. Great Britain—History—James II, 1685–1688—Fiction.
2. Monmouth's Rebellion, 1685—Fiction.   I. Title.
PR6052.E4474F35   1990
823'.914—dc20                          90-37117
                                              CIP

First published in Great Britain by Random Century Group

First U.S. Edition: November 1990
10  9  8  7  6  5  4  3  2  1

For Hugh
who grew with this book,
but entered the world much earlier.

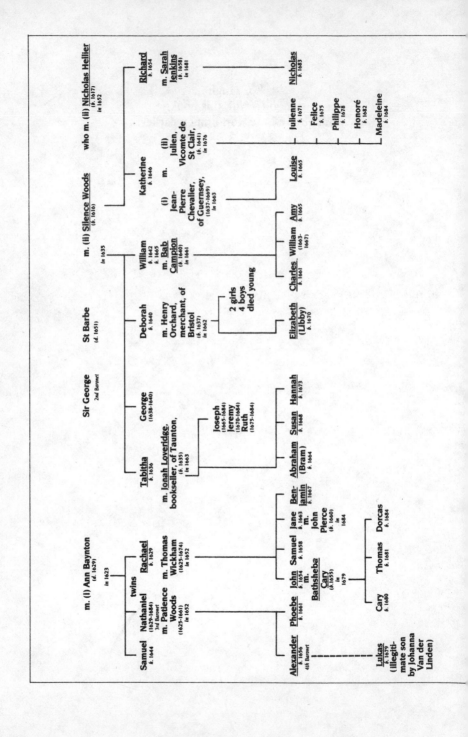

*A Falling Star*

# PART I

*'Sagacious, bold, and turbulent of wit'*

# I

## 'Harden'd in Impenitence'

It was so much smaller than he remembered.

Strange, that a place that had loomed so large in his life, that had driven him away, that had called him back, should be so insignificant. Low, gabled, built in the grey-gold stone that still thrust like bones through the earth in the surrounding fields, it seemed hardly more than a farmhouse. He had seen the palaces of Europe, he was familiar with great houses in four or five countries, and beside them, Wintercombe was nothing.

And yet ... it had been the home of the St Barbes for nearly two centuries, and now it was his, possessed by right of inheritance. He had been born here, passed his childhood within and without the rough grey walls, had known a little of happiness, and rather more of its opposite. It had not been able to hold him, and as soon as he could, he had escaped.

Home. Home was here: not Amsterdam, nor Den Haag, nor Aunt Kate's pretty château by the wild Loire. And after nearly fifteen years, he had come home for good.

Or had he? There was no one about, save a couple of men chopping up a wind-blown tree down by the Wellow Lane. He could still change his mind, deny his past and his destiny, and defy his father for the last and most decisive time. He could turn his horse about, and ride back to Bristol, to take ship for his old life, his regiment, and for Johanna and the careless debauchery of the other English exiles, voluntary and involuntary, who crowded the towns and cities of Holland. If he did ...

If he did, Charles would have Wintercombe by default. And he was damned if he would make a gift of his inheritance to Cousin Charles.

The decision, after all, had already been taken, long since. He smiled rather grimly, and twitched the horse's reins.

Henry Renolds, the most junior stable boy, had doubts, and expressed them nervously. Surely Mistress Louise should not be riding Shadow? If she must venture out on this chilly February afternoon, why not take Nance, her usual mount?

Louise Chevalier stood unmoved in the centre of the stable yard, tapping her whip gently against the thick dove-grey folds of her French

3

riding habit, and let the boy's thick Somerset dialect trail away into confusion. 'I told you, Henry,' she said calmly. 'I wish to ride Shadow. Go saddle him at once, if you please.'

The boy, faced with vastly superior tactics and weaponry, gave up. 'Aye, mistress,' he muttered, and scuttled into the stables. Louise waited, now and then glancing at the sky, which was high and white today, threatening neither rain nor snow. If only the wretched child would hurry, before someone discovered what she was about.

But no one shouted from the windows looking down over the stable yard, no one came bustling officiously out to ask her what on earth she was doing, going riding alone, and on the most notorious horse in the stables into the bargain. She knew that she should be sitting decorously indoors, stitching, or talking French to her cousin Amy, but today the prospect appalled her even more than usual. She had to break free, or suffocate, and once this wild mood was on her she would brook no opposition.

Shadow appeared, already frothy around the bit and under the girth. He was a big, well-made gelding, young and fast and hot-headed, and emphatically not a lady's ride. Young Henry, who was only fourteen, struggled to hold the horse's head as he danced and fretted, cooped up, like Louise, for too long, and desperate to run. She admired his looks, the dark, almost black hide, the white blaze on the proud head, the curving, well-muscled quarters and white-splashed legs. She loved all horses for their power and grace and beauty, but Shadow was the pick of Wintercombe's stables.

With some difficulty, Henry persuaded Shadow to stand still by the block for the few vital moments necessary for Louise to mount him. She arranged her skirts, made sure that her small, dashing hat, in the latest French fashion, was perched securely on her head, and grinned at the boy, letting the wild bubbling excitement surge out of her at last. 'All right, Henry – let him go!'

Shadow, released at last, found that he was not, after all, in control. His rider had a confident seat and a firm grasp of the reins. Moreover, she carried an efficient-looking whip, and would undoubtedly use it. He subsided with a wicked, rolling eye, and Louise, well aware that the slightest slackening of her hold would reap the whirlwind, steered him briskly out of the stable yard, with a smart tap to remind Shadow who was in charge.

There was another rider ahead, coming up the hill from the Wellow Lane. Curious, Louise narrowed her eyes. The horse, though obviously weary, was a magnificent animal, a big strong-boned dappled grey, its mane and tail a pure and flowing white. She tightened her grip on

4

Shadow's head, having no wish to be deposited ignominiously at the visitor's feet, and urged him into a brisk trot, the quicker to investigate. Personable strangers were rare at Wintercombe.

And this man, she saw as she drew nearer, was rather more than personable. Like the horse, he was uncommonly tall and strongly made, with wide shoulders and a slouching, easy posture that betrayed the habitual horseman. He wore an unadorned dark suit and a hat decorated only with a single plume, and the black hair that drifted untidily in the gentle wind was plainly his own, and no periwig. And Louise, now close enough to have a good view of his face, knew his identity with a sudden jump of her heart.

She had not seen him since . . . Thirteen, she had been, a wild skinny hoyden with a passion for horses and a direct and belligerent manner that had been the despair of her governess, and now, nearly seven years later, made a more sophisticated Louise blush to recall it. He had seemed almost godlike, her splendid cousin, descending on her stepfather's château and turning it upside down with a breathtaking ease that had delighted the rebellious child. And her wayward, mischievous mother had seemed to revel in the disruption of her usually well-ordered household, had laughed off her husband's complaints and the outraged appeals of the senior servants, and entered into an unholy alliance with her disruptive nephew that had scandalised the district. Louise, in some ways more adult than her mother realised, had known that there was nothing improper in Kate's behaviour, however much the neighbouring aristocracy might gossip and whisper. There had been no lingering glances, no touched hands, no secret assignations. Louise had seen such things before, when her stepfather had been her mother's secret lover while his first wife, ailing and jealous, was still alive. No, it had simply been that Kate, still young and lively, had relished the arrival of a kindred spirit whose inventiveness, audacity and brilliance had dazzled almost everyone around him.

He had dazzled Louise too. Her vivid memories still had the power to make her giggle at inopportune moments. The time he had ridden his horse into the dining room . . . the day when the entire household had been smoked out of doors by his unauthorised alchemical experiments in the stillroom . . . the race, involving riding, swimming and running, that had ruined everyone's clothes and nearly drowned her stepfather's young cousin, although Alex, godlike in this as in all else, had brought him miraculously back from the dead.

That wonderful summer, seven years ago, had coloured her behaviour for months after his departure. She had wanted so desperately to look like

5

him, to have the sapphire-blue eyes and lively, lazy features, the black hair which he wore thick and long, scorning a periwig, an affectation entirely characteristic and the subject of much adverse comment amongst people whom Louise thereafter despised. She was his cousin, his mother's sister's grandchild: why had she failed to inherit his beauty?

All that she saw in her mirror was the same Louise, with her narrow pointed face, rather lifeless in repose, unfashionably olive-skinned and dominated by a nose, alas, that already threatened to become aquiline. Her eyes were good, being like her mother's, large, and an unusual shade of chestnut brown. Louise, unaware of the sparkle that transformed her expression when she talked or laughed, had long ago decided that she would never, despite all her longing, look as glorious as her English cousin Alex, for she too greatly resembled her Guernsey father's family.

She could ride like Alex, though, and she had set herself to excel in the saddle, bruising herself severely in the process, breaking her arm and acquiring a reputation for daredevilry throughout the district. When he returned, as he surely would, she could dazzle and impress him with her skill and dash.

But he had not come back. Whispered family gossip spoke of scandal in England, both political and amorous, hasty exile in Holland, a string of mistresses, and service in the army of the Dutch, enemies of France. And Louise, to her horror and indignation, was sent away to school near Blois, protesting until the moment her stepfather pushed her into the coach, to acquire, as her mother pointedly told her, some polish and sophistication. If Alex had visited during her enforced absences, she had never come to hear of it.

And now here he was in the flesh, riding towards his polished and sophisticated little cousin, and she was tolerably certain that, seeing her here in England, hundreds of miles from her mother's family, he could have no idea of her identity.

She reined Shadow in with a flourish just in front of the grey's nose, judging the distance to a nicety, and raised her eyes to Alex St Barbe's face.

Amusement, Louise had expected, perhaps even interest: she might not be pretty, but she was confident of her attractions. What she had not thought to see was his hostile blue stare, nor to hear the hard voice full of malice. 'What the devil do you think you're doing, madam?'

Submission and decorum had never been amongst her long suits. Louise's chin came up dangerously. 'I might ask the same of you, sir. Whom do you wish to visit at Wintercombe?'

Shadow, balked of his extended gallop, was beginning to sidle and fret,

6

chewing at his bit. Specks of froth splattered the ground, and she gave him a warning tap with the whip. The inimical eyes surveyed her and her restless mount. 'Hardly a lady's ride, is he?' said her cousin, in the sort of contemptuous drawl that had always infuriated her when she heard it employed by aristocratic Englishmen.

'Perhaps you think you can manage him better?' she suggested, with a withering glare that indicated her thoughts as to the likely outcome of such a situation.

'I intend to,' said Sir Alexander St Barbe, 'since he is, I assume, my horse.'

Louise gave him the haughty stare down her undoubtedly aquiline nose (it did have some uses, after all) that she had practised before her mirror for the quelling of an impertinent young vicomte. '*Your* horse, sir? How strange – I was under the impression that it belongs to Sir Alexander St Barbe, and you surely cannot presume to an acquaintance with him.'

For a moment their eyes met, mutually antagonistic, and it took every scrap of her bravado not to flinch from the unpleasantness in his gaze. All her expectations, and her disappointment, had crystallised into her swift-rising anger, and she would have given anything now to call those words back, instead of leaving her insult hanging between them like a cleaver.

'I think you know very well who I am,' he said softly. 'As to who *you* are, madam, making free with my property –'

'*Moi?*' said Louise. She had annoyed him, the cousin she had once worshipped, with a few ill-chosen words fuelled by her quick temper, and she did not intend lingering to make matters worse. She gave him a brilliant smile, full of false mischief, and employed the French he must speak almost as well as she did '*Moi, Monsieur? Vous me connaissez bien – je suis une Guernesiaise!*'

And she gave Shadow his head at last, and sent him flying down the hill towards the Wellow Lane, heedless of the mud that her mount's hooves might scatter all over the man who had once, in another and more innocent lifetime, been her childhood hero.

'M'lady! M'lady!'

She had been plain Mistress Hellier for more than thirty years, and there was no one now at Wintercombe, save Jem Coxe the gardener, who had served in her employ, but to the servants here she suspected that she would always be 'M'lady St Barbe', subject of legend and respect far beyond what she had always felt she deserved. The real Silence Hellier was a quiet, ordinary woman who had once been forced into the danger

7

and terror of extraordinary events. Somehow, with good fortune and stalwart support, she had survived the horrors of war. But she had always felt that anyone in her position would have struggled, like her, for the safety of her home, her children and the household which was her responsibility. The whispered, admiring stories, the wide-eyed marvelling of the younger servants, she had always felt to be misplaced and rather embarrassing. She had only done her best, and her duty, after all: and besides, what would they think of her if they knew the entire and unvarnished truth?

But that was all forty years in the past, and Wintercombe was no longer her home. She was only a visitor here, an interloper, summoned from her husband and family in Chard, as so often before, to solve problems that were none of her making, to comfort where none could be given, to neglect her own concerns because once more the St Barbes had need of her wisdom, her common sense and her ability, honed over her long life by experience and trial and learning from so many mistakes, to soothe ruffled feathers, apply balm to injured feelings, and to suggest compromise and co-operation.

She had thought that she had succeeded. She had had to fight her own appalling grief at her beloved stepson's sudden and untimely death – he had only been fifty-five – and her worry about her son's wife, Sarah, suffering a difficult pregnancy at Chard, and negotiate with people who, if they had not been tied to her by blood or marriage, she would not have wished to help. And now, just as she was hoping that her task was done, and that she could make the long and tiring journey back to Chard and those she loved best, it seemed that another crisis was looming.

'M'lady – oh, m'lady!' The white-capped head of Betty Barnard, the Wintercombe housekeeper, appeared around the door. Silence Hellier, once Silence, Lady St Barbe, put down her sewing and pushed her spectacles to the end of her nose, the better to see her. She had accepted her deteriorating sight, as she had all the other gradually encroaching infirmities of age, with her characteristic wry resignation, and had even laughed at her stepson's teasing comment that she looked like a wise but rather worried old owl . . .

He was dead, her dear Nat, laid in the cold vault of the church in Philip's Norton, all that love and laughter and loyalty vanished, and she felt quite bereft, as if she had lost a part of herself.

And here was Betty, whom he, a widower, had chosen to keep house for him, a fussy hen of a woman, small and plump and plain, with bright red cheeks and thinning, greying hair. Silence suspected that she had been chosen because her unprepossessing manner and appearance would hardly invite scandal. And, to give her her due, she was a perfectly competent housekeeper, though the other servants did not seem to hold her in overmuch respect.

'Yes, Betty? What is it?'

As an afterthought, the other woman bobbed a hasty curtsey. 'M'lady – Sir Alexander has come home!'

An extraordinary feeling of delight, of relief, swept over Silence. At last, he had returned – Nat's black sheep of a son, disgraced, exiled, trailing clouds of disruption and scandal wherever he went – at last he had realised the extent of his responsibilities, and had come back to take up his inheritance.

And at last, Wintercombe and its inhabitants would become someone else's problem, and she could go home.

'That's wonderful news, Betty,' she said. 'Where is he now?'

'Still in the courtyard, m'lady, when I came to tell you. He's brought no servant with him, and no baggage either, by the look of it,' said Betty, her face avidly curious. 'Shall I instruct Twinney to bring him to you, m'lady?'

'When he is warmed and refreshed after his journey,' Silence said, finding a certain irony in the housekeeper's attitude to the man who now owned Wintercombe, as if he were the visitor, and she the lady of the house. She added, feeling that the other woman should be reminded, 'Remember, he is master here now, Betty.'

'Of course, m'lady,' said the housekeeper, a look of surprise on her round dumpling features. She ducked another curtsey, and withdrew.

At last, Silence thought, leaning back in her chair, her sewing forgotten on her lap. At last, Alex had come back. It should not have been a matter for such surprise and comment: any other heir in foreign parts, informed of his father's unexpected death, would have hastened home at once to take charge. But her nephew had always been wayward, contrary, a law unto himself, and it was entirely in character for him to arrive now, unannounced, unceremoniously alone, and nearly two months after her sad letter telling him that he was now fourth baronet, and master of Wintercombe.

He had been away for several years, and infrequently at home before that, so it was a long time since they had last met. She remembered him best as a child, in the topsy-turvy way of elderly recollections, so that the little boy of five, mischievous and enchanting, was etched more clearly in her mind than the man he had become.

Twenty . . . nine, he was, she realised with a certain shock. His mother, her beautiful sister, had been dead for twenty-four years, after a difficult, agonising childbirth that had produced Alex's sister Phoebe, a poor

9

misshapen scrap who had, astonishingly, been stronger than she looked, for she had failed then, and ever since, to follow her mother to the grave. Looking back, Silence could see, with the bitter clarity of hindsight, how that tragic early death had wrought the change in Alex, leading him through the years from the enchanting child, intelligent, loving, to the unpredictable and cynical libertine whose exploits had appalled his entire family.

He had even antagonised his father: Nat, a worldly cynic himself, had had to admit the failure of his relations with his only son. And Silence, who had loved her stepson very dearly, and mourned him still, had found it hard to forgive Alex for the pain and grief he had caused his father. On the whole, she was glad that she could go home to Chard and leave her nephew here to wreak his havoc and raise hackles and cause the shock and scandal that Alex had always engendered, these past twenty years and more, ever since . . .

She suddenly found herself suppressing a smile at the memory of his first truly appalling act. At the age of eight, he had taken his fragile, crippled little sister, just three years old, into the garden one April day. And there, he had attempted to plant her in a hole in the ground and water her, because, he had explained with just enough earnestness to be plausible, he had wanted to make her grow.

They had believed him, because the alternative was too dreadful to contemplate. Phoebe, covered with earth, soaking wet and screaming, had taken a chill on the lungs and nearly died from it. And Silence, wise in the ways of most children, but not this one, had never really known, from that day to this, whether Alex had genuinely meant well, or had acted with malicious intent.

Considering his intelligence, not to mention his subsequent history, she rather inclined to the latter view.

Dreadful as this opinion of her nephew's character was – had he *really* intended to do Phoebe actual harm? – there was something in Silence, a wild, rebellious recklessness buried deep beneath the decorous, unfashionable Puritan exterior, which responded to such outrageous deeds with shocked amusement. Nat, closer to the boy, more involved, feeling so much more for him than he could allow himself to show . . . Nat had not been able to take that attitude.

She felt her eyes watering, as they did so often now whenever she thought of her stepson, and pushed the spectacles aside to mop the tears away. And when she had finished, she looked up, and saw Nat's son standing on the threshold.

She had forgotten how big he was. Nat himself, frail and undersized in childhood, had never attained great height, and the St Barbes tended to the stocky, rather than the tall. But Alex had started to grow at the age of twelve, had overtopped everyone else in Wintercombe by the time he was fifteen, and had passed six feet a year later. Most of the doorways were too low for him, and he had acquired several cracked heads before becoming accustomed to his unusual height.

This was not that gangling boy, though, all legs and arms and strength without any idea of what to do with himself. This was a man, still rather with the air of untidiness she remembered, filling the room suddenly with his presence. He had Nat's colouring, the dense black hair, pale skin and vividly blue eyes, but his features reminded her, sharply and painfully, of her long-dead sister Patience, who had also been wilful and wayward. And like Patience, she realised with some foreboding, he was much too attractive for his own good.

'Hullo, Aunt,' he said, unsmiling, unwelcoming. He looked as if he had had a long and difficult journey, and no hopes of greater comfort now. 'Somehow, I might have expected to find you here.'

The child Alex, like his mother, had been generously endowed with charm. This man might never have known the word. He pushed forward into the room, and cast himself sprawling into the other chair by the fire, his long legs stretching out to the warmth. Silence thought of all the things she might say, discarded them, and contented herself with a long survey over the top of her spectacles. 'Has something put you out of temper, nephew?' she enquired at last, mildly.

Alex glanced at her, and she wondered if he would explode. Then, completely unexpectedly, he grinned, and ran a hand that was, she saw, rather dirty, through his untidy hair, disarranging it still more. 'Not something,' he said. 'Someone. A young lady by the name of, at a guess, Louise Chevalier.'

'Louise? But I thought she was with Amy.'

'You err – I should imagine that she is, at this moment, galloping hell-for-leather towards Wellow, on a horse that even I would think twice before riding. What is she doing here, anyway? I thought she was in France.'

'So she was, until last August – but Kate decided that she needed to spend some time in England, for the good of her education, so she was sent to Wintercombe.'

Alex gave her a shrewd glance that reminded her overwhelmingly of Nat, but made no other comment on this extremely expurgated account. He said, suddenly mischievous, 'It seems to be high time that someone took her in hand. Have you been saddled with the task, Aunt?'

'Now that your father is dead, yes,' Silence said, reflecting that it would be most unwise to leave her granddaughter here at Wintercombe when she returned to Chard. True, she would hardly be alone with Alex: the presence of the other St Barbes, not to mention a houseful of servants, would ensure that. But the combination of Louise, passionate, reckless and already the cause of scandal in France, and Alex, whose name was a byword in north Somerset for debauchery and excess, was certain to damage her granddaughter's already fragile reputation. Kate had sent her to England so that an English, and Protestant, husband could be found for her, someone blissfully unaware of the gossip that had flowed like floodwater up and down the Loire last summer. And malicious talk, whether unfounded or not, must not be allowed to damage Louise's chance of a good marriage.

Besides, she did not trust either of them an inch.

'So you will take her back to Chard with you?' said her nephew. 'An act of some bravery, it would seem.'

'Nonsense,' Silence said, with brisk asperity. 'Louise is a delightful girl, if a trifle . . . independent.'

For the first time, Alex laughed. It was a surprisingly carefree sound. 'I've not heard wilful and wanton disobedience called that before.'

'Independent,' Silence repeated severely. 'She is a lively girl, and the company of her cousins has not been especially inspiring . . . particularly since your father's death.'

The unspoken questions wreathed gently in the air between them like smoke. Why did it take you so long to come home? Why did you cause Nat so much grief? Why, oh why, did you spoil all that early promise and spend most of your life drinking and whoring around Europe, flirting with treason as carelessly as with women?

But for Nat's sake, and for those who would have to share Wintercombe with his son, she kept her peace.

'Cousins?' said Alex. There was a knock on the door, and Abigail, the senior housemaid, appeared with a laden tray. A pause ensued while it was set down, a table drawn up, and the platter of steaming pie and the flagon of wine placed within his reach. Abigail, in her early thirties but still pretty, curtseyed and withdrew. As soon as the door closed behind her, he added, 'Apart from you and Louise, who else lives at Wintercombe? Tell me what has been happening here.'

'Do you want me to take all night about it, or will an hour or so suffice?' Silence asked, rather tartly. It was strange, because Alex was so different from his father, and yet she found herself slipping, without noticing it, into their old comradely habit of speech, just as if he were Nat. And for a moment, her grief, renewed, rose and caught her by the throat.

12

But it was all in vain: Nat was dead, and so was her lovely sister Patience, laid at last in peace together beneath the chilly flagstones of the church in Philip's Norton, and their unlikely love had produced this cynical, impolite and dissolute man, sprawling in his chair and swallowing the wine rather faster than the pie.

'A few minutes,' he said. Silence tried not to glance too obviously at his hand as he poured out a second measure and drank it off, and her housewife's mind began to review the barrels stored in the buttery, assessed their number, and estimated how long it might take him to work his way through them. Then, returning with an effort to his question, she marshalled her thoughts carefully, thinking of the people who lived here, who must co-exist in some sort of peace with Alex when she was no longer available to mediate.

'Bab is still here, of course,' she began cautiously. There was no discernible reaction from the man opposite, so she went on. 'And Charles and Amy, too. Charles has gone to Frome today, but he should be back before dusk. Amy is upstairs sewing – and I had assumed that Louise was with her.' A thought occurred to her, and she added, 'Was Louise *alone* when you encountered her?'

'Save for her horse, yes.'

'Perhaps I had better send one of the grooms after her,' said Silence reflectively. 'Not that I fear some footpad might appear from behind a tree, but if she should meet with an accident, or be thrown . . .'

'Quite likely, on the horse she was riding,' Alex said, through a mouthful of pie. He washed it down with a gulp of wine, and added, 'On the other hand, probably a return to earth with something of a bump would do her no harm. Your granddaughter, dear Aunt, seems to delight in showing off her skills – and you know what they say about pride.'

Nat would have uttered that last remark as a joke. From Alex, it sounded as if he welcomed the prospect. Silence, her mouth tightening, rang her bell and issued instructions to Abigail to send a groom in immediate pursuit of Mistress Louise, to find her and escort her until her safe return to Wintercombe. Then, her duty done, she glanced at her nephew, who had taken the opportunity to ask Abigail for more wine. Nat had always been notably abstemious, so it was hardly his influence that had encouraged Alex to drink. He had been expelled from the Bath Grammar School at the age of fifteen, for drunkenness and whoring, and his family had felt the disgrace very keenly. And it had not been just a youthful indiscretion, soon forgotten as more responsible behaviour was acquired. Instead, it had signalled the pattern for the future.

'They'll have to go, of course,' said Alex, so casually that for a moment

Silence did not grasp the import of his words. She stared at him stupidly, and received the full malice of those very disturbing blue eyes in return. 'Who?' she said in bewilderment.

'My Aunt Bab – who else? And her precious offspring. Doubtless Cousin Charles had hopes of inheritance – I'm sorry to have to disappoint him.'

'I don't believe he thought anything of the kind,' said Silence sharply. There were times, and this was one of them, when she positively disliked her nephew. To hear him speak with such contempt of her grandson caused her real distress. She added, 'I am sure he would not wish to stay where he is not welcome. But Bab . . . she has nowhere else to go.'

'So what? She has sucked on my father like a leech for nearly twenty years, and I'll be damned if she'll milk my generosity as well. Where she's concerned, I don't possess any.' He smiled, not very pleasantly. 'She's your daughter-in-law, after all. Why not invite her for an extended stay down in Chard?'

The thought was so preposterous that Silence might have laughed, had not it also been so ghastly. She had never really understood why her beloved son William, so frank and generous and open-hearted, should have married, at the age of nineteen, without anyone's knowledge or consent, a lovely but brainless young woman two years his senior, without a penny to her name and, worst of all, an enthusiastic Papist. But she, and Nat, had tried to make the best of it, to support William and his wife and, later, the inevitable children, in something a little better than the genteel poverty to which his soldier's pay had condemned them. Then, to his mother's great grief, William had been killed, slain at the age of twenty-three during the sea-battle of Lowestoft, and his pregnant widow and infant children left destitute.

To do her justice, Bab had not at first importuned her late husband's family. She had struggled on alone for several years, surviving with money sent both by the St Barbes and by her own family, the Campions. But the poor lodgings and difficult life had affected her own health, and her children's. Little William, aged four, died of a fever that nearly carried off his brother and sister as well, and Nat, six years widowed and with children of his own, had written to Bab, suggesting that she and her remaining offspring take up temporary residence at Wintercombe.

And there they had stayed. Bab had earned her keep by managing the house for a while, until a mild suggestion from Nat to the effect that she should perhaps remove to some congenial dwelling in Bath, or Wells, had caused her to succumb to the first of a lengthy series of mysterious and debilitating ailments. Her brother-in-law, recognising after the second such attack that he was being gulled, had nevertheless refused to harden his heart. As he had once explained to Silence, Bab might be an addle-pated Papist who would have made a notable actress, given the chance, but the children, Charles and Amy, were of his blood, and for William's sake he would not brutally eject them from the ancestral home. Besides, Wintercombe was large enough for all of them, and his purse sufficiently long to keep them in comfort. Charles would be company for Alex, as Amy would be a friend for Phoebe.

It was unfortunate that the temperaments of the four children were hardly inclined to such a convenient state of affairs. Alex, wild, moody and rebellious, was openly contemptuous of Charles, who was nearly six years younger and a quiet, reserved child with none of his dead father's golden exuberance. And Phoebe, with her crippled leg and the sharp, bookish mind that was so akin to her father's, proved to have nothing whatsoever in common with giggling, feminine Amy. Nor had matters changed over the years, and Silence had wondered how these disparate young people would manage to live together at Wintercombe in something approaching harmony.

But to have Bab at Chard . . .

'There'd be murder done, inside a week,' she said. Alex smiled. 'Precisely my point. And if she has such an effect on you, my dear and saintly Aunt, imagine how I must feel at the prospect of living under the same roof – *my* roof.'

'I can, all too well,' said Silence, wondering how her husband, Nick, and their son, Richard, would react to the suggestion, for both of them cordially detested Bab. And besides, there was Richard's wife Sarah to consider. She went on, firmly. 'I can quite see why you don't want her to stay at Wintercombe. But your father leased a house in Bath – could she not be installed there, with her maid and her children, and given a small pension to keep her in comfort?'

'Perhaps,' said Alex. His smile broadened wickedly, and he glanced at her, assessing her reaction. 'Or perhaps not. I would be perfectly within my rights to compel her to rely on her son for support. He's a man grown, after all – or, at least, I suppose he is.'

'But they have very little money,' Silence said, wondering if that simple fact had occurred to her nephew. 'They are to a large extent dependent on your charity. Bab's family were never wealthy, and they are all dead now. William was not properly provided for by his father's will, and had to make his own way in the world. Nat made some small provision for them, and Amy will at least have some dowry. I suppose that Charles could take a position as someone's steward or secretary, but he will achieve nothing without your recommendation.'

'And they are both Papists,' said Alex. 'That is the nub of the matter, is it not? Only another Papist would consider employing Charles, or marrying Amy. Oh, I can see the choice well enough – keep them at my coat-tails for the rest of their lives, or turn them out to fend for themselves. But on one thing, like you, Aunt, I am adamant: I will not have any of them under my roof.'

And since Abigail chose that moment to return with the wine, Silence was forced to relinquish the argument, for the present.

In happy ignorance of his cousin's unheralded return, let alone his plans for the future of Wintercombe and its inhabitants, Charles St Barbe rode leisurely towards Wintercombe in the fading light of a February afternoon, humming gently under his breath. The business at Frome had gone well, a couple of recalcitrant tenants brought to heel, and he carried a heavy and clinking bag at his saddlebow.

It was beginning to seem to Charles as if this very pleasant situation would continue for ever. Nat had for some years employed him as his secretary and man of business, and there was little that Charles did not know about his late uncle's possessions, both around Wintercombe and further afield. He was accustomed to dealing with tenants who failed to pay their rent, or who cut down timber without permission, or neglected to repair buildings or maintain the land in good heart. His meticulous keeping of the accounts had noted every item of expenditure, from a packet of pins to the purchase of a valuable brood mare, and the income from possessions which included not only the Wintercombe lands and sundry manors scattered all over north Somerset, Wiltshire and Gloucestershire, but property in Bath, Wells and Bristol, mines for lead and coal in the Mendips, and interests in merchant ventures instigated by one of Nat's brothers-in-law, Master Henry Orchard of Bristol. The many profits, the losses, rather fewer, the results of speculation and the returns on prudent investment, all had been set down in the huge book, bound in red leather with the St Barbe arms stamped in gold on the cover, in Charles's beautifully elegant hand, with his uncle's scrawled signature attesting to the accuracy of every page.

Over the past few years, Nat had allowed Charles to take a greater and greater part in the day-to-day management of his property, and his nephew, a sensitive young man extremely conscious of his awkward situation, had discharged his duty with considerable competence, and thereby achieved a modicum of self-respect. He was no longer the poor relation, an object of charity and pity, dependent on his uncle's generosity. Now, he had earned his place at Wintercombe, and could with justice say that his assistance and expertise had contributed to the smooth running of the estate, so that not even Nat's unexpected death had greatly disturbed the even, peaceful garnering of wealth.

For Charles in particular, the ague which had carried off his uncle so suddenly had been a disaster. For five agonising days, his whole future hung in the balance, and was then cast into the abyss. And, bitterest pill of all, the man who had, Charles felt, treated him almost as his own son – and after all, he had indeed served him more loyally and faithfully than his own son – had failed utterly to recognise his invaluable assistance. Land, goods and silver worth some three or four hundred pounds had been his only reward in Nat's will, little more than was left to all the other young nephews and nieces: and Wintercombe, which he had grown to love with passion, had gone to Nat's only son and heir, who had not set foot in England for years, and had paid his family only flying, acrimonious visits for some time before that. By right of law and inheritance, true, Wintercombe now belonged to Alex. In justice, however, Charles knew bitterly that it should have been his.

But Alex, summoned home, had not replied, had not even appeared. As the weeks crawled past, Charles had allowed himself to hope. His cousin had never spoken of Wintercombe with anything other than contempt. Perhaps he did not wish to leave his comfortable, dissipated life in the Low Countries. Perhaps his inheritance meant nothing to him, save as a source of ready coin with which to buy drink and women. Charles, as abstemious as his uncle, had always regarded Alex's more dubious activities with deep distaste. It would certainly suit him very well, and everyone else at Wintercombe too, if his disreputable cousin were to remain in Holland, indulging his vices with the income from his inheritance, while the rest of his family lived peacefully under Charles's eye, unmolested and in blissful ignorance of Alex's debauches.

Nat had died in December. It was now February, and Charles was increasingly certain that his cousin would not return. He had even permitted himself, once or twice, the luxury of making some decision that directly affected the estate, as if he were master here in truth. The Frome tenants had grovelled and apologised as if to their landlord, not his deputy. A reminiscent smile spread over Charles's broad face. For once, he had been given the respect which was his due.

He was passing the mill: Wintercombe was not far now, just out of sight on the crown of the hill to his left. He urged his chestnut gelding to a trot. It would soon be dark, and he smelled rain in the air. Warm fires and hot spiced ale and a hearty supper filled his mind, so that he hardly noticed the figure on horseback waiting for him in the dusk under the hedgerow, until it moved abruptly into his path.

'Louise!' he said in surprise, and reined his horse abruptly to a halt. 'What are you doing here?'

'Waiting for you,' said his cousin. She was wearing her favourite riding habit, a soft dove-grey woollen coat and waistcoat like a man's, frogged and banded with gold braid, an extravagantly long skirt draped elegantly over her legs, and a very fetching beaver hat, also in a masculine style, placed apparently precariously over her dark brown curls. With her olive-gold skin and haughty nose, she was as alien and exotic as a popinjay in the mundane Somerset countryside, and her French accent, faint but unmistakable, only heightened that impression. 'Charles . . . I have some news for you, and I don't think that you will like it.' She gave him an affectionate, encouraging smile. 'I don't, either. Charles . . . Alex has come home.'

And all the hope and happiness drained out of him. He sat stupidly on his tired horse, staring at her in appalled disbelief. '*Alex* – Alex is here?'

'Yes. I met him as I was going out for a ride. I was rather rude to him,' said Louise, with a flash of sudden mischief. 'I don't think he liked it very much.'

Charles was still staring at her, his mind rattling with confused questions, while another part of him noted that, though not at all pretty, his cousin was delightfully attractive. And that had been another hope gradually insinuating itself, the growing friendship between them, and his desire for something much more.

And now Alex was back, and all his dreams were dust. He said in bewilderment, 'Why *now*? Why did he wait so long? He should have come weeks ago, he should at least have written . . . Why didn't he let Grandmother know what his plans were?'

Louise shrugged, a very Gallic gesture. 'The Lord knows. Alex is not exactly predictable, is he? But he has obviously made up his mind to prefer Wintercombe to the fleshpots of Europe. Only . . . he does not seem too delighted at the prospect.'

Far from encouraging Charles, as she had hoped, this news seemed only to anger and depress him further. In the six months since her arrival at Wintercombe, Louise had come to know her cousin quite well, and to hold him in considerable affection and regard. But this sudden look of black, wild despair was quite alien to the reserved, thoughtful young man who had been such a pleasant companion.

'If he doesn't want it,' said Charles savagely, 'then he should have stayed in Amsterdam with his whore.'

'Charles!' Louise was shocked, not by the word itself – she had heard, and used, many worse when her temper got the better of her common sense – but by hearing it from her sober, moderate cousin, who had always managed to control his tongue. Control – that was the word that described Charles's nature best, she realised. Everything he did had always been so cautious and considerate. And now, even before meeting him, Alex had wrenched him out of his composure and into this bewildered and unhappy travesty of the Charles she had grown to like and to value, despite his apparently staid and steady character.

'I'm sorry,' Charles muttered, blushing suddenly like a schoolboy, and dropped his eyes to his horse's withers. 'I shouldn't have forgotten myself – forgive me, Lou?'

'Nothing to forgive,' she told him stoutly, wondering what he would think of her if he ever discovered the half of what she had done in France. 'He made me lose my temper, too. If he has the same effect on everyone else, we should prepare ourselves for a very interesting few weeks.'

'You don't like him, then?' said Charles, raising his head to stare at her in some surprise. 'But I thought . . . you were always telling those stories about him, when he stayed with your mother in France . . . he seemed to be your hero.'

'He was then,' said Louise, briskly dismissing all that childish longing and emulation as if it had never existed. 'But I was only twelve or so – and too young to know any better. Now that I've met him again, I can see exactly why my stepfather detested him so much.' She smiled at Charles, trying to give him heart. 'Don't worry – he *is* obnoxious, but once he finds out how much you helped poor Uncle Nat, I'm sure he'll be only too glad to return to Holland and his . . . lady friend.' The smile turned, dazzlingly, to pure, joyous mischief. 'And leave you here in peace, to look after Wintercombe for him . . . well, isn't that what you want, then?'

Charles, aware of a painful feeling somewhere beneath his ribs that threatened to dry the tongue in his mouth, nodded helpless agreement. For months, Louise had enchanted him, as she had everyone at Wintercombe, with her mischief, her sparkle, the vibrant and heedless life that bubbled within her like a young cat, all charm and claws and energy, unknowing of the damage she did or the hearts that were broken. And now, the knife twisted within him, for he knew, as surely as if struck by lightning, that he was in love with this bewitching, infuriating young woman, as helpless as if snared, or drowning.

And he wondered if she would ever think of him in that way, or if she would always see him only as a friend or a brother. But he could not declare his feelings to her, because of his craven fear of her probable rejection, her laughter and amazement. And he would have to stand by and watch Alex, with that arrogance that is the mark of a man who has never known a moment of self-doubt, crook his finger and have Louise and all her grace and wit and innocent mischief fall adoringly at his feet, the latest dupe in an appallingly long and disreputable line.

The thought of it, that Alex might casually steal not only his home but the girl he loved, caused him to clench his fists in fury. He saw Louise looking at him in bewilderment, and strove to order his expression. 'Yes, and let's hope that's his plan. After all, someone of his, er, proclivities will not want to stay very long in a quiet little backwater such as this.'

'I wouldn't have thought so, either,' said Louise. She steered her horse closer to his, and he realised suddenly that she was riding the forbidden Shadow, but wisely made no comment. 'Charles – please don't worry. In two weeks he'll probably have returned to Amsterdam, and we won't see him again for years.'

'I wish I shared your certainty,' he said, unwilling to reveal any optimism, for life had so often tempted him with glowing prospects, only to snatch the cup from his lips at the moment of greatest hope. 'I'll believe it when I see it.'

Louise looked at him with compassion, and on impulse put her gloved hand on his, as their horses stood quietly together. For a moment, their eyes, chestnut brown and pale blue, met and held, and a faint line appeared between her brows. Uncharacteristically, she hesitated, and then said quietly, 'I don't think it will be easy. Not with Alex here – somehow he always manages to turn everything downside up.' She grinned at Charles, realising her mistake: it was not often that her command of her mother's tongue deserted her. 'But, Charles – whatever he does – remember that I'll be on your side.'

And he treasured the thought of her smile and her handclasp and her words, all the way back to Wintercombe.

# CHAPTER 2

## *'Prodigious gifts in vain'*

'Phoebe?'

She did not hear him at first, so completely had the book held her attention. She sat in her chair, the one with the arms and the high, cushioned seat, from which it was so much easier to rise, her thin face bent down towards the page, every line of her angular, awkward body expressive of her utter absorption. He had to say her name again, more loudly than he intended, before it penetrated her concentration, and she realised that there was someone else in the library. Slowly, reluctantly, as if returning from another and infinitely preferable world, she lifted her head, and saw her brother standing in the doorway.

Damn him, thought Phoebe St Barbe, and it was not only because he had disturbed her from her book. Damn him – now we shall never have any peace.

Not, of course, she reminded herself ruefully, that peace had exactly filled Wintercombe over the past few months. The arrival of Louise, Nat's unexpected death, the inevitable shock and grief and mourning, Bab's complaints and Amy's tears, Charles's attempts, very deliberately and obviously, to assume the mantle of master of the house, all had taken their toll of Phoebe's health, never good, and her temper, always somewhat acerbic. Her Aunt Silence, with her gentle wisdom and her refusal to take sides, or to lose that air of ageless serenity, had removed some of the burden from Phoebe's narrow, uneven shoulders, but nothing could replace her father, his dry humour, his shrewd cynicism, and above all, understated but never, ever doubted, his love.

Just as Louise, when feeling suffocated by her cousins, was impelled by the urge to flee Wintercombe on horseback, so Phoebe, lacking her physical strength, found her escape in books. From a small child, often confined to her bed, deprived of the outdoor activities enjoyed by her brother and cousins, she had devoured everything; poetry, histories, romances, theological works, plays, farming treatises, all the fruits of her father's collection, and far older volumes bought by the long-dead Sir Samuel St Barbe, the first baronet, whose ruffed portrait, stiff and starched as the wooden dolls with which she had scorned to play, hung in the dining parlour. Nat, seeing in his frail daughter perhaps an echo of his own ailing childhood, and more certainly the seeds of just such a curious, incisive and thirsty intellect as he possessed, had encouraged her to the hilt. With his help, she had learned Latin, graduated to Greek, flirted with Hebrew and then decided, with a pragmatism that made her father's eyes gleam, to study the languages of the living rather than the dead, since her chances of meeting Julius Caesar or Socrates were distinctly slender, in this life at least. Almost casually, she had acquired French, German, Italian and Spanish, with the assistance of Nat's scholarly friends, and at the time of his death, enlarging her horizons somewhat, she had been studying Arabic.

The book that lay before her now, however, was no scholarly work, but a translation of *Don Quixote*. And the man walking with that long, easy stride up to where she sat at the round, gate-legged oak table that stood in the centre of the library, bore no resemblance to the hero of Cervantes's romance. Phoebe watched him with a wariness born of many years' unhappy experience. Being forcibly planted and watered in the garden at the age of three had been only the first incident in a shared childhood notable for the quarrels and the constant feuding between her and her brother. He had been physically far stronger and possessed of a nice line in invective. Phoebe, nearly six years younger, had lost no time in honing her own tongue in emulation. She had envied him so much: his masculine freedom, the casual charm that had undeservedly extracted him from so many appalling scrapes, and above all the strong straight legs that could carry him wherever he wished to go. As a child, bursting with energy, he had been the kind of boy who could never stand still, he had run everywhere, dancing fleet of foot across her sight while she, twisted and damaged beyond repair, was confined to bed and chair and could only walk hobbling with a stick. Frustrated and helpless, she had raged at her limitations, and still more at her brother's cruel, callous mockery of them.

But adolescence had brought compensations. Alex, after that sensational end to his schooldays, had been sent to Oxford, and became, as their father had despairingly pointed out, the bad company that everyone else's sons got into. And Phoebe, very like Nat in so many ways, had been without at first realising it the substitute for his deeply unsatisfactory son and heir. She absorbed Nat's philosophy, his pragmatic outlook on life, and his encouragement and approval of her unwomanly scholastic endeavours, as readily as she had absorbed his books. And she knew now, with the absolute certainty of those who are deeply loved, that in almost every way possible, by the time of her father's death, she had replaced Alex in his affections.

It would have been a more than adequate revenge for all those years of her brother's unkindness, save that she was tolerably certain that Alex did not give a toss for his father's feelings, or hers, and never had.

'Hullo, Alex,' she said, her level voice devoid of any hint of welcome. 'What brings you here so late in the day?'

Dusk was falling, and the beautiful room, lined with shelves and books, was in deep shadow save for the sphere of amber light around her branched candlestick. The soft glow imparted a deceptive gentleness to Phoebe's rather harsh face, lined and hollowed beyond its years by long, accustomed suffering. Her brother did not answer her question directly, but walked round to glance at the thick, open volume between her hands. 'Oh, Phoebe, Phoebe, I'm disappointed in you. Not in the original Spanish?'

'It would be, if Father had been able to obtain a copy,' Phoebe snapped, and regretted it immediately. She had learned long ago that the only way to deal with Alex in this mocking, argumentative mood was to remain completely calm, and in icy control of her temper. Allow him to think that he had made a chink in her armour, and he would show her no mercy.

'But you are, of course, continuing with your studies, despite the enforced departure of your tutor? Which language is it this week? Dutch? I can help you there. Or Sanskrit? Some savage tongue from the New World, perhaps?' He picked up the book and closed it, thereby losing her place. 'Come on, little sister, after all these years, aren't you going to give me a kiss?'

'If I must,' said Phoebe, in tones of weary resignation that effectively disguised her annoyance. 'But I hope you will forgive me if I do not stand up.'

'Of course,' Alex said magnanimously. 'How could I forget your infirmities?' He bent his head and gave her a cool, distant kiss, merely brushing his lips against her cheek. It confirmed what she had already suspected, that he had been drinking, but she had no intention of giving him the satisfaction of admitting that she was aware of it. And besides, she thought bitterly, what does it matter? If he's chosen his own route to the devil, let him take it, and leave us and Wintercombe in peace.

'What remarkable restraint,' said her brother, regarding her with some amusement. 'I wouldn't have thought you capable of resisting the temptation to enumerate my sins to me yet again.'

'There wouldn't be any point,' said Phoebe, with her habitual waspishness. 'I'm sure that's one of the main reasons why you transgress – to give yourself the satisfaction of shocking us. Unfortunately, I don't think you can shock me any more.'

'A pity,' Alex observed. He pulled up one of the leather chairs that surrounded the table, and sat down. Phoebe studiously ignored his feet, cased in plain black shoes, which suddenly appeared on the board beside her, narrowly missing her book. Her brother tipped the chair on to its back legs and linked his hands behind his head. Taking her by surprise, he grinned at her, and she had to stop herself from responding. In their adult years, during their infrequent meetings, he had often been able to draw her out of her usual prickly reserve, to charm her and make her smile in reply to his outrageous wit, and, reluctantly, she had to admit that she enjoyed these encounters. But such times habitually left a sour taste in her mouth, as if her privacy had been invaded against her will.

'How long do you plan to stay?' she enquired. In the past, her brother's visits to Wintercombe had been brief, usually just of sufficient duration to upset expectations and plans and sensibilities, to offend and disturb and disrupt, before waving his family goodbye with casual contempt and going on his way, leaving the inevitable chaos in his wake. Often, Phoebe had wondered how, despite his dreadful behaviour, everyone seemed to be enlivened by his presence. She had come to the conclusion that, with all his faults and vices, Alex did at least bring a little excitement into their otherwise rather dull and humdrum lives.

'For good,' he said, glancing at her.

This time, she was quite unable to control her reaction. '*What?*'

'You heard me, little sister. I've had enough of my wandering, footloose existence. I think that it's high time I faced up to my responsibilities and settled down to the life of a country gentleman.'

'*You?* Settle down? Flying pigs are more likely,' said Phoebe, startled out of her usual composure. 'Alex – you can't.'

'Why not? This is my inheritance, my home. I intend to exploit my advantages to the full. Where is your objection?'

Phoebe stared at him, her blue eyes, very like his, wide with shock. She thought of a hundred excellent reasons why not, and voiced the first and most obvious. 'What about Louise? And Amy? It's their home too.'

'What about them? Afraid I might seduce them?'

Phoebe continued to stare at him. 'To be brutally honest – yes. And even if you do not, your reputation will ensure that the whole of Philip's Nortion, not to mention Somerset, will think that you have.'

'Unlikely. Aunt Silence has said she will take Louise back to Chard with her – a shame, for she's in possession of rather more spirit than I remember Amy having. Is she still the same simpering little miss?'

'How long is it since you were here last? Five years?'

'Nearly four.'

'Then you will find that she has grown up a trifle,' said Phoebe drily, with an image of her cousin Amy, golden-haired and lovely, rising in her mind to mock at her own deficiencies. 'But doubtless you will meet her soon, at supper if not before.'

'Doubtless. And her mother, of course. How is dear Aunt Bab?'

'The same, but worse,' said his sister gloomily. 'She has made as thorough a study of her ailments as any physician, and airs her diagnoses with as much authority, and at far greater length.'

Dislike of their Aunt Bab, a burden to her brother-in-law and an embarrassment to her family, was apparently one of the few things that Alex had in common with Phoebe, for he laughed. 'You're right, she hasn't changed. Does she still keep to her chamber in state?'

'For much of the time, yes – and then she'll make an appearance, leaning on Amy or Charles or her maid, and expecting everyone to defer to her years and ill health. And in fact,' said Phoebe waspishly, 'she's only forty-four, and as fit as a fiddle.'

'Well, you need not suffer her any longer,' Alex said, and once more sent her a grin nicely calculated to soften her hostility. 'I'd already determined on it, and what you say merely confirms my decision. Bab must go – and her offspring with her.'

For the second time in a few minutes, he had astonished and appalled her. Phoebe gaped at him. '*Go?*'

'Go, leave, depart – have you never heard the word? Close your mouth, little sister, it's hardly flattering, and as far as I know, you're not related to a fish.'

Phoebe snapped her lips shut so abruptly that her teeth knocked together. 'You can't,' she said, infuriated to find her voice hoarse with surprise. 'This is her home – Alex, you *can't!*'

'Why ever not? Father may have been willing to tolerate her bloodsucking ways, and support her and her children in idleness. I am not Father, and I refuse to be exploited by a witless Papist who'd give Monsieur Molière ample material for several plays.'

'Bab as "*la malade imaginaire*"?' said Phoebe, amused despite herself. 'You wouldn't happen to have a copy of the play in your baggage, would you?'

'Alas, no – I travel very light. Most of my baggage, including one very luscious piece, remains for ever in Amsterdam. This is a fresh start, little sister, pastures new, and I fully intend to be the proverbial new broom. Hence my determination to evict the detestable Bab.'

'But she's lived here for nearly twenty years –'

'Seventeen and a half, to be pedantic.'

25

'It's still a very long time,' said Phoebe angrily, while one part of her stood aside with cynical detachment and wondered why she should be defending someone whom she had always disliked, and rather despised. 'Wintercombe is her home – she'll be heartbroken. And what of Charles, and Amy? Charles *hasn't* been idle – he has assisted Father very ably these last few years.'

'To his own profit, no doubt.'

'Profit? Charles? How dare you?' said Phoebe, with the brutal forthrightness that only she, alas, had ever employed to her brilliant brother's face. 'I'm sure his only desire was to earn his place here, somehow, and becoming Father's steward was an excellent way of achieving it. And he can't have profited at all – he only received quite a small sum in Father's will, about four hundred pounds in all.'

'That's hardly small,' Alex pointed out. 'Although I suppose it might seem so to someone who expected far greater rewards.'

It had grown quite dark, but in the candlelight the expression on his face was brutally unambiguous. Phoebe studied him in silence for a moment, seeing with sisterly clarity the subtle lines that debauchery had wrought, unfortunately not affecting his good looks, on a face that had always been startlingly attractive. There was, for all his vices, a life in Alex, a vitality and energy that drove him as powerfully and variously as the wind. Restless, undisciplined and wayward, trailing chaos like an earthbound Lucifer, he would never cease to surprise her with some chance remark, tossed aside as if of no account, that yet revealed how quickly his wits worked, and how acute was his perception.

For it was true. She was fond of Cousin Charles, an affection that had begun in their childhood when they had both been the unhappy objects of Alex's mockery, Phoebe for her inability to run and jump and ride, Charles merely for being quiet and unadventurous. She liked her cousin, and so, though normally as detached in her judgement as her father, she had turned a blinkered eye to his growing and evident desire for Wintercombe.

And now, callously, Alex was planning to remove every vestige of Charles's hope, kick the prop of family support from under him and his mother and sister, and thrust them forth into a colder, harsher world, to sink or swim as they might.

'He will be desperately disappointed,' she said slowly, her eyes on her brother's face.

Alex laughed, and got to his feet in a characteristically swift explosion of movement, to prowl with insulting ease around the room. Phoebe, too mature now to feel the old corrosive envy at his strength, turned her head

26

to watch him in the gloom. After a while, she added, 'Why not install Aunt Bab in that house of yours in the Abbey Green in Bath? Then she could take the waters to her heart's content, and indulge her ill health to the full. And, who knows, perhaps she might even get better.'

'Unlikely,' Alex commented. He had come to a halt by the fire, which was banked with Mendip coal and glowing a hot and sullen red. He bent and thrust a poker into the heart of it, and the new flames sprang up, eager and greedy. 'That woman's ailments are all that makes her life interesting, and she knows it. If she were well, she'd fade away to nothing. And if I were you, little sister, I'd abandon any attempt to tell me what I ought to do. You should know better than most that for some strange and unaccountable reason I always decide on the exact opposite.'

It was true. However forcefully she marshalled the arguments of sense, of compassion and family feeling, Alex would do precisely as he had intended to all along. But if he had originally decided to pension Bab off to comfortable seclusion in Bath, he would be far less likely to do so now that she had suggested it. She had never decided whether it was a sign of maturity, or its opposite, that Alex was always so adamantly indifferent to persuasion.

She shrugged briskly, admitting defeat and reserving her judgement, as she usually did. 'Then I'll say no more, and retire battered and bloody from the field.'

There must have been too sharp a note of bitterness in her voice, for Alex left his position by the fire, which was now blazing uncomfortably hot after his interference, and came to stand by her chair. He said, his tone not noticeably softer, 'We've talked of what I plan to do – but what of you, little sister? You must have some thoughts about your future.'

Once more, he had taken her aback. Phoebe tried, and failed, to remember when her brother had ever shown any concern whatsoever for her prospects – which she had always considered, in view of the limits of her abilities and the unconventionally wide bounds of her education, to be exceedingly restricted. Unlike Amy, lovely but almost dowerless, she had never yearned for what, realistically, she knew would never be hers. Even with the handsome sum of money that her father had left her, she was no man's ideal wife. It would be an extraordinary suitor indeed who would be prepared to overlook her crippled state, her ignorance of even the most basic aspects of domestic duty, her fearsome intellectual accomplishments, her plain face and blisteringly honest manner, for the sake of two thousand pounds. And she knew that, when her father had drawn up his will, he had not been intending that legacy to serve as her dowry. It was what he knew that she wanted, a sum sufficiently large to set her up in an independent establishment, in some comfort, for the rest of her days. She was of age, and could do as she pleased: and no man, least of all her brother, had the power to prevent her.

But something – fear of his ridicule, perhaps – held her back. She would not parade her small fierce dreams of freedom under his mocking gaze. She said tartly, 'You know as well as I do what my prospects are. Don't tell me you have half a dozen eager suitors lined up at the door, begging for my hand.'

She had brought a grin, curiously and incongruously boyish, to her brother's face. He sat down beside her once more, and took one of her thin, ink-stained hands in his. 'Little sister, I know full well that I may have been less than kind to you in the past –'

'So do I,' she said, an answering smile pulling at her unwilling mouth. 'You used to call me Feeble.'

'I remember it only too clearly. How you could tolerate it, I can't imagine.'

'I didn't have much say in the matter, did I?' Phoebe pointed out. 'I could hardly hit you over the head, which is what I wanted to do. So I learned to defend myself with words, just as Charles retreated into his shell for protection. But there's no point to any bitterness or recriminations or apologies – what's past is past, and cannot be changed.'

'Perhaps so. But just the same, I would like, now I have come home, to make amends. Whatever you want, little sister, whatever your dreams are, I will do my best to provide for you. Within reason, of course.'

Phoebe gazed at him incredulously. For a moment, her anger stuck fast in her throat, rendering her speechless. And then, blisteringly, it forced itself into words, the words with which, as so often before, she would attack her brother. 'You – *you* – want to make amends? I won't believe it's to salve your guilty conscience, because you don't possess such a thing, and nothing on earth is going to convince me that you've changed in any real degree from the child who used to make my life a misery!' She saw the alteration in his face, knew that she had struck home, and went on, showing him no mercy, as ruthless as he himself could be. 'And what is even more repellent than your belief that you can saunter back to Wintercombe as if you'd never left it and order people's lives like some petty interfering heathen god, with no regard whatsoever for their feelings or hopes or desires – what really *sickens* me, Alexander St Barbe, is your arrogant assumption that you can give me something that Father could not! Well, do you want the truth, brother? The truth, the honest unadorned truth is, that given the choice, I would rather he had lived two months ago, and you had died!'

The silence was appalling. I have done damage, Phoebe thought, looking at his face, and was not sorry for it: in fact, she exulted in her victory. For, God knew, some plain speaking was needed to force some of that obnoxious, careless arrogance out of him, and let in a little healthy self-knowledge and doubt. He had always been so infuriatingly sure that he was right, so determined on his own way, so oblivious to the hurt he did to others, and above all to their father. Now he knew the extent of her dislike, and, no doubt of it, had been shaken. As if, thought Phoebe venomously, some weak and fragile little kitten, condescendingly and pityingly petted, had suddenly turned into a full-grown panther, and rent him with its claws. Well, serve him right.

And besides, she realised, careful to keep her triumph from her face, the very fact that I have hurt him means that he cannot be entirely beyond redemption – unless, of course, the injury is purely to his pride.

'You may live to regret saying that.' Her brother's voice was soft and menacing. 'I had no idea you loathed me so much, Phoebe. And since you do, there's no point in making amends, is there? Good day, sister.'

He bowed, mockery and malice all over his face, and shut the door behind him with deliberate moderation. Only Phoebe, who possibly knew him better than anyone, could guess at the efforts he had made not to slam it, or shout at her, or otherwise abandon his self-control.

'So you do have a soul after all, do you, Alex?' she said softly to that firmly closed door. 'Well, with any luck, I might yet transform you into a civilised human being.'

'Supper is ready, my lady,' said Abigail, putting her head round the door rather nervously, as if expecting that one of the occupants might bite. The new master of Wintercombe, however, was conspicuous by his absence from the warm, cosy winter parlour, and Silence gave her a reassuring smile. 'Thank you, Abigail. Is Mistress St Barbe coming down, or is she taking her food in her chamber?'

'She be coming down directly, my lady,' said the maid, in tones of mild wonder. 'She d'want to welcome Sir Alexander, I suspect.'

Privately, Silence thought this unlikely, to say the least. Curiosity was one of Bab's besetting sins, and it was far more probable that she wished to see the monster of depravity that her notorious nephew had become, according to rumour, in the years since he had last graced Wintercombe with his presence. With foreboding, Silence contemplated the coming meal and the wealth of antagonism gathered in one confined space.

She walked with the sedate dignity of age to the dining parlour. The table where once she had presided as lady of Wintercombe was neatly laid for seven, with her own place – by right of seniority, she thought wryly – at the head. Alex would occupy the other end, with Bab and her children on one side, Phoebe and Louise on the other.

Only Alex's sister was already there, sitting composedly with her stick unobtrusively propped beside her. Silence had always kept a special place in her heart for Nat's daughter, loving her not only for her spirit and humour, so similar to his, but for the determination and utter lack of self-pity with which she overcame her disadvantages. She smiled at Phoebe, and said, 'Has everyone else taken fright?'

Her niece did not return the smile. She said quietly, 'I think they'd be wise. I've told Alex certain home truths, and he didn't like them at all.'

'Oh.' Silence surveyed Phoebe, noting that the girl did not seem unduly disturbed by the experience. Like her father, she combined physical frailty with a toughness of spirit that took many people unawares. 'Is that why he has spent all evening shut away in his chamber?'

'Probably,' said Phoebe. She gave her aunt a wicked sideways glance, very reminiscent of Nat. 'You're the soul of discretion. Aren't you all agog to find out what I said?'

'It was probably very similar to what I told him myself, but in a manner considerably more forthright.' Silence sat down at the head of the table. From old habit, she glanced at the pewter plates and bowls, seeing that they were well scoured and polished, and at the gleaming silver cutlery laid out in front of her. Each place boasted a fork, although her pompous, elderly first husband had condemned the things as newfangled gewgaws that had no place on an honest gentleman's table. Needless to say, Nat had seen the manifold advantages of such an implement, and had lost no time in ordering a dozen from London as soon as he had entered his inheritance.

'It was more than forthright,' said Phoebe thoughtfully. 'I was hurtful, brutally so. And I didn't think that Alex *could* be hurt, did you?'

Silence gave her a rather bleak smile. 'No. In fact, the impression I received was that he cares very little for anything. Certainly not for us, nor for Wintercombe. He left a mistress behind in Holland, or so I believe.'

Phoebe, whose wide education had early dissolved any girlish inno-cence, said slowly, 'Oh, I don't imagine he cares about her, either. Not from the little he let slip . . . You know, Aunt, I wish he had never come back.'

Silence gazed at her niece, and shook her head in resignation. 'I think we may all come to regret it . . . This house is not ours, but his, however much we would like it to be otherwise. And whatever happens in the next few hours, and days, and weeks, I think we would do well to remember that.'

'That we're all here on his sufferance?' said Phoebe, the wry twist to her mouth a replica of her father's. 'At least you're lucky, Aunt – you have a home of your own, and you can return to it any time you want.'

But Silence, thinking of the people who would become Alex's victims, without her age and authority to temper his excesses, knew that, for the present at least, she could not leave Wintercombe.

'Good evening, Grandmother, good evening, Phoebe.' The door had opened, effectively killing any further discussion about Alex, for here, handsome and golden-haired and smiling rather tentatively, were his cousins, the children of that unfortunate, doomed alliance between William St Barbe and Bab Campion.

William had been very dear to Silence, a sunny, open child, free of deceit or malice, easy to like and to love. She had suspected, though, that the impoverished Bab had fixed her expectations less upon his friendly smile and his yellow hair than on the fact that, after the child Alex, he had been the next heir to Wintercombe. The truth – that William had only ever wanted to be a soldier, was completely lacking in any other ambition, and was quite content to live in comparative poverty so long as he could pursue the trade he loved – had never penetrated her rather limited intelligence. He was handsome, charming, and brother to a baronet, and probably the last attribute counted for more in her mind than the other two.

Fortunately, Charles and Amy resembled their father more than their mother, who possessed the rather kittenish prettiness which looked well at eighteen, and rather less congruous on a lady in middle age. Charles was not tall, and had William's stocky build, his corn-fair hair, and frank, open face. His eyes, though, were not William's warm dark brown, but the paler blue of his mother. Amy, beside him in her best gown of deep blue silk, had made considerable efforts with her appearance. The abundant golden locks were neatly curled and shining, her stays had evidently, to her grandmother's amused and observant eye, been laced several inches tighter than usual, and a filmy lace tippet rather inadequately covered her shoulders. Her eyes, brown like William's, sparkled with excitement, and Silence knew exactly what she was thinking. There was no denying that Amy, with her tilted nose and peach-cream skin, was a delightful-looking girl, full of liveliness and chatter. But with Alex, who had never suffered fools gladly, she was undoubtedly wasting her time.

Hard on their heels came Louise, dark and somehow alien amongst these pale English people. Her French clothes and Gallic gestures and accent would always make her exotic at Wintercombe, despite the fact that her mother had been born here. With an increasing presentiment of disaster, Silence saw that she also had taken great pains with her dress. The mantua gown in striped golden-yellow silk was of a fashion so new that it had hardly yet crossed the Channel, and her hair, teased into dramatic shadowy ringlets all around her head, gave her an aura of extreme, brittle sophistication. Nor did the face below, subtly enhanced with powder and paint and two small, heart-shaped patches, dispel her grandmother's foreboding. Beside Louise, Amy, pretty as she was, seemed like an immature schoolgirl, trying on adult attitudes for the first time. And whereas Amy, despite her looks, was still essentially innocent, Louise knew exactly what she was doing.

Silence unwarily caught her eye, and her suspicions were immediately confirmed by her granddaughter's slow, deliberate wink.

'Mother is coming down,' said Amy breathlessly. She darted a glance at Louise, plainly envious of her glamorous cousin, who, quite effortlessly and without even being beautiful, had stolen her thunder.

Louise saw the look, and smiled inwardly. She had no particular grudge against Amy but an inability to endure more than an hour or so of her exclusive company. Since her cousin's one wish at the moment was to learn French, the language of fashion and polite society, and as much about modes and manners as she could possibly extract from Louise, relations between them were at present rather strained. It was not so much that they disliked each other, but that they had no interest whatsoever in common besides Amy's urgent desire to become more French than the French. And since her accent, even after several months of Louise's impatient instruction, was quite execrable, her vocabulary limited and her grammar hopelessly confused, even that point of contact had almost expired.

Strangely enough, considering Louise's love of activity, her delight in riding and outdoor pursuits, she had liked Phoebe from the start, and the feeling had been returned.

'No one has seen Alex, I suppose?' Silence asked gently.

Amy and Charles exchanged significant glances, the girl with anticipation, her brother looking as if she had mentioned some name of ill omen, certain to bring bad luck. 'A man arrived just after I came home,' Charles said, in his quiet, rather diffident voice. 'He had some baggage with him, on a pony, that he said belonged to Alex, so I sent Abigail to find him before I went upstairs to change. He's taken up residence in the East Chamber.'

It was obvious, of course, that he would choose the best room in the house, used in recent years for important guests. Once it had belonged to Silence, and she had regarded it as her kingdom, the place where she hoarded all the things she loved: her books and flowers, her pets and her children. Even her first husband, George, had grudgingly asked her permission before coming to her bed, puffing up the spiral stair that led only to that chamber and the two closets just off it, and she had done her duty, though always feeling his unwelcome presence to be in some way a violation.

Somehow, to think of Alex, careless and arrogant, treating that lovely room as casually as he seemed to view everything else at Wintercombe, upset her considerably. But, as she had said to Phoebe, he was master here now, and he could do as he pleased.

'What sort of baggage, Charles?' Louise asked, feeling the familiar bubble of mischief beginning to fizz inside her.

Her cousin shook his head. 'I have no idea, save that it was bulky, and some of it apparently fragile. It was piled in the Hall, but it wasn't there just now, so he must have ordered it moved.'

'How exciting!' Amy said, clasping her pale, soft hands together. Phoebe fixed her with a sardonic blue eye. 'Really? Does a gentleman's baggage usually enthral you so much?'

'No – no,' Amy stammered, suddenly confused. 'I – well – it's exciting to have him home again from foreign parts. That's what I meant.'

Even Charles, who was very fond of his sister, looked exasperated. He said, with some annoyance, 'Oh, do stop rattling on, Amy. Do you want him to think you're a ninny-head? Where is he, anyway? I would have thought it only common courtesy to have made his presence felt in person, instead of skulking in his chamber.' Try as he would, he could not keep a rather peevish note from his voice. He had longed to take that room for himself, so much larger and grander than the chamber above the winter parlour which had been his for years.

'I expect he was tired from the journey,' said Silence, quietly soothing, as she had done for so long. 'He rode straight here from Bristol, after all, as soon as his ship tied up. And I'm glad to hear his bags have arrived – he could hardly appear for supper in travel-stained garments. There is no one here who has clothes that would fit him.'

At that moment the door opened, and five pairs of eyes turned in expectation. They were, however, doomed to disappointment, for standing there, triumphant on the arm of her maid, was Bab St Barbe, making her grand entrance.

She had not left her chamber for some weeks, and Silence, even though she had visited her daily, had forgotten how very fat she had grown. Bab adored sweetmeats and cakes, and every morning the cook, Nan Stevenson, baked a special batch which would be sent up, each delicious spiced pile glistening with crumbled sugar, for Mistress St Barbe's afternoon delectation. The results of such indulgence were plain to see in the rolled fat, the numerous chins, the obesely bulging line of her waist, and in her pink, puffed face, perspiring with the effort of unaccustomed exertion. Her maid, Beck Richeson, a sturdy and conscientious girl from Frome, seemed to be wilting somewhat as she supported her mistress's weight.

Bab's faded, blue-grey eyes searched in vain amongst the five faces already gathered in the dining parlour, and a look of peevish disappointment sagged her face as she realised that she had been denied the opportunity to make a dramatic entrance in front of her infamous nephew. 'Where is he?' she demanded. 'He's late!'

Both Charles and Amy, Louise saw, looked distinctly embarrassed by their mother's appearance. Bab's silly foibles and foolish talk were much easier to tolerate, and ignore, when in self-imposed isolation in her chamber, than aired before the entire family and the servants. It's just as well poor Uncle William was killed so soon, thought Louise, regarding his widow with some irritation. He'd have been driven mad, or to drink, by now, if he'd lived.

'He shouldn't keep us waiting,' Bab continued, as if she herself had not done just that. 'He should be here to greet us. Has he spoken to you, Charles, dear?'

'I haven't so much as clapped eyes on him,' said her son, rather more curtly than usual. 'He will doubtless appear, in good time.'

'And sooner rather than later, I trust,' said Bab. 'Help me to my chair, Beck . . . so inconsiderate . . . doesn't he realise that I'm a sick woman? I shouldn't leave my chamber . . . the effort exhausts me . . . my heart, you know . . . he really should be here.'

A movement behind her ample shoulder attracted Louise's attention, as her aunt manoeuvred, wheezing and panting, towards her place at the table. Alex was standing in the gloom of the passage outside the door, undoubtedly able to hear every word that she said. Before Louise could glance away and pretend that she had not noticed him, he had caught her eye and smiled. It was not a particularly warm expression, and boded no good whatsoever for the immediate future. Once more, Louise felt the fizz of anticipation begin to bubble up. Between Bab and Alex, not to mention Phoebe and Charles, this was likely to prove a memorable evening.

If anyone else had seen him, they gave no sign. Charles was busy helping his mother to sit down, and her stertorous breathing was punctuated by a stream of complaints about her health, her nephew, and the dangerous paucity of candles to light the stairs. In the middle of this, Alex stepped into the room.

He had changed out of his riding clothes and was wearing a suit of blue-grey velvet, trimmed with blue and silver, whose understated elegance immediately drew Louise's appreciative eye. His black hair lay combed and sleek on his shoulders, as long and thick as a periwig, and his blue eyes gleamed with malice and laughter. 'Good evening, everyone.'

The hush was instant, save for the soft plumping noise as Bab, released from her son's grip, dropped solidly down on to her chair. His gaze swept them all, lingered a while on Amy – who blushed and lowered her eyes – and returned to her mother. 'Hullo, Aunt. I am so sorry that I have kept you waiting. It was most discourteous of me to do so, and I present my profound apologies.'

Bab, the wind stolen from her sails, could only gape at him. Alex swept them all a flourishing bow, a courtesy variously echoed, after a fractional pause, by his kin. Then, still with that untrustworthy smile, he indicated the vacant place opposite Silence. 'This is my chair, I take it?'

Silence, who found Alex in this mood frankly terrifying, regarded him with her usual composure. 'It is indeed. If you would all be seated, I will ring the bell for supper.'

A procession of maids, clad in the neat, plain dark blue that all Wintercombe's servants wore, with decorous white linen cuffs and aprons, caps and collars, bore in the steaming dishes. Once, long ago, the St Barbes had employed the best cook in the West Country, justly famous for his sauces, but poor Nan Stevenson, though very competent, entirely lacked her predecessor's flair. There was a pigeon pie, a roast fowl somewhat past its first flush of youth, a winter pottage made of leeks and beans and gobbets of salt mutton, and a rabbit hash in the French style, after a recipe which Louise had provided from memory, it being a favourite of her stepfather's cook in France. The maids, with the same air of suppressed curiosity and excitement that had infected Amy and Louise, bustled round the table, their eyes sliding sideways to the new master of Wintercombe, who sat at the end of the table, his expression impassive. At last, all the steaming dishes had been laid before the assembled St Barbes, along with jugs and bottles of beer and wine, and Silence motioned to the servants to stand in a row by the door. 'Sir Alexander, may I present these members of your household?'

'By all means, Aunt,' said Alex, in a lazy drawl that made her wonder, suddenly, how much he had imbibed in his chamber this past hour. 'There are one or two faces that I recognise, but pray refresh my memory.'

Silence gave him a considering, warning stare. The uncomfortable sapphire eyes gazed blandly back. She decided that the servants had best be dismissed from the room as soon as possible, and waved her hand. 'Twinney has been with us for four years – he is butler and footman both. Abigail you must surely remember.'

The senior housemaid bobbed a curtsey, her round Somerset cheeks suddenly fiery.

'And Edith Grant – she too has been four years in service here.'

It was plain that Edith, pockmarked and possessed of a nose of truly heroic proportions, would not attract her employer's eye.

'Lydia Jordan will have been here two years come next month.'

Lydia, seventeen and as thin as a rail, with a sharp high colour and a barking cough that could often be heard all over the house, was not likely to tempt Alex either.

'And this is Tamsin Pearce, who came to Wintercombe last August, I believe.' The girl, scarcely fourteen, was normally a likable little chatterbox, her round childish body still weighted by puppy fat. Under her new master's sardonic eye, she flushed deep crimson, and stared at the floor.

'How tedious,' said Alex, still in that infuriating, inebriated drawl. 'Four maids, and variously all too old, too ugly, too young and too sickly to entice me. Was it deliberate, Aunt, or unfortunate coincidence that conspired against me?'

Louise, staring round at the appalled faces of her kin, felt that bubble of laughter well again in her throat. 'By design, Cousin, of course,' she said, the French intonation in her low, rather throaty voice very pronounced. 'All the pretty ones have been sent away to Bath – and if you ask at the sign of the Cock in Walcot, you'll find them there.'

'Louise!'

'Well, Gran'mère, how else could Amy and I ensure that we were noticed?'

Silence stared at Louise in astonishment, hardly knowing whether to laugh or be angry at the girl's outrageous wit. Belatedly conscious of the proprieties, she wrenched her gaze from her granddaughter's suddenly wicked grin, and spoke hastily to the servants. 'You may all go, and bring in the tarts and cheese when I ring the bell.'

'Yes, m'lady,' said Twinney, his handsome face a wooden mask of rectitude, and he and the four maids filed from the room, doubtless eager to relay every detail to a shocked and delighted audience in the servants' hall.

'And what else will I find at the sign of the Cock?' Alex enquired of Louise, who was sitting on his right. Ignoring Charles's horrified face, she

36

let her lips curl up in guileless innocence. 'Why, Cousin, what would you be expecting to find?'

'I hardly think it's a fit subject for this table,' said Silence severely, resolving to give her granddaughter a blistering reprimand as soon as opportunity offered. Alex in this mood, half drunk and motivated by malice and mischief, was by himself as dangerous as a cask of gunpowder, without Louise lighting the fuse. 'Now, I shall say our grace, and then I suggest we eat before all this delicious fare spoils.'

For a while the room was deceptively peaceful, as the seven diners obediently addressed their supper. Bab, as usual, attacked the food with dedication, eating efficiently and greedily, and every morsel, even the more gristly pieces of mutton, was swallowed with audible relish. It was so long since she had attended a family meal that Louise had forgotten how her aunt's single-minded gluttony could disgust her, and tried not to watch or listen. At least the presence of Alex, almost at her elbow, was a distraction. She knew that in bantering oblique bawdry with him, she had indeed attracted his notice, and despite her earlier anger and her pact with Charles, part of her, the wild and wayward part that had been her stepfather's despair, exulted in her success. There had been no mistaking the look in those very blue eyes as she had challenged him, for she had seen it before. A strange feeling settled somewhere in the pit of her stomach, compounded of excitement, danger and daring, and also an extraordinary sense of kinship. Nearly ten years, and a vast gulf of experience, separated them, but she recognised in him just such a wilful and reckless nature as she herself possessed.

But she was no green girl to be swept head over heels by a practised seducer. She had played with fire before, and been scorched, and had learned her lesson. Besides, she had no intention of allowing her chances of ensnaring a wealthy and well-born husband to be damaged by ruinous scandal.

It was, all the same, a very welcome excitement. She glanced surreptitiously at her cousin, who had wisely eschewed the mutton pottage in favour of the rabbit hash. Even slouching back in his seat, his neckcloth askew and his legs sprawled under the table so that she had to tuck her own beneath her chair to avoid touching him, there was a casual, powerful elegance about him that was disturbingly attractive. She found herself wondering idly what his qualities as a lover might be, and sternly brought her reflections to an abrupt halt. That way lay a great deal of unpleasantness, whatever delights his experience could offer her, and she would not be so foolish.

Besides, there was Charles to consider. She had already seen the bewildered, angry hurt that he had done his best to hide, and was torn between affection and a mild, but unworthy contempt. He had never displayed anything other than a proper cousinly fondness for her, but intuition told her that his real feelings were considerably stronger. She did not need his devotion, nor any man's, nor did she want to see his dismay every time she uttered the most mildly *risqué* remark. All she required from life was amusement, and the freedom to do as she pleased. Flirting with her debauched and dangerous cousin would undoubtedly provide the former. It was very unlikely that allowing Charles to declare his adoration would give her the latter.

Really, sometimes everything was altogether too complicated. She glanced again to her left, noting that Alex had been drinking steadily throughout the meal. Already, the two bottles of wine at their end of the table were all but empty, and yet both she and Charles, opposite, had taken just a glass each.

Whatever happened, this supper was unlikely to be boring. Like her bewitching, mischievous mother Kate, Louise thrived on argument and excitement. Even the frequent quarrels of her mother and stepfather, as noisy and crackling as a thunderstorm, had never frightened her, for somehow their fury, with the vivid ferocity of a lightning bolt, seemed to fuel their undoubted passion. They had been seven years illicit lovers, then for nine years happily married, with two sons and three daughters, and yet their ardour for each other seemed undimmed. Louise, realistically, knew well enough that she was most unlikely to find such a match for herself, and certainly she had met no one in all France – save one – who could spark her into flame, as the Vicomte de St Clair had set her mother ablaze. From what she had heard, and seen, of English men, she would undoubtedly be even less lucky in Somerset.

The meal progressed in uneasy quiet. Bab was too busy eating, and Amy too shy and bashful, for either to indulge in casual chatter. Charles, pointedly offended by Louise's earlier remarks, ignored everyone. It was as if they were all too frightened of Alex to say anything, Louise thought impatiently, looking round the table as the cheese and tarts were brought in by Twinney and Abigail, both of them distinctly uneasy. Even her grandmother had not spoken, beyond requests to pass various dishes, and the salt.

'Another bottle of wine, Twinney,' Alex said suddenly, and the butler bowed and turned to leave the room. The servant's face remained impassive. 'Very good, sir. The sack, or the claret?'

'Is there any other choice?'

Louise, aware of a movement to her right, concentrated on cutting herself a piece of cheese, and did not dare to catch Phoebe's eye.

'There is some Malaga, sir, and beer and cider, of course.'

'Something of a Hobson's choice,' said Alex, leaning back in his chair and surveying his butler through half-closed eyes. 'Another thing I'll have to change. A bottle of the Malaga, Twinney, and if you can avoid taking all night over it, I'd be grateful.'

Silence waited until the unfortunate servant had hurried from the room, before she spoke. 'Alex, do you not consider that you've had enough?'

Up and down the table, movement froze. At each end, only Silence and her nephew seemed unaffected by the sudden, palpable tension. For a long moment, hazel eyes stared into blue, and neither gave way. Then, suddenly, Alex smiled. 'Your memory must be failing, Aunt. I am no longer fifteen, and I think I'm capable of judging my own capacity – I've had enough practice, after all. And besides, have you not forgotten something else? This is my house, and in it I may do as I wish, and direct the servants as I please, without interference. And you'd all of you do well to remember it.'

His gaze swept around the table. Louise met his eyes boldly, wished she had not, and from pride and anger would not look away. For what seemed like an eternity, she suffered his unspoken malice, and then said, spuriously innocent, 'But what if we forget, Cousin?'

'Then you can go elsewhere,' said Alex shortly. 'Do I need to say it again? Wintercombe is mine. If I have a fancy to tear it down, or keep a brothel here, then I will. I do not intend to alter my habits or desires to suit any of you. If you do not like it, you can go back to France, and good riddance.'

'And if I do like it?' said Louise coolly, looking down her long nose with what her six-year-old half-brother Philippe had called her '*expression de duchesse*'.

Alex laughed. 'Then you, my sweet and deceptive cousin, can warm my bed with pleasure.'

'Alex!' It was Phoebe, not Silence, who spoke. Her face white with anger, she had never looked more like her brother. 'Alex, you're drunk.'

'It makes no difference – the truth will out, so they say. And as for you –' He swung his attention abruptly to the other side of the table, to the considerable alarm of the three St Barbes sitting there. 'As for you, dear Aunt Bab, you can go too.'

'Go?' Bab stared at him in horror, her several chins quivering. Scattered across them, a trickle of gravy and several crumbs bore witness to her greed. 'Go? Where?'

'Anywhere but here. You've lived your ease off our charity too long, and it's plain that Wintercombe has fed you more than adequately. I suggest you take yourself off to Bath, and indulge your hypochondria there.'

Bab had no idea what the word meant, but the venom in his voice was quite unambiguous. She stared at him for a moment longer, and then dissolved into wailing tears.

'Alex!' said Silence sharply, from the other end of the table. She had risen to her feet, but her face seemed deceptively calm still. 'For shame – did you have to air your views quite so unpleasantly?'

'Certainly I did – she's so witless, she wouldn't understand me, else.'

Bab had sunk her head in her hands, and was rocking to and fro. Disjointed phrases – 'Our home . . . can't go . . . sick woman . . . so cruel . . . heartless!' – emerged between her sobs. Amy, in tears herself, was attempting to comfort her, while Charles, speechless with impotent rage, stared at his cousin. Alex smiled evilly back. 'What's the matter? Wondering if you can muster the courage to protest? Or are you too frightened that I'll throw you out as well, so you won't be able to feather your own nest any more?'

'I – ' Charles, faced with his childhood tormenter, swallowed and then said, his voice hoarse with the effort to keep calm, 'I do not wish to bandy abuse with a drunkard. There'd be no point in defending myself or insulting you, for you'd only have forgotten it, come morning.'

'I didn't think it *was* possible to insult me. Ah, there you are, Twinney. Bring the bottle over here.'

The unfortunate butler had been hovering, aghast, for some minutes in the doorway. Louise felt rather sorry for him, but at least he would be able to regale the servants' hall with the details of this latest example of their new master's depravity. He had been well trained, however, and stepped forward, past the weeping Bab, to place the bottle of Malaga at Alex's elbow. 'Is that to your liking, sir?'

Slowly, with excessive deliberation, Alex poured a trickle of the pale sweet wine into his glass, inhaled, and then drank. Save for Bab's sobs, there was utter quiet. Louise risked a glance at Phoebe, to her right, and surprised a look of cold and profound contempt on the girl's thin face. She is Alex's sister, Louise thought. Surely she cannot dislike him so much?

Louise, intelligent and unashamedly curious, had made a study of the strangely assorted people with whom her mother and stepfather consorted, and learned early to distinguish the flatterer and the depraved, the honest and the virtuous, and to keep Kate's healthy sense of the absurd and the ridiculous. She had turned the same clear eye upon the denizens of Wintercombe, until liking, or irritation, had clouded her view and her judgement.

But then Alex – Alex had, in a few short hours, turned everything upside down. And if it had not been for her regard for Charles, and for Phoebe and her grandmother, she might have relished his arrival still more.

However, Louise thought wryly, attraction in this case is entirely separate from liking – for I have never yet encountered a man so intent upon alienating everyone around him. The Alex she remembered from her childhood, mischievous and inventive, might have been a different person altogether from this arrogant and offensive man who seemed to take a perverse delight in hurting his own family. But why had he changed so much?

'Tolerable,' he remarked, having finished the glass of Malaga. 'But the contents of the buttery will have to be extended a trifle, Twinney. One of a long list of things to be discussed in the morning. Meanwhile, you may go.'

'Very good, sir,' said the butler, bowing with an expression perilously close to relief on his face, and beat a hasty retreat.

'There are other things that will be better discussed in the morning,' said Silence, rising abruptly to her feet. 'When you are in a condition to think clearly –'

'I hate to disappoint you, Aunt, but my thoughts are perfectly clear, and a tun of Malaga would make little difference to them. Besides, I am acquainted with gentlemen whose habits make mine seem positively moderate. Perhaps I should invite them here to enliven you all – what else is there to do in this godforsaken little backwater but to eat, drink and be merry?'

'If you dislike it so much, why in God's name did you ever come back to plague us?' It was Charles, goaded into an uncharacteristic rage, his voice cracking with sudden anguish.

Alex leaned back in his chair, one hand curled round the graceful stem of his wine glass, the lax line of his body utterly at odds with his cousin's tense, fraught posture. 'Shall I tell you why, dear Charles? Because Wintercombe is mine. Mine, and not yours. Now do you understand?'

'I think it is best if we leave,' said Silence. She glanced at Amy, caught the girl's eye, and motioned to her to rise. 'If you want to drink yourself into a stupor, Alex, you may, but I for one do not particularly wish to witness such an unedifying spectacle, and I doubt anyone else does either. Charles, perhaps if you would assist your mother? She is still very distressed.'

41

'You could always stay and drink with me,' Alex suggested, grinning suddenly. 'Or are you still too much the milksop to risk it?'

Louise, watching, wondered for a moment if he had at last achieved his obvious aim and provoked the younger man to lose control. She saw Charles's hands clench into fists, and his jaw tighten, and felt suddenly ashamed of herself. She had promised her support, and she had failed him. She got to her feet with a rustle of silk, and said pointedly, 'It is not the action of a milksop to refuse to behave like a repellent boor. He probably finds you quite as disgusting as I do.'

Bab, still sobbing, had already waddled out of the room on her daughter's arm. Silence waited by the door, and Phoebe, awkward but determined, had struggled to her feet and was hobbling doggedly towards her. Louise walked round behind Alex, taking good care to stay well out of his reach, and stood beside Charles. To her distress, she saw that he was trembling, and touched his arm. 'Come, Cousin. Let's go, and leave him to pickle in his own wine fumes.'

Alex laughed, a brutally contemptuous sound that seemed to bring Charles back from a very great distance. He started, and stared at Louise as if she had appeared beside him by magic. 'Lou?'

'Let's leave,' she said and, taking his arm, led him from the dining parlour. Silence, her usually serene face almost unrecognisably grim, shut the door behind them, and the sound of Alex's derisive, mocking laughter followed them all the way up the stairs to the safety of their own chambers.

It had, indeed, been a most memorable evening.

# 3
## 'Who from faults is free?'

'I won't go – I *won't*! This is my *home*!'

Louise and Silence exchanged glances over the top of Bab's lace-capped, quivering head. For an hour or more, they had attempted to calm her, but all their efforts, the soothing words, the cup of hot sweet chocolate, the sedative limeflower cordial, had been to no avail. And despite her dislike for her aunt, Louise could not help but feel pity for the broken, distraught woman sobbing in her bed. Away from Alex's charismatic presence, the scene in the dining parlour seemed neither amusing nor exciting, but left a sour and bitter taste in the mouth. I hope his head hurts tomorrow, she thought savagely. I hope he feels like death.

'I'll speak to him,' Silence said softly, Bab's soft, plump white hands encased within her own, wrinkled and veined with age and long labour in garden and stillroom. 'Bab, he may listen to me. I can't promise anything, but he may listen. And even if he doesn't, is it so bad? A house in Bath, perhaps, convenient and cosy, you'll have Amy and Charles with you, and Beck too – think of it, Bab, your own little house!'

'I don't want it – I want to stay here!'

Silence looked down at her daughter-in-law and shook her head sadly. 'Oh, Bab – we'll do our best for you. But in the end, you know, it is his decision, and his alone.'

'So cruel!' A fresh convulsion of sobbing rippled along the massive rolls of fat. 'Cruel and heartless!'

'Well, yes, I think we'd all agree with you there,' said Silence drily. She gently removed her hands, and got stiffly to her feet. 'In this damp weather, I'll swear my joints creak. Beck?'

Bab's maid came forward, her face tense with concern. 'Yes, m'lady?'

'Have you mixed up the poppy draught?'

'Here it be, m'lady.'

At last, Bab was persuaded to drink the bitter potion, and gradually her sobs died away into the regular snores of a deep and apparently peaceful slumber. Silence watched over her until she was sure that her daughter-in-law slept, and then ushered Louise from the large, pleasant chamber above the library which Bab had occupied for many years.

The house around them was dark and hushed. Silence stood listening for a moment, her face, in the soft flattering light of the candle, lent a deceptive illusion of youth, so that Louise saw how she might have looked forty years ago, when this house had been garrisoned by enemy soldiers, and she alone had stood between Wintercombe and destruction. It was hard to connect this gentle, serene old woman, with her aching joints and spectacles and silver hair, with that Lady St Barbe whose heroism was still a legend in Philip's Norton, and who had saved her home, her servants and her children from the evil Colonel Ridgeley. But Louise, who over the past two months had come to love and admire her grandmother very much, had also discerned the core of steel beneath that apparently soft exterior.

'Goodnight, Gran'mère,' she said, but Silence put out a hand to detain her. 'No, not yet, Louise. I want to talk to you. Come to my chamber.'

Their eyes met: the older woman's a warm, greenish hazel, not yet faded, and the girl's the same unusual chestnut brown possessed by her mother Kate, and also by the man who had once, forty years ago, been Silence's secret lover, and was now her husband. Louise smiled, bright with mischief and exactly like Kate. 'Are you going to take me to task, Gran'mère?'

'Of course I am,' said Silence, smiling in response, and steered her wayward granddaughter briskly within her chamber.

It was a large and comfortable room, with an old-fashioned steeply pitched ceiling, heavily beamed, and a grandiose fireplace surmounted by the St Barbe arms. At this late hour, the coals were smouldering quietly in the grate, and Silence's maid, Fan Howard, had placed a warming pan in the bed and a pot of spiced chocolate on a trivet in the hot ashes of the hearth, before retiring to her closet.

Louise took the cup of chocolate that her grandmother handed to her, and sat down in one of the chairs by the fire. This chamber had belonged to her Uncle Nat, and he had died in that bed, with his grieving stepmother and beloved daughter by his side. She had felt almost excluded by their sorrow, as if she herself had had no right to mourn him. Yet in her brief months at Wintercombe, she too had come to value and to love him. She had thought it a little strange at the time that Silence had moved into this chamber only a week or so after Nat's death. Now she wondered suddenly if, by so doing, her grandmother had sought to become closer to her stepson's departed spirit.

With the cup of chocolate warm between her hands and the rich thick taste of it on her lips, she said, 'Are you intending to warn me about Alex?'

Silence gave her a startled glance, then laughed rather ruefully. 'Yes. Am I becoming so easy to read, then, in my old age?'

44

'It was the obvious thing for you to do,' Louise pointed out. 'And I know exactly what you have in mind to say, Gran'mère. He is dangerous and dissolute, a libertine who is ruthless and selfish and will quite probably attempt to seduce me. Am I right?'

'Well,' said Silence, surveying her forthright granddaughter in some surprise, 'yes, you are – though I doubt I'd have spoken so bluntly.'

Louise grinned at her. She did not much resemble Kate, save in those chestnut eyes, and more brilliantly in her wide, three-cornered, mischievous smile. The long, brown-skinned face, the aquiline nose and thin spiky brows had looked very handsome on her seafaring father, less so upon Louise. Silence found herself wondering afresh why Amy should be so much lovelier, and yet could appear so bland and insipid beside her lively cousin.

'I feel I can be blunt with you, Gran'mère,' Louise said, in explanation. 'You arc like my mother – the truth does not shock you.'

'Unlike your poor stepfather,' said Silence drily. 'Let us hope that his own daughters do not have half your capacity for mischief, or they'll drive him into an early grave.'

'I doubt it – Felice was thinking about becoming a nun when I left.' Louise shook her head, smiling. 'I am glad that Maman insisted that I did not turn Papist – even though life is being made so difficult now in France for Protestant people. I don't think I would enjoy life in a convent very much.'

Silence, looking at her granddaughter, thought that something of an understatement. She forced her mind sternly back to the task she had set herself, and said quietly, 'I doubt that you would. But, Louise, I am serious. You cannot flirt with Alex, or bandy words with him, as if he were some callow boy. He isn't like Charles – I have seen his sort before, and he is *dangerous*, Louise – he is quite capable of ruining you.'

'Gran'mère, listen. I realise that I may seem very young to you – I am only nineteen, after all. But my life in France was nothing like this. Here it is very quiet and rural, and even though Amy is only a little younger than I am, she has done nothing, seen nothing, been nowhere, save to Bath. I have been presented to King Louis, I have danced at the French court and welcomed my parents' friends in their absence – and,' Louise added, with that sudden, delightful grin, 'I have been rude to more importunate sprigs of nobility than either you or Amy have ever met in your life. I'm not a green girl, Gran'mère – I can look after myself.'

'I don't doubt it,' Silence said, with truth. 'But . . . Alex is no importunate sprig of nobility, either. All his life he has been able to get whatever he wants, by fair means or foul. If you should for any reason give him cause to notice you, to think that you might not be averse to his advances, then whatever your intentions, or your feelings, you might find him very hard to resist.'

'He is very attractive,' said Louise, and grinned again. 'Like Master Milton's Lucifer, too much so for anyone's ease or comfort.'

'I didn't know you had read *Paradise Lost*,' Silence said in surprise, for Louise, active and horse-loving, had seemed as little addicted to books as she was to sewing.

'I haven't – but Phoebe described the plot to me,' Louise told her candidly. 'She's given me a nodding acquaintance with most of the books in the library – with her as my tutor, I've no need of any further education!' She paused, her smile fading, and then added, 'Phoebe isn't very fond of her brother, is she?'

'It would be surprising if she was,' Silence pointed out. 'Alex spent his entire childhood treating her with disdain at best, and outright unkindness at worst. Whatever small affection she may feel for him now he has had to earn from her – and Phoebe, I know, has made him work very hard for it. And she isn't afraid to tell him exactly what she thinks of him, whereas the rest of us, I feel, tend to skirt round him rather gingerly, in case we provoke an explosion.' She glanced at her granddaughter, and Louise gazed blandly back, her face spuriously innocent. 'Present company excepted, of course.'

Louise laughed softly. 'I am sorry, Gran'mère. I don't *wish* to make him angry, but somehow I seem to say the things that do. Maman always said I was an impertinent little minx . . . Why are you smiling?'

'Because she was just the same as a child.'

'Yes, I expect she was.' Louise thought of her vivacious mother, her dazzling smile and captivating ways, and was assailed with a sudden pang of longing for home, for France, where the company was so lively, and life full of excitement and laughter, and she understood the rules of all the games.

But she was here in England, and so was Alex, unpredictable and wild, and perhaps Wintercombe would not prove so dull in the future. She said slowly, thinking aloud, 'When he visited us at the château, he was never so . . . malicious. He was amusing, he made everyone laugh, even my stepfather, although everything he did was so outrageous and unconventional – we called him "*l'anglais fou*". And now . . . now, it's almost as if he's another person, someone quite different, he's changed so much.' A small, self-mocking smile curled her mouth. 'He used to be my hero, when I was thirteen.'

'And is he still?'

'No!' said Louise, with a vehemence that surprised her. 'No, not at all. I don't much care for Bab, but she didn't deserve such treatment, and Charles certainly doesn't.' She stared thoughtfully at Silence. 'Why? Why has he changed so much?'

Her grandmother was quiet for a long moment. She sipped her chocolate, slowly and deliberately, and gazed unseeing into the fire as she pondered the problem. Louise finished her own drink and set it down carefully among the warm, gentle grey ashes at the edge of the hearth. The slight clunk as the thick glazed pottery met the stone flags seemed to rouse Silence from her reverie. She gave a little start, and turned to face Louise, an apologetic smile on her face. 'I'm sorry – I was years away. A common fault, I'm afraid, in the old.'

'I can never think of you as old, Gran'mère,' said Louise, with perfect truth. 'I *know* that you are, but you don't seem to *feel* it, somehow.'

'Good,' Silence said briskly. 'Because I don't feel it either, despite the legions of my grandchildren, and even step-great-grandchildren. One of the greatest burdens of advancing age is to feel as young as a girl in your heart, and to see only wrinkled flesh when you gaze in your mirror . . . but then I've never been known for a beauty, only for my common sense, and increasing years are an excellent enhancer of the latter, though not the former. So you could say that I am lucky.' She paused, and her eyes were suddenly sad. 'Patience would have hated to be old. If she had not died bearing Phoebe, she would be sixty this year. Oh, no, age would not have sat lightly on her shoulders, she was much too lively and pretty for such indignities.'

'Was she much like you?' Louise asked. She had heard very little of Patience, Lady St Barbe, Nat's wife, mother of Alex and Phoebe, and her grandmother's sister. Her own mother had spoken of her occasionally, and from her anecdotes Louise had received an impression of a rather flighty but enchanting woman, not a little resembling Kate herself. And Kate, it was plain, had in childhood adored her.

'Not in the least like me,' Silence told her, smiling reminiscently. 'She was nine years the younger, to begin with, and as warm and pretty as sunlight. We always used to joke about our names; that I could not be silent, and Pru could not be careful, and Patience . . . well, she was always known as Impatience, or Imp. Everyone loved her, even our father, who mistrusted laughter and levity – she learned to twist him around her finger before she could walk. My own children were enslaved, too. And Nat . . . Nat saw everything so clearly, he always did, he could see straight through her wiles, and still he loved her . . . more than anything or anyone else, I think.'

The chamber was quiet, save for the soft sounds of the fire, and a buffeting noise outside the curtains: the wind was getting up. Silence leaned forward and placed a log firmly at the back of the grate, where the glow was brightest. She added, glancing up at Louise, 'And she loved him. Gossip may come to your ears from time to time, for she was so lovely, and flirting was as natural to her as breathing – half the gentry in these parts, from boys hardly old enough to shave, to gatfers in their dotage, fancied themselves in love with her. But she was never unfaithful, she adored Nat to the end, and he likewise. And he was so proud of Alex when he was a child, very like Patience, a delightful little boy ... she had difficulty conceiving, several babes miscarried, before Phoebe ... and then she died. Nat was distraught – nothing in his philosophy could accept her death.' She smiled sadly. 'He attended church, he spoke with the vicar, he did nothing to upset people, but he never believed, he never had faith. I think he thought at heart that it was all an empty mummery, with no more significance than a child lighting a candle because it is afraid of the dark. And when Patience died, his darkness was impenetrable. He shut himself away, and became very distant. He didn't seem to care about the baby, or about Alex, he didn't even seem to notice them. Of course to Phoebe, being so tiny and so frail, it meant nothing – she had to struggle so hard just to survive. But Alex – I think he felt that he had been orphaned twice over. I took him to Chard for a while, I thought he would be happier there than at Wintercombe, and Nat didn't object – and he was like a little ghost, so quiet and wan you hardly knew he was there. He'd been so close to his mother, all children adored her. And now she had gone for ever, and his father had turned his back on him, or so it must have seemed, and all he had in return was some wailing useless scrap for a sister. Small wonder he was so unkind to her – and small wonder that when he returned to Wintercombe, his behaviour deteriorated so markedly.' She sighed. 'At first, I think he was trying to make Nat notice him. When it didn't work, he became more and more outrageous – and to be honest, I'm sure he enjoyed it, too. Mischief is so much more amusing than obedience, after all. Oh, there's no point in futile regrets, and it's such a very long time ago, but if Patience had not died, I think Alex now would be very different.'

Louise thought of her grandmother's sister, all that vitality and laughter so cruelly snuffed out, leaving as legacy only her husband's grief, and two children who were, in different ways, crippled by the premature loss of their mother. A sense of her own immense good fortune crept over her. True, she had lost her own father, drowned in a shipwreck, but so early that she barely remembered him. Soon after his death, her mother, still very young, had attracted the attention of the Vicomte de St Clair, saddled with an ailing and barren wife, and had very swiftly captured his heart. He, and not the shadowy Guernsey sea captain, had been the father of her childhood, a handsome, intense, passionate man, accustomed to his own way, yet curiously conventional. Alex, the mad Englishman, unbound by aristocratic restraint, had taken him completely aback. The vicomte's money, his status and security, and above all his love for Kate, had provided the haven of her early years. She had never suffered great loss, and her rebellions had been almost light-hearted, springing from her own nature rather than from repression. She had been loved, tolerated, even indulged, surrounded by a growing brood of young half-brothers and half-sisters, and given a splendid home when the vicomte's wife at last died and he was free to marry his mistress Kate.

But Alex . . . Alex had been alone.

'Don't feel too sorry for him,' said Silence, who had been watching her closely. 'We are none of us entirely children of circumstance – we are also what God, and our own nature, make of us. And cruelty is something which I will never, ever condone in someone who is old enough to know better, no matter what the excuse.'

Louise knew that she was thinking of Bab, a foolish, irritating woman, but one who was, surely, too insignificant a target to merit the quantity of vitriol which had been poured over her. She shook her head, still unable to reconcile the present Alex, so liberally unpleasant, with the young man who had enchanted her and Kate nearly seven years ago. She was sure that her admiration had not entirely been due to the uncritical and impressionable ignorance of youth.

In any case, that cruelty had not yet been directed at her: and when, if, it was, she knew that she was more than capable of defending herself.

'But he was so different before,' she said, almost to herself. 'He was not nasty, or unkind, or brutal. He was so amusing, such good company – it was a wonderful summer. What has happened to him since then, Gran'mère?'

For a while, Silence did not speak, the cup of chocolate cold in her hands. Finally, she said slowly, 'I don't know, Louise, I really don't know. When was it?'

'I was thirteen, so it must have been six years ago last summer.'

'Sixteen seventy-eight,' said Silence thoughtfully. 'The year of the Plot.' She saw her granddaughter's look of puzzlement, and explained. 'Have you not heard of the Popish Plot, that had all London, if not England, in a ferment? Discovered, or invented, by a singularly unpleasant man called Titus Oates.'

'Ah,' said Louise, on more certain ground. 'I have heard of him.

Charles spoke of it once. I must admit I did not pay very much attention, but he did say that the whole affair was fabricated by this man Oates.'

'Charles would say that,' Silence pointed out. 'He is, after all, a Papist himself, and felt threatened by such talk of plots.' She hesitated, unwilling to enter into all the tortuous and tangled complexities of the infamous Plot, of which, she suspected, no one save Oates and his fellows would ever know the exact and doubtless unsavoury truth. Moreover, Louise, for all her English blood, had been reared in France, and doubtless had little interest in stale English political scandals. Finally, she said, 'Charles was only a boy at the time, and until then I don't think he had taken his mother's faith very seriously. The Plot made him examine his beliefs closely, and he became committed to popery. A shame, since he could not then go to Oxford, and so many opportunities were barred to him.' She smiled sadly. 'I was reared to hate Papists, but I failed in my duty, it seems. Unlike almost anyone else, I cannot see that they pose a threat – even when the new King is one of their number. They are misguided and stubborn, perhaps, but surely not dangerous. Alex, though – Alex seemed to think otherwise. When he returned to London, some while after his visit to your family, he became mixed up with a faction called the Whigs, and was a friend to the Earl of Shaftesbury, amongst others, and the Duke of Monmouth. So deeply enmeshed, that he was soon one of the leaders of the Green Ribbon Club, and implicated in the design to have the Duke of York, as the King then was, excluded from the throne because he was a Papist. Of course, the plan failed, and King Charles was no fool. Even his bastard son Monmouth, whom he loved, was exiled to the Low Countries, and Lord Shaftesbury died there. Alex went too, ostensibly because of some scandal concerning a married lady, and joined the Dutch army. But I think it is quite possible that he would have been imprisoned if he had stayed in England.'

Louise wished, suddenly, that she had paid more heed to all the confused references to recent English politics. Those of France, despite the wars and the shifting alliances and the persecution of Protestants, seemed to be much simpler. She said, 'Presumably, since he has returned openly, he is no longer in any danger of it.'

'The old King is dead, and the new one may wish to heal old wounds, despite being a Papist,' Silence said. 'Alex may still have influential friends in London ... I don't know.' She smiled ruefully at her granddaughter. 'He is twenty-nine, and since he left Wintercombe at sixteen to go to Oxford, I doubt if he has spent more than a few months altogether here. We have seen so little of him. But if you want to know why he has changed so much ... perhaps the answer lies in those years of exile. He was not poor, he had the money his mother left to him, but he may have grown bitter.' She put her cup down, and surveyed Louise. 'I don't doubt that you are quite able to look after yourself, but you are young, and unmarried, and even in these dissolute days, reputation is a fragile thing. Don't throw away any chance of a good match because you find Alex too tempting.'

If anyone other than Silence had spoken, Louise would have said something impolite. But because she loved her grandmother dearly and did not wish to upset her, she bit back the rude response that rose impulsively in her mind. And besides, the older woman's insistence on the obvious attraction between her and Alex, even in their brief and stormy exchanges at the supper table, was beginning to have a subtle influence on Louise. So thoroughly had she been warned not to contemplate succumbing to his advances, that it now seemed almost inevitable that she would.

And in her heart there was no denying that attraction. He was unpleasant, arrogant, callous and inconsiderate, and she did not even like him: in fact, on the strength of her two encounters with him today, she could fairly say that she detested him. But there was something about his face – the clear strong lines and angles of bone under the pale, taut skin, the blue eyes, the eccentric fact that he wore his own hair, the way his body moved with that prowling, casual grace, the size of him, a presence that dominated the room and imposed itself on everyone there – something that turned her bones to water just thinking of it.

She would not think of it. He was dangerous, ruthless and completely unscrupulous, and if she had any sense, she would have nothing whatsoever to do with him. And if she wanted to be in control of her own life, instead of submitting always to the commands and wishes of others, she must first prove that she could be trusted. There were few men, in France or in England, who would be prepared to wed a young woman with a string of notorious love affairs in her past. They would want to be sure that their heirs were their own.

'Don't worry, Gran'mère,' she said reassuringly. 'What is the phrase? I know which side my bread is buttered. But,' she added drily, 'if I am to marry some wealthy gentleman – and that was the reason I came to England, *n'est-ce pas?* – then where am I to meet them? Since Uncle Nat died, we have had few callers here, and we have not visited anywhere save Bath.'

With a pang of guilt, Silence acknowledged the truth of what she said. She realised suddenly how dull this place – lovely but small, rural, indeed a backwater – must seem to a lively, sophisticated young woman accustomed to the glittering aristocratic life of the St Clairs. No wonder Louise was driven to ride out unaccompanied; no wonder she was attracted to Alex, a gust of fresh and exciting air ripping through the sleepy calm of Wintercombe. And it was tolerably certain that the new baronet would not be entertaining any suitable, eligible bachelors. She had a very good idea of the sort of men who would be Alex's friends, and she did not wish her granddaughter to be ensnared by an impoverished soldier, a dubious cardsharp, or a dissolute drunken wencher.

'Well,' she said, with an air of resolution, 'I intend to change all that. I cannot promise you a husband, Louise, but at least I can ensure that you are introduced to a wider circle than you have known here. You have cousins all over Somerset – there are the Loveridges in Taunton, the Orchards in Bristol, the Wickhams in Glastonbury, as well as my own family at Chard. As soon as Alex has settled in here, shall we do the tour?' Her eyes sparkled in the firelight. 'And who knows . . . you might meet someone interesting.'

'I might indeed,' said Louise, conscious of conflicting emotions. It was true she had fretted and chafed at Wintercombe for the last few months, feeling restricted and bored by this quiet rural life, with nothing to do save ride and sew and read. It was not her home; her uncle, into whose care her mother had entrusted her, was dead, and now her grandmother had assumed responsibility for her. She had heard enough about all these other cousins to make her look forward to meeting them, and only a few hours ago the prospect of riding round Somerset, even in February and March, would have seemed a splendid one, full of interesting possibilities.

So why was her first reaction one of disappointment?

She knew very well, but had no intention of revealing it to Silence, who was looking at her with those wise eyes that were altogether too perceptive. So she expressed her heartfelt pleasure at the idea, and hoped that she had thereby allayed any suspicions that her grandmother might have entertained as to her sincerity.

It was late and she was tired, so she thanked Silence for the advice and the chocolate, and, not without a mild feeling of guilt, kissed her goodnight. She closed the door softly behind her, and stood for a moment in the dark passage outside, her candlestick in her hand, listening to the silent house. Not so quiet tonight, though, for the wind was audible even here, tugging at the stones and howling round the hill on which Wintercombe stood, harbinger perhaps of a wild day on the morrow. In the dark, Louise heard too the muted scuttling and creaking and rustling of an old house at rest: and something else.

Below her, someone was singing very softly. She stood absolutely still, straining her ears to distinguish the tune, but it eluded her. Suddenly curious, she crept to the head of the spiral turret stairs that led to the ground floor, set her candle down at the top, and slipped down the first few steps, feeling her way in the shadows with a hand against the cold, smoothly curved stone of the outside wall, until she could hear more clearly.

It was a song that she knew, that her village maid Christian Birt often sang or hummed as she worked. And there was no doubt about the singer, either, although she had not realised until now that he possessed any interest in music. Crouched still and intent in the dark, Louise listened to her cousin Alex's voice, slurred and roughened but drunkenly tuneful, meandering through the aching, agonised sadness of a ballad so old and so true that it was familiar everywhere:

> 'The water is wide, I cannot cross over,
> And neither have I wings to fly,
> Bring me a boat that will carry two,
> And I will sail my love to you.
>
> Against the stream I dare not go,
> Because the stream it runs too strong.
> I'm deadly feared I'm one of those,
> Who loved an unkind maid too long.
>
> There is a ship that sails the sea,
> She's loaded deep as deep can be,
> But not so deep as the love I'm in,
> I know not if I sink or swim.
>
> I leaned my back unto an oak,
> I thought it was a trusty tree,
> But first it bowed and then it broke,
> And so my true love proved to me.'

There was no more, though she sat on the step for a long while, waiting, a forgotten, thoughtful smile on her face. Then she heard the door of the dining parlour open and close, and the careful, unsteady footsteps passing the foot of the stairs. Not until they had long gone did she rise stiffly to her feet, suddenly conscious of the cold and hardness of the stone and the draught from the narrow little window above her. In the Hall, the longcase clock in which her uncle had taken such pride and delight began to chime

53

the hour. She counted to eleven, and no more: high time she was in bed, enjoying what Amy called her beauty sleep.

Louise grinned to herself, well aware that she would never be beautiful, even if she slept for a hundred years. She turned and crept back up to her shrinking candle and the warm embrace of her bed, snug against the cold gale outside. It was not long before she slept: but even so, the sound of that unexpectedly melodious voice, drunkenly singing of false love and unfaithfulness, echoed in her ears until slumber overtook her.

The wind had abated by morning, leaving a scattering of leafy and twiggy debris heaped in corners of the courtyard. In the stables, the grooms had been up since the cold first light of dawn, feeding and tending their charges. There were fifteen of these, ranging from stout brood mares, heavily in foal, through the various riding horses belonging to members of the family and the slightly less handsome animals placed at the disposal of the servants, to the beautiful and exalted creature which the new master of Wintercombe had brought with him from Holland.

When Louise entered the dim, aromatic stables, the entire staff, three in number, were gathered by the loosebox at the far end. As she walked down the narrow cobbled passageway between the stalls, the heels of her boots clopping sharply on the stones, and the vast trailing skirt of her habit draped over one arm, the familiar heads, brown, bay and chestnut, swung out to greet her.

'So this is where everyone is! Good morning, Dan.'

'Good day to ee, Mistress Louise,' said Pardice, the head groom. He was a small, wiry man in his forties, with thinning sandy hair and shrewd blue eyes. He had originally set Louise down as just another aristocratic nincompoop, certain she knew best and always insistent on the most spirited mounts, and had told the stable lads that she was unquestionably riding for a fall. In less than a week, he had discovered that Mistress Kate's French daughter was a skilled and confident horsewoman, knowledgeable about the strengths and weaknesses of the animals she rode, well versed in effective remedies and not afraid to put on a saddle and bridle for herself, nor to brush out mud and dust and prepare feeds and poultices. During her six months at Wintercombe, each had come to recognise the other as an expert, perhaps with some difference of opinion upon the finer points of horse management, but with a considerable amount of mutual respect.

'What do ee think of en?' Pardice asked her, and added to the two boys, short Renolds and long Earle, 'Do ee stand aside, lads, and let Mistress Louise looksee!'

Hastily, they leaped back, and gave her a clear view of the occupant of the loosebox. She walked right up to the bars which stretched from the wooden partition up to the ceiling. The area enclosed was some twelve feet square, a generous size – many poor families had less space in which to live – and held a manger, well filled with hay, a leather bucket of water, a considerable quantity of straw, and a horse.

She had already seen this particular beast, of course, plodding exhausted and mud-stained up the hill to Wintercombe the previous afternoon. Even then, she had marked its quality. Now, clean and groomed, fed and rested, the grey stallion stood beneath the one small, rather cobwebby window, and accepted their admiration as his due.

Louise rested her elbows on the top of the partition and put her right hand through the bars, palm upwards, a piece of carrot temptingly displayed. She clucked softly in her throat, and the horse, interested, swung his head and studied her with large, intelligent eyes, the silvery ears pricked. He stepped leisurely to the partition, blew gently on her hand, and took the carrot with evident enjoyment.

'What a beauty!' said Henry Renolds, his round ruddy face glowing with adoration. 'Be he a Turk or a Barb, Mistress Louise?'

'He has the blood, certainly,' she said, running a finger down the silky dark muzzle, feeling the warm life beneath the velvet smoothness. 'See his dark skin? That's a sure sign of a Barb. But I don't think he's purebred, he's too tall. Have you measured him, Dan?'

'Sixteen hand and an inch,' said the head groom. 'And five year old, to judge by his teeth and his colour. That dappled grey allus turn white by the time they see ten. And sweet-tempered as a baby, so he be.'

'I can tell,' said Louise. She held out another piece of carrot, purloined from the kitchen where it had been intended to form part of a warming winter pottage. 'He must be a wonderful ride.'

'Oh, no,' said Dan Pardice at once. 'Oh, no, Mistress – Sir Alexander, he said most particular last night – nobody to ride him save hisself.'

'I see,' said Louise thoughtfully. More than anything, she longed to feel this big, powerful horse beneath her, to blend with the rhythm of his gallop, to sense the wind in her face and exult in the knowledge that she was in control of the swiftest and most beautiful horse in all Somerset. For no other animal she had seen, in all her time in England, could compare with the lovely, gentle grey stallion, who had taken the carrot from her hand without touching her skin. Even her stepfather's purebred chestnut Barb, all fire and brimstone – he had been dubbed 'Petard' with reason – was no more splendid than this magnificent creature.

55

'Has he a name?' she asked Dan. The groom shook his head. 'No, Mistress Louise, not that I know of.'

'He is called Pagan,' said her cousin's voice, so close behind her that it took a considerable effort to conceal her surprise. Deliberately, eyebrows raised, she turned and surveyed him. He was dressed for riding, in the same dark clothes he had worn on his arrival the previous day. As she had noticed before, his garments seemed to have been shrugged on without much care, and his neckcloth was loosely and hastily knotted. That, and his coiling dark hair, gave him a distinctly slovenly appearance, at odds with his immaculate attire at supper. Louise, not without satisfaction, noted his pale face, the taut shadowed lines around his eyes, and the frown between his long level brows. He looked exactly as she would have expected after a night of drinking, and he undoubtedly had a headache.

'Good morning, Cousin,' she said, with her best and falsest smile, and inclined her head. 'We were admiring your horse. Is he indeed part Barb, or Turk?'

'His sire was an Arabian from the Prince of Orange's stables, and his dam was a Spanish mare,' Alex said. 'And I trust you were not thinking of climbing on his back.'

'Nothing could have been further from my mind,' said Louise, archly and with transparent innocence.

Undeceived, he raised his eyebrows and turned to Pardice with a curt list of enquiries concerning Pagan's well-being. Louise, unaccountably annoyed, caught young Henry's eye. 'Can you saddle Nance for me?'

The bay mare was standing by the mounting-block, Louise checking girth and breastplate, when Pardice emerged from the stable, leading Pagan. The big stallion looked almost asleep as he ambled after the groom, but she saw the length of his stride, and knew that the grey's somnolent manner was deceptive. It was likely that he was in fact possessed of considerable speed, and likely, too, that within a short time all those sporting gentlemen who raced their fastest horses on the wide bare downs above Bath in the summer would be bringing their best mares hopefully to Wintercombe.

She mounted Nance while Henry held the bay's bridle, and arranged the heavy, soft dove-grey skirts of her riding habit. When she looked up, Alex was there, Pagan's reins looped over his arm, his hat pushed on his head at an angle, his face unsmiling. 'Are you riding alone, Cousin?'

Damn him. Louise kept her voice level and cool. 'It is my usual practice. Do you object?'

'Not at all – if you are happy to risk lying undiscovered in a ditch all day, who am I to gainsay you? But it seems churlish to ride out at the same time and go our separate ways – so, Cousin Louise, will you accompany me?'

A small red devil gibbered temptingly on one shoulder, and on the other, her conscience, freshly burdened, urged her to decline. She was no green girl, however, and she was well aware that she was risking her good name, at the least, by consorting with him.

There was, however, an easy remedy for that. 'Of course,' she said, resisting the impulse to comment that he was eminently qualified to judge churlishness. 'If we can just wait for the groom . . . Henry! Hurry and saddle up, will you? We shall be riding along the Wellow Lane – you can catch us up.'

'Yes, Mistress Louise,' said the boy, startled but willing, and scuttled back into the stable.

Louise, her honour safeguarded, glanced sideways at her cousin, and surprised a look of amusement on his face. 'Very wise,' said Alex approvingly. 'Although I always find February so *cold* for an outdoor rape, don't you? Far better to wait for warmer weather – or to do the deed in a nice soft, comfortable bed. Though of course one misses the thistles and nettles – they always add a certain *je ne sais quoi*, don't you think?'

'I wouldn't know,' said Louise coldly, praying that her suffocating urge to laughter was not nakedly displayed on her face. She turned Nance, largely so that she could hide her expression from him, and rode out of the stable yard and on to the track which ran past Wintercombe on the crest of the hill.

To her left lay the huddled miscellany of buildings collectively known as the Barton farm; to the right, down in the valley, the muddy lane along the Norton Brook, where she usually rode. She turned Nance's head that way, wishing that she had Shadow beneath her instead of this sedate, lazy old mare. But perhaps, given Alex's presence, it was as well she did not. She had already decided not to mention anything concerning last night, if possible, and to avoid arousing any of that blistering ire. He had expressed a wish to ride in her company: that boded well, and she wanted, with surprising force, to rediscover the Alex she had known long ago and never forgotten. Even now, even after the unpleasant scenes at supper, she could not believe that it had all been a childish illusion. With Henry's presence, albeit at a distance, she could preserve a semblance of decorum, even if their talk was less proper. And if it was, Louise, her wit and conversational skills honed in her mother's company, knew that she was more than a match for her cousin.

Hoofbeats sounded lazily behind her, and a silver-grey nose drew alongside. Still looking sternly ahead, she asked, 'Where did you acquire him?'

'Pagan? He was owned by an acquaintance of mine,' said Alex. 'And "acquired" is probably the right word. He was payment for a debt.'

'A debt of dishonour?' Louise enquired, and had the reward of a laugh.

'Of course. My extraordinary luck at cards is one of my more respectable attributes.'

'Really? Then you don't cheat.'

'Not unless it's absolutely necessary, no.'

'A very useful skill,' Louise said reflectively. She risked a turn of her head, and saw his profile, pale and faintly smiling, edged in the wan light of a feeble February sun. 'Perhaps you will teach me, when we have the leisure? I would dearly love to beat Amy at piquet.'

'By all means, sweet Cousin – though I would have thought it was unnecessary to cheat in order to beat Amy at anything.'

'Believe me, at piquet she is a demon.'

'Perhaps she cheats.'

'Perhaps she does.' Louise shrugged. 'Since I've never lost more than pence to her, it doesn't seem to matter.'

'Still, you may well find yourself playing for higher stakes one day.'

'If the stakes included Pagan, I would cast all my scruples to the wind,' said Louise. 'Those which I still possess, of course.' She glanced behind: Henry, on a fat shaggy brown cob, had come into view, trotting doggedly down the hill. She turned back to Alex, and met his vivid blue gaze, bent unwaveringly upon her. It was a mistake: somehow, she could not look away, nor would her pride permit her to do so.

'Scruples,' said her cousin softly. 'I was unaware that you were familiar with the word, sweet Louise.'

'On the contrary,' she said instantly, despite all her earlier good intentions. 'My command of English is quite excellent. From all the evidence, yours is more deficient.' And she forced herself not to flinch under the intensity of those brilliant eyes, already regretting her words.

But Alex had always been unpredictable. The storm failed to break: he gave a sudden wild shout of laughter that brought Pagan's head up like a startled stag's. 'No, Cousin, I dance to no one's music but my own, and I'll warn you, it's a morning too pleasant for picking quarrels. Is this lane fit for a gallop?'

They had reached the end of the Wintercombe track and the road, muddy and narrow, running between Philip's Norton and Wellow. Louise nodded. 'Yes – it's rather wet at present, but not enough to be risky. Not many people use this route – the highway on the hill may be longer, but it's drier, and more convenient.'

'Excellent,' said Alex. He smiled at her suddenly, startling her; before she realised it, she had bestowed on him the same glowing, mischievous grin that only her close friends usually saw. 'You go ahead,' she told him, as if, given the quality of her mount, she had any choice in the matter. 'Henry and I will jog along behind.'

'Without a chaperone? For shame, sweet Louise,' said Alex, and twitched Pagan's reigns. 'See you in a mile or two.'

She had been right: the grey was surpassing swift. She held Nance firmly in check as he exploded away from her, the silver mane and tail flying and Alex crouched over his back, his coat whipping behind him, heedless of mud and water, cold and wind.

'Lord a' mercy!' said Henry's high voice in amazed admiration. 'That horse d'have wings, I reckon.'

'I wish he did – he wouldn't throw up so much mud,' said Louise, glancing down at her besplattered skirts. 'Well, Henry, I suppose we'd better follow on, in case they end in a ditch.'

Nance was no Shadow, but Louise had ridden her regularly all winter, and she was fit, hardy and willing. She needed little encouragement to break into a brisk but uninspiring canter, and even to extend, on firmer ground, to a gallop. Louise kept her eye on the lane unwinding in front of them, guiding the mare away from the deeper puddles and ruts, aware of Henry, toiling distantly behind, and more so of Alex, somewhere ahead. A part of her, the malicious part, would have relished his coming to grief in a ditch, but it was most unlikely, even in this soft chancy ground. He had always ridden like a centaur.

And sure enough, he was waiting for her, a mile or so further on, where the hills crowded in on either side, and trees grew close to the lane. Pagan, mud-splattered and gently steaming in the cold air, was sampling the scanty contents of the hedgerow, while his rider sat relaxed on his back, his feet out of the stirrups, and watched her approach. Nance blew hard as she pulled up, and Louise was guiltily aware that she would not usually have ridden her so fast and so far.

'I can see why you were riding that big dark bay yesterday,' said Alex, as the mare came to a breathless halt beside him. 'This old nag sounds like a pair of leaking bellows. I take back all I said to you then – you may take the gelding in future.'

'For the pleasure of fishing me out of a ditch?' Louise enquired caustically.

'Of course. Though I can see that you are not usually at risk of such an accident.'

It was the nearest to a compliment that he had yet offered her. Once, long ago, the child Louise would almost have died to earn those words, and hearing them, would have blushed and said something distracting and silly. The adult Louise gave him her wide, cool stare, and inclined her head in graceful acceptance. 'I do prefer to ride Shadow. He might at least make a show of keeping up with you. Do you plan to race Pagan?'

'I might – though my need of the prize money is not so acute these days. But my main purpose in bringing him here was to improve the Wintercombe stock. My late father was more concerned with cattle and sheep than horses, as I remember. Is there a stallion here at present?'

'There was, until about a year ago – or so Dan told me. A bay called Red Robin. He was Nance's sire.'

Alex's rather disparaging gaze travelled along her mount's undistinguished and mud-splattered bulk. 'Not the most shining example of his progeny, I trust?'

'Dan says that Nance was one of his best.' Louise patted the mare's russet neck with affection. 'She's a good, willing horse, she'll plod along all day and she's never been lame in her life – but she's hardly in Pagan's class, is she?'

'Hardly – but, you never know, she may prove to be an adequate brood mare. I have plans for the Wintercombe stables,' said Alex reflectively. 'Pagan forms the chief part of them, but I may have need of your advice and expertise, Cousin.'

'Mine?' Louise, startled, looked round.

'Yes, yours. I have not passed my brief hours here entirely in drunken debauch. I spent a while talking to Pardice last night. He has a high opinion of your horse sense.'

To her extreme discomfiture, Louise felt herself blushing. She said coolly, 'Does he, indeed?'

' "Mistress Louise d'know more about horses than the rest of they put together," ' Alex said, his mimicry of Pardice's gravelly voice wickedly exact. 'Apparently, you are the best judge of a nag's qualities in this part of Somerset, and if I need an opinion on the finer points of a stallion or a brood mare, "Mistress Louise d'have a sound eye and a sure touch." '

'I'm flattered,' she said, trying not to laugh. 'But I don't think such abilities rate very high on any list of suitable ladylike accomplishments, do you?'

'Lady?' said Alex, opening his eyes very wide. 'Who said anything about ladies?'

'I certainly didn't – and I had no idea you had a wide acquaintance with the breed,' said Louise drily. 'I thought your, er, friends were of a different sort altogether.'

'Of course they are – life is then so much more amusing,' Alex said. He

60

glanced at Henry, looking bored and faintly bewildered some distance away, and added wickedly, 'And what of you, sweet Louise? Are you a lady, or a well-disguised *fille de joie?*'

It was long past time to end this conversation, but she could not resist one last sally. 'It depends on the company I keep,' she said. 'But unfortunately for you, Cousin, I'm not yet tempted to progress beyond idle banter. Come on, Nance!'

There was, of course, no hope of outrunning Pagan. Before the bay mare had had time to cover more than a few yards, she heard the stallion's hoofbeats, loud and squelching in the mud, and then he was flying past her as if she and Nance were standing still. She had a brief glimpse of his hand, raised in salutation, and the flash of his smile, before man and horse had vanished round a twist in the lane, with only the faintly diminishing sound of their progress, and her mired and besplattered skirt, to indicate that they had ever been there.

Honour had been maintained, and satisfied. Smiling reminiscently, Louise turned Nance and sent her jogging unhurried back to Winter-combe, with Henry Renolds, bemused and uncomplaining, a few paces behind.

# 4

## 'Wild ambition'

'Ah, Charles. That was very prompt – come in.'

Charles, faced with Alex at his most spuriously expansive and charming, stood solid and suspicious just inside the library door. He had never really liked this room, despite its handsome proportions, the splendidly capacious fireplace, and the four wide windows giving a tantalising glimpse of the neat, formal terraced gardens that stepped down to the orchard and stream on Wintercombe's southern face. It was only thirty years since his uncle, who had leanings to the scholarly and was something of a bibliophile, had added it to the existing medieval building, and already the new stonework was virtually indistinguishable from the old. Charles had always considered it to be badly sited: surely it would have been better to have extended another part of the house, perhaps along the courtyard. But family legend, usually reliable, held that since an addition to any other part of the house would have meant sacrificing one of the lovely oriel windows, or, worse, part of the terraced garden, Silence had put her foot down. So the library now had a dark little antechamber, once a stillroom and buttery, with two arched openings, previously windows, leading into the library itself, which had been built over a large part of the dispensable kitchen garden.

He walked forward, under the left-hand arch and into the light. Alex sat at the central table, which was piled and scattered with papers and account books. Charles's eye, less acute than that of Louise, failed to discern any signs of the previous night's debauch. He stared at his childhood tormenter with stony dislike, and Alex, quite unaffected, smiled breezily back. 'You look as if you've lost a guinea and found a groat. I apologise unreservedly for my behaviour last night, and particularly for the distress I caused your mother. In explanation, I can only say that "drink, sir, is a great provoker".'

Charles, ignorant of most of the works of Shakespeare, said stiffly, 'I find it hard to forgive your words at supper, but I shall make a sincere effort to do so. And I trust that you will moderate your excesses from now on? Remember, my sister and my cousins are of tender and innocent years.'

'I doubt I will forget that fact,' said Alex, in a drawl which did nothing to allay Charles's suspicions. 'However, I haven't asked you here to discuss my habits, repellent though you may find them. I understand you've been greatly concerned in the management of the estate, and I shall benefit considerably from your opinions and advice.'

His cousin stared at him in amazed disbelief. 'You want *my* advice?'

'Of course. You've lived here for most of your life, have you not? Whereas I have been, up until now, something of a fleeting bird of passage, "flying upon the wings of the wind".'

Charles did recognise that quotation: he thought it was from one of the psalms. Since he had never encountered anyone so ungodly as Alex – at least Uncle Nat had had the decency to hide his doubts from public view – his suspicions were increased. He took the chair which his cousin pushed towards him, and sat down as gingerly as if taking tea with Lucifer.

'I'll give you a long spoon if you like,' Alex said, grinning maliciously, and so aptly that Charles almost jumped. 'But I promise, for what it's worth, that I am, at present, stone cold sober and unlikely to bite. Now, I've skimmed through the account books, and all seems to be in order and very healthy indeed, but there are one or two questions I'd like answered. Tell me about William Crowe.'

'Crowe?' said Charles, surprised. 'He's the bailiff, lives in the cottage by the new barton, just up the lane. Uncle Nat engaged him last year – he'd been with the Horners before, I believe. He's very well thought of in the village – devout, conscientious, likely to be elected churchwarden very soon, from all accounts.'

'Trustworthy?'

'I would have thought so,' Charles said. 'I've never had cause to doubt him, and neither did your father.'

'Good. A reliable bailiff is an invaluable asset, don't you think?' said Alex, with that smile that had always raised the hairs on the back of his cousin's neck. 'Does he know anything about horses?'

'Well, no more than anyone else here,' said Charles, a small puzzled frown between his rather heavy brows. 'Pardice is the expert – and Lou, of course. Crowe is more interested in growing these newfangled crops – turnips, French grass, that sort of thing. Why do you ask?'

'Because I plan to breed from the stallion I brought with me from Holland. From what I've seen, the quality of the stable here is abysmal, but if I purchase a half-dozen good brood mares, and perhaps another stallion close to Pagan's class, it won't take too long to make a marked improvement in the stock. Do you know if any other gentlemen hereabouts breed horses?'

Charles looked at him blankly. 'Well, of course almost everyone does, in a small way, riding horses for their own use mostly, but round here there's little more. Down in the Levels, though, near Bridgwater or Glastonbury, that's the place to go. Cousin Wickham is a noted dealer – your father used to go to him, or his friends, if he needed new blood.'

'Then I shall seek his advice too,' said Alex. He shuffled through a few papers, and came up with a small neat piece of parchment, trailing a red seal. 'I found this amongst the other deeds. It's the lease of the Bath house.'

There was a small silence. Charles, to his fury, found his heart pounding ominously beneath his thick winter waistcoat. 'Yes?' he said, with an effort at unconcern.

'According to this, a man called Thomas Barlow has rented it from my father for a twelvemonth, from Michaelmas last year to Michaelmas this, and if the agreement is to be terminated earlier, by either side, a quarter's notice is required.' Alex lifted his head and smiled at Charles. 'It seems that you are safe from eviction for a little while, since I cannot ask Master Barlow to leave until midsummer at the earliest.'

'And you aren't going to turn us out on the street?' his cousin said, with more bitterness than he intended.

Alex laughed. 'No, I wouldn't dream of it. If I implied otherwise, it was the wine speaking and not me. Surely you didn't think me so unfeeling?'

I will not lose control, Charles said to himself, urgently and silently. It's obviously what he wants – and I will not, I will *not*, give him that satisfaction. Aloud, he said, 'No – I knew that you would be open to reason. But you caused great distress to my mother and to Amy, and I would be grateful if you could offer them your sincere apologies at your earliest convenience.'

'Do you always talk like a letter from a damned lawyer? Yes, I will,' said Alex. 'And in return, could you possibly try to convince your dear mother that a little house in Abbey Green, along with the pension my father left her, is all she has ever wanted in life? I doubt very much if I could withstand her reproachful looks, otherwise. I think she will see sense eventually. After all, the sort of bachelor establishment I have in mind for Wintercombe will hardly be suitable for Amy's tender innocence, will it?'

'I doubt it very much,' said Charles, trying not to clench his teeth. 'I agree with you – my mother and sister will be infinitely better off in Bath, well away from your activities.'

'Perhaps not as far as you might think – do you know the Cock in Walcot? No, I didn't think you would, somehow. Rest assured, Charles, I won't come knocking on your door demanding to ravish your sister, however delicious I find her. And besides, if you are all in Bath, you will be able to entertain Father Anselm with perfect discretion.'

'I see,' said Charles. It was becoming increasingly difficult to contain his anger, but he managed it with a supreme effort. 'The reason you don't want us to remain at Wintercombe any longer is because we are Catholic.'

Alex smiled, and slowly shook his head. 'Oh, no, Cousin. Your popish beliefs have nothing to do with it. Wintercombe is mine now, and although it may seem selfish, I wish to enjoy my inheritance unencumbered by stray relatives.'

'Save for Phoebe, of course.'

'Save for Phoebe – though I should imagine she has her own plans for her future. At any rate, I don't intend to have my style cramped by any of you. Louise and Aunt Silence will go to Chard, you and your entourage to Bath, and Phoebe . . . well, who knows?'

'You can't drive her away from Wintercombe too! She's frail, unwell – what would such inhuman treatment do to her?'

'My sister, in all the ways that matter, is as tough as an ox. I expect, knowing her, that she has some desire to set up an independent establishment of her own.'

'She can't!' Charles was genuinely horrified. 'Alone – unmarried – without even your dubious protection –'

'Thank you for that generous compliment.'

'– she'd be prey to any passing fortune hunter.'

'Phoebe? I pity any fortune hunter who casts his lure at her. She'd clap his head between two volumes of philosophical treatises, and push him out of the door at the end of her stick. No, Cousin, Phoebe is not destined for matrimonial bliss, and is sensible enough to be well aware of it. She has a very handsome competence from our father, she is of age, and free to do as she pleases. Who am I to trample heavy-footed over her wishes with talk of brotherly duty and polite convention?'

'There seems to be no further profit in this conversation,' Charles said tautly, and got to his feet. 'If you will excuse me, Cousin –'

'No, I will not. Sit down, for Christ's sake – I haven't finished with you yet.'

Charles found himself firmly pushed back in his seat, as if he were a recalcitrant schoolboy. His fury threatening to choke him, he glared at his tormenter, and Alex gazed benignly back. 'Yes, I do know I'm behaving badly – but then I always do. If we are to remain under the same roof for three or four months, then we had best learn to rub along together.'

'I don't see why –'

'Shall I spell it out for you plain? I shall need a secretary, a man of

65

business. There is a great deal to do here, and I suspect a great deal for me to learn. For that, I shall require your help.'

'I refuse to be treated like a parasitic fool,' said Charles, through clenched teeth. 'If you want my assistance, you'll have to pay me for it.'

'As much as my father did, certainly. But only until you move to Bath. After that, you'll have your own way to make. There must be plenty of Papist gentlemen who'd appreciate your services.'

'Doubtless there are,' Charles said. Fury and resentment were seething within him, but the childhood years of forced control in the face of Alex's malice stood him in good stead now. He wanted to shout, to rage and blaspheme and punch that cool, mocking, infuriatingly handsome face to a bloody pulp. But he was nearly half a foot shorter than his cousin, and by the look of Alex, despite his drinking and other, even less respectable vices, distinctly inferior in strength and fitness. He might be twenty-four, only five years or so younger, but beside his cousin he felt like a child again, helpless and cornered by a being whose arrogant assumption of superiority struck unerringly at the heart of Charles's confidence and self-esteem. Uncle Nat had valued him, taught him, encouraged him. But to Alex, he was at best an irritation, a minor obstacle to be swept relentlessly aside in spite of his feelings, and ignoring any question of family obligation.

Deep beneath his solid, apparently acquiescent exterior, Charles's heart began to beat out the sullen, remorseless rhythm of hate. It was as well that he was so skilled in hiding his emotions, for he would have died rather than give Alex cause to gloat over this victory. He kept his voice carefully neutral, to disguise how greatly the answer mattered to him. 'What . . . what do you plan to do with Wintercombe?'

Alex looked surprised. 'What do I plan to *do* with it? I hadn't really considered the matter. I'll stay here, of course, for much of the time. The life of a country gentleman, encumbered with wealth and not over-burdened with responsibilities, is peculiarly attractive at present. The house is lamentably old-fashioned, of course, but could easily be remodelled, or even torn down and rebuilt in the latest style. It would give me something to exercise my mind – in between debauches, of course.'

Charles's sense of humour, as Louise had already discerned, was a trifle underdeveloped. He missed the glint in his cousin's eye and said, rather more hotly than he had intended, 'You'll have Grandmother to reckon with, if you do.'

'Really? I was not aware that this house was any concern of hers now – or of yours, come to that. As I have said, time and again, and will probably have to repeat until it's dinned into your collectively thick skulls,

Wintercombe is mine, and mine alone, and I shall do as I please with it. If I choose to tear it down and erect a miniature Versailles, if I fill it with choice harlotry or set up a gaming den, it is no business of yours, or my aunt's, or anyone else. But you can rest assured of two things, Cousin.'

'What?' said Charles, with admirable restraint.

'Firstly, that I shall have a deed drawn up, as soon as may be, assigning the lease of the Abbey Green house to your mother for the term of her natural life, at a peppercorn rent – perhaps one Ave Maria to be said yearly for my imperilled soul? Perhaps not. She will not be able to move before midsummer, but at least her future will be secure. And secondly, until such time as she does leave Wintercombe with you and your sister, I will moderate my naturally boorish and disgraceful behaviour, in consideration of Amy's tender years and innocent nature, and promise not to fondle the serving maids in her presence, nor to get drunk more than three times a week – which, considering that there's precious little else to do in this place, I think demonstrates astonishing self-control on my part. And,' Alex added, with the sudden grin that many, but not Charles, found so disconcertingly attractive, 'I'll have it signed and sealed on parchment too, if you like.'

'No,' said Charles stiffly. 'That will not be necessary. Your word as a gentleman will suffice.'

His cousin leaned back in his chair and laughed. 'And if you rely on that, dear Charles, you're a bigger fool than even I took you for.'

At which point, dear Charles, not trusting himself to remain calm any longer, took his leave tight-lipped, and escaped.

He went in search of Silence, and found her in the winter parlour with Louise and Amy. It was a peacefully domestic scene, his grandmother sewing by the fire, her round spectacles firmly on the bridge of her nose, her plain dark gown the conventional garb of a Puritan wife. In contrast, the two girls, in silk and ribbon and lace, resembled frivolous flowers. Louise was reading aloud from a large and deceptively serious-looking tome in her exquisite and expressive French, and Amy listened intently, a frown of concentration between her fair, arched brows. As Charles hesitated at the door, unwilling to disturb them, his sister asked, with painstaking deliberation, '*Cousine Louise? Dites-moi encore, Cassandre, est-elle la sœur de Hector, ou de Paris?*'

Charles saw a fleeting look of irritation cross Louise's face, but she said, clearly and patiently, '*Cassandre est la soeur de Hector, et de Paris aussi. Dites-moi, chère Amy, qui est le père de Cassandre, de Hector et de Paris?*'

Amy had noticed Charles. With a certain pride, she answered in that rather plodding, and unmistakably English accent, '*Priam est leur père. Il est le roi de Troie.*'

67

'*Et qui est leur mère?*'

'*La mère de Cassandre, c'est Hecuba,*' said Amy. She smiled triumphantly at her brother. 'Isn't my French good now! I've made such progress, haven't I, Louise? And it won't be long before I can read *Cassandre* for myself.'

'A little while yet,' said Louise. She put the book down with some relief. There was a limit to the quantity of this weighty and convoluted romance which she could read at one sitting without becoming bored or, worse, for Amy was absolutely enthralled, openly disclosing it by yawning. 'Hullo, Charles. You look remarkably out of sorts.'

Charles opened his mouth to declare that indeed he was, and with good reason. Then he closed it as he remembered that in fact, Alex had, astonishingly, been almost generous. It had not seemed like that at the time, and so arrogant and infuriating had been his cousin's manner that the gift of the Abbey Green house had passed almost unnoticed, and certainly unthanked. And yet to Charles, who had spent the earliest years of his life in conditions of poverty, despite his mother's efforts, Wintercombe was, and always would be, the palace of his dreams, the yardstick by which all other places were measured, and the home of his heart. He had lived here for nearly eighteen years, he belonged here, he had worked to enhance it and had come to think of it, however mistakenly, as his own. And now this interloper, who in all justice had no right to it save by inheritance, had supplanted him, threatened to turn him and his mother and sister out of doors, and finally offered him, with gracious condescension, the lease on a poky little house in Bath with a back yard overlooked by an inn of dubious reputation, as if it were the answer to all his prayers. True, it was better than nothing, and at least Bab and Amy would have a sound, if restricted, roof over their heads. But Charles would, at that moment, have given anything for the audacity, or the foolhardiness, or even the opportunity, to throw Alex's patronising and spurious generosity back in his face.

'What is it, Charles?' his sister asked, rising gracefully to her feet, her lovely face anxious.

Hastily, he pulled his mouth into something resembling a smile. 'Oh, nothing bad, I promise you. In fact, the reverse. Alex has told me that he is prepared to assign the lease of the Abbey Green house in Bath to Mother for her lifetime.'

Amy gave a little gasp, and put her hands to her mouth. 'But that's not good news! He *is* going to turn us out – out of our own home! Oh, Charles, can't you persuade him to let us stay? We've lived here for so long, I can't even remember anywhere else. And poor Mother – it will break her heart if we have to leave.'

'You try arguing with him,' said Charles grimly. 'You might as well turn the wind around. Oh, Amy, please don't cry. At least we'll have a house to call our own, and you can visit the shops or stroll round the Baths whenever you like.'

Amy's tears stopped in mid-flow. 'I hadn't thought of that,' she said ingenuously. 'I don't want to leave Wintercombe, I *don't*, not really, I love it here, and so do you – but to live in *Bath*, and see all the Quality, every day . . .'

'Only in the season,' Charles reminded her. 'Out of it, the place is almost as quiet as any other small country town.' He drew a deep breath, and gave her an encouraging smile that did not in the least reflect his true feelings. 'Don't worry, Amy, we'll be happy, you'll see. Mother has her pension, enough to keep us in modest comfort, I have the money which Uncle Nat left to me, little though it is, and you have the dowry he gave you – we'll catch a husband for you yet.'

Amy had brightened all the while as he spoke, and at his last words let out a squeak of delight, and cast her arms about him. 'Oh, Charles, *Charles* – thank you, thank you so much!'

'It's Alex you should thank, not me,' said her brother reluctantly. He disengaged himself from her embrace and stood holding her hands lightly in his, looking down into the lovely, flawless face. 'And it isn't – of course it isn't – the *best* solution. In a perfect world, we would stay at Wintercombe – I would like that beyond anything, anything at all. But we don't appear to have much choice in the matter, and so we must be cheerful, and make the best of it.'

'Of course,' said Amy. It was apparent to Louise, watching, that an excitingly frivolous life in Bath was already eclipsing the more worthy, but tedious, rural beauties of Wintercombe. For one whose mind was taken up with fashionable fripperies, new gowns, dancing, the latest styles of hair, and everything modish from French romances to ivory fans, the opportunity to exchange this dull backwater for the hurly-burly of the town, where everyone who was of the Quality came to take the waters, to promenade and to mingle with those of like degree, was irresistible.

'I'm glad, Charles,' said Silence, who had listened to his words with approval, her sewing laid aside. 'I knew that Alex would not be so callous as he appeared – and I'm sure it's the best possible solution for everyone. Have you told Bab yet? Because I think it would be a good idea to make sure that she knows of this as soon as possible, to set her mind at rest. And although Alex should really be the one to speak to her, I think it might be kindest if you did.'

Charles gave her a rather apprehensive smile. 'Yes, Grandmother – I

69

suppose it would. She has been much better today. Perhaps her good night's sleep has removed all memory of what happened at supper, for she hasn't mentioned it to me at all, and she seemed quite cheerful, didn't she, Amy?'

'Yes, she did,' said his sister. 'Shall I come with you?'

'No need – I think it might be best if I saw her alone,' he told her, to her evident disappointment. 'Despite Alex's . . . generosity, she may not take kindly to the idea at first, and you would only be upset. Let me tell her, and you can come up later, in an hour or so perhaps, when she's had time to become used to it.'

He left them with a rather formal bow, disguising his nervousness, and both Silence and Louise came independently to the conclusion that it was somewhat optimistic to expect that Bab, apprised of the imminent and complete disruption of her life, could be brought to calm acceptance of it in less than a week, let alone an hour.

'Ah, dearest – come in, come in!'

Charles had been steeling himself for some time before actually raising his hand to tap on the door which led into his mother's rooms. His tentative knock had been swiftly answered by Beck, Bab's maid, a plump, stalwart young woman who seemed genuinely fond of her mistress. She conducted him through the dark little closet to the wide, lovely chamber that lay above the library and shared its generous proportions. These, however, were disguised by the clutter all around: ribbons, pins, books, the painted guitar which she had once strummed to captivate William St Barbe, unplayed now for years, jars and bottles of remedies and physic, jars and bottles of ointments, unguents, scented waters, creams for the skin and colours for the face, and a prie-dieu, always ablaze with candles, partly screened off in a corner.

Any conversation with Bab in her chamber was invariably punctuated by the snores, snuffles and ill-tempered growls of her tiny red and white spaniel, Floss, who was no respecter of persons, and could nip with astonishing ferocity for a dog of his diminutive size. His grape-round eyes bulging belligerently, he struggled out of Bab's arms to stand yapping on the edge of the bed, his stout body, from snub nose to plumed tail, stiff with ridiculous aggression. From long and bitter experience, Charles gave him a wide berth. He resisted the temptation to speak sharply to the little dog, who was still growling defiance, and greeted his mother with a kiss on her plump, powdered cheek. Bab called Floss back to her, with much cooing persuasion, nonsense talk and endearments, as if, Charles thought irritably, the wretched creature were a human infant. At last the little dog

70

was tucked up inside her robe, his pop eyes fixed unwaveringly on the intruder. He allowed himself the luxury of one more warning growl, and then subsided.

'Are you feeling better, Mama?' he asked, wondering how he was going to broach the subject of their forced removal from Wintercombe without inducing further hysteria.

'Oh, a little, dearest – as much as one can expect when my heart is so bad. But I think that when I have eaten my dinner, if I feel well enough, I just might, *might* be able to take a little turn about the chamber – with dear Beck's help, of course.'

'And mine,' said Charles at once. It was strange: away from his mother's overwhelming presence, or even if he was beside her in company, he found her embarrassing and ridiculous, with her dramas and crises, her headlong rush from one extreme of emotion to the other, and her obsession with the condition of her undoubtedly quite healthy heart and lungs. But here in her chamber she seemed neither suffocating nor foolish, but the devoted, adored and adoring mother of his childhood.

He took a deep breath and put his hand, broad and square, on her soft plump fingers. 'Mama, I have some good news for you.'

'Good news?' Bab looked at him fondly, an indulgent smile on her face. 'Oh, Charles, how wonderful! I knew that dreadful Alex would let us stay after all!'

With a sigh, Charles shook his head. 'No, Mama – no, I'm afraid not. But he has promised to lease you the Abbey Green house for your lifetime, at no more than a peppercorn rent – and really, I do think that it's the best solution.'

As he had dreaded, his words opened the floodgates. Bab threw herself, flesh quivering, into a paroxysm of grief and rage. Wintercombe was their home, they had always been made welcome, Nat had been so kind, and now Alex, cruel and vindictive, was going to cast them out of the only real home they had ever known, the only place where, said Bab, sobbing into a lace-edged kerchief, she had ever known true happiness. 'And it's so unjust, so unfair!' she wailed, as Charles put his arm across her shoulders in ineffectual comfort. 'When you did so much to help your uncle while that man was wenching in London and Holland and couldn't have cared less about Wintercombe – you worked so hard and now he's taken it all away from you, and it shouldn't even be his, by rights!'

'I know,' said Charles, who was of the same opinion. 'But unfortunately he has inherited it from his father –'

'His father? Nat wasn't his father!'

Astonished, Charles stared at her. Bab's eyes were red and swollen

71

with weeping, but her face was implacably hostile. He glanced round and saw Beck, out of earshot he hoped, looking anxiously at her mistress. He gave the maid a reassuring smile and turned back to his mother. 'What do you mean? Of course he's Uncle Nat's son!'

'I doubt it,' said Bab. The tears had vanished, to be replaced by a look of vindictive satisfaction. 'He doesn't look in the least like him. Nat was not a tall man – not as tall as you, in fact – and very slender. Think about it, dearest. Alex is more than two yards high. Is it *likely* that he is Nat's son?'

Put like that, it did seem rather improbable. Charles collected his churning thoughts and tried to muster some rational argument from them. 'But Uncle Nat never doubted it, I'm sure,' he pointed out. 'And he was a very clever man.'

'Perhaps – but besotted with his wife, nonetheless. And *she* was no better than she should be. The talk of Somerset, she was, with her flirting and her frivolity, and he, poor man, could never see the truth. Even when we came to Wintercombe and she'd been dead for years, there was still gossip about her.'

Gossip to which Bab, evidently, had listened greedily. Charles felt a twinge of distaste, but his own curiosity overcame it. 'Do *you* believe it, Mama?'

'Of course I do,' said Bab. She dabbed at her eyes once more, and the expression on her plump face became more openly malicious. 'Nat's wife was a lightskirt, and known for it. Alex was born after nearly four years of barren wedlock, and bears little resemblance to his supposed father. Five more years without a child, then Phoebe – who, I grant you, does look more like Nat. And there's no smoke without fire. Oh, I'm sure of it, dearest. And if *that* is the case, then that man has no more right to Wintercombe than the King of France.'

Charles stared at her stupidly. 'But his father – Nat – he bequeathed it to him in his will.'

'But would he have done that if he'd known the truth? I don't think so,' Bab said. 'And if Alex is not his son, then the next male heir, dearest, is *you*.' She smiled in gleeful triumph. 'Wintercombe should be yours, but instead that man has stolen it from you.'

The implications of what she had said were too enormous, too overwhelming, for him to comprehend all at once. He passed a hand across his brow, still bewildered. Eventually, he said doubtfully, 'Even if it is true . . . we can't do anything about it. In law, he is his father's – Nat's – heir, and his mother has been dead for well over twenty years. How can we possibly prove it? And without proof, the law will not help us.'

Bab looked at him peevishly. 'Oh, Charles, dearest, don't make such difficulties. There must be something we can do. It isn't *right*, it isn't *fair*, what that man has done. Are you just going to stand by and let him steal your inheritance from you, let us be turned out of Wintercombe when it should be ours? Charles, for my sake, for Amy's sake, you *cannot* just let him do that!'

'But I must,' he said, seeing with dismay the tears beginning to flow again as she clutched at him urgently. 'Oh, Mama, can't you understand? We're helpless. We have no money to speak of, and certainly not enough to mount a lawsuit. And even if we did, to claim Wintercombe purely on the basis of malicious gossip more than twenty years stale ... We'd never win, Mama, we couldn't. Our claim would be laughed out of court.'

It took him a long time, with repeated explanations, before he could convince her of it. She sat like a disappointed child, sulking, her precious schemes spoilt, and glowered at him as if he were the architect of their doom. 'You don't believe me, do you? You think I'm just a foolish old woman.'

'No, no, of course I don't,' Charles said hastily. 'But you must understand, Mama, that proof is needed before anything can be done – and proof, after all this time, will be impossible to obtain. I know it is a very bitter pill to swallow, but we can do nothing.'

'Perhaps not,' Bab said, sniffing. She grabbed Charles's arm suddenly, with a strength that was almost painful. 'But, dearest, please, please, promise me something.'

'If I can, I will,' said her son.

'Promise me – if ever an opportunity offers to turn the tables on that man, to obtain justice for us – you will take it, won't you? Promise me, Charles dearest – *promise* me!'

Ashamed of his doubts and his carefulness, he promised her, knowing that such an opportunity would be most unlikely to occur. What she had told him was no more than spiteful lies, surely: it did not seem possible that Nat could have been cuckolded so openly by the wife he had adored.

And yet, and yet, the idea, once implanted in his mind, could not be ignored. For if it was true, then Alex was indeed an interloper at Wintercombe, enjoying the fruits of an inheritance to which he had no rights at all, and which should belong to Charles. And how could he live in acquiescent obscurity in Bath, and ignore the terrible injustice that had been inflicted upon him, and his mother and sister?

It was perhaps fortunate that Alex chose the next day to visit Bath and the attorney who, with his father before him, had looked after Nat's affairs. In the meantime his behaviour, although still caustically infuriating, had not again reached the depths of that first night. He spent much time going through papers, and was closeted for some hours with the bailiff, William Crowe, greatly surprising him with the speed of his understanding and his grasp of estate management. He rode out twice, in Crowe's enthusiastic company, to inspect the lands which lay immediately around Winter-combe. He even apologised to Bab with an insouciant charm which did nothing to alter her opinions, either of his character or of his origins.

In consequence, mealtimes were ostensibly calmer, though as the rest of his family remained on tenterhooks in case of further unpleasantness, they were no less dreaded. Louise, mindful of her grandmother's words, behaved with impeccable decorum, as demure as a schoolgirl, or as Amy. Only Phoebe, always a rather detached and ironic observer of human frailty, might have offered some lively conversation, but as she was confined to her chamber with a severe cold, Alex was deprived of the acid comments of the one person who had never minced her words to him. When he left for Bath, on a cold raw morning with promise of later rain, the inhabitants of Wintercombe breathed a collective sigh of relief, and looked forward to a peaceful day or two, undisturbed by his presence.

The attorney, Philip Cousins, lived in a pleasant house in Westgate Street, with a wife and several children whose presence, unseen but not unheard, could be discerned from the sounds of juvenile dispute and distress which filtered down from the upper part of the house. He was a young man, his rising status indicated by the elaborately curled wig, the gold lace on his coat, and the cosy, elegant warmth of the room in which he received his clients. Cousins had liked and respected Sir Nathaniel, and regretted the division that had arisen between him and his only son. He had never met Alex, having served Nat only in recent years, since his own father's death, and on receiving the message that the new master of Wintercombe was to visit him, had spent no little time imagining, somewhat luridly, what manner of man he would prove to be.

The reality was quite, quite different. This was no flabby, pouch-eyed drunkard, full of oaths and uncouth manners, but a very personable, and physically impressive man, uncommonly tall and dressed with a casual, almost slovenly elegance that revealed wealth, taste, and a certain individuality of mind. Apart from his densely black hair and very vivid blue eyes, there was no resemblance to his dead father that Cousins, accustomed to sizing up his clients from acute observation at first encounter, could readily discern. His bow was courteous and correct, from a gentleman to a professional almost his equal in prestige, and surpassing him in learning. Cousins, not usually susceptible to charm, found himself the recipient of a remarkably disarming smile.

'You see before you the prodigal son,' said Alex, taking the chair that the attorney had indicated. 'But rest assured, sir, I have neither tail, horns nor a direct route to Hell, whatever you may have heard to the contrary.'

Cousins was nothing if not discreet. He coughed deprecatingly. 'Rumour, Sir Alexander, is notoriously unreliable, and I would never place any credit in it. I prefer to judge a man from my own observations of his words and deeds, and not by his reputation.'

'Then I shall have to ensure that I am on my best behaviour whilst in your presence,' said his client, the smile growing wider. 'Well, sir, shall we to business? There is much that I wish to discuss with you, but you can oblige me first by describing the details of my late father's will, and the full compass of my inheritance.'

It took some time. A maid, young and shy, brought mulled wine, very welcome on such a cold day even in the glow of Cousins's roaring fire, and a plate of small hot pies filled with spiced dried fruit and dusted over with sugar. Both men sipped and ate as the lawyer's unemotional legal voice listed the various provisions of Sir Nathaniel's will: the sum settled on his daughter Phoebe; the rather lesser amount bestowed on his niece Amy St Barbe for her dowry, and the lands, goods and silver bequeathed to his sister-in-law Barbara St Barbe and his nephew Charles St Barbe, which would supply them with a regular income for their maintenance; the fifty pounds left to each of those nieces and nephews who were not dependent on his charity; the various mementoes and small items of plate, books and so on for his sisters and more distant relatives; a guinea apiece for the Wintercombe servants; and land worth the princely sum of five pounds a year, the proceeds to be used to pay for poor but able boys from Philip's Norton to attend the Bath Grammar School.

The wry smile on the face of the master of Wintercombe, as this act of charity was described, reminded Cousins that he was that unfortunate establishment's most notorious pupil in recent years. Alex said drily, 'I hope the brats appreciate such benevolence.'

'Undoubtedly they will, Sir Alexander,' said the lawyer. 'Apart from these many and generous bequests, and after all outstanding debts have been paid – a remarkably trifling amount, I may say – there is, of course, the residue of the estate. The house itself, that goes without saying – Wintercombe, and all the lands lying about it – property in Bath, in Wells and Frome, the Mendip mines – most profitable in recent years – and of course, your father's interests in Bristol, including his share in the ships *Deborah*, *Silence* and *Patience* of Bristol, in the ownership of his brother-in-law Master Henry Orchard – all these pass absolutely to you for your lifetime, and after you to your heirs.'

There was a small, significant pause. Alex said softly, 'Is there something that I have not been told?'

Cousins sighed rather apprehensively. He was well aware that this particular aspect of the inheritance might not be welcome to his client, but there was no altering it: everything had been sealed and settled two years ago, and certainly, by his lights, Sir Nathaniel had been entirely justified in taking such a step. He said cautiously, 'The legal circumstances of the estate have been changed, yes. I do not know if your late father informed you of this.'

'I doubt it – we hadn't been in communication for some years. He could have mortgaged everything to buy an island in the West Indies, and I wouldn't have known.'

Cousins wisely refrained from comment. 'I must emphasise that your father acted from the best of motives. He was very conscious of the fact that Wintercombe has been in the St Barbe family for some two hundred years, and that changing fortunes might put such an ancient and valuable heritage in jeopardy. In order to safeguard it for future generations – his heirs and yours – he arranged for the core of the estate – Wintercombe and the lands around it, lying in the parishes of Philip's Norton, Wellow, Charterhouse Hinton, Wolverton, Rode, Beckington, Farleigh and Wingfield – to be subject to entail in the male line. This means that the land cannot be mortgaged nor sold. And should you die without direct heirs, that portion of your possessions will then pass to your nearest male kin – which is at present your cousin Charles St Barbe. The order of inheritance is complex, but it is clear that if there should be no more male St Barbes to inherit, the property reverts to the nearest in the female line – that is to say, your daughters, if you have any, and failing them, your sister Phoebe and her heirs. After that, since your grandfather Sir George had rather more daughters than sons, the situation becomes more complicated still, but is arranged basically in order of seniority. However, since you are young, and will undoubtedly take a wife, and have every expectation of siring sons in plenty, and your cousin Charles the same, the problem should not arise. Have I made it all quite plain, Sir Alexander?'

'Tolerably so,' Alex said. He was lounging in his chair, the Venetian glass, empty now of wine, disregarded in his hands, and if he was angered or perturbed by the news, he gave no sign of it to the lawyer's watchful gaze. 'If I die without male issue, Charles will inherit Wintercombe as a matter of course. Does he know this?'

'I think he does – indeed, since in recent years he has taken such a prominent part in managing the estate, I would be very surprised if he did not.'

'Then I'd best watch my back,' said Alex lightly. He set the empty glass gently down on the table between them, and crossed one leg over the other. 'So, this entail means that I cannot in any way dispose of that part of my inheritance?'

'Since it is in essence held by you in trust for your heirs, yes, that is correct. You may do what you please with the rest of your property, but Wintercombe and the lands around it must be kept intact.'

'What did my father imagine I'd do with it otherwise?' said Alex. He sounded, to the attorney's relief, no more than amused. 'He must have thought I'd waste it all in riotous living.'

'I'm sure the thought didn't enter his head,' said Cousins mendaciously.

His client gave him a disconcertingly shrewd glance, and laughed. 'You're too damned discreet, even for a lawyer. In fact, he had no reason to worry. Entail or no entail, I am fully aware of the burdens and responsibilities of my inheritance, as well as the benefits, and I have no intention of dissipating it. But it does begin to seem as though I should look round for a wife.'

'That might indeed be wise, Sir Alexander. And since I have a wide acquaintance with the gentry of these parts, and their affairs, I may be in a position to act in some sort as broker, should the need arise.'

Alex grinned suddenly, and Cousins found himself, somewhat to his surprise, almost liking the man. He was so different from what he had expected, and displayed an assurance and a shrewd intelligence that was comforting. The lawyer had been very concerned that such a fine estate should pass into the hands of a notorious wastrel, and had urged the entail on his father. However, it did now seem as if his worries might have been groundless.

His hopes were dashed by his client's next words. 'I'll tell you my requirements now, if I may. She should be young, handsome, of good fortune, and above all meek. I'll have no scold to rule my life and take exception to all my assorted peccadilloes and vices. After all, I do have a certain notoriety to keep up.'

'I do not think it is a matter for jest, sir,' said Cousins with some severity.

Alex snorted derisively. 'I hadn't thought you so prim. Nine-tenths of your clients are in all probability no better, and no worse, than I am. My chief crime is that I make no secret of my sins. If that offends you, or anyone else, well, I must confess that I do not greatly care.'

Which, thought Cousins, certainly puts me in my place. He was beginning to get the measure of Sir Alexander St Barbe. He might be the family's black sheep, long estranged from his father because of an outrageous series of misdeeds, and a man with an unsavoury reputation for drunkenness, loose living, scandal and even more sinister behaviour, the perennial subject of whisper and gossip in north Somerset, despite his long absence from England. But he was also gifted with charm, intelligence, wit, and a formidable air of determination. This was no idle, weak-willed wastrel, but someone who had decided upon his course in life, and did not seem likely to be thwarted in achieving his desires, whether for a meek and mild wife, or something much less respectable.

He listened attentively to his client's wishes concerning the Abbey Green house, and went so far as to express his approval. It was arranged that the lease assigning it to Bab should be drawn up by the following morning, when Alex, who planned to stay in Bath that night, would be able to collect it. Then he made his courtesies and went on his way, leaving Philip Cousins feeling at once drained and exhilarated by such an abundance of energy. The lawyer wondered ruefully which of the young gentlewomen of good fortune at present residing in Somerset or Wiltshire could possibly make a fitting wife for this formidable, disreputable and individual man.

There were probably none, but he would do his best. Smiling, he went in search of his own wife, who was neither meek nor mild, but no less beloved for that, and beside whom, in his eyes, all the women in Bath would not be noticed.

# 5

## *'He sought the storms'*

'How do I look, Charles?'

It was a question which Amy St Barbe directed at her brother, on average, at least once a day, and he, fond of his sister, usually took care to make a proper answer rather than a noncommittal masculine grunt. He was very conscious of his own apparel, paying particular attention to the neatness of his appearance, and was careful to choose garments that enhanced his status and self-esteem. Today, he wore a suit of sober dark green cloth, adorned with silver buttons at cuff and hem and pocket, and his cravat was edged with intricate, ice-white lace. The suit was only some six months old, chosen to be neither outrageously fashionable nor dowdily outmoded, and he knew he looked well in it.

Amy, in contrast, would not care if she looked ridiculous, so long as she dressed in the height of fashion. Her skill with a needle and her undoubted flair for such things had transformed an old gown of sky-coloured silk into a handsome mantua in the latest French style, as copied from one of Louise's garments. She had made a tippet, too, to cover her shoulders, using a length of fine holland stored in the linen cupboard, with a deep border of rich lace removed from an old petticoat. With her honey-coloured hair arranged in heavy curls around her face, her eyes sparkling, she was lovely indeed, and Charles, sincerely, told her so.

'Oh, thank you, brother!' Amy cried, and gave him a delighted kiss. 'Now we can go down to supper.'

She fairly danced from his chamber, and he followed, not without misgivings. An unwelcome memory rose in his mind, concerning Alex's return from Bath earlier that day. He had arrived not only with the deed assigning the Abbey Green house to Bab and her children, but in the company of several hired men and laden packhorses. Their burdens, a number of large and interesting-looking packages, had been unloaded and stacked in the Hall, and Amy, insatiably curious, had hung over the gallery above, wondering whatever they might contain.

Alex, who seemed to be in a mood of some hilarity, had seen her watching, and had called up to her with a wildly dramatic gesture. ' "But

79

soft! What light through yonder window breaks? It is the east, and Amy is the sun!" '

To his evident amusement, the girl had looked behind her to see who was being thus addressed. When she realised that, in fact, she was the recipient of such an extravagant salutation, she had blushed and put her hands to her mouth, prompting another outburst. ' "Oh, that I were a glove upon that hand, That I might touch that cheek!" '

'You are mocking me, Cousin,' Amy said, rather coyly, and blushing more rosily still.

Alex shook his head reprovingly. 'Oh, no. Would I mock such an ethereal vision of loveliness?'

The vision's response was a delighted giggle. She peeped over the rail and said, greatly daring, 'Please will you tell me, I'm dying to know – what have you brought with you from Bath?'

'Do you really want to find out? Very well, on your own head be it. Item, one runlet of best French brandy, containing some three gallons, at a cost of three shillings and eightpence a gallon. Should last me at least a week, with care and moderation. Item, several parcels of books, upon a variety of subjects, some of which will not be fit for one of your tender years, so I'll spare you the details. Item, a parcel of tobacco and six dozen pipes, the better to smoke you all out of doors. Item, several bundles of lace, ribbons, buttons, pins, and so on – but not, alas, intended for you, my pretty cousin. Item, various articles, still, I hope, intact, which may also smoke you out of doors.'

'What are they?' Amy had asked, while Charles, standing superfluous in the middle of the Hall, wished that his sister would not behave quite so boldly with her lecherous cousin.

Alex laid a finger to his nose, and winked. 'You'll see, in time. Have you by any chance some gold about your person?'

With his energy and malice and wild, unpredictable moods, he both frightened and fascinated her, but like this, cheerfully expansive, he did not seem so dangerous. Impulsively, she fumbled in her bodice and pulled out the little cross on its delicate chain which she always wore. 'There is this.'

He gave a shout of laughter. 'Perfect! When all is set up and ready, I'll promise to transmute your Papist gold into purest heretic lead.'

Dismayed by her own immodesty, Amy had beaten a hasty retreat. But thinking about it now brought a renewed blush to her cheeks. He had called her pretty, and addressed her as an ethereal vision of loveliness. In her limited, sheltered experience, she had met no one remotely like him, and one smile, one glance of those compelling blue eyes, one moment when she had attracted his undivided and admiring attention, was quite enough to turn her head. She had hugged the memory to herself all afternoon, occasioning some tart comments from Louise, and had dressed with great care for supper. Wild, romantic thoughts filled her head. She had undoubtedly attracted him – she was, as he had said, pretty – and she had advantages that none of his other women possessed. She was well born, his cousin, his equal in rank if not in fortunate, and he was surely the most eligible bachelor for miles around. Her mind leaped forward to the inevitable embraces, the wedding, the deference and wealth and freedom that would be due to her as Lady St Barbe, no longer the poor relation dependent on charity. Her inadequate dowry – for the four hundred pounds which her Uncle Nat had left to her for that purpose did not now seem a great deal – would mean nothing if Alex fell in love with her, for he was rich enough not to need it.

With these delightful daydreams entrancingly in her mind, she waited at the foot of the stairs for her brother to offer her his arm. She failed entirely to notice his anxious, thoughtful expression, and allowed herself to be led into the dining parlour, where the rest of the family, with the exception of Bab, were already gathered.

All her excitement and satisfaction drained abruptly away at the sight of Louise. Her cousin was wearing a garment which she had not seen before, of a dull red figured damask that set off her rather olive skin to perfection and clung to her slender, graceful figure. Amy's plumpness might be more modish, but her generous curves were entirely concealed beneath that demure, fashionable tippet, whereas the low neckline of Louise's mantua enhanced her modest proportions. With that convex nose and rather long, thin face, she was not beautiful, nor even pretty, but her poise and sophistication more than compensated for her lack of conventional good looks, and her expressive eyes, Gallic gestures and sudden, brilliant smile reflected a vivid, lively and humorous personality. Amy's heart sank. She might indeed, in Charles's brotherly eye, be lovely, but beside Louise she felt like a silly, simpering schoolgirl.

And of course Louise she was talking to Alex. Phoebe, whose health was never good, was still confined to her bed with a feverish cold, and so the only other person in the room was Silence, who was standing by the fireplace, watching her nephew and her granddaughter with a distinctly thoughtful, not to say disapproving expression. Amy realised suddenly that she was not the only one to be displeased at the sight of Alex and Louise apparently enjoying each other's company and conversation.

But, gratifyingly, her entrance changed everything. Alex broke off in mid-sentence, and came forward to greet her with the generous smile that raised yet another fiery blush to her face. 'Amy! I didn't recognise you for a moment – you look quite delightful.' And he raised her hand to his lips, his eyes seeking hers.

Suddenly confused by the strength of her feelings, she said, in the voice that always sounded too girlish after Louise's husky drawl, 'Th-thank you, Cousin. You – you're very kind.'

'For once, it is kindness to speak the truth,' said Alex, keeping hold of her hand. She was acutely aware of her grandmother's scrutiny, and Louise's raised eyebrows, and Charles's displeasure almost tangible beside her. She blushed still more deeply, and dropped her eyes. His fingers were long and fine, the calluses betraying a life spent much on horseback, and her small soft white paw lying in his seemed to belong to another species.

'Haven't you ever seen a hand before?' Alex enquired. Startled, she looked up and saw that he was grinning at her. Too confused to tell if it was with malice or not, she giggled nervously.

'Allow me to escort you to your place,' said her cousin, and under Charles's hostile and disapproving gaze, she was conducted to the sanctuary of her chair. The sight of Louise's rather superior smile did nothing for her confidence. It's no good, Amy thought miserably, as the servants trooped past to set the dishes on the table. How could I ever have thought that I might attract him?

But he continued to be attentive, talking to her, making her laugh with some ridiculous tale of a man and a bear in Amsterdam, while her grandmother sat as quiet as her name at the other end of the table, and Louise and Charles applied themselves ostentatiously to their food. Under the warming, encouraging influence of the claret in her glass, she found herself chattering on in reply, and if she bored him, he gave no sign of it. She was acutely disappointed when Silence, rising at the end of the meal, indicated that she and her granddaughters should leave the two men to sample the bottle of brandy which an impassive Twinney had already brought to the table. And for the rest of the evening, she relived again and again in her memory the words she had exchanged with Alex, hardly believing her good fortune, and certainly unable to concentrate on her cards: so that, for the first time, Louise was able to beat her at piquet.

Below, in the dining parlour, Charles was tasting good French brandy for the first time, and heartily disliking it. His cousin seemed to have no such inhibitions: he sat sprawled comfortably in his chair, a long clay pipe balanced in one hand and his glass in the other, wreathed in fragrant smoke like a sorcerer. Charles, feeling acutely uncomfortable, sipped at the fiery brown liquid and tried not to splutter.

'More?' Alex suggested, pushing the bottle towards him: he had already begun his second glass. Charles, afraid of once again being branded a milksop, surreptitiously wiped his eyes and poured a less than generous measure with foreboding. He had never been drunk in his life, and found the idea of loosening his taut self-control deeply disturbing.

'She's a very pretty little thing, your sister,' said Alex, blowing a rather ragged ring of smoke. He watched its erratic progress towards the ceiling, and shook his head. 'My powers must be failing – I used to be able to achieve a perfect circle.'

Charles refrained from pointing out that the brandy might have something to do with it. He took a reluctant sip, determined to ignore the reference to Amy. The girl's conduct at supper had angered him. The man was their enemy, an interloper, and by talking to him with such eagerness, she had betrayed both her mother and her brother.

Alex, on the other hand, obviously had no intention of letting the matter rest. 'And she has a very fetching innocence.' He blew another ring, a little more neatly, and studied it, frowning. 'Very fetching indeed. Have you found a husband for her yet?'

Charles, astonished, stared at him. 'No – no – well, I haven't – we haven't really thought about it.'

His cousin shook his head reprovingly. 'For shame, Charles. What is she now? Eighteen? Nineteen?'

'She'll be twenty in October.'

'And not even a betrothal arranged? That's very remiss of you.'

'It didn't seem important,' said Charles, recovering himself with an effort. 'And now, so soon after Uncle Nat's death, it would hardly be fitting. Besides, there's the question of her dowry.'

'She has four hundred pounds from my father, has she not? Quite generous, in the circumstances. What's more to the point,' said Alex, finishing his brandy, 'is her religion. You'd be surprised how many Papists can crawl out of the woodwork, given the opportunity. I know for a fact that there are several families hereabouts and in Bath, and surely Father Anselm knows of an eligible young man or two. Unless, of course, Amy is not so scrupulous in her beliefs as to insist on a husband of her own persuasion.'

'I'm sure that she has no intention of considering anyone who is not a Catholic,' said Charles, although he knew that his sister's devotion to her religion was much weaker than their mother's, or indeed his own. She would undoubtedly need very careful direction and guidance when the time came to find a husband for her.

'That's a pity,' Alex observed. 'Damned inconvenient to be a Papist,

83

quite apart from any other considerations. Barred from the Universities and the Inns of Court, and all public life – at present, at any rate, although given the beliefs of the new King, probably not for much longer. For myself, I'd find it much too restricting to stay a Catholic – but then, unlike you, Cousin, I am undeniably not a man of principle.'

'I was aware of that,' said Charles, unable to keep the bite from his voice. His cousin glanced at him and smiled. It was not a particularly encouraging expression, and Charles's heart sank. He found that he had finished his brandy, and that the bottle had been pushed his way again. He wondered if he dared refuse it, saw Alex's face, and gloomily filled his glass once more. By taking small sips, he could at least keep his eyes from watering, and his throat from rebellion. How Alex could toss the liquor back as if it were water, he could not imagine.

'Anyway, Papist or Protestant, a husband should be found for her,' said Alex. 'She's such a lovely girl, you shouldn't have much trouble – her looks should outweigh the minor disadvantages of her religion, if she holds to it, or, of course, her poverty.'

'Amy's not poor!' said Charles indignantly.

'Perhaps not, but she's not richly dowered either, is she? You'll have to find someone who's so besotted with her golden curls that he's willing to overlook everything else. Who knows?' Alex said, and smiled wickedly at his cousin. 'Perhaps even I might be tempted.'

It must have been the brandy, robbing him of his usual caution and self-control. Charles felt a great surge of fury rise within him, clenching his hands and closing his throat. For one wild moment, he moved in his mind to the heavy silver candlestick at the centre of the table, picked it up and smashed it across Alex's malicious, arrogant face, ruining those deceptive good looks for ever. So vivid was this rare flight of his imagination that for an instant he thought that he had actually done it, until his cousin's laughter forced him brutally back to reality. He said, hoarse with shock, 'You wouldn't want to marry Amy.'

'Wouldn't I? How do you know? Though of course you don't want me to marry anyone at all, do you? At present you're my heir, and it doubtless suits you very well to be in that position.'

Charles, floundering, could think of no adequate reply. Alex's eyes, unnervingly direct and clear, were bent on his. He studied Charles for a very long, very uncomfortable moment, and then said, 'I take it you do know about the entail which my father placed on the estate?'

'I was his secretary,' said Charles, aware that he sounded belligerent. 'I could hardly avoid knowing of it. Phoebe does too – in fact,' he added, recalling something which still rankled, 'I believe that Uncle Nat consulted her first.'

'Well, since he was basically disinheriting her, I expect he felt that it was only fair to do so,' Alex pointed out, with some sarcasm. 'I cannot imagine that Phoebe has any great attachment to Wintercombe, beyond the books that it contains – and in any case, as I have already remarked, she has been handsomely compensated. Besides, I can't think of anything she would hate more than to be an heiress, and have her hand sought for that reason alone. But we weren't talking about her, were we? We were discussing your pretty sister's need for a husband, and mine for a wife. Indeed, only yesterday Philip Cousins reminded me that it was my urgent duty to marry, and produce a string of heirs for Wintercombe. He promised to keep his eyes and ears open, and hunt me out a suitable young lady. One of tender years, I think, docile and attractive and eager to fall so desperately in love with me that she – or her family – is willing to overlook my dubious reputation and my lack of fidelity, scruple and sobriety for the sake of my face and my fortune. But of course, if such a paragon were to be found under my own roof . . .'

His voice tailed away suggestively. Charles stared at him in horror. The idea of marriage between his sweet, innocent little sister and this debauched rake was so repulsive that his mind quailed to think of it. And yet Amy was undeniably attracted to him, she had almost flirted with him that evening, the silly little fool – did she not realise that she was playing with a fire far too strong for her? He said thickly, 'Amy wouldn't marry you if you fell down on your knees and begged her – I'll make sure of that.'

Alex looked at him and laughed. 'Have some more brandy – it's certainly altering you for the better. And understand this, my prim and proper cousin. You may be my heir at the moment, and you may have certain hopes for the future. But I have no intention whatsoever of letting that situation continue for much longer. I mean to have a male and legitimate heir of my body to continue my father's line at Wintercombe. And if I wish to marry your sister to do it, then I will, and I very much doubt if you, or anyone else, can stop me.'

And Charles, his fingers locked around the stem of his glass, saw the implacable arrogance on Alex's face, and prayed, mutely and fiercely, that the justice of God would bring his vain and vicious cousin to his knees in humility.

The arrival of a consignment of books, reported by Martha Jones, the maid who served both Phoebe and Amy, was enough to raise Alex's sister from her sickbed. The cold had been severe, and she still suffered

85

headaches, a dry throat and an infuriating tendency to sneeze at the most inopportune moments. Her mirror showed a thin, wan face, deathly pale save for the dark rings round her eyes, and the raw shiny red of her painfully sore nose. Phoebe glared at her unlovely countenance, slapped on some soothing ointment, and made her halting way, with determination, to the library.

Mattie had been quite right. The central table was piled high with volumes, most of them already bound, a few still loose in sheets. The familiar, faintly musty aroma hung in the air, penetrating even her temporarily blocked and insensitive nostrils, and Phoebe sniffed with deep appreciation. Then the dust tickled her, and she sneezed loudly and explosively.

'Don't do that,' said her brother. 'You'll frighten me to death.'

'Frighten? You? Don't be ridiculous,' Phoebe told him briskly. She clumped round the table and saw him sitting behind the largest pile, evidently making a catalogue, for pen and ink and a blank ruled book lay in front of him. She said, 'Are these what you brought back from Holland, or did you buy them in Bath?'

'Both. That heap there is a lifetime's collection – I doubt you'd find many of them for sale in this country, without going to a great deal of trouble. The others I bought from various booksellers in Bath, yesterday and the day before.'

Phoebe was peering at the second pile. 'Boccaccio?' she said.

'That self-righteous tone ill becomes you, sister. Rest assured, it will be placed on the highest shelf.'

'Then I shall have to get you to lift it down again for me – I don't think anyone else at Wintercombe is tall enough,' Phoebe told him. 'As you well know, I'm quite beyond any normal notion of female propriety – and besides, I suspect that you and I are the only ones here who can read Italian. This is interesting – I would like to study this very much, when you can spare it.'

'The *Micrographia*? I've been looking for that for years. I mean to order a microscope from a maker in London,' Alex said, glancing at her. 'And a telescope, as well – one made to Newton's design, with a reflecting mirror. Would you like to watch the stars? Perhaps we can emulate Halley, and make a chart of the heavens, or discover a new comet.'

'I would like to see Saturn's rings,' Phoebe said, enthusiasm kindling on her drawn face. 'And the mountains of the moon, and the Milky Way and all the constellations . . . and I know where we could set up the telescope, too – on the top of the tower in the courtyard.'

'We'd have to evict the doves. I do not relish the thought of wading up

86

those stairs with my precious, delicate and highly expensive instruments through a mass of bird droppings, dead fledglings and bits of nest.'

'Then have it cleared out – you're the master here, after all,' Phoebe pointed out.

Alex gave her a cool, surprised stare. 'Am I? Well, well, I'd never have thought it.'

Unwillingly, Phoebe smiled. It faded very quickly as she saw the book at the bottom of the pile. With some difficulty, she heaved the rest off, and opened it.

The title page stared up at her. A king, crowned and sceptred, made up of many smaller individuals, reared up beyond a range of hills, whether benevolently or in threat was not entirely clear. '*Leviathan,*' she said quietly. 'Have you read it?'

'Of course – I've had it for years, as you can probably tell by its well-thumbed condition. Have *you* read it?'

'Father bought a copy, some while before the University authorities at Oxford ordered it to be burned,' Phoebe told him. 'So, since I've read every book in his library – yes, I have. Are you an atheist?'

The bluntness of her question might have surprised him, but Alex did not show it. He smiled. 'It's dangerous, and perhaps no longer fashionable, to admit as much – even in jest. I might very well ask the same of you – and somehow, people seem to think such opinions far more shocking in a young unmarried woman than in a debauched old libertine like me.'

'I have no intention of discussing my private beliefs with you, brother,' said Phoebe, but her smile robbed the words of any sting. 'Any more than you have yours with me, I suspect. Anyway, in the eyes of most devout people, merely to possess *Leviathan* is to be a Hobbist, and therefore, by extension, an atheist. Charles would be horrified.'

'I don't intend to give Charles the run of my library. You've read Hobbes – have you also read this?'

'*Oceania*, by James Harrington. Is he connected with the Haringtons at Kelston?'

'Distantly, I believe. Do you know it?'

'Only by repute,' said Phoebe. 'Are you also a republican, as well as an atheist?'

'I shall admit to nothing,' said Alex, turning on her that sudden, charming, brilliant smile. 'As I said, such things are dangerous in these times – not to think, perhaps, but to profess openly. It's tantamount to treason, after all, to believe that a republic or a commonwealth is the ideal solution to this country's problems. That's why poor Algernon Sidney was executed, a few years ago – not so much because of his plots, but because of the republican writings that he'd made, which were found in his study. Rest assured, little sister, if – if – I had republican sympathies, I would not be so foolish as to commit them to paper, nor to air my opinions to the vicar, for example.'

Phoebe gave a snort of laughter. 'I doubt he'd hear you. He's grown very deaf.'

'God's bones, is Pigott still alive? He must be well into his dotage.'

'He's eighty-one this year, and just as determined to carry out all his duties,' Phoebe told him. 'Even though his voice is grown so thin that those at the back of the church can hardly hear him speaking, let alone follow the thread of his sermons.'

'A situation for which all the poorer sort weekly thank the Lord, and the gentry curse him,' Alex commented. 'Since I shall doubtless be expected to occupy the foremost pew, I shall not look forward to Sundays with any particular enthusiasm.' He stretched, and yawned, and smiled, reminding Phoebe vividly of a very self-satisfied cat. 'Perhaps I'll call up a troop of demons. That should enliven the proceedings.'

His sister, resolutely refusing to be shocked, glanced at him quizzically. 'Is that within your capabilities?'

'Well, if it's possible to summon demons, or angels, or ethereal spirits, then I have a mind to attempt it – purely from curiosity, you understand, just as I might also try to determine the nature of matter, or the structure of the eye, or any other example of natural science which takes my fancy. I am one of the new breed of enquirers, my dear sister – I'll take no man's, or woman's word for anything, no matter how eminent my informant. If I can discover truth by experiment, then I will – and if I fail to establish the existence of demons, then I shall draw the obvious conclusion.'

'That there are no such creatures?'

'Precisely.' Alex grinned at her, disarming all her doubts. 'Have no fear, sweet sister, I do know what I'm doing. After all, what disciple of Hobbes could fail to consider any supposed denizen of Hell – or of Heaven, for that matter – as pure superstition?'

'From my limited reading on such matters,' Phoebe said drily, 'an angel summoned by an unbeliever is most unlikely to appear, whereas a demon is sure to turn up just to spite you. And,' she added, becoming severely practical, 'where precisely at Wintercombe do you plan to perform your, er, experiments? The stillroom?'

'Next to the servants' hall? I'd be the subject of wild conjecture for ever more. No, one of the closets off my chamber will suffice for the present.

My servant, Gerrit Tijssen, is the soul of discretion – and besides, I doubt he knows enough English to gossip.'

'Your servant?' said Phoebe, startled. 'But you didn't bring him with you.'

'Nor I did – how observant of you. I do in fact possess one, a most capable man, who's been with me for some years. But I left him behind in Holland to clear up one or two items of business which I had to leave unfinished. He'll arrive here eventually.'

'Well, I hope he is discreet – to have you taken up for a warlock would do nothing for the family's reputation,' said Phoebe tartly. She glanced down at the *Leviathan*, and then up at her brother. 'Alex . . . why is everything that interests you so dangerous?'

'Is it?'

'Of course it is! Talking about raising demons, even if only in jest . . . to be a republican is to commit treason by definition – and atheism is hardly popular, and not a little inconsistent with wanting to conjure devils.'

'I prefer to believe the evidence of my own senses,' Alex said, smiling up at her from his chair. 'I'm not one of these gullible souls who glean all their experience from books. I have the greatest admiration and respect for the views of Master Hobbes and his mechanical philosophy, but I would like to put it to the test myself. Much of what he says I know already to be true, from what I myself have observed and concluded, but how can I assert that there are no such things as demons or angels – and by extension, Heaven or Hell – unless I attempt to summon them in the approved manner, and fail?'

Phoebe looked at him narrowly. 'I don't believe that such things are dangerous in themselves – they're just mummery practised out of curiosity, or malevolence, or greed. But if anyone should find you conjuring spirits, the punishment is death. And that's what is dangerous – not the act itself, but the penalty.'

'But I don't intend to be caught,' Alex said, grinning. 'And I suspect, as you do, that I'll go no further than discussing the possibility with you.'

'I'm glad to hear it,' Phoebe told him. 'And Alex, please . . . don't air any of your views in front of Aunt Silence? She would be very disturbed and upset.'

'As a good Puritan surely must . . . No, rest assured, I have no intention of subjecting her to such horrors – although I doubt that our father's opinions were unknown to her, and she still seems to hold him in high regard.'

'Father was a scholar and a sceptic, but his conduct gave no one any cause to doubt his principles – and he kept his true beliefs to himself and his family,' Phoebe reminded him. The ache in her joints had become almost intolerable, and with the aid of her stick she moved awkwardly over to the nearest chair, and sat down. 'You seem to make no secret of them at all. You were concerned somehow in that affair with Shaftesbury – and don't look so innocent, brother, you *know* it's true – and Father had it on good authority from one of his friends in London that if you hadn't fled to Holland three years ago, you would have been clapped in gaol – or faced the hangman.'

'If they had ever found the proof – but unlike poor Algernon Sidney, I have never committed my thoughts to paper. Do you think, if they had, I would have come home now, when there is a new King even more intolerant of such things than the old one? They may suspect, but there is no proof. My reasons for going to Holland so suddenly were quite different.'

'And female, no doubt,' said Phoebe astringently.

'No doubt,' Alex agreed, straight-faced. 'Of course there is danger in it, little sister – as there is danger in any new idea or philosophy until the adherents of the old come to see that they cannot stem the tide by repression or argument. The truth can't be for ever denied, and will out, one day, despite all the efforts of the Tories and the churchmen to force men to think as they do. That is why the new philosophies are dangerous – because intolerant, blinkered people are frightened of them, and of the world changing, being turned upside down as it was in Cromwell's day.'

'But is that why they interest you?' Phoebe enquired acidly. 'Because they are forbidden?'

'Perhaps,' said her brother, grinning at her. 'I do admit to some of the old schoolboy impulse to shock. Immature, I grant you, but not an uncommon trait.'

Phoebe would have liked to shake him as he sat there, armoured in arrogance and certainty, shaken some sense and responsibility into that altogether too handsome head. She wondered why she should feel so concerned for his welfare, for she had never met anyone less in need of care and protection, nor known anyone else who prompted such feelings in her. She had thought that she disliked, even hated Alex, and certainly she envied him most deeply, for his health, his maleness, his assurance and wide experience, whilst also feeling contempt for the way he had dissipated his gifts and promise over the years. In his place, what could she not have done? For certain, she would not have frittered away her freedom and her intellect in wine, women and treason, playing with new ideas as if they were toys for an afternoon's amusement, and laughing at the peril involved. He was impossible, infuriating and undoubtedly riding for a fall – and yet blood must still be thicker than water, for she supposed that she loved her brother.

But she would have died rather than admit it to him, who, as she had good reason to know, could be quite ruthless in his dealings with his family. So all she said, lightly, was, 'Be careful. It's not impossible that you may have enemies, who'd leap at the chance to do you harm.'

'Enemies? Legions of 'em,' said Alex, grinning wider. 'It's lucky, isn't it, that I haven't been much in Somerset recently. Most of the people most urgent to murder me were left behind in Holland.'

'Aren't you ever serious about *anything*?' Phoebe cried, suddenly exasperated. 'Do you *never* think about the consequences of what you do?'

'Invariably – but only after I've done it. The air is thick with the sound of all my chickens winging home to roost.' Alex got up with one of his characteristic abrupt explosions of movement, and came to stand by her chair. His face, looking down at her, was suddenly thoughtful, and hauntingly reminiscent of his father. 'Little Phoebe – is it by any chance possible that underneath all that prickly dislike you actually might harbour some small sisterly affection towards me?'

'For you? Unlikely,' said Phoebe scathingly, and met his eyes without flinching. 'But I have some sense of family honour, and no wish to be pointed out by the common sort as the sister of the notorious Sir Alexander St Barbe.'

For a moment longer, their eyes, the same brilliant sapphire blue, held. Then he smiled and turned away, with the cat-like ease surprising in such a big man. She watched him take up the nearest pile of books and place them in a gap on the long shelves that had been built on either side of the huge fireplace. He dusted his hands and said, looking at her closely, 'Do you want to stay at Wintercombe for a while, or are you desperate to set up your own establishment?'

'Not until I've plundered your book collection,' said his sister. 'How else am I to equip myself to argue with you?'

'Then I shall look forward to a long and disputatious spring,' Alex said with satisfaction. 'You are one of the few people with whom I can actually cross swords. Somehow, I don't quite know why, most people seem to back down when the debate becomes at all serious.' He gave her that boyish, wicked grin, daring her to say anything.

Phoebe regarded him with a deceptively mild expression on her thin face. Then she said casually, 'Louise is not averse to battle, is she?'

'Louise? I had an argument with her before I ever reached Wintercombe,' Alex said reminiscently. 'No, she is *not* one of those milk-and-water madams without a thought in her head beyond her appearance

– though she takes more trouble with her dress than most, I'll grant you.'

So he had noticed her. Phoebe was very fond of her cousin, seeing in her quick wits and sharp speech the reflection of a good, if untrained, mind. She had never before envied Louise for her looks – striking, if not pretty – and still less for her beautiful clothes. But now she felt suddenly and acutely conscious of her old black gown, shiny along the seams, discreetly patched by Mattie Jones, and undeniably dowdy. But she could not imagine Alex with any woman other than some languishing, voluptuous, comfortable female who would be submissive and adoring enough to attend to his every need, and turn a blind eye to all his misdeeds, without complaint.

'What you need,' she said, thinking aloud without her usual circumspection, 'is a nice meek little wife.'

Alex gave a shout of laughter. 'Oh, no – not you too!'

'Why – who else has suggested it?' Phoebe asked, already regretting her words.

'Philip Cousins has taken it upon himself to look me out some sweet young virgin of good birth. Aunt Silence has hinted as much. And I don't need a book of divination or prophecy to see what's in Amy's mind.'

'*Amy?*'

'Of course, you were ill yesterday, so you didn't see her behaviour at supper. Yes, Amy has been blushing and simpering enough for fifty wise virgins, let alone a hundred foolish ones.'

'For a confessed atheist, you use a lot of Biblical allusions,' Phoebe could not resist pointing out. She added firmly, 'And if, God forbid, you have any intention of marrying her, I shall set up my own establishment forthwith.'

'Isn't she meek and submissive enough?'

'That isn't the point. She's your cousin – she doesn't possess two wits to rub together – and she's a sweet-natured little innocent and you'll make her miserable, you know you will.'

Alex grinned cheerfully. 'Rest assured – lovely and tempting though she is, I have no intention of succumbing to her rather cloying charms.'

'Yes,' said Phoebe brutally. 'But does she know that? It's hardly fair to encourage the child to fall in love with you – she can't be expected to know the rules. And besides, it's easy for you to say that now. But now, you're sober.'

'Are you implying that I'll rape her when I'm drunk? What a very intriguing prospect. Ah, Aunt! Do come in. Phoebe and I were having a most interesting discussion.'

Phoebe wondered how much her aunt had heard of his last remark. She stood below the arched entrance to the main part of the library, still and calm as ever, showing no signs of shock or outrage. But then, she was uncommonly skilled at hiding her feelings and thoughts, when she wished. Phoebe suspected that even if she had discerned Alex's words she would be determined not to give him the satisfaction of revealing it.

Louise, however, was standing just behind her, and from the curve of her mouth and the sparkle in her eyes, Phoebe decided that she, with her sharp young ears, had certainly heard it. As ever, she was beautifully dressed, in the flowered tawny-yellow mantua she often wore during the day, with a fur tippet around her shoulders for warmth. Alex's eyes lingered on her, and his sister noted that she had not imagined his interest.

'I hope we are not disturbing you,' Silence said, walking forward. Her brisk stride was that of a much younger woman, and her quiet vigour legendary. Phoebe, prey to every stray infection, wondered if she had ever known a day's illness. Louise, tall, energetic, as narrow and taut as a whip, was at first glance nothing like her grandmother, but they shared that same indomitable spirit, even if their ways of expressing it were utterly different, and Phoebe knew that in Louise, Alex had found another adversary to rival herself.

'I see that you are sorting the books,' Silence was saying, her hands straying over the heaped volumes, lingering on the smooth worn leather of their bindings as if she delighted in the sensation. 'And making a catalogue? Nat was always saying that he would, but that he bought new books so frequently that any list would be out of date before it was finished.'

'It's certainly a very wide collection,' Alex said, sweeping a hand in the direction of the bookcases which lined the room, and which his father had ordered to be constructed in the latest manner. Not so long ago, Wintercombe's library had been housed, like most others, in a large wooden chest. 'There are probably at least a thousand here, apart from my own. Making a list will keep my dear sister busy for some time.'

Phoebe, who had not been consulted about this latest imposition, glanced at him wryly, and said nothing.

'I expect you'll enjoy it,' Silence told her, with a brief smile that revealed how much she understood. 'Especially if you spend as much time reading the books as you do in making a list of them.'

Reluctantly, her niece grinned. 'Probably *more* time reading.'

Louise had walked over to the range of shelves to the right of the fireplace, and was studying the gold-lettered spines. 'Do you read Italian?' she asked suddenly, in that language.

'Tolerably well,' Alex told her. 'Have you discovered the Boccaccio?'

'Indeed I have,' Louise said, with that wide, dazzling grin, and rejoined Silence. 'We've come to tell you that we shall not be troubling you much longer. Gran'mère has resolved to take me on a Grand Tour of Somerset, and all my cousins.'

'In February?' said Phoebe, startled. 'But the roads will be appalling – you can't be thinking of it!'

'It will be March in a few days' time,' Silence reminded her. 'And the winter has been comparatively dry and mild – it will be easier now than in some years. I think I've been here long enough, and besides, Louise wants to meet her grandfather, and her cousins.'

'All of them?' Alex said. 'It'll take you most of the year – Chard, Taunton, Glastonbury, Bristol – Somerset is crawling with your descendants, Aunt.'

'I suppose my children should not have been so prolific,' Silence said drily. 'But my mind is made up. I have been absent from my own family for far too long, and Sarah is near her time and will need me soon. I'm sure that you are quite capable of managing Wintercombe in my absence. You will find Betty a competent housekeeper, quite able to run everything smoothly.'

'Don't tell me that I need a wife,' Alex said. 'Everyone else seems to be.'

Silence looked at him. 'The thought had not crossed my mind,' she said mildly. 'You know perfectly well, Alex, that I would not dare to presume to tell you what you do or do not need – you are perfectly capable of deciding that for yourself.'

'I'm glad you think so highly of me, Aunt,' he said, with one of his most infuriating grins. 'When are you and Louise planning to tear yourselves away from this delightful place? Today? Tomorrow? No, I forgot – tomorrow is Sunday. Monday, then.'

'We had thought Monday, yes,' said Silence gravely. 'I really don't think you can be rid of us any sooner.'

'Of course we don't want to be rid of you,' Phoebe said at once. 'Or at least – I don't.' She glanced meaningfully at her brother. 'Perhaps he doesn't either – although he may think that your presence will, er, cramp his activities somewhat.'

'He would undoubtedly be right,' Silence said. She added, 'If there are any messages or invitations which you might wish us to take – I had thought of calling on your Aunt Rachael first, at Glastonbury, and thence to Chard. Later in the spring, I think, when Sarah has had her baby, we'll go to the Loveridges at Taunton, and then perhaps up to Bristol.'

'I spoke with Uncle Orchard when I landed there last week,' Alex said.

'He is well, and Aunt Deb too – their daughter is staying with her cousins in Taunton, I gather.'

'She often does – they are all much of an age, and it is lonely for Libby, being the only one,' Silence commented. She glanced at Louise. 'You will like the Loveridges, though the girls are younger than you, and still at school.'

'If you intend to visit the Wickhams first, then perhaps I will escort you,' Alex said. As both Silence and Louise looked at him in surprise, he added, 'Cousin Jan breeds horses, and I have a mind to consult him on various matters, and perhaps buy some brood mares. And I'm sure that you would appreciate an escort.'

'Somerset is hardly crawling with footpads and highwaymen,' said his aunt. 'And you will surely supply us with a groom. Do not consider accompanying us on our account, for I assure you, we do not need it.'

Even that, Phoebe noticed with amusement, did not discourage her brother. He said with a smile, 'Don't worry, I'm not proposing to go all the way to Glastonbury on your account, but on mine. I'm sure that Wintercombe can survive without me for a couple of days – and Pagan needs the exercise.'

It was evidently not a prospect that greatly delighted Silence. But Phoebe, ever the observer, noted the brilliance of Louise's smile, and knew that for her, at any rate, the prospect of Alex's company on the road to Glastonbury was not at all unwelcome.

# 6

## 'Poor pitied youth'

To her surprise, Louise felt a pang of real regret as they left Wintercombe, on a cloudy, mild, late February morning. She had thought that only leaving Alex behind would cause such feelings, but since they were to have the dubious benefit of his company as far as Glastonbury, that could not be the reason. She must, after all, feel some real affection for the home of her mother's family.

Almost everyone in the place, it seemed, had turned out to bid Silence goodbye, and to wish her Godspeed. Only Bab, as usual pleading ill health (palpitations of the heart this time), was not on the doorstep waving a kerchief. Amy gave her grandmother an effusive and tearful hug, and another for Louise, rather to her embarrassment. 'And you will come back soon, won't you?' she said breathlessly, her eyes overflowing. 'Please say you will!'

'I'm sure I will,' Louise promised her, with a glance at Silence. 'Early in the summer, perhaps, when travelling is easier and more pleasant.'

'Wonderful!' Amy cried, with an enthusiasm that Louise found distinctly irritating. Surely her impatient French lessons had not made such an impression? 'I shall look forward to it *so* much!'

Charles was rather more restrained, but the look in his eyes as he approached her made her feel a little uncomfortable. On the surface, her cousin was so quiet, so mild and pleasant, but recently, since Alex's return, she had become acutely conscious of another side to Charles, a side that he usually kept hidden, something much deeper and darker and more intense than the affable companion whom she regarded as her friend. From what Phoebe had occasionally revealed, Louise had gained some idea of the possible reasons for this, some knowledge of the torment that Alex had inflicted on his cousin and his sister, long ago in their shared childhood. There was no doubt of it, the new master of Wintercombe was not a particularly pleasant character, and yet one glance of those vivid eyes could send chills up her spine, make her wonder what it would be like to kiss him, even to share his bed . . . and it would be possible, too. She had absorbed her instincts in such matters with her mother's milk, and she was well aware that he was attracted to her, perhaps as strongly as she was to him.

But these people were her cousins, not the light-hearted, amoral French, and here in Somerset very different standards prevailed. Much though she was tempted, she would not fling herself at him, to the ruin of her reputation and the scandal of all about her. She would restrict herself to the brittle, delightful game of flirtation, saying with her eyes and her gestures what she would not say in words, keeping it all on the level of a complicated and empty dance. And if he thought that she might be easily seduced . . . well, she was well versed in the wiles of men, even men such as Alex, and more than capable of dealing with him.

Charles, though . . . Charles, with that air almost of desperation, as if he yearned for something utterly out of his reach, was another matter. He would not play by the rules she knew, because his simplicity and lack of sophistication precluded it. And she had seen that look in his eyes too often, in other men, to mistake it. Her intuition never lied: he was, or fancied himself to be, in love with her.

Poor Charles, Louise thought, with regret for the sincere friendship they had shared all through the autumn and winter months, and which now, inevitably, must be laid to rest. For she was fond of him, she liked him – but only as a friend. He was good-looking, with his honey-blond hair and blue eyes, well-spoken, pleasant – but there was none of that sense of risk and danger, no *frisson* of the hidden desire that she felt whenever she looked at Alex.

'Don't look so sad,' she said to Charles now, as they kissed each other, cousin-fashion, on the cheek. 'I've already promised Amy that I'll come back to visit – in early summer, perhaps, if I can persuade Gran'mère on to her horse again.'

'Do you promise?' he said, holding her hand, and his eyes said what his reserve could not put into words.

'I promise,' said Louise, knowing that it was better to be cruel than kind, but unable to disappoint him.

By contrast, her farewell to Phoebe was notable for an utter lack of emotion. The older girl looked far from well, though she had supposedly recovered from her cold. She leaned much on her stick, and even the bulky folds of her shabby black gown could not disguise her twisted body, or how painfully thin she had become. So fragile and insubstantial did she seem in the wan pale light of early morning that Louise found herself wondering, in some distress, whether she would see her cousin again, even if she kept her promise to return in May or June.

But Phoebe must be much tougher than she looked, or she would have been in her grave long ago. She smiled at Louise, a rather sardonic expression that was very reminiscent of Alex, and produced a folded piece

97

of paper. 'If you are going to Taunton soon, could you give this to Uncle Jonah? He is a bookseller, and often keeps volumes by for me. If he can obtain these, I would be most grateful – and either send them to me by the carrier, or, if you are coming back in two or three months, could you bring them with you, if that is not too inconvenient?'

'Of course it's not,' Louise said warmly. She liked Phoebe, respecting her formidable intellectual abilities while having absolutely no desire to emulate them herself, and she also admired her cousin's complete lack of self-pity. 'I would be happy to do it – and I do hope to visit Wintercombe again, if Gran'mère will let me.'

She grinned, but achieved no similar response from Phoebe. The older girl glanced around, and then said, very quietly, 'Louise . . . you may well think this presumptuous of me, and I will quite understand if you are offended . . . but I should be very careful of Alex.'

Louise felt a sudden surge of anger. She was not a child, and she was quite capable of conducting her own life. But she held back her annoyance, because she liked Phoebe and did not wish to spoil their friendship. She said, equally softly, 'Don't worry. I know he is dangerous. But so were half the men my parents knew in France, and I learned how to handle them in my cradle.'

Her assurance seemed to thaw some of Phoebe's reserve, and at last she smiled properly, with warmth. 'Good. Where my brother is concerned, you'll need such skills. I know, none better, how charming and pleasant he can be when he wants – and he has great gifts, no denying it, even though he does his best to waste and squander them. But I have never forgotten, even when he is at his most entertaining, that he is completely without scruple.'

'Don't worry,' Louise repeated. 'I can take care of myself – and of him.'

Alex was already mounted, on the handsome dapple-grey stallion that had aroused the admiration of the grooms. Pagan, despite being an entire horse and therefore potentially just as dangerous, though in a slightly different way, as his master, was, as Dan Pardice commented, as docile as an old sheep, his only discernible bad habit being a tendency to chew at the wooden framework of his manger. Louise eyed the snowy fall of Pagan's magnificent tail, and wished, not for the first time, that she too could possess a horse as fine as that. But her sweet little mare Étoile, the companion of her wildest rides, had been left behind in France to produce her first foal, and all she had now was solid, uninspiring, comfortable Nance, the sort of animal the English considered to be a good safe lady's ride.

Still, perhaps she could persuade Alex to put her saddle on Pagan for a little while, before they reached Glastonbury, although it required some effort of her imagination to visualise her cousin, in exchange, perched on top of the stout bay mare.

Henry Renolds held Nance for her as she mounted, shook out her skirts and looked around at her travelling companions. Wintercombe did not yet boast a coach – the roads in these parts were generally so poor and steep as to render such an expensive purchase a useless luxury – and so they must travel on horseback. This, of course, was far more welcome to Louise than an uncomfortable ride in a jolting, enclosed coach, insulated from life and fresh air by leather and glass. But Silence, who at her age might have been expected to prefer a less taxing method of transport, seemed quite happy to ride, to Louise's relief, rather than to hire a coach or even to be carried in a horse litter, the last resort of the ancient or infirm. Her maid, Fan Howard, sat on one of Wintercombe's lesser nags, with Louise's maid Christian riding pillion behind her. The group was completed by Henry Renolds, who would help with any horses that Alex might purchase from Glastonbury, and the gangling Lawrence Earle, the other stable lad, who would accompany the women to Chard and take their borrowed mounts back with him.

There was a chorus of farewells from the residents of Wintercombe as they rode out of the courtyard, and Louise smiled and waved to them for as long as they were still in sight. Then, with a sudden rush of happiness and a sense of freedom and adventure, she turned her face to the road that lay ahead, and Glastonbury, the first stop on their Grand Tour of Somerset.

In summer, in good conditions, the journey would probably take a day, or even less, for it was only some twenty-five miles. But in February, even if the weather was kind, the roads were clogged and soft with mud, and dusk came soon in the day. Besides, Silence had announced that she did not have it in mind to travel at a great pace. They would stop at Frome for dinner, and hope to reach Shepton Mallet by nightfall, leaving an easy ten or eleven miles to Glastonbury the next morning.

Louise had hoped for an opportunity to ride alongside her cousin, perhaps to discuss horses in general and her next mount in particular. But Alex, with a certain lack of courtesy, set Pagan off in front of them at a speedy gallop, and they did not see him again until a mile or so outside Frome, where he was sitting waiting for them. 'Come on, my sluggard aunt! At this rate, we won't reach Glastonbury until next week.'

'At my age,' Silence said, putting back the soft dark hood which protected her hair, 'I reserve the right to plod on at my own pace, irrespective of your youthful dash and fire. Besides, my poor old horse really isn't capable of anything faster than an amble. If you really want to gallop that magnificent beast to and fro until he founders, that's your affair – so long as you pay for our rooms and our meals, you can do as you please.'

Alex laughed, running a gauntleted hand along the stallion's dappled, sweat-darkened neck. 'Rest assured, I won't leave you stranded. But Pagan was in sore need of a gallop, and I want him looking his best tomorrow for Cousin Jan's inspection – which he won't if he's still fat and out of condition.'

'You're not planning to sell him, are you?' Louise asked.

Alex shook his head. 'Christ, no – he's worth half a fortune. He'll stay at Wintercombe to improve our own stock. No, I need our cousin's advice, since he appears to be the family expert on all aspects of horse breeding. I shall need to purchase brood mares who will match well with Pagan, to produce foals with his stamina and temperament, if not his speed – although it would be pleasant if one or two of his progeny proved capable of racing. Do they still hold matches up on Lansdown, above Bath?'

'I believe so,' said Louise, who had heard Charles, some time ago, make reference to such meetings. She added, seizing her opportunity, 'I would also appreciate Cousin Jan's advice. Nance is a good enough horse, but –'

'You wish for something with a bit more fire and brimstone? I can't say I blame you.'

'I had a little mare in France, as sweet-tempered as Pagan, and almost as swift – a lovely dark chestnut, like copper, with a star on her forehead, so I called her Étoile.'

'And what happened to her? Did she break a leg out hunting?'

'I have never,' said Louise, quietly and forcefully, 'never, ever killed or injured a horse under me – all my mounts have retired, or been outgrown, or, as in Étoile's case, been put to breeding. Do you think me such a reckless rider, then?'

'Reckless, certainly – but perhaps not in the saddle,' said Alex. He had guided Pagan so close, as they began the steep descent into Frome, that his right leg was almost touching her. Silence was some paces behind, although not, Louise thought, quite out of earshot. 'So, Cousin Louise, sweet Louise, do you never ride for a fall?'

'Never,' she said, with a sly sidelong glance.

His eyes, that disturbing sapphire blue, were intent upon her. He brushed a stray hair from her face, so deftly that, a second afterwards, she wondered if she had imagined the gesture. 'Oh, Louise – surely rumour has not lied?'

'It's known to be a lying jade,' she pointed out coolly. There was no doubt that if he had heard even the half of those tales that had been bandied up and down the Loire valley last summer, he would think her ripe for the plucking. A tiny voice of warning, deep in her mind, kept whispering to her in words remarkably like Phoebe's: but she was adult, sophisticated, experienced in such things, and she could take care of herself. Determined to keep the conversation on a safer footing, she added, 'There is a favour I would like to ask of you, Cousin.'

'Oh?' His eyes sparkled wickedly. 'Is this my lucky moment, I wonder?'

'Hardly, with Gran'mère as chaperone,' said Louise firmly. 'No, this is a favour which you may not wish to grant, and I will quite understand it if you do not. If you agree, I would very much like to ride Pagan for a space on this journey.'

'Really? And how do I know that you will take good care of him?'

'You trust me,' said Louise, looking him full in the face. 'You have seen me in the saddle several times – you must have formed some idea of my competence. If you doubt me, then, as I have said, you are quite free to refuse, and I will bear you no malice.'

'Oh, I have every confidence in your skills on horseback,' said Alex. 'But have you considered the figure I shall cut, perched on that bulbous old nag with, no doubt, my feet dragging the ground?'

'Nance is fifteen hands,' Louise pointed out. 'Hardly a pony. Are you so afraid of looking ridiculous, Cousin?'

'Of course,' said Alex, and grinned, giving his words the lie. 'Well, sweet Louise, I have a mind – a mad, lunatic impulse – to trust you. I'll have Earle change the saddles over after dinner, and you may try Pagan's paces. But – one word of warning.'

'Yes, Cousin?'

'If harm comes to him through your lack of any thought, or care, or your recklessness, then I shall not readily forgive, or forget,' said Alex, quite pleasantly. 'Understood?'

'Understood,' Louise told him coldly. 'And I further understand that you do not trust me, or you would not have found those words necessary. Well, I shall just have to make you eat them, shall I not?'

The inn at Frome was warm, welcoming, and supplied an excellent early dinner. Lawrence Earle hid his astonishment at his master's request, and put Louise's side-saddle on the big grey stallion. He knew her for a very competent rider, but Pagan was, surely, not for a mere woman to ride. He watched her progress with interest as they clattered out of the inn yard and up the hill towards Shepton Mallet, but to his covert disappointment, she showed no signs of falling off.

Louise was thoroughly enjoying herself. Pagan had a mouth like melted butter, and a beautiful gait, a supremely smooth and comfortable trot that, after Nance's jolting, graceless stride, was like riding on a feather bed. He had fidgeted a little when she mounted, unused to the novel distribution of weight and the flapping skirts of her habit trailing down one side, but showed no sign of embarking on the battle of wills which she had fought with Shadow. She tried out his paces, noted the enthusiasm of his response and the equanimity with which he greeted such hazards as a furiously barking dog, a sheep stuck in a ditch, and a piece of rag fluttering in the hedge. Finally, she chose a wide straight stretch of road, bordered with a strip of smooth-looking emerald grass, and without waiting for permission from Alex, gave Pagan his head.

It was like riding the wind. The grass was rutted and wet, but the grey stallion negotiated all obstacles with a sureness and agility that aroused her wonder and respect. Shadow would have refused to stop at the end of it: Pagan accepted her increasing pull on the reins, and allowed his stride to shorten to a canter, then a trot and, finally, to a halt. Breathless and exhilarated, she turned him, patting the sleek dappled neck which, despite his exertions, was barely damp with sweat, and waited for the rest of the party to come up.

Alex had somehow persuaded Nance into a lumbering canter. She hoped that his saddle was secure: the length of girth had proved almost inadequate to describe the mare's extensive circumference, although she was a full hand and more smaller than Pagan. Despite the incongruity of horse and rider, the long lean man and the short stout mare, he did not look in the least ridiculous. She watched him as he approached, savouring his appearance, at once untidy and ill-disciplined with his black hair streaming behind him and his coat flying, and yet also powerful, almost menacing. The burgeoning feeling within her, the suffocating, heart-juddering sense of desire, of lust, was at once dangerous and enjoyable. She might revel in the overwhelming effect that his presence seemed to have on her, but she must not surrender to it, or her fragile reputation would be smashed as if with a hammer.

You were wrong, Phoebe, she thought, careful not to let her hunger show in her face as her cousin pulled Nance up a few yards from Pagan. It is not Alex who is the principal danger: it is I, myself, and my response to him.

She smiled graciously. 'Shall we change the saddles back? I would not keep you any longer from such a paragon of equine virtue – and besides, I fear that if I'm allowed to sit on his back for much longer, I'll never relinquish my position.'

'He is to your liking, then?' said Alex, removing his hat. The clear light suited his face, with its sharp, bleak lines unaffected by experience and debauchery. Louise felt her heart begin to pound, a slow remorseless rhythm which she fought down. It was lust, pure (or not so pure) and simple, for she did not even like the man, and certainly did not trust him.

'Assuredly he is,' she said, letting her delight in Pagan disguise other, less innocent feelings. 'Worth half a fortune, as you said.'

'So long as he proves capable of passing on his talents to his progeny,' Alex pointed out. 'And not every stallion has that ability. I was only shown one foal that was said to be his, and that was a most promising colt, but chestnut like his dam, and could just as easily have been another's. It will take three or four years before I can judge whether he will be a good foundation for the improved breed of St Barbe horses which I have been planning.'

'If he sires a filly like himself, dapple grey, will you sell her to me?' Louise said. She kicked her foot from the stirrup, and vaulted lightly to the ground. 'And I will use her as the foundation mare for the Chevalier and St Clair breed.'

'Then you plan to return to France?' Alex asked, still sitting the blowing Nance.

Louise, her long fingers busy with the girth strap, glanced up at him. 'Perhaps. Perhaps not. It depends on a great many things. Life is not easy for Protestants there, at present.'

'And you would not turn Catholic? Has not your mother done so?'

'Yes – but then it matters little to her, she did so to please my stepfather. She is determined, though, that I shall stay Protestant – she says it was always my father's wish. And so – she sent me to England.'

Alex dismounted and began to unstrap his saddle. Louise noted with amusement that he was more than a head taller than Nance. He said, with a sudden smile, 'So that was why you were despatched here. I did wonder.'

'Where else would I find a Protestant husband? And I am half English, after all, even if I am also a Guernesiaise.'

'By blood only, of course, since your father was drowned when you were . . .'

'I was four. I can just remember him,' said Louise. She finished unhooking the breastplate, and felt Pagan's soft, velvety lips nibbling at her hair. Laughing, she pushed his head away. 'No – it's grass you eat, idiot!'

'He likes you,' said Alex. He had taken the saddle from Nance's broad back, and came over to Pagan. 'Can you lift that off?'

'I may be a woman,' Louise said frostily. 'But I am not so weak and feeble as you might suppose.' She pulled the saddle off Pagan with an ostentatious lack of effort. 'Here you are, sir – you may have your horse back, with my grateful thanks and my deep green envy.'

He laughed as she passed him, and in a companionable silence, broken only by the cawing rooks in a nearby stand of elms, they secured their own saddles. Behind them, on the brow of the hill, her grandmother had appeared, with the servants just behind her, ambling along in no hurry. Louise looked around for a log, a fence, a gate, something which would serve as a mounting-block, but the thick bristly hedgerow promised no such help. There was only one alternative: she checked the tightness of the girth, and said to her cousin, 'Will you assist me to mount?'

'Of course,' Alex said. He left Pagan snatching mouthfuls of grass, and came over to stand by her, very close. She was tall, with her father's height, but she had to tip her head back to look into his face. He made no effort to help her into the saddle: instead, he bent his head and kissed her.

It needed an almost superhuman effort of will not to respond, when every separate sense screamed at her to give in to the flood of desire weakening her resolve. Her arms ached to pull him closer, to bend her body pliantly against his, to return the kiss with all the passion she had so far kept hidden. But her grandmother would be watching – had he delayed the moment until he was certain that Silence could see what he did? – and Louise had much liking and respect for her. Deliberately, she pushed her leg forward and trod as heavily as she could upon his foot. Then, as he checked, she ducked and twisted smoothly out of his grasp and stood a few feet away, smiling, her hair only a little disarrayed and her breath just slightly disordered. 'I asked you to help me mount,' she said, putting as much acid as she dared into her voice. 'Not to try and mount me.'

She had thought he would be angry: instead, to her surprise, he laughed, and turned on her the enchanting boyish grin which she had never received before, and which made her catch her breath with sudden, cheated regret. 'My apologies, sweet Louise – but you don't exactly seem unused to gentlemen taking liberties.'

'They don't usually try more than once,' she said pointedly. 'Believe me, Cousin, I have dissuaded more importunate would-be wooers than there are stars in the sky, and I am quite capable of doing damage, if necessary. And I would not wish to hurt you, unless forced to it.'

Alex was looking at her with a rather quizzical expression. 'You're lucky I don't laugh in your face. I'll grant, you're tall and strong for a woman, but when it comes to sheer brute force, you surely couldn't prevail against a man, however puny he was?'

Louise looked him up and down, and smiled. 'My mother taught me a trick or two – and she broke a man's arm once, when he tried to force himself on her. But I would not have it come to such a pass between us, Cousin – I had much rather we were friends. Now, will you help me mount?'

'Trouble,' said Alex unexpectedly, and grinned. 'Something tells me you bring nothing but trouble – but then the same could be said of me. If I promise not to try and rape you for at least an hour, will you let me assist you to mount, sweet Louise?'

And, laughing despite her misgivings, she allowed herself to be helped into the saddle. And whether Silence, riding up at that moment with her face set in the calm, mild mask that gave nothing away, had seen her nephew's embrace of her granddaughter, could not be discerned.

For the rest of the way to Shepton Mallet, during all their stay at the comfortable and welcoming inn, and the short miles to Glastonbury the next day, Louise took good care to keep close to her grandmother, and to avoid any chance of being alone with Alex. She was not a fool, after all, and would not let her heart – or baser feelings – rule her essentially practical head.

It was not easy to ignore the lift of her spirits when he rode alongside her, or entered the room, or to repress the power of her response to his presence. But she was strong-willed and determined, and rode the last stretch of highway to Glastonbury with perfect decorum, chatting to her grandmother, and watching the astonishing, tower-capped cone of rock that was Glastonbury Tor grow ever closer.

The Wickhams lived on a manor farm called Longleaze, west of the town, with many acres of lush pasture land reclaimed from marsh, on which the horses grazed, and a long low house built on the side of a hill, well above flood level, and surrounded by barns and stables. This family were the only other relatives that Louise had so far met, for they alone had lived close enough to attend her uncle's funeral, and Rachael – whom she called 'Aunt', though in fact they were no blood kin at all – was Nat's twin. Her husband, Tom Wickham, had died some years ago, leaving her with four surviving children. The eldest, John, known to his family in Somerset fashion as Jan, now managed the farm, and his wife, Bathsheba, attempted without much success to assert herself over her three small children and her forthright mother-in-law. The second son, Samuel, had run away to sea on a Bridgwater ship eight years ago, to the great grief of his mother, and the youngest, Ben, who had not attended the funeral, was only eighteen and apparently a simpleton. There was also a daughter, Jane, who was married and lived in Wells.

Alex had sent Lawrence Earle on ahead to warn of their arrival, and the entire family were waiting for them at the gate. Rachael, gaunt and unsmiling, stood at their head, wearing a dark grey gown whose stark severity was only emphasised by her old-fashioned and distinctly Puritan cap, collar and apron. Beside her, Jan's wife Bathsheba, plain, plump and pleasant, attempted to keep Cary and Tom, aged four and three, in check until the horses had stopped. Hovering in the background, his broad face oddly distorted, was undoubtedly the lack-witted Ben.

Jan was in his thirties, and despite the closeness of their relationship, he did not look like Alex at all, being brown-haired and much shorter, with a rather diffident expression in his blue eyes that was very far from the other man's habitual arrogance. He walked with a noticeable limp, the result of a bad kick some years ago. He reminded her a little of Charles, although to judge from his worn and serviceable russets, he did not share Charles's love of good clothes.

The horses were whisked away for a rub down and a drink, and Jan's eyes followed Pagan as he was led towards the stables. Then Silence and her companions were drawn into the warm, inviting comfort of the farmhouse, and a savoury mixture of aromas announced that dinner would soon be ready. Louise relinquished her bags to a tiny smiling maid, and allowed herself to be shown to her chamber by Jan's wife.

Over dinner, which was plentiful and delicious, she was able to study the Wickham family in greater detail. Rachael was a rather forbidding woman, who rarely smiled: it was difficult to remember that she was Nat's twin sister, for there was little resemblance in her thin, rather bitter face, save in the brillance of her blue eyes, which Nat, Alex and Phoebe also shared. Clearly her sons, even Jan, went in some awe of her, and her daughter-in-law and the two small grandchildren – there was a baby too, whose cries had occasionally resounded through the house – seemed quite cowed in her presence. Curiously, it was the simpleton, Ben, whom Rachael seemed to treat with indulgent kindness. She did not scold him when he interrupted her almost interminable grace, or slobbered his food, or leaned across Bathsheba to reach a dish he wanted, knocking over a glass of wine in the process. He's like a child, Louise realised with sudden clarity, an overgrown child who will never be adult. But there was nothing pathetic about Ben. He was obviously as strong as an ox, short and thickset with bulging muscles, and yet from his smiles and laughter and thick, almost incomprehensible speech, he was both loving and loved. Louise thought of another idiot, the child of the baker in the village nearest to the château, who was stoned and taunted by the children, abused and ill-treated by the adults, and she knew that Ben was fortunate indeed.

He had greeted her with a wet, slobbery small boy's kiss, and had said several times, 'Louey. Pretty Louey!' Really, she had thought, smiling in return – he had Rachael's blue eyes, rather puzzled, but determined, and a shock of dry dusty-looking brown hair – he was just like her little brothers. It was not easy to understand what he said, but he had taken her arm and uttered several urgent words, of which only two came clearly. 'See horses!'

'They're his pride and joy,' Jan had told her, coming to her rescue. 'Ben is so good with them – he treats them like children, and they thrive on it. You show Cousin Louise the horses after dinner, Ben?'

'After dinner, yes,' said his brother, grinning widely, and revealing irregular and rather discoloured teeth. 'Show Louey horses – foal!'

No one had made excuses for Ben, or tried to hide him away: he was simply accepted for himself, and the two small children seemed to regard him as a larger version of themselves. They, however, were obviously not granted the same licence at mealtimes, and sat bolt upright on their stools at the end of the table, unnaturally well behaved.

It was plain, too, that Rachael thoroughly disapproved of Alex. She must have known, from Lawrence Earle, that he was one of the party, and yet a look of surprised dislike had been very plain on her face when she saw him ride up to Longleaze. Louise, munching a very tasty meat pie, watched with amusement as Alex set himself to charm his aunt. It was beautifully done, obvious but not blatantly so. He drank only in moderation, his wit and flights of fancy were at no one's expense, and his manners impeccable. Once, Louise caught her grandmother's eye. Silence gave her a tiny, secret smile, let her eyes slide sideways to Alex, sitting next to her, and very slightly winked. Louise felt a niggling jab of annoyance. If he was capable of such courteous behaviour, why did he not employ it more often?

She knew the answer already: because he did not care. Nothing seemed to penetrate that carapace of wit, intellect and arrogance. Even in his cups, he gave nothing away. Then she remembered suddenly that song sung drunkenly and desolately to a sleeping, unheeding house. Perhaps that showed that he could be hurt: but if there was a way through his armoured outer self to a different, softer Alex within – if indeed such a person existed – she had no idea of how to find it.

After dinner, she would have liked to have joined the others in the warm, snug parlour, to rest and digest the meal, but Ben was insistent, and she did not want to disappoint him. At Silence's suggestion, she put on the heavy Brandenburg coat that she wore for riding in cold weather, for it was chilly outside and would be dark in a couple of hours. Then she followed Ben outside to the stable yard that lay alongside the house, around three sides of a square. It was obviously new, and handsomely built, with stalls and looseboxes within, plenty of windows, and a hayloft above. Louise looked around her with pleasurable anticipation. This was all evidence that Jan Wickham was an extremely competent and knowledgeable breeder of horses.

Ben towed her inside. Like the stables at Wintercombe, there was a passage running all round the three sides of the block, with stalls ranged alongside, and looseboxes at either end. He stopped at once by Pagan, who was pulling hay from his manger with his usual lazy elegance. 'Beautiful – Alex's horse – beautiful!'

'His name is Pagan,' said Louise. She had realised that Ben, although rather deficient in speech, was by no means lacking in understanding. 'Isn't he lovely? I rode him yesterday, and it was like being carried along on a cloud.'

'Fast?' said Ben eagerly. Without waiting for her reply, he pushed past her into the stall. Pagan's ears flickered, but he continued to munch hay. Louise, hoping that Ben was aware of the dangers of entering a stallion's space, even that of a gentleman like Pagan, stood warily just outside, ready to take action.

She need not have worried. With a grace surprising in such a clumsy-looking person, Ben stepped up to Pagan's head, moving slowly and smoothly, crooning under his breath. The grey ears twitched again, and then the stallion, his interest aroused, abandoned the hay and swung round to investigate. Ben's stubby hands reached up to stroke the soft, whiskery nose, and then drew the lovely head down so that they were face to face, almost touching, while that wordless sound went on and on, lifting the hairs on the back of Louise's neck.

'See – friends!' said Ben suddenly, and turned on her a wide, joyous smile. 'Pagan and Ben – friends!'

And to judge from the sleepy, silly look on the big stallion's face as the underside of his jaw was gently scratched, he spoke the truth.

Most of the Longleaze horses kept indoors at this time of year were mares heavily in foal, awaiting the birth. One or two had already been born, beautiful long-legged, delicate-looking creatures surely destined for a gentleman's stable. Ben knew the names of them all, and proved also to have a pocket full of sugary sweetmeats, congealed into a sticky lump which he carefully pulled into pieces and gave to each eager animal. It was plain that the horses were his life, and plain also that, despite his supposedly limited intelligence, he was far more skilled in handling them than many grooms or stable lads with all their wits about them.

She was leaning over the partition of the last loosebox, admiring one of Jan's two resident stallions, when a not unwelcome voice said, just behind her, 'He's good, I'll grant you – but not as good as Pagan.'

Trying not to appear startled, Louise turned. Alex stood just behind her, clad in the pale grey suit he had worn for dinner. He smiled at her, and nodded in the direction of Ben, who was sifting tangles out of the chestnut stallion's flaxen mane with his stubby fingers. 'Does he disconcert you?'

'No,' said Louise, quietly but indignantly, and hoping that Ben had not heard. Since he was utterly absorbed in his task, and singing to himself, it was unlikely, but she had already conceived a great affection for him, and did not want him hurt. 'Of course not,' she added, with genuine admiration. 'He is wonderful with the horses – almost as if he were one himself.'

'He birthed his first foal when he was ten,' said Alex. 'Most people would dismiss him as of no account, a beast, something less than human. But the prosperity of Longleaze is due in no small measure to his skills. Jan was telling me about the bay mare two stalls down, with the chestnut colt foal – it was a breech birth, and both would have died if not for Ben.'

'Perhaps if a foal is born while I am here, I can watch,' said Louise thoughtfully. 'They would never let me, at home – it wasn't considered proper for a lady to see such things.'

'You may find that Jan thinks the same.'

'Well, if he does, I'll just have to convince him that I'm no lady,' Louise said, with a flashing, flirtatious smile. She was having some trouble controlling her breathing, and her hands were prickly with sweat, although the warmth of the stables was not to blame. She turned away from him, afraid that, despite all her care, the strength of her desire for him would show in her face, or voice, or gesture. 'Ben?'

'Yes, Louey?' said the boy, swinging round eagerly. 'Oh, Alex – hullo, Alex – Pagan my friend!'

'You've seen him, then?' his cousin said. 'What do you think of him?' His manner was easy and friendly, as one expert to another.

'Good,' Ben told him, his head nodding enthusiastically up and down while his overlarge tongue tripped over the words. 'Good foals – better than Amber – better than *any*!' He glanced at the chestnut, who was standing quite calmly beside him, looking bored, and added, 'Sorry, Amber.'

The stallion blew heavily and stamped a foot. Ben drew down his golden head, whispered something in one large furry ear, which flicked attentively, and then released him with a gentle pat. He returned to the door of the loosebox with a broad and beaming smile. 'Like Amber. Ben's favourite. Good horse – good foals.'

'Perhaps I'll be able to buy some of your young mares,' said Alex. 'For Pagan to serve. I've already spoken to Jan about it, and he suggested I discuss it with you. Are there, say, four or five fillies who show promise?'

They were soon deep in horse talk, and despite the limits of Ben's powers of speech, seemed to understand each other very well. Louise listened for a while, unwilling to be excluded, yet also reluctant to leave Alex's presence. Which, she told herself with sudden annoyance, is quite ridiculous – he will be gone tomorrow, and you probably won't see him again for months, by which time, with luck, this inconvenient infatuation will be past and gone.

With sudden resolution, she turned and walked out of the stables, noticing, with some exasperation, that neither Alex nor Ben seemed to be aware of her departure.

He left the next morning, having reached an agreement with Jan to the satisfaction of both parties, and of Ben, and with him went Henry Renolds and three fine fillies, two bays and a brown, that would, with luck, be the foundation mares of the new breed of St Barbe horses. Pagan curvetted and pranced skittishly, as if well aware of his own destined role, and relishing it. And despite all her good intentions, Louise felt a real, sharp sense of loss as she watched Alex diminish, surrounded by horses, into the distance of the road back to Wintercombe.

Quite apart from anything else, life would be tolerably dull without his company.

She found it difficult to converse with Bathsheba, and her Aunt Rachael, though perfectly courteous, did not possess the warm friendliness of Silence, or indeed of Amy. The children, however, were delightful when away from their grandmother's intimidating presence. Louise, who missed the younger members of her own family more than she cared to admit, greatly enjoyed playing with them and teaching them silly songs and rhymes in French. She also spent much time talking horses to Jan, and to Ben, and conceived a plan which, at the end of five rather hectic days, finally brought its reward, in the shape of a very pretty mare, a golden dun with black points, mane and tail, five years old and as gentle and willing a mount, said Jan with pleasure, as any lady could wish for.

Such quality, of course, did not come cheap, but Louise had a substantial allowance from her generous stepfather, besides her own small inheritance from her father, and could well afford it. Indeed, she thought, as she rode the mare at a decorous canter around the damp home paddock, savouring her smooth action and responsiveness, the wonder of it was that she had put up with the deficiencies of poor Nance for so long.

She thanked Jan profusely for his efforts on her behalf, and he waved her away with a diffident, shy grin. 'No trouble, Cousin. It's a pleasure to see you suited so well – and she's a fine mare, she'll give you many years of willing service, and good foals too if you've a mind. Do you plan to put her to Pagan?'

'I might,' said Louise. 'But for the present, I think I will just enjoy riding her.'

She debated what to call her new acquisition. The Longleaze horses had all been given descriptive names – Amber, Blackbird, Brown Bess, Whitefoot – and she supposed something similar would be most suitable for her yellow mare. And as Ben seemed to have christened most of them, she went in search of his advice.

He was in the stables with a mare, one of the grooms told her, and she found him gentling and soothing a young, nervous iron grey in the process of birthing her first foal.

There was no one to tell her what was and was not proper for a lady. Ben turned his big grin on her as she came to the door of the loosebox. 'Louey! Come – come see! Almost there!'

She entered the box cautiously, her skirt snagging on the thick yellow straw. The mare lay, sweat-streaked and bulging, her ears laid back and her head low. A convulsive heave twisted her flanks. Ben stroked and soothed her as the pain passed, and then turned to Louise again. 'Foal – see, Louey, foal hooves!'

And, sure enough, she could see them under the mare's tail, small, dark, pointed. Another contraction shook the horse, and she grunted in pain. Ben left her head and came round to inspect. He looked thoughtful, and then glanced up at her as she stood, fascinated. 'Louey hold her head – Ben pull.'

It was surprising how authoritative he sounded. She obeyed the instruction of an expert, and knelt by the mare's head, whispering encouragement to her as she braced herself for another push. Ben undoubtedly knew what he was about – he had probably helped more foals into the world than most midwives had birthed babies – but she could not help but feel some anxiety. So often, matters went awry, and mother or foal, or both, were lost. She would have liked to watch the entire process, but Ben had given her a vital task to perform, and she would do it willingly.

With hand and voice, she tried to soothe away the pain and dumb bewilderment in the young mare's soft dark eyes, and reminded herself that this sort of agony and danger was the likely outcome of indulgence in the feelings that Alex had aroused in her. The horse squealed in sudden pain, and she tightened her grip as the mare gave a final, shuddering convulsion. There was an exclamation of satisfaction from Ben, and Louise peered round the horse's bulk. There was a dark, shapeless bundle huddled in the straw beside Ben, and she saw the sudden flash of his grin. 'Louey – see, come see!'

She unwound her cramped fingers from the mare's head collar, surprised that she seemed to have gripped the leather so tightly. The horse, freed, at once swung her head round towards her offspring. Ben was wiping and cleaning it with a hank of straw, and suddenly the amorphous shape resolved itself into the component parts of a foal, head and body and astonishingly long, crumpled legs. It shook its head, the large soft ears flapping, and uttered an experimental bleating cry. The mare whickered in response and tried to struggle to her feet. With Ben's help, she managed it, and turned, narrowly avoiding Louise, to push her nose enquiringly at the foal.

'Good,' said Ben. 'All well now – now stand, then drink.' He got to his feet, wiping his hands on straw, and in the half-light his ugly, unformed face was soft, and almost beautiful with pride and happiness. 'Colt foal. Thank you, Louey – thank you!'

'It was my pleasure,' Louise said warmly, smiling at him. 'I was glad to help. I've never seen a foal born before.'

Ben's mouth dropped in comical astonishment. 'Never? Never, Louey? But . . .' His voice trailed away into incoherency.

She was not sure what he meant to say, but could guess. 'Yes, perhaps it is strange, but my mother and stepfather do not approve of such things. They think that ladies shouldn't see – that it's improper.'

Ben's response was a derisory snort that entirely won her approval. She grinned at him, and he grinned back, the two of them remarkably united despite the unbridgeable gap in ability and experience. 'Not a lady,' said Ben, with rich scorn. 'You much better – you *Louey*!'

It was a compliment which she would cherish for the rest of her days.

# 7

## '*A fiery soul*'

Their time at Longleaze expired, Louise and Silence and their maids packed their bags, said their farewells to the Wickham family, and rode southwards to Chard, the home of Silence and of her husband Nick Hellier, Louise's grandfather, whom she had never met.

All her life she had wondered about the man who had, once, been her grandmother's illicit and adulterous lover. Kate, their first child, had been born while Silence had still been the wife of Sir George St Barbe, and he, ignorant of his wife's brief affair with a Cavalier captain, had unquestioningly accepted Kate as his own. It was only after Sir George's death, when Silence and her lover had met again and married, that the truth about Kate's parentage had been acknowledged. She herself had made no secret of it, either to the vicomte or to her daughter, and had spoken of her father and mother in the fond but rather distant tones of a woman who had far outgrown her background. Louise had always taken the whole tale – romantic or shameful, according to the morals of whoever heard it – very much for granted, a part of ancient family history that had happened long before her own arrival in the world. But then she had met her grandmother for the first time, and the ensuing weeks in her company had prompted her curiosity. It was so very difficult to imagine Silence, calm, wise, old-fashioned, as a young Puritan wife willing to risk reputation, home, husband and children for a penniless Cavalier adventurer.

But if she had not, long ago, indulged in a recklessness that her granddaughter could not possibly see in her now, then Kate would never have existed, and nor would Louise herself, a thought at once fascinating and appalling. The episode did not seem sordid, not as Kate had described it, with her admiration for Silence's wild behaviour glowing in every word. But still Louise's imagination failed to envisage her grandmother as a furtive adulteress.

The house at Chard was old, but had been very much refurbished in recent years. It was small, surrounded by a walled garden with an imposing gateway, and the farm buildings tucked well out of sight down the lane. Louise rode the dun mare, whom Ben had named Saffron, up to the gates, and saw that they had a welcome. The family that was closest to her, after her own, had all come to greet her.

The slight, brown-haired man with the soft smile must be her uncle, Richard, her mother's brother. The blonde woman beside him, bulky in the last months of pregnancy, would be his wife Sarah, and the little boy, perhaps two years old, peeping round her skirts with a shy curious grin, was their son Nicholas.

And his grandfather, and hers, for whom he had been named, was this lean, brown-skinned, white-haired man in a countryman's plain russets, coming forward with an amused, lazy smile on his mouth. She was as tall as he was, and could discern little resemblance to herself in his neat-featured face, the lines of laughter reassuringly pale around his mouth. Then she saw the colour of his eyes, the warm chestnut brown of her own and Kate's, and of her five half-brothers and half-sisters.

'So you're Louise,' he said, sizing her up with a shrewd expression. 'My eldest grandchild – which makes me feel positively ancient. Welcome to Chard, dear girl – and I hope you won't find us too quiet and provincial after Wintercombe.' And he grinned suddenly and disarmingly, and she saw where Kate's smile had come from.

For her, he had a friendly kiss on each cheek. For Silence, Louise noticed with affection, there was an embrace that would not have seemed out of place between a pair of betrothed lovers. Whatever the truth of their long-past adultery, there was no doubt that thirty years of marriage had not quenched their love for one another.

Silence had told her that the Chard house had once been a dark, unwelcoming place which she had heartily disliked. Sir George had left it to her for her widowhood, and she had not wanted to live there. But Nat had transformed it, as a wedding present to her and Nick, and now it was a delightful home, light and sunny, filled with the fragrance of dried flowers and beeswax, and even on this, the fourth day of March, the garden glowed with clumps of purple crocus, the rather battered pallor of snowdrops, now almost over, and the first splashes of daffodil yellow. The love and labour of more than thirty years showed plain in every neatly clipped hedge, the walks and arbours, the fruit trees trained bare and knobbly against the ancient stone walls, and in the immaculate tidiness of the gravel, with not a weed to be seen or a leaf out of place anywhere.

Her chamber was tiny, whitewashed, with a dormer window giving an excellent view of the garden. There was a half tester bed, cosily piled with quilts and blankets, an old-fashioned clothes press at its foot, a table with a jug and basin and a bowl of sweet-scented dried flower-petals, and two cane-seated chairs.

'It's not very big, I'm afraid,' Sarah told her apologetically. 'There's little spare room here – your maid can have the closet next door, which is even smaller, if that is possible. But I've tried to make it comfortable.'

'It's lovely,' Louise told her. 'Thank you so much – I shall be very happy here.' She looked at her uncle's wife – it did not somehow seem right to call a girl only a few years older 'Aunt' – and saw the air of contentment, the smile in her eyes, her general appearance of health and fertility, and was surprised to find that she envied her. Sarah lived in a world very different from her sister-in-law Kate, an apparently narrow existence bounded by husband, home, children, but that limited life had given her, it was plain, great happiness and security. With a sudden flash of insight, Louise wondered if her mother, moving with bright gaiety in her fashionable and frivolous château, could really claim such bliss.

But Kate, whether happy or not, could certainly never be so in such a restricted environment: indeed, she had escaped from Chard at the age of seventeen, eloping with the Guernsey sea captain whom she had met at her half-sister Deb's house in Bristol, and had never returned. And now her daughter, coming for the first time to the house where her mother had grown up, meeting her father and her brother, could not imagine Kate, with her reckless laughter and wild ways, ever being content in this sleepy little house.

And yet she herself had no sense of being trapped here, not yet: there was, in the simple, refreshing little room, only peace, and homecoming. She knew herself: she knew this feeling would not last and that, as at Wintercombe, she would soon crave difference, excitement and freedom once more, just as Kate had. But she could also see so clearly, as perhaps her mother had not, the grief Kate had caused when she ran away twenty-two years ago, without explanation or farewell, for love of a tall, olive-skinned sailor with dark greedy eyes, who knew so much more of the world than she did. And he had given her freedom, and Louise, and unhappiness and ecstasy in equal measures, until his death in a shipwreck off the rocky Guernsey coast when Louise was four.

She sat thoughtfully on the soft feather bed, one part of her mind pondering what to wear, the rest acutely conscious of her origins, her own past and that of her family, here in this small unassuming Somerset house.

And, she realised as she decided on her tawny-yellow silk, with the sable tippet, she had not thought of her cousin Alex for almost a day.

March slipped by, mild and full of birdsong. Louise lived quietly, enjoying the peace while her restless spirit would allow her, talking to her grandparents, helping Sarah, coming to know her Uncle Richard. He was not at all like Kate in character, being quiet, thoughtful and reserved, in contrast to his energetic wife and bouncing small boy: in fact, he was, Louise realised quite soon, rather shy. But she charmed him sufficiently for him to teach her backgammon and chess, and to take her out riding on her mare Saffron, and little Nicholas, a fair-haired imp of mischief just two years old, provided much amusement.

She found herself in sole charge of her small cousin when Sarah, rather earlier than had been expected, was delivered of her second child, a girl with a very loud and healthy-sounding pair of lungs. Louise held Nicholas as he peered in fascinated disgust at the red wrinkled scrap in the cradle and announced firmly, 'That's not a sister, that's a *prune*.'

There was some discussion over the baby's name. Sarah and Richard wanted to call her Silence, for her grandmother, but that lady reacted with horror to the suggestion. 'Oh, no – you can't in all conscience saddle the poor mite with my name! Why not Sarah?'

'I think it would be too confusing,' said her son's wife, smiling up from the pillows: it had been a comparatively easy birth, and already the colour was back in her cheeks, despite her evident weariness. 'Why do you not like your name? I think it's quite lovely, and so unusual.'

'And very inappropriate for that noisy infant,' said Nick Hellier drily, gesturing at the cradle, which was at present quiet, though not likely to remain so for long.

'The reason,' Silence said briskly, 'is that I would not want my grandchild to suffer the same teasing and taunting that I endured, all my childhood and after. When I had Kate and Richard, I deliberately chose good plain names for them, rather than make them ridiculous. Puritan names such as mine are no longer the fashion. It's outlandish enough now – how peculiar will it seem when she's reached my age?'

'I doubt it will – instead, it will seem lovely and rare, just as your name is now,' said Nick fondly.

Silence looked at him, and smiled and shook her head. 'No, I forbid it, Sarah – *please* don't call her after me, poor little thing.'

'Well,' said her daughter-in-law from the bed, 'Richard and I wanted to do it to please you – and since it doesn't, we won't, don't worry.'

'It'll make little difference anyway, I suspect,' Nick pointed out, 'since Nicholas will undoubtedly insist on referring to her as Prune.'

In the end, the baby was christened Rebecca, after Sarah's mother, but her grandfather's prediction proved quite correct, and soon everyone in the household called her Prune. But her birth heralded a change in Louise's comfortable, quiet life. Sarah was almost entirely occupied with the baby, and Silence, of necessity, with managing the household.

Richard was busy on the farm, where cows and sheep were producing their young with the usual frequency of springtime, and Louise found herself largely left to the company of her grandfather.

She was not disconcerted by this. He might be close on fifty years her senior, but he was neither distant nor censorious, unlike most men of his generation whom she had met in the past. Louise found him very easy to talk to, and he in turn had a large fund of stories, some exciting, others amusing, from his days as a Cavalier captain in the civil wars. And it was from Nick that she learned a great deal more about her other Somerset relations, both those he knew, and those she had not yet encountered.

It was certainly a diverse group, scattered like leaves across the West Country – Bristol, Taunton, Chard, Glastonbury and, of course, Wintercombe. She inferred, from Nick's descriptions of them all, that, surprisingly, only one of Silence's children or stepchildren had made a conventionally 'good' match, and that was her Aunt Deb, who had married the only son of a wealthy Bristol merchant. And she, it seemed from what Nick let slip, was perhaps the least fortunate in her choice. The moral in all this, Louise decided, was that a spouse with money and position alone was unlikely to provide happiness.

'And you?' Nick asked her, during one of their conversations. 'I understand from Silence that you're on the catch for a husband.'

'Perhaps,' Louise said, smiling. They were walking in the garden, warmer now as March had given way at last to April: the grass was growing, the sun shining, and there was blossom already on the plum and cherry trees. 'But I'm in no particular hurry. And besides, I'm far too fastidious to seize on the first man I see.'

'And have you seen any yet?'

She was holding a pale pheasant's-eye narcissus to her nose, sniffing its delicate fragrance. 'None that measure up to my exacting requirements, I regret to say.'

'Which are?'

'Wealth – health – youth – and tolerance,' said Louise, ticking them off one by one on her long, elegant fingers. 'Above all, tolerance of my foibles. My future husband must allow me to spend vast amounts of money on clothes, so I am quite à la mode – he must not throw up his hands in horror when I urge my horse into a gallop – and above all, he must indulge all my whims. If I could find a man who would do that, then I would marry him tomorrow.'

'Unless he is married already,' Nick pointed out. 'So – you have found no one? Well, as you said, there is plenty of time, and two more sets of cousins to visit. Who knows – you may find the man of your dreams amongst them.'

'I doubt it,' Louise said drily. 'I'm beginning to doubt that he exists.' She glanced sideways at her grandfather, and flashed him that sudden, triangular grin that was so like her mother's. 'Perhaps I shall reject marriage altogether, and become a pampered *fille de joie*, kept in luxury by a succession of wealthy noblemen.'

She had read him right: he was not in the least shocked, but amused. 'Hardly your style, Louise – you are much too independent-minded to follow such a servile path. Can you imagine yourself telling some fat marquis in his dotage what a wonderful lover he is, for the sake of his money and jewels?'

She laughed. 'No, to be honest, I can't. Besides, jewels have never really appealed to me. I would prefer a string of horses to a string of pearls. And since ladies of pleasure are not supposed to be interested in anything outside the boudoir, I think a husband is inevitable.'

'Alex is interested in breeding horses, so your grandmother tells me.'

Louise felt a betraying flush seep up under her skin, and hoped that he had not noticed it. She was ashamed of herself, behaving like an infatuated schoolgirl. She was not sure of the exact nature of her feeling for her cousin – perhaps lust was the nearest word for something so dark, and overwhelmingly powerful, and based entirely upon his physical presence. But the strength of it did not go well, in her eyes, with her self-esteem. She should be able to play the game, to flirt and act the coquette as she had done so many times before, without revealing how deeply he affected her. And to have her grandfather, friendly and pleasant though he was, guess at her thoughts about Alex was to make herself vulnerable.

She said, her voice held casually level, 'Yes, he is. He has a magnificent stallion that he brought with him from the Low Countries, and he bought some mares from Cousin Jan in Glastonbury.' She let the enthusiasm for his project creep into her voice, hoping that Nick would think that it was the horses that attracted her, and expounded at some length upon the opportunity that Pagan's arrival presented for the future of horseflesh at Wintercombe.

Nick Hellier was not deceived, and later that evening, alone with his wife in the chamber that they had shared for the thirty-three years of their marriage, he mentioned his talk with Louise, adding casually, 'She seems very taken with Alex.'

Silence looked up sharply from the table where she was making notes of the seeds sown that day in the garden. 'Alex? Oh, dear.'

'She did her best to hide it,' said Nick. 'And she did very well – almost, but not quite, as good as you. But I received the impression that she has . . . a certain fondness for him. Why did you say "Oh, dear": Don't we want to find her a wealthy husband?'

'You haven't seen him for years,' Silence pointed out. 'Yes, he is wealthy – but that is about the only suitable qualification which he possesses. If you really want your granddaughter shackled to an offensive drunken libertine with the arrogance of Lucifer and the instincts of a tom cat, then Alex will do admirably.' She removed her spectacles and stared at him earnestly. 'It grieves me greatly to think that Nat's only son has turned out so bad – and I would not wish Louise to marry him, if he were the last man in Somerset.'

Nick shook his head. 'Silence, Silence, it's not like you to be so vehement. What is it about Alex that has upset you so much? He is Nat's son, and Patience's, he was such a charming child – I know he has a wild past, but surely he cannot have gone so far beyond redemption?'

'He seems to have done,' she said sadly. 'Oh, I can see only too clearly why Louise is attracted to him. He has his mother's looks, and his father's intelligence, even if he does misuse it. And he can still be charming, when he chooses – he made himself very pleasant at Glastonbury, he even succeeded in mollifying Rachael, and as you know, that's no easy task. But I have seen the other side of him, which I suspect, alas, to be the real Alex. And believe me, it was not pleasant. Louise is a delightful girl, full of life and happiness, but she's as headstrong as Kate, I think.'

'She can't be – she's still unwed, and she's nearly twenty.'

Silence smiled wryly. 'Unwed, yes, but perhaps not wholly innocent. That, after all, was apparently the reason Kate sent her to Wintercombe – there was considerable scandal in France, concerning the attentions of a certain gentleman, and the more so since he was married, and twice her age.' She sighed. 'Reckless, wilful – it must be the Hellier blood in her.'

'More likely to be from your own family,' said Nick, gently teasing her. 'How else to explain Patience, and Alex, and Kate, and Louise – not to mention you yourself? There's a wildness in you, my love, for all it's buried so deep that no one else suspects it. Perhaps Louise and Alex are well matched.'

'Then I shudder to think of their offspring!' said Silence caustically. 'Any such would doubtless be quite ungovernable. But Nick, I do mean this seriously. I cannot in all conscience allow Louise to enter into any kind of connection with Alex. She may seem to be an independent girl of strong character, well able to take care of herself – but if she becomes infatuated with him, she will be so vulnerable. He'll use her, and cast her aside – and she deserves so much better than to be the leavings of such a man.' She smiled rather bleakly. 'She needs someone her own age, or just a little older, to laugh with her, and –'

'And indulge and tolerate her foibles, she said to me,' Nick told her. 'There is a very practical streak in your granddaughter, have you noticed? She seems exceptionally level-headed, and quite clear-eyed about the whole business. I don't think her feelings for Alex are within her control, or even very welcome to her. And she's certainly in no hurry to wed – she told me so herself.'

'She's young, and there's plenty of time – so long as Alex doesn't leap in first and ruin her reputation,' Silence pointed out. 'Still, I have an idea or two still in hand. Perhaps it's time for her to visit Tabby in Taunton.'

Nick looked at her, and began to laugh. 'I know exactly what you're thinking! But surely he's too young?'

'Bram is twenty-one, he's clever, good-looking and a very nice boy indeed. Of course, he is her cousin, but that need be no bar. And he will inherit Jonah's business, and doubtless expand it to great profit – he may forever have his head in a book, but he has a great deal of sense.'

'He'll have to cultivate an interest in horses to attract Louise,' Nick told her. 'In fact, I suspect that she has more in common with Alex than with Bram.'

'And what did I have in common with you, pray?' Silence enquired, smiling at him, and in the soft, buttery light her face looked for a moment as young and fresh as her granddaughter's. 'The shy Puritan wife and mother, and the roistering Cavalier captain? There is no accounting for love. Anyway, I have no intention of suggesting anything to Louise, or of trying in any way to influence her. She can go to Taunton, and meet Tabby's family, and I will let matters take their course, or not. But nothing would give me greater pleasure than to see her come to an understanding with Bram.'

In complete ignorance of her grandmother's hopes for her future, Louise welcomed the suggestion that she spend a few weeks with her Loveridge cousins in Taunton. The old restlessness had attacked her again, prompting her to wonder whether she would ever be truly happy confined in one place with a limited circle of friends. She was surrounded by affection, she was indulged, allowed to ride out whenever she pleased, able to do exactly as she liked, but somehow it had all become rather flat and unexciting, even, she dared to admit to herself, a little tedious. There was little to engage her interest at Chard, no surprises, no handsome and eligible young men, although several neighbours had been invited to dinner to meet her. She was bored, and felt decidedly guilty for feeling thus, for she was well aware of how kind her grandparents had been, and of how much she owed them. But the sense of peace and homecoming that had made her first weeks with them so pleasant had now evaporated, and she was ready for a change.

So she packed her bags with a light heart, consoled her maid Christian, who had developed an affection for one of the Chard grooms, said goodbye to Sarah and Richard and their children, and to Silence, who would not be escorting her the dozen miles or so to Taunton. Then she mounted her yellow mare, with Christian sniffing mournfully on the pillion pad behind her, and set off, with her grandfather as escort, to meet her Loveridge cousins in a mood of considerable anticipation.

She had learned quite a lot about them over the past few weeks. Tabitha Loveridge was Silence's eldest and, probably, favourite daughter, who had once been one of the loveliest girls in Somerset, and much sought after by nobility and gentry alike. But she had spurned them all, however good-looking, rich and well-mannered, and at the age of twenty-seven, almost an old maid, she had married Jonah, a Taunton bookseller with radical views and very little money, and had lived happily ever since. They had had seven children, but only Bram, the eldest, and the girls Susan and Hannah, aged sixteen and eleven, had survived. Despite his father's comparatively humble origins, Bram had been sent to Oxford, where he had apparently distinguished himself as a scholar, and he had returned to help his father in his business, making regular trips to London to consult others in the trade and to buy books. The two girls were still at school in Taunton, and had been joined, for her education and companionship, by another cousin, Elizabeth Orchard, who was fifteen and usually lived with her parents in Bristol. The prospect of four young people in the house was a pleasant one, and, much as Louise loved small children, the Loveridges had no squalling babies or demanding two-year-olds.

Taunton lay in the green, lush vale of Taunton Deane, the paradise of the West Country, thick with orchards and bees and apple blossom in the sunshine of early May. It was prosperous place of several thousand people, famous for its cloth and cider, its markets for cattle and horses, and as a nest of Dissenters and radicals. Forty years ago, during the war, the town had been twice besieged, unsuccessfully, by the Royalists, and had suffered greatly for it. Less than a third of the houses had remained standing by the time Taunton was relieved, on the eleventh day of May, 1645, a date remembered with rejoicing ever since, despite the attempts of Tory mayors to ban public ceremony.

But there were no signs of such devastation now, although, Nick told her, all the eastern side of Taunton had been a smoking ruin. The houses no longer had the raw, naked look of the absolutely new, but lay on either side of the broad highway known as Eastreach, as if they had been there for centuries. They were built mostly of timber and plaster, with some of brick or the dark red local stone, and had a neat, prosperous air, like the people thronging the street.

Jonah Loveridge lived in a tall, narrow, half-timbered house just where East Street joined Fore Street, opposite the marketplace and Cornhill. It was, Louise thought as she dismounted, a prime site for any shop, although the quiet reflections of those browsing amongst her uncle's stock would probably be rudely disturbed on market day. There was apparently no stabling behind the house, so, by long-standing arrangement, the horses were given into the keeping of the Red Lion, which stood almost directly opposite. Nick assured her that they would be well cared for, but Louise could not help casting a concerned eye over the stable yard, visible through the arch. Everything seemed neat, clean, and in good order, so she followed her grandfather across the street to the Loveridges' shop.

It was immediately apparent why no one had come out to greet them, for the bookseller was occupied with a customer, and both men were deep in conversation over a large volume open on a table in the centre of the book-lined front room. One of them, a spare, grey-haired man of fifty or so, raised his head, peered at them through the gloom, and said briskly, 'If you'd care to browse amongst my shelves, sir, madam, I will be able to attend to you shortly.'

'By all means, Jonah,' said Nick, smiling.

The other man blinked, and fumbled in the pocket of his plain dark coat, producing a pair of spectacles which he hastily balanced on his rather beaky nose. 'Nick! A hundred apologies, man – I did not recognise you. Pray excuse me, sir,' he added to the customer, a well-dressed and portly man who was obviously of some substance. 'This is my wife's stepfather, come from Chard – and my niece, on her first visit to Taunton, and I must give them welcome.'

'Certainly,' the customer said, in lordly fashion, and favoured Louise with a keen, lingering and appreciative stare, before returning to his perusal of the book. Evidently, the dusty ride on a warm morning had not had too detrimental an effect on her appearance.

'Welcome to Taunton, Louise,' Jonah Loveridge was saying to her with a smile. He was not, and probably never had been, a handsome man, for his nose was too prominent, his mouth too thin and his eyes bright and shrewd, despite the spectacles, beneath rather bushy brows, but she liked him at once. 'I hope you have had a good journey,' he added. 'I don't know where Tabby is – she knew you were coming, but she seems to have vanished, and Bram is out on an errand to the Grammar School, and the girls are at school themselves, of course.'

'She hasn't disappeared – I can hear her,' said Nick, glancing up at the uneven plaster ceiling. And Louise, listening, heard sweet and faint, threading through the busy noise of Taunton at midday, the sounds of a keyboard instrument being played with uncommon skill. She felt an unworthy stab of envy, for she had never possessed the patience, still less the ability, to master any kind of music. She could not even sight-sing, apparently an accomplishment which many English men and women took for granted, although she had always enjoyed the private concerts which her stepfather had organised at the château for the family and their guests and neighbours. But her grandfather played the fiddle, well enough to provide evening entertainment, and her Uncle Richard had a fine voice and a sure touch on the virginals. If the sounds drifting down from above were any guide, her Aunt Tabitha had a gift to outshine them both.

'We'll go up and surprise her,' Nick said. 'You attend to your customer, Jonah – don't worry about our bags, one of the grooms at the Red Lion is bringing them over.'

As Louise climbed the narrow stairs, her skirts held well clear of her feet – a fall now would not be pleasant – she heard the swift torrent of music come to an abrupt end, and footsteps approaching. A door opened as she reached the head of the stairs, and her Aunt Tabitha stood there to welcome them.

She had once been known as the loveliest girl in Somerset, and enough remained of that famous, ethereal beauty for Louise to see that the tale was true. Tabby Loveridge was tall, slender still, with an unusual face, pale and delicate of feature, that must have been quite exquisite twenty years ago, and a mass of thick, curling hair, honey-coloured and well streaked and frosted with silver, loosely knotted at the back and showing signs of surprisingly youthful rebellion. 'Hullo, Louise,' she said, taking her hands with a smile. 'You're not in the least like Kate.'

'Oh, but she is,' said Nick. 'Wait until you see her eyes – and her smile. Not to mention her sense of mischief.'

And Louise, feeling that she was going to enjoy her stay in Taunton, was drawn into the sunny, west-facing parlour that lay above Jonah's shop, and looked out on to the bustling marketplace. She had a brief impression of chairs, a settle piled high with cushions, a comfortably upholstered squab couch, a table covered with books and sewing, shelves loaded with more books and pottery, a black and white cat regarding her unwinkingly from a window seat in the sun, and a small hexagonal keyboard instrument, obviously the source of the music, and so similar to the *épinettes* that Louise had seen in France that she supposed it must be a spinet.

'You were playing that?' she said to her aunt. 'It was absolutely lovely – I've always wished I could play, but I haven't the gift, or the patience.'

'I owe any skill I have in such things to Nick,' Tabby told her. 'He taught me to play, as a child, and somehow I have managed to keep in practice, despite all the distractions of domestic life. Now, you must be in need of refreshment after your journey – what would you like? There's coffee, chocolate, cider, beer, even a little tea, if I can find the key to the caddy. And dinner should be ready in an hour, if you can wait that long.'

When a very young maid had brought beer for Nick and a pot of steaming, fragrant coffee for the two women, they settled down in the comfortable chairs around the table for a family gossip. The cat left its window seat and came to investigate Louise's lap: it was evidently satisfied, for it settled down with a contented sigh on the thick folds of her riding habit, and began to purr.

'That's Jezebel,' said Tabby, smiling. 'She's Pye's great-great-great-great-great-granddaughter – has Mother told you about Pye? She was the cat we had at Wintercombe, when Nick and the other soldiers were garrisoned there. Since then, Mother has always had one or two of her descendants, and so have I, and the rest are catching mice and rats all over Somerset. I called this one Jezebel because she's such a brazen hussy – and she has that rather smug look I always imagine that Jezebel would have, before her unfortunate end, of course.'

Jezebel, sleek and glossy with paws of a deceptively pure and innocent white, purred modestly under Louise's stroking hand. She listened, sipping the strong dark coffee, while her aunt and her grandfather exchanged titbits of family news, reports on Sarah's baby, the doings of the Loveridge daughters, and the recent events at Wintercombe. She tried not to look too interested as Alex's name was mentioned and the rather awkward situation of Bab, Charles and Amy discussed. She wondered suddenly what had happened there, in the two months she had been away. Surely, if Charles and Alex had come to blows, they would have heard of it? Bab, who seemed to regard Silence as the family's mentor, to be summoned at every crisis, would surely have sent news of any disaster. She felt guilty about poor Charles, who had been forced into an almost impossible position, compelled to rely for survival on the good will of a man he detested. There was no doubt of it, he was a much more sympathetic and pleasant character than Alex.

124

The mystery of it all was, why did Alex attract her so strongly, rather than Charles?

A thunder of footsteps up the stairs roused her from her thoughts, and Jezebel woke with a jerk. The door opened, and a young man stood there, flushed with exertion, his eyes going at once to Louise.

'This is Bram,' said her aunt, rather unnecessarily.

Louise hoped that he was not the only one of the family to inherit his mother's looks: if his sisters had not, it would be very unfair. He had the honey-gold hair, sufficiently thick and curling to render a wig unnecessary, the fine-featured faun's face and the hazel eyes, fringed with lashes that would have seemed long on a girl. There was a certain look of Jonah about his mouth, but the rest was all Tabby's. The effect should have been weak and effeminate, but was emphatically not: there was a fierceness in his face, an eagerness that was at once invigorating and very attractive. She got to her feet, forgetting Jezebel, who slid off her knees with an indignant squawk and retired to the window seat, shaking her paws as she went to make her point.

'And you must be Louise,' he said, and made an abrupt, almost jerky bow, very different from Alex's insolent grace. 'Have you come to stay with us? How brave of you! I hope you like books – and sleeping in cupboards.'

'Bram!'

'Well, forewarned is forearmed, Mother. Shall I show it to her now? You see, Cousin, this house was probably built for a race of dwarfs. These rooms have ceilings high enough, but on the next floor even Hannah has to bend her head to get through the doorways, and she's eleven. As for the two floors above, well, I leave that to your imagination.'

'Bram, you're exaggerating shamelessly,' said his mother with a rather rueful laugh. 'Take no notice of him, please, Louise – your chamber isn't very large, I'll be the first to admit, but it's certainly not a cupboard.'

'Perhaps not,' said Bram. He pushed his hair out of his eyes and grinned. 'Is that a pot of coffee I see before me? More to the point, is there any left? I've run all the way from the Grammar School – and it must be all of two hundred yards – and I'm parched.' He walked over to the pot sitting on the table, and peered inside. 'Alas, just the dregs. Never mind, perhaps I can twist Moll's arm and she'll make me some more.'

Louise sat down, trying not to smile, so infectious was this irresistible whirlwind of a cousin. Strangely, he reminded her a little of her mother in one of her wild moods – or, indeed, of Alex, long ago in that enchanted summer. More than ever, she looked forward to the next few weeks. With the lively Bram for company, they were most unlikely to be dull.

And so it proved. The three girls, Sue, who was sixteen, her younger sister Hannah, and their cousin Elizabeth Orchard, always known as Libby, were still giggling schoolgirls, eager for news of French modes and fashions, and Louise, finding them more congenial company than the empty-headed Amy, was happy to oblige them. Sue was very skilled with the needle, and there was a chest full of unused materials, from woollens to expensive silks, in her parents' chamber. Under their cousin's direction, the two sisters stitched enthusiastically, making mantuas and aprons and tippets, while Libby, who was plump and rather quiet, curled in the window seat, with Jezebel on her lap, and read her way voraciously through her Uncle Jonah's stock.

Bram was usually busy, helping in the shop, or delivering orders to outlying customers, for his father had arrangements with many book-sellers and printers in Bath, Oxford, Bristol and London, and almost every day saw the arrival of another heavy parcel of volumes that had been requested by Jonah's clients. Louise, who had never taken much interest in books save as a pleasant diversion to while away a wet afternoon or a dark evening, found herself falling under the spell of Bram's enormous enthusiasm for his family's stock in trade. Books in a dozen languages, on an endless multitude of subjects, from pompous histories and earnest theological works, through treatises on the natural world and the turgid romances that Amy had loved, to the small cheap chapbooks that appealed to the poor, the young and the unsophisticated, all jostled on the crowded shelves of the shop, and even tottered in piles on the floor. Somewhat to Louise's surprise, the local merchants and gentry were by no means Jonah's exclusive customers. Many of the people who came to look, to browse, and even to buy, were not wealthy, in fact sometimes seemed to be living in abject poverty, to judge from the condition of their clothes. Puzzled, she had said to Bram, 'But surely such people aren't able to read?'

'Some of them, no, I grant you,' her cousin told her, brushing the hair out of his eyes, with what she had come to recognise as a characteristic gesture. 'But you'd be surprised how many people in towns like Taunton – *especially* in Taunton – have had a little education. Learning is seen as . . . as a way of bettering yourself, but also as a means to bring people closer to God.'

Louise looked at him, her eyebrows raised. She had only lived in the Loveridge household – in a chamber somewhat larger than a cupboard – for a few days, but that had been enough to tell her that these cousins, while intelligent, thoughtful people, did not place the same emphasis on prayers and religion as the Wickhams, under her Aunt Rachael's aegis, did at Glastonbury. They attended the parish church of St Mary Magdalene, a magnificent building just round the corner off Fore Street, but without notable enthusiasm, and she had assumed that this family, like her own in France, did not allow their religious beliefs to rule their lives. She said curiously, 'Is that what you think?'

They were alone in the shop, for Jonah had taken a selection of books on Roman history to a valued customer at present sick at home, and business was slow just now: only one person in the last hour, and he had left without buying anything. Bram sat on the edge of the table on which his father laid out books for inspection. In the dusty sunlight filtering through the window, his face had an almost unearthly, angelic look. The illusion was shattered by the impudent grin which he sent her. 'Not necessarily. I think that learning is essential for everyone – rich, poor, male, female – because it's only through books that most people can discover the word, and be shaken out of all their prejudices and complacencies and forced to think for themselves. And of course, people who form their own opinions are not always welcome to those who govern them – or to the churches.' His face became suddenly serious. 'I believe in tolerance above all, and freedom. I don't want anyone, whether priest or parson or presbyter, telling me how to think or where to worship. My beliefs are my own business. The trouble with Papists and Presbyterians, and some Anglicans, is that they always want to rule your life as well as your religion. And the new King is a Papist.' He glanced at her as she stood on the other side of the table, a feather duster in her hands. 'You are a Protestant, yet you lived in France under Papist rule. You must have some understanding of the problem.'

'A little,' Louise said apologetically. 'But my situation was very different to that of most of the Huguenots, who tend to be the poorer sort, craftsmen, small farmers and so on. Wealth and influence can do much to shield a Protestant from the full force of persecution. I was sent to a Huguenot school at Blois, I was allowed to attend Protestant services – even though my stepfather is Catholic and my mother converted.' She smiled. 'That's partly why she sent me to England – because she wanted me to make my home in a Protestant country. Life is becoming more and more difficult for Huguenots in France, even the wealthier ones.'

'My point exactly,' said Bram. 'The Catholic church, like most churches, cannot tolerate any dissenting opinion – even if it does believe that heretics will fry in Hell. The Hugenots are being persecuted for their religion in France. Now, we have a Papist King in England. Already it's obvious that he favours other Catholics – his household is full of them. Within a few years there'll be Papists in all sections of government, from the village to Whitehall. And he's not famous for his tolerance, either. How long will it be before he persecutes English Protestants and enforces his Papist beliefs with an army, just as King Louis is doing in France?'

'I can't believe that he would,' Louise said. 'England is a Protestant country with a few Catholics. France is a Catholic country with a few Protestants.'

'And England was a Catholic country once, then Protestant, then Catholic again,' Bram reminded her. 'Oh, it would take years, I grant you – and the King has no Papist heir, nor does it seem likely after so many years without one. But imagine if the Queen were to bear a son now, a Papist son to inherit his father's crown – I think there'd be a revolution.' He grinned. 'After all, we English have disposed of one unsatisfactory king, less than forty years ago. Why not another? Regicide can become a habit.'

'King James has heirs – his daughters.'

'Yes, but they're Protestants, and most unlikely to turn Papist to please him. And Mary, of course, is married to Dutch William, and a more fervent Protestant never breathed. Of course,' Bram said, his eyes shining, his voice dropping to a conspiratorial hush, 'there's an heir who's more satisfactory still, and one who some would say has been unjustly deprived of his right.'

'Who?' asked Louise, puzzled. Her knowledge of English politics was even more sketchy than her interest in French affairs of state, and that was small enough.

Bram glanced round at the empty shop, the bustle in the sunny street beyond the window, and said softly, 'The Duke of Monmouth.'

'Oh, you mean the last King's natural son?'

'Well, officially his natural son,' said Bram. He leaned forward, his face transformed from angel to hawk. 'But there's been talk for years now that King Charles and Monmouth's mother were married. It's quite possible – they were in exile, very young, poor – there was no certainty that he would ever become King. There's talk of a black box which is supposed to hold the marriage certificate. And if that tale is true, then Monmouth is the rightful King of England!'

She liked Bram very much, but at moments such as this he seemed very young and idealistic, and she felt herself aeons older and wiser. Choosing her words carefully, Louise said slowly, 'But that isn't very likely, is it? Surely, if Monmouth were King Charles's lawful son, he would have acknowledged him?'

'He might have been ashamed of the marriage,' Bram said. 'By all accounts, Monmouth's mother was little better than a whore. And he quickly tired of her. But he always showed Monmouth much greater favour than any of his other bastard children, and that's surely significant.'

'Perhaps he just liked him better,' Louise said. In her heart she doubted very much whether the Duke was indeed the late King's legitimate son. It seemed most unlikely that King Charles, whose shrewdness was legendary, would have failed to acknowledge Monmouth if he had in fact been married to his mother – particularly since his next heir was his Papist and unpopular brother. But she kept her counsel, for she had no intention of entering into an argument with her cousin concerning anything so unconnected with their own lives.

'I saw him, five years ago,' Bram was saying. 'He made a progress through Somerset, and stayed at Master Prideaux's house near Chard, and the whole of Somerset seemed to have turned out to see him. I was at Oxford then, but it was August, so I was at home, and we all rode over to cheer him. Sue was only eleven or twelve, but she fell deeply in love.' He grinned. 'If you wish to learn more about our Protestant Duke, consult Sue. She has a stack of pamphlets and books under her bed, all exceedingly well thumbed.'

'Perhaps I will,' Louise said, flicking at stray motes of dust. 'So you've seen this Duke? Is he like his father?'

'Like enough to leave no one in any doubt as to whose son he is,' her cousin told her. 'He's tall, and dark, and uncommonly handsome, which is what attracted Sue. But what impressed me most was his manner. He was easy, friendly and pleasant to everybody – he looked every inch a prince, and yet he had the common touch. The people loved him – indeed, we all did. If he should ever return from exile to claim his right, the whole of the West Country will rise behind him.'

Louise frowned, the duster ignored in her hands. His eagerness and enthusiasm shone out like a lantern, but it struck no answering flame in her. Common sense told her that if Monmouth ever did leave Holland to challenge his Papist uncle for the throne, he would need rather more than the fervent loyalty of the people of Somerset to sustain him. And she could not, by any stretch of her imagination, picture this green, lush, placid country overset once again by civil war.

'I hope you choose your audience carefully,' she said, trying to keep the lightness in her voice. 'What you've just told me is probably treason, after all.'

'So it may be, but they can't arrest nine-tenths of Taunton,' Bram said cheerfully. He slid off the desk and came close to her. 'Dear Cousin, can you keep a secret?'

Louise was beginning to feel worried. Whatever else she had expected in this conversation, it was not treason, nor the possession of knowledge that was undoubtedly dangerous. And it was becoming obvious that her uncle's bookshop, outwardly so prosperous and respectable, might well harbour within its walls some very dubious opinions indeed. Politics and religion had never really concerned her: so long as she was free to ride, with money to spend and friends to laugh with, affairs of state had no relevance to her life. What did it matter who sat on the throne, or how he governed, so long as she had the means to enjoy herself? Even the plight of the Huguenots, persecuted and harassed for their beliefs, seemed remote and unreal.

'I can,' she said, doubtfully.

He whispered very quietly, almost in her ear, 'Argyll has sailed for Scotland!'

It meant absolutely nothing to her. She stared at him in bewilderment. 'I don't understand.'

'Of course, I keep forgetting, you've lived so long in France.' Bram did not seem annoyed by her ignorance: instead, with a patience that was most endearing, he explained. 'The Earl of Argyll is one of the exiles in Holland. Apparently, he set sail for Scotland last week, with three ships and three hundred men, arms and ammunition. It's been a year in the planning. And now Monmouth must follow him and invade England.'

'Invade?' She managed to keep her voice as low as his, with some difficulty. 'Invade England? How do you know?'

Bram smiled. 'Well, a man of his pride would hardly sit back in idleness while others went out to claim his throne for him, would he? It will be a matter of honour for him to launch his own invasion as soon as possible. And even if that were not so, suffice it to say that the Loveridge family has an unimpeachable source of information in Holland.' As Louise looked at him enquiringly, he added, 'Well, I'm sure you can guess. Which of our cousins has lately resided overseas?'

There was a man outside the window, peering in as if to ascertain whether or not the shop was attended. Louise glanced at Bram, aware that this period of undisturbed conversation was about to expire. She said, hardly able to believe it, 'You mean – do you mean *Alex*?'

'Who else? He was in the Low Countries for three years – he's served with the English regiments in the Dutch army and he knows many of the exiles there, including Monmouth. He's been sending my father information for years – *and* pamphlets, political ones that you can't buy in England. Don't look so surprised, Louise – Cousin Alex plots as naturally as he breathes.'

'I thought he drank as naturally as he breathed,' she said caustically.

'Oh, I knew he'd had to leave England quickly because of some scandal, but I thought it was something to do with a woman.'

'And with his supposed involvement in the Rye House Plot,' said Bram. 'Mind you, I think that was pure speculation. Alex is much too clever to have mixed himself up in an affair as incompetently managed as that. I don't know if he's changed, but he used to be a republican. And an atheist.'

She knew enough about English politics to realise that to adhere to just one of those two philosophies was to invite trouble, and to profess both was decidedly dangerous. 'Are you?' she asked, unwillingly.

'Certainly not an atheist. Possibly a republican,' said her exuberant cousin, grinning at her. 'Louise, don't look so serious! It's quite safe – our network is very well organised. And even though Alex has left Holland, we're still kept well informed by the contacts he arranged. That's how I know that Monmouth will invade very soon.'

It all seemed ludicrous and pointless, games played by children for monstrously high stakes. The King sat securely on his throne, the country was at peace: what possible chance did some penniless bastard adventurer have of overturning the established government?

But she could not reveal her derision to her idealistic cousin, all shining with enthusiasm for his chosen cause. And the involvement of Alex gave her food for thought. She knew him well enough, enigmatic as he appeared, to have considerable respect for his intelligence. If he was involved in this possible plot – and she only had Bram's word for it that the invasion plan even existed – then could it be more sure of success than it appeared?

She wished, suddenly, that she was back at Wintercombe, despite Amy's chatter, and her confused feelings about Charles, and above all the glittering, beckoning temptation of Alex. If he was plotting treason and insurrection, she wanted to be there, not here in this rebellious little town with her other kin, two of whom at least were not at all as they seemed. Apart from anything else, thought Louise, suddenly and grimly practical, it would be such a waste if I had resisted temptation so virtuously all this time, and Alex was then taken up for a traitor.

The memory of him, of his kiss and the feel of that long, hard, overpowering body against hers, warmed her suddenly with desire.

'Don't say anything more!' Bram hissed, and she realised that the shop door was opening and a customer was about to enter. She smiled, and touched her finger conspiratorially to her lips, and began decorously dusting the shelves while her cousin attended to the man, who was in search of a particular book of sermons. But inside, the old restlessness was growing again, insistent, urging her to saddle Saffron and ride out of Taunton, north-east, back to Wintercombe, and Alex, and whatever was happening there.

# 8

## 'In his son renewed'

The man rode up to Wintercombe late on a sunny afternoon, very early in June. There were cuckoos calling from the woods over towards Wellow, and clouds of bluebells, achingly vivid, drifting in the hedgerows. He was plainly dressed, with a broad-brimmed hat pulled well down over his straggling hair, and his blunt features and ruddy complexion showed little interest in his surroundings.

In contrast, the small boy who rode pillion behind him was looking about him with an air of quiet but devouring interest. As they passed the mill, he said something to the man, in a language not English, and received a smiling but weary reply in the same tongue. The child did not smile, but his small pale face, smudged with travel stains and fatigue, took on an expectant look, and he peered round the rider's broad back, eager for a first sight of their destination.

As luck would have it, only Phoebe was at home when Twinney, the butler, came to tell her of the visitors. Alex and Charles had gone to Bath on business, and Amy, never one to waste the opportunity of a shopping expedition, had accompanied them. Bab, of course, was in her chamber, sleeping off the latest excess of cakes and sweetmeats. Wintercombe was warm, sleepy and quiet, and Phoebe had seized her chance and gone to ground in the library. With a whole day in which to work, free of disturbance, she was cataloguing the more interesting volumes in Alex's collection of books.

Twinney's apologetic knock was not welcome. Phoebe hastily closed the *Leviathan* so that its distinctive title page was not visible, and said with thinly disguised impatience, 'Yes, Twinney? What is it?'

'I beg your pardon, Mistress Phoebe – but there are visitors, come to see Sir Alexander. Foreigners, Mistress.'

'Not English?' Her curiosity aroused despite herself, she stared at the butler, frowning. 'Have they given any name? What are they like?'

'No, Mistress Phoebe, there's no name. The man's a servant, most likely, and dressed very plain. Not a Frenchman, that I do know. And he has a child with him.'

'A *child*?' Phoebe said, startled. 'Boy or girl? How old?'

'A little lad, Mistress, five or six years old perhaps. He looks proper exhausted too, poor little mite.' Twinney, despite his correct and punctiliously official air, had a notoriously soft heart.

'I'll come and see what they want,' said Phoebe, although a monstrous suspicion was already waking in her mind. She rose with some difficulty, for she had spent some time in the chair, and her joints had as usual become very stiff. 'Show them into the winter parlour, Twinney, and bring some refreshment for them.'

He bowed and went out. She found her stick and slowly, doggedly, made her way to the door. Outside, she could hear Twinney's voice, and the gruff tones of the stranger, speaking haltingly and in strongly accented English. Not a Frenchman, Phoebe thought, smiling grimly to herself. Of course, all at Wintercombe were familiar with the delightful and French-flavoured voice of Louise. This man, she would lay odds on it, was Dutch.

They had reached the winter parlour by the time she entered. The man at once doffed his hat and bowed, and the child beside him followed his example. As Phoebe stood, breathing rather raggedly and trying to ignore the pain in her legs, she looked at the boy and knew at once that her suspicions were correct. His face was soft and round, of course, but already there were the marks of a very unchildlike maturity, the indications of suffering, in the level set of his mouth and the shadowed, sapphire-blue eyes.

'Hullo,' she said, putting a welcoming warmth in her voice. This sudden, unheralded arrival was not their fault, but Alex's, and she would vent her anger on him when he returned from Bath. 'I very much regret that Sir Alexander is not here at present – he is out for the day, but should have returned in time for supper. I am Phoebe St Barbe, his sister, and I bid you both welcome to Wintercombe.'

The man grunted unintelligible thanks, and bowed again. The child stared up at her thoughtfully, and then said in a high, clear voice, in impeccable English, 'I believe, madam, that you must be my aunt, for Sir Alexander St Barbe is my father.'

This will set the cat amongst the pigeons with a vengeance, thought Phoebe, with unworthy glee. She smiled at the boy. 'Yes, I can see that he is – you are very like him. What is your name?'

'Lukas, Aunt Phoebe,' he said, without any flicker of an answering smile.

'Well, Lukas, welcome to Wintercombe. Have you come from Holland?'

'Yes, Aunt Phoebe. We came in a ship from Amsterdam to . . .' He

134

turned to the servant for help, and the big Dutchman answered him. 'Bristol.'

'Yes, that was it, Bristol. Then we stayed in an inn last night, and today we rode here.' The boy looked up at her, and for the first time a wobble of uncertainty entered his voice. 'When will my father come home?'

'Very soon, I promise you, Lukas,' said Phoebe, as reassuringly as she could. She had no experience of children, but it was obvious that her nephew was, as the butler had observed, exhausted by the journey. She added, 'Twinney will bring you food and drink – you must be very hungry and thirsty.'

'Thank you, Aunt,' said Lukas. 'We did stop at an inn for dinner, but that seems a long time ago. I expect that Gerrit would like some beer.' He turned to the servant. '*Wilt U bier, Gerrit?*'

Dutch was not amongst Poebe's languages, but that at least was quite intelligible. So was Gerrit's reply. '*Ja, graag, Luikje.*'

As if on cue, Twinney appeared, bearing a laden tray which he put on the table at Phoebe's direction. There was indeed beer, a pottery mug of hot chocolate – in view of its expense, evidence that Twinney's soft heart had certainly been touched – and a variety of small pies and cakes. When the man and the boy had been supplied with their refreshments, Phoebe told them to sit down, and with a hidden sigh of relief, sank gratefully into her own chair. A hundred questions jostled in her mind, but she could hardly ask them of a six-year-old boy. She thought without much relish of Alex's likely response to her enquiries, the foremost of which would be that if Lukas was indeed his son – and the resemblance made it entirely likely – then why had they not been told?

A little colour was returning to the boy's wan face as he ate. She said, smiling, trying to make it more than just polite conversation, 'It must have been very frightening for you, to have come all the way from Holland to Bristol on a ship.'

'Frightening?' Lukas stared at her, surprised. 'No, Aunt Phoebe, I wasn't frightened at all. Gerrit was with me, you see, and he's my friend. He helped me to escape.'

Phoebe stared at him in astonishment. '*Escape?* Surely you were not in *prison?*'

'Oh, no, Aunt Phoebe – no, Gerrit helped me to escape from my mother.'

Whatever else she had expected, it was not this. The whereabouts of Lukas's mother, of course, was one of the first questions which she had planned to ask Alex, but had not wanted to raise with the child – after all, he might well have been sent to Wintercombe because she had recently died. She said thinly, 'Forgive me, Lukas, but I don't understand – why did you have to escape from your mother?'

'Because my father wanted me to,' said the boy, staring up at her solemnly. 'He had to come to England, but he left Gerrit behind to help me. But my mother thought that my father would want to take me away, so she tried to hide me. Gerrit found me, though, and set me free.' He glanced at the servant with trusting affection. 'And he brought me here.'

Phoebe gazed speechlessly at this extraordinarily self-possessed child. There were so many things she could say, and needed to ask, but only one question forced itself past her tongue. 'But what of your poor mother? She must be very unhappy – she can't have *wanted* you to be taken away from her. What grief must she be feeling now?'

'She didn't like me,' said Lukas. 'And I didn't like her. She used to shout at me, and hit me, and lock me in cupboards. She said I was in her way. She only kept me because she hated my father.' He spoke in the same flat, unforgiving voice as Alex had used, long, long ago, to the fragile little girl who had tried to join in his games. 'Go away, Feeble, we don't want you.'

'Is truth, Juffrouw,' said Gerrit earnestly. 'She is very bad woman – very bad. Best to bring boy here, safe.'

But once, it seemed, this woman had loved Alex enough to bear him a son. Was she his wife, or merely a mistress? She could not ask the boy such questions, nor the servant, whose command of English appeared in any case to be very limited. And why, oh why, had Alex said nothing of the child's existence, when he must have been well aware that Lukas would probably arrive at Wintercombe sooner or later? Knowing her brother, she doubted very much that she would obtain a satisfactory answer, but she nevertheless intended to subject him to a very thorough inquisition when he came home. After all, if she did not do it, no one else would dare.

The only bright spot in this impossible, ridiculous and somehow tragic situation was the thought of what Bab would say when she found out.

Alex, Charles and Amy returned to Wintercombe later that afternoon, earlier than they usually did, but not early enough for Phoebe. She had spent an initially difficult hour or so with Lukas, whose manner, unchildlike, unemotional and chillingly polite, was most disconcerting. She had suggested that Gerrit should join his English fellows in the servants' hall until his master returned, an event for which she was waiting as impatiently as he must be, and Twinney had imperturbably taken the Dutchman under his wing. Then, wondering about nursemaids and tutors, she had led the child up the spiral stairs to the chamber lying over the dining parlour, once his grandfather's, that Silence had occupied on

136

her last visit, and which seemed, for the moment, to be the best room for him.

He looked very small as he stared round at the huge four-poster bed, the high, timbered ceiling, the lovely oriel window, twin to the one on the eastern side of the house, in Alex's chamber. Phoebe felt a pang of acute compassion for this reserved, lonely child, surrounded by adults, with an absent father and a mother who, apparently, had ill-treated him. No wonder he turned for affection to the servant who had rescued him.

'You can sleep in this room for the present, Lukas,' she said. 'Do you like it?'

'It's very nice,' the boy said, looking round him. 'Aunt Phoebe, what is that?'

She followed his gaze to the hole cut in the wall, just beside the bed. 'Oh, that's the squint. It looks down on to the Hall below – you can see and hear everything that goes on – it's for spying on people.' She added hastily, 'There's no need for it now, of course.'

'Why not?'

Under the steady, assessing blue gaze, Phoebe was beginning to feel distinctly uneasy. She said briskly, 'Because when the house was built, times were dangerous, and there were robbers everywhere. If soldiers or thieves entered the Hall, it would be useful to keep an eye on them. There are two other spy-holes too, hidden behind faces on the wall high up on the far side of the Hall. If I lift you up, you'll be able to see them.'

For a child so slight in build, Lukas was surprisingly heavy. Phoebe, already taxed by the unaccustomed climb upstairs – she kept as much as possible to the ground floor – felt her leg give way, and nearly fell. Lukas, freed abruptly from her grasp, stared up at her, and she saw the concern in his face and felt unaccountably touched. 'Are you hurt, Aunt?'

'No – no, I'm all right,' said Phoebe, although for a moment the swift shaft of agony had made her feel faint and dizzy. 'I have a bad leg, you see, which is why I usually walk with a stick. I should not have tried to lift you up, it was very careless of me.'

'Have you always had a bad leg? My father had one once, when he fell from his horse, but it soon mended. Will yours mend too, Aunt?'

'No, it won't, for I've had it all my life,' Phoebe told him. She added rather brusquely, 'Don't worry – I'm quite used to it after all this time. Would you like to see the garden? There is a little summerhouse, and a pond with fish, and knots and terraces, and an orchard with a stream running through it, where you can play. Would you like to do that until your father comes home? He should not be very long.'

'I would like it very much, Aunt. Will you come with me? Shall I help you down the stairs?'

His care for her might have been ridiculous in so young a child, but somehow was not. Phoebe allowed herself to be assisted with good grace, and was escorted by her diminutive nephew down the steep, twisting stone steps to the ground floor, and then out into the warm garden, soaked in golden light from the westering sun. As they walked slowly together down the terraces, she ascertained that he was six years and two weeks old; that he had lived in a very tall thin house in Amsterdam overlooking a canal, with stairs so steep and narrow that furniture had to be hoisted in and out of the windows, suspended on ropes; that he had not been seasick at all on the voyage, but that many of the other passengers had; and that what he would like more than anything else in the world would be a pony of his own to ride.

'I'm sure your father will give you one gladly,' said Phoebe, quite unable to visualise Alex as an indulgent parent. He must set some store by the child though, or he would surely not have gone to the trouble of removing him from his mother, but simply left him behind in Holland, just another by-blow of no account. And doubtless, given Alex's history and tastes, there were a number of those scattered around England and Europe.

But, a small chilly voice reminded her, what if Lukas had been abducted, not for his own sake, not in a spirit of uncharacteristic paternal love, but because he was the legitimate heir to Wintercombe?

She thrust that thought from her – although it would certainly remove the problem of finding her brother a suitably unshockable and complaisant wife – and said to the small boy at her side, 'Do you like books? Can you read yet?'

'No,' said Lukas, in a small, regretful voice. 'My father said he would teach me, but then he had to go away. And Mama always said it would be a waste of time, because I was stupid.'

Phoebe, shocked, stopped and stared at him. 'Oh, Lukas, that isn't true! How could she say a cruel thing like that?'

'But it *is* true. I was always getting in her way, and dropping things, and coming into her chamber when she didn't want me there.' The boy suddenly went red, as if the memory was shaming. 'That's why she was always shouting at me. I'm glad I'm here, Aunt Phoebe. My father doesn't shout.'

'Well, not at you, at any rate,' said Phoebe, with a crowd of recent images, vivid and outrageous, rising unwelcome in her mind. Alex drunk, Alex objectionable, Alex fondling one of the dairymaids, a notorious lightskirt, in a corner of the barn, Alex returning from Bath, unshaven and unrepentant, after two days, obviously, spent in debauch. What sort of father was this for a young, observant and impressionable boy?

'Don't you like him?' Lukas was asking, in that curiously matter-of-fact voice. 'You don't sound as if you like my father.' He glanced up at her warily. 'My mother didn't like him either.'

'I do like him,' said Phoebe. 'He is my brother, after all.'

Lukas gazed at her for a moment. 'I like him too,' he said at last. 'I'm glad I'm here.'

'I'm glad you are too, Lukas,' said Phoebe, and found, to her surprise, that she was speaking no less than the truth. 'Look, here is the orchard. Why don't you run around and play for a little while?'

Lukas stood at the top of the steps that led down into the long grass and the apple trees. He hesitated, and looked back at Phoebe.

'Go on,' she said. 'It's all right. You can make as much noise as you want to.'

There was a pause. It was as if, Phoebe thought, the boy was almost afraid of that lush green expanse of space. She wished that she could run with him, play with him, encourage him to behave as, surely, all small boys naturally behaved when freed from adult restraint. Even the quiet and obedient Wickham children, Tom and Cary, had galloped in and out of the trees, two small counterfeit horses neighing and snorting and stamping, on their visit last December for their Great-Uncle Nat's funeral.

Lukas took two steps down, and glanced at her again. Phoebe wondered suddenly if he knew how to run wild. After all, he had been born and reared in the confines of Amsterdam, and his mother evidently had regarded him as a nuisance best kept as much out of her way as possible. She smiled at the boy. 'See if you can see the big pike in the stew-pond – he likes to bask in the sun in the warm shallow water at the edge. I'll sit down here and wait for you – I don't want to come any further.'

At last he smiled back. It was a tentative, almost experimental curve of his mouth, very different from his father's impudent grin. 'Will you be all right on your own, Aunt Phoebe?'

'I think I will,' she told him. 'Go on, Lukas – go and say hullo to that evil old pike.'

One last look, and then he walked down the remaining steps and set off through the grass, looking around him rather as if he expected wild beasts to drop from the branches, or leap out from behind the gnarled old cider trees. Phoebe watched until he had disappeared amongst the crowded

139

trunks and blossom, and then walked painfully over to the stone seat by the sundial. The sharp shadow showed that it was already six o'clock. Soon, with luck, Alex would be home: perhaps, since Lukas unaccountably seemed to worship him, that would set a proper smile on the child's face. She had left instructions with Twinney that she was to be informed as soon as her brother returned. Meanwhile, she could rest here and ponder the rise of a feeling that she had never thought to encounter within herself.

Crippled, intellectual and unsentimental, Phoebe had early realised that she was not, by nature or circumstance, destined for the conventional female progression of betrothal, marriage, children. And not for one moment had she regretted it, preferring the satisfaction of the fulfilled mind to the more dubious and perilous indulgence of sense and emotion.

Until now, when Lukas had smiled shyly at her, and revealed to her some tiny glimpse of what a child of her own could mean.

In this, as in so much else, Alex had won, and she had lost.

There was no sound from the orchard. Evidently Lukas had been unable to shed his inhibitions, even when alone. Phoebe, with the ruthlessness of long practice, expunged all tendency to self-pity from her mind. To have a child was, as a matter of course, to ally herself with a man, and the undeniable, long-accepted fact was, she knew, that no man would look at her twice. If her twisted leg and plain face and shrewd, forthright tongue did not discourage hopeful suitors, then her learning and erudition undoubtedly would. Nor, if she were honest, did she wish for marriage. To sacrifice her independence, her integrity and her selfishness would be more than she could tolerate.

She had thought her emotions inviolate, long withered from lack of use. But now, in the space of half a year, her father's death, Alex, and now his six-year-old son had proved her wrong. It was an unexpected Achilles' heel which she regretted, and determined never, if possible, to reveal to her brother, thereby risking his merciless mockery.

'Mistress Phoebe!' It was Twinney, calling from the top of the terrace. 'Sir Alexander is back!' He came briskly down as Phoebe pushed herself to her feet, gripping the sundial firmly for support. 'They've just ridden into the courtyard, Mistress.'

'Thank you, Twinney,' Phoebe said. She thought quickly. 'Could you tell my brother that there is a visitor to see him, in the garden, and ask him to come down here? Thank you.'

The butler bowed imperturbably, and turned back to the house. Phoebe limped to the balustrade, grateful for the support which the warm, worn stone gave to her aching body, and called down into the orchard. 'Lukas! Lukas, come up here!'

For a moment there was no response at all. In sudden, uncharacteristic fear, she imagined him drowned, or lost, or fallen from a tree and hurt, and berated herself for her carelessness. Then a small, welcome figure burst through the trees, running as if wolves were behind him, his hair flying, his face blazing with a joy that took her breath away. He flew up the steps and stopped himself with difficulty from cannoning into her. 'Oh, Aunt Phoebe, is it – is –'

'Yes, your father is back. I've sent him a message to come into the garden – you'll see him in a moment.'

There were voices from the house, the sound of footsteps on stone, and she looked round and saw Alex, still in his riding boots and dusty from the journey, standing on the flagstones of the top terrace, just outside the house. His eyes narrowed suddenly, and he said, with a delight in his voice that Phoebe had never in her life heard before, 'Lukas?'

'Papa!' the boy shrieked, and hurled himself past her towards the steps that climbed up the two lower terraces. He tripped on the last, went sprawling on the gravel with a force that would have left most children howling, picked himself up undaunted, and ran the last few yards into Alex's arms.

Phoebe watched, despising herself for the depths of her jealousy, as her dissolute, callous brother swept up his son into a joyous hug. The child's dark head burrowed into his father's shoulder, and on Alex's face, as he held Lukas close, was an expression that prickled the hairs on her neck, for she had never before seen his emotions so openly and vulnerably on display.

There was after all, it seemed, one person on this earth whom he loved, and cherished, and for whom he would fight.

With her usual slow, relentless determination, she negotiated the steps up which Lukas had sprung so exuberantly only a moment before. There was movement in the screens passage, through the door: she saw Amy standing there, her face inquisitively alight, and behind her was Charles, looking bewildered. There were specks of blood on the gravel, and she saw a dark stain on her brother's grey sleeve. At once unwilling to spoil their reunion, and wishing it to end, Pheobe said, 'He hurt himself when he fell.'

Alex's blue eyes shifted to meet hers, after a pause, as if returning from a great distance. Lukas, clinging to him as tightly as ivy to a tree, did not move. He said, in something akin to his usual manner, 'I know. But you wouldn't want to fuss over him now, would you? It's not like you, little sister, to be so concerned.'

Phoebe was not so easily squashed. 'I'm concerned for your coat,' she said waspishly. 'If you're not careful, it'll be ruined.'

'And it's not like you to be so domestic, either,' said Alex, with a curl of his lip. 'Or is the real reason that you're jealous?'

Blue eyes, the colour of sapphires, met those of an identical blue, and held. But it was Phoebe, humiliated by the acuteness of his judgement, who dropped her gaze first. 'I'll leave you in peace, brother,' she said coldly, and limped past him into the sanctuary of the house.

It proved poor refuge, however, for Amy pounced on her before she had gone three steps across the floor of the screens passage. 'Phoebe! What's happening? Who's that child?'

'His name is Lukas, and he's Alex's son,' she said curtly.

Amy's jaw dropped, comically aghast. 'His *son*? But – I didn't know he had one!'

'Neither did I,' said Phoebe drily. She saw Charles's face, stark with a horror that was plain even in the dim light, and knew what he was thinking. A cruel impulse prompted her to add, 'The child's mother is in Holland, apparently. Alex had the boy taken away from her and brought here.'

'The boy's mother?' Charles stared at her, swallowed, and in a voice barely recognisable, said, 'Do you mean his *wife*?'

'I have no idea,' Phoebe told him. 'Whether she's his wife or mistress, whether the boy is his legitimate heir or his bastard, well, your guess is as good as mine. Knowing Alex, it could be either. The only certain facts are that Lukas is his son – the resemblance, in looks at any rate, is quite marked – and that his mother is alive and living in Amsterdam.'

Both brother and sister looked appalled. Losing impatience, Phoebe added briskly, 'As to the truth of it, I suggest you ask Alex himself – although not, of course, in the presence of the child. And the best of luck.' She stumped past them with as much speed as her determination could force from her inadequate limbs, and crossed the Hall towards the sanctuary of her own chamber. As she went, she heard Amy's voice, high with disbelief and distress. 'It can't be true – he can't have a wife – he *can't*!'

The world won't wag the way you want it to just because you want it, Phoebe thought with sour satisfaction, and closed her door with a bang.

There was only half an hour or so to supper, so she would have no chance to question Alex in the mean time. Doubtless he would be taken up with his son: indeed, as she wondered whether or not to wear a slightly more respectable garment than her accustomed shabby black in honour of the occasion, she heard the sound of booted footsteps passing across the stone floor of the Hall, and the unmistakable voice of Lukas, the only child at Wintercombe. Despite her mood of envy, malice and self-dislike, Phoebe thought of that touching moment of reunion, and smiled reluctantly. Who would have thought that her disgraceful, unfeeling brother could have revealed himself to be so unexpectedly and endearingly vulnerable?

Later, Mattie Jones came to help her dress, all a-twitch with unasked questions which Phoebe resolutely failed to answer. She showed some surprise at being asked to take out the grey figured silk, a gown which Louise would doubtless consider to be hopelessly outmoded, and which she had worn perhaps twice in the past year. It hung on Phoebe in unflattering folds, confirming what she had suspected, that she had lost weight since her father's death. She made no other concessions to her appearance, instructing Mattie to dress her hair in its usual plain, uncurled style. No jewels or fans or fripperies enlivened her severe attire: Phoebe studied her drawn face in the mirror, and wondered suddenly, with surprise, what it must mean to be beautiful, like Amy, or vibrantly self-confident in one's powers of attraction, like Louise.

It was no use: she had chosen her path, or had it chosen for her, long ago, and it was too late, and entirely inappropriate, to change it now.

'Thank you, Mattie,' she said. 'That will be all. Have you dressed Mistress Amy yet?'

'Yes, Mistress Phoebe.' Mattie hesitated, and then added, 'She be tarblish overset, Mistress, she were a-sobbing fit to burst when I went to her.'

If she had thought that this information would provoke a flood of confidences, she was mistaken. 'I trust that she is quite recovered now?' said Phoebe, with an air of mild enquiry, and rose to her feet. 'Good. I will see her at supper. Thank you, Mattie.'

When she arrived in the dining parlour, Charles and Amy were already there. As usual, he was beautifully dressed, in the dark green suit he often wore, with not a button out of place, the buckles on his shoes polished shiny and the lace of his cravat impressively arranged. It was obvious that Amy had indeed been crying, for her usually lovely face was red and puffy around the eyes, and she kept dabbing at her nose with a damp-looking handkerchief. Phoebe, studying them both with a jaundiced eye, wondered how deep her cousin's foolish fancies had led her. Surely she could not seriously have imagined that marriage with Alex was even possible, let alone likely.

From her first words as Phoebe came in through the door, it seemed that she had. 'How could he?' Amy wept, wringing her kerchief between trembling fingers. 'Why didn't he tell me?'

'If it's any consolation, he didn't tell anyone,' Phoebe said, trying to conceal her irritation. 'Anyway, do I take it that your distress is wholly due to the fact that he is married?'

Charles was looking angrily at his sister: evidently he had not encouraged her in her ambitions. Amy nodded, sniffing.

'And yet,' Phoebe pointed out tartly, 'you have no reason at all to think that he is – except for Lukas's arrival, of course. Isn't it much more likely, given my brother's history and, er, proclivities, that the woman in Holland is in fact his mistress, rather than his wife?'

Amy looked up at her with pathetic, tear-sodden eyes. 'I – I d-don't know.'

'Of course it is, you lack-wit,' Phoebe told her roundly, wishing that she could knock some sense into her cousin's golden head. She added, turning to Charles, who was standing beside his sister with an expression of some indignation on his face, 'As for you, don't you think you should have discouraged this nonsense? She's no more hope of marrying Alex than she has of marrying the Pope, and if you told her straight, she might listen to you. What would my brother want with a little innocent like Amy? He needs someone who'll play him at his own game and have a chance of winning, but if Amy is so besotted with him as to offer herself up on a plate, I wouldn't put it past him to take advantage of her – if he hasn't already done so.'

Charles flushed angrily. 'Of course he hasn't and, by God, if he ever tries, I swear I'll kill him.' He rounded on his sister. 'Do you hear me? You can put any ideas of snaring Alex out of your mind for good. I wouldn't let you marry him if he were the last man on earth.'

Outside, the childish voice of Lukas, enquiring, reminded them that this was hardly the time or the place for such a quarrel. Phoebe said quickly, 'Charles – please remember, Lukas is only six, and he isn't to blame for any of this. If you want to confront Alex, please wait until the boy has gone to bed.'

He looked at her, and she realised suddenly that she had no idea of what he was thinking. Charles – quiet, devout, neat and conscientious to the point of obsession, the absolute antithesis of Alex – had always seemed to be an open book to her, an uncomplicated young man with whom she had grown up, and whom she had thought she knew through and through. And now, with new, unwelcome insight, she found that she did not know him at all, and that his deepest thoughts and feelings had always been quite opaque. In fact, Phoebe thought with a sense of shock, in his own quiet way he's as enigmatic and unpredictable as Alex.

At that moment, her brother entered the dining room with a flourish, escorting the small, frail-looking figure of his son. Both had changed, Alex into a suit she had not seen before, crimson and gold and resplendent, quite unlike his usual rather slovenly style of dress, save that his cravat had been swiftly and casually knotted, in contrast to the painstaking neatness of Charles's attire. Lukas wore blue, and the sleeves were noticeably too short for him.

'Well, good evening, everybody,' said Alex, glancing round at the three other adults. 'Is Bab not gracing us with her presence today?'

'No, Cousin – she is keeping to her chamber,' said Charles, with considerable self-control.

Alex smiled brilliantly. 'Well, I shall have to take Lukas to meet her tomorrow.' His hand rested lightly on his son's shoulder, and the boy glanced up and met his eyes. A look of understanding passed between them, and Phoebe, watching it, wondered suddenly if he had warned Lukas about the various inhabitants of Wintercombe.

'But for now,' Alex was saying, 'your Aunt Bab's son and daughter must suffice. Amy, my dear, and Charles, may I present my son Lukas. Lukas, this is your Cousin Amy, and your Cousin Charles.'

Without prompting, the boy bowed carefully, one leg before the other, very low in the French manner. Amy, with a last despairing dab at her overflowing eyes, so far overcame her distress as to manage a rather watery smile. Charles inclined his head with stiff politeness, obviously unwilling to make himself pleasant to a child who might well prove to be his supplanter.

'And your Aunt Phoebe, of course,' Alex finished, turning to her. 'But of course, you have already met.'

A small but sunny smile curved Lukas's mouth, making him seem very like his father. 'Hullo, Aunt. Thank you for looking after me this afternoon.'

'It was a pleasure,' said Phoebe warmly. The least she could do, with Charles standing there glowering, and Amy dropping tears into her kerchief, was to make it plain to the child that he had another ally at Wintercombe, besides his father.

As she had feared, this supper was an exceedingly awkward affair. The atmosphere was so thick with unvoiced recriminations, accusations and urgent questions, that she could almost see the words floating above their heads. 'Why have you brought the boy here?' 'Is he your legitimate son?' 'Who is his mother – your wife or your mistress?' 'Why, why, *why* didn't you *tell* us?'

Characteristically, only Alex seemed entirely at ease. He devoted much attention to Lukas, ensuring that he had enough on his plate, talking to him, making the boy smile and even, once, provoking a laugh. And as Phoebe, ever the observer, watched them together, the dark heads so alike, she realised why her brother had gone to the dramatic lengths of abducting Lukas from his mother's care. Whether Lukas was his legitimate son, or merely his bastard, counted for nothing beside the unlikely truth that became more and more obvious as the meal progressed. For it was clear to her, who saw him perhaps more plainly than anyone else, that Alex loved his son very dearly.

She noticed, too, that in marked contrast to most other suppers since her brother's arrival at Wintercombe, his wine glass remained almost untouched.

When Lukas, almost painfully polite and restrained, had finished the raisin tart and tansies that ended the meal, his head evidently growing too heavy for his neck to support, Phoebe said briskly, 'That child should be in bed. Shall I see to it?'

'No need,' Alex told her. 'Gerrit will perform that task perfectly adequately, he has done all the way from Amsterdam.'

'But you are planning to engage a nurse to look after him, I trust?' Phoebe said, glancing at Lukas, who was very nearly asleep.

Alex shrugged. 'Perhaps. He's used to Gerrit. I would not want him turned into a baby again.'

'If you choose the woman carefully, that should not happen,' she pointed out. 'A child so young, it's hardly fitting that he should be tended by your manservant.'

'Why not? What are you afraid of? Gerrit only likes women, if that's what you're implying,' Alex said bluntly. He leaned forward and touched his son's arm, just as the child's eyes were closing, so missing Charles's smothered exclamation of disgust. 'Lukas! Wake up, it's time for your bed.'

The boy jerked upright, and stared round with a bewildered expression. 'Oh, please, Papa, can I stay a little longer?'

'Any longer, and you'll have your plate for your pillow,' said Alex, smiling. 'Now say your goodnights to your aunt and your cousins, and Gerrit will show you to your bed.'

'Papa?' said Lukas hesitantly, his blue eyes very wide in his pale face. 'Papa, do I have to sleep in the chamber Aunt Phoebe showed me?'

'What was it, a dungeon?'

'No,' Phoebe said, feeling suddenly very sorry for this brave, woe-begone child. 'It was the guest chamber – but perhaps it is rather big and comfortless for his first night.'

'Gerrit can make up the bed in the other closet off my chamber, for tonight at least,' Alex said. 'So if you wake in the dark, Lukas, I shall be just the other side of the door. And tomorrow, as Aunt Phoebe suggested, we will find a kind woman to come and take care of you until you are a little older. Would you like that?'

146

Lukas's doubtful face indicated he was not at all sure, but he nodded politely. 'Yes, Papa. And – and can I have a pony, please? I've always wanted a pony of my own.'

'In the morning, rascal,' Alex said, laughing. 'And all in good time. At this moment, you need your sleep more than a thousand ponies. Now, say goodnight to everyone.'

The little boy obeyed, despite his evident exhaustion, with his accustomed impeccable manners. Whatever the faults and vices of that unknown mother in Amsterdam, she had certainly taught him all the essentials of polite behaviour. Then he bowed very low at the door, while Gerrit, summoned by his master, waited to escort him to bed.

And of course, once he was gone, the storm would be free to break. Almost before the door closed behind him, Phoebe saw Alex reach across for the second bottle of claret. He filled his glass to the brim and drank it off in one swift, practised gulp before pouring another. Phoebe, the hairs rising on her neck like a dog sensing imminent menace, glanced meaningfully at him.

'It's called Dutch courage, I believe,' said her brother. He leaned back in his chair and surveyed the other three at the table, Phoebe wary, Charles hostile, Amy fearful. 'Well, what do you think of him? He's a pleasant child, is he not?'

'Is he yours?' Charles asked. All his habitual caution seemed to have dropped off him like a discarded cloak, to reveal a hard core of black and implacable hatred.

'Of course he's Alex's son,' Phoebe said quickly. 'The likeness is obvious.'

'Thank you, little sister, but I don't need you to fight my battles for me. What's troubling you, Amy? Don't you feel well?'

Amy had always hated confrontation and dispute. The tears flowing again, she rose to her feet. 'N-no,' she stammered, flushing with embarrassment under his unpleasant stare. 'No – yes – I feel faint. Goodnight, Alex – Charles – Phoebe –' And she stumbled hastily from the room.

'Good,' was the callous response of the man she had hoped to marry, as the door closed. 'A few minutes more and we'd have been up to our necks in salt water.' He smiled at Charles, who glared back. 'Well, Cousin? Do you accept that he is my son?'

'I'll agree that he is – that fact is plain enough,' said Charles. 'What I want to know is, which side of the blanket?'

'And there's the rub, eh, Cousin Charles?' Alex said softly, taking another mouthful of wine. 'If legitimate, your sister's foolish daydreams are shattered – and don't look so surprised, I guessed what was in her mind, if you can call it that, from the moment the silly little chit threw herself at my head. And you, of course, would no longer be the heir to Wintercombe. Whereas if his mother is not my wife, then of course Lukas is not my heir, and I remain the most eligible bachelor in Somerset.'

The silence after he had finished speaking threatened to stretch out to infinity. Alex filled his glass again, and pushed the bottle, now half empty, towards Charles. 'Are you going to drink a toast with me?'

His cousin stared at him. 'Well?' he demanded urgently, ignoring the suggestion. 'Is the boy your bastard, or isn't he?'

'Ah,' said Alex, evidently disposed to be annoying. 'That would be telling, wouldn't it? Come on, Cousin, let's drink to Lukas.'

'I'm damned if I'll drink to him,' Charles said. Outwardly he seemed almost as calm as Alex, but Phoebe sensed the rage seething just below the surface, ready to erupt. 'Tell me – *tell* me – is he your bastard?'

'Perhaps he is,' said Alex, musingly. 'And then again, perhaps he isn't. Greater men than I have fallen into that trap. Is the Duke of Monmouth the legitimate King of England, or not? Is there really a black box with Lucy Barlow's marriage certificate inside? Does Johanna Van der Linden keep such a paper under her pillow? Wouldn't you dearly love to know?'

'Johanna? Is that the name of Lukas's mother?' Phoebe asked hastily, hoping to deflect some of the awesome malice emanating from both men. 'What is she like, Alex?'

'A bitch,' her brother said concisely. 'A beautiful, bewitching, unfaithful, cruel, callous, malicious bitch.'

'Then like called to like, did it?' Charles sneered.

Phoebe hurried into the breach. 'Lukas said that she was unkind to him. He seemed to regard you and Gerrit as his saviours.'

'He has an entirely unrealistic opinion of me,' said Alex. 'Of necessity, his illusions must be shattered at some time, but later, I hope, rather than sooner . . . And if I find anyone, *anyone* attempting to open his eyes to the brutal truth about me, then I swear I'll strangle them with my bare hands. Do you understand me, Cousin?'

Charles stared at him down the long length of the table crowded with empty plates, bottles, glasses and the abandoned wreckage of the meal. Phoebe glanced from one pair of blue eyes, vivid and compelling, to the other, paler and altogether less distinguished. It was Charles who dropped his gaze first, and his voice came quietly, though no less hostile. 'I understand you.'

'Good. I knew you'd see sense. Now, are you going to drink that toast, or shall I finish the bottle?'

'I'll not drink to any brat of yours, legitimate or not,' said Charles.

'A wise move – you really haven't the head for more than a glass or two of wine,' said Alex, with transparently contemptuous concern. 'Well, all the more for me – I fancy getting drunk tonight.'

'There's nothing new in that,' Phoebe pointed out frostily. 'How many nights since your return have you not been drunk?'

'More than you might think,' Alex said, turning his most charming smile upon her. He emptied the contents of the bottle into his glass, and drank.

Charles watched him, loathing printed plain on his face. 'For the last time – for God's sake, put us all out of our agony and tell us – who is that boy?'

'You know already – he is my son. As to his status – well, I don't feel like telling you yet, one way or the other. Dear little sister, you're looking tired – why not go to bed?'

'Not yet,' Phoebe said grimly. She had no intention of leaving the two men alone in the dining parlour: in their present mood, murder would probably be done if she did. She added, trying to draw the conversation away from dangerous waters, 'If Lukas is six, you must have known his mother when you were in Holland in 'seventy-eight.'

'Your mathematics is excellent,' Alex told her, smiling. 'And a sweet thing she was then – blonde and round and beautiful, just like a peach. Shame she went rotten so quick.'

'If you deserted her when she was expecting your baby, I'm not surprised,' Phoebe retorted. 'But whatever her faults, Lukas does not seem to have suffered too much.'

'How do you know? Have you asked him?'

'No, of course not. But . . . he's a delightful child.'

'And small thanks to Johanna for it, I would say,' Alex commented. 'The truth of it is that she did not want him, and I did. And such was her love for me, that because I wanted him, she refused to let him go.'

'You wanted him?' Charles said. 'Then he must be your legitimate heir! Why else would you want to be saddled with a child?'

Phoebe knew, but if Charles was too hostile and obtuse to see it, she would not enlighten him. Alex merely smiled lightly. 'Why not? As Phoebe says, he is a delightful boy. You'll learn the truth in due course, Cousin – but for now, why don't you take yourself off to bed, since you obviously can't bear the sight of me, and leave me in peace?'

'I can't win, can I?' said Charles softly, and the bitterness in his voice took Phoebe aback. 'Whatever I say, whatever I do, whatever I want, you have all the answers, and you go your own way. It's like banging my head against a wall.'

'Then why don't you stop?' Alex leaned forward, his indolent manner evaporated. 'I have arranged a house for you, and you and your family have a more than sufficient competence under the terms of my father's will. I owe you nothing else. Don't whine for the moon, Charles – I should think even Lukas has grown out of that.'

For an instant, Phoebe, alarmed, thought that Charles would so far forget himself as to hurl something at his cousin. But somehow he held on to the shreds of his dignity, and with bitter pride got to his feet. 'I see there is no arguing with you – no compromise, no family feeling. I think I had better leave before you disgrace yourself further. Goodnight, Phoebe.' And he bowed to her, correctly if not so low as Lukas, turned, and walked stiffly from the room.

Alex began to laugh before he had shut the door. 'Poor Charles! As he so rightly says, he cannot win.'

'It's hardly a fair contest,' Phoebe pointed out acidly. She paused, waiting until her cousin's footsteps had diminished into the distance and there was no chance that he would hear her. Then she said softly, 'Lukas's mother – Johanna – she was your mistress, wasn't she, not your wife?'

Alex glanced at her over the top of his wine glass. 'How very astute of you, Phoebe. What are your reasons for coming to that conclusion?'

She stared at him steadily. 'Firstly, if you remember, you told me that you had asked Philip Cousins to seek out a suitable wife for you. I doubt even you would be brazen enough to do that if you already had one alive and well, if not exactly satisfactory, in Holland. Second, I can't see you becoming ensnared in matrimony by some heartless little Dutch trollop. You're quite capable of enticing women into your bed without going to those lengths. And thirdly, your reason for taking Lukas away from his mother has nothing to do with whether he is your heir, or otherwise.' She held his gaze sternly. 'You had him brought to Wintercombe because you love him.'

In the utter silence that followed her last words she heard the soft distant sounds of a busy house winding down into the peace of evening: footfalls, voices, the remote clatter of crockery from the kitchen. Then Alex laughed. 'That sounds very unlikely. You've said often enough yourself in the past that I am, in your words, a callous heartless bastard.'

'And so you are – I don't dispute it. But a man often has a soft spot for his only son, whether legitimately begotten or not. And if half the stories that Lukas has told me are true, he is far better off here than in Amsterdam.' She smiled thinly. 'Whatever your defects, you are unlikely to lock him in cupboards or call him stupid.'

'Instead, for my sins, I have agreed to give him a pony, and to teach him to read,' Alex said. He sat still for a moment, smiling, and the incongruous, unaccustomed tenderness on his face told her that he was thinking of his son. 'Or perhaps you could help there? You have more time than I do, and perhaps more idea of how to set about it.'

Phoebe opened her mouth to deny and decline, and found herself saying, 'Yes, of course I will.' Somewhat surprised at herself, she added, 'You need not worry. I have no axe to grind where Lukas is concerned. I don't know very much of children, but he is a charming boy, and I think we will get along very well.' She hesitated, unwilling to reveal her vulnerability to her merciless brother, and then added quietly, 'I am fond of him already. He is too quiet, too reserved – I would like to see him run, and laugh, and get into mischief. It's a shame there are no other children here. Perhaps he could stay with the Wickhams for a while.'

'I can't see Aunt Rachael allowing one of my by-blows to taint her house,' said Alex drily. 'Although I could, of course, always invite Jan's children here. Cary is a year younger than Lukas.' He glanced at his sister, and smiled suddenly, with a warmth that almost equalled his expression when he had spoken of his son. 'Thank you, Phoebe. Have you noticed that whenever we talk, somehow all the hostility seems to disappear? Blood must be thicker than water, after all.'

'It can't be,' Phoebe pointed out. 'Since Charles looked as if he would dearly have liked to slaughter you just now.'

'Good for Charles. He always was a milksop – perhaps this awkward situation will put some backbone into him. And anyway, in a month's time, with luck, he and his watery sister and preposterous mother will move to Bath, and you and I and Lukas will have Wintercombe to ourselves – for a while, at any rate.' He grinned. 'Until I acquire this wife that everyone is so anxious to saddle me with and thereby take Charles off his tenterhooks. Rest assured, dear sister, when I do enmesh myself in matrimonial coils, I won't choose a weepy little flibbertigibbet like Amy. Nor will she be a venal bitch like Johanna.'

'I'm glad to hear it,' said Phoebe. She was feeling very tired all of a sudden, and the thought of the warm horizontal surface of her bed was very enticing. She got to her feet, fumbling for her stick, and surveyed her brother sprawled negligently in his chair, his neckcloth loose, his black hair untidily over his shoulders. 'You don't deserve Lukas,' she said suddenly. 'Don't – please don't do anything to hurt him.'

Alex stared at her in surprise. 'I'd hardly do that, if all the feelings you so generously imputed to me just now are genuine.'

'No, not intentionally,' Phoebe told him. 'But, as you yourself have pointed out to me, in your cups you become someone else. Goodnight, Alex – and sleep well.'

As she limped out of the room with his laughter following her, she realised suddenly that she had committed herself to beginning her nephew's education, and thereby delayed, for the foreseeable future, any attempt to set up her own, independent household elsewhere.

Somehow, when she thought of that lonely, serious child, it did not seem such a terrible sacrifice.

# 9

## 'Scanted by a niggard birth'

Silence St Barbe surveyed her five grandchildren, three Loveridges, an Orchard and a Chevalier, crowding the parlour of the Taunton house, and was conscious of a very warm feeling of love and satisfaction. They were all such pleasant children – though Bram and Louise, of course, were hardly children now, being twenty-one and twenty (Louise had celebrated her birthday at Chard) respectively. Sue and Hannah were sweet girls, although they took after Jonah in looks, rather than their lovely mother, and Libby, although too plump and rather plain, was very clever – a waste in a girl, her father Henry had said – and had a dry, wicked sense of humour. But there was no denying that Bram, with his vivid manner and youthful idealism, was her favourite, and Louise, too, had become very dear to her in the months she had known her – for half a year now, Silence thought, with some surprise. And nothing would delight her more than to see these two young people come to an understanding.

But Louise had only been staying with the Loveridges for a month, so it was early days yet. And besides, Silence knew, none better, that such things took time. Still, she seemed very happy and lively, laughing with the girls, and exchanging banter with Bram and Jonah, and there was no sign of the almost feverish restlessness that had afflicted her at Glastonbury, and then at Chard. Perhaps, Silence thought optimistically, she has forgotten all about Alex and his dubious attractions. And certainly this household, full of young people and surrounded by the bustle and interest of Taunton, was a far more suitable place for a vivacious and sophisticated young girl than the sleepy peace of her grandmother's home at Chard.

Of course today, being market day, was especially busy, and the cries of the vendors, the lowing of cattle and the frantic bleating of terrified sheep, filtered intrusively through the tightly closed windows at the front of the house. The small dining parlour at the back, facing north-east with a fine view over sunlit gardens and outbuildings to the splendid tower of St Mary's church, was both quieter and cooler, and it was here that the table had been laid with nine rather cramped places for the monthly market-day dinner which Tabby always gave for her mother and stepfather. Normally, Richard and his wife would also have been present, but Sarah was still unwell from the birth of her baby, and Richard had stayed behind to keep her company.

Wonderful aromas ascended from the tiny dark kitchen below, where Nan the cookmaid regularly performed culinary miracles. Silence glanced across at Tabby, caught her eye, and smiled. Her eldest daughter had always been the closest to her, and she was glad that she lived only a few miles away so that this regular dinner was an easy matter to arrange. It was many months since she had visited Deb, Libby's mother, who lived in Bristol: and as for Kate, she had not seen her youngest daughter since the day of her elopement with Louise's father twenty years ago.

The older members of the family took their seats at the table, while the five young people, with much laughter and joking and, from the sound of it, some danger of spillage, brought the dishes up the narrow stairs from the kitchen. Jonah lived comfortably, but he was not a rich man, and the household boasted only Elias, the young apprentice, the cookmaid, and two maidservants, all of whom lived out. The girls dressed each other's hair, and it was noticeable that, since the arrival of Louise, their appearance had grown considerably smarter. Sue, rather thin and lanky, with her father's lean face and straight brown hair, looked quite different swathed in a mantua that Silence was sure she remembered last as a set of blue striped bedhangings, and with her hair properly curled and shining. Hannah, who was only eleven, had also evidently had recourse to curling papers, and even Libby, who took very little interest in her appearance, seemed to have acquired a waist under her old-fashioned dove-grey gown.

Bram, with his usual extravagance, waved a hand at the steaming spread. 'To delight the palate – a chine of beef, well roasted – a leg of lamb, ditto – a baked trout – a mutton pasty – and two sallets from our own garden! Pray fall to and enjoy our humble repast, ladies and gentlemen.'

In the laughter that followed, the urgent entrance of Elias, Jonah's apprentice, went almost unnoticed, and it was some time before he could make himself heard. 'If ee please, Master Loveridge, there be a man below asking for Mistress Hellier – he've rid over from Chard with a letter for her, and he say as how tis despeard important, sir.'

'A letter – for me?' Silence said, and her face creased with sudden anxiety. 'Oh, dear – I hope it's not bad news.'

'Shall I show him up, sir?' the boy persisted, and Jonah, as perplexed as his mother-in-law, nodded. 'Yes, of course, Elias.'

The young man who came puffing red-faced up the stairs was no stranger: it was Lawrence Earle, the lanky Wintercombe groom, dusty with riding and looking as if he had had little respite on his journey. He bowed to the assembled company, and then fumbled in his travel-stained coat. 'Sorry, m'lady – Mistress Hellier – but Mistress St Barbe give me this letter and told me to bring it to ee as quick as I could, and when they told me at Chard where you was, I thought I'd best come on here.'

'You did very well, Lawrence – thank you for your trouble,' Silence told him. She took the outstretched rectangle of paper and searched in the pocket of her gown for her spectacles. 'If you go downstairs, Elias will show you the kitchen, and the cookmaid will find some food for you.'

When Lawrence had clattered down the stairs again, his duty done, a small uneasy quiet fell around the table. Silence balanced her spectacles on her nose, and pushed her thumbnail under the seal. 'I think it's from Bab, not Phoebe – I do hope it's not bad news!'

'There's only one way to find out,' Nick pointed out, and Louise, watching with a suddenly thudding heart, saw his hand touch his wife's, reassuringly.

Silence unfolded the letter and peered at it. No one spoke as she studied Bab's rambling scrawl. It was heavily blotched, both by ink and what seemed too be tearstains, and all but illegible. Her family waited in suspense as the food steamed its heat away towards the ceiling, uneaten despite their hunger.

'Well?' Nick asked, when his wife seemed to have had ample time to read several letters, let alone one. 'Is it bad news?'

Silence was frowning in perplexity, and his words seemed to rouse her from deep thought. 'Thanks to Bab's appalling writing, I can't tell whether it is or not,' she said drily. 'What is certain is that she is considerably distressed, and implores me to go to Wintercombe immediately, and "discover the truth", she says – that much at least is quite clear.'

'The truth about what?' Nick enquired in bewilderment. 'And why does she always assume that you have the leisure and inclination to go gallivanting about the countryside at her beck and call?'

'She has no one else to turn to,' Silence said. She peered again at the letter. 'I think – although it hardly seems credible – that Alex's son has arrived at Wintercombe.'

Louise sat quite still, although the sudden surge of her heart seemed so strong that she wondered no one else appeared to have noticed it. But her relations were too astonished, too busy clamouring with questions, to pay her any attention.

'His *son*?' Tabby was saying in disbelief. 'I didn't know he had a son.'

'No one did – I certainly had no idea,' Silence said. 'There's no word here of his mother – perhaps she has sent him to Alex to bring up. The boy can't be very old.'

'Any mention of whether or not he is legitimate?' Jonah asked, mindful of the bright curious faces of his daughters and Libby.

'I can't discern any, but that doesn't mean anything – half of what she's written is completely illegible,' Silence said. 'Perhaps that's the truth she wants me to discover. Presumably she thinks that I'm more likely to wring it out of Alex than she is – which is undoubtedly true, but why should he not tell her whether the child is his heir or not, since, if I know Bab, it means so much to her?'

Louise could guess, but kept her counsel. It was Nick who put the unpalatable truth into words. 'If all you've told me about your nephew is true, he probably has every intention of keeping her in suspense for as long as possible.'

'I'm afraid you're probably right,' Silence said, sighing. 'Oh, I have very little time for Bab – such a tiresome woman! And I know that Alex likes her even less. But she does deserve a little consideration – more than she'll ever have from him, I fear.'

Louise had not thought about Alex for hours, days even, so immersed had she been in this cheerful, friendly, lively household. But now, listening to her grandparents discussing him, his image stood bold and clear and insolent in her mind, the brilliant eyes assessing her with an open and lecherous invitation that she had found increasingly difficult to resist. If her grandmother went to Wintercombe in response to Bab's desperate plea, could she persuade her that she should come too? There were Phoebe's books to take, and her promise to Charles to return in the spring was already overdue: it was now Saturday, the sixth day of June.

And besides, she was intensely curious. Who was this mysterious child who had arrived apparently unannounced out of nowhere? Was his mother Alex's wife, or his mistress? Why had he come to Wintercombe? Accompanying Silence would ensure that she found out as soon as possible. And she would see Alex again, enter once more into that strange game, composed of desire and hostility, danger and mischief, that she had played in the winter. She liked the Loveridges, especially Bram, but he seemed very young, still only a boy, beside Alex's powerful self-assurance.

'So what will you do?' Tabby asked, her tone indicating exactly what she herself thought. 'Will you drop everything and go rushing off to Wintercombe?'

'There have been many times during the last twenty-five years,' Silence said drily, 'when I have wished with all my heart that poor William had never set eyes on that woman: she is stupid, selfish, meddling; she likes to parade her helplessness when in fact she is quite capable of looking after herself – as witness how she managed for several years on her own after

William was killed; she likes to lean on poor Charles, and manipulate him, and it *cannot* be good for him to be still tied to her apron strings – he's nearly twenty-four now, after all. And yet . . . and yet, Alex has been very unkind to her, far more than she deserves. Besides,' she added, smiling suddenly with a mischief that reminded Louise vividly of her own mother, and made her look many years younger, 'I am all afire to see this child, and if he is indeed Alex's. Curiosity always was one of my most besetting sins.'

'So you'll go?' Tabby said. 'Oh, Mother, you can't!'

'Why not? The weather is very good, it's an easy road, and I am still hale and hearty even if I am nearly in my dotage. And I'm sure that my household can cope very well without me for a week or so.'

'I'll come with you,' Louise said quickly. 'I promised Phoebe and Charles and Amy that I would go back to see them. I expect Libby will be glad to have her cupboard back,' she added, smiling at her cousin, whose chamber she had usurped, and who now had to sleep with Sue and Hannah in their own rather restricted quarters.

Silence surveyed Louise thoughtfully. If she was dismayed at her granddaughter's suggestion, she gave no sign, but said quietly, 'You need not think that you have a duty to accompany me across Somerset at my elderly snail's pace, Louise. Stay here by all means, if that's what you wish.'

'No, Gran'mère, I would *like* to come.' Louise glanced apologetically at Tabby, who had made her very welcome, and added, 'I know Charles would be very disappointed if I didn't, and Amy too. And Phoebe asked me particularly to bring those books to her. Bram and I have found all of the ones that she wanted, save for two that are very rare, and I would like very much to take them to her in person.'

So ostensibly simple a request, so ordinary the reasons, with all the family present Louise knew that Silence would find it difficult to refuse, for she could hardly announce that she did not wish her granddaughter to accompany her for fear that Alex might seduce her. Louise did not miss the quick exchange of glances between her grandparents, and waited, suddenly tense, for the decision. Although, of course, since she had her own horse, and plenty of money, there was nothing to stop her going in spite of any prohibition, even if to do so would greatly distress and worry her family.

'Well, that is very kind of you, Louise – I shall be glad of your company,' Silence said, with a smile of warmth. 'And if Tabby and Jonah can spare you – I've been hearing all about your invaluable help in the shop.'

'Of course we can – though you must feel free to return at any time,' Tabby told her. 'You'll always be welcome here, Louise – even if you do have to sleep in a cupboard!'

157

And as she joined in the general laughter, Louise felt the old familiar wild bubble of excitement rise in her throat. She was going back to Wintercombe: and despite her affection for her Loveridge cousins, she suddenly could not wait to leave Taunton.

Four days later, on a beautiful June evening, she rode with Silence, their two maids, and Corbett, one of the Chard grooms, up the familiar track to Wintercombe. She had left in March, when the air was cold and the trees bare, and the luxuriant green landscape around her was so fresh and new that it was almost like coming to a completely different place. She imagined riding her mare Saffron across the lovely meadows, and her heart quickened in joyous anticipation. Merely travelling from one place to another, though a welcome change from the confined bustle of Taunton, was really just a chore. To run free with her horse for the love of speed, along lanes thick with hawthorn flowers and through grassy fields, was heaven indeed.

'I wonder how the garden looks?' Silence said, smiling up at the house she loved so much. 'June is always the best month, so many flowers – Jem Coxe does wonders, but I can never resist the temptation to poke and pry and interfere.' She glanced at Louise, and voiced the thought that had been left unsaid between them, all the way from Taunton. 'You haven't come with me just to see Charles and Amy and Phoebe, have you?'

Louise, startled, laughed. 'Oh, Gran'mère, you know I haven't! Apart from anything else, I too am very curious to see this child.'

'And Alex?'

'I will be careful,' Louise said, anticipating Silence's next question. 'I know what is at stake, after all. And I am a woman, Gran'mère, not a silly little flirt like Amy, or a schoolgirl like Sue and Hannah and Libby. Can you not trust me?'

And Silence, with an ominous sense of impending disaster, looked at her exultant, glowing face, and said, without much hope, that she would.

Lawrence Earle had gone ahead to warn of their arrival, and as they dismounted in the courtyard, Henry Renolds came running to take their horses, and the housekeeper emerged from the porch, her face split into a broad, welcoming smile. 'Oh, m'lady – Mistress Louise! Have you had a good journey?'

'A very pleasant one, thank you, Betty,' Silence said, moving a little awkwardly towards the front door on Louise's unobtrusive arm. She did not mind her granddaughter's assistance but hoped that Betty, who did tend to fuss like a broody hen, would not notice how stiff and tired she was after the long day's ride from Glastonbury, where they had stayed the night with the Wickhams. 'Who is at home, Betty?'

'Everyone, m'lady,' said the housekeeper. 'Sir Alexander is over at the farm, I believe, but Mistress Phoebe and Mistress Amy and Master Lukas are in the garden, and Master Charles is working in the study, and Mistress Bab in her chamber, of course. Supper will be served an hour before sunset, as usual, and doubtless you will both wish for refreshments after your long ride?'

They were shown to the chambers which they had occupied during their previous stay at Wintercombe, and Silence, with the quiet efficient help of her maid Fan Howard, changed out of her dusty russet riding habit that had never been in the forefront of fashion, and into a plain silk dress, one of her favourites, with a lace-edged tippet and a light scarf draped over her grey hair. The reflection that Fan showed her in the hand mirror stared back, the familiar face, calm and faintly smiling, an effective disguise for the doubt and apprehension that she actually felt. 'Thank you,' she said to her maid. 'I will go pay my respects to Mistress St Barbe. I'm sure that you have plenty to do before supper.'

'Indeed I do, madam,' said Fan, and she was already brushing the dust from the skirts of the riding habit when Silence left the chamber.

She would much rather have spent these moments resting on the bed with a cup of hot chocolate to restore her strength after the journey. Nick was right: she was undeniably too old to be jaunting round Somerset on horseback, although she suspected that the purchase of a coach, even one of the most modern design, would not make her travels any more comfortable or less exhausting. Besides, the many steep hills in Somerset, particularly those around Bath, made such a vehicle rather impractical. Soon, as old age, that she had for so long kept valiantly at bay, crept inexorably up on her, she would be confined by infirmity to Chard and Taunton, and her vigorous young descendants would have to come to her.

Since almost everyone she loved lived within those two towns, it would be no real hardship. But the thought that this might be the last time she stayed at Wintercombe, the house she loved more than any other, even Chard where she had been so happy with Nick, caused her real pain.

She put the sadness resolutely from her mind, and paused outside the door of Bab's rooms, collecting her thoughts and marshalling all her resources of calm, wisdom and restraint. Then she knocked.

The maid Beck, surprised, ushered her through her own antechamber and into the big, light room beyond. It was as cluttered and frowsty as ever, the range of potions and vials on the windowsills seemed to have doubled, and the musty aroma of Bab's little dog permeated the stale air. He leapt up, yapping belligerently, and snapped and swirled officiously around her skirts.

Bab reclined on the comfortable squab couch by the fire, which was lit and blazing even on this warm June evening. To Silence's assessing eye, she seemed to have lost some weight, and her face, which had once, plump and powdered, at least preserved a small semblance of her youthful health and beauty, was now grey and drawn under the thick paint. To her mother-in-law's secret annoyance, she showed no pleasure at her entrance, but put a large, lace-edged kerchief to her eyes and began to weep loudly.

The maid, for whom Silence had always felt great sympathy – tending Bab was a task equivalent in difficulty to any of the labours of Hercules – sighed heavily. Silence walked forward and touched the younger woman on the shoulder. The lace layers of Bab's elaborate tippet quivered with emotion, but there was no other response. She said quietly, 'You sent for me, Bab, and here I am. What do you want of me?'

Beck was busy amongst the ranks of potions and cosmetics. She returned with a small glass, from which a bitter but refreshing smell arose. 'Drink this, madam, it'll do you good.'

It was some time before the cordial did its work, and Silence waited patiently for the sobs to subside, aware all the while of the acute inward irritation that always afflicted her when she came into close contact with her daughter-in-law. She knew well that it was not for Bab's sake, but for her dear, long-dead son William, that she humoured this foolish, pathetic woman, and did as much for her as for her own children, who by virtue of love and ties of blood had the first claim to her help and support. They themselves could not understand why she should concern herself with Bab: indeed, there were many occasions when Silence could not understand it either. But she remembered, as if he were the subject of an old painting, William's young face glowing with love, and then Bab, worn and desperate with grief for her dead son, pleading for refuge for herself and her surviving children; and finally Charles and Amy, golden-haired and angelic in clothes that all too obviously had been worn to shreds, patched, then worn again. Yes, she was a silly, meddling, idle woman, and a Papist into the bargain. But she had been genuinely fond of William, and had suffered greatly after his death: and to Silence, she was irrevocably part of the family.

'Oh, dear Mother,' said Bab at last, tremulously. She had always addressed Silence thus, despite her attempts to prevent her. 'Thank you for coming so soon. I don't know what I would have done if you had not – oh, the shock was terrible, terrible!'

'Tell me,' Silence said patiently. 'Your letter was not very clear – what was the shock?'

'That child, of course, arriving here out of the blue – his son, so he says, but won't say anything else – Charles *asked* him if he was married to the child's mother, over and over again, but he just laughed,' Bab said, in an anguished torrent.

'So – you assume the child is Alex's son? And he's admitted as much?'

'Yes,' said Bab. She was calmer now, and her eyes had dried. 'The boy adores him – I can't imagine why.'

Silence could not envisage Alex as the subject of childish worship either, but doubtless she would be able to see for herself soon enough. 'And what of his mother? Presumably *she* hasn't arrived here too?'

'Oh, no – no – she's in Amsterdam, I think. There was some story of his servant – such a big uncouth Dutchman – of him abducting the boy from her care. But surely not even *he* would be so cruel? And if the boy isn't his heir, why take him away from her?'

Why indeed? Silence thought for a moment, and then said quietly, 'She might be a bad mother. He may be fond of the child. How old is he?'

'Five – six – I don't know.' Plainly, Alex's son had no significance for her in his own right, only in his possible status. Bab added, twisting her wet kerchief, 'He will listen to you – he will tell *you* the truth. If the boy is his legitimate heir, it changes everything, everything!'

Silence stared at her. 'But Bab, that is hardly your business, is it?'

'You don't understand!' her daughter-in-law wailed. 'Charles had hoped – and Amy, the foolish child, it seems she's besotted. God knows what she's done, she may be ruined!'

She dissolved into tears again, and Silence resisted the sudden base temptation to slap her soundly across her fat raddled face. She said, her rare anger rising suddenly in her throat, 'Do you mean to say that he has seduced Amy – *Amy* for Heaven's sake?'

Bab snivelled into her kerchief. 'I don't know – not for certain – the poor child's in love with him, he may have taken advantage of her, it's the sort of thing he would do – I don't know! But if he's got a wife already, if Amy proves with child . . .'

Silence set a hand on each plump shoulder and shook her, none too gently. 'What do you mean, you don't know? Have you no communication with your daughter at all?'

'I thought she was a good girl!' Bab wailed. 'A good, sweet, innocent girl – how could a man like that not take advantage of her?'

'But you don't *know* that he has,' Silence pointed out, keeping her temper in check. 'And surely all you have to do is to ask Amy outright – she

161

would not lie to you.' For one thing, she thought grimly, the girl lacked the wit to deceive anyone, even Bab.

Bab, between sobs, confessed that she had not asked her. With a sigh, Silence set herself to extract all the information that she could from her daughter-in-law, and very soon came to the conclusion that Bab was in fact making a very large mountain out of a very small molehill. Certainly, Amy was infatuated with him, and Alex, from the sound of it, had unkindly encouraged her to flirt with him. But Silence doubted very much that it had gone any further than that. Amy was very pretty, but she was much too insipid and prone to tears to interest Alex for very long. And besides, she suspected that if her nephew had in fact laid more than the very lightest of fingers on innocent Amy, the child would have screamed for help at the top of her voice. But Bab had convinced herself that Alex had taken advantage of her daughter, that Amy's reputation lay in tatters, and that her only remaining hope of matrimony, however distasteful, was with her seducer. And of course, if he proved to be already married, this would be impossible.

The whole situation was so ridiculous that Silence did not know whether to laugh, or to lose her temper altogether and knock some sense into Bab's silly head. But she restrained both impulses, and questioned the other woman closely. Did Amy have a chaperone? Did Mattie Jones accompany her at all times? Could she ensure that the girl was never alone with Alex?

To this stream of enquiry, Bab had no real answer. But at any rate, at the end of a tearful ten minutes Silence was tolerably certain that her naïve and innocent granddaughter would be very much better protected in the future. And she hoped devoutly that this was not a case of locking the stable door after the bolting horse.

Still, a brief conversation with Amy should settle it one way or the other. Silence left Bab's cluttered chamber in a mood of considerable exasperation. If the foolish woman had not spent the last few years virtually confined to her chamber by supposed ill health, but kept a proper watch over her daughter, then the girl would have been in no danger at all. She could not feel much pity for someone so resolutely opposed to helping herself: her sympathy was reserved for poor, naïve Amy, neglected by her mother, and cruelly misled by Alex, and for Charles, whom she liked, and whose future seemed lamentably uncertain.

She met him in the screens passage on her way to the gardens. His rather broad, fair-skinned face, at first glance so like William's, broke into a surprised and delighted smile. 'Grandmother! I knew Mother had written to you, but I had not expected you so soon. Will you help us?'

This place, so public, was hardly the best location for a discussion of intimate family affairs. 'I have just spoken to your mother,' said Silence briskly. 'I'll do all that I can – but I can't promise you success.' She reached up to kiss him affectionately on the cheek. 'So don't build your hopes too high. Have you seen Louise?'

The expression of sudden, overwhelming joy, gone as quickly as it had appeared, told her something of his feelings. 'No, Grandmother, I haven't – is she here too?'

'She did duty as my escort – she insisted on coming, she said she'd promised you and Amy that she would,' Silence told him. 'And she has a bundle of books for Phoebe, too, so I believe.' She smiled at him, while assessing the implications of that fleeting look of delight. It seemed that Charles had no little affection for Louise – and she was certain that her wayward and lively granddaughter would look on him as a friend, but no more.

Poor Charles: through no fault of his own he seemed to be forever doomed to be second best. Silence wished that she could do something about his plight, but he was a man grown, and quite capable of breaking free of Bab's clinging tendrils and making his own life. And despite her secret hopes and fears for them, she had never made it a habit to interfere too greatly in the lives of her children, or grandchildren. A little gentle steering was all that she usually allowed herself to do.

'I expect she's gone to the garden to see Amy and Phoebe,' she added, taking his arm. 'Shall we go and find her?'

But there was no sign of Louise among the scented, sunlit flowers. Silence heard voices, and walked with Charles along the middle terrace towards the upper gardens that lay on the eastern side of the house. She was pleased to see the box hedges neatly clipped, and the flowers making a goodly display, yellow marigolds, blood-red wallflowers, the first roses, columbines and forget-me-nots all in glorious and colourful profusion, and not a weed to be seen. Two boys were working industriously on the knots along the lower terrace, and just beyond them an older man was raking gravel. Silence breathed deeply, savouring the richly scented warmth of the air. It was worth the journey, the exhaustion and discomfort, and the unpleasantness with Bab and, probably before the day was out, with Alex, to be here in the place she loved best, at her favourite season of the year.

'There they are,' said Charles, and she saw, with her long sight – her spectacles were only used for close work, such as reading or sewing – two girls, one fair, one dark, sitting on the stone bench that lay between the terraces and the pond garden. As they drew nearer, she discerned Amy and Phoebe conversing quietly, while beyond them, in the centre of the wide rectangle of knots and gravelled paths that lay beside the house, a small figure hunched, utterly absorbed, above the still oval of the pond.

Amy turned her head and saw them approaching. She leaped to her feet, something sliding from her lap on to the gravel, and ran pell-mell down the steps and along the path towards them. 'Oh, Grandmother, you're here! How wonderful!'

Amy might have the least sense of any of her grandchildren, but there was no denying her warm heart or her genuine affection. Silence thought grimly that if Alex had indeed seduced her she would never be able to forgive him. She smiled in welcome, and kissed her, admired her new gown in a pale and impractical rose silk that set off her flawless face to perfection, and observed the girl closely as she chattered. Amy had always been very fickle in her moods, easily cheered, easily brought to tears. But Silence thought that if Bab was right she would not be able to hide her misery. This lovely smiling girl was surely still an innocent, even if she had, naïvely, fixed her affections on a confirmed and unscrupulous rake. And the blush silk outlined a smooth, plumply perfect figure that had none of the clumsiness of pregnancy.

It was just as well, Silence thought. Married to Alex, her life would have been one of miserable luxury. Surely even Amy, who read romances so voraciously and doubtless believed that love would conquer all, could not be so foolish to imagine that, once wed, Alex would become a reformed character?

Phoebe had risen to her feet, her sharp pale face unflatteringly illuminated by the westering sun, a thin smile on her lips. 'Hullo, Aunt. Have you been summoned to sort out our problems once again?'

'It does appear so,' Silence said, undeceived by the coolness of her niece.'How are you? Better for the warm weather?'

From anyone else, Phoebe would have given such concern for her health even shorter shrift. She shrugged, a gesture curiously reminiscent both of Alex and of Louise. 'No worse than usual, thank you, Aunt – certainly I'm glad to see summer here. And you,' she added, with a sudden, unaccustomed smile. 'But I'm under no illusions as to whom you have really come to see. As you must have guessed, that is Lukas, by the pond.'

'Lukas? Is that his name? No one,' said Silence drily, 'has referred to him as anything other than "the boy" or "the child", until now. I presume it's the Dutch form of Luke. Does he speak English?'

'As well as he speaks Dutch,' said Phoebe. 'Apparently, he learned both languages from his mother – and from Alex, of course. Shall I call him over?' As Silence nodded, she cupped her hands and shouted. 'Lukas! Can you come here, please?'

The small boy scrambled almost guiltily to his feet, although he had been doing nothing wrong, and turned round. Then he walked hastily towards them, his shoes crunching on the gravel. Silence glanced at Amy, standing beside her. She was looking at the boy with an almost warm expression in her eyes. Evidently, even if the existence of Lukas's mother had endangered her hopes, she had acquired some affection for him in the few days he had been at Wintercombe.

Charles, however, was frowning, his mouth compressed: clearly, Lukas was not at all a welcome arrival. He said abruptly to his sister, 'Have you seen Louise?'

'No, I haven't – is she here too? Oh, I'm so glad,' said Amy, ingenuously. 'I shall be able to practise my French.'

'I expect, if she is not here, she is in the stables, seeing to her horse,' Silence told her. 'You know Louise, after all.'

'I'll go and find her,' said Charles abruptly, and walked away. Silence, disturbed and a little annoyed at his rudeness, found it hard to escape the conclusion that he was avoiding Lukas, as much as searching for Louise. She would have to talk to him: the child's parentage was no fault of his own, after all, and she did not like to see Charles led by his prejudice into being unfair.

'Lukas, here is someone to see you,' said Phoebe, and Silence turned back in time to see the little boy's deep, impeccable bow. 'Mistress Hellier,' her niece added formally, her normally serious eyes dancing, 'may I present your great-nephew, Lukas Van der Linden?'

Silence inclined her head graciously, and then stared at the child. She had expected to find a replica of Alex at the same age, before his mother's death clouded his spoiled, happy charm. What she had not imagined was to see again the small, solemn, assessing face of Nat, who at five years old, long, long ago, had watched his new stepmother intently for several months, before telling her gravely that he liked her. It had been the start of a deep and rewarding friendship that had lasted nearly fifty years until his death, and she wished now, with the intensity of renewed grief, that he could have lived to see this, his first and only grandson, return to Wintercombe.

'So you are Lukas,' she said, smiling, hoping that no one would notice the tears that had suddenly filled her eyes. 'Do you like it here in England?'

'Oh, yes, thank you,' he said at once. 'Much better than in Holland. Aunt Phoebe is teaching me to read, and Papa says he will buy me a pony!'

Clearly, this was the summit of his desires. 'You will have to ask your Cousin Louise to teach you to ride,' Silence told him. 'She is very good – she has a lovely yellow mare called Saffron.'

'My father's horse is called Pagan,' Lukas said. He stared up at her, frowning. 'Please, Mistress Hellier, if I am your great . . . nephew, what are you?'

'I'm your great-aunt,' said Silence, laughing. 'Your father's mother was my sister.'

'I haven't got a sister,' said Lukas. 'I wish I had – and a brother too.' He paused wistfully, his blue eyes thoughtful, and then added more cheerfully, 'Would you like to come and see what I've found in the pond, Great-Aunt? There are lots of little black things that wriggle everywhere, and I don't know what they are.'

And Silence, who loved children and felt great sympathy for this serious, lonely little boy, allowed herself to be taken by the hand and led towards the pond to look at tadpoles, as if they were the rarest and most remarkable of creatures.

As her grandmother had suspected, Louise had indeed gone to the stables, leaving her maid Christian to unpack her clothes and brush the dust from her riding habit. She did not feel in the mood for a meeting with Amy just yet, or with Charles, and although she trusted the Wintercombe grooms, she always checked herself that her horse was well tended at the end of a long ride. Saffron would need hay and water, a good grooming to remove the dirt of the journey from her yellow hide, and a thorough inspection of her legs and hooves for signs of lameness or trouble with her shoes.

And besides, it was three months since she had last seen the inhabitants of Wintercombe's stables, and she was looking forward to a long talk with Dan Pardice about her cousin's horse-breeding plans.

She wore a gown that was not her best, of a flowered tawny-yellow, with the long overskirt looped into the narrow belt at her waist to keep it out of the dirt. Her hair could have been better dressed, and Christian, who prided herself on her skills, had urged her not to go out until it had been brushed and scented and rearranged into the bubbling dark curls on either side of her head, with a long single ringlet to trail seductively over one shoulder, that she usually wore. But there would be time for that later, before supper: time, too, to put on the peacock-coloured silk which she had had made in Taunton, extravagantly low, that emphasised and enhanced the slender curves of her body. She was looking forward to seeing Alex's reaction to it, and to the next moves in the dangerous, exhilarating game which she had not played for too long.

The stables were the same as ever, dim and welcoming, and cool after the heat of the evening outside. Daniel Pardice greeted her with sincere warmth, and led her to the stall where Saffron was tethered, with Henry Renolds, whistling a ballad cheerily and tunelessly through his gapped teeth, combing out her black tail while she munched the hay bundled into the manger. 'As nice a little mare as I'd ever wish to see,' said the head groom appreciatively. 'Where did ee find her, Mistress Louise?'

She explained about Jan Wickham's efforts on her behalf, and the talk turned naturally to the young mares that Alex had brought back from Glastonbury. All were doing well, and with luck would throw a fine crop of foals next spring, Pagan having performed his appointed task with enthusiasm. The big grey was at present running with his mares, but Daniel led her along to the loosebox at the end of the stable block, to show her the new young stallion that her cousin had bought only a few weeks previously.

He was as tall as Pagan, but much more lightly furnished as yet, being, as Dan pointed out, only four years old. Louise eyed him rather warily, warned by the rolling eye and restless feet that this horse was rather more lively, and less gentlemanly, than his older rival. But he was a handsome animal, a rich bright russet bay, with a broad white blaze and a proudly carried tail.

'A proper handful, that one,' Dan observed. 'Saddlebroke, or so twas said, but Sir Alexander d'have the devil of a job to keep on his back sometimes – only don't ee tell him I said so, Mistress.'

'I won't,' she promised. At the same moment, her cousin's voice intruded. 'What am I not to be told, Dan?'

Louise caught the groom's eye, and he winked. Laughter bubbling up, she turned to face Alex, standing a few feet away with his eyebrows raised. 'Apparently your new purchase is somewhat spirited,' she said sweetly.

'Does his best to fling me off into the nearest ditch, you mean. Fortunately, he hasn't yet succeeded, though God knows that's not for want of trying, eh, Dan? He's young yet, though, and should settle down in a year or two – and meanwhile, I plan to advertise his prowess by racing him on Lansdown. Hence the need to impress upon him the advantages of obeying his rider.'

'Rather ee than me,' said Dan drily. 'Well, I've a-plenty to do, so if you'll excuse me, sir – good evening to ee, Mistress Louise.' And he walked away down the passage alongside the stalls, turned the corner, and was gone.

'Well, well – so you've come back,' said Alex. In the dim, aromatic light he seemed very big, the dark coat and hat emphasising his height and size.

'And what brings you to Wintercombe, sweet Cousin?' He leaned casually against the wooden partition wall of the loosebox, and folded his arms. 'Curiosity?'

'A family visit only,' said Louise lightly, though her heart was thudding, and she did not dare meet his eyes. Even with her face turned away, she was as aware of him as she was of the sun's power, warming her body and trickling desire through her veins. 'I escorted my grandmother.'

'And why is *she* here? Something to do with Bab's letter, perhaps, and Lawrence Earle's little errand?'

'It could be,' Louise said cautiously. She turned to look at the bay stallion, who had arrived at the door of the loosebox, and was regarding her lacy tippet with undisguised and greedy interest. 'He's a fine horse. What is his name?'

'He has several, none repeatable. His manners are abominable, and it'll be some time before he's capable of civilised behaviour – but I feel I'm winning the battle.' He came to stand beside her, and the bay's ears flicked rather apprehensively at his approach. 'Would you like a closer look?'

'I thought you said his manners were atrocious.'

'They are – with a rider on his back. In his box, he's as gentle as a lamb. Don't look so doubtful – I thought you were quite fearless where horses are concerned.'

'I am,' said Louise, rising to the bait. 'What are you waiting for?'

He grinned and opened the door of the box. At once, the bay pushed forward, ears pricked, and Alex took a carrot from the pocket of his coat, and offered it to him. Louise, her skirts pulled clear of the thick layer of clean yellow straw, slid past through the gap, and into the box. She watched warily, trusting neither man nor beast despite his words, until the carrot was finished and the bay, his white nose inquisitive, began to nuzzle Alex for more.

'You see?' said her cousin, with that unexpectedly splendid smile that had the power to dwindle all her resistance away to nothing. 'Like a lamb.' He ran his hand down the smooth, muscular red curve of the bay's neck. 'And a coat like silk – Henry's done his work well. No, greedy one – no more!'

The stallion leaned his head against Alex's coat, and slobbered at one of the big silver buttons that adorned the front. His owner laughed, and pushed him away. 'You've hay and oats in plenty – there's no need to eat my coat as well.'

So obviously sulking at his rejection that Louise laughed, the bay gave Alex one last indignant glance, and then turned round, as bidden, to attend to the contents of his manger. Louise had to move out of his way, and her two brisk sidesteps brought her much nearer to Alex than she had intended: so close, in fact, that her laced, ruffled sleeve brushed his coat. Immediately she tried, without making it too obvious, to slide backwards, but too late. His hands came out to rest on her shoulders and turn her to face him. 'You haven't given me a welcoming kiss, sweet Louise. Will you oblige me now?'

There was no point in refusing, when she wanted it as much as he did. 'Of course I will,' she said, smiling, and, lifting her hands, drew his head down for the embrace.

Charles, walking up to the loosebox where Dan Pardice had told him that Louise could be found, did not see them at first, and looked around, puzzled, wondering if she had slipped out of the stables by another door. Then he heard a sound, a soft sigh of desire, and glanced curiously into the loosebox.

Their shapes, black and tawny gold, imprinted themselves on his appalled mind until long afterwards. Louise, pressed back against the whitewashed stone wall of the loosebox, the long clear lines of her throat and jaw pale against the darkness of his hair, her arms, wound round his neck, almost as white as the rich lace ruffles falling below her sleeves: and Alex, stooped above her like a predator, devouring her with his kiss.

For what seemed like an eternity, Charles stared at them, trying desperately to refute the evidence of his own eyes. Then, unable to bear it any longer, he turned and, not caring whether they heard him, almost ran, retching, for the nearest door and the clear untainted air outside.

'I've changed my mind,' Louise said to her maid, Christian. 'I shan't wear the blue tonight. This will suffice.'

Christian, who was no fool, eyed her mistress. She had had her suspicions ever since Louise had arrived in her chamber, flushed and bubbling over with laughter and excitement, but this was surprising. If Louise wished to impress her lover – and Christian had a very good idea as to his identity – then the peacock silk was the ideal choice. The tawny yellow, less fashionable, less daring, was also much less likely to inflame his desire – if, indeed, thought the maid with amusement, it needed inflaming any further.

She knew better than to argue, however, for Louise was not accustomed to having her wishes questioned. So she merely said calmly, 'Very well, Mistress,' and set about dressing her hair.

Louise sat at the table, looking at her reflection in the mirror. Her skin was as brilliant and glowing as if she had painted it, and her eyes stared back, huge and dark with remembered passion. Not love – though his touch melted her bones, though she wanted far more of him than one long kiss in a stable, she was under no illusions. Lust, and nothing more, would be her undoing, if she allowed it.

And she would not – yet – hence the change of gown. The peacock blue, which all but exposed her breasts, was hardly fitting for a quiet supper *en famille*, after all, even with the addition of her best lace-edged tippet, which revealed almost more than it hid. She had no intention of surrendering to Alex yet, anyway, if at all. That lingering embrace in the loosebox – she smiled at the aptness of the term – had whetted both their appetites, and left her in no doubt whatsoever as to the force of his desire, as well as hers. The knowledge was intoxicating: she, Louise Chevalier, who had once been a skinny, ungainly hoyden, the despair of her mother, had attracted this formidable and experienced man.

*Fool*, she upbraided herself, and wrinkled her nose severely at the glowing face in the mirror. *He is a rake, which means that his powers of discrimination are less well developed than those of other, more scrupulous men – so is that any tribute to your charms?*

No, she would not surrender, even in the face of the overwhelming, suffocating temptation which she had felt in the stable. But it would do no harm to let him think that she would, to keep him dangling, doling out a kiss here, a hurried fondle there, and perhaps deflate a little of that overweening arrogance in the process.

With a smile of pleasurable anticipation, Louise smoothed the folds of her bodice, adjusted her overskirt, and patted a stray curl into place. Then, as full of self-satisfaction as a cat, she stepped lightly down to supper.

Her grandmother, in ignorance of events in the stable, had not been looking forward to the meal. A variety of possible scenarios, all of which featured her nephew at his most drunkenly offensive, had filled her mind, and she was deeply worried about Charles. He, it seemed, had not been able to find Louise with the horses, but instead looked as if he had been vouchsafed a vision of Hell. Even Amy, hardly the most perceptive of souls, had commented on his strange looks and almost monosyllabic speech, and had been curtly rebuffed. And then there was Lukas, so small and alone amongst his warring adult relations, and as sensitive as all children to atmosphere and mood. She hoped, but somehow doubted, that Alex would repay the adoration which shone in every word that his son spoke about him.

She was astonished and pleased to find, as the supper progressed, that she had done her nephew an injustice, in this matter at least. Alex, very tall and imposing in his crimson and gold, took his accustomed place at the head of the table, with Lukas on his right and Phoebe on his left, Amy, Louise and Silence distributed beyond them, and Charles at the other end, in grim and lonely splendour, saying very little. It was Lukas, with his engaging chatter, at once polite and very direct, who held their attention. He talked about the tadpoles, and the pony he had been promised, and Louise was once more suggested as a tutor. 'After all,' Phoebe pointed out, 'she is our equine expert.'

'I'd be delighted to,' Louise told Lukas. 'But there are two problems. Firstly, I do not think that Gran'mère will be here for very long – a week or so, at most, and that's hardly time enough. Learning to ride takes months, even years of practice. And secondly, your father has not yet bought you a pony.'

The boy's small face fell, and he stared unhappily down at his plate. Louise touched him lightly on the shoulder. 'But I'll do the best I can, I promise you that.'

'There's a farmer at Combe Hay who often has ponies and small horses for sale, or so Dan Pardice tells me,' Alex said. 'You and I can ride over tomorrow and see if he has one that would suit you. It's not far, and the weather seems set for another sunny day.'

The transformation of Lukas's pale, rather pinched face was breathtaking. A less inhibited child might have leaped up to hug his father: he only smiled, but it was the pure joy in it that brought a ridiculous lump to Louise's throat. 'Oh, can we  can we? Can I ride Pagan with you?'

'I was planning to take the bay – Pagan is still keeping company with his mares. But I'm sure one of the grooms will let you ride pillion behind him. What sort of pony would you like?'

The rest of the meal was given over to equine topics, and became almost a three-cornered conversation between Alex, his son, and Louise, with occasional comments from the other three women. Charles, at the opposite end of the table from his enemy, sat miserable and savage in front of food that tasted of nothing, and wine that might have been water for all the savour it had. His mind, bewildered and disgusted, was still reliving, over and over again, the stark little scene in the stable, the man and the woman wound so close together that they might have been one flesh, united by the corruption of lust.

He loved Louise: the friendship between them, growing in the months of her first sojourn at Wintercombe, had changed, almost without him being aware of it, into something far stronger. There were few young women in his circle of acquaintance, and the two he knew best of all, Amy and Phoebe, were so dissimilar as to seem almost members of different species. Louise, with her confidence, her wit, her sophistication and, above all, the open, friendly honesty of her manner, had enchanted him as if she were a creature from another world. His head knew that in this imperfect life she was not, and never would be, for him: she was destined for a good marriage to some wealthy Protestant, not to an impoverished Catholic without any prospects save the hopes and schemes which Bab and circumstance had sown in his mind. But his heart, so used already to yearning for things which he would never have, thought differently, and supplied his dreams with bright, joyous pictures in which Louise, with the lively innocence of her youth, consented lovingly to be drawn into his embrace.

And instead, she had apparently chosen Alex, the debauched un-principled libertine, doubtless riddled with foul disease (although, most unfairly, his appearance gave no sign of it), the man who had deprived Charles of his inheritance and his future and his home, and laughed about it: and the man who had apparently already attempted, fortunately without success, to seduce Amy. In his heart, he had come to look on Louise as his, and her betrayal struck deep into his soul.

But perhaps Alex had seduced her. This thought, compared with those that had preceded it, was almost comforting. Charles toyed with the stem of his wine glass, watching the rich crimson claret, the colour of Alex's coat, swirl delicately in the bowl. Might not his dear Lou, young and trusting and innocently friendly, have unwittingly led the older, un-scrupulous man into believing that she would not repel his advances? And although his brief glance, all he could bear, had not shown him any signs of resistance, she was only a weak female and Alex a big man, over two yards high and powerfully built.

This idea was a very attractive one. Charles lifted his gaze to the face of his enemy, twelve feet away at the other end of the table. Alex was talking to his wan-faced little bastard: in the week since Lukas had arrived at Wintercombe, Charles had been unable to address any more than the most brief and stilted phrases to him, to the child's evident bewilderment. In the flattering yellow candlelight, it was possible, grudgingly, to admit the man's attractions. No wonder poor, deluded Amy had been so distressed at the thought that he might already be married. The question gnawed evilly at Charles's mind. He had always been mild and cautious, eschewing violence as the mark of an uncivilised brute, but the status of Lukas's unknown mother now loomed so large in his thoughts that, given the equipment and the opportunity, he would have racked the truth from Alex without compunction.

A plump, cheerful and very plain girl with the face and figure of a good-natured pig, who had been engaged as Lukas's nursemaid, appeared to take him to bed. The child's face fell, but he went with her docilely enough. Twinney brought more wine, bowls of sweetmeats, and a bottle of brandy. Usually, at this time, the women were accustomed to withdraw and leave Charles and Alex in lonely and hostile splendour. Silence, however, accepted more wine, put two sugar plums on her plate, and glanced round the table at her grandchildren and her niece. She waited until Twinney had left the room, and then fixed Alex with a stern and unwavering eye. 'He's a very nice little boy, and his manners are beautiful – a miracle, given his parentage and upbringing. It's obvious that he's your son – but on which side of the blanket?'

Alex, the constraint of Lukas's presence removed, had already poured himself some brandy. His blue gaze, equally implacable, rested on his aunt. 'Is that any business of yours?'

'Perhaps not directly,' Silence said mildly. 'But it *is* the business of people whose lives and expectations are affected by it – not to mention those who are, with the most selfless motives, endeavouring to procure you a wife.'

The irony in her tone was not lost on Alex, who raised his eyebrows at her. 'Oh? And who might they be?'

'Philip Cousins, for one,' Phoebe said unexpectedly. 'You told me yourself that he had offered to trawl Somerset for suitable ladies. I'm sure it's his business if he's unknowingly helping you to commit bigamy.'

'Philip is a competent enough lawyer to be quite alive to all the possibilities,' Alex pointed out, in the lazy drawl which always raised Charles's hackles. 'Besides, he already knows about Lukas. I went to Bath two days ago and told him.'

'The truth?' Silence enquired.

'Of course. Certain alterations to certain documents were required.'

'Then if you're prepared to tell him, why in God's name won't you tell us?' Charles demanded suddenly.

'Mischief,' said Alex, behind his glass. He took a swallow of brandy and continued. 'The pleasure of seeing you all squirming on the hooks of your own greedy ambition. And I may as well inform you now, pretty Amy, that whatever ideas you may have allowed into your silly little head, I have no intention of marrying you, though you were the last woman on earth.'

There was a stunned pause. Amy gasped and got to her feet, her face suddenly distorted by disbelief and anguish. She stared at Alex, and he smiled, inclined his head, and raised his glass to her. 'You'll find a husband, my sweet, who's far more to your liking. Look on it as a pleasurable interlude. And at least you're still virgo intacta.'

Amy gazed at him in acute distress, her full red lips trembling uncontrollably. Then she gave a sudden, convulsive sob, and fled to the door. Her desperate running footsteps died away into the evening quiet. Louise, appalled by Alex's behaviour, and disgusted with her own, avoided looking anyone in the eye.

'That was remarkably cruel of you,' Silence said, and her voice, abruptly, showed the steel so rarely displayed beneath that deceptive air of calm and ancient wisdom. 'I doubt you did it for her own good, so I can only imagine that for some obscure reason you enjoy hurting those who cannot defend themselves. Your great-grandmother was the same – not an attractive trait. And I would like very much to know, as I am sure Charles would, whether you spoke the truth concerning her virginity.'

Alex laughed derisively. 'Of course I did. Credit me with a little sense, Aunt. Would I so readily give Charles an excuse to murder me? I merely stole a few kisses, that's all. Is it my fault that she built such a palace of illusion on very sandy soil? I thought it best to curb her rampant daydreams before they grew to unmanageable proportions, that's all.' He gave his aunt the sudden, impudent smile that was so charming, to the susceptible. 'Amy is not the wife for me, and you know it. Far better to nip her pretensions in the bud now, and save much greater grief in the future.'

'We have strayed somewhat from the point,' Silence said, aware that it would be impossible to win this particular argument, which, unless ended now, threatened to continue all night. 'You have yet to tell us about Lukas. And, in case it concerns you, I'll say that to my mind, whether his mother is your wife or not should make no difference to our attitude to Lukas himself. His parentage is hardly his fault, after all.'

'I agree,' Alex said. He leaned back, surveying her, his face a little flushed. 'But while you are unlikely to visit the sins of the parent on the child, Aunt, there are others at Wintercombe, I regret to say, if not further afield, who will not be so generous. And, as you say, he is a charming child, and I will not have him hurt.'

'Nor will he be,' said Louise suddenly. 'Do you think it makes any difference to me, whether he is your legitimate son or not? He is Lukas, and that alone should matter.'

'*Should* – but in this bigoted country, it is often the child who suffers,' Alex pointed out. 'A more enlightened attitude prevails on the other side of the Channel. Here, even though our late King made bastards the fashion, the mentality of Cromwell's time tends to prevail outside the Court. If the world believes Lukas to be my lawful heir, not only is he saved from malice and wagging tongues, but I am saved the bother of finding myself a wife.'

'Your argument's spurious, and you know it,' Silence said roundly. 'You've never given a toss for gossip, and Lukas is too young to be affected by it – though I admit that in five years or so it might be different. Meanwhile, we are all of us, for our different reasons, most concerned to know. Is that woman in Amsterdam your wife?'

'What do you think?' Alex said immediately.

By this time Louise, were she in her grandmother's place, would have been hard pressed not to wring his neck. But Silence only looked at him, a long, assessing stare tinged with an expression that was almost one of regret. 'I don't think that even you would be fool enough to marry such a creature,' she said at last, consideringly. 'Phoebe has heard a little about her from Lukas. And marriage in haste, repentance at leisure, has never seemed to be your style. So, on the balance of probability, I would say that she was your mistress, rather than your wife.'

Alex laughed. 'Oh, dear Aunt Silence, your reasoning does you great credit.'

'Well?' Charles demanded urgently. 'Is she right?'

Alex looked down the table at him, the smile fading suddenly. 'Of course she's right, you half-wit,' he said derisively. 'Johanna is a lady who is very pleasant to view, but not at all nice to know. In her eyes, Lukas was a mistake, whose sole advantage was as a pawn to tie me to her permanently. Unfortunately, she did not realise that I would not stoop to such depths, even to gain a legitimate son. I provided for Lukas and for her, more than generously, but I refused to marry her, despite her entreaties.'

'There are some who would say,' Silence pointed out coldly, 'that you had an obligation to marry the unwed mother of your child.'

'If I had, she'd have set horns on my head before the week was out. Johanna is incapable of virtue or faithfulness,' Alex said, a glint in his eyes showing that he was well aware of the irony. 'Both before and after the few months when she was my mistress, she enjoyed a string of lovers to keep her in her accustomed style of lavishness. Lukas was an inconvenience, a nuisance, and she treated him disgracefully, as Phoebe will attest – he has confided in her a little.'

'But if she didn't want him, why did she not send him to you?' Silence asked.

Alex shrugged. 'She is jealous, perhaps. The child hero-worships me – God alone knows why – and she did not want to make him happy so easily. I don't know. She is a fiery and unpredictable woman. And also, I think, she still entertained some hope, while Lukas was in her keeping, of enticing me back to her bed.'

'Even though she obviously dislikes you?' said Phoebe, in tones of some doubt. Alex glanced at her, and smiled. 'Any feelings we had for one another began and ended in her bed. It's not a particularly flattering testimony to my prowess, either, when you learn that none of her other lovers was a day under fifty.'

Louise stifled a mad impulse to laugh, took too big a gulp of wine to cover it, and choked. At once Alex, pleasantly solicitous, leaned across Lukas's empty chair and gave her a buffet, not in the least gentle, across her shoulders. It hurt, but it achieved its purpose. She coughed, swallowed, and wiped her streaming eyes. Charles, staring at her with all his yearning agony displayed, sat unnoticed at the end of the table.

'Are you all right?' Silence said to her granddaughter. As Louise, still speechless and gasping, nodded, she turned to Alex, who was downing the rest of his brandy. 'It's not a particularly edifying tale, but I believe it. If the stories that Phoebe has been telling me are true, and since they came from Lukas rather than from you, I have no reason to doubt them –'

'Thank you,' said Alex, with a generously insolent smile.

'If they are true,' Silence continued, ignoring his interruption, 'then you have one thing to your credit, and that is your removal of Lukas from his mother. Let us hope that here he will find the happiness that has so far been missing from his life. And perhaps the presence of a young and impressionable child will prompt you to put some long-overdue restraint on your behaviour.'

'I shouldn't wager any money on it, Aunt,' said Alex, and grinned wickedly, apparently quite unaffected by her stern tone. 'You saw for yourself how early he goes to bed. And I do not intend taking him with me to visit Bristol Nan's, or any of my other haunts in Bath. Rest assured, Lukas will see nothing that he hasn't already seen in his mother's house.'

Unwarily, Louise met Phoebe's eyes and almost disgraced herself again. Silence, unaware, pushed her chair back with some force, and stood up. 'I think it is time I retired,' she said, the anger still plain in her voice. 'And doubtless Louise and Phoebe will accompany me. Goodnight, nephew – goodnight, Charles.'

Left alone, the two men stared at each down the long crowded length of the table. Alex poured himself more brandy, and pushed the bottle a little way towards his cousin. 'D'you want some? You look in some need of it.'

'I thank you for your concern, but no,' said Charles between his teeth. His hands longed to smash the leering mockery from Alex's face, with a force that threatened to run beyond his usual control. It was distinctly alarming, and he must at all costs keep his dignity, however much his cousin tried to taunt him.

'Good,' Alex said. 'All the more for me.' He stared menacingly over the rim of his glass. 'Why the long face, dear Cousin? You've learned the truth about Lukas, and it's surely good news for you – you're still my heir, and I'm still wifeless, and your virginal sister will no longer wish to throw herself at my head. Although perhaps I'll change my mind about her – she really is a very pretty little thing, despite being so waterlogged. I wonder whether that plump body will seem so tempting when I've taken her clothes off?'

'If you lay another finger on her,' said Charles, exploding to his feet, 'I'll kill you, I swear it!' He wanted to mention Louise, but quailed at the thought of admitting what he had seen in the stable. Instead, ignoring the amused, goading face of his cousin, he blundered to the door, and slammed it forcefully shut behind him.

With no one to watch him, Alex sat still for a moment, smiling reflectively, his thoughts obviously elsewhere. Then he drew the brandy bottle towards him, and set about finishing it.

# 10

# 'Youth, beauty, graceful action seldom fail'

The following day dawned, as predicted, fine and sunny, in marked contrast to most of the inhabitants of Wintercombe. Lukas, however, with the promise of a ride and a pony before him, was in high spirits, and could hardly sit still even while eating his breakfast: a meal from which his father was, as usual, absent.

Louise, who had also risen early, had her own strategy to put into operation. She finished her bread and cold bacon, and smiled at the little boy. 'Are you looking forward to choosing your pony, Lukas?'

'Oh, *yes*,' said Alex's son, with a huge and uncharacteristic grin that was very like his father's. 'Very, *very* much. I wish I could ride on Pagan, though.'

'Pagan is busy with his mares, and besides, your father wants to take the bay stallion,' Louise told him. 'And you can't ride on him, it would be dangerous. He's young, and hasn't learned good manners yet, apparently.' She paused, and then added, as if the thought had just occurred to her, 'Why don't I come with you, and then you can ride on my horse Saffron? She's a lovely little yellow mare, very sweet and gentle and comfortable, but she can run like the wind when I ask her to. Would you like that?'

'Oh, yes, please!' Lukas said, his eyes round. 'That would be lovely, Cousin Louise – thank you very much.'

'And perhaps you can ride your own pony home,' suggested Phoebe, who was the only other person at present in the dining parlour. She smiled fondly at her nephew. 'Let's hope the farmer at Combe Hay has a suitable one for you. If Louise goes back to Taunton soon, she will only have a little time to teach you.'

'But Papa can when you are gone, Cousin.'

'Your father has a great deal to do – he might be too busy,' Phoebe said gently. 'Still, if you are as quick to learn to ride as you are with your letters, you'll be a proper little centaur in no time.'

'A centaur? Please, Aunt, what is a centaur?'

'A mythical creature – one that doesn't really exist, save in stories,' Phoebe told him. 'It has the body of a horse, but a man's, or a woman's, head. So, if you say that someone rides like a centaur, it means that they ride very well.'

'I would like to,' said Lukas. 'Do you think I will, Cousin Louise?'

'There's no reason why you shouldn't,' she said. 'It's good to start young, on a pony that's kind and safe, and we'll find you one of those to ride if we have to scour three counties for it.' She pushed her plate away, and got to her feet. 'If I'm to come with you, I shall need to change into my riding habit. I'll meet you in the stable yard – don't go without me!'

It took only a few minutes to pull off her gown, with Christian's bemused assistance, and to change her long, stiff stays for the looser and more comfortable pair which she wore for riding. The French habit, consisting of a ruffled linen shirt and neckcloth like a man's, the long dove-grey coat and waistcoat, also of masculine style, and the extravagantly cut skirts, was soon slipped over the top, and the maid pinned the little hat at a rakish angle over the abundant, freshly curled hair.

With a grin of satisfaction at her reflection in the mirror which Christian held, Louise made an exuberant pirouette, whistling a French tune, and ran downstairs to join Alex and Lukas.

It was obvious that her cousin had not yet appeared, for Lukas, looking rather forlorn, was sitting on the mounting-block in an otherwise empty stable yard. As she entered from the door in the long wing of the house that formed the eastern side of the stable quadrangle, he looked up hopefully, and then jumped down and came to meet her. She had already noticed that, compared with her half-brothers, Lukas was a very quiet and reserved child, almost unnaturally polite, even when allowing his enthusiasm to get the better of him. Philippe and Honoré would have run across the cobbles, shouting in joyful welcome. Lukas walked carefully, and saluted her with a bow that was almost comical in its correctness. 'Hullo, Cousin Louise.'

She inclined her head in graceful acknowledgement. 'Hullo, Lukas. Have you seen Pardice? The head groom?'

'He has gone to saddle Papa's horse, I think. Ah, here he is.'

Dan Pardice emerged from the stables leading the bay stallion. The big red horse was restive and fretting, prancing stiff-legged and tugging at the rein. Lukas stared at the animal, which from his diminutive height must have seemed gigantic. 'I'm glad I'm going to ride with you, Cousin.'

'You'll certainly be safer,' said Louise. She was studying the bay, who in the warm clear light of a June morning seemed even more handsome than he had appeared in the stables, and twice as large and fiery. He was no Pagan, though, and despite his good looks, she mistrusted his eyes. This horse would make a good stud, if he passed on his handsome lines to his progeny, but his temperament was distinctly suspect.

Pardice tied the horse securely to one of the rings set in the wall of the barn, and came over to her, noting the significance of her riding clothes. 'Do ee wish I to saddle the yellow mare for ee, Mistress Louise?'

'If you would, Pardice, thank you – and can you put a pillion pad on her for Master Lukas?'

'Very good, Mistress,' said the groom, and disappeared into the stables once more. The girl and the child waited in companionable silence, enjoying the sunshine and the breeze, until Lukas, gazing in awed fascination at the big bay, said, 'Must you go back home so soon, Cousin Louise? Before you've had time to teach me to ride?'

Before we've had time to become friends, she thought, feeling regretful herself. 'If it were up to me,' she said, 'I'd stay for much longer. But I came here to keep my grandmother company, and it wouldn't be fair to her to let her go all the way back to Taunton on her own, would it?'

Slowly, reluctantly, Lukas shook his head. 'No, I suppose not.'

'But I shall come back later in the summer, perhaps, and see you all again, and stay for longer then. And, I promise you, I'll teach you to ride, and to do all the tricks my brother Philippe has learned.'

'Your brother? Have you got sisters as well? Are they in Taunton too?'

Louise explained, clearly and simply, that her mother and stepfather and her five half-brothers and half-sisters lived in France. Lukas, it was plain, was enchanted by the thought of so large a family, and demanded details. She told him about Julienne, who was fourteen and as wild a hoyden as Louise herself had been at that age, and Felice, four years younger and at present, to her mother's alarm, desperate to become a nun. Then the boys, Philippe and Honoré, imps of mischief both, and Madeleine who had been only a tiny baby when Louise left for England. Lukas listened, wide-eyed, to her stories of Philippe, who could already stand on his pony's back while it walked around the field.

'Could you teach me to do that?' the boy asked wistfully. 'Is it very difficult?'

'By the time you're seven, the same age as Philippe, you should be able to do that – but I warn you, it's very easy to fall off,' Louise told him. 'Ah, here comes Pardice – and there's my little Saffron. Isn't she lovely?'

Lukas admired her sincerely, from a safe distance. Louise led him up to the yellow mare, and let him stroke the soft, sensitive nose. 'She isn't *very* little,' he said doubtfully.

'Nor could she be, and still carry my weight,' Louise pointed out. 'But your pony will be much smaller, don't worry.' She turned to Pardice, who was holding Saffron's reins. 'Have you seen Sir Alexander this morning?'

'No, Mistress Louise. He gave me the order to saddle the bay last night, and for Henry to go with him and take the little lad, but I haven't seed him since then.'

It was a lovely morning, and she knew the way to Combe Hay, and Henry Renolds, now leading his own undistinguished mount from the stable door, would go with them. Alex could catch them up, if he was coming, and she hoped very much that he would. Not only did she wish for his company, and the sensations of power and desire and danger it brought, but he had promised Lukas, and already the child's rather wan face was showing the beginnings of disappointment and an awareness of betrayal. She wondered where Alex was, and decided that he must be in bed still, sleeping off the previous night's probable indulgence.

'No matter,' she said to the groom. 'We'll go now, rather than keep all three horses waiting – not to mention Master Lukas.' She grinned at the boy, and was rewarded by a rather hesitant smile. 'Tell Sir Alexander that we've taken the Wellow Lane, and we won't be hurrying – he can easily catch us up. Come on, Lukas – if you take Saffron's reins for me, can you lead her over to the mounting-block?'

Flushed with responsibility, the boy held the thick leather straps and gently pulled. Saffron, who had a mouth as silken as her buttery hide, followed him willingly, with Louise alongside, unobtrusively ready to intervene if necessary. She showed him how to stand at the horse's head, making sure that she was still, and then mounted with her usual graceful ease.

'But how do I get on?' Lukas asked, rather anxiously. Pardice, smiling, took his place, and the child, following Louise's instructions, climbed the mounting block, stood hesitantly on top, and then, awkwardly but full of determination, climbed on to the pillion pad. She made sure that he was comfortable and holding on tightly round her waist, and then grasped the reins. 'Are you ready, Lukas? Here we go.'

And slowly, steadily, the mare Saffron walked out of the stable yard, with Henry Renolds, grinning, following sedately behind on his nag.

On a day like today, bright and breezy, she would usually have cantered the mare along the lane, enjoying her speed and the feeling of freedom and release which it gave her. But with Lukas, brave but nervous, clinging tightly to her, she could not, yet, progress beyond a walk. He said nothing as they descended the hill on which Wintercombe stood, and Louise suspected that all his concentration was devoted to staying on the mare's back. But once they were dawdling along the narrow, winding lane, the steep slopes and sheepwalks on their right, and the water meadows, the brooks and the humps of Hassage Hill and Baggridge on their left, his grip relaxed, and she could sense that he was beginning to enjoy himself. Behind, Henry, who appreciated such expeditions, was whistling some bawdy ballad with great cheerfulness but a marked lack of tune. Suddenly light-hearted, Louise said to Lukas, 'Do you like singing?'

'I don't know,' said the boy, after a startled pause. 'I don't think I know how.'

'Oh, Lukas, you must – everyone sings, even if the sound isn't always very pretty. Shall I teach you a French song that my brothers like?'

'Yes, please, Cousin Louise. But I don't know any French.'

'You don't have to. Just listen to me, and I'll hum the tune first, and then I'll sing the words, over and over again, and you join in when you feel ready. Henry? I'm going to teach Master Lukas a French song, and you can learn it too, if you like.'

Henry was a good-natured boy, and took the hint. Into an air suddenly devoid of all music save birdsong, she hummed a jaunty tune several times, and then began to sing, in a voice that was rather throaty, but essentially accurate.

> *'Alouette, gentil alouette,*
> *Alouette, je te plumerai!'*

On the third repetition, she heard Luke's small, piping voice joining in behind her. Twice more, and he had words and tune perfectly, which was more than could be said for Henry Renolds.

'That was excellent,' Louise said, pausing for breath. 'Shall we go on to the next bit? It's a little more complicated – do you think you're ready?'

'I think so,' Lukas said. 'But, Cousin Louise, what does it mean? What's an al-oo-etter?'

'An *alouette* is a lark, and the words say, "Lark, pretty lark, lark, I will pluck you."'

There was a pause, and then Lukas said, in tones of pity, 'Oh, poor lark.'

'It's all right, it's only a song, and a very silly one, too. If you don't want to sing it any more, you needn't. Would you like to trot instead? We can go very gently to start with.'

'Yes, please,' he said from behind her.

'Good. But hang on to me tightly, and tell me to stop if you want to. Are you ready?'

They had reached a comparatively straight stretch of road, where the left-hand hills, now wooded, were coming closer to the lane. Louise, sure that Lukas was firmly attached to her, clicked her tongue softly and urged the mare on with a tap of her heel. Saffron needed no second bidding. She broke at once into a brisk, steady, surprisingly comfortable trot, and the boy's hands tightened convulsively again. 'Are you all right?' she called, glancing swiftly behind, and heard him say, in between jolts, 'Yes – thank you – Cousin –'

It happened so suddenly that they were both completely unprepared. One moment the mare was striding out, ears pricked, her dark mane bouncing on her yellow neck, eager and willing. In the next she shied abruptly to her right in one single violent movement. Louise, caught utterly unawares, lost her balance and the reins, clawed frantically and vainly for a handful of mane, and fell sideways, taking Lukas with her.

She hit the hard earth of the lane with a crash that knocked all the wind and half the senses from her. From a long way off, she heard Henry's voice shouting in alarm, and, rather nearer, someone gasping and crowing. For an instant, bewildered, she thought it was Lukas, until she realised that the sound coincided with her own desperate attempts to draw breath.

'Cousin! Cousin Louise, oh, Cousin Louise, are you all right?'

That was unmistakably Lukas. She seemed to be lying on her back. Muzzily, she peered up and saw his small, worried face veering in and out of focus just above her. She felt sick, and closed her eyes, trying to concentrate on breathing. It hurt, but she persisted, dragging huge painful gasps of air into her lungs

'Mistress Louise!' That was Henry, just as anxious as the child. 'Be ee hurt? Oh, Mistress Louise, do ee say summat, please!'

'Saffron?' she managed.

'She be fine, Mistress, and a grazing just over there. Summat frit her, Mistress, but I don't know what it were. Can ee sit upright, Mistress? I'll help ee.'

She had thought she was only winded until she attempted to move her left arm. Then a vast shrieking agony speared through her shoulder, and she fell back, gasping with pain. 'No,' she managed to say, somehow. 'Something's wrong – my shoulder – think it's broken.'

'Oh, Mistress!' Henry cried. She opened her eyes and saw his round Somerset face looming above her, grey with horror. 'Oh, Mistress Louise, whatever shall we do?'

At least her breathing was easier, and the pain in her shoulder had died abruptly to a sharp, nagging ache. She said, as clearly as she could, 'Help me to sit up – *carefully*, Henry, please – take my *right* shoulder, that's it.'

It was not broken, she realised as soon as she tried, with great care, to move her left arm again. The fall had put it out of joint: even concealed by the layers of clothing, she could see how awkwardly it hung, and the slightest movement was agony. She tried to lean her uninjured shoulder against Henry's chest as he knelt beside her, but he was not expecting it, and moved away. Only the quick use of her right arm, supporting her weight, stopped her from falling back. She swore savagely and fluently in the idiomatic French she had learned in her stepfather's stables, and said afterwards, 'Henry – for Christ's sake take my weight – there – that's it!'

He looked very embarrassed, kneeling in the road with his mistress sprawled lopsidedly against him, as if they enjoyed a much closer relationship. Louise, finding the relief from pain overwhelming, ignored his flushed, anxious face, and glanced round for Lukas.

He stood just beside her, with grass stains all down his blue coat and breeches, and his hair matted with bits of leaf and twig, evidently very frightened indeed. She gave him a reassuring smile, and said, 'It's all right, I don't think it's broken after all. But my arm has been wrenched out of joint, and it's rather painful, and someone will have to put it back. Is there a bonesetter in the village, Henry?'

'One of the Pearces d'have some skill,' said the boy. 'But I can't leave ee here, Mistress, not all alone. Sir Alexander should come up with us soon, for certain.'

Louise did not like to say in front of Lukas that she doubted it. 'I think you should go,' she told Henry firmly. 'I shall be all right, and Lukas can look after me. And I expect you'll meet Sir Alexander on the road.'

'I can't leave ee,' Henry repeated, with frightened obstinacy. He was only fourteen, after all. 'What if footpads d'come by?'

'Footpads? On this little lane? Henry, you're lucky if you see more than a shepherd or two,' Louise said. She twisted round unwisely, flinched, and moved back to her original position with extreme caution. 'Help me to get up, and walk over to that tree there, and I can lean against it. Henry, please do as I say.'

It took far longer than she had thought, even to get to her feet, and by the time she managed it, she was drenched in sweat. Her legs seemed to be undamaged, but had the strength of straw stalks, and she was forced to lean heavily on Henry's slight body for support. It must have been an incongruous sight, she thought to herself, trying to wring some glimmer of humour from the situation, for the undersized stable lad barely came up to her shoulder. But very slowly, for she dared not risk falling, he helped her to walk the few yards to the verge of the lane, and the trunk of the young elm tree that sprouted sturdily out of the hedge.

'That be what frit that mare of yourn, I d'reckon,' Henry said, and indicated the brambles just by the tree. Caught in them, and fluttering pale and brave in the breeze, was a long strip of pale cloth. 'She wouldn't have seed it till she came anunt en, Mistress, and if she had just a glimpse, well, it'd frit any horse.'

'I expect you're right,' Louise said, although at this moment, with her legs threatening to give way altogether, she could not have cared less. 'Help me sit in the grass, Henry, *gently*, for Christ's sake, please – that's it. Now I can rest.'

'You look tarblish green, Mistress,' said the boy, with deep concern. 'Be ee all right? I don't want to leave ee –'

'And if you don't, we could be here all day,' Louise said, more curtly than was kind. She closed her eyes for a moment, struggling with nausea and faintness and the renewed pain in the distorted joint, and then opened them and tried to speak coolly and with authority. 'Henry, listen carefully, and do exactly as I say. Ride back to Wintercombe, and tell them what has happened. You may need to bring a litter or a hurdle back – Pardice will know what to do. And then someone must find a bonesetter, as soon as possible.' She tried to keep her voice calm, but a sudden awful memory had assailed her, of one of her stepfather's friends who had put his shoulder out in just such an accident, but who had been mended too late, so that the bones and muscles were twisted and all but useless. 'That's very important, Henry – as soon as possible. The bone has to be put back in the socket very quickly. Do you understand? If you can bring him out here, so much the better. Now *go*, Henry, please – ride as fast as you can, but be careful.'

'Yes, Mistress – I'll be back as quick as thought,' the boy promised. He still hesitated, but Louise waved her good arm at him urgently. 'Go *on*, Henry – for the love of God, *go!*'

Stung at last into action, he ran for his nag, sprang into the saddle, and urged it back down the lane towards Wintercombe with frantic, flapping hands and heels. As he vanished round the corner, Lukas came over to kneel by her side, his pale face pinched with fear and anxiety. With a gesture that she found very touching, and also comforting, he slipped his hand into hers. 'Does it hurt *very* much, Cousin Louise?'

'It's worse when I move,' she told him. 'If I sit quite still, it's not too bad. But aren't you hurt? You fell too, after all.'

'I landed on the grass, and it was soft,' Lukas explained. He ventured a small smile, looking up at her. 'My nurse Griete used to say that I bounced. I fell out of a high window once, when I was little, and I wasn't hurt at all.'

'Adults don't bounce so easily,' Louise said drily. 'I certainly don't – this is the second time I've hurt myself falling off a horse. At least on this occasion I don't seem to have broken anything. Last time, it was my arm.'

'Oh,' said Lukas, looking very doubtful. Louise laughed, and squeezed his hand. 'Don't worry. Everyone falls off when they're learning to ride, and usually they bounce. But I usually fall off when I'm doing something stupid, I'm afraid – and I'm old enough to know better.' She grinned, rather wanly. 'I think you'll be a much more sensible rider than I am. And besides, there are so many things in life that hurt – like aching teeth, or stomach gripes, or the megrims – and they can't be avoided, so you have to learn to bear a little pain now and again.'

She sounded rather priggish to her own ears, and hoped that Lukas would not think so. But he had turned, and was looking eagerly down the lane towards Wintercombe. 'Oh, Cousin, there's a horse coming – listen!'

Above the quiet birdsong and the breeze sifting through the leaves above her head, she could indeed hear distant, approaching hoofbeats. Lukas leaped up and ran towards the sound, his coat and dark hair flying, a miniature of Alex in his untidiness, shouting something. It was the first time she had seen him move faster than a walk, or raise his voice. She hoped that whoever was approaching knew something about dislocated bones: she did not think that she could bear much more of this, even though the pain was almost tolerable if she kept absolutely still.

It was Alex. The bay stallion, galloping at breakneck speed, thundered round the bend in the lane, and for one awful, heart-stopping moment she feared that Lukas, in the middle of the road with his arms flapping, would be run down. But the boy had some sense of self-preservation, and dived for the verge in plenty of time, while Alex brought his horse to a hard-fought, foam-flecked halt only a few yards from where she sat against the elm. He jumped down, hitched the reins to the broken branch of a sapling in the hedge, and came over. 'I met Henry Renolds on the road. He's gone up to the house for help. Which shoulder is it?'

'The left,' said Louise, staring up at him. The insolent manner, the arrogance and malice, had vanished utterly, replaced by an air of competent, unfussy concern that took her completely by surprise. She added, 'It's out of joint – I told Henry to find a bonesetter –'

'No need. I've watched our surgeon in the Dutch regiment deal with this many a time – and put back a few myself, too, when he couldn't be found. It has to be done quickly, or worse damage will come of it. But, I warn you, it'll hurt more than a little.'

'I know. It hurts already when I move.' Louise shifted her position a little, and added, 'It's all right, Lukas, don't look so worried. Your father seems to know what he's about.'

'If I didn't, I wouldn't be here, I'd be riding for the bonesetter or the nearest surgeon,' Alex said. He kneeled beside her, and began to undo the numerous gilt buttons of her coat. 'This will have to come off, I'm afraid, and your waistcoat as well – I'll need to feel your shoulder, see how it should go back in. Can you move your arm at all?'

She had imagined the moment when he first undressed her: it had not been anything remotely like this. The thought almost made her smile; then she had to clench her jaw as he gently pulled her away from the tree so that her coat could be drawn off, one arm at a time. Even the slightest movement agonised the stretched, distorted muscles around the misplaced joint, and she gave a smothered gasp of pain.

'I'm sorry,' Alex said, giving the garment to Lukas, who was crouching next to him, his eyes vast with fright and horror. 'I'll have to hurt you more than that in a moment. Are you ready for the waistcoat?'

'Get it over with,' said Louise, doggedly. 'I've known worse.'

She had not, in fact: her broken arm had been a mere discomfort compared to the shrieking pain his actions were causing her, but she knew he despised feeble females like Amy, and was determined not to show any weakness. Her resolution faltered as the waistcoat slid from her shoulders, for it fitted more tightly than the coat, and was correspondingly more difficult to remove without affecting her injured arm. Alex was surprisingly deft and gentle, but she was very glad indeed when he had finished. Lukas clasped the dove-grey garments tightly to his chest, as if they were in some way both a help and a protection.

Alex was talking to her: she forced herself to listen carefully through the fog of pain and dizzy nausea that had suddenly descended on her. 'I'm going to kneel beside you, on your left side. You'll have to move away from the tree. Then I'll take your arm, and pull it gently, so that I can twist and slide it back into the socket. I won't lie to you – it'll hurt like hell. Scream as much as you like – I know I would.'

From some depth, she managed a grin. 'I'll probably scream much louder. Lukas – don't worry – it has to hurt, or it won't be mended properly. Are you all right?'

The little boy nodded mutely. She felt Alex's hands, gentle and efficient, guiding and supporting her away from the tree, manœuvring her until she was in the right position. She waited, tense with predicted agony, as he took her misplaced arm in his right hand, supporting her shoulder with his left, assessing the position of bone and joint. 'Ready?'

'As I'll ever be,' Louise said, between clenched teeth. And then he lifted and wrenched her abused arm, and twisted it round so that she cried out at the tearing red-hot pain, and then suddenly bone grated on bone, she could feel and hear it, and as if cut off with a knife, the agony ceased, and she was left with a sharp, throbbing ache.

It was over. She swore, in French, and saw Lukas's appalled face and tried to smile at him, although she was feeling most peculiar and everything seemed suddenly remote. Then Alex said, his voice concerned but very distant, 'Louise! Are you all right?'

She must have fainted. It was something which she had never done before in her life, not even after her broken arm had been set when she was fifteen. One moment she was sitting under the tree, supported by her cousin: the next she was lying on her back on something rough and jolting and uncomfortable. Her head seemed to be pillowed on something, her stays had been loosened, and her injured shoulder firmly bandaged, the arm strapped tightly to her side so that movement was impossible. She lay there, her eyes closed, listening to the sounds of tramping feet, the Somerset voices – amongst which she could certainly distinguish those of Pardice and Henry Renolds – and, more distantly, the hooves of at least two horses. Brought home on a hurdle, Louise thought ruefully. What an ignominy!

She felt still more foolish when the hurdle was set down in the front courtyard, and Wintercombe seemed to explode into activity. People rushed out, bleating and fussing, asking her if she was all right. It was with some difficulty that she persuaded the housekeeper, Betty, that she did not need to be carried, there was nothing wrong with her legs, and she could walk perfectly well.

Inevitably, Alex took charge. He shooed away the gaggle of clucking servants, said something to Silence, and then came over to Louise, who was sitting up on the hurdle. She hoped that her shirt was not in any way transparent, and that her coat and waistcoat were not creased and crumpled beyond redemption. He stood in front of her, tall and capable, and gave her the friendly, encouraging smile of a comrade, not an adversary. 'Can you walk?'

'I think I can,' Louise told him. 'But I shall need help to get up – and to climb steps and stairs.'

'Does it hurt much?'

'It still aches,' she said concisely. 'But since you've swaddled me up so tight, I've no chance to test it by moving.'

'Good – that was my intention. Hold out your hand and I'll help you – then you can lean on me. And don't worry, I won't let you go.'

He was as good as his word. She found that her legs were still weak and shaky, and there was a pain in her ankle which she had not noticed before and which must have been caused by the fall. But with his steady, reassuring strength lending her support, she successfully negotiated both the steps up to the porch and, much more difficult, the twisting narrow stairs that led to the first floor and the sanctuary of her chamber.

Christian was there ready with a pile of linen strips, several pungent-smelling jars, and an anxious expression. She started forward as Alex guided Louise through the door, but he said quickly, 'Don't worry – I'll help her to the bed. Mistress Hellier will bandage her properly and make sure no lasting damage has been done. I'm just the bonesetter.'

Despite her earlier protestations, Louise was very glad to sit down on the soft feather mattress of her bed. Alex settled her, and withdrew a little way. Exhausted and suddenly trembling, she remembered even so to look up and smile. 'Thank you, Cousin – thank you for all you've done.'

'I only hope I've done it right,' Alex said. He grinned suddenly, a boyish and entirely amicable smile that was devastatingly attractive. 'I didn't like to tell you at the time, but yours was the first shoulder joint I've ever put back.'

'But you said –'

'Oh, I *said* I'd done it several times – because I didn't want to worry you,' Alex told her candidly, grinning wider. 'I have watched the surgeon, though – that part was true enough. Still, I seem to have put it back in the right place. Here is your grandmother, who undoubtedly knows far more than I will ever do – I'll abandon you to her tender mercies.' And he sketched a bow, suddenly full of the old insolence, and left.

Apart from the occasional headache or cold, various minor childhood fevers and the broken arm, Louise had not suffered a day's illness or pain in her life. She did not know whether to laugh or to protest at the solicitous concern of her grandmother and her maid as they gently removed her remaining garments and the rough and ready bandaging which Alex had applied over her shirt, and which proved to be made from his neckcloth.

Given the force of her fall, the damage was surprisingly slight. Her shoulder, of course, the abused muscles and tendons already hot, swollen and very, very sore. The left ankle must have been wrenched out of the stirrup, and was also puffy and painful. Otherwise, save for the spectacular bruising, and the wan, drawn look on her face, Silence considered that Louise had been very lucky. She asked how the accident had happened, and her granddaughter told her, adding, 'I couldn't have prevented it, or expected it – it was so sudden. But it could have been so much worse – at least Lukas isn't hurt, nor is Saffron, and I'll mend in good time.'

'It'll be a week or two before you can climb on a horse again,' Silence commented, opening a large jar containing a thick murky red paste. 'This is an excellent remedy for bones out of joint – it should take away most of the pain and bring down the swelling. Morello cherries, egg yolks and sheep's milk – nothing unpleasant.'

'At least it smells nice,' said Louise, as Silence gently rubbed the stiff sticky ointment on to her shoulder. 'Some of your medicines stink like the devil, Gran'mère.'

'I'd be the first to admit it,' Silence said, her fingers steadily massaging. 'Am I hurting you?'

'No,' Louise told her, untruthfully. There was worse to come, however: once the ointment had been applied, her shoulder and arm were strapped up so firmly that movement was impossible. 'For it's well known,' Silence said, tying the last knot with expert efficiency, 'that a shoulder once dislocated will spring out more readily in future, doing yet more damage, and so it goes on. If it is tightly bound now, and the arm kept from use for at least a week, perhaps longer, then you will mend very much more quickly. So – no riding, no violent exercise, nothing more than a leisurely stroll in the gardens. Can you survive such a restricted regime?'

'I shall have to,' Louise said. 'But no riding – that will interfere with your plans for a quick return to Chard, will it not?'

'I can stay a little longer,' Silence told her. 'But we'll discuss that later. For now, I suggest that you keep to your chamber today – wear that pretty silk nightrobe if you wish to receive visitors – and rest. In fact, I think you could begin now – you look exhausted.'

Louise opened her mouth to deny it, and found herself yawning. Without protest, she was tucked up in bed with a pile of feather-soft pillows to support her abused and aching shoulder, given a bitter-tasting drink which was apparently certain to send her to sleep, and was deep in slumber before Christian had had time to draw the bedcurtains.

She slept until the afternoon, and woke refreshed, still sore and very stiff, but ravenously hungry. A light repast – a fricassee of chicken, an egg tart and a handful of early strawberries with a frothy syllabub of new cream – arrived on a tray, and as soon as she had eaten her fill, a stream of visitors appeared. First Amy, noticeably subdued, and full of silly questions, which Louise, feeling surprisingly magnanimous, endeavoured to answer with as much patience as she could muster. Then Lukas, still rather pale around the mouth, bearing an armful of books which, he explained, his Aunt Phoebe had recommended to alleviate the boredom of being kept in bed. Phoebe herself sent her good wishes and apologies, but did not feel able to climb stairs today. Christian arranged the volumes on the table, smiling as Louise assured the little boy that she was perfectly well, unlikely to die just yet, and was merely resting because her shoulder would mend quicker if she did.

'You never taught me the rest of "*Alouette*",' Lukas said, his face at once serious and imploring. 'Please, Cousin, could you teach me now, if it won't make you tired?'

'It won't, I promise,' Louise said reassuringly, wishing that she could hug a smile into that too solemn face. 'Sit on the bed and we'll try – if Christian can tolerate our singing, that is.'

They were in the middle of the first verse when there was a tentative knock on the door. Christian opened it to admit Charles, his handsome face pale and anxious, a small package in his hand. Lukas, sitting shoeless on the bed, singing in his high, rather tuneless child's voice, had not seen him. Louise, in full flight, touched her finger to her lips briefly as she sang alternately with the boy:

*'Je te plumerai la tête.'*
*'Et la tête.'*
*'Et l'aile.'*
*'Et l'aile.'*
*'Alouette, gentil alouette,*
*Alouette, je te plumerai!'*

'Hullo,' said Charles awkwardly, seizing his chance as the verse ended. 'I was very sorry to hear of your accident, Lou. What a terrible thing to happen. Are you all right?'

'As you can see,' Louise told him, smiling. She seemed to remember his face, grey with horror, amongst the crowd in the courtyard as Alex helped her from the hurdle, and she was uneasily aware that this cousin, unlike the other, had an exalted and probably sentimental regard for her. But the silk nightrobe, in a soft blue with intricate embroidered designs that were allegedly Turkish, was perfectly proper, even if informal. She added, 'I shall be stiff and sore in the arm and shoulder for some days yet, and I won't be able to ride for a week or more. But it could have been much, much worse. Lukas was riding pillion behind me, and he escaped with just a bruise or two.' She smiled at Alex's son, who had retreated abruptly into his shell at Charles's entrance. 'I'm sorry you haven't been able to choose your pony today, Lukas. Perhaps your father will take you tomorrow.'

'He said that he might,' Lukas told her, so quietly that she could barely discern the words. 'I – I must go, Cousin. Can I come and see you again later?'

'Of course you can – and we can sing some more songs,' Louise said. She watched as the child slid off the bed, found his shoes, and made his usual faultless bow before leaving her chamber in subdued silence. It was plain that he was uneasy in Charles's presence, and she knew why. She waited until the door had shut noiselessly behind him, and then said approvingly, 'What a very pleasant child.'

'Is he?' Charles said curtly. 'I haven't taken much notice of him. Lou – this is for you.'

She caught sight of Christian's surprised face. It was not perhaps quite seemly to accept a gift from a man who so evidently wished to court her. But she liked Charles, she felt sorry for him, and she knew that, compared with Alex, he was a sincere and honourable person. Yet despite his feelings for her, that he had never openly admitted, she had no sense at all of that dangerous, passionate and overwhelming desire that Alex, despite – or perhaps because of – all his vices, could inspire in her. Charles would always be a friend, but nothing more, and she did not yet have the heart to strip him of his illusions and tell him so.

'Thank you,' she said, and smiled at him. 'That's very kind, Charles. Whatever can it be?'

If her voice sounded false and even condescending to her own ears, he did not seem to notice it. 'Open it and see,' he said, with a rather hesitant smile, and handed it to her.

It was soft, and flexible, and light. She undid the ribbon one-handed, and folded back the cloth, and stared at a pair of riding gauntlets, beautifully made, of leather much too fine to be practical, embroidered sparely around the edge of the cuff.

Gloves. A lover's gift. She felt an unworthy prickle of irritation. If his feelings were so strong, why could he not tell her plainly?

But of course he had, using the package on her lap instead of words. She looked up and saw his face, at once anxious and apologetic. 'I hope they fit,' he said.

She gave him her best smile, hoping that it would not encourage him too far. For how could she explain her own feelings towards him, when he would not, from caution or shyness or inexperience, reveal his own? 'I'm sure they will,' she said, laying her good hand over one of the gauntlets. 'But I don't think I can try them on until my shoulder mends.'

He looked disappointed, so she dutifully admired the workmanship and the softness of the leather. 'Thank you so much, Charles,' she added. 'They're lovely. I shall keep them for important occasions.' She took a deep breath, acutely aware of Christian, the perfect servant, unobtrusive and long-eared in the background, and looked up at him. 'Charles, I know that you hold me in high regard, and I hope that we will always be friends.'

But no more than that: her unspoken words hung between them. He frowned a little, and then his face cleared. 'Of course we will, Lou, you can count on that.'

'Of course,' she said. 'Now, if you could be a real friend, Charles – I'm feeling very tired, and I've been told to rest as much as possible. Thank you for the gloves, and your visit, and I will see you tomorrow, when I hope I'll be feeling much better.'

'I'm so sorry,' he said at once, looking stricken. 'I didn't mean to tire you – of course, I'll go at once. I do hope you feel better soon. Goodbye, Lou.'

'Goodbye,' she said, and watched him leave, with a last wave and that tentative smile. Christian, attempting to set right the grass-stained, crumpled remains of her mistress's riding habit, kept her head bowed and ostentatiously said nothing. With a sigh, Louise settled down amongst the pillows, and found herself wishing that she had someone, preferably a female of her own age, station and tastes, in whom to confide. Many years ago, her grandmother had enjoyed the service and companionship of a redoubtable woman, her maid Mally Merrifield, who had been a true friend, far more than just a servant. Louise had met Mally, who had married a Taunton merchant, and was now a respected mother and grandmother, and wished that she too had such a maid, loyal and reliable and yet unafraid to speak her mind. Christian was a pleasant girl, and very capable, but lacked Mally's abrasive intelligence. Nor did Louise, whether justifiably or not, feel inclined to trust her with her deepest secrets.

For there was trouble coming, she knew it in her heart. She was caught between Charles's yearning love and Alex's open lust, and from soft-heartedness and her own desires, she would not discourage either of them: two men who despised and hated each other, despite the fact that they were kin. And she feared that, if Alex continued to taunt and belittle his cousin at every opportunity, he would push Charles to a breaking point whose effects would be completely unpredictable. For there were depths in Charles that she sensed, but had never begun to fathom. Goaded by Alex into proving, once and for all, that he was no feeble milksop, what might he do?

She could not tell anyone about her feelings for Alex: it was decidedly improper for a respectable young English lady to admit such desires even to herself, never mind to a friend or confidante. Any discussion that involved such matters would bring, inevitably, shock, horror and disapproval. Even Phoebe, with her dry dispassionate mind, would not understand. And Louise, who was essentially realistic and practical, had no intention of having to justify to any prim English cousin, or even to her

193

grandmother, those unladylike urges that were accepted in France as a matter of course. In such matters, she knew that discretion and secrecy were vital.

But Charles . . . that was another matter. For Charles's intentions, she felt sure, were entirely honourable. For him, it would be marriage or nothing. And since he was, patently, such an unsuitable husband for her, because of his religion and his lack of wealth and prospects, she could probably discuss the problem with Phoebe, who, after all, had known him for most of her life, or even with Silence. Alex, and Charles's hatred for him, was a complication that need not be mentioned.

But how to tell Charles, whom she liked, that she could not, would not marry him? However gently she broke it to him, he would be desperately distressed and hurt. And if he suspected anything at all about her feelings for Alex, she feared that her rejection of him might bring him to that breaking point sooner and more disastrously than she had feared.

It had all begun as an enjoyable flirtation, with a man who had been her childhood hero and who had turned into something much less heroic, and more dangerous, and almost irresistible. Now Louise looked back over her recent actions with a clear and unprejudiced eye and recognised, with foreboding, that it was no longer a game. Carelessly, without forethought or any end save the gratification of her own pleasure and desires, she had sown the seeds of disaster for herself, and perhaps for two other people at least. If she was wise, she would return to Chard at once, tail between her legs, and stay there.

But she could not. No riding for at least a week, possibly two, so Silence had said. And so she must face up to her responsibilities and try to remedy her thoughtlessness before it was too late.

It was not a particularly enjoyable prospect, and she did not see how it could be done without hurt or unpleasantness. But done it must be, or more would suffer.

Something would occur to her, some way out, some method of rectifying the damage. Meanwhile, she had been ordered to rest, and Phoebe had sent her some books.

Louise selected the first in the pile, found it to be Gervase Markham's treatise on horses, and was soon so utterly absorbed that Charles St Barbe and his rakehell cousin Alex might never have existed.

# PART II

*'The madness of rebellious times'*

# *'The Good Old Cause reviv'd'*

At the same time as Louise was accommodating herself to her enforced rest, some seventy or eighty miles to the south, in the little Dorset port of Lyme, there was a certain amount of curiosity amongst those with the opportunity to survey the sea. Three unfamiliar ships, one large, the others little bigger than fishing vessels, had appeared off the coast. They flew no colours, but the men of Lyme, whose livelihood lay in shipping, could tell from their appearance that they were of French or Dutch build.

All day, the three strange ships hovered a league or so off the shore, while rumours swept the town. News came that two men had been landed on a beach a few miles away, spoken mysteriously of rebellion, and then vanished inland. Nor had the customs officer, who had earlier been rowed out to investigate the ships, returned for his weekly bowls match, an occasion he never normally missed.

The mayor of Lyme was unfortunate in being loyal to the present King, James II, and to the established church, in a town as famous as was Taunton for rebellion and dissent. The arrival of a newsletter from London containing an account of the three ships which had left Holland on the first day of June, believed to be carrying the Duke of Monmouth and his adherents on their way to launch rebellion in England or Scotland, confirmed his suspicions. But he could do nothing, for he had virtually no support for his views in Lyme. When boats full of armed men put out from the ships and began to row to shore, the mayor chose the better part of valour, and rode hastily out of the town to warn those in authority that Lyme had been invaded.

Close to sunset, borne in on the high tide, the seven boats landed on the pebbled beach near to the Cobb, and disgorged their passengers. The curious, eager people who had come to investigate, fired by rumours and hope, saw a tall, dark-haired man, splendidly dressed, kneel on the round stones of the beach to pray. Above him, unfurled and drifting gently in the dying breeze of evening, the motto on his deep green colours glittered plain in the sharp gilt light of the sinking sun: 'Fear Nothing But God'.

Rumour had not lied. The crowds gathered, mobbing him, laughing and crying and shouting as he and his intrepid band of followers made their way up the track to the town. 'Monmouth! Monmouth, and the Protestant religion!'

He had come at last, their saviour, their rightful monarch, to free them from persecution and from the terrible future presaged by the accession of a Papist king, and to bring once more to the West Country, for the second time in forty years, the dread spectre of civil war.

Bram Loveridge had books to deliver, newly arrived with the carrier from London. Men and women in Pitminster, Corfe and Stoke St Mary were eagerly awaiting a miscellaneous collection of works on history and affairs of state, the latest romances, and three copies of a recent and rather scurrilous pamphlet, printed in Amsterdam, concerning the past and present occupants of the throne. These last had been slipped discreetly inside his shirt, in case he was stopped and questioned. Ever since the last rebellion scare, two weeks ago, the militia had been garrisoned in Taunton, filling the taverns and alehouses to capacity and making a nuisance of themselves to no discernible purpose. Even such an innocuous errand as delivering books to the local gentry might earn the scrutiny of those set to watch the highways, but Bram was confident that he could talk his way out of trouble.

As usual, he had hired a lively chestnut cob, feather-footed and willing, from the Red Lion, the inn opposite the bookshop, whose landlord, William Savage, was a friend of Jonah's and a well-known republican. Savage had been one of those rounded up as a precaution after letters had been found in the Taunton postbag hinting at imminent rebellion. He had been languishing in the Bridewell by the River Tone for nearly two weeks, while his wife and his son John managed the Red Lion in his absence. Bram, well aware that only his father's extreme care and discretion had kept him from a similar fate, hoped that the militia, notoriously bored, incompetent or just drunk, would live up to their reputation.

He was challenged twice, but his explanation satisfied them, and even if they had discovered the pamphlets, he doubted if they could have read them, let alone realised their import. It was near to dinner time when, the last books delivered and his bags, and his person, once more quite innocent, he turned the cob's head for home and the baked mutton he had smelled from the kitchen before he set out.

He rode into Taunton along Eastreach, whistling, and noticed something unusual at once. Everywhere, on street corners, in doorways, even, perilously, in animated conversation in the middle of the highway, were knots of people. Someone was running along in front of him, shouting something that he could not catch. Plainly, news of considerable importance had arrived in Taunton that morning: but what was it?

There were a number of possibilities, but Bram had his suspicions. He saw a friend, who had been at the Grammar School with him, and called to him. 'Tom! Tom, what's happened?'

Tom Dinham, the son of a brewer, waved in acknowledgement and ran across, his pale, pockmarked face flushed with excitement. 'Haven't you heard? Everyone's talking about it!'

'I've been out on errands since an hour after dawn,' Bram told him, leaning down from the saddle, his hazel eyes eager. 'What is it, Tom?'

'Monmouth!' said his friend, and a huge, involuntary smile suddenly split his face. 'The word is that Monmouth's landed at Lyme, and raised his standard to overthrow the King!'

It was wonderful, amazing, too good to be true. Bram found an answering grin stretching his mouth, and he gave a shout of pure joy. 'Monmouth! Oh, Tom, are you sure?'

'Of course I'm sure,' Tom said indignantly. 'News came three hours ago, and several have confirmed it since then. He landed at Lyme yesterday evening, and they're saying men are flocking to join his army.'

Bram was thinking, calculating. It was obvious that Lyme, well known for sedition, had been chosen for that very reason. And it lay only twenty-five miles or so south of Taunton. Surely, surely, the rebel army would march this way, through the country where Monmouth, beloved and fêted on his last visit to these parts, would be assured of greatest support?

'Where will he go, do you suppose?' he asked. 'Any word of that?'

'He's bound to come here,' said Tom promptly. 'He knows how loyal Taunton is to the Protestant cause. And we'll give him a welcome fit for a king, you can be sure of that.'

'Even though there are two regiments of militia here?'

Tom laughed. 'And the whole of Taunton against them! You've seen them – they're little more than a rabble of peasants, and half of them favour Monmouth anyway. There are supposed to be thousands gathering at Lyme, and the whole country will rise, you can be sure of it. What can two regiments do, in the face of that?'

'Or the King's army,' said Bram, his eyes shining. 'Are you going to join them, Tom?'

'Of course I am! Are you?'

Bram looked down at him. Tom was impulsive, and young for his age, which was the same as Bram's. As a boy, he had been so regularly beaten that, the joke went, he had taken to wearing leather breeches for better protection against the justifiable wrath of his elders. Where trouble went, there followed Tom Dinham: and despite his own passionate opposition to the Papist, absolutist King, and his espousal of Monmouth's Protestant cause, a small, alien voice in Bram's mind urged upon him his father's natural caution and discretion.

'Perhaps,' he said, unwilling to commit himself to Tom. 'But I'll wait till they come here. Apart from anything else, I expect the militia will be on the lookout for people going to Lyme. By the time Monmouth reaches Taunton, he'll have an army with him, and with luck the militia will just melt away like snow in summer.'

'That's not like you to be so faint-hearted,' Tom said indignantly. 'If everyone thought as you did, Monmouth would have no army at all. If you believe in a case, you must be prepared to fight for it, or you're just another windbag who talks loud enough in the tavern, but won't back his fine words with action.'

Bram stared at him for a moment, and the sudden fierce fury in his face made Tom blink. He had forgotten their schooldays, when Bram, small for his age and with those embarrassingly girlish looks, had been taunted unmercifully by a group of bigger boys. In rage and self-defence he had learned to fight back, to use words and fists and heels as his weapons, and once his strength had caught up with his intentions there had been no more trouble. Now Tom, seeing his friend's suddenly whitened face and compressed mouth, regretted his hasty accusations. 'I'm sorry,' he said, rather sheepishly. 'I didn't mean to imply – of course you're not a coward.'

Bram stayed unmoving in the saddle, one fist on his hip, his eyes still hostile. 'I'm glad to hear it, Tom. And if I were you, I wouldn't go rushing off to Lyme just yet. You'll undoubtedly run the risk of being taken up for a suspected rebel before you've got as far as Chard, and you won't be much use to Monmouth in prison.'

'Perhaps I'll wait,' Tom muttered reluctantly. 'But when Monmouth comes, I'll be the first in line to join – and so should you.'

'By then, it'll make sense,' Bram pointed out. 'There's no point in taking up arms in a rebellion if there are so few of you that there's no hope of success. If all these people here are willing to risk their lives for the Protestant cause, then I'll do no less, and gladly.'

'So will I,' said Tom with fervour. 'Monmouth!'

'Monmouth, and the Protestant religion,' Bram said, and they clasped hands. Then, with a friendly wave, he urged the chestnut further up East Street, seeing everywhere the crowds of excited, eager people, drawn from work and duty to discuss this astonishing and longed-for news with friends and neighbours.

Despite his cautious words to Tom, he was sorely tempted to turn his horse's head around and gallop for Lyme, to offer his services to the man who had come to deliver them from popery. But he had a duty to his parents, as well as to the Duke of Monmouth. He was their only surviving son, for his two younger brothers, Joseph and Jeremy, and a sister, Ruth, had died in the terrible fever that had killed so many in Taunton only two years ago. His father, he knew, had plans to set up a printing press in the town, with Bram to manage it, to expand the business and to make the name of Loveridge synonymous with bookselling in Somerset, perhaps even further afield. There had also been talk of opening up a shop in Bath, where the fashionable gentry who flocked to the waters every summer would doubtless prove much more generous buyers of books than the sober, thrifty and earnest merchants and craftsmen of Taunton. Without Bram to inherit, all this glittering and enticing future fell to dust: the business would be sold off, and the proceeds divided between Sue and Hannah.

And yet, and yet . . . what, indeed, was the point of talking sedition, of wishing the King to his Papist devil and campaigning for the freedom of every man to worship as he wished, when he was not prepared to hazard his life and his future in support? If not, he was, as Tom had said, just a tavern windbag, and no amount of secret and treasonous pamphlets smuggled from Holland could pretend otherwise.

Both his heart and his head knew what he should do. The trouble was that they each urged quite different things.

Caught on the horns of his dilemma, he left the chestnut at the Red Lion, and was drawn despite himself into a most animated conversation in the taproom, surprisingly crowded despite the absence of the militia, who were doubtless elsewhere, stopping potential rebels from running off to Lyme. It was with difficulty that he extracted himself, his head ringing with joyous words of treason, and ran across the busy street to his father's shop.

Jonah had a customer, a portly and periwigged gentleman in the black cloth and plain bands of a clergyman, and both were bent over a book lying open on the table as Bram burst in, his enthusiasm fired by the talk at the Red Lion. Just in time, he recognised the jowled red face, and air of fussy disapproval. Master Axe was entirely loyal to the King and the Anglican church, and had no time at all for Dissenters, or for any who might favour rebellion. Despite Jonah's reputation as a supporter of the Whig view, Axe was a regular customer, for the shop was the largest of its kind in Taunton, and the only one that could boast regular links with printers and booksellers in London.

'Ah, Bram,' said his father, as he sketched a breathless bow to Master Axe. 'You have doubtless heard the news?'

'Dreadful,' said the clergyman, with an angry shake of his head that almost dislodged his wig. 'The rabble, of course, are overjoyed – let us hope that Colonel Luttrell and his militia succeed in preventing them from flocking off to Lyme to join in treason and rebellion.'

'I expect they will,' said Jonah, noncommittal as ever. He glanced at Bram and gave a very slight, significant jerk of his head.

His son knew what he meant, but had no intention of disappearing upstairs just yet. He said innocently, 'I thought I had seen no soldiers in the street. Is that where they have all gone, Master Axe?'

'There will be plenty left here to keep the town in good order,' said Axe. He fixed Bram with a protuberant and faintly fishy eye. 'And what of you, young man? Which side of the fence do you fall, eh?'

'I have no intention of rushing off to join Monmouth in Lyme, sir,' Bram told him, with perfect truth. 'My father has much work for me to do here.'

'I don't doubt it,' said the reverend, with a sharp hostile glance that showed all too clearly how much he did doubt it. 'Well, Loveridge, I'll be on my way. I'll take the *Exposition* but not the *Commentaries* – I fear that man's ideas are sadly suspect. Pray have it sent round to my house later. Good day to you, sir – and to you, young man.'

They waited in silence until the shop door had banged uncompromisingly shut behind him. Then Jonah put the despised *Commentaries* back in its allotted place on the shelves, and gave his son a rather grim smile. 'If that man had his way, I'd be in the Bridewell with poor Savage – and probably so would you. At least you have the sense to keep your mouth shut in his presence.'

'Of course,' Bram said cheerfully. He cast the empty bags down on the table, and added, 'Everything delivered, and no trouble at all – though for a while I felt as if I must have a sign above my head reading, "This man carries seditious pamphlets". I met Tom Dinham, and he told me the news.'

'Did he, now?' said Jonah. He picked up his pipe and began to fill it, absently, with tobacco, and then looked for his tinderbox. Bram found it for him under a pile of loose sheets, and watched as he lit the tobacco, puffing intently until the weed was well alight. His father dearly loved a smoke, but Tabby had asked that he restrict its use to the shop.

'We agreed that Monmouth was certain to march this way, and that the militia are unlikely to stop him,' said Bram, after a pause filled with clouds of blue smoke. 'He also accused me of being a tavern windbag, because I didn't share his burning ardour for the cause. I had to persuade him not to go to Lyme then and there.'

'Good for you,' Jonah said. He stabbed the stem of the pipe towards his son. 'I hope you've more sense than to listen to that harum-scarum young fool. There are other ways of serving the cause than dying for it needlessly. And of course you could hardly tell him that distributing seditious pamphlets is as treasonable, and as dangerous, as actually taking up arms.'

'Not very well,' said Bram, with a reluctant grin. 'And then John Savage was trying to persuade me to join him. He's leading a band of a dozen or so down to Lyme tonight, he said.'

Jonah put the pipe down and looked him in the eye. 'And did you succumb? I know you – there's a deal of sense in your head, but not enough to resist the tide when it's flowing in the right direction.'

'I'm not a child to be dictated to, Father,' Bram reminded him, trying not to reveal his sudden anger. 'I'm of age, and a man, and I've held responsibilities for several years now. Whether I decide or not to join Monmouth is my own affair, and not yours.'

'That's where you're wrong,' Jonah said. The pipe forgotten, he walked up to his son, so like his beloved wife, and laid his hands on his shoulders. 'It's my affair, too, and Sue's, and Hannah's, and your grandparents', and above all your mother's. Think on her face, boy, when she discovers you've ridden off after a pretty courtier who seems to have appointed himself the saviour of the Protestant cause.'

Bram had flushed with annoyance. 'You're talking as if I'd already gone. I haven't even decided yet, one way or the other. And don't you think I'm old enough to make my own decisions as to what's right and what's wrong – whatever you and the rest of the family think?'

Loud girlish voices sounded outside, and the door was flung open. Sue, Hannah and Libby, flushed and laughing, tumbled through it, giggling and clutching each other. When they saw the sober faces within, they made an effort to be serious, and Sue, the eldest and supposedly responsible for the others, untied her hood, smoothed her plain everyday apron, and made a little curtsey which Hannah and Libby, rather belatedly, copied. 'Hullo, Father. We have been excused school, on account of the good news. Mistress Musgrave has said that we need not come back until tomorrow.'

'And she's asked us to make colours for the Duke's soldiers!' Hannah added breathlessly. 'We have to have a piece of silk, as large as possible, with a motto that's suitable, and a picture embroidered on it –'

'We're all going to work on it,' Sue said. 'Even Libby. Mistress Mary Blake suggested that we do a Bible, with a sword coming from it. I think "The Protestant Religion" would be very appropriate, don't you, Father?

And Mother has plenty of oddments of silk and scraps of material – it should be easy to find plenty to work with, and if we all three do it, I'm sure we'll have it finished by the time Monmouth marches into Taunton!'

Something in the quality of her uncle's face must have given Libby pause, for she glanced at her exuberant cousin and nudged her. Bram, standing beside Jonah, could not see his expression, but could sense the force of his feelings. There was a brief silence, time for the girls' blazing enthusiasm to splutter and fade; then Jonah banged his pipe down on the table, with such force that the stem broke, and said in a low, furious voice, 'Do I hear you aright? Is Mistress Musgrave – the woman I appointed your teacher in matters moral as well as educational, the woman whom I trusted to set a good example to her pupils – is she planning to involve you all in *treason*?'

'It's not only her,' Libby said. 'Mistress Blake and her sister are just as hot for the cause. When Monmouth comes, we're to present him with our colours, and of course Mary Mead is working on a special one, with gold thread.' She sounded rather contemptuous: Mary was the senior pupil, a little older than Sue, and favoured for her beauty, grace and undoubted skills of needlework, despite her unfortunate lack of sparkle or intelligence.

'I don't care if half of Taunton is embroidering colours for Monmouth,' said Jonah. 'But I do care if people who should know better encourage those who do not in an act of treason, and I shall call on your Mistress Musgrave this afternoon and tell her so.'

'Oh, please don't, Father!' cried Hannah, who worshipped her teacher.

Sue, who was old enough for more reasoned argument, said more quietly, 'But you used to go to the meeting-house, Father, until they closed it. You've always spoken up for the freedom to worship as we please, and for the Protestant religion. So does Monmouth. Surely you cannot go against him?'

Bram, a memory of those seditious pamphlets acute and vivid in his mind, added quickly, 'And you've been peddling treason yourself for years. Don't play the hypocrite now.'

'Hypocrite?' Jonah stared at him, his lean face flushed with unaccustomed anger. 'There's a world of difference, my boy, between spreading the Word of God and Justice by quiet, peaceful means, and fomenting open rebellion. And what if, by some unbelievable miracle, he does succeed, and King James is overthrown? All we'll have is another King James, of Monmouth, and within a few years you won't be able to tell them apart – save that one is a fanatical Papist, and the other a fanatic Dissenter!'

'Are you a republican, Father?' asked Sue, in the same tones in which she might have asked if he were a bigamist or a murderer.

'In the sense that I don't believe that one man by right of birth has any more authority over his fellows than another, yes,' said Jonah. Bram grinned to himself: his father's weakness, if it could be called such, was that even if he tried to lay down the law, his offspring could always tempt him into a spirited and sometimes heated debate. 'And that the government of a country by a group of men who have been elected by their fellows to rule is, in justice, far preferable – since I believe that to be true, then yes, I suppose I am a republican. But I do *not* believe in force of arms and might, with power to the strongest. The will of the people should be enough to prevail – change should come about by peaceful means.'

'And if it doesn't? If rebellion is the only possible way to overthrow a tyranny?' Bram asked. 'What would you do then, Father? Groan under the yoke, but refuse for conscience's sake to do anything to improve your lot?'

'I would do all I could, short of taking up arms,' Jonah repeated. He looked at his rebellious and treasonous children, and sighed. 'And if I were in your shoes, I'd think more than twice before throwing in my lot with a penniless adventurer who is as likely to be his father's legitimate son as I am to be the King of France.'

'But everyone knows –' said Sue, Monmouth's passionate partisan.

'Knows what? That he's a pretty lad with nice ways and the knack of making himself agreeable to all, high and low? He was just another wild courtly rakehell until he fell in with Shaftesbury and the Green Ribbon Club. Don't you think his father would have acknowledged him if he had been his legal son? And don't you think, also, that if Monmouth had been any more than a handsome lightweight, he would have given him high office and real responsibilities in government? King Charles had the measure of him, right enough, and to follow such a man now would lead to certain disaster.'

'You're wrong,' said Sue fervently, her round eyes shining. 'The whole country will rise – he's the hope of the Protestant religion and all Dissenters – give us just a few weeks, Father, and we'll see you eat your words!'

Jonah surveyed them, frowning. He said at last, 'Perhaps I will – or perhaps you'll eat yours. Oh, make your colours if it pleases you – I can hardly object after all. But if – if – Monmouth comes to Taunton, you will not see me amongst the first to welcome him. Just because I support the cause which he has appropriated does not mean I support him. But I would bid you, all of you – be careful. You may think your Protestant

Duke is bound to triumph, but from where I stand, matters look a good deal less certain.'

The Protestant Duke, hope of all who feared King James and Papists, raised his standard at Lyme, and the countryside rose in enthusiastic response. The King in London received the news of the invasion with some surprise, for it had been assumed that Monmouth would sail for Scotland, or Cheshire. He hastened to put the south-west into a state of greater readiness and defence. Warrants went out to the Lord Lieutenant of Somerset to raise the militia and march upon the rebels. Troops of horse and dragoons and companies of foot from the regular army were ordered to Salisbury, to add expertise and equipment to the local soldiers under the command of the Duke of Albemarle, who was instructed to prevent people going to Lyme to join Monmouth, but not to attack him unless from a position of great advantage, until the professional forces should arrive.

There was little chance for the more hot-headed inhabitants of Taunton to hurry off to Lyme. Colonel Luttrell, in charge of the despised local militia, had already summoned his troop commanders to muster their men, armed and ready, in the marketplace of Taunton, and their chief task would be to watch the roads and highways to the south for intending rebels. The Bridewell and the castle were full of suspicious travellers, and the town waited in an atmosphere of high expectancy for the imminent day when their saviour should march up East Street and deliver them from the impositions of Bernard Smith, the mayor, and the menace of Colonel Luttrell and his militia.

In Lyme, Monmouth and his officers were busy consolidating their precarious position. As the word spread round the countryside, hundreds of men came to join them, evading the militia, and twenty-four hours after the Duke's landing, he was in command of almost a thousand foot, and perhaps a hundred horse. Guards were posted behind the hedges lining the highways into the town, in case of attack: but the militia, obeying instructions, held back until the forces from London should arrive. There was a skirmish in Bridport, though, between a small force under the command of Lord Grey, Monmouth's friend, and a band of Dorset militia. The rebel horses, unused to warfare, proved unmanageable and bolted, and the foot was brought off under fire by Nathaniel Wade, who had no military experience but an abundance of coolness and common sense. They had taken several prisoners, however, killed two militia officers and, most important of all, seized thirty or so horses. First blood had been shed, and the rebellion had begun in earnest.

All over the West Country, the news spread, related with joy or disgust or indifference or foreboding, according to the inclination of the informant. It was not very difficult to evade the militia, especially for men with local knowledge of every short cut and trackway, and a steady stream of intending rebels, mostly travelling at night, managed to slip past the part-time soldiers watching the roads, and to join Monmouth and his growing army at Lyme. Soon his force would be sufficiently large and strong for him to leave the town and begin his march through Somerset towards Bristol, the second city of the kingdom, noted for its Dissenting opinions, and a certain source of men, money and support. With Bristol taken, the west would be his, and with such a firm base at his back, he would strike at London, and the King.

The news of the invasion arrived at Wintercombe two days after it had happened. By this time, Louise had recovered from the first shock of her fall, and was no longer confined to her bed. But her left shoulder was still intensely painful, the flesh and muscles around it much bruised and inflamed, and her grandmother bandaged and strapped up her arm every morning, with a fresh application of a pungent embrocation which Louise suspected had been originally intended for equine use. It did seem to lesson the pain and swelling a little, but she was still forced to move with extreme caution, creeping round the house in a loose gown and tippet like an elderly invalid. Riding, of course, would be out of the question for at least ten days, if not longer.

But Lukas had his pony. The day after the mishap, Alex had taken him over to Combe Hay, the boy riding pillion behind Henry Renolds, as originally planned. They had returned with a small, fat, amiable beast, mostly white with a haphazard collection of russet patches, unprepossessing but with a kind eye under the shaggy mane. Lukas, it was plain, was utterly besotted: he described his new friend to Louise in such glowing terms that when she first saw the skewbald pony in the flesh, the day after its arrival, she was hard put to recognise it. The narrowness of his escape from injury, and the severity of Louise's hurts, had not discouraged the boy, and if anything, he seemed more eager to learn to ride. An ancient felt saddle was exhumed from the furthest, dustiest corner of the tack room, and Louise, rather stiffly and with considerable care, made her way to the little paddock beside the stables, to give her first lesson.

Alex had forestalled her. He was showing Lukas the mechanics of saddle and bridle, while the pony stood sleepily in the afternoon sun. His face showed some surprise as Henry opened the gate for her. 'What are you doing here? I thought you were still resting.'

'I should be,' Louise said. She had not encountered him since he had helped her to her chamber after the accident: seeing his unwelcome expression, she wondered now if that brief glimpse of a friendly, unthreatening Alex had been purely a product of her imagination. 'But I did promise Lukas that I'd come and see his first proper ride,' she added. 'Don't worry – if the need arises, I shall return to my bed forthwith.'

'Just so long as I don't have to rescue you from your own folly again.'

'My own folly! Saffron shied, and there was nothing that anyone could have done to prevent it,' said Louise indignantly. 'It was completely unpredictable, and unavoidable.'

'Perhaps it was,' said Alex, raising a disbelieving eyebrow. 'However, that need not concern us now. You may stay and watch, if you like.'

'But Papa, Cousin Louise promised that she would teach me to ride!' Lukas objected. He walked round the pony's head to confront his father, his face crinkled with puzzlement. 'Why can't she?'

'Because I'm all strapped up like an Egyptian mummy, and not much use for the task,' Louise pointed out reasonably. She was annoyed with Alex, but did not intend to embark on an argument with him now, in the child's presence. 'Your father is a much better rider than I am.' She gave Lukas a friendly, teasing grin, and extended it, deliberately, to Alex. 'For a beginning, he doesn't fall off so frequently as I do!'

The little boy giggled, the first time she had heard him give a proper laugh. 'And now,' Louise added, assuming her haughtiest expression, 'I shall retire to my chair of state, and watch over the proceedings.' And to the sound of renewed amusement from Lukas, she swept grandly over to a sunny spot by the gate, where Henry had placed an upturned wooden tub with a piece of clean sacking carefully folded on top for her greater comfort.

Alex did not seem in the least disconcerted by her presence. Indeed, for the next half-hour or so, he ignored her completely. She watched as Lukas, his coat and waistcoat discarded, was shown the proper way to mount, and the correct posture and grasp of the reins. Then Alex led the pony several times around the field at a gentle walk, explaining to Lukas as they went how to direct his mount, how to use his hands and heels to urge it faster, and the reins to make it stop. The expression on the child's face was an infectious mixture of joy and concentration that brought an answering smile, unawares, to Louise's mouth. And she had no fault to find, so far, with the method of teaching: in just this gentle way she had given her little half-brother Philippe his first lessons, at the same age. But it was very difficult not to interfere, to pass comment or praise, when every impulse directed her to add her own skill and knowledge to that of her cousin. She clamped her lips shut and watched, determined, for the sake of Lukas who adored his father, and also seemed to have conceived some fondness for her, not to intrude.

Henry Renolds, however, had no such scruples. As Alex was explaining to Lukas the difficulties of the trot, he arrived panting at the gate. 'Sir! Man here to see ee from Frome, he d'say he have despeard important news!'

'He can wait five minutes,' Alex told him curtly. 'Take him to the kitchen, and Twinney can find him some beer – I'll come see him when I'm ready.'

Henry opened his mouth as if to protest, shut it again, and ran back to the stable yard. Louise wondered curiously what the news could be. Whatever it was, it was probably just as urgent as Henry seemed to think.

She glanced at Alex. His back to her, he was showing Lukas how to move with the rhythm of a trotting horse. Incorrigibly inquisitive, and also filled with a sudden and childish desire to hear the news before he did, she rose unobtrusively to her feet, opened the gate with her sound arm, and slid through it, shutting it behind her. It took only a moment or two to walk briskly down the lane, out of his sight, and to turn into the stable yard.

They had also heard the news, it seemed, for there was a knot of servants standing by the water-trough, deep in discussion. Ignoring the throbbing ache in her shoulder, engendered by the swift movements, she went up to them, addressing Pardice. 'What's happened?'

The head groom doffed his hat at once, and the others followed suit. 'News have just come, Mistress Louise – the Duke of Monmouth have landed in Lyme!'

'Monmouth?' She stared at him, wondering for a moment what the name signified. Then a sudden, vivid memory returned of Bram in his father's bookshop, talking about the bastard son of the late King, as if he were the only bulwark of the Protestant religion against popery and arbitrary government.

'Yes, Mistress – the Protestant Duke!' Henry Renolds said, as if the description were all that was required for her enlightenment. 'He've come to save us all from they Papists.'

'Oh, don't ee be such a lack-wit,' said Lawrence Earle, scathingly. 'Do ee know any murdering Papists hereabouts?'

Henry looked blank for a moment. Pardice took pity on him. 'Mistress Bab and Master Charles and Mistress Amy be Papists every one. Do they seem like bogles to ee? All most such folk want be to worship as they d'please, and not to plague the rest of us. Now do ee get back to work, both of ee, afore I lose my temper.'

The two boys scuttled into the stables. Pardice turned to Louise, his sunburned face crinkling with amusement. 'They bain't bad lads, Mistress, but they d'need a firm hand most times. As if anyone in this house would think Papists be a threat to us!'

'They are to the Protestants in France,' said Louise, recalling the forced conversions, the brutal harassment and terror that King Louis had recently inflicted on the French heretics. 'But England isn't France, nor likely to be. Where is Lyme, Pardice?'

'Down on the south coast, Mistress, just on the border between Dorsetshire and Somersetshire. All those parts are full of Dissenters, Baptists, Anabaptists, Quakers and the like. He'll find plenty to join his army there, I reckon.'

'Army?' Louise stared at him, wondering why she had not realised this before: perhaps that fall had addled her wits in addition to damaging her shoulder. 'You mean – he has *invaded*?'

'Well, he haven't come to kiss King James's hand,' said Pardice drily. 'Let's hope the militia d'know what they be about, eh, Mistress? Or there'll be war back in Somerset again, if this vlother bain't knocked on the head quick.'

By supper time, everyone at Wintercombe, from its master down to Jeffery Combe the gardener's boy, had heard the news of Monmouth's landing. Opinions, not unnaturally, varied wildly. Philip's Norton, like most of north Somerset, was strongly Protestant, and several of the villagers attended a Dissenting conventicle that met regularly four miles away, in Beckington. Many of the younger servants, male and female, had some sympathy for the rebels, although one or two were more cautious, pointing out that King James, despite being a fanatic Papist, had occupied the throne a scant five months, and had hardly yet proved himself an enemy, or indeed a friend, to the Protestant religion. Moreover, his heir was his daughter Mary, married to the Prince of Orange, and both of them as stout a pair of Protestants as ever breathed. To these, Monmouth's invasion seemed a ludicrous miscalculation, pointless and much too soon, before the King had shown himself to be a villain – if, indeed, he was one. Why had the Duke not waited until support for a Protestant rebellion would be fervent and spread throughout the country?

'Perhaps he knows something we don't,' Twinney said darkly. 'There's rebellion in Scotland too. Perhaps this is 'forty-two, come again.'

And the group of excited, chattering servants fell silent, for even those who had not been born when the last war began had heard so many tales about it, from parents and grandparents, that it seemed as if they had almost lived through it themselves. And while some secretly relished the chance of future danger and excitement in their humdrum, narrow lives, the majority hoped devoutly that such times would never be repeated.

In her chamber, Bab St Barbe prayed, with equal fervour, for the defeat of the rebel and treasonous heretic, Monmouth. He would doubtless claim to act in support of freedom of worship for Dissenters and all the numerous, ridiculous Protestant sects. That he would extend such toleration to Catholics seemed most unlikely. Already, so Charles told her, their priest, Father Anselm, was able to hold masses openly in Bath, without hindrance or restriction, for if the King himself was one of their number, they need no longer fear repression. She had no reason to welcome Monmouth, and every reason to fear him.

Beside her, Charles and Amy prayed too, certain that God would not allow such a disreputable adventurer to prevail against the rightful King and government. But her son at least, aware of the strength of Protestant feeling in Somerset, and of the deep mistrust that many had for the Catholic King, knew uneasily that Monmouth might prove a much bigger menace to the peace of the West Country, if not the entire kingdom, than his mother and sister appeared to think, however dubious and self-seeking the Duke's motives might be.

There was, in consequence, a most lively discussion at supper. Louise, whose knowledge of English politics, despite four weeks in Bram's company, was still very sketchy, listened with interest to a civil war in miniature around the table. Charles and Amy, of course, took the King's part, and treason was a word frequently mentioned. Phoebe, as dispassionate as ever, pointed out that His Majesty was not a man noted for his soundness of judgement, unlike his late and lamented brother. He was known to admire his cousin, Louis of France, and she found it quite easy to understand the fears of the people that King James would apply the methods of King Louis to return his country to the Catholic worship.

Louise noted that Alex took no part in the debate. Often, he addressed a few words to Lukas, sitting as usual by his side and looking at once bored and bewildered by all the adult argument. But for the rest of the time he remained quiet, eating and drinking in moderation, and wearing a distinctly sardonic expression. Louise hid her amusement, certain that once Lukas had left the table, his father would make his opinions known. Since, according to Bram, he had been supplying the Loveridge bookshop for some years with seditious pamphlets from Holland, there was little doubt as to which side of the fence he would favour.

'To be honest,' said Silence, entering the conversation for the first time during a momentary lull, 'I do not care overmuch for either side. His Majesty is our lawful king, but that does not make him infallible, nor does it necessarily mean that it is treason to oppose him, whatever he does. I believe that there are times when a monarch, or a government, must be resisted, if their actions are abhorrent to any reasonable man or woman. But King James has yet hardly had the chance to prove himself a good or bad ruler. And as for Monmouth – what does he hope to gain from this rebellion? He can hardly be aiming to right injustice, for there has not yet been any. He is judging the King purely by his religion, which is a most dangerous practice. I suspect that, whatever his avowed intentions, he means to make himself king.'

There was a brief pause, broken by Phoebe. 'If you're right, Aunt, then I doubt the gentry will give him their support. The ordinary people, yes, because he is their hero, and they love him. Remember those thousands who came out to welcome him, five years ago? It was said that he had touched a woman for the king's evil, and cured her, and in their eyes, that proves him to be his father's rightful heir.'

'Ridiculous!' Charles said, shifting angrily in his seat. 'Only the most gullible could possibly be taken in by those stories about a black box, and his mother's marriage certificate. It's purely wishful thinking.'

'I'm inclined to agree with you,' Phoebe said, her clever face thoughtful. 'But there's a third actor in this play that none of you have yet mentioned – and his role is the most mysterious of all. What of the Prince of Orange?'

'He's married to James's heir,' Silence pointed out. 'I doubt he would wish Monmouth to succeed, especially if the Duke plans to claim the throne. But he doesn't seem to have made any attempt to stop him sailing for England. Perhaps it's not himself that Monmouth will proclaim King if he succeeds, but William of Orange!'

They had finished the second course, and Lukas's nurse came to take him to bed. He was obviously most reluctant to go, but with his usual obedience made his bow, politely wished them all goodnight, and left.

As Louise had expected, Alex entered the conversation as soon as his son had gone. 'The Prince of Orange is a very subtle and cautious man. You can be sure that his intentions will be kept a close secret – probably not even his wife knows what he really thinks about Monmouth, or about anyone else, for that matter. I doubt, though, that he has any thoughts of claiming the English throne at present. My guess is that Monmouth is a stalking horse, allowed to mount his little invasion to test the waters. But William would never lend his name to such a foolhardy expedition.'

'And of course you know him personally,' said Charles, unable to keep a sneer out of his voice.

Alex smiled, his hands clasped round his glass, which was full of his customary brandy. 'To tell the truth, yes, he and I are acquainted – although the Princess Mary has been a better friend to me, recently.'

'Really?' said Charles, an expanse of innuendo in his voice, worthy of Alex himself. 'How very interesting.'

Before his cousin could respond in his usual offensive manner, Silence stepped into the breach. 'I have something to tell you which cannot very well wait, and this will be my last chance to speak to all of you together. I am planning to return to Chard tomorrow.'

'You can't!' Charles's shocked voice coincided with Phoebe's. 'Don't be ridiculous, Aunt.'

'I am not being ridiculous,' Silence said patiently. 'What danger could there possibly be from either side to an old woman travelling back to her home? I shall have my groom and my maid for company, and I expect you have a brace of pistols which you could lend us, Alex, to set your mind at rest.'

'But Chard is very close to Lyme,' Charles objected. 'You'd be riding right into the fighting.'

'If there is any, which I doubt. Can you see the militia devastating their own countryside? Nor will Monmouth dare to molest ordinary people, when he relies so much on popular support. Yes, I do admit that perhaps such a journey at such a time might be considered foolish. I may be old, but I am not yet senile, and there will be chance enough for you all to rule my life when I am truly in my dotage. I only intended to stay here for a few days, anyway. And although I do not think that they are in any real danger, I do feel most strongly that, much as I love you all, my place is with Nick and Richard and Sarah and the children, at Chard.' She folded her arms and looked round at her family, benign but utterly determined. 'And short of tying me to my bed, there is no means you can use to prevent me.'

They stared at her, apparently stunned. Then Louise said slowly, 'You have remembered that I can't come with you, Gran'mère?'

'As I said, I am not yet in my dotage,' Silence remarked drily. 'Of course you can't ride with me – and for the moment you should stay here, until this Monmouth affair has ended, one way or the other. Wintercombe is as safe as any place in Somerset, after all – and probably a good deal less dangerous than Chard. And although I know that you don't relish taking advice, I would tell you now – and you, Amy, and Phoebe – not to go gallivanting about the countryside alone. I have very vivid memories of what soldiers can do, and I doubt that their habits have changed very much in forty years.'

Louise grinned mischievously. 'It's all right, Gran'mère, I have no intention of being raped. And besides, I know a trick or two that my mother taught me.'

Silence smiled, ignoring Amy's shocked expression. 'Well, it's best to avoid unpleasant situations altogether, and be careful until the danger's over. But I doubt very much if Monmouth will come within twenty miles of Wintercombe. Exeter, or Bristol, are probably his immediate targets, always assuming that he is allowed to advance so far. And in any case, Alex and Charles are perfectly capable of ensuring the safety of everyone at Wintercombe. You are all adult enough now to manage without me.'

She had effectively disarmed all opposition, but Louise, much though she admired Silence's indomitable spirit, could not help feeling a little uneasy. Her grandmother was old enough, though of course hardly frail, for any journey across Somerset to be an arduous undertaking for her, let alone at a time of rebellion and, possibly, open warfare. But she was utterly determined, and, as she had so forcefully pointed out, not to be dissuaded. And it did seem unlikely, on the face of it, that soldiers of either side would consider her a threat. After all, Monmouth would hardly be so short of support that he was likely to draft seventy-year-old ladies into his army.

And if Silence returned to Chard, she would be left at Wintercombe. At present, she was severely restricted by her injured shoulder, but surely in a week or so, she would be able to indulge her longing for freedom once more?

'Of course we are,' she said, smiling at her grandmother. 'Don't worry about me – Christian can strap up my shoulder every morning, and I don't intend to put myself at any sort of risk. If you want to go home, then of course you must go.' She added drily, 'And I would like to see anyone try to stop you, Gran'mère.'

And she hoped, as the people around the table smiled, that Silence's suspicions would not be aroused. For not only did freedom beckon, once her tiresome injury had healed: there was also the delightful prospect of a sojourn at Wintercombe, and the continuing temptation of a flirtation with Alex, without the inhibiting presence of her grandmother.

## 12

## *'Disobedient son'*

'You must be mad!'

Jonah Loveridge confronted his eldest, only surviving son across the parlour, his face white with anger. His wife, daughters and niece sat mute, watching and listening intently, as the battle, that had been threatening like a thunderstorm for upwards of five days now, was finally and explosively joined.

'Then if I'm mad, most of Taunton is too,' Bram said furiously. With his wild hair, and his beautiful face sharpened and glowing with rage, he had never appeared more handsome, and Libby, fifteen and just the right age for hero-worship, thought him far better looking than Monmouth, over whom Sue and Hannah had swooned sentimentally on his triumphant entry into Taunton, earlier that day.

'Probably they are. The whole of Somerset has lost its wits, by all accounts,' said Jonah. He made a visible effort to calm himself, although he was shaking with the force of his feelings. 'You say you want to leave your home – your future – your family – your mother – and follow this adventurer? He'll come to a sticky end without a doubt, and if you join his so-called army, you run the risk of doing the same.'

'He's for the Protestant religion,' Bram said, through thinned lips. 'So are you – or so you've always said. You've brought us all up to wish for toleration and freedom of worship, to think for ourselves, and make our own decisions. Well, I've made mine, and if you're too cautious to fight for the cause you've always said you believed in, Father, well, I'm not!'

Hannah, who tended to let her own tongue run away with her, opened her mouth. Sue, sitting next to her, reached out a foot and prodded her warningly into silence.

'Do you consider me a coward?' Jonah asked, with deceptive mildness. 'I would like to know.'

'I wouldn't go so far as that, but you're certainly a hypocrite!'

'That's enough,' said Tabby, getting to her feet. She too was pale with fury, an emotion which, in the twenty-odd years of her marriage, had very rarely mastered her. She loved both husband and son, but at this moment she dearly wanted to knock their obstinate heads together. 'You should

215

both be ashamed of yourselves, arguing like this in front of the girls. I suggest that you go to our chamber or somewhere else that's private, and conduct your quarrel well away from the rest of us.'

Jonah stared at his wife as if she had suddenly donned sword and armour. When he had married her she had seemed a gentle, retiring, graceful young woman, possessed of rare beauty and a substantial dowry, and as far beyond his reach as the stars. That she had even noticed him, let alone returned his passionate adoration, was a miracle which still stopped his breath when he thought about it. And yet it had not taken many months of wedded bliss to realise that, behind the lovely face and glorious hair, she harboured an astonishingly powerful will, and a fierce sense of rightness and justice that seemed altogether inappropriate in such an apparently delicate creature. And Jonah, by nature dry, discreet and ascetic, hopelessly in love for the first and only time in his life, had at last come to accept that his wife was a much more forceful character than he was. She did not dominate him: theirs was an equal partnership. Yet the only time he had ever felt her to be the weaker was when their children died in the fever epidemic two years ago, and she had wept furiously in his arms, heartbroken and railing against the cruelty of fate. But always, in front of their remaining offspring, they had preserved, by tacit consent, the fiction that Jonah was the unquestioned master of the household. Now, with a few hasty words, she had shattered that illusion. And the worst of it was that she was right: there was a time, and a place, to argue with his obstinate son, but this assuredly was not it.

And Bram, of course, so like Tabby in many things, not least that fierce sense of right and wrong, knew her well enough to capitulate immediately. 'I'm sorry, Mother,' he said, with an apologetic smile certain to melt her anger like ice in sunshine. 'I was carried away – I should have known better.'

'We'll finish this discussion later,' said Jonah severely, trying to give the impression that he shared his wife's disapproval, rather than being one of the subjects of it. 'Now, Hannah, were you not about to read to us?'

In an atmosphere of some apprehension, his younger daughter opened the big Bible that lay on the table in front of her, turned the pages, and began in her clear sure voice to describe the youthful exploits of David. Tabby sat down, already regretting her loss of temper. It was just as well that Jonah was slow to anger, or the argument with Bram might quickly have become little better than a brawl. She sent her husband a quick, rueful smile, to reassure him that she was still on his side, and carefully avoided her son's eye. In her heart, she could not help but be sympathetic to his wish to join the rebels, but for the sake of family peace she would not reveal her true feelings, not yet.

Three days previously, Monmouth had left Lyme at the head of some three thousand eager but completely raw and untrained recruits, many of them armed with whatever they could lay their hands on. They had been divided into four regiments, the Red, the White, the Yellow and the Green, and the very few experienced officers that their leader could muster had been sprinkled amongst them. But he, a competent soldier, was well aware that his cavalry was the weakest element in his burgeoning army. Horses were desperately needed, and those that they did have were for the most part inferior animals, straight from the farm or the cart, with only a few of better quality. Already, an argument over a fine mount had cost the life of one of his adherents, a Taunton goldsmith who had come with him from Holland, and forced him to send the killer, a professional soldier whom he could ill spare, back to the ship in disgrace. And his great friend, Lord Grey, who commanded the cavalry, was, like the horses, completely inexperienced. Monmouth did not want to replace him with someone more competent, both for their friendship's sake and because Lord Grey was his only aristocratic supporter and therefore vitally necessary to encourage the wealthy Somerset gentry to join the rebellion. The common people had flocked to him, and their love and joy warmed his heart: but he needed the landowners of the West Country, their wealth, their horses and their prestige, if the rebellion was to have any chance of success.

There was a skirmish, brief and confused, as the rebel force approached Axminster from one direction, and the Devon and Somerset militia, under the command of the Duke of Albemarle, from another. The Somerset men, already half-hearted and reluctant to fight against their neighbours, friends and Protestants like themselves, abandoned their arms and fled, leaving the rebels in jubilant possession of the town and an invaluable quantity of weapons, coats and equipment, not to mention several militia men who had decided to join them.

The next day, Monmouth advanced to Chard. News of the militia's flight at Axminster had already reached Taunton, and the soldiers there, deciding likewise for the better part of valour, marched out during the night, leaving most of their armour and weapons behind, locked in St Mary's church. As soon as word spread that they had gone, a group of the more passionate townspeople broke in through the windows at dawn, opened the doors from the inside, and carried out their booty in triumph, shouldering aside a few loyal spirits, including the Reverend Axe, who had tried to prevent them. As one of their number forcefully pointed out, Taunton now belonged to Monmouth's supporters, and those who opposed him had best beware. The prisoners were released from the castle and the Bridewell, amid much jubilation, and when word came that Monmouth had reached Chard, every one of his adherents who could beg, borrow or steal a horse, rode the twelve miles south to welcome him.

The militia was in disarray, fled or defeated, while their despairing commanders wrote increasingly frantic letters to the authorities in London, begging for the regular soldiers who alone, it seemed, would be able to hold back the irresistible swelling momentum of Monmouth's army. And at midday on Thursday, 18th June, he entered Taunton at the head of his men, now numbering above four thousand with more joining every hour.

Every man, woman and child in the town, so it seemed, had gathered in East Street to greet him. The windows dripped greenery, and young girls and women threw flowers and rose petals and sweet-smelling herbs, so that the scene resembled a wedding procession rather than an army's march. The bells of St Mary's and St James's clashed joyfully overhead, and so great was the press of people all around, shouting and cheering and trying to touch his horse or kiss his hand, that the Duke's progress towards the marketplace was slow, and at times almost nonexistent. Despite the clamour and the crowds, he had a smile for everyone, was not reluctant to embrace the screaming, ill-wrapped babies lifted up to him every so often to kiss, and waved frequently to those hanging out of windows or even, perilously, clinging to chimneypots to obtain a better view. And in every hat and cap and hood was the bunch of greenery, colour of life and new growth, that was the rebel badge.

The Loveridge family watched from their parlour window overlooking the marketplace as the hero was conducted to the neighbouring house of John Hucker, one of the wealthiest merchants in the town. He had been an officer in the militia, but, like so many others, had swiftly deserted them for Monmouth. So huge and dense was the crowd that the Duke was almost lost amongst them, only the white plumes on his hat marking him out. Sue and Hannah all but lost their balance leaning out of the window to obtain a better view, and even Libby, quiet and observant, seemed to be infected with the riotous enthusiasm below, and went so far as to wave her kerchief and cheer with her cousins.

It was the sheer size of the welcome and the intoxicating joy all around him which persuaded Bram that he must join the rebels. His cautious words to Tom Dinham, just a few days ago, seemed now to be the speech of a timid hypocrite. The thousands of men who had already joined

Monmouth, the hundreds more in Taunton who undoubtedly would, were proof positive that this wave of popular acclaim was invincible. With the West Country behind him, Monmouth would sweep to London, overcoming all obstacles: Whigs and republicans and Dissenters in Cheshire, Scotland and London itself would all rise in his support, and the hated and feared King James would flee for his life, abandoning the throne to his nephew. With that wonderful future assured, what young man of spirit, a fervent believer in the rights of Protestantism and the rule of Parliament and the law, would not choose to be part of such glory?

His heart had arrived at that decision as soon as he beheld the welcome that the people of Taunton gave to the Protestant Duke, although his head still argued, with less and less conviction, that this was a foolhardy enterprise, inevitably doomed to failure. By evening, Monmouth's force had been settled in a camp in Paul's Field to the west of the town, and outposts placed to guard the roads with the four cannon that were all that the Duke could boast in the way of ordnance, and crowds still lingered outside Hucker's house opposite the Three Cups Inn, hoping for a glimpse of their hero. And Bram's mind was made up. Tomorrow, he would join the rebel army.

His sisters, of course, would be wholeheartedly approving. For days they had laboured over the colours that Mistress Musgrave and Mistress Blake and her sister had instructed them to make, taking the precious square of green silk with them to school every day, working on it with the other girls instead of the more usual lessons in reading, writing, Bible study, history and arithmetic, and bringing it home again in the evening. Now it was almost finished, and Sue, nearly bursting with pride and joy and excitement, had told him that Mistress Mary Blake had arranged for all the colours to be presented to Monmouth the next day, after his proclamation was read out in the marketplace. At last, she would meet her idol.

'And are you going to join them?' she added, her plain face glowing. 'Oh, Bram, you must!'

He was very fond of Sue, though they had grown apart from the close companionship of childhood, and he would not lie to her. 'Of course I will,' he told her, and saw the surge of pride fill her face most gratifyingly. 'How could I not? I've made up my mind, and I shall go to the rebel camp tomorrow and offer my services.'

'Oh, Bram, you're wonderful!' Hannah cried, and flung her arms around him with childish enthusiasm. It was left to Libby, clever, and surprisingly more mature than his sisters, to point out the obvious. 'But what will Uncle Jonah say?'

Of course, Jonah had said a great deal, and so had Bram. Tabby had stopped them before the argument could descend to the completely unforgivable, but after the girls had gone to their chamber to put the final touches to their flag, she took her husband aside.

Bram had gone with his sisters to inspect their work, so they were alone, for the moment, in the parlour. There was still a little light in the marketplace below, and Jonah stood at the window, looking at the people who still thronged the street, restless and unwilling to return to their homes after such a stirring day. Tabby joined him, slipping her arm companionably through his. She said quietly, 'Do you think he means it? You said the other day that he'd seemed to show some sense in the matter.'

'He did – but he's changed, for some reason,' Jonah said, without looking at her. A hard knot of despair had settled round his heart. He loved all his children, those who had died so tragically, and those who lived, but this surviving son had always been his favourite. And now, it seemed, he would lose Bram as he had lost Joe and Jeremy and Ruth, but to battle, not to disease. Being as usual honest with himself, he did not see how he could bear it. He added bleakly, 'Yes, he does mean it. You know Bram. Once his mind is made up, he's implacable.'

Like you, he might have remarked, and Tabby was well aware of it. She laid her head on his shoulder. The spare evening light fell kindly on her face, smoothing out the lines of laughter and caring so that she seemed to regain for a moment the gazelle's beauty which she had passed to her eldest son.

Jonah said suddenly, desperately, 'He can't go – he can't! What will happen to them? The fate of all rebels – exile, or death in one form or another, all horrible. I can't let him march away with them – not Bram.'

'But you must,' Tabby said, her voice calm, her eyes fierce. 'He was quite right. We have reared our children to love freedom, and hate tyranny – we have taught them to reach their own decisions, and encouraged them to be independent. Can you not see that if Bram listens to you now, we have failed?'

Jonah was silent, fighting his angry grief, his impulse to deny what she said, which was unquestionably the truth. Finally, he turned to her, and saw for the first time the distress in her face, matching his.

'Of course I don't want him to go, any more than you do,' Tabby said. 'My dear, of *course* I don't – but you must see that he is adult, he is of age and his own man, he isn't a child – and this is something that he alone must decide. And besides,' she added drily, 'when have you ever known simple persuasion move him when his mind is set on something?'

'Then if persuasion won't, perhaps force will,' Jonah said in anguish. He saw her face change, and added hastily, 'I'm not suggesting that we knock him on the head or tie him up – but there is a key to his chamber, is there not?'

Tabby stared at him for a long moment, as if he were a stranger. Finally, she said, 'You would do *that*? You would imprison your own son, rather than let him do what he wants?'

'Yes!' Jonah cried, his expression distorted by grief and the desperation of his dilemma. 'Yes, I would, if nothing else will work. Oh, dear Tabby, he is the only son we have left – I can't let him go with the rebels, I can't, I *can't*! And surely, if you love him, and me, you must agree.'

His wife's large and remarkable hazel eyes, direct and unflinching, searched his face. 'Of course I love him,' she said, a little impatiently. 'But can you not see that if you stop him from joining the rebels, you run the risk of forfeiting his regard for you, for ever?'

'To have him safe, it's a price that I am prepared to pay,' said Jonah stubbornly. 'But perhaps it won't be necessary. Perhaps he will listen.'

Tabby's expression showed her doubts. She said at last, 'My dear, please reconsider. I know you'll regret it if you don't.'

'I'll regret it if I do let him go,' said her husband bitterly. He paused, and then said quietly, 'Tabby – please – don't tell him. Not yet, when it may not be necessary. Nothing would drive him into the rebels' arms faster.'

'I won't,' she promised him, and smiled rather wanly. 'But remember when you talk to him that he is not a child. He is adult, just like you and me, even if he has not yet had the benefit of our experience of the world.'

But when Jonah knocked on the door of his son's chamber under the eaves, there was no reply, and the room was empty. Sick with fear that the boy had somehow overheard his conversation and run already to the rebel army, he hurried to his daughters' chamber. They were sitting on the bed with their cousin, industriously edging the expanse of green silk with a handsome red braid border, and looked up in surprise and dismay at his intrusion. To his hasty question, Sue said mildly, 'Didn't he tell you? Tom Dinham came a few minutes ago – they've only gone to the Red Lion.'

He thanked her, and went back to the parlour. Pride forbade him to go running across the street to check that the story was true, and he spent the rest of the evening in an agony of apprehension, trying to read, trying to stay calm, listening to the sounds of joyful revelry outside, and wondering whether his beloved son would return.

At least he would not be the worse for drink: Bram was a young man of most unusual moderation, unlike his notorious cousin Alex. But when he did appear, long past the supposed curfew, flushed and elated and whistling some jaunty tune that had been much in the air in Taunton that day, Jonah took one look and realised the impossibility of reopening the argument. His son was simply not in the mood for persuasion, or for dispute: reasoning with him would be hopeless.

He sat long in the parlour after everyone else had retired to bed, wrestling with his conscience. He knew that Tabby was right, that Bram was an adult, quite capable of directing his life, and that, having brought him up to make his own decisions, his parents could hardly complain if they were not to their liking. And he knew also, chillingly, that if he carried out his intention, Bram would never forgive him.

Which was to be preferred? A son dead, who had loved him, or a son living, who would turn against him?

In the last extremity, there was no case to answer. He could not let Bram march away to probable death. And once the decision had been made, it was easy. All the chambers in the house could be locked, but none were: the keys, long disused, were kept on a hook in the corner of the kitchen. Slowly, stiff and heavy with misery, Jonah got to his feet and made his way down the stairs, carrying the one guttering candle. The house was quite silent: it was past midnight now, and everyone else must have been asleep for an hour or more. He lifted the keys from their hook. All were different, but he knew Bram's: it had a very thick barrel and only two notches in the ward. He ignored the miaows and sinuous greeting of the cat Jezebel, and climbed the stairs as quietly as he could, given the many creaks and ill-fitting boards, to his son's chamber.

No sound came from within, and no light showed under the door. Jonah took a deep breath, inserted the key in the lock, and turned. It was stiff and jerky with disuse, and the noise of metal grating on metal seemed shatteringly loud. But the key had done its work: Bram was now a prisoner.

With care, still surprised that his son had not been roused by the sounds, Jonah withdrew the key. He had wondered if he should drop it down the well – after all, any competent locksmith would have the door open in ten minutes – but he had discarded the thought. He had no idea how long it would be necessary for the boy to remain a prisoner, but it might be days, even weeks, and he would have to be given food and drink. He slipped the key into the pocket of his breeches, and, with a sense of having burned all his bridges behind him, crept sadly down the stairs to his own bed.

Bram slept very soundly that night, aided by weariness and several

222

tankards of beer, and heard nothing. He woke refreshed at dawn, with a lift of his heart. Today, he would defy his father, and doubtless his mother too, and join the rebel army. The girls, presenting their precious colour, would have their moment of glory, and then he would seize his.

He jumped out of bed, whistling 'England's Darling', a ballad they had all been singing in the Red Lion last night. The morning was bright, and full of promise, and the sparrows chattered unmusically above him on the roof as he dressed, and sang.

> 'Young Jemmy is a lad
> That's royally descended,
> With every virtue clad,
> By every tongue commended:
> A true and faithful English heart,
> Great Britain's joy and hope,
> And bravely will maintain their part,
> In spite of Turk and Pope.'

Today, no garments would do but his best, however unsuitable for soldiering. So he took out his fine holland shirt, and the breeches, coat and waistcoat, in gleaming tawny satin, that he wore when visiting important customers. His Sunday cravat, frothing with expensive Devon lace, completed the picture. He dragged a brush through his long, curling, honey-gold hair, so thick that a periwig was an unnecessary expense, singing the final verse of the ballad.

> 'Let all good men implore
> For Jemmy's restoration,
> Whose conduct must restore
> The ruins of our nation:
> That he to Charles's praise may live,
> Our freedom to maintain, ·
> When Jemmy shall his fame retrieve,
> And be in grace again.'

He had a good voice, rich, powerful and well tuned, and the sounds rang through the house. Sue and Hannah and Libby, likewise dressing in their best, combing each other's hair and fastening their gowns, heard it and smiled. Jonah, afflicted by pangs of conscience, knew that his son could not yet have discovered that he was a prisoner. But there was no going back now. He waited nervously for the inevitable reaction.

Still humming cheerfully, Bram went to the door, lifted the latch, and pulled. Nothing happened. He tried again, and again, with increasing force, but in vain: the door remained firmly shut. Puzzled, he stared at it for a moment. It had never jammed fast before, although it was prone to stick in damp weather.

The truth came to him abruptly, and with it a devastating flash of anger. He kicked at the door, and yelled at the full pitch of his lungs. 'Father! What have you done?'

Footsteps, many of them, came tumbling up the stairs to his door. He heard Sue, suddenly sharp, and Hannah saying something in bewilderment. Through them all, Jonah's voice came, at once defiant and apologetic. 'Bram? I'm sorry, but this was the only way to stop you.'

'You've locked him in!' Sue cried indignantly. 'Father, how *could* you?'

'This is ridiculous,' Bram said, through clenched teeth. 'Father, please, see sense and let me out.'

'No,' Jonah told him, very close on the other side of the door. 'No, I cannot let you join the rebels. You'll rail against me now, but I promise you'll thank me later.'

'I doubt it,' Bram said grimly. He wished that he had the strength to force the door, but he was not tall, and slightly built compared with, say, his cousin Alex. He added, trying not to plead, but to speak to Jonah man to man, 'Look, Father, this is so petty, so stupid. If you feel this strongly about me joining the rebels, then for God's sake let me out, and we'll discuss it reasonably.'

'No,' Jonah said, with finality. 'No, no, and no. I have the key safe. You need not worry – you can have food and drink, anything you want except your freedom, until Monmouth has gone and all this is over.'

Bram was tempted to put all his energy, and all the tumultuous fury boiling inside him, into one last assault on the door. But he was no longer a child. Brute force was not the answer. For the moment, his father seemed to be implacable, but he wondered whether he would still be so adamant after the rest of his family had had the chance to soften him. From the other sounds outside the door, he guessed that his imprisonment was as much a surprise to his mother and sisters as it was to him.

'Your breakfast will be brought to you soon,' Jonah told him. 'Books, too, if you want them. Is there anything else you might need?'

'Yes,' said Bram bitterly. 'If it isn't too much trouble, Father dear, I would like my freedom back.'

There was a brief silence on the other side of the door, and then the noise of retreating feet. At once a hubbub of female voices broke out, diminishing as they followed Jonah down the stairs. With no one to hear him, Bram aimed a last, futile kick at the door, and then hurled himself down on the bed.

His black mood lasted all morning, while below him, and outside, his family and Taunton prepared for the greatest day of their lives. Jonah, perspiring and looking nervous but determined, brought a tray with hot frumenty, bread, cheese and beer, put it down just inside the door, and retreated hastily in the face of his son's glare, as if he thought that Bram would push past him and make a dash for freedom. Then the door was firmly shut, and the key turned in the lock with brutal finality.

Much to Bram's surprise, he was hungry. He finished it all, every crumb, and then sat for a while on the bed, a brooding frown disfiguring his face, trying to find a way out of this impossible, ludicrous and undignified situation.

He had been there for what seemed like hours when sounds of increased activity beyond the window roused him from his thoughts. He jumped to his feet, and went to look out.

The marketplace around the Cross was crowded thickly with people, and the cheers that rose from them were distinctly derisive. Bram opened the casement and leaned out. He saw some of the members of Taunton's Corporation, clad in their robes of office and visibly frightened, being hustled through the throng at the point of sword and pistol, to the steps of the Cross. They huddled there in a group, conferring, and there was an interval of some minutes, accompanied by a crescendo of hisses and whistles from the crowd, before one of their number turned to the group of Monmouth's soldiers standing below them. Even from this distance, his words lost in the noise of the crowd, his posture and gestures indicated vehement refusal. Bram, his own situation temporarily forgotten, watched with a grin on his face as the worthy people of Taunton, infuriated, jeered and threw objects that appeared to range from mud and stones to rotten fruit, and less savoury missiles. The cacophony died away only when one of the rebels sprang up on to the steps of the Cross, and loudly and forcefully appealed for quiet.

The noise faded gradually, like a receding wave, ebbing outwards towards the fringes of the marketplace. One lone voice, just below Bram, bawled into the comparative silence, 'Why don't you just string up the Papist-loving bastards?' To laughter, he was hastily hushed by his friends, and the rebel officer took a paper from one of his comrades and began to read.

It was some kind of proclamation, and continued at inordinate length. Bram, hanging out of the window at a perilous angle, could not distinguish more than about half of it, but that portion was inflammatory enough. King James, described therein as the Duke of York, was accused of burning London, fomenting the Popish Plot, furthering war with

Protestant Holland and friendship with Catholic France, planning to place England under the yoke of a Papist tyranny and, for good measure, poisoning his brother King Charles. To each of these charges, a roar of approval rose from the crowd, who evidently agreed wholeheartedly with all of it, however unlikely. Then the officer went on to declare that they were fighting this 'murderer, and an assassinator of innocent men, a traitor to the nation, and tyrant over the people', in order to bring him to justice for his crimes. They wished to preserve the Protestant religion, and repeal all laws against Dissenters from the established church. Nor did they intend to persecute Catholics, so long as they worshipped in peace and did not seek to subvert the law. He finished by announcing that the Duke of Monmouth at present wished only to lead the Protestant forces of the kingdom, 'assembled for the end aforesaid', and would not insist on his title, but left that decision to 'the wisdom, justice and authority of a Parliament legally chosen, and acting with freedom'.

So he was not, yet, openly claiming the crown. Listening to the deafening cheers which erupted from the people as the officer ended, Bram wondered how long that stand would last. His sisters, with schoolgirl jealousy, had waxed envious the previous evening about Mary Mead's splendid banner, embroidered and fringed all around with gold, bearing a crown and the letters JR. It could hardly be intended to glorify the present incumbent of the throne. The inhabitants of Taunton were for the most part Dissenters, not republicans, and they would undoubtedly want Monmouth for their King, not the Papist James or foreign Dutch William.

The rebel officer stepped down from his makeshift pulpit, and vanished into the press, to rapturous acclaim. There was a stir on the far side of the marketplace, and Bram, craning his neck, saw a procession forming up there on the fringe of the crowd. The people parted to make passage for them, and he saw the principal of his sisters' school, Mistress Musgrave, place herself at the head of a file of girls, all dressed in their best. She was a small, frail-looking woman in middle age, so to see her bearing a drawn sword in one hand (there was a Bible in the other) was somewhat incongruous. Behind her came the lovely Mary Mead, proudly bearing her precious colour, the sunlight glinting on the gold, and some twenty of the younger children, also carrying their banners. They were followed by the two Mistresses Blake, the other teachers, with the older girls. Bram saw Sue, pacing slowly and stiffly with the green colour draped from the pole which she held firmly in her grasp. Hannah and Libby, probably as deep a green with envy, came empty-handed behind.

He watched as the procession made its way to Hucker's house, some doors down from the Loveridge shop. By leaning dangerously far out of the window, he could just glimpse what was happening. To loud applause, the Duke emerged, followed by his entourage. Mistress Musgrave delivered a brief speech, so softly that few could hear her. Monmouth, more used to speaking before a large crowd, was more audible in reply. He thanked her for the Bible, and went on, pitching his voice to reach as many onlookers as possible. 'I come now into the field with a design to defend the truths contained in this book – and I shall seal it with my blood, if there should be occasion for it.'

There was more cheering, a little hoarse by now, and then the girls were led forward to be presented. Each, even the smallest, sank into a reverent curtsey, and were raised up and kissed on the cheek by the Duke, and by his friend Lord Grey. Bram grinned, knowing that they would never hear the end of this from his sisters. Libby, though she had entered into the spirit of the rebellion with Sue and Hannah, so far did not equal their enthusiasm for the handsome Duke.

Someone brought horses, and Monmouth and Lord Grey mounted. The children formed up their procession again behind, lifting up their colours proudly, and each escorted by a soldier. Then, following the rebel leaders, they made their way back through the jubilant crowd towards the High Street and Paul's Field where the rest of Monmouth's forces were encamped. Presumably, the precious fruits of all those frenzied hours of needlework would be handed over ceremonially to the various companies and troops of the rebel army.

Most of the crowd followed their Duke and the schoolgirls, shouting hurrahs and flinging their hats in the air. There was nothing more to see, but Bram lingered at the window, looking for some means of escape. The Loveridge house was tall and narrow, like the others around it, with a single gable in which his window was placed. In the trough between their own gable and the next, a gutter ran, and rainwater fell from that into a pipe fixed to the wall. He was fit and agile, he had often climbed trees and on rooftops during his schooldays: if the downpipe was close enough, it would be possible to descend it.

He measured it with his eye, and tried an experimental stretch, but however hard he tried, the pipe remained tantalisingly out of reach. And there was a potentially lethal drop to the stones of the marketplace below.

He was prepared to take risks, but he was not foolhardy. It would do the rebel cause no good at all to have one of its intending adherents maimed or dead in such a futile manner. He would have to think of something else. Frowning, deep in thought, Bram went back to the bed, and gave himself up to the problem.

'Bram! Bram!'

He must have fallen asleep, for the sun no longer shone in through the south-facing window, although it was many hours yet from setting. He sat up with a jerk, wondering what was happening. The voice called again, and he realised that it was Sue, just the other side of the door.

At once fully awake, he scrambled off the bed and ran across. 'Sue! What is it?'

'Were you asleep?' she asked, in tones of disbelief. 'I'd have thought that you'd have found a way out by now.'

'Your faith in me is touching, but I'm not some hero out of a romance,' Bram told her drily. 'For a start, I'm unable to fly.'

Sue giggled. 'Can't you? That's odd, I was convinced that you could.'

'Don't be silly. What do you want?'

'Well, I was going to tell you about Monmouth's camp, and what he said to me when I presented the colour, and all the other wonderful things that have happened to us today while you've been languishing in idleness in your chamber,' Sue said infuriatingly. 'But as you obviously don't want to know about that, or where Father's put the key, then I won't tell you.'

'I wasn't very interested anyway, I saw it all from . . . Where Father's put the key? Do you *know*?'

'Of course I know. He's hidden it inside the spinet, he didn't know I'd seen him,' Sue said triumphantly. 'Do you want me to fetch it? He's down in the shop at the moment, and Hannah and Libby are in our chamber, and Mother is in the kitchen talking to Nan about supper, so I could get it now if I'm quick, and let you out and put it back and they'd think you *could* fly!'

'Well, don't waste any more words,' Bram said, his jaw clenched with sudden impatience. 'Go and get it!'

He heard Sue's hasty heels clattering down the stairs. His handsome tawny satin was now sadly crumpled by his hours on the bed, but there was no time to change.

For agonising moments he waited, pressed against the door, for the sounds of Sue's return, praying that the parlour would still be unoccupied, that no one would see her lift the lid of the spinet, that the key was still there . . .

She was coming. The smart rap-rap of shoes on the stair was unmistakable, and the harsh metallic grating of the key in the lock was all the answer he needed. She muttered something, and he distinguished a word he had not thought that she knew. There followed the sounds of a wrestling match with recalcitrant iron, and then the latch lifted and the

228

door swung open on her triumphant face. 'It was so stiff that I didn't think I could turn it,' said his sister jubilantly. 'But I managed it in the end.'

'You're wonderful,' Bram said, and gave her a grateful, delighted hug. 'And you have my heartfelt thanks. Is Father still in the shop?'

'Yes, and busy with a customer.'

'Even better. Right, if I lock this again, can you put the key back so that he won't know it's been touched? The longer it takes for anyone to notice that I'm gone, the better.'

'Of course,' Sue told him, her eyes shining. She watched as he locked the door again – she was quite right, it was so stiff from disuse that he wondered how she had mustered the strength to turn the key – and then reached forward and gave him a swift, sisterly kiss. 'Hurry, or he'll find you've gone – and good luck, and Godspeed!'

Together they ran down the two flights of steep wooden stairs to the parlour. At the door, he saw her slip inside, the heavy rusty key in her hand, and waved his thanks.

Only one more obstacle to freedom. He looked down to the hallway, empty and bare. The street door was open, but that which led to his father's shop lay firmly closed.

Well, it was now, or never. Bram took a deep breath and descended the stairs, trying to tread lightly so that it would sound like Sue, or Hannah. The door on his right did not open. With sudden joy, he took four huge strides to carry him to the street, and the warm June air, and freedom. Then, knowing that it was too late now to be stopped, he began to run across the marketplace, aiming, as his sisters and the other girls had done that morning, for Monmouth's camp in Paul's Field.

# 13

## 'Arms for public liberty'

The day after Mary Mead had so pointedly presented the Duke of Monmouth with her colour bearing a crown and the letters 'JR' worked in gold, the rebel leader bowed to the forceful arguments of his advisers. Although the people of Dorset and Somerset had come in gratifying numbers to join his army, there were almost no gentry among them. Some of them, well-known Dissenters or republicans, had been hauled into custody as soon as rumours of invasion had reached the King's ears, but there were many, many squires and baronets who had welcomed him on his triumphant progress through the West Country five years ago, and who were now conspicuous by their absence. Only with the support of those with wealth and prestige could he hope to succeed without a bitter struggle. His lieutenants pointed out that his declaration, drafted by a renegade clergyman called Ferguson, might have been construed as too republican in sentiment, harking back to the days of Cromwell and the Commonwealth, and thus hardly likely to encourage the local gentry to flock to his standard. But if he proclaimed himself King, then surely men of quality would be persuaded that it was worth risking life, land or liberty to join him.

Accordingly, on the 20th June, the people of Taunton gathered once more in the marketplace, crowded with stalls and hucksters and all the appurtenances of market day, to hear 'The most illustrious and high-born Prince, James, Duke of Monmouth, son and heir-apparent of King Charles the Second', declared 'lawful and rightful sovereign and King, by the name of James the Second'. And among the onlookers were Jonah Loveridge, his wife, niece and daughters, trying to pretend that Bram's enlistment in the rebel army was something that the whole family had supported and encouraged from the start.

It had been a terrible blow for Jonah, the discovery that his son had escaped. Ignorant of Sue's part in the affair, he assumed that the boy had somehow climbed out of the window and negotiated the drainpipe. This terrible risk that Bram had taken, even before joining the rebels, made his blood run chill, and he now bitterly regretted his misguided attempt at imprisonment. Sue, determined not to tell anyone, not even her sister, of her part in the escape, did not enlighten him. At present, she had very little sympathy for her father, even though he showed gratifying signs of remorse. He had accepted the situation, though, despite his anguish, and did not, to his family's great relief, announce any intention of descending on the rebel camp to persuade Bram to change his mind. He knew his son well enough to be certain that he could not be deflected, once set on his course.

And so he put a brave face on what had happened, and tried to look appropriately proud when his friends and neighbours congratulated him on his son's commendable zeal for the cause. Then he smiled and applauded King Monmouth's second proclamation as if it did not confirm his terrible fear, deep and unspoken in his heart, that this rebellion was doomed to ignominious and tragic failure, and that when the army left Taunton, all brave and bright under the colours that the schoolgirls had sewn for them, he would never see his beloved only son again.

The next day, Monmouth marched out of the town towards Bridgwater, amidst the cheers, blown kisses and rose petals that had attended his entry along East Street three days earlier. He should have had every reason for joy, for the army that tramped haphazardly but enthusiastically behind him was now some six thousand strong, and he had high hopes of adding to their number at Bridgwater, Glastonbury, and all the other towns in northern Somerset on his way to take Bristol, another place where he could rely on much fervent support. And yet, it was noticed by some of the more observant that he seemed thoughtful, dejected even, as if he felt in his heart that this triumphant leave-taking would prove to be the highest point of the rebellion.

Bram, marching in the Blue Regiment, composed entirely of Taunton men to the number of six hundred or more, did not notice. He wore his stout old suit of blue serge, the famous local colour and weave, that his mother and sisters had brought to the camp at his request, it being very much more appropriate for campaigning than the tawny satin, however splendid. As the son of a respected and wealthy shopkeeper, and related to one of Somerset's more notable gentry families, he had been honoured, to his surprise and delight, with a commission as ensign, and one of the colours presented by the girls of Mistress Musgrave's school, somewhat indifferently stitched and rather uneven round the edges, waved gently from the pole he carried. Ensign Loveridge sounded very well, and Bram stepped out proudly in the sunshine, a joyous and hopeful smile on his face, at one with his comrades, and a great sense of glory, of fate and destiny, filling his heart. Monmouth and his army would save England from the depredations of a Papist tyrant, and he was fortunate indeed to be one of their number.

Once more, armies were marching across Somerset: once more, war had come to this serene, fertile, abundant country. And as Monmouth left Taunton, early on that Sunday morning, the second-in-command of the King's forces was only a dozen miles to his rear in Chard, in command of several troops of dragoons and horse guards, a regiment of foot under Colonel Kirke, and the remnants of the militia, those who had not fled back to their homes, or joined the rebels.

Chard itself, having welcomed Monmouth's men only a few days previously, lay sullenly docile under the occupation of the King's troops, and many of the more sensitive officers were conscious of a distinct itch between their shoulderblades. They were enemy invaders in a hostile land, and supplies, assistance and accommodation were given most reluctantly by the country people.

Several officers of the horse guards were quartered in the comfortable, if cramped, manor house belonging to Master Nicholas Hellier, and were greeted with courtesy by its owner, his wife, who had only just returned from a journey visiting relatives, and their son. It was obvious that this family were far from being rebels, or even sympathising with them, but the officers were nonetheless aware that they were quartered only on sufferance. They were not to know that, for Mistress Hellier, this uneasy situation brought back terrible memories, with a clarity unobscured by forty intervening years, of the time when Wintercombe had been occupied by brutal Cavalier soldiers bringing fear, destruction and murder to a small and peaceful community. Silence knew, rationally, that half a dozen civilised and well-behaved officers of breeding were hardly to be compared with the villainous Ridgeley and his crew, but she could not help loathing their presence in her pleasant house.

Nor was there any remedy for her other worry. Monmouth was in Taunton, and so, of course, was her beloved Tabby and her children. Knowing the Loveridges so well as she did, Silence was well aware that they would support the rebels. Indeed, she suspected that for years Jonah, in his quiet, discreet way, had been assisting those who were opposed to the government. And, if she examined the evidence too closely, she knew also that her nephew Alex would not be so innocent, either. The news of Monmouth's invasion had, by the look of it, come as no surprise to him: had the Dutch servant who had brought Lukas to England brought information as well?

Such speculation could only result in anxiety and unease, and she tried to avoid thinking about such things. She could not send to Taunton for word of her daughter and her grandchildren, not while officers of the Royal army were under her roof, but she feared for them, and above all for Bram, idealistic, impulsive, and as adamant as his mother for right and justice. Perhaps he had, after all, inherited some of his father's caution and circumspection, but she knew, with a sick sense of doom, that she was only clutching at straws.

There was a skirmish between a troop of the horse guards, led by one of the young officers quartered with them, Lieutenant Monoux, and a band of rebel cavalry, at Ashill, only a few miles away towards Taunton. Several of Monmouth's men were killed, as well as the young lieutenant, shot in the head. His body was brought back to Chard and buried in the church on Midsummer Day. He was the first casualty of the rebellion whom the Helliers had known personally, a smiling, cheerful, capable young man, who had talked at supper, the night before his death, of the girl he hoped to marry. How many more, Silence wondered despairingly, would be slain on both sides before this apparently futile and ridiculous rebellion was brought, one way or another, to an end?

Nick held her close at night as she whispered to him the fears that she would never, ever dream of revealing to another living soul. And because he, alone of the people at Chard, remembered the nightmare of forty years ago, he understood the depths of her anguish as she saw war return to Somerset, and her grandchildren, this time, at risk.

That Sunday, Midsummer Day, was hot and loweringly oppressive: it was plain that the fine, dry weather that had lit the country with sunshine for weeks, would soon break. The news came from Taunton that Monmouth had marched out that morning, and Lieutenant-General Churchill, still considerably outnumbered by the rebel army, gathered his forces together and left Chard in distant, cautious pursuit.

They were free, and at once Richard Hellier took horse and rode over to Taunton, late in the afternoon, to obtain news of his half-sister's family. He listened to the excited gabble of Sue and Hannah, Tabby's bleak acceptance, Libby's hero-worshipping pride and, unspoken but quite evident, Jonah's anguished despair. He stayed the night, and the next morning, under a glaring blue-grey sky like molten steel, he rode back to his parents to report.

It confirmed Silence's worst, most dreadful fears. Bram was with the rebel army, and his sisters and cousin had taken part in some charming but treasonous procession that would, if the rebellion ended in failure, doubtless be recalled to their detriment. She said, trying to conceal her distress, 'How is Tabby? Is she very upset by what has happened?'

Richard, despite his own misgivings, said drily, 'Tabby? I think in her

233

heart that she feels that Bram was right to join the rebels, if their cause is one in which he believes, but of course she'd never say that openly – especially since poor Jonah is so obviously devastated by his going. And the girls, of course, knowing no better, think he is a hero.' He smiled unhappily at his mother. 'There is nothing we can do, except wait for news, and hope and pray for him.'

Outside, the sky had grown suddenly and menacingly dark. A distant, ominous growl of thunder followed his words, as if in comment, and Silence unobtrusively took hold of her husband's hand. Something cracked once against the west-facing window of her parlour, like a pebble: she glanced round, eerily afraid, and saw the first rain for weeks, the drops as hard and heavy as stone, begin to batter her beloved garden.

Monmouth's brave army, that had left Taunton in high hopes and sunlight, would find their march towards Bristol very much more arduous now.

In torrential rain, their spirits dampened despite themselves by the sudden and virulent deterioration in the weather, the rebel soldiers left Bridgwater, where they had been given a tumultuous welcome and had gained many more recruits – so many, in fact, that there were not enough conventional arms to equip them, and five hundred men wielded an ingenious and deadly weapon, a scythe blade firmly fixed to an eight-foot pole. Others, less fortunate, bore clubs, axes and other implements, humble, but still capable of doing much damage to human flesh and bone.

Through mud and puddles they trudged doggedly along the long low ridge of the Polden Hills, clear of the soggy green marshland below, towards Glastonbury. Here, soaked and exhausted after a march of some fifteen miles in appalling conditions, the rebels set up camp in the largest open space available, amongst the ruins of the great abbey that had once been the splendour and marvel of the West Country. The local people, sympathetic, brought food and firewood, and huge bonfires blazed in the dusk amongst the tall stone pillars and empty arches of the abbey church.

Bram, however, was not there to witness this strange and eerie sight. He had made sure that the men under his command, if that was the right word, were fed and settled steaming around the fire, and then went in search of Colonel Bovett, the commanding officer of the Blue Regiment.

The Colonel was at the George, Glastonbury's chief inn. Bram knew him, for, like most men of standing and education who lived in Taunton, he was a regular visitor to Jonah's bookshop, and his daughter, Catherine, attended the same school as Sue and Hannah Loveridge. He greeted Bram with a rather preoccupied smile, which quickly turned to genuine

234

interest as his ensign explained his purpose in seeking him out. He listened with approval, nodding and asking occasional questions, and clapped Bram on the shoulder when he had finished. 'Well done, young Loveridge. We're still desperate for horses, and although I'm told that forty men rode in an hour ago, their mounts were pretty indifferent, apparently. Can you ride? Yes, of course you can, you've delivered books to my house at Bishop's Hall often enough. Well, if you can obtain half a dozen or more horses of some quality from your cousin, save one for yourself and join Captain Hucker's troop. Better than wearing out your shoe-leather, eh?'

'Yes, indeed, sir – thank you,' Bram said, with delight. A thought struck him, and he added, 'But I have no riding boots, Colonel, nor any pistols.'

'Perhaps we can provide you with the weapons,' said Bovett. He was a big, upright man, about the same age as Bram's parents, who had been a Colonel of Militia during the Commonwealth, and wore now a stout buff coat, rather worn and lovingly cared for, that he had probably owned during the heady days of Cromwell. 'But I don't doubt that your cousin – Wickham, did you say? – will be happy to provide you with a pair of boots. Now, we must rouse Captain Hucker, and he'll give you some men for an escort.'

'One last thing, sir,' Bram said diffidently. This was a difficult request to make, and would probably be denied: already he was aware, like most of his comrades, of the drastic shortage of coin and equipment in the rebel army. As Bovett looked at him enquiringly, he added, 'I would not wish these horses simply to be taken, without any form of redress. My cousin breeds them for his livelihood, not as a pastime, and he won't be very happy if we do not give him at least some payment for them.'

'Then he is not sympathetic to our cause?' Bovett said sharply.

Bram shook his head. 'Oh, he favours Dissent, sir, I know that for a fact. But he is not really interested in affairs of state, his horses are his whole life. And frankly,' he added, with a rather guilty smile, 'I would feel myself to blame if we took all his best horses at my suggestion.'

'And you don't wish to antagonise your cousin? I can well understand that,' said Bovett, to Bram's secret relief. 'I'm sure we can find some coin, or at the very least the Duke, I mean King, can sign a promissory note, for payment after our victory. I can't say fairer than that, can I?'

Bram, agreeing wholeheartedly, thanked him profusely, and within half an hour, as the sun was setting, found himself on a borrowed horse, an ill-behaved nag with feathery plebeian heels, in the company of five troopers, all Taunton men, and Captain Hucker, in whose house Monmouth had stayed while in the town. Like Colonel Bovett, he knew

235

Bram well, and was full of praise for his suggestion. This was heartening, for Bram himself was beginning, now that they were actually on their way to Longleaze, to have considerable doubts. What would his Cousin Jan say when this band of rebel soldiers arrived on his doorstep and demanded a tithe of his best horses? And, much more to the point, what of Aunt Rachael's reaction?

Well, he would know soon enough. The lights of Longleaze flickered through the trees ahead, the outline of the house long, dark and gabled in the diminishing dusk. Bram brought his horse up level with Captain Hucker's, and said quietly, 'Sir – perhaps it would be most tactful if I were to speak with my cousin first.'

'Break the news gently, you mean?' said Hucker, who was a thin cynical stick of a man, surprising amongst all the fervent Dissenters who made up the bulk of Monmouth's army. 'Well, I've no objection – so long as you remember, lad, that none of us will be best pleased if we've come out here on a fool's errand when we could have been snug round a fire with hot food in our bellies.'

'I'll remember,' Bram said. It was still raining fitfully, and cold water was dripping off his hat and trickling uncomfortably down the back of his neck. They rode through the gate and up to the porch, and as their horses, tired from the day's march and as empty-bellied as their riders, came to a grateful halt, he saw the door open, and the gaunt, unwelcoming and suspicious figure of his Aunt Rachael stood unmistakably outlined by the light behind her.

With a feeling of dread that, he suspected, no enemy armies would have the power to instil in him, Bram dismounted, throwing his reins to a trooper, and went to meet the woman of whom he and his sisters had always gone in awe.

'What's this? What do you want?' His aunt's voice cut like a whip. She was dressed in the black she had worn ever since her husband's death, ten or eleven years previously, and the two engraved lines between the fierce grey brows were even deeper and more threatening than usual. Behind her, he saw the big, amiable figure of Jan, a chicken leg held in his hand, and his wife Bathsheba, nervously peering round his shoulder. Anxious not to give them any more cause for alarm, he called out, 'Don't worry, Aunt – it's me, Bram!'

'Abraham? Abraham Loveridge?' said Aunt Rachael, rather as if he had announced that his name was Lucifer, son of Beelzebub. 'What are you doing here? Who are these men? Are they rebels?'

He was close to her now, his hat doffed, and what he hoped was a charmingly apologetic smile adorning his face. 'I'll explain everything,

Aunt Rachael, but perhaps I'd better come inside for a moment, rather than talking on the doorstep.'

She stared at him with hostile, suspicious blue eyes. Then she said brusquely, 'Very well, if you must,' and held the door wide.

It was not the most auspicious of welcomes. Feeling like an invader and a traitor, he sent a hopeful glance over his shoulder to Hucker, still sitting on his horse, with an expression on his face that Bram could interpret only too readily. The number of horses that the army could obtain would, as everyone knew, be vital to the success of their cause. Hucker had a bag full of coin at his saddlebow: some local gentleman, cautious with his tenants and his horses and weapons, had been a little more generous with his money. Monmouth, moreover, had expressly forbidden the stealing of horses by his overenthusiastic supporters, for he wished to keep the undoubted good will of the local people. But even so, Bram suspected that Hucker, given the chance, was quite capable of defying his commander and stripping the Longleaze stables and paddocks bare, giving no redress.

It was some while since he had last stood here in the low, panelled dining parlour, with its huge stone fireplace, burning on this cold rainy June night, and candle sconces lighting the walls. A shelf displayed pieces of decorative slip-ware, fine pewter, and a handsome silver vessel that had been part of Rachael's dowry from Wintercombe, long ago. He looked at his aunt's severe face, aware of his rain-sodden clothes, his shoes, hardly suitable for riding, and the green favour, badge of Monmouth, decorating his hat. Jan appeared mildly puzzled, with Bathsheba clutching his arm, while Ben stood by the table loaded with the half-eaten remains of their interrupted supper.

'I'm sorry to intrude like this,' Bram said awkwardly, all his customary assurance and banter disappeared like smoke. 'Very sorry I –'

'Are you with the rebels?' Rachael asked baldly.

No use at all trying to break it gently. Bram nodded, smiling apologetically. 'Yes, Aunt Rachael, I'm afraid I am.'

'Afraid?' she snapped, and suddenly, so abruptly that he was taken aback, her hard face cracked into an answering smile. 'There's no reason to be afraid, Nephew. The best thing you've ever done, I'd say, joining the Protestant Duke. With a Papist on the throne, we'll never know rest.'

Rachael, of course, was a practising Dissenter, who alone of all her family attended conventicles and prayer meetings in defiance of the law, and had not set foot inside her parish church for years. Even Jonah, whose family were Baptists, was not so fanatical, but had always compromised when circumstances were against him. For Rachael Wickham, there would never be any compromise, but she had not yet managed to persuade any of her family to follow her determined path. Jan was only really interested in horses, and Bathsheba, even though she went in awe of her mother-in-law, dutifully followed her husband's lead, and accompanied him to worship at the church of St John in Glastonbury. And Ben, of course, understood only the simplest matters of religion, and his faith was childlike and uncomplicated.

Bram realised that he should have foreseen, knowing all this, that in fact Rachael would be his ally. He smiled gratefully back at her. 'I'm glad you think so, Aunt. But I have not come here to exchange pleasantries, much though I'd like to stay and talk. I've come on an errand.'

'Oh?' said Jan, and in his broad, fair-skinned face there was, suddenly, a glimmer of apprehension. 'Why are you here, Bram?'

'The army is very short of horses,' he said. 'When we reached Glastonbury, I thought of you at once. Have you any spare that we could take back with us? We'll pay good money for them,' he added hastily, seeing Jan's horrified expression.

'Even if you had not the means, we would give them gladly, for the cause,' said Rachael, with a quelling look at her eldest son. 'Would we not, John?'

'Er . . . if you say so, Mother,' Jan said unhappily. He looked at Bram, his eyes anxious. 'You haven't come at a very good time. Most of the colts that might have been suitable for your needs have been sold on – the paddocks are full of mares with young foals at foot, and I *cannot* let you take them, for the foals would sicken or die. But we do have seven horses in the stables that I was intending to school and sell on this autumn, and those you may have. Is that sufficient?'

He looked so worried that Bram was quick to reassure him. 'Of course it is, Cousin – more than we'd hoped for. Are you sure you can afford to let us have them?'

'If you'll give me their value, yes,' said Jan, with a rather wary smile.

Bram gave him his most wholehearted one in return. 'Captain Hucker outside has the money. It may not be enough, but I promise on my own account that you won't lose on this transaction. After all, coming to you for horses was my idea, so I feel responsible.'

It was plain that Jan was still very reluctant, but his mother's adamant approval of the idea seemed to persuade him. A lantern was found and lit, and Bram walked with his cousin and Captain Hucker to the stables.

Ben followed them, his eyes shining. He had already questioned Bathsheba in an excited, barely intelligible gabble, but her reply had been clear enough. 'Yes, Cousin Bram's a soldier now – a soldier in the Duke of Monmouth's army.' And the boy's crowing sound of excitement and envy

238

had, strangely, affected Bram more than his sisters' enthusiasm, days ago in Taunton. Like all the family, he was very fond of Ben, and respected his judgement as one might that of a favoured and intelligent hound. The simpleton's obvious hero-worship was no embarrassment, despite Hucker's raised eyebrows at the sight.

The seven horses, all geldings, young and saddlebroken but rather skittish, were led out by Ben and a clutch of surprised stable boys. Hucker professed himself well pleased, and at Bram's gentle reminder, untied the bag of coin with a flourish that did not disguise the fact that he had obviously hoped to get away with paying nothing. 'My heartfelt thanks, Master Wickham. I'll give you five guineas apiece for them– less than they're worth, I know, but I'm sure you will not grudge this small donation to our cause.'

Jan's face was a picture. Bram dug him gently in the ribs, and gave him what he hoped was a reassuring smile. He did not know much about the trade in horses, but was well aware that thirty-five guineas for seven animals of promise was a derisory sum. The best amongst them, schooled and suitable for a gentleman's saddle horse, might fetch that amount on its own.

Despite his amiable appearance, Jan was capable of driving a very hard bargain, but in this awkward situation, between the implicit threat of these armed men on the one hand, and Bram's urgent eagerness on the other, he could do very little. With a rather forced smile, he nodded reluctantly. 'Very well, sir. As you say, it's less than they're worth, but for the cause . . .'

'Good man. Your cousin knew that we could rely on your help,' said Hucker cheerfully. 'And while you're being so generous, you must have noticed that the lad hasn't any boots to his name – have you a spare pair he could use?'

Jan, the bag of coin weighing down his hand, still looked somewhat bewildered. 'Yes – I should think we have. Come with me, Bram, and Bathsheba will find you something.' He gave orders to the little knot of stable lads standing with the horses, and then, his hand companionably on his cousin's shoulder, guided him back to the house.

'I'm sorry,' Bram said, as soon as they were within doors. 'He told me he'd give you a fair price for them, and I was fool enough to believe him. How much are they really worth?'

'If I'd kept them until the autumn, anything up to twenty or thirty pounds apiece,' Jan told him. 'But of course there's their keep, four months of it, and the efforts expended in schooling them, so it's not as bad as it seems. I'll send down on to the Levels for some more – if your

239

Protestant Duke hasn't stripped all the farms in Somerset bare of horses, that is.'

'Not yet,' Bram said, wondering how he could find the money to reimburse his cousin. 'But cavalry is our biggest problem – our horses are too few, and those we do have are completely untrained for war – they turn and run at the first shots. We need more time, time to be able to stop and train them, and the foot as well – but the tale runs that Churchill and the regulars and the militia are on our heels, so we can't afford to stop. Not until we reach Bristol, anyway.'

Jan studied him thoughtfully. A big man, with warm eyes and mouse-brown hair, he did not in the least resemble his mother. He said quietly, 'How did your father take it when you joined the rebels?'

'He accepted it,' said Bram. The imprisonment in his chamber still rankled, but it was not a subject for family gossip and comment. 'He was not happy, but he knows that I am of an age to make my own decisions.'

'Well, you're – what? Twenty-one? I keep forgetting,' Jan said. 'Time passes so quickly. Still, I suppose we'd best find you some boots, and send you on your way. Bathsheba? Sheba, where are you?'

It took some time to unearth a suitable pair of riding boots. Bram's feet were not as big as Jan's, and the only ones that could be found to fit him belonged to Sam, the black sheep of the Wickham family, who had run away to sea eight years previously, and had last been heard of as the mate of a merchantman plying between Bristol and the West Indies. They had been kept dry and oiled, but were still so stiff and unyielding that they stood upright on their own like logs. By the time we get to Bristol, Bram thought, though without much hope, perhaps they'll have softened a little with wear. Riding in them would be uncomfortable enough, and when he put them on, he clumped round the kitchen like a carthorse, while Jan grinned and even quiet Bathsheba giggled.

He had lingered long enough, loath as he was, suddenly, to leave this familiar, welcoming place, so full of memories, and venture back into the alien military world into which he had so impulsively plunged himself. He thanked Jan profusely, kissed Bathsheba and his aunt, and took his reluctant leave. Behind him, candlelight and warmth and the savoury aroma of roasted chicken: in front, the cold wet night, and a damp bed, and a supper that was as uncertain as his future.

The soldiers were ready, each with a led horse, and Hucker waved at him impatiently. 'Come on, lad – what were you doing, making them?'

'I'm sorry, sir – a suitable pair was not very easy to find,' said Bram. He came up to his horse and found that Ben was holding its reins, a lantern in the other hand. 'Thank you,' he said to his cousin, and the boy's face creased into a huge grin. 'Bram? Take Ben – take Ben with you.'

His tongue had always been too big for his mouth, and it was hard to discern what he said. But the gist was clear enough, and Bram stared at him, dismayed. 'Oh, Ben, you can't! I'm a soldier now, and it's no place for you.'

'Soldier,' said Ben, pronouncing the word carefully and with pride. 'Bram's a soldier. Ben wants to be a soldier too.'

'Well, you can't,' Bram told him firmly. 'It's quite impossible, Ben – you really can't come too – this isn't a *game*, Ben, it's real, it's *war*, and people get hurt or even killed in war. What would your mother say if something happened to you?'

He had expected petulance, anger, sulks. But Ben just stood there at his nag's head, the reins slack in his big blunt fingers, and his face crumpled like a child's. 'P-please,' he muttered, staring at the ground.

Bram hastily hardened his heart. He pushed one of the big clumsy boots into the stirrup, and swung up on to the horse's back. 'No, Ben,' he said again. 'No, no, and no. You stay here with Jan and the horses – you're needed here at Longleaze.'

He felt like a traitor as he rode with the others into the night, leaving his cousin sobbing like a baby in the middle of the stable yard. Ben had fixed upon the imagined glory and excitement of being a soldier, but a rebel army was no place for a simpleton, even one whose skill with horses amounted almost to the magical. If things went wrong, God forbid, the fact that Longleaze had supplied the rebels with horses would look bad enough, without Ben joining them as well.

But nothing would go wrong. They had men in plenty, and the country supported them. Once Monmouth took Bristol, success was quite possible, even likely. And Bram had done his small part, and provided his commander with seven much-needed horses. As a reward, he would be made a cornet, a post of greater prestige than ensign, part of the cavalry, the élite of any army, even one such as this.

His spirits high, he whistled all the way back to Glastonbury, and refused to be cast down, even at the prospect of an uncomfortable night in a makeshift straw bed inside one of the few parts of the abbey that still had a roof on it. Once, it had been the abbot's kitchen, and the huge fireplace was exceedingly welcome. He slept surprisingly well, woke a little stiff and sore, and ready, even eager, for the day's march.

His cheerful mood did not last long. It was still raining, a thin penetrating drizzle that insidiously soaked everything. Breakfast consisted of a huge hunk of dry bread and some old cheese with mould thick upon it, and a taste like the interior of his riding boot. And just as the men were ready to mount up and move on, a trooper he did not know came hurrying up. 'Be ee Bram Loveridge? Someone here d'want to see ee.'

And there behind him, a dogged, sheepish grin on his broad face, was Ben, sitting on a solid bay gelding that usually pulled carts at Longleaze.

Bram's heart plummeted. He said, with a forced, bright smile, 'Hullo, Ben. Have you got a message for me from Jan?'

No one could call Ben a graceful rider: his slouched posture strongly resembled a sack of meal. But he never fell off, and he could persuade the most recalcitrant beast to behave beautifully, with the manners of a high-bred Arabian. 'No message,' he said, grinning. 'Ben's coming with you.'

Bram had been afraid of this. Childlike, Ben was prey to intense obsessions that would fill his mind to the exclusion of all else. At the age of five or six, barely able to speak, apparently little more than an animal himself, he had become devoted to horses, even sleeping in the stables, riding, grooming, schooling them so that he became an expert before the age of twelve. But that was somehow natural, the attraction understandable: the horses loved Ben because, it seemed, they sensed that he was nearer to them than the other, supposedly more intelligent humans who handled them but lacked true insight. Sometimes, Bram had wondered fancifully if Ben thought that he was a horse himself.

But this desire to be a soldier, when he could have no idea at all of what it meant, what would be required of him, was impossible. The thought of gentle, loving Ben in charge of the implements of death was almost enough to make Bram weep. He would have to go back.

He tortured his fine-featured face into a hideous frown, and glowered at his simple cousin. 'No, Ben,' he said severely. 'No. Go home. Do you understand me? You *must* go home.'

'No,' Ben protested. 'No, *no*, Bram. Soldier now, with you.'

'You can't!' his cousin cried despairingly. They were ready to march, his men were giving him curious looks, gaggles of pretty Glastonbury girls had come to wish them Godspeed, despite the drizzle, and he was forced to stand here arguing with his simple-minded cousin, a situation as likely to bring success as persuading a rock to sprout wings. 'Ben, please. You can't stay, you can't come with us. We might have to kill people, Ben – *kill* them! You wouldn't like that, would you?'

For the first time, an expression of doubt appeared on the boy's face. He slowly shook his head.

'Then go home, Ben, please,' Bram begged him. The horse was beginning to move out, and people were cheering them. Out of the corner of his eye, he saw Captain Hucker urge his mount towards him. 'Go on, Ben – home!'

Stubbornly, his cousin shook his head. 'Not kill,' he said, and then added, as if he had just thought of it, 'Horses! Ben look after horses! Come with Bram!'

'What's this, Loveridge? Problems?' Hucker had come up, his lean face impatient. 'Hurry up, lad, we can't linger here all day. Who's this?'

'My cousin, Ben Wickham, sir. If you remember, we met him last night.'

'Oh? Has he come to persuade you to go home?' said Hucker.

'No, sir – he wants to join us.'

The captain's face cleared. 'Oh, is that all? Then why the delay? Anyone who can ride is welcome, half-wit or no.' He added to Ben, with a smile, 'Welcome to the army of King Monmouth, Ben Wickham. Keep him by you, is my advice,' he said to the horrified Bram, and turned his horse to shout at a ragged and dilatory knot of horsemen.

'Me a soldier? Ben a soldier?' The boy's face was all one huge smile, and the joy in it stabbed to Bram's heart. 'Ben stay with you – that man said so!'

One or two of the troopers, who had been curious onlookers, gave voice to cheerful words of approval. Ben, beaming, looked all round at them like a child receiving birthday greetings. It was too late, Bram realised, with a boulder of guilt and unhappiness weighting his heart: much too late to return him. He wished with all his heart that he had never thought of asking Jan for horses. If he had not, none of this would have happened, and Ben would be safe with his mother and brother on the farm where he had lived all his life.

'Mount up!' Hucker shouted, and he realised that there was nothing he could do to alter the situation. It would take too long to explain to Ben, and he knew that a month of persuasion would not be enough to make him change his mind. Nor could he take him home himself. Instead, he must find someone to take the message back to Longleaze, which was not on the line of march to Shepton Mallet.

From the cheerfully good-natured words which they were addressing to his cousin, much to Ben's delight, he could not have found anyone prepared to do anything so brutal and apparently unnecessary as to drag his cousin back to Longleaze. Ben had wanted to join the army, and here he was, admitted to their ranks, and his delight was hugely evident. Where, then, they would say with Hucker, was the problem?

The problem would come at the end of all this, at Longleaze, for Bram doubted very much that his aunt, fervently though she approved of the

243

rebel cause, would have wished her beloved, protected and simple-minded youngest son to join them. And he, Bram, would certainly get the blame for it.

But Ben, with that ridiculously happy smile, was a soldier now, a green favour already in his hat, and it was too late to do anything about it. With a resigned but heavy heart, Bram mounted, and led his cousin and his troopers out of the ruins of Glastonbury Abbey, to follow the rest of the army along the road to Shepton Mallet: and beyond that to Bristol, and the hope of victory.

# 14

## 'Rebellion may be thought a crime'

'You'll be able to ride soon, I reckon, Mistress Louise,' said Christian with satisfaction. 'Do it pain ee much, now?'

Louise sat on her bed, cautiously revolving her injured shoulder. Beside her lay a heap of linen bandages, with which she had been strapped so tightly that her left arm was quite immobile. It had been uncomfortable, to say the least, and the skin below the rough, scratchy linen had itched abominably, with no hope of remedy. She rubbed the red marks, delicately printed with the weave of the cloth, with heartfelt relief. 'No, Christian, it hurts hardly at all. Not even when I lift my arm – so.'

Her maid watched with a certain pride, as Louise's pale, blotched limb waved energetically above her head. 'Do ee take care, Mistress,' she said. 'Twouldn't do to undo all our good work.'

'No, indeed, it would not,' said Louise fervently. The thought of being able to dress without that stiff strapping, of being able to use her arm and to be rid of that terrible itching, and above all to be able to *ride* again – after nearly two weeks of inactivity, the prospect was wonderful. She lowered her arm, feeling the stiffness of the muscles, noting every tiny stretch and protesting ache. There were very few. Another two or three days, perhaps, and then she could once more sit a horse in safety. Freedom beckoned enticingly, but she would have to be careful. Everyone at Wintercombe – in particular Charles, Amy and Christian – had treated her these past weeks as if she were made of glass. At first such solicitous concern had annoyed her, but then she had regained her sense of humour, and turned it all into a joke. She knew, though, that they meant it, and that if she were seen to enter the stable yard before popular opinion considered her to be ready, she would instantly be surrounded by a dozen polite, caring people who would gently take her arm and lead her firmly back to the cocooned safety of the house.

'I'll leave the strapping off for today, and see how I fare,' she said to Christian, who was shaking out her blue mantua. 'It will be pleasant to be able to lift a fork again. It isn't until you're prevented from using one that you realise how convenient they are.'

'Yes, Mistress,' said Christian, who had never handled one of these

245

effete, newfangled implements until she arrived at Wintercombe and found, to her alarm, that even the servants were provided with them so that she had had perforce to learn their proper use. 'Shall I help ee dress?'

'Well, I can't appear in public like this,' Louise said, grinning. She wore only her chemise, pushed down round her waist, so that the bandages could be removed. With care, Christian helped her to slip her arms back into the bulky, ruffled sleeves. She had not, for obvious reasons, worn stays since her fall, and fortunately her figure, lean and slender, did not need their support. The silk mantua was arranged over the chemise, a stomacher in a similar fabric, heavily decorated with ribbons, pinned between the edges of the bodice, and a narrow dark blue belt encircled her waist. With deft, judicious hands, Christian arranged the folds of the mantua, tweaked at the chemise ruffles that showed above the sky-coloured silk, looped up the heavy, trailing overskirt, and finally pinned up her hair.

Louise looked at her reflection with considerable satisfaction. No longer was her arm bound to her side, like a casualty of battle, and the absence of stays was hardly noticeable under the stiff silk. For the first time in thirteen days, she felt like her usual, vibrant self again. With a lively spring in her step, she swept downstairs, her head high.

Lukas was the first to notice. As she entered the dining parlour, he leaped up and ran to her. 'Cousin Louise, you're not strapped up any more!'

'Nor I am,' she said, in mock surprise. 'How strange. I wonder why not. Oh, Lukas, you must be careful – don't hug me too tight!'

The weeks at Wintercombe, where he had been loved, taught, cared for and noticed, had wrought a considerable change in Alex's son. Gone was the wan, over-polite little puppet who had arrived from Holland too scared to step out of line. Now he laughed, he ran, he had even, once or twice, very daringly disobeyed his nurse. Alex, Phoebe and Louise he never disobeyed. There was colour in his cheeks, and he had grown and put on weight. Every morning, save for the Sabbath, he retired with Phoebe to the library for his lessons, and had made considerable progress. In the afternoons, when the weather was fine, he rode the brown and white pony, called Tubs, round the paddock under Louise's eye. Already he could trot and canter, although the pony was rather reluctant to exert itself, and he was daily gaining confidence in the saddle. Once Louise was able to ride again, she had promised him that they would go out together and explore the surrounding countryside.

The only cloud on Lukas's sunny blue horizon, though, was Alex. Since the news had come of Monmouth's invasion, he had hardly been seen at Wintercombe. Every day, he rose early and was away before anyone else was up, to Frome, or Bath, or Bristol, or closer to home, all apparently on estate business. Louise, her sphere of activity drastically curtailed, had barely exchanged a word with him for days. So much, she had thought wryly, for Grandmother's fears!

For Charles's sake, though, she was glad. Her cousin had enough to worry about, with the house in Bath shortly to become vacant. With a generosity that seemed lamentably unappreciated, Alex had left him a free hand to order and repair and refurbish as he wished, and Charles had frequently sought her advice on decoration, furnishings and other supposedly feminine matters. Louise was not very interested in such things, but did her best to suggest items that were fashionable and tasteful, without being too expensive. She suspected, though, that her opinions would not much matter in the end, since Bab was certain to submerge the whole house in a sea of carnation ribbon and silk.

Charles had seemed very anxious and preoccupied, and she worried about him. He was so much more vulnerable than Alex, and so painfully distressed by her accident. And it was just as well that Alex seemed to be so little at Wintercombe these days, for Charles was very fervently opposed to Monmouth's invasion, and she remembered Bram's words to her in Taunton. If Alex was as sympathetic to the rebel cause as his young cousin had implied, then any supper-table discussion of the progress of the invasion was bound to end in bitter words, if not worse.

But, so far, it had not happened. Their suppers were free of Alex, and correspondingly quiet, although Bab made several appearances at them. It pained Louise to see how she and her son treated Lukas so dismissively. He was no threat to them, after all: he was not the legitimate heir to Wintercombe, and the circumstances of his birth were hardly his fault. He had asked Phoebe once, in tones of bewilderment, why his Aunt Bab and his cousins did not seem to like him very much: and she, treading the knife edge between honesty and cruelty, had answered sadly that he was not to blame, that he had done nothing wrong, but that perhaps his aunt felt that he should not have come to Wintercombe.

'Oh,' was all Lukas said, frowning thoughtfully, and Phoebe leaned across to hug the nephew whom she had come to love very dearly. 'But your Aunt Bab doesn't rule this house, and besides, she and Charles and Amy are due to remove to Bath very shortly. Lukas, you have never been less than heartily welcome here – and I'm very glad that you came, and so is Louise, and of course your father.'

And Lukas had seemed to accept her explanation, although it was noticeable that in the presence of Charles, in particular, he reverted to the subdued unchildlike little boy who had first arrived at Wintercombe. But Amy, from sheer good nature, had obviously found it difficult to preserve her brother's air of cold disapproval, even after Alex's unkindness towards her. She had several times smiled at the boy, and even exchanged a few words with him, when Charles was not present.

It was an attitude that Louise found very hard to understand or excuse in her cousin. She had not thought Charles so petty or vindictive, but it seemed that the rift with Alex ran so deep that no amount of common sense or the conventions of decent behaviour could bridge it. She had asked Charles about his stand once, and he had rudely turned on his heel and walked away: almost as Alex might, she thought unhappily. And, like Alex, in the end the only person he hurt by this behaviour was himself.

Phoebe was also at breakfast, as ever the early riser, thoughtfully chewing bread and soused herring. She smiled at Louise. 'Almost back to normal. When will you ride again?'

'Oh, in a day or two, I expect,' Louise said casually. 'Is there any news this morning?'

For a fortnight, since Monmouth's landing, 'news' had consisted of only one topic. Wintercombe, lying in a quiet valley well away from large towns like Bath or Frome, nevertheless received information from a wide variety of sources. The St Barbes, with differing degrees of interest, had learned of the Protestant Duke's march to Taunton, heard wild reports of the vast numbers who had risen in his support, and reacted with interest or dismay, according to their sympathies, to the news that he was proceeding northwards towards Bristol, by way of Shepton Mallet and Pensford, some five miles from the city.

'The word, apparently, is that the rebels crossed Keynsham Bridge yesterday morning,' Phoebe said. She illustrated her words with a hasty disposition of breadcrumbs and cheese. 'This, here, is Bristol – and here's Keynsham, about halfway between Bath and Bristol. According to Alex, it's probable that Monmouth plans to attack Bristol from the north – he says it's less easy to defend it from that side.'

'Alex says? When have you spoken to him? I haven't seen him for days.'

'He was here until about ten minutes ago,' said Phoebe. 'Then he said something about riding to Frome this morning – but he did promise he'd be back for supper tonight, didn't he, Lukas, so you needn't look so downhearted. Have you finished your breakfast?'

'Yes, Aunt Phoebe.'

'Then you may go wait for me in the library, and until I come you can practise writing your name, until you have it perfectly – and I will be with you directly. Off you go.'

Lukas, with a quick grin at Louise which reminded her sharply of his father, left the room. When he had gone, Phoebe said quietly, 'I don't wish to talk too much in front of him – his wits are so sharp, and he listens to everything. Yes, Alex has been saying a great deal – fortunately, Lukas only heard a small part of it.' She grimaced. 'I've been here almost since dawn, talking. God knows where he gathers his information – though I have my suspicions.'

Phoebe was the one person at Wintercombe to whom Louise felt that she could speak freely. She swallowed her cheese, and said, 'Bram told me that Alex was in contact with the exiles in Holland – that he was a supporter of Monmouth.'

'Well, rumour has said such things for years, but he's always been very careful not to provide any evidence – my brother has the cunning of Lucifer, as I expect you've noticed,' Phoebe said drily. 'Believe me, if there *was* anything known against him for sure, he'd have been hauled off to prison weeks ago. This rebellion has been threatened in Somerset for some time, and all the known agitators and enemies of the government were taken into custody as a precaution. The Tower of London is full of them, apparently. But Alex was a major in one of the English regiments serving with the Dutch army, and he must have convinced the authorities long ago that they had nothing to fear from him – even if he was once a member of the Green Ribbon Club, and a friend of Shaftesbury. He did leave England very suddenly, three years ago, but that was supposed to be as a consequence of an entanglement with a married lady in possession of an inconveniently and violently jealous husband.' She smiled wryly. 'Knowing Alex, of course, I could well believe it – but there's no doubt that he was plotting very deep at one stage. Unlike most of his fellow-conspirators, however, he was much too clever to be caught.'

'But that was three or four years ago,' Louise said thoughtfully. 'Bram told me that he'd been supplying Jonah with all his seditious pamphlets that had been printed in Holland and smuggled in through Bristol, or Lyme.'

'It wouldn't surprise me in the least,' said Phoebe. 'Nothing would surprise me where my brother is concerned. If he arrived back from Frome this evening at the head of a hundred horse shouting "For Monmouth", I wouldn't turn a hair.'

'Is *that* what he's doing?'

Phoebe nibbled her bread with small, pale, rather pointed teeth that made her look disconcertingly fierce. 'I doubt it, actually. Alex has his inheritance, and an heir whom he loathes, and I can't really see him putting such a prize in jeopardy, especially when Charles is hovering expectantly, waiting to pick it up if he miscarries. Don't, by the way, say anything at all of this to Charles. Being a Papist, he has no love whatsoever for Monmouth or Dissenters. I don't think he realises the full extent of Alex's political involvement, now or in the past. And if he did know, I would not put it past him to use his knowledge against Alex.'

There was a small, shocked silence. Louise struggled with the implications of Phoebe's statement. It was very difficult to reconcile such a betrayal with the Charles she knew and liked, apparently upright and decent. She said, finally, 'Surely he wouldn't do such a terrible thing.'

'Wouldn't he?' Phoebe fixed her with an intense, sapphire-blue stare disconcertingly akin to her brother's. 'Think about him. I know he is not dishonest, nor is he vicious or evil. But nor is he a paragon of virtue, although when he compares himself with Alex, he must think that he is! If he suspected that Alex was giving any support to Monmouth, however small, he would consider it his duty to tell the authorities. And because over the past few months Alex has gone out of his way to taunt him, and made no secret of his contempt, I doubt very much whether Charles would have even the smallest twinge of conscience in denouncing him.' She smiled bleakly. 'And of course, the fact that he inherits Wintercombe if anything happens to Alex is another reason, although I suspect that Charles would rather die than admit it, even to himself.'

Louise thought of her two cousins, so very different, and so utterly at odds. Yes, it was difficult to think of Charles, usually so reserved and courteous and pleasant, betraying his own flesh and blood. But once Phoebe had put the dreadful possibility into words, she could understand that there was indeed a danger of it. And if Charles was tempted, she could also see that, to most men who opposed Monmouth's rebellion, he would only be doing his duty as an honest and loyal supporter of the King. The ties and obligations of kinship would not enter the bargain at all.

'Don't worry,' she said, chilled. 'I won't breathe a word.'

'Good,' said Phoebe. 'Disreputable and disgraceful though he is, he is still my brother, after all. And his care for Lukas has done much to redeem him, in my eyes at least. That child has blossomed since coming to Wintercombe.'

'Your doing as well,' Louise pointed out.

Phoebe shrugged. 'Perhaps – and yours. I would never, I must say, have believed that a child snatched away like that would not miss his mother, but he is completely happy without her. From what he has let slip, she seems to be a most unpleasant woman. I wonder whatever Alex saw in her?'

'I can guess,' Louise said drily.

Phoebe laughed. 'And if I'm honest, so can I.' She glanced shrewdly at her cousin. 'How sits that wind in your quarter?'

'Not at all,' Louise said. 'I won't deny I am sorely tempted. He is very attractive, despite his unlikable qualities. But don't worry, I'm as well aware of the dangers as you are – and besides, there has hardly been the opportunity lately.' She looked directly at Phoebe, who had pushed her plate away and was staring thoughtfully into space, her sharp chin propped on her linked hands. 'What do *you* think he's doing, to be gone so long every day?'

'It could be any one or more of a number of things,' her cousin said. 'He could have found a new and enticing mistress – very probable. That slut from the dairy, I notice, has recently been subject to the sulks. He could be gathering information – certainly, he seems to have a remarkably complete picture of what is happening in this rebellion. He could be buying horses, or selling land, or raising money, or just drinking himself into a stupor away from my beady eyes – he had certainly been drinking when he came home last night. But despite what I said earlier, I don't seriously think that he is organising open support for Monmouth. He has too much to lose.'

Louise had not missed the qualification. '*Open* support? Do you think he might be helping them secretly?'

'With Alex, nothing is certain,' Phoebe said. 'He could be. He could not be. I don't *know* – I only suspect. But pray God he is careful. I would not see him throw away all this for the sake of a futile little uprising that's doomed almost certainly to failure.'

'*Failure?* But I thought that half of Somerset was behind Monmouth!'

'So it is – but it's the wrong half. No gentleman to speak of has joined him. His army must number several thousands by now, but they're mostly small men, by all accounts, weavers and farmers and suchlike, no one of any consequence. Like Alex, the gentry of Somerset have too much to lose. I suspect they're all watching each other, waiting for the first one to move. It might only take one or two with courage, and the rest would follow. But so far, the one or two have not shown themselves. And few would wish to be associated with an army they probably consider to be a rabble, with a disgraced royal bastard at its head.'

'Put like that, it does sound very unlikely,' Louise said. She looked at the array of crumbs on the white linen tablecloth, representing the towns and cities of the West Country. 'So where are the rebels now? Still at – what was it called? Cansham?'

'Keynsham. They were there yesterday.' Phoebe crumbled a lump of cheese, and distributed the pieces. 'The King's commander, Feversham,

251

is in Bath, apparently, with a few horses. Lieutenant-General Churchill is following the rebel army, a few miles to their rear – say they're here, at Glastonbury. The Duke of Grafton is bringing several foot regiments from London, with the artillery train following slowly behind, and he's probably quite close to Bath now – say here, a few miles away, near Chippenham. So Monmouth can't very well linger too long where he is. He must take Bristol as soon as possible, or the King's men will fall on him, and all his advantage will be lost.'

'I hope he comes nowhere near Wintercombe,' Louise said. 'If he doesn't take Bristol, where will he go?'

'Anywhere,' Phoebe said, picking up the piece of bread that rather inadequately represented the handsome person of the late King Charles's favourite bastard. 'North, into Gloucester, and well away from us. Eastwards, towards Bath, and London – though he risks a pitched battle if he does, or south again, back into Somerset, which would undoubtedly be an admission of failure. But if Bristol is out of the question, then he will surely go wherever he has, or thinks he has, most support waiting to rise in his favour. And where that might be, well, I am not Monmouth, so I have no idea.'

Louise studied the makeshift little plan. She had been long enough in England – nearly a year now – to have a fairly accurate picture of the lands around Wintercombe, the positions of the larger towns, and the steep hills and valleys that folded the countryside. She had no knowledge of military strategy, but Monmouth's plight was obvious, even to her ignorant eyes. The King's forces were closing in, and he must run, or turn and fight.

She had thought that she cared nothing for either side: such things held no interest for her, unless they touched her directly. But rebellion, possibly even a battle, lay so close, no more than a dozen miles away, that she could not help but wonder what would happen. She said, 'How many are the rebels?'

Phoebe spread her hands. 'I don't know, and neither does Alex. Perhaps as many as seven or eight thousand, but of course they're not soldiers, and I don't think all of them are properly armed. But Monmouth has military experience, so they may well prove to be a formidable fighting force. If the two sides were to meet, who knows what the outcome might be?'

Who, indeed? Louise stared at the scattered, apparently meaningless crumbs in front of Phoebe, as if she were a buzzard wheeling above the land between Bath and Bristol, studying real armies, real people, with a bird's beady and dispassionate eye. But at least it did not seem very likely that any of the forces involved would come near Wintercombe. And her emotions were not engaged, anyway: she knew no one who marched with the rebel army.

'Good morning, Lou – good morning, Phoebe.'

It was Charles, stocky and fair, in the doorway. He bowed punctiliously, a courtesy that in the informal family intimacy of Wintercombe seemed rather superfluous, even pompous. Louise was thankful that Lukas was no longer in the room, and that she and Phoebe had just been discussing the rebel army in general, not Alex in particular. She smiled, and returned his greeting. Phoebe, with a quick significant glance at her, indicated the apparently random scatter of crumbs. 'We were debating the position of the rebels and the King's army, Charles. Have you anything to add? Monmouth was at Keynsham yesterday, apparently.'

'I can't imagine what Feversham thinks he's doing, letting them march up and down Somerset as they please,' Charles said, coming over to the table. He peered at Phoebe's makeshift map. 'Is that Bristol?'

'Yes, and Bath is here – this is Frome, and Shepton, and Wintercombe. Now do you see it clearly?'

'I think so,' her cousin said, frowning. 'And this piece of cheese is the rebel army, I take it?'

'Yes, and this is Lieutenant-General Churchill, and the Duke of Grafton here. I don't think you'll find that Monmouth will be allowed to progress freely for very much longer,' Phoebe told him.

'I fervently hope not,' was Charles's comment. 'I shall pray that the traitor and all his followers receive the penalty they so richly deserve. They have sacrificed the peace of the kingdom to their own selfish ends, and to my mind no punishment is too harsh.'

There was a brief, uneasy silence. Louise, remembering Bram on the subject, said mildly, 'Perhaps if those who are Dissenters could be sure that they would not suffer further persecution, they would not be so ready to take up arms against the King.'

Charles looked at her as if she had suddenly sprouted horns. 'Louise, there is no excuse, none whatsoever, for treason and open rebellion.'

It would have been more sensible if she had meekly agreed with him and kept her thoughts to herself. But something about the unshakable self-righteousness of that statement had raised her hackles. She looked up at him, and said provocatively, 'Oh, do you really? So all those poor Huguenots, persecuted in France, have no justification for resistance, even though their maidservants are dishonoured, their children taken away from them, and they are subject to daily abuse, injury, harassment and even death?'

Charles looked distinctly uncomfortable. 'That is in France. You know as well as I do that the Dissenters here in England do not suffer any such persecution.'

'I agree, they don't,' Louise said. 'Not at present. But they *fear* it.'

'They have no reason to,' said Charles indignantly. 'None at all. His Majesty has every intention, I am sure, of protecting the rights of all his subjects to worship as they choose, without persecution.'

'Then perhaps he would be well advised to make his thoughts on the matter absolutely clear,' Louise pointed out tartly. She did not like arguing with Charles, but his obvious intransigence had goaded her into taking the opposite side.

'Sit down and take some breakfast,' Phoebe said, indicating the chair next to her.

Charles shook his head. 'No, thank you, Cousin. I have just remembered something I must do. Pray excuse me.' And he went out with rather less than his usual courtesy, banging the door.

Louise made an expressively ugly face. '*Hélas!* I seem to have put him out of sorts.'

'Well, what did you expect?' Phoebe began to search about for her stick. 'Charles's chief fault is that he always knows that he's right. Damn, it's fallen on the floor.'

Louise bent down to pick it up for her. 'I know that I was unfair to him, but I couldn't help it. It was as if I wanted to be rude.'

Phoebe took the stick from her, and prepared to rise from her chair. She gave her cousin a shrewd glance, and observed drily, 'You have noticed that he is devoted to you?'

Unusually, Louise flushed. She glanced down at her plate, and then up at the other girl. 'Yes, of course I have. Poor Charles – he's never *said* anything, but there's no mistaking that look.'

'And doubtless,' Phoebe said, getting with difficulty to her feet, 'you have seen it frequently before.'

Louise gave her a dry glance. 'Yes, I'm afraid I have. But Charles . . . I know I was unkind just now, but that was unusual. It isn't easy to be the subject of feelings that I can't return. I . . . I have never given him the slightest encouragement, all I want from him is friendship, and yet he looks at me so imploringly sometimes, and I feel guilty because I can't give him any hope, nor do I value his feelings so lightly that I can just dash them to pieces with the truth. How can I tell him, without hurting him, that he will never be any more than a friend to me, and that his hopes are futile?'

'In the long run,' Phoebe observed, 'it may be kinder to tell him so, soon. Then he will no longer be prey to unrealistic expectations.'

'If I find the right moment, I will try,' Louise said thoughtfully. 'But nothing has been said, no declaration, and that makes it very difficult.'

'And meanwhile, you have to live under the same roof,' Phoebe pointed out. 'I am truly grateful that my defects make me safe from such dilemmas. Desirability, it seems, is a double-edged sword.' She smiled self-mockingly, and inclined her head. 'I will go and find Lukas – he should have covered several sheets of paper by now. Doubtless I will see you later. *Au revoir, ma chère Louise.*'

'*Au revoir,*' said her cousin, and watched as Phoebe made her halting, indomitable progress from the dining parlour.

It was true, of course. She ought to make it quite clear to Charles that his yearning adoration, never voiced, absolutely obvious to anyone with half an eye, was hopeless, and certain to remain so for all time. It was not his lack of money, nor prospects: she would marry for worldly reasons, certainly, but she wanted also a man who would be a friend and a lover, someone with whom she could laugh and enjoy herself. Charles, conventional, cautious and strait-laced, might be in love with her, but as a husband he would drive her mad with frustrated tedium inside a month. She suspected that her sophistication and self-assurance and her flavour of the exotic attracted him: and her wildness, that he would never tolerate in a wife.

Perhaps the quickest, easiest and most brutal way to shatter the scales over his eyes would be to tell him the truth about herself. But no one in England knew of it for certain, although her grandmother must suspect. And she feared his inevitable revulsion and hurt, and also the power over her that such knowledge would give him. She desired no more scandal.

It was raining again: even if she had wanted to risk her scarce-healed shoulder, this was emphatically not riding weather. She thought of Monmouth's army, somewhere near Bristol, doubtless miserable and dispirited in such a downpour, and of Alex, who, unlike poor prudish, loyal Charles, attracted her like a moth to a flame, and would singe her sorely if she let him.

The thought of his face, his hands, his kiss, made her blood sing and all her resolution falter. She put him with determination from her mind, and rose to go in search of some diversion, whether a book or conversation, to while away the dull morning.

The endless rain, that seemed to have fallen without ceasing ever since they left Bridgwater, had somewhat sapped the enthusiasm of Monmouth's motley band of soldiers. It seemed to the weavers of Taunton, as they tramped under a sky as lowering and depressed as their spirits, that this would never end, that they were doomed to march eternally around Somerset until their feet rotted, pursued at a distance by enemy forces that might choose any moment to launch a surprise attack.

They had made an early start from Pensford, and reached Keynsham later that morning, the day before Louise's conversation with Phoebe over the breakfast table. From there, so it was said now, up and down the ranks, an attack would be launched upon Bristol, second city in the kingdom, and, like Taunton, a hotbed of Dissent and rebellion. That information was enough to raise the army's hopes, and the line of tramping men buzzed with rumour as they straggled down the hill, under a weeping grey sky, to Keynsham in the Avon valley below.

Bram was very glad to be part of the cavalry now. The rain had turned the highways into quagmires, with ruts and puddles a foot deep and more, and the foot soldiers were plastered in mud to the waist. Their shoes, too, had often failed to withstand the long arduous marches, and many men were limping, their toes exposed between flapping, disintegrating pieces of sodden leather. He was, like them, cold and wet, but at least his feet, in his cousin Sam's old boots, were dry and protected from the elements, and even in those terrible conditions most of the mud had not reached him, his horse having taken the brunt of it.

There was singing as they entered Keynsham. A troop of rebel horse had driven off a band of militia the previous night, and had repaired the bridge over the Avon that would give Monmouth and his army access to Bristol's relatively undefended eastern and northern sides. Beside Bram, Ben began to whistle tunelessly, beating time with his hand on his saddlebow, a broad smile on his face. His evident glee was infectious: Hucker's troop took up the tune as they rode over the bridge and drew up in the meadow beyond in which the army would muster for the attack on Bristol. It was still an hour or more until noon, and they sat their wet, steaming horses expectantly, hoping that the heavy rain threatening in the western sky would hold off, at least until they were given the chance to fall on Bristol. Cheerfully, the men around Bram talked of the dry beds they would occupy tonight, and the welcome they would receive as they entered the city. If the godly citizens could be organised to rise at the right time, they might not even have to fight for it.

It was very easy to be swept away by their enthusiasm, and to join in the excessive hope all about him. But Bram could not believe that Bristol would fall so easily – it was much too important for that. There would be guns, militia, perhaps a detachment of the regular army. Surely, surely even the King, who had seemed very unprepared for his nephew's invasion, would not have left such a prize undefended?

They waited for what seemed like hours in the meadow, in a light, intermittent drizzle. The people of Keynsham brought bread and cheese, refusing payment, and, even more welcome, the landlord of one of the inns arrived with a small cart, laden with barrels of beer, which he and his tapsters decanted into leather jacks, to be passed around the tired troops. Monmouth had set up temporary headquarters at the abbey, home of Sir Thomas Bridges, who had fought for the King forty years previously, and there he and his council of war discussed the strategy for taking Bristol, while their men waited, bored and urgent for a decisive move, in the meadow beside the Avon.

Early in the afternoon, the menacing heavens finally opened, and torrential rain drenched the soldiers. Soaked, shivering and miserable, they huddled together under makeshift and inadequate covers made of blankets or coats thrown over their weapons. In this weather, the powder would be damp, and matchlock muskets useless. No one was really surprised when the order came to return to Keynsham for shelter, and the weavers and clothworkers of Taunton, used to working indoors and unaccustomed to prolonged rain, hurried gratefully back into the town, to find quarters where they could.

It took some hours to settle everyone. The horse, needing stables, occupied all the inns, of which Keynsham boasted several. Bram tended his weary animal, trying to rub down the worst of the mud, with indifferent success. Ben had already earned the respect of the men for his unrivalled knowledge of horses, and he spent all afternoon moving from stall to stall, soothing, advising, begging medicines and poultices from any likely source, and administering them to suffering mounts. His own horse at last made comfortable, with water and a full manger, Bram went in search of his cousin, and found him at the centre of a good-humoured huddle of troopers, explaining, in his thick, almost unintelligible speech, why purging pills compounded of tar, butter, liquorice, aniseed and garlic were an infallible remedy for all manner of ailments.

It was plain that the soldiers regarded him with a curious mixture of comradely friendship, condescension, and a certain amount of super-stitious awe, rather as if he were a small child with incongruously magical powers. Bram hovered on the outskirts of the group, smiling. Ben, wise and innocent at once, would always find friends, save amongst those who feared people thus afflicted in their wits. Already, the men of Hucker's troop seemed to have adopted him almost as a mascot, someone who would bring them good fortune. Since many lack-wits led a miserable life, persecuted and abused, Bram knew that his cousin was exceptionally lucky. Or perhaps his warm and sunny nature was responsible, for it was impossible to dislike him.

There was a sudden alarm outside, a great confused noise, and several shots, shatteringly close. The untrained troopers stood, staring in bewilderment, until Bram shouted, 'It's an attack! To horse!' And then the chaos was instant, men running for their mounts, flinging on saddles and bridles in frantic haste, while a soldier ran down between the stalls, his boots banging on the rough cobbled floor, bawling, 'Attack! Attack!'

Bram dragged his reluctant, startled horse out into the inn yard, jostling with others. It was still raining, though not so heavily as earlier, and the sky was dark. In this light, the scene was an inextricable confusion of shapes, all struggling to mount and ride out into the long main street of Keynsham. There was a great noise of drums and trumpets that terrified the horses, and Bram's chestnut flung up its head and banged him painfully on the nose, making his eyes water. And then he and a dozen others had burst into the street, to see more of their horse engaging furiously with several score of Royal troopers, distinguished by their back-and-breast armour and scarlet coats.

Bram was never sure, afterwards, of exactly what happened that evening, nor was anyone else in his troop more certain. There seemed to be two separate parties of the King's horse, for there was fighting along the length of the street, and utter confusion, the clash of swords, shots, the smell of powder and the screams and neighs of injured men and frightened horses. Any concerted action was impossible, and none of the rebels appeared to have any idea of what to do, save to charge at the enemy, shouting 'Monmouth!' and waving their swords. And their maddened, terrified mounts, wrenched abruptly from their warm quiet stables to face this nightmare, were almost beyond all control.

Bram thought that he might have slashed someone with his sword, but it was so dark, and happened so quickly, that he was not sure until afterwards, when he found blood dried like rust on the blade. It was almost impossible to keep his seat, and direct his frenzied mount, and fight, all at the same time, and using his pistol was quite out of the question, even if it had been loaded. There were bodies in the gutter, his horse trod on one and nearly unseated him, and he lunged at a man wearing the back-and-breast armour of the enemy, only to find that the man was one of his own: fortunately, his sword-thrust had missed by a foot or more.

And then it was over, as suddenly as it had begun, and the only evidence of the skirmish, apart from the drumming, retreating hooves of the Royal cavalry, was the debris scattered up and down the street, dead men, wounded men, loose horses, dropped weapons, discarded hats and helmets.

It was over, and he was still alive, and untouched. Bram drew a shuddering breath, and found that his hands were shaking. He sheathed his sword with some difficulty, and looked round for Ben.

There was no sign of his cousin, although he walked his nervous, wild-eyed horse up and down Keynsham's street four times, amongst the knots of bewildered soldiers and excited cavalrymen. Everywhere was the sound of victory: they had put the King's men to flight!

Hucker encountered him, and gave him his orders. He was to return to his quarters, and await the night attack on Bristol that had already been planned. He added, with a smile of satisfaction, 'We did well, lad. Several of theirs killed and prisoners taken, so perhaps we'll discover something of their plans and dispositions.'

'I hope so, sir,' Bram said. He added, as Hucker seemed to be moving on, 'Have you seen my cousin, sir? I have been searching for him up and down this past hour, and there is no sign of him.'

'Your cousin? You mean the lack-wit? No, I haven't,' Hucker said. 'Don't worry – his sort were born under a lucky star. You'll doubtless find him safe in your quarters.'

Sick with anxiety, Bram rode back to the inn, and was relieved and delighted to find Ben there, just as Hucker had suggested. He was tending a horse that had been slashed across the rump, applying an evil-smelling mixture that made the animal shake and twitch, despite his soft, crooning voice. He looked up as Bram approached, and gave his huge, disarming grin. 'Hullo, Bram – safe!'

'I'm safe, but what of you?' He looked more closely at Ben, and saw that his hair was dry, and his garments no more mudstained than they had been earlier. He said slowly, 'Did you fight, Ben?'

'Fight? Ben don't fight,' said his cousin stoutly 'Ben don't *like* fighting – not killing, either. Stayed here, safe, looked after horses.'

For any normal soldier, that would have been an admission of rank cowardice. But Ben was not normal, and Bram knew that no one would object to him staying out of the action. He would be little more than a sitting target for enemy weapons and bullets, being quite unable to defend himself, or to use the sword with which he had been issued: no one had thought fit to waste precious pistols or carbines on him. It came to Bram that this attitude of Ben's was something to be encouraged. Certainly, any value he might have to the rebel cause lay not in his fighting ability, but in his skill as a horse doctor.

Gradually, the men returned to the stables, in varying degrees of elation, proud that they had apparently repulsed the attack of the Royal horse, relieved to have survived it. One or two had minor sword cuts: the light had been too bad for much effective use of pistols. Two men, limping, mud-covered and horseless, admitted sheepishly that they had been unseated by their undisciplined mounts early in the fray. Only Bram, remembering the wild, total chaos in Keynsham High Street, the complete lack of organisation and discipline, seemed to harbour any doubts. They had faced, at the most, two or three hundred men, who had withdrawn in good order, leaving utter confusion behind. Until Monmouth could snatch the time to train the cavalry he did have, or to recruit men and horses of better quality, his troopers had little chance of withstanding a full-scale onslaught from the King's forces, better armed, horsed and trained.

They were in the middle of supper, the men in the big inn kitchen, the officers in one of the larger parlours, when Hucker appeared, his face lacking its usual cynical cheerfulness. 'There's no time for that – we march within the hour.'

'The attack on Bristol?' Bram said eagerly.

Hucker shook his head. 'No. He has decided against it. One of the prisoners we took earlier told us that the King's army – the regular army, not the militia – are very close at hand. And certainly the troops that attacked us were not part of the militia, but the Lifeguard, so I am told. So the attack on Bristol is out of the question. There was a choice – to march into Gloucestershire, and thence to our friends in Cheshire, or to go into Wiltshire, where we have been assured that there are five hundred armed horse ready to rise in our support. It has been decided that we march for Bath, and then to Wiltshire, where we can join with these horse and be ready to match with the King's army before it grows larger.'

'Why not Gloucester?' one of the other officers demanded. Hucker shrugged. 'It's four days' march, and the men's shoes are in a parlous state. Besides, we can expect more attacks and harassment from the horse who fell on us today, delaying our march until the main body of the King's army can come up and give battle. You know as well as I do, after that fiasco out there, that it's good cavalry that is our most desperate need. These five hundred men will make all the difference.'

Bram glanced at the faces of his brother officers. On them were written a variety of expressions: bewilderment, anger, frustration, misgivings, disbelief, despondency. Someone said sharply, 'But we have many friends in Bristol, and people with us who are natives of the city – people who know the garrison and the dispositions of the defences. These enemy forces, where are they? Where are they supposed to be? Have scouts been sent out to find them?'

Hucker looked at him, and shrugged again. 'That is the decision which

260

His Majesty has made, and which he and his council believe to be the best and most expedient, in the circumstances.'

'Northering vlother!' someone near Bram muttered.

'But if we turn into Wiltshire, to find these five hundred horsemen, who may or may not be as imaginary as any of the other support promised to us – if we turn away from Bristol, we have lost all chance of taking it,' said Tom Chadwick, who had been a gentleman volunteer in the King's Lifeguard, and had left London to join Monmouth, one of the very few to do so.

'The five hundred are no illusion, but reality,' said Hucker, rather with the air of a man convincing himself. 'We have been assured by Captain Adlam, who rode in today, that they wait only for our army to come into Wiltshire to rise – but they will not do it without our presence, for the militia in those parts is still very active. Once they have joined us, we will march on London. That is the situation, gentlemen,' he added, looking round the dubious, silent faces with something like a sneer on his own. 'Well – are you still with us, or are you too faint-hearted?'

'Of course not – we are with King Monmouth, to the death!' said William Savage, landlord of the Red Lion in Taunton.

With fervour, the others echoed him. 'Monmouth!' 'King Monmouth!' 'To London, and victory!' 'Monmouth, and the Protestant religion!'

Hucker surveyed them, with that oddly cynical, worldly smile. 'Excellent, gentlemen – I knew we could count on you. Make haste – we must be ready to march within the hour!'

There was no more time for rest, for eating or drinking. The men had to be roused, and the purpose of the march explained to them: not Bristol and glorious victory, but the uncertain promise of a body of horse somewhere in Wiltshire. There was much astonishment, rage and grumbling, and Bram, looking at the sullen, disappointed faces as they saddled their horses, wondered uneasily how morale would be affected by this devastating blow to their pride.

But no one was missing from the cavalry when they rode out of Keynsham in the darkness of night, the moon cloud-obscured and giving hardly enough illumination to show their way. Behind them tramped the foot, damp, still sadly lacking adequate shoes, and unhappy that their backs were turned on Bristol. And if a man, here and there, decided that he had had more than enough of all this marching in the rain, and slipped away unseen in the dark to return ignominiously to hearth and family and safety, then few were surprised.

It was still raining, and the road eastwards towards Bath was thick and cloyingly muddy, so that their progress was slow and miserable. They made their way along the course of the River Avon, until in front of them, dim in the half-light of dawn, rose the honey-gold walls of Bath.

There was no sign of the four thousand enemy troops that the Royalist prisoners had assured Monmouth were close at hand. There were only sentries peering over the walls, and they plainly belonged to the militia. The sodden, bedraggled rebel force lined up outside the south gate, safely beyond the river and out of range, while Monmouth, well aware of the demoralised state of his followers, sent a trumpeter over the Avon bridge to demand the city's surrender.

It was an act of pure bravado, born of desperation: with the King's army perhaps only a few miles distant, there was no time for an assault, and they only had four small field guns, totally inadequate for such a purpose. One of the sentries showed his derision by shooting the trumpeter dead.

Bath was impregnable, in their present circumstances. There was no help for it: somehow, their best hope was to swing into Wiltshire, join up with Captain Adlam's promised horse, and slip past the Royal army to reach London, now empty of troops and undefended.

But either Feversham, the Royal commander, or the Duke of Grafton, who led the foot, must surely block the main road that climbed the hills to Chippenham, and then on towards London. There was another route, however, more arduous, but also more likely to avoid the King's forces: and it would take them quickly into Wiltshire, and the promised meeting with Captain Adlam's horse.

Obediently, the rebel soldiers turned away from Bath, and began the long climb into the bleak downs that lay above the city to the south. Weary and footsore and miserable, they made very slow progress through the sticky mud and driving rain.

Behind them, Feversham, at the head of a small force that included the Lifeguard, left Bristol in haste and arrived at Bath some hours after the rebels had gone. On the great flat-topped hill of Kingsdown, where on a clear day half of Wiltshire could be seen, he gathered the separate elements of his army. The Duke of Grafton, another of the late King's bastards, with the foot; lieutenant-General Churchill with a further contingent of horse; and the men of the Wiltshire militia, a rather shabby and ill-equipped crew, slouching beside the regular soldiers. The rebels were almost within their grasp, and now at last they had the numbers to make a full-scale attack. Feversham heartened his men, put them in order of battle, and then marched them back down the hill towards Bath, and the pursuit.

Monmouth and his army toiled along the steep slippery valleys, as yet in ignorance of the King's army, strong and at last united, following hard upon their heels. And ahead of them, a comfortable place to rest and spend the night, was the village of Philip's Norton, in which Wintercombe lay.

# 15

## 'War in masquerade'

For once, Alex kept his promise to his son, and was back at Wintercombe well before supper time: in fact the sun, which had made a feeble and tentative appearance that afternoon, was still high in the sky when he rode into the stable yard on the bright bay stallion, who now went by the name of Blaze. To Pardice, who came out to take the horse from him – none of the younger grooms was allowed to tend such a valuable and volatile animal – he said briefly, 'Make sure he is comfortable, and then assemble all the servants in the Hall. The Duke of Monmouth's army is at Midford, and heading this way.'

Predictably, this astounding news flew round Wintercombe as quick as thought, and was brought to Phoebe, walking in the damp garden with Louise, Amy and Lukas, by the housekeeper, Betty.

She came hurrying up the steps to the pond garden, calling in a voice of extreme urgency, 'Mistress Phoebe! Oh, Mistress Phoebe, such terrible, dreadful news – whatever will become of us? We'll all be murdered or shot to pieces, for sure!'

Amy gasped, and put her hands to her mouth. Phoebe, more robust, leaned on her stick and said briskly, 'Whatever has happened, Betty, I'm certain it can't be as bad as that. What is it?'

'Those wicked rebels are at Midford, and marching here – they'll be at our door directly!'

'Oh, no,' Amy cried. 'They'll kill us all, they hate Papists!'

'Well, they won't kill me – I'm an honest Protestant,' said Phoebe. 'Oh, Amy, don't be ridiculous – they wouldn't dare to lay a finger on you, and nor, I should guess, would they want to. Anyway, this house is not entirely defenceless. There is a small store of weapons, and the men to use them.'

'Sir Alexander is back – he brought the news,' Betty said, apparently calmed by Phoebe's common sense. 'I expect he'll tell us what he's heard.'

Lukas, his blue eyes wide, was looking up at the adults. 'Please, Aunt, what is happening? Is it bad news?'

'I hope not,' Phoebe said. She glanced at Amy, who was very pale, and then at Louise. 'Your father is back, and we must go hear what he has to say. We can trust him to do the right thing, whatever happens.'

But she glanced significantly at Louise as she spoke, and her cousin knew that in reality, she did not think that Alex could be trusted at all. It was an opinion with which she was in full agreement. But, Louise thought, as they made their way slowly, at Phoebe's pace, back to the house, whatever happened over the next few days, it was unlikely to be boring.

The great Hall at Wintercombe, lit by the high arched windows, three to the south and three to the north, was full of servants, all betraying various feelings: fear, excitement, anxiety. One of the little kitchen maids, who was only twelve, was snivelling into her apron. Phoebe, whose legs were aching in the unseasonably wet weather, sat down solidly on one of the chairs around the long central table, and after a pause, Louise and Amy took their places next to her, with Lukas standing very close behind. The assembled servants, by tacit and common consent, moved gradually to the back of the Hall, around the fireplace and the entrances to the eastern part of the house, so that the three girls and the child formed the front rank.

Louise had guessed where Alex, with his flair for the dramatic, would stand to address his household, and she was right. He appeared suddenly on the gallery above the screens passage, with Charles, surprisingly, just behind him. The muted talk died away below as his arrival was noticed, and more than a score of anxious faces turned up towards him. He folded his arms on the gallery rail and leaned over, his manner informal and comradely. Louise tried to ignore that suffocating, sensual longing that had as usual swept over her as soon as she saw him. Aware of Phoebe's shrewd glance, she concentrated, with some success, on projecting an air of cool curiosity.

'I'm glad to see you all here so promptly,' said Alex, without preamble. His voice was slow, almost drawling, and not especially loud, but something in its tone commanded attention, and he continued amid complete silence. 'You've probably heard by now of the reason for this meeting, perhaps somewhat exaggerated in the telling. The simple truth is that the rebel army, under the command of the Duke of Monmouth, was at Midford not an hour ago, and is heading this way along the Bath road. I can tell you this with absolute certainty because I saw them myself. They'll be in Philip's Norton before nightfall – they're not moving very fast. I have called you here to keep you informed, and to tell you what to do should any rebels arrive at Wintercombe. They may demand food, shelter, even arms or horses. If any appear, fetch me. If what they require is comparatively trivial, and easy and convenient to provide, we shall give it to them rather than provoke trouble.' He paused, to let this sink in, and then added drily, 'This last does not apply to demands for horses, or weapons. Whatever they may threaten, or ask for, they must deal with me, and me alone – it is my responsibility, not yours. If rumour is correct, the King's army is not far behind them, so I doubt they will linger very long in Philip's Norton. While they are here, it would be wisest to avoid any confrontation.' He surveyed the anxious faces below him, and smiled suddenly. 'And I need not tell you that any attempt by any of you to do something so foolish as to join the rebel army, will receive the appropriate punishment.'

He did not sound, to Louise's over-sensitive ears, as if he anticipated that punishment to be particularly severe. She looked at Phoebe, and saw a small crease of disapproval between her thin dark brows. The same expression, rather more prominently, was also visible on Charles's face as he stood in the background behind his cousin. She remembered what Phoebe had said, and felt a distinct sense of unease. Then she recalled another part of that conversation, and relaxed. Phoebe was right: her brother would be careful, whatever the impression he gave to the contrary, for he had too much to lose.

He dismissed the servants briefly, with a series of pungent witticisms which raised a wave of laughter, and then left the gallery as they began to disperse back to their duties. Charles remained for a while longer, looking down as the men and women filed from the Hall, talking earnestly amongst themselves. Then he turned abruptly and followed in Alex's wake.

Phoebe glanced at Louise with significance, and then picked up her stick. 'It's raining again, by the look of the windows,' she said. 'Shall we adjourn to the parlour?'

At the foot of the stairs, just before the door that led to the study and the winter parlour, they found Alex waiting for them. With a smile and an expansive flourish, he whisked his sister's stick out of her hand, and substituted the support of his arm so swiftly that she scarcely faltered. 'Allow me to escort you, Mistress St Barbe, to the comfort and safety of a chair.'

'I'll need it, after that,' was Phoebe's dry comment. She let him guide her into the winter parlour, which had a small fire burning brightly, an indication of the sudden unseasonable dampness and chill of the weather. Grateful for the warmth, she settled herself comfortably in the chair nearest the hearth. Lukas curled up on the window seat and peered out at the dismal sky, once more threatening rain, while Amy and Louise, one expectant and fearful, the other expectant and excited, took their places next to their cousin.

Alex remained standing: as usual, his sheer size and physical presence, not to mention the force of his personality, dominated the room. Louise glanced surreptitiously at Amy, who was still very pale, and had clasped her hands together so firmly that her knuckles stood out white. She was looking up at Alex as if, despite his brutal rejection of her, he still filled all her world and vision: no need to guess at her feelings for him, they shone from her face as clearly as if written across her forehead. With some irritation, Louise hoped that she herself did not appear so naïvely transparent. Amy, shy, sheltered and immature, was a victim only of calf-love. Louise, far more worldly and experienced, knew her own passions and desires to be of an entirely different order.

'I haven't a great deal to add to what I said just now,' Alex told them. He leaned against the mantelpiece, thereby blocking off a goodly proportion of heat, and kicked a stray, smouldering coal back into the embers. 'There are several thousand of the rebels, mainly foot, but also some rather ragged horse, and all making very slow progress. The rain seems to have dampened their spirits more than a little. But some of them were singing quite cheerfully, so I should not write them off as a spent force just yet. And Monmouth himself is no mean soldier – it's not at all certain who would win, should it come to a pitched battle.'

'But why are they heading this way?' Phoebe asked, frowning. 'I was under the impression that they were marching to attack Bristol.'

'So were they,' Alex said drily. 'I had the opportunity of a quick talk with some of them, and it was most illuminating.'

'You *talked* to them?' Amy said, in astonishment. 'But they are the enemy!'

'No, they are not,' Alex told her. 'They are ordinary people possessed by ordinary, but on the whole admirable motives – fear for themselves and their families, for the future of their country and their religion, a desire for justice and an end to persecution. Can you blame them, in all honesty, for taking up arms?'

'But they are rebels,' said Amy unhappily. 'However good their reasons are, isn't it treason to rebel against the King? We could have a civil war again!'

'We could,' Alex said. 'But somehow, I doubt it. There doesn't seem to be much support for Monmouth outside the West Country, and remarkably few of the gentry have joined him. That's another reason for the rebels' gloomy spirits. They know they need success to breed success, and so far there have been only a few scrappy and inconclusive skirmishes. They need a battle, and quickly, with the King's forces – and they must win it.'

'And if the Royal army catches up with them too quickly, then you think

267

that the battle may well be here?' Phoebe queried. 'And don't mince your words, brother – I, at least, am quite stout-hearted enough to take the truth, and so, I suspect, is Louise.'

Amy said nothing, but her knuckles whitened still further. Alex did not look at her: his attention was fixed on his sister. 'It's a possibility, certainly, but a remote one, I think. Monmouth may not even stay the night – although, since they've marched from Keynsham and taken half the night and all day to do it, they're undoubtedly in need of a rest, if the Royal army allows them to have one. And the King's men are not exactly snapping at their heels just yet – from what I've heard, they're still gathering outside Bath.'

'They'd best hurry up, then,' Charles said. He had entered the parlour in time to hear his cousin's last words. 'What Feversham can be doing, to allow the rebels to rampage unchecked all over the West Country, I cannot imagine. The sooner he falls on them, the better.'

'So soon that the battle is here in Philip's Norton, or very close at hand?' Alex enquired acidly. 'I thought not. However much bloodshed your thirst for justice and retribution requires, Charles, I doubt you would want it spilled quite so close to your own doorstep. The further away the better, eh, so you don't actually have to witness it?'

Predictably, the younger man had flushed at his cousin's derisive tone. He said defensively, 'The rebels cannot be allowed to go unpunished. Where would this country be if treason and rebellion were permitted to flourish?'

'But perhaps the King has created a climate in which such things find fertile soil? There's no surer way to provoke a man into open revolt,' Alex said, 'than to threaten him and all he holds dear – or, through blundering obstinacy, blindness and sheer stupidity, to make him *think* that he is threatened. Don't you agree?'

Charles said angrily, 'I gather that you are attempting to be offensive. Perhaps I had better go. After all, someone should be seeing to the defence of this house, and Twinney has no idea what to do. Amy?'

His sister rose reluctantly, gave Phoebe and Louise an anguished, despairing glance, and followed him out of the room. When their footsteps and voices – Charles's angry, Amy's pleading – had safely retreated, Alex turned to his son. 'Lukas. There are important matters we three must discuss in private, and quickly. Can you go play in the garden for a while?'

'But it's just started to rain, Papa,' Lukas objected: he was plainly yearning to be allowed to participate. Alex smiled. 'Well, if it has, then you may go to the library. We won't be long, I promise. Now off with you, before someone else comes to disturb us.'

'Very well, Papa,' said the boy, who knew an incontrovertible decree when he heard it. He slipped off the window seat, made his old-fashioned bows to the two remaining women, and walked, with a certain reluctance still evident in the drag of his feet, out of the parlour. At once, Alex left his position by the hearth, pulled Amy's chair closer to those of Louise and Phoebe, and sat down. 'We probably haven't much time before some fool comes to ask where the gunpowder is kept, so I'll be as brief as possible. I didn't want Charles, or Amy, to know of this just yet, although I suspect that it won't be a secret from them very long. I spoke to the rebels, as I said – and, more specifically, to one rebel in particular. Cousin Bram is with them, one of the horse.'

'*Bram?*' Louise almost shouted the name in her astonishment, but hastily modified it to a more subdued tone. 'Bram is with the rebels?'

'Are you surprised?' said Alex. 'Surely you learned *something* about the Loveridges during your stay in Taunton – or did you spend the entire time talking frippery with Sue and Hannah?'

'No, I did not,' Louise hissed, with some vehemence. 'I had several long talks with Bram – we accorded very well – and he told me some things that *did* surprise me – your part in his father's activities, for instance. But I must say, I'd assumed that he would have more sense.'

'Oh, he may give that appearance,' Alex told her drily. 'But Bram has a very absolute idea of right and wrong. If he conceived Monmouth's cause to be just, and worth fighting for, then I doubt anyone could prevent him joining – although I imagine poor Jonah tried quite hard. He worships the boy – he's his only surviving son, after all.'

'Let's hope Charles doesn't hear of it,' Phoebe commented. 'Though, as you say, it can hardly remain a secret with Bram marching through Somerset in Monmouth's wake for all to see. Let's hope he keeps some sense of self-preservation.'

'He has more hope of survival than the foot,' Alex said. 'At least he has a horse, and a fair chance of outrunning pursuit.'

'Bram wouldn't run away!' said Louise, with indignation.

'He might not *intend* to – but the rebel cavalry are little more than a barely trained, badly organised rabble,' Alex told her. 'He might well have no choice in the matter – have you ever tried to pull up a terrified, bolting horse, let alone influence its direction? But at least he has all his wits about him, and can have some care for himself. Ben is quite a different matter.'

There was an appalled silence. Phoebe said, softly and forcefully, each word low and distinct, 'Ben? You mean – you *cannot* mean – Ben Wickham is with them too?'

Louise, stricken, thought of the lack-wit boy, his good nature and warmth and his one, astonishing skill, a true innocent going to war with no more idea of what he was about than a babe in arms. She felt suddenly sick, and fearful, with an awful presentiment of disaster. 'Oh, not Ben,' she whispered, and found tears in her eyes.

'Yes, he is with them,' said Alex, with a grimness neither girl had seen before. 'He seems very happy, and he rides with Bram. I had no time to enquire as to how he came to join the rebels, but I'm sure that Bram did not persuade him – he seemed very unhappy about the situation, even if Ben was enjoying himself.'

'Aunt Rachael would never have let him go willingly – he's the apple of her eye,' Phoebe said. 'Alex – if they do camp here in Philip's Norton tonight – even if they just march through – could you not speak to Ben and try to persuade him to leave the rebels? It wouldn't be desertion, it's plain for all to see that he's a simpleton, a child who doesn't know what he's doing – in a battle he would have no chance, no chance at all.'

'You surprise me,' Alex said, looking at his sister. 'Sentimentality has never been a vice of yours. Would not most people feel that such a lack-wit is beneath notice, and better off dead?'

Phoebe stared at him as if she could not believe what she heard. 'If you think that, brother, then I have nothing left to say to you.'

'What a shame it is that I don't – then I might have some peace from your scold's tongue.' He smiled at her, but her anger was undiminished, and a red patch had appeared on each sharp cheekbone. 'It's no matter for jest,' Phoebe said. 'Why do you always insist on saying whatever is most offensive?'

'Perhaps I enjoy arousing passions – of all kinds,' Alex said, unrepentant, and with a fleeting glance sideways at Louise that was as blatantly suggestive as if he had asked her to remove her clothes.

Louise hoped earnestly, but probably in vain, that Phoebe had not noticed it. He was sitting between them, so close to her that their legs, encased in fine grey wool and in blue silk, almost touched. She could make out every long dark hair curling on his shoulders, and the faint shadow of the black stubble under his pale skin, and the slight but ineradicable lines around mouth and eyes that betrayed his experience and maturity, and his way of life. The urge to reach out to touch him became so strong that she clamped her hands together in her lap, as Amy had done, but from a different kind of fear that she did not, at present, care to analyse. She said, ignoring her own feelings and the sudden hostility between the people on either side of her, 'Phoebe's suggestion makes sense – will you act on it?'

He turned his head to study her, immaculate as ever in the slippery sapphire silk, and she saw herself reflected, blue upon blue, in his eyes. 'Perhaps,' he said, in a conversational tone. 'Perhaps not. What is certain is that I refuse to be dictated to. Now, since there is no point in further discussion, I will leave you two ladies to your sewing, or whatever takes your fancy, and go to impose a little order on the chaos that is undoubtedly reigning outside.'

Phoebe and Louise were left to stare at each other across the chair he had so abruptly vacated. The older girl laughed reluctantly, and shook her head. 'He is utterly impossible! Doesn't he care for anything *at all?*'

'He cares about Ben,' Louise said, for that fact, despite Alex's manner, had been quite plain to her. Phoebe nodded slowly. 'Yes, you are right – he does, in his own strange way. And for Lukas, of course – and for Wintercombe too, I think. But as for the rest of us – well, I fear we might as well be blocks of wood or African savages for all the affection he shows us.' A wry grin appeared on her face. 'Perhaps it's just as well. He causes enough trouble already. Think of the turmoil and upset, were he to find some deserving object for all his passions.'

'Apart from the ladies at the Cock in Walcot, of course,' said Louise tartly, wondering if Phoebe were hinting at something. But it was lust, no more, that aroused those powerful feelings in her body, and, evidently, in his: lust, soon slaked, soon dead. She was in search of something a little more lasting, and whether it was with one of her cousins – Bram, perhaps? – or with a man yet unknown to her, waiting somewhere all in ignorance as she waited for him, she knew that, eventually, she would find it. And be damned to the temptations offered so provocatively by Sir Alexander St Barbe.

The Duke of Monmouth, at the head of his ragged, footsore army, at last entered Philip's Norton after a march that had taken half the previous night, and all of that day, to cover a scant fourteen miles. At Midford, the highway had been so muddy that the four small cannon had become bogged down, and several of the baggage waggons as well. The men, exhausted and suffering from lack of sleep, had toiled doggedly up the terrible steep road out of the village, and on to the high windswept hills above, thankfully drier underfoot than the sodden valleys. It had rained every so often, heavily, and even the Duke was soaked to the skin. He rode alone, speaking to no one, dejected and hunched on his handsome grey horse, and more than one of the officers wondered at the mood of their leader, who in adversity no longer seemed so inspiring, or so dashing.

An hour or more before sunset, they entered the small town of Philip's Norton. Here, the weary men and horses could rest, eat, and above all sleep. The villagers turned out to watch the vanguard march in, but there was, fortunately, no repetition of the regrettable incident that had happened a little earlier.

A countryman, holding a gate open for a party of scouting horse further down in the valley, had been asked by one of the troopers whose side he supported.

'Why, the King, sir,' the peasant had responded, with a cheerful smile that changed to bewildered astonishment as one of the horsemen drew his pistol, cocked it, aimed and fired. The yokel disappeared abruptly behind the hedge, while his assailant, a young man with a notably arrogant and quarrelsome attitude, blew some stray powder nonchalantly from the weapon's muzzle, and thrust it back into the holster.

'Have you killed him?' demanded Cornet Loveridge furiously. 'What the devil are you playing at, you fool? We want the people to help us, not to run and hide when they see us coming, in case we shoot them out of hand.'

'He deserved a lesson,' said the trooper, a Shepton man called Taylor, whom Bram had disliked from the start. 'So I gave him one. If he's not dead, he'll remember it.'

'He *is* dead, sir,' said one of the other troopers, who had gone to look. 'Shot through the heart.'

Taylor preened himself. 'A good clean hit. So may all our enemies end. Well, Cornet? Are we or are we not going to seek assistance from yet another of your cousins?'

Bram stared at him wearily. There was no doubt of it, being an officer – even a lowly cornet – was not the position of unalloyed privilege that he had assumed. He preferred to treat his fellow-men as equals, in friendly fashion, and had still not become used to giving orders. Most of the dozen or so men who had been detailed to accompany him down into the Norton Brook valley, and so to Wintercombe, were pleasant and amenable enough, but Taylor, who obviously thought that he, and not Bram, should carry the sad, soaking colour that hung damply above its bearer's head, had expressed resentment and disaffection from the outset, culminating, now, in outright insolence.

'That's quite enough from you, Taylor,' he said, trying to sound authoritative. 'I'll report your conduct to Captain Hucker, when we rejoin the army. Now follow me.'

They made their way rather cautiously down the hillside, scattering flocks of curious sheep. There was no sign of anyone else to help or impede their progress: hiding in the hedges, if they have any sense, thought Bram unhappily, wishing that he could put a bullet, with similar brutal despatch, through Taylor's unrepentant heart. Up on the hillside at

272

their backs, they could hear the endless rumbling noise of the army's creeping progress, five thousand foot, a thousand or more horse, forty waggons and four cannon, all streaming into the small town where his mother had been born, and which he knew well from numerous happy visits. It did not seem possible, or right, that this tranquil, lovely place, bound to the changing seasons for countless centuries, should be thrust so abruptly into turmoil and war.

But it had happened before, forty years ago. Was he now about to become the unwilling harbinger of destruction and death to Wintercombe, as once his grandmother's husband, Nick Hellier, had been?

He almost missed the right turn up the hill to Wintercombe, and had to call two of the men back. Ben, riding at his side, had cried out and put his hands over his ears at the gunshot earlier, although he did not seem to understand its implications, or the fate of the victim. Now, he gave a crow of joy and pointed. 'There – Wintercombe – home!'

And so it was home, Bram thought, as their tired horses squelched and slipped up the muddy track in a light drizzle: home to all their family, however far-flung. He felt far more for this house than for the narrow little building in Taunton where he had lived all his life: even his grandmother, so happy at Chard, seemed to hold Wintercombe dear above all else. He looked round for Taylor, and addressed him with as much menace as he could muster. 'These are my kin, and I will *not* have them harmed or frightened in *any* way, understand? One threatening move on your part, and I swear I'll put a bullet through you with as much mercy as you showed to that poor man just now.'

He had no idea whether or not he would actually be able to strike the man down in cold blood, and from the sneer on Taylor's face, he did not consider it very likely either. But if you do try anything, Bram thought grimly, with a glare at his adversary, you never know – you might get an unpleasant surprise.

There was another, waiting for them at Wintercombe. The great wooden gates into the stable yard, never to his knowledge closed since the last war, were barred against them, and a voice Bram recognised shouted through a gap in the dilapidated boards, 'Do ee go away! We don't want none of ee here!'

Out of the corner of his eye, Bram saw Taylor fingering his pistol. He called urgently, 'Pardice! It is Dan Pardice, isn't it? Don't you remember me?'

There was a startled pause. Then the voice said dubiously, 'Be ee Master Bram?'

'Of course it is, Pardice – and Master Ben, too. We come as friends, and we wouldn't dream of harming you. Can we speak with Sir Alexander, please?'

A slightly shorter pause, interrupted by running feet. 'Henry have gone to fetch him for ee, Master Bram. I daren't open up to ee till he tell me to – I hope as how you'll understand, sir.'

'Of course I do,' said Bram warmly. 'It's only sensible, in these times.' He grinned at the unseen Pardice. 'You never know what riff-raff might appear at the gate.'

Taylor still had his hand resting lightly, threateningly, on his unfired pistol. With a sudden rush of apprehension, Bram hoped that Alex would come quickly, although he was not looking forward to this second meeting of the day. His cousin had always been a rather remote, intimidating figure, unpredictable of mood, sometimes friendly, at others downright hostile. And Bram, moderate in his own habits, even at Oxford, had heard family gossip about Alex that was, to put it mildly, hair-raising, and culminating in the unheralded appearance of a six-year-old bastard son whose existence no one had previously suspected. Until today, he had not encountered his cousin for years, and despite their earlier, quite friendly conversation, he wondered uneasily if the older man would treat him, in front of the men, as if he were still a callow youth.

There was the sound of a bar being pulled back. Slowly, with much geriatric creaking and groaning, one of the gates opened. Bram saw a cluster of curious faces, and, in the forefront of them, his cousin. Slowly, deliberately, Alex came out of the gate to confront him. Bram was reminded again of how tall he was, the tallest of all the St Barbes, and was glad of the extra altitude of his horse. He smiled rather warily, and held out his hand in greeting.

Alex did not take it. He walked up to the horse's head and said bluntly, 'What the devil do you want?'

After their comparatively amicable talk at Midford, this was a little disconcerting. Bram said, trying not to seem anxious, 'I'm sorry to appear unannounced like this, Cousin, but I'm acting under orders. Captain Hucker has sent me here to ask for your help.'

'And what makes you think I'll give it?' Alex spoke clearly and with hostility, but there was quite a different message in his face, unseen by the members of his household peering curiously out of the gate.

'I'm asking as your cousin, your kinsman,' said Bram, hoping urgently that Taylor would not be tempted to do anything rash. 'Our need is desperate – not for quarters, we can be accommodated well enough in the village, but for food, coin, and above all, horses. And all those things you can readily supply.'

There was a pause. More people were crowding the gate, or peering over the low wall that bounded the courtyard lying in front of the house. Out of the tail of his eye, he saw a little group of women, and amongst them, Louise. She gave him a cheerful wave, and he raised his hand briefly in reply. He thought he saw Phoebe beside her, and the pretty blonde curls must belong to Amy, but there seemed to be no sign of her brother Charles, who would, of course, as a Papist be entirely opposed to the rebel cause.

'I have no intention of voluntarily giving aid to a pack of rebels,' said Alex. His eyes met his cousin's, and he gave a tiny significant jerk of his head. With something of a shock, Bram realised what he meant.

Louise, watching, saw the two men meet, and heard the brief and unpromising exchange of words. It did indeed appear, as Phoebe had said, that Alex would be careful. And although by coming boldly up to the door, Bram had announced his membership of the rebel army to Wintercombe, and thus to all the world, that was his own choice, and while she feared for him, it was impossible not to admire his courage. She herself had seen enough, in France, of how a Papist king could treat his Protestant subjects, not to have a strong feeling of sympathy with the rebels, however foolhardy they might be.

Ben was there, sitting a bay cob she vaguely recalled as being one of Cousin Jan's, with a slumped, almost somnolent posture, looking eagerly at Wintercombe. She waved at him, and at once his broad flat face creased into a vast grin, and he mouthed her name and flapped his hand as energetically as a child. Lukas, peering over the wall beside her, fingers clinging to the edge like a crab, followed her gaze and said, 'Is that Cousin Ben?'

'Yes, it is.'

'He looks strange,' said the boy, slowly. 'Is he nice?'

'Yes, he is, and very good with horses,' Louise told him, deciding not to attempt any explanation of Ben's particular difficulties. 'But he shouldn't be with the rebels – he can't fight, it's wrong to see him in an army.'

'Why can't he fight?' Lukas asked, with that courteous curiosity that was so hard to resist. 'Is he hurt?'

'No – it's just that he wouldn't know how – he doesn't like killing people,' Louise said, feeling herself floundering. 'Ssh – I want to hear what they're saying.'

But there was no sound from the two men outside the gate. Bram, rather impressive on his chestnut horse, his abundant hair, darkened and coiling with rainwater, streaming on to his shoulders, held the sorry flag, its colours run and the material much crumpled and shrunken. Alex, by

275

contrast dry and immaculate in the grey suit he often wore for riding, stood in front of him, protecting the house and its inhabitants at his back. For a moment, Louise thought that Bram and his men would turn round and ride away, leaving Wintercombe safe and undefiled.

The little confrontation altered so quickly that she could never be quite sure, afterwards, what had happened. One moment, Alex and Bram and the soldiers were standing as stiff and unmoving as a woodcut, and the next, there was utter confusion. A shot exploded, and the household of Wintercombe, incredulous and bewildered, stood staring. People screamed or shouted, a horse whinnied frantically, and another shot, terrifyingly loud, sent everyone diving for the shelter of wall or gate. Louise, crouched low to the ground, Lukas huddled beside her, wondered in terror if anyone had been hit, and above all, if Alex was safe. The hubbub on the other side of the wall gave her no clue. Cautiously, she unfolded and pulled herself inch by inch up the rough stones of the wall, until she could peer over the top.

'You fool, get down!' Phoebe said angrily, but Louise saw at once that the danger, although not past, did not involve her. Bram, controlling his nervous, frightened horse with an effort, had a smoking pistol in his hand. Alex, his back to the gate, was being guarded by a trooper with a most menacing, ruthless expression, and a pistol, two feet long, pointed ominously at his heart. To Louise's relief, he seemed quite unhurt, even unruffled, and the look on his face was not one of alarm or anger, but amusement. No one appeared to have been hit, so presumably the two shots had gone wide.

'I told you, we are desperate for horses,' said Bram, his voice pitched loud to carry to everyone in the courtyard and the stables. 'And we will take them, whether you wish it or not. Trooper Taylor has already killed one man today, and believe me, Cousin, he'll have no compunction in killing another. Now, may we have those horses?'

Silence. Louise, looking aghast at Bram, remembered the talkative, endearing idealist whom she had liked so much in Taunton, and could not recognise him in this grim, threatening young man. The trooper glowered at Alex, and took a step closer. Even if Bram were not murderously inclined, and she could not believe that his rebellious fervour would possibly go so far, the man Taylor seemed quite willing, indeed eager, to slaughter Alex in cold blood. Give in, she prayed silently, willing him with her eyes and heart. For God's sake, let them have whatever they want – nothing is worth your death.

As if he had heard her, he smiled up at Bram, and spread his hands. 'It seems that for once you hold all the cards, Cousin. There is nothing I can do, is there? I suppose that some half-dozen horses can be found for you, but do not feel tempted to take the bay stallion – he's barely broken to be ridden, let alone to war, and he'll kick someone's head in if mishandled. The saddle horses will be adequate for your needs. Pardice?'

The head groom's agitated head appeared very cautiously around the gate. 'Yes, Sir Alexander?'

'Bring out some horses for these gentlemen, so that they may choose those that are to their liking,' Alex told him, in tones of some sarcasm. 'And if I were you, be quick about it – I've no wish to be perforated unnecessarily.'

'Of course, sir,' Pardice said hastily and vanished. Alex shouted after him. 'And make sure everyone keeps their heads down – we don't want any unfortunate accidents.'

'If you all do as we say, there'll be no need,' said Bram. He gestured at the trooper, whose finger still lingered itchily on the trigger. 'Put your weapon away, Taylor. I will ensure that my cousin does nothing stupid.'

With an insolent, disbelieving stare, the man very slowly returned the pistol to its holster. Louise, who had been watching Bram very closely, saw him relax, and an astonishing possibility leaped into her mind. Taylor was obviously a murderous rogue, who would have liked nothing better than to put a bullet through anyone who crossed him, with very little excuse. But how could Bram be so certain that Alex would not cause him trouble – unless this confrontation had been arranged beforehand?

Appalled and incredulous, she glanced at Phoebe, who had struggled to her feet with the help of Amy and Lukas and had dusted off her gown. Alex's sister shared his devious nature, after all, and knew him better than anyone. With a sick feeling of dismay, Louise saw that the same idea seemed to have occurred to her too.

The horses, wild-eyed and alarmed, infected by the air of panic, were led out by the two stable boys. The bay Nance, who had once been Louise's mount, was amongst them, but not, she was relieved to see, her pretty mare Saffron. Each horse was briefly approved by Bram, who still stood guard over Alex, and handed to a trooper. Ben, his face still displaying the bewilderment that had filled him when the pistols were fired, took charge of the skittish Shadow. Louise was surprised to see him amongst the animals whom Pardice was prepared to sacrifice: but the gelding was too difficult a ride for anyone at Wintercombe, save for herself and Alex, and had been intended for sale. It would be something of a two-edged gift to the rebels, she thought wryly, for Shadow, although a quality mount, was by no means suitable for cavalry work. Even the gentle Ben, whispering and stroking and soothing, could not succeed in calming him.

'This will suffice – we don't want to strip your stables bare, after all,' said Bram, with the sudden wide grin that Louise remembered so well, and which convinced her still further that all this was no more real than a play. 'I thank you, Cousin, for your forbearance and your generosity – it's a pity that your conscience could not allow you to join our just cause. King Monmouth, and the Protestant religion!'

'King Monmouth!' his troopers echoed with spirit, and their cheers rang briskly around Wintercombe's stone walls and blank windows. Then they turned their horses and, with the six purloined mounts in tow, made their way at a fast trot back down the hill towards the Wellow Lane, and Philip's Norton.

If it had all been prearranged, and Louise was still by no means certain of it, then both Bram and Alex had played their parts with uncommon skill and conviction. It had failed to convince either her or Phoebe, though they were both Alex's friends, and would not betray him. But how many of the household, perhaps not so loyal to the master of Wintercombe, had also somehow seen through that elaborate charade?

And, even more to the point, where was Charles?

Darkness fell with summer tardiness upon Philip's Norton, the sun setting a little while after the church clock, comparatively new and maintained with loving pride by the churchwardens, had struck nine. Monmouth had roused himself a little from his despondent mood to order a barricade placed across the Bath road where it entered the village at North Street, and had grunted assent when his senior officers suggested that guards should be posted in the hedges beyond. But it was almost impossible to get further orders from him: instead, he lapsed into a dejected silence, emerging only to rail against the perfidy of the promised five hundred Wiltshire horse, none of whom had yet appeared, and of those officers in his old regiments who, he had hoped, would desert to his side. He sat in the handsome chamber he had taken at the George, staring miserably out at the darkening marketplace below, lost in thought and self-pity, while his officers, aware of their increasingly desperate situation, disposed their forces around the village as best they could, and ensured that they would not be surprised in the night.

The foot were encamped in two fields to the north side of the town, and made themselves as comfortable as possible with fires, makeshift shelters and the food which had been brought by the villagers. Philip's Norton had always been strongly Protestant, even Puritan, and Parson Pigott was over eighty and unable to give any lead to what little Royalist feeling lurked in his parish. Even Henry Prescott, the landlord of the George and a pillar of the established church – he was on the vestry committee – was so far disaffected as to turn a blind eye to his tapsters, who appropriated several barrels of beer from the cellar and rolled them along the muddy streets to the camp for the refreshment of the soldiers. And he had welcomed the Protestant Duke and his senior officers to his hostelry with apparently genuine warmth, and had supplied a handsome and lavish dinner for all his guests, disclaiming any suggestion of payment.

The horse, fewer and more fortunate than their foot-bound comrades, had found billets in the village, their mounts – including the six obtained, apparently under duress, from Wintercombe – stabled in barn or outhouse or shed or, in the absence of shelter, tied up in gardens and orchards. With commendable aplomb, the few hundred inhabitants of Philip's Norton fed their uninvited guests, asked eager questions about their adventures, and expressed their good will and good wishes for future success. Bram and Ben, taken in along with several others by a family called Sloper, who inhabited a large and prosperous house just off South Street, found themselves made welcome, given beds and pallets in the warmth of the kitchen, and plied with hot pottage, beer, and three sizzling roasted chickens. After the miseries and exertions of their march from Keynsham, such evidence of kindness was a marvellous restorative for their depressed spirits, and the rapt attention which the servants – and the daughters of the house, who were close in age to Bram's sisters – gave to them as they spoke nonchalantly of marches, skirmishes and battles, made them all feel like heroes.

But for their leader, no such remedy seemed possible. He remained in the comfortable best chamber above the porch of the George, while below him his officers bustled tirelessly to ensure that their men were settled and well defended. His dinner congealed, almost uneaten, and Master Prescott's best and strongest brew remained untouched, as he sat silent, apparently contemplating the depths of despair. His steward, William Williams, had given up his vain efforts to cheer him, for nothing, it seemed, could lighten his master's desperate mood. Not only had the Wiltshire horse failed to appear, and they were the only reason that he had marched in this direction at all, but the news that King James had set a bounty of a thousand pounds on his head had put him in fear of his life. He would eat nothing that Williams had not tasted or prepared, in case it had been poisoned, and he was afraid that some traitor amongst his followers, greedy for gold, might try to shoot him. At last Williams, despite all his efforts, had to acknowledge defeat, and left the Protestant Duke alone in his chamber to bemoan his fate, while he went down to the taproom to vent some of his own despairing fury on

Monmouth's officers, who were likewise growing somewhat impatient with their leader.

Had Williams known it, the danger that his master feared was more real than he himself had suspected. Yet it did not come from within his army, but from outside.

Night settled on Philip's Norton, crowded with ten times its usual number of inhabitants. The guards at the barricades and along the Bath road peered uneasily into the dank, moonless gloom, and several times a false alarm was sounded as nervous soldiers took fright at owls, sheep, cattle or the movements of their own comrades. But they were looking for an army: it was quite a simple matter for one man, who had heard of the price on Monmouth's head, to slip across the fields and tracks, through gates and over ditches, to reach the village unseen.

The Duke was quartered in the George, as everyone knew: likewise, it was most likely that he would be ensconced in the Porch chamber, the best in the inn. The man, watching in the shadows by the Market Cross, saw that lights still burned in the window of that chamber, despite the lateness of the hour. It was a desperate stroke, but if it worked, his fortunes would be changed for ever. His pistol was already loaded and primed: he saw a shadow move within the chamber, and a man approached the window, perhaps to draw shutters or curtains.

It was the Duke, his tall figure unmistakable against the light within, a perfect target. The watcher lifted his weapon, cocked it, and aimed with agonised care. For a moment longer Monmouth remained motionless, staring out into the dark, and the assassin had the strange, unsettling illusion that he had seen him, watching and hungry in the night. He cast aside all scruples, and pulled the trigger: and at the precise moment that the flint hit the steel, the Duke turned away.

The pistol shot sounded like cannonfire in the quiet village. At once, every dog in Philip's Norton set up a cacophony of barking, and the sounds echoed around the narrow streets amid a torrent of shouting, alarmed voices.

He had failed. Monmouth was still alive, and the thousand pounds would never be his, for he knew that he would not have another chance so good.

Officers and men were pouring out of the George, and he had no illusions as to his fate should they discover him. With alacrity and bitter disappointment, he turned and hurried into the safe anonymity of the enveloping dark.

# 16

## 'Unfortunately brave'

By dawn, every member of the Duke's forces had heard, often in highly elaborate detail, of the attempt on their leader's life. Plainly, the hand of God had preserved him from death, and although the escape of the would-be assassin was very unfortunate, at least the Duke was alive and unharmed. And, strangely, the pistol shot, which had shattered the window glass and buried itself harmlessly in the panelling, seemed to have wrenched Monmouth out of his despondent spirits. He had organised a vigorous search for his assailant, and when it failed had toured the guardposts around the northern perimeter of the village, heartening and encouraging his men. He had gone to bed well after midnight, slept soundly, and woken refreshed and much restored, ready for the day's march to Frome, where further reinforcements, according to confident report, would surely join them.

Bram, saddling his horse, and making sure that his pistols and those of his men were loaded and ready, looked up to see a familiar figure approaching. The last person he might have expected to see walking across the yard, with its piles of quarried stone ready for building – Master Sloper was a mason – was his cousin Alex, whom he had robbed at gunpoint not twelve hours previously.

The other troopers had also seen him, and there was a mutter of surprise. Bram pinned some sort of smile to his face, and said pleasantly, 'What brings you here, Cousin?'

'A private matter, which need not detain us long,' Alex said. 'Is there somewhere we can talk?'

'Hullo, Cousin!' Ben cried, rushing over. He made a clumsy bow and beamed in welcome. 'Good seeing you, Alex.'

He, at least, appeared to have forgotten the confrontation yesterday. Bram still broke out in a sweat when he thought of it. Alex smiled, and said, 'This concerns you as well, Ben. Shall we talk? Bram will find us somewhere private.'

'We'd best be quick,' his cousin said. 'The orders are that we march within the hour, and we are to cover the foot. There's a small garden where we won't be overheard – come with me.'

Mistress Sloper's herbs and marigolds were still bowed down with the night's rain, which had died away before dawn, but seemed likely to return soon. The three cousins stood amidst them, their heads close. Ben's attention seemed inclined to wander, and Alex's first words were addressed to him. 'The army's no place for you, Ben, and your mother and Jan must be very worried about you. Why don't you go home now, before the fighting starts?'

'Fighting?' said Ben, and a grin spread over his face. 'Ben won't fight. Ben looks after horses. Won't fight.'

'I know,' Bram said, guilt once more assailing his tender conscience. 'He shouldn't be here – he's no more aggressive than a lamb. I tried to dissuade him – I did my best. But he wouldn't go home, and no one could take him, and anyway I was the only one who seemed to see something wrong in him joining us. And,' he finished, with a glance at the tall man beside him, unsmiling in the grey dawn light, 'he's not a child – it wouldn't be right to use force, even if I had the means.'

Alex looked at him, and Bram wondered whether he would ever, if he lived to be a hundred, be able to discern what his cousin was thinking. After a pause, he said, 'I take your point. And I understand, too, that there was nothing you could do to stop him coming with you. But perhaps he will come back to Wintercombe with me.'

As Louise had previously noticed, Ben's understanding was considerably in advance of his speech. He had followed Alex's words closely, and said at their conclusion, 'Wintercombe? Ben go to Wintercombe?'

'That's right,' Alex said. 'You can come home with me now, and stay for a day or two – then I'll take you back to Longleaze. I expect your mother will be overjoyed to see you safe.'

'No,' Ben said. A mulish expression, which Bram had seen before, pushed his lower lip out. 'No, no, no. Ben's not going. Ben wants to stay here with Bram.'

'But you shouldn't be in the army at all – you shouldn't *be* here,' Bram told him forcefully. 'Ben – please go with Alex, please.'

The lower lip came out still more, and the boy's ungainly head began to shake from side to side. 'No, no, *no* – stay with you, Bram, stay with you!'

It was quite evident that persuasion was not going to work. And Ben, while far shorter than Alex, was stocky and heavily built, more than capable of putting up considerable resistance. Bram's imagination quailed before the scene that would inevitably follow should Alex try to force him back to Wintercombe: Ben screaming and blubbering like a child, dragged through the streets of Philip's Norton to make a public spectacle for villagers and army alike, the appalling loss of his dignity and self-respect, the laughter and pointing fingers ... The idea was utterly repugnant, and he was certain that Alex must share his feelings. Their only possible tactic was persuasion, and how could Ben be brought to understand that the real reason for wanting him at Wintercombe was that in battle or skirmish he would be utterly defenceless, and an easy target for slaughter?

My father tried to prevent me from joining the rebels by force, Bram thought. He would have denied me the choice, and that action will always form a barrier between us, hereafter. How then can I deny Ben his free will, even though he's a simpleton?

'It's all right,' he said to his cousin, who was still shaking his head obstinately. 'It's all right, Ben, you can stay – no one's going to force you to go with Alex.'

Ben seemed at first not to understand. He backed away from Bram's soothing touch, the obstinacy still plain on his face. 'No! No!'

'Ben, listen,' Alex said, capturing a large, spatulate hand. '*Listen*. You – don't – have – to – go – with – me. You can stay with Bram – stay!'

Eventually, his words had some effect. Ben stood still, gazing from one man to the other, slack-jawed. 'Stay? Ben stay?'

'You can *stay*!' Bram assured him urgently. 'Don't worry, Ben, it's all right. Go and saddle your horse – quickly now, we march as soon as possible.'

Still confused, the boy stood rooted, staring in bewilderment at his cousins. It took some minutes more before the fact that he would not be parted from Bram penetrated his mind, and then the change on his face was dazzling, like the sun coming out. Crowing wordlessly, he embraced his cousins and capered back to the yard, overcome with joy.

'I wish all our problems were so easily solved,' Bram said drily. He glanced at Alex, who was gazing thoughtfully after Ben, his mind evidently somewhere quite different. 'Your generous gift yesterday was but a drop in the ocean of our needs.'

Alex turned and grinned suddenly, a friendly conspiratorial smile that caught Bram by surprise. 'It took you long enough to realise what I intended, didn't it? I didn't think you were usually so slow to understand.'

'After a march like that, Descartes himself would be hard-pressed to collect his thoughts,' Bram pointed out. 'Did anyone suspect?'

'Phoebe, perhaps – but she's hardly lacking in guile herself, so can more readily discern it in others. As for the servants, I am sure they saw only what was obvious – that I was robbed at pistol-point, and in peril of my life.'

'You certainly were, with Taylor guarding you. He's like a wound-up spring, with murderous intentions.'

Alex laughed. 'I did gain the impression that he would have been delighted to have had the slightest excuse to put a bullet through me. Fortunately, I failed to give him one – and anyone watching would have been in no doubt of my danger.' He grinned again. 'With Cousin Charles probably likewise eager to fasten on any good reason to denounce me as a traitor, it's just as well.'

Bram glanced at him, knowing that he must go, but unwilling to leave his cousin before the one vital question had been put. It was now or never, and Alex's mood seemed congenial enough, although he knew how volatile he was. He took a deep breath, and said quietly, 'Then you have no thoughts of joining us?'

The blue eyes opened very wide. 'I was wondering when you were going to ask me that,' Alex said. 'It would be quite a coup for your Protestant Duke, would it not? So few of the gentry have joined him, and he must be desperate for their support, coin, horses, prestige ... I'm sorry, Bram. You know where my sympathies lie, none better, and if my father were still alive, or under other circumstances, I might agree ... but I have too much to lose, and Wintercombe depends on me.'

'You have heirs,' Bram said, made waspish by disappointment, although, realistically, he knew that he could have expected no other response. 'The St Barbes do not end with you.'

'I know they don't,' Alex said sharply. 'But I'll be damned if I'll do anything to make Cousin Charles a gift of the inheritance he's always considered to be rightfully his.' He studied Bram thoughtfully. 'And what of you? You are Jonah's only son. Surely you did not join the rebels with his blessing?'

To his annoyance, Bram flushed. 'No,' he said. 'He did his best to dissuade me, but, as you can see, it did not work.' Not for anything would he reveal to Alex the humiliation of being locked like a naughty child in his own chamber, freed only with the help of his sister.

Alex gave a wry shrug of his shoulders. 'It was your decision – and you are certainly more competent to make it than Ben. But I understand why you would not force him. Half-wit or no, he has his dignity. I do not have to ask you, though, to have a care for him?'

'Of course you don't,' Bram said. 'I feel in some sense responsible for the fact that he is here – we visited Longleaze to obtain horses, and he was seduced by the thought of soldiering, even though he has no idea of what it means, and would not willingly hurt a fly. I'll look after him as best I can, and at least Captain Hucker seems quite happy to have him in charge of the horses and kept well away from any fighting. But . . .' He looked up at

Alex, and his hazel eyes were haunted. 'But you do realise, I can't promise anything.'

'I was a soldier for three years – I know that, none better,' Alex said. He smiled at Bram, and the younger man saw that, in his cousin's eyes, he was plainly no longer an untried boy. 'Good luck,' he added. 'I'll hope for your success, though I think you know as well as I do that your chances may be limited – unless Monmouth wins a spectacular victory.'

'He is a soldier – he's wrought miracles with us,' Bram said stoutly. 'It isn't impossible, and the odds against us are not so great, despite our sorry cavalry. At least our men are convinced of the justice of our cause.'

'Oh, your cause is right enough,' Alex said, very softly. 'It's your choice of leader that I would quarrel with. His heart's not in it, and never has been. I suspect he only agreed to lead the rebellion because Argyll had already decided to invade Scotland, and his pride and honour would not allow him to stand by while lesser men fought for what he considers to be his inheritance. And that's a view I can readily understand. But, competent soldier though he undoubtedly is, I don't have much faith in his powers of leadership. Oh, I know what you're going to say – that he has inspired thousands of men to follow him, and I'm not denying that. But it's the men of authority, the gentry, the justices, he needs to attract – and, like me, they are not going to risk all they hold dear for a man whom many see as little better than a rabble-rouser.'

Bram, stung, said indignantly, 'Well, who would you follow?'

'Not Monmouth,' Alex said. 'I am too well acquainted with his faults. But there is another man in Holland, not so beloved or so well known, whose right, should King James prove disastrous, is unassailable, and whose competence and suitability alike are unquestionable. And that is William of Orange.'

'Dutch William? But he's a foreigner!'

'He is also James's nephew, half a Stuart, he's married to James's daughter, he is an excellent soldier, a capable ruler, and above all, staunchly Protestant. If *he* came knocking on Wintercombe's door for support, I would gladly give it. But not, I fear, to King Charles's spoilt bastard with delusions of grandeur and kingship beyond his ability to obtain.'

'I see,' said Bram: and the trouble was that he could, very clearly. He wanted to defend Monmouth, to deny what Alex had said, but somehow it stuck in his throat, for he saw the essential truth in his cousin's words, and confirmed what he had already suspected, that the Duke was essentially a fair-weather leader, heartened and inspiring when matters were going well, disproportionately low-spirited and ineffective at the least sign of a

285

reverse. And his disconsolate mood of the previous day, although now vanished, had had its inevitable effect on his followers. Morale was slipping, and more had deserted last night.

But he would not readily admit as much to Alex: he lifted his head proudly, and smiled. 'Well, you are entitled to your opinion, as I am to mine. Shall we agree to differ, Cousin, and part friends?'

'We have never been anything else,' Alex said, holding out his hand. 'Goodbye, Bram, and keep yourself and Ben safe.'

They turned to leave the garden together. In the doorway that led to the yard, through which Ben had danced a little earlier, a young woman was standing, wearing a plain dark green gown overlaid with a loose heavy Brandenburg coat, of masculine style and cut, and a black hood pushed back from her dark curling hair. She was much too well dressed to be one of the Sloper daughters, but Bram did not recognise her at first: it was only when Alex said sharply, 'What the devil are you doing here?' that he realised that it was Louise.

She gave them both her huge, dazzling smile, quite unrepentant, and came towards them. She was not wearing riding clothes, so she had probably walked from Wintercombe. Alex said, 'You shouldn't be here – it's too dangerous.'

'Where's the danger?' Louise gestured at the peaceful little garden. 'I've met with nothing but courtesy and helpfulness all the way up South Street. And if you're wondering why I walked, well, it isn't far, and my shoulder is not fully mended yet, and anyway I don't want my sweet little mare brought to the attention of a notorious horse-thief.' She grinned at Bram. 'Hullo, Cousin. I didn't want you to leave without speaking to you, to wish you Godspeed at the least.'

'And I'm glad that you have,' he told her. 'But what has happened to your shoulder?'

'Oh, I put it out of joint in a fall from my horse, and Alex employed his skill as a bonesetter to mend it,' Louise explained, with a mischievous glance at her older cousin. 'But for some time, I have had to be very careful, and riding is still forbidden, so I'm afraid I cannot join your army, even if I had thoughts of disguising myself in breeches.'

'You'd probably be more use to us than some of the men under my command,' Bram said drily. 'But I doubt that Captain Hucker would accept you, even if he did allow Ben to join us.'

'I've just seen him,' Louise said. 'I gather that you haven't succeeded in persuading him to leave the army.'

'No, I haven't,' Alex said curtly. 'And I don't think anyone could.'

'I tried,' Louise said. 'He likes me, so I thought I stood a good chance of success. But as soon as I suggested he come back to Wintercombe, he started shouting, "No!" So I thought I'd best leave well alone.'

'A wise decision – pity you don't make it more often.'

Louise glared at him. 'I'm not a child, Alex.'

'No, I can see that all too clearly.'

'I can't waste time standing idly by while you two argue,' Bram said. 'We have to march soon – in fact, I think I can hear the vanguard beginning to move out now. Thank you for coming to see me, Louise – I hope it hasn't got you into trouble.'

'With him?' She cast a scornful glance at Alex, who was frowning at her. 'Both of you should know by now that I am quite ungovernable, by coercion at any rate. Witty and charming persuasion always works much better where I am concerned. Goodbye, Bram, and God go with you – I shall think of you always.' And, to his surprise and delight, she gave him an affectionate, cousinly salute on both cheeks. 'Good luck!'

'Good luck,' Alex repeated, and Bram, knowing that he must leave at once or neglect his duty, gave them a last wave, and ran from the garden.

'Have your wits quite deserted you?' Alex demanded, as soon as he was out of sight. 'The village is full of soldiers, Feversham and the Royal army could arrive at any moment, and you take a casual stroll from Wintercombe?'

'There is no danger,' Louise said angrily. Because of the muddy terrain she had put a pair of sturdy wooden pattens over her shoes before setting out, and the extra three inches put her almost at his height, a considerable boost to her confidence. 'I walked as far as Lyde Green before I met a single soldier, and since I was obviously not part of the King's army, he let me pass. Then I came past the manor, which is full of horse, and the officers were very pleasant, and told me where Bram might be found, and then up West Street to the Market Cross, and so to this house, and never met with even a frown, until you, let alone any danger, despite the fact that everywhere is thick with soldiers. And,' she added with a grin, 'I have to confess that I did linger by the George, to catch a glimpse of Monmouth. He's quite as handsome as they say, although he looked rather tired and pale.'

'Since someone apparently took a pot-shot at him last night, that's not altogether surprising,' Alex told her. 'Well, let's not linger here – as it is, we'll have to fight our way back against a tide of marching rebels. Come on, madam, and no more dawdling to ogle handsome soldiers.'

He took her arm. Louise, by now thoroughly annoyed at his manner, jerked it away. 'Get your hands off me!'

'How unusual. I was under the impression that your wishes were quite different.'

They stood glaring at each other amongst the marigolds. For a moment anger, and something else, almost crackled and scorched the air between them. She held his gaze defiantly, determined not to be the first to back down, and at last he made an impatient exclamation and turned away towards the gate. With a secret smile of triumph, she walked unhurriedly after him.

The mason's yard was full of jostling horsemen being harangued by a spare, middle-aged man on a very good bay horse. She paused beside Alex, watching. Bram, once more with the colours in his grasp, was easy to spot, and so was Ben, squat and ungainly just behind him. In ragged, confused order, the troopers filed out of the yard and into South Street. Her cousins waved farewell, Bram simply lifting one hand, Ben flapping his energetically. And then they were gone, and she wondered, bleakly, whether she would ever see either of them again.

'Sir Alexander!' It was Robert Sloper, the owner of the house. He had emerged from one of the outbuildings ranged around the yard, and came quickly towards them, a big well-muscled man in early middle age, and a respected and prosperous village elder. 'Forgive me, I had no idea that you were here – and Mistress Chevalier, too. Will you take some refreshment, sir, before you go? My wife is brewing some tea.'

It would have been discourteous to decline, and Alex accepted the invitation graciously, with the warning that it might not be wise to stay very long. Master Sloper, delighted at the prestige of entertaining the notorious Sir Alexander St Barbe within his pleasant abode, ushered them inside to a warm and pleasant parlour, where his wife presided over a steaming silver pot that was obviously her pride and joy.

Louise was glad of this interlude, although she had hoped to catch a last glimpse of the army as it left Philip's Norton. Still, it would take some time for all six thousand or more of them to leave, so she probably would not miss the spectacle entirely. And she doubted that Alex's anger with her would survive a quarter-hour of Mistress Sloper's cheerfully relentless conversation. His moods were intense, but she had realised that they did not last very long. Besides, he had that saving grace, a keen sense of humour and the absurd. She did not like it when he was angry with her, as if she were some wayward child in need of chastisement: that was why she could never meekly absorb his criticism, but always responded too readily in kind. I wish, Louise thought, as she settled herself gracefully in a cane-seated chair, that he could make up his mind whether I am a little girl to be corrected, or a desirable and attractive woman.

At last, after a dish of tea and some rather stilted conversation, Alex rose with thanks and apologies to Mistress Sloper, and the advice to stay within doors until the rebels were safely clear of the village. Then he escorted Louise out of the house, and into the hectic bustle of South Street.

It was still full of rebel soldiers, making their weary way towards Frome, and presenting a rather pathetic sight. Louise, held at the gateway by her cousin's restraining hand, watched the slack, exhausted faces of men who had been tramping across Somerset, to no discernible purpose, for upwards of two days without regular rest or food or shelter, mostly in direly inhospitable weather. All were bearded, there being no opportunity to shave, and their clothes were damp, mud-covered and ragged. She noticed that several men had bound their feet with rags, their shoes having presumably disintegrated, and although most carried muskets or swords, there were several groups armed only with scythe blades, lashed to eight-foot poles.

'Don't be misled,' Alex told her, seeing her staring at these makeshift implements, eloquent of poverty and desperation. 'They can be extremely effective – quite capable of taking limbs off, if wielded with enough gusto. But there's no doubt, muskets would be of more use. Monmouth spent so much money on his ships that he had not enough arms for his supporters – and he hasn't been able to seize sufficient on his marches to make up the difference.'

'How do you know all this?' Louise asked cautiously. Alex laid a finger alongside his nose. 'Never you mind. Let's just say that I keep my ear close to the ground. Now, there seems to be a gap in the traffic – shall we go?'

Further down South Street, waggons were visible, apparently tangled, holding up the march. Louise wondered how many men had already left the village, and whether her cousins, and the horse, were with the vanguard or part of those in the rear. Since it was unlikely that even Alex knew the answers, she said nothing, and allowed him to escort her down the street towards the Market Cross, keeping well to the side to avoid the mud, ruts and puddles, not to mention the stranded waggons, in the centre of the road.

They had almost reached the George when a loud crackling sound rattled the air. Almost before she had realised what it meant, she found herself being dragged unceremoniously sideways into a doorway that afforded precious little shelter. Outside the George, people were running to and fro, shouting, and a rider on a wild-eyed horse galloped almost into the inn's porch before he pulled up, yelling something frantic and unintelligible.

'Attack?' she said, trying to appear calm, despite the sudden and furious hammering of her heart.

Alex nodded, keeping himself between her and the street. Urgent to see something, she peered round his shoulder, and beheld only confusion and chaos. More shots snapped rapidly, and she realised that they were not nearly so close as she had supposed. The same thought had evidently occurred to her cousin. He said curtly, 'Keep hold of me, and well out of the way of the horses. We'll take refuge in the George until we can find out what's happening.'

Her pattens slipping awkwardly on the rough slippery stones and mud, she followed him to the yard that lay on the inn's left side, surrounded by stabling and outbuildings. Not surprisingly, it was seething with men and horses, and she caught a glimpse of Monmouth himself, conspicuous on a milky-grey horse, giving a stream of orders. The sudden promise of action seemed to have enlivened the Duke, who looked years younger than he had earlier, and much happier. Then Alex propelled her in through a side door to the warm and comfortable shelter of the George.

There was almost as much chaos inside as out, but at least they were safe from stray bullets. Louise sank breathless on to a bench in the corner of the taproom, beside a fierce fire that was never allowed to go out entirely, even in the warmest weather, and Alex went to find Master Prescott.

He returned instead with the landlord's son, Harry, a high-coloured young man with, already, an incipient paunch, and addressed her briskly. 'Apparently the King's army – whether the whole force or just an advance party isn't yet known – has attacked the barricade at the end of North Street. Those rebels who have already marched out will be recalled – a man's just been sent to tell them to turn back – and it's likely there will be heavy fighting at the least, if not a full-scale battle. And of course, returning to Wintercombe would mean venturing far too close to the action for safety. There's no question of you being able to go back there just yet.'

He did not say, 'I told you so', for which she was profoundly grateful, although she had no doubt that he thought it. She said tartly, 'If there is fighting in North Street, the George is hardly safe either.'

'Perhaps not, but it's certainly less dangerous than trying to pick our way through a battlefield.' Alex surveyed her, his arms folded, and she saw the twitch of a smile. 'Harry's wife, Mistress Mary, is upstairs in her chamber, with the children, and she would be delighted, so Harry says, to have you join her. It faces west, towards the church, so you need not fear stray bullets coming through the window – not yet, anyway.'

'We've had enough of that already,' Harry observed grimly. 'And God alone knows what the rest of this day will bring. If you'll come with me,

Mistress Chevalier, I'm sure Moll will be pleased to see you, and you can stay as long as is necessary. Would you like some refreshments? The Duke and his men have virtually eaten our larders empty, but I will see what my mother can provide. A little chocolate, perhaps? I know we had some last night.'

'That would be delicious,' Louise told him. She rose, clasping her Brandenburg around her, and glanced at Alex. 'What are you going to do, Cousin? Will you join me and Mistress Mary and the children?'

'Hardly,' Alex said, with a grin. 'I, of course, am going to put myself, in typically foolhardy fashion, in the path of danger – but before that, perhaps a fortifying tankard or two of Harry's strong beer. I'll let you know what's happening as soon as I've found out. Meanwhile, I suggest you stay with Mistress Mary. Apart from any other considerations, I would be cast even further into your grandmother's black books were you to do anything stupid while under my care.'

'Don't worry,' Louise told him shortly. 'I have no intention of it.' And she gave him a brief curtsey just short of insolence, and followed Harry from the taproom.

Despite her misgivings, Mistress Moll proved to be a pleasant young woman, plain and plump, and obviously much harassed by the lively presence of her three small sons and their nursemaid. She made Louise welcome, poured chocolate, and asked her anxiously as to the progress of the fighting, of which in fact Louise knew little more than she did. The sound of musket fire could be heard quite plainly through the small window, and continued relentlessly as they talked. The children, especially the older two, were fretting with impatience, wanting to know what was happening, and Louise had some sympathy. She asked Mistress Prescott about the soldiers who had stayed at the George: had she spoken to Monmouth?

'I was presented to him,' said the other woman. 'No more than that, alas – Harry's parents had much more to do with him than I did. He's a charming man, as they say, though rather melancholy and preoccupied – and who can blame him?'

As a fresh burst of musket fire rattled in the distance, Louise rose to her feet and prowled restlessly to the window. The green lush slope of Church Mead and Fair Close, sweeping down to the low wall surrounding the churchyard at the bottom of the hill, and more empty fields climbing the rise along the Wells road, were all that was visible. Frustrated, she turned away from this deceptively peaceful vista, and cast herself down in her chair. She was not worried for Alex: he was not a soldier, he would not become involved in the fray, and he was doubtless at this moment enjoying Master Prescott's best beer with his usual excess. But Bram and Ben were another matter. Were they fighting, perhaps hurt, perhaps already dying, or dead?

'You seem anxious, Mistress Chevalier,' said Moll, with a sympathetic look. 'Are you worried for Sir Alexander?'

'The devil will probably look to his own,' Louise told her. 'No, I have two other cousins with the rebel horse, and I have no idea if they are concerned in the fighting, or whether they are safe.'

'I didn't know that,' said Moll Prescott, with a gleam of curiosity. 'With the horse? How did they come to join the rebels?'

It was a relief to talk about Bram and Ben, as though it would somehow preserve them from harm. Louise told her the little she knew of why they were with Monmouth, and was rewarded by the rapt attention of Moll, her children and the nursemaid. As she finished, the other woman sighed. 'So young – and so brave. What a pity they could not have chosen a more hopeful cause.'

Louise glanced at her, and said softly, 'What is your opinion, then?'

'I think as Harry does – that there is no reason, yet, to rebel against King James, and that Monmouth and his men are probably rash and foolhardy – but I cannot help but have some sympathy for them,' said Mistress Prescott frankly. 'God knows how it will all end – in disaster, I fear. Let us hope that your cousins are safe and well!'

At that exact moment, Bram was riding, with some hundred or so other horse, towards the thick of the fighting. They had in fact left the village in the vanguard of the army, and had been recalled when perhaps a half-mile or so down the road. Cantering back in haste towards the sound of musket fire, past files of bewildered foot crushed into the hedges to let them past, he hoped that Ben, lumbering along in his wake, could be persuaded to stay in the village: and also, that Louise and Alex were by now safely returned to Wintercombe.

A barricade, composed of an overturned cart and waggon, gates, sheep hurdles and wood, had been erected at the end of North Street, where the houses ended. Beyond, the road to Bath ran along the side of the hill between thick hedges, with fields of pasture and corn on either side. Sixty musketeers, under the command of Captain Vincent of the Red Regiment, had seen enemy soldiers approaching fast, and with a tempting lack of caution, along the road towards them. Hastily, they had made ready, and Vincent had sent a score of men along the hedges to provide flanking fire. The Royalist advance guard, tramping confident and eager up the road, wondering where the rebels could be, found themselves facing a hail of bullets, from three sides. Several men fell, and the King's general, Feversham, seeing all too clearly what was happening, ordered his grenadiers and cavalry to advance in support.

There followed an hour or more of close and vigorous fighting. Vincent's musketeers, quickly joined by more of their comrades, kept up a hot and withering fire from behind the cover of the hedges. The rest of the Red Regiment, under the command of Nat Wade, one of Monmouth's most able officers, hurried down West Street, along which the famous fair was held in happier times, cut through the outbuildings and barton surrounding the manor house, and turned right to rush up the little lane that met North Street at the site of the barricade and the heaviest fighting. Behind them, urging on their reluctant mounts, came a ragged body of horse, Bram and Ben amongst them.

It was far more terrifying than the brief skirmish at Keynsham. The untried horses fought against their riders' heels and spurs, and several whipped round and bolted. To Bram's dismay, Ben was still with him, quite unarmed, shouting gleefully until they came near to the shooting. Then, as realisation dawned, his face crumpled with sudden fear. His horse, sensing the sudden loss of control, seized its opportunity to turn and flee, and Bram was utterly relieved to see him go. Now, he could concentrate on his duty to his comrades, without always having to be looking out for Ben as well.

Afterwards, he reflected ruefully that his cousin might just as well have stayed beside him, for all the danger they encountered. The horses, maddened with fear, could not be forced more than a few yards up the lane, and those men who had enough control and skill to bring their mounts to a halt, rather than allow them to flee, saw the men of the Red Regiment, determined to come to grips with the enemy at last and prove their worth, run headlong into the fray. The force of their charge surprised the King's soldiers, and the narrow Bath road became an inextricable tangle of fighting men, with the rattle of musket fire giving way, as the risk of shooting comrades increased, to shouts, cries and the clash of swords. In such enclosed ground, it was no place for the horse, and Bram could see, if he peered above the hedge, the enemy cavalry, some five hundred of them, waiting helplessly further up the hill, well to the rear.

'Bram!'

He turned in amazement to see Alex, threading his way through the restive, nervous horses. He was on foot, bare-headed, and, as far as could be seen, without weapons. To venture undefended within a scant few yards of vicious hand-to-hand fighting was little short of lunacy, and

Bram, forgetting his cousin's eight-year seniority, said in astonishment, 'What in God's name are you doing here? You must be mad!'

'No – just curious,' Alex said. His face was flushed, and the blue eyes brilliant. 'Well? Are you winning?'

'It's not as easy as that,' Bram told him, still incredulous. 'The fighting's very close and fierce – it's too enclosed for the horse. Feversham's are up on the hill, with the rest of his army behind. If they advance, you'll be caught up in it.'

'Oh, I can run fast enough,' Alex said carelessly. For someone who had seemed so concerned about Wintercombe's ability to manage after his demise, he seemed remarkably casual in the face of considerable danger: at any moment, the fighting could spill down the lane and engulf them. Bram hauled one of his pistols from its holster and thrust it at him. 'Here – at least take this.'

Alex shook his head. 'No, it'll only mark me out as a target. And I'm not the only one to venture out to view the spectacle – look behind you.'

Bram obeyed, and saw several curious villagers peering round the hedge at the bottom of the lane, where it turned into the manor barton on the left, and the Wellow Lane, that ran past Wintercombe, on the right. He said doubtfully, 'Where's Louise?'

'Don't worry, she's quite safe. I left her with Mistress Prescott at the George.'

'And you sampled some of the landlord's beer before coming out?' said Bram, suddenly realising the reason for his cousin's elated mood.

'Only a jug or two. You have a remarkably exaggerated view of my vices,' Alex told him, grinning. 'Oh, and I saw Ben. He's with the rest of your horses, milling about by the church. Are you and your fellows here the only ones with a proper government of your mounts?'

His pointed question was overheard by several of the men around Bram, and some looked at this unwanted and objectionable interloper with active resentment. Taylor, just loud enough to be heard, made his views plain. 'Well, if you think you could do any better, I'd like to see you try, if you aren't too high and mighty for it.' And several others muttered in agreement.

Alex gave no sign that he had heard, but Bram flushed with embarrassment, annoyed that his cousin had aroused the dislike, not to say the contempt, of his comrades. He said indignantly, 'If you're not going to join us, then you'd better go. You can do no good here, you're only in the way – and one unarmed simpleton is quite enough for me to look after, thank you.'

The fighting just beyond them was increasing in intensity. The Royalist advance guard had been all but cut off by the weight of the Red Regiment's attack, and now more of Feversham's foot, and a troop of horse grenadiers, were advancing hastily to the rescue. Alex sent his cousin a wild, flyaway grin that made him resemble no one so much as Louise, plotting mischief. 'Very well, Cousin, I'll beat a tactical retreat – and the very best of luck to you!'

And then suddenly Bram heard the tramp of hundreds of marching feet, and much shouting. He whipped round in the saddle to see a torrent of rebels, the musketeers and scythemen of the Green Regiment, with some pikes, pouring round the corner from the direction of the manor, with Lieutenant-Colonel Holmes, who had fought with Cromwell, at their head. The lane was very narrow, and there was hardly room for them to pass the little knot of horsemen occupying the way. Bram's chestnut reared and snorted, and Holmes yelled something as he pushed past. For a moment there was utter confusion, frightened horses, swearing men, and one of his comrades yelled, 'Let's go with them! Monmouth! Soho!'

Tangled up in the Green Regiment, infected by their urgency, Bram and the rest of the cavalry, some three dozen or so in number, were swept along with them. Too busy controlling his horse and drawing his sword, he did not have time to see what had happened to Alex: and then they were in the thick of the fighting.

The next hour or so was a chaotic nightmare, as the men of the Green and Red Regiments, fighting doggedly and with great courage, forced the Royal soldiers back from the barricade with pike and scythe and musket, and the very limited assistance of those few cavalry who could persuade their mounts into the fray. Bram's chestnut proved obdurate, and in the end he hovered with the rest on the edge of the battle, discharging his pistols at obvious targets, without notable success, and riding down stray enemy fugitives. But in these narrow lanes and thickly hedged fields, they were almost useless: it was the foot soldiers who bore the brunt, and at push of pike the fighting swayed to and fro across the pasture, while men fell underfoot, or crawled away wounded to die in the unripe, rain-battered corn, and the steep muddy slope of the little lane leading up to the barricade flowed with a liquid that ran redder than water.

Rain was beginning to fall: the pearl-grey morning sky had darkened from the west, and now the more distant hills were almost hidden behind the curtain of water pouring down. In such weather, matchlock muskets were all but useless, and powder became damp and unreliable. Grimly, knowing that they must take advantage of their superiority in numbers if not in weaponry, the rebel soldiers fought their way forward from hedge to hedge, the enemy falling back before their dogged, relentless advance, until at last they had retreated beyond the last barrier that separated them from the main body of the Royalist army, drawn up in the wide ploughed expanse of Hinton Field. Breathless and exultant, the rebels lined up behind the hawthorns, glad of the chance to rest and take stock, and those of the cavalry who had joined the attack halted a little to their rear.

Bram looked round at his fellows, and met, in the faces of each one, the expressions that must be mirrored on his own: exhaustion, relief, and above all gladness that they had survived so far. There had been several killed, almost all from the foot, and it seemed that the Royal forces, victims first of that initial murderous musket fire, and then of the bitter hand-to-hand fighting, had lost a considerably larger number. Desultory shots were still being fired, despite the downpour, but then a much vaster, flatter sound shattered the air, and something large and dark sailed over their heads, to bury itself with a splattering thump in the close behind their field. The horses, utterly weary, were hardly in a state to protest at this new horror, but the man next to Bram swore ferociously. 'Field pieces, by God's bones! Why weren't they used before?'

'Perhaps they got bogged down at Midford, as ours did,' Bram said. 'Let's hope their aim continues so poor – for our pathetic little two-pounders can hardly make an adequate reply to that.'

Another deep boom, and a cannon ball landed much further down the valley towards the mill, to a few derisive cheers from the rebel ranks. Bram soothed his horse, who stood unmoving and uncaring, its wet and muddy head hanging to its knees, and steam rising from its flanks. Taylor, who had earlier expressed his contempt for Alex, glanced at him and said, 'Your friend wasn't so high and mighty after all.'

'What do you mean?' Bram stared at his least-liked trooper, suddenly alarmed. He had given no thought to Alex for some time, and had assumed that he had returned to the safety of the village, or Wintercombe.

'He must have heard what I said,' Taylor told him smugly. 'I saw him later in the thick of it, waving a sword about him, just by the barricade, and yelling "Monmouth" and "Soho" with the best. I'm glad to see that no friend of yours is a coward,' he added slyly.

'You saw him *fighting*?' Bram said in appalled astonishment. 'But he didn't have a sword!'

'He did when I saw him,' Taylor said with satisfaction. 'And putting it to good use, too. Couldn't say what happened to him after that, though – haven't laid eyes on him since.'

'Thank you,' Bram said, through his teeth. A cold dread feeling had settled on him that seemed to be a certain intimation of disaster. Ben was probably safe, but he had given no thought to Alex. Was his one of the huddled lifeless bodies littering the northern outskirts of the village?

He had to find out. He peered through the rain at the ranks of foot sheltering behind the thick hawthorn hedges, their hats pulled well down against the weather. No one was bare-headed, and their motley collection of soaked, ragged, homespun garments bore no resemblance to Alex's fine grey wool. His urgency, fuelled by that terrible foreboding, made him pull his weary horse around, to ride along the lines of soldiers, seeking the unmistakable height of his cousin, while the King's guns kept up their intermittent fire.

He had gone perhaps a quarter of the way along the hedge when Colonel Wade caught at his bridle. 'Cornet! What's your name?'

'Loveridge, sir, of Captain Hucker's troop,' Bram said, with respect. Wade was well liked by the rebels, who admired his determination and ability. 'I'm seeking my cousin, sir –'

'Oh, yes, the half-wit. Well, you can seek him in Norton, and fetch the rest of the horse up, all you can find, as quick as you can – now off with you, man!'

There was no chance to explain, or argue. Bram turned his exhausted horse and urged it into a shambling trot across the lumpy pasture towards the village. He made his way through a gap in the hedge bordering the lane, and at once the chestnut shied wildly away from a corpse lying in the ditch beyond. It clattered in a panic down the lane towards Lyde Green, while Bram heaved vigorously at its reins.

The horse's fright, however, proved more potent than its weariness, or his strength. It galloped into the manor barton, and shuddered at last to a halt, brought up short by a body of horse coming the other way. Hastily, he shouted the password, 'Soho!', and was disproportionately relieved to recognise Captain Hucker, although the likelihood of any Royalist horse being so far in advance of their lines was remote, to say the least. 'Message from Colonel Wade, sir!' he added briskly, to disguise his precipitate arrival. 'He wants all the rest of the horse to advance up to our position, as quickly as possible.'

'We're on our way,' Hucker told him. 'I tried to send your cousin up to the George, but he'd have none of it, so he's here, somewhere behind me. I suggest that he attaches himself to you. The rest of the horse are gathered in the meadow above the church, under Captain Tucker.'

'Thank you, sir,' Bram said, and pulled the chestnut out of their way. Ben, his broad flat face crumpled with bewildered distress, was in the last rank. He gave an inarticulate cry of joy, and pushed his horse across to his cousin's, tears running down his cheeks.

'It's all right,' Bram told him, as the boy sobbed his name over and over.

'It's all right – we're both safe and unharmed, thank God.' And so much for us, he thought anxiously: but what of Alex?

With Ben's horse close behind, he rode through the barton and into West Street. People were peering out of doorways, some, more boldly, standing in the road. A woman ran up, weeping, demanding news, and he said hastily, 'There's been some fighting, but we've beaten them back, with some loss.'

She wailed something, her husband's name perhaps, although he knew that very few Norton men, if any, had joined the rebels. There was no comfort that he could give her, and guiltily he forced the chestnut into a trot, turning into Fair Close through an open gate, and to Church Mead beyond, to deliver his message.

# 17

## *'Seduc'd by impious arts'*

Louise had been watching, and waiting, for hours, while the distant sounds of battle filtered muffled through the window of Mistress Prescott's chamber. Fretting with powerless impatience, she had longed to run downstairs, to ask the first person she met, anyone, the Duke himself, what was happening. Harry Prescott had come up, perhaps an hour or more after her arrival, to give them what news he could: that the fighting was thick at the barricade at the end of North Street, and that some of the Royalists had briefly broken through but, in grave danger of being cut off, had retreated with considerable losses. He had added that Sir Alexander had gone out to discover more, and would doubtless be able to tell her all the details when he returned.

But Alex had not returned, and Louise, cooped up with a stranger, however pleasant, had grown increasingly restless. When some of the horse began to straggle into Church Mead, and little Henry shouted the news from his post by the window, she rushed to look. But amongst the increasing numbers of ill-assorted cavalry, she could see no sign of Bram, or Ben: and indeed, at this distance, she knew that she could have little hope of doing so.

But she stayed by the window, with the two small boys, Henry and Tom, on either side of her, agog to see the soldiers and any fighting. The minutes and hours ticked by, counted by Mistress Prescott's handsome clock, and although more horsemen entered the mead, and some left, there was no real activity. The far-off musket shots diminished in number, and then came a much louder, flatter sound that rattled a loose pane of glass and made the children jump.

'It must be cannon,' Louise said, as Moll Prescott leapt to her feet and came running, and the nursemaid picked up the youngest child, who had burst into frightened tears. 'But I didn't know Monmouth had any.'

'He has three or four – I saw them going past this morning,' said Moll Prescott doubtfully. 'But they were very small – only two-pounders, so Harry said. Surely they wouldn't sound so loud as that?'

Another explosion gave point to her words. The baby wailed louder, and his mother turned to take him from his nurse's arms. Louise, gazing intently through the greenish glass, saw the cavalry in the mead begin to split up. A considerable number of them were leaving, while the rest were being grouped in some sort of order by an officer with a fervently waving arm.

The bombardment continued, still distant, but loud and fierce enough to intrude. Louise watched avidly as the first group disappeared out of her view, and two men rode into the field. From this distance, the first could have been anyone, but the second, slouching ungracefully in the saddle, was quite unmistakable. With a gasp of relief, Louise swung round from the window. 'Mistress Prescott, I've just seen my cousins – I'm going to find out what is happening.'

'Is that wise?' the other woman asked anxiously, rising to her feet. 'There must still be fighting, we don't know where or how fierce –'

'Don't worry, I won't venture outside unless I'm sure that it's safe,' Louise assured her. 'But I do want to see my cousins – they may know what's going on, and where Sir Alexander is.' She gave Mistress Prescott a confident smile that did not exactly reflect her true feelings, and fairly ran from the chamber before her hostess's frantic protests could delay her.

She found Jem, one of the tapsters, tapping a barrel. In stark contrast to the crowded confusion earlier, the George now seemed quiet and empty. A man of few words, he nodded to her. 'A'ternoon, Mistress Chevalier.'

'What's happening, Jem? Where is everyone? Have you seen Sir Alexander?'

'Not since he were sat over there drinking beer with Master Prescott.' Jem finished his task, and straightened. 'Haven't been outside, Mistress – can't tell ee much, save that all the wounded have been brung back to our stable.'

'Thank you,' Louise said, with equivalent lack of ceremony, and peered cautiously out of the door which led to the small inner courtyard. This was crowded with men, many wounded and groaning, being helped to the stable building at the end. She glanced to her right, under the archway and out into the marketplace. Some of Monmouth's waggons still stood there in the driving rain, with a curious assortment of plough-horses and oxen drooping in the shafts, and from North Street came a group of rebel soldiers, supporting more wounded amongst them. As she watched, they were carried past her, to join their fellows outside the stable. On the cobbled stones, blood lay in a bright spattered trail.

Wherever the fighting was taking place, it was plainly not in the immediate vicinity of the George, and the intermittent cannonfire seemed, even here in the open, to be quite distant. Louise pulled her

Brandenburg coat on over her gown – she had left off her pattens, in which it was difficult to walk quickly – and hurried out into the marketplace.

There were plenty of village people about, standing and staring, so she did not feel conspicuous, or in any danger. Indeed, their curious, avid faces were more appropriate to a fair or some other holiday spectacle, rather than the presence of two warring armies. As more groups of wounded emerged from North Street, she ran down West Street through the rain, hoping that she would not be too late to find Bram.

The last of the horse were coming briskly through Fair Close, and trotting up towards her. She drew in to the side of the road, already regretting the pattens, for her skirts were soaked and spattered with mud. At last, her searching eyes located Bram, almost unrecognisable as the confident, handsome cavalryman with whom she had conversed that morning. He was coated with mud and soaking wet, his hair snaking from under his hat, and his face beneath the dirt was grey, weary, and sick with worry. From the look of him, the day had not gone well for the rebels.

She hailed him urgently, and at her second call he turned his head and saw her, standing by the wall that bounded Fair Close. At once he brought his chestnut to a halt, waited until the men on either side had passed him, and then steered the horse towards her. Behind him, to her relief, was Ben, grinning a welcome.

'Louise! I thought you were supposed to be safe in the George,' Bram said. 'What are you doing here?'

'I came to see what was happening,' she said breathlessly. He seemed so different, so changed from the cheerful, exuberant companion of those carefree days in Taunton, only a scant few weeks ago. Now, with rebellion and warfare erupted in the West Country, that time seemed inexpressibly distant, and the Louise and Bram who had discussed Monmouth so lightly in Jonah's bookshop to be different people entirely.

'There's been a battle – well, a fight, really,' Bram told her. 'We've driven them back, though, thanks to Wade and Holmes, and now they're drawn up in a field about a quarter of a mile along the Bath road, and our men are lined up behind the hedge, facing them. It's too wet for musket fire now.'

'But I can hear cannon.'

'It's easier to keep their match dry, or so I believe,' Bram told her: he knew nothing at all about the arcane mysteries of artillery. He added, with a renewed surge of anxiety, 'Louise – have you seen Alex at all?'

'Alex?' She stared up at him, bewildered. 'No – no, I haven't, not since he left me at the George, hours ago.'

The look on Bram's face made her blood run suddenly cold. 'He met me,' her cousin said quietly. 'He spoke to me, in the lane that runs up from Lyde Green. He seemed strange . . . and then one of my men saw him, in the middle of the fighting, and he had a sword.'

'A *sword*? But he wasn't wearing one,' Louise said in disbelief. 'Are you sure it was him?'

'I didn't see him, so I only have another's word for it – but he's not exactly inconspicuous, is he? Of course,' Bram said, clutching at hope, 'he may be with our foot, up by that hedge – I only had time to look for him amongst a few of them before Colonel Wade sent me back to collect the rest of the horse. But . . . it's foolish, I know, and he would be the first to mock me for it, but I can't help being anxious.'

'They are bringing the wounded from North Street to the George,' Louise said. Her mouth had gone dry, and her mind reeled in horror from the thought of Alex, whom she had thought safe, inviolable, lying dead or hurt, perhaps only a hundred yards distant from where she was standing.

'Then can you go and look for him there?' Bram asked her. 'And somehow get a messge to me – Ben, go with Louise, look for Alex, and you follow me and tell me whether you've found him. I'm sorry, Louise, I have to go – but I won't give up if I can help it, and I'll let you know if he's safe.'

She looked up at him, narrowing her eyes against the steady rain, and managed a brave smile. 'Thank you, Bram. And – good luck!'

Ben followed her meekly enough back to the George. By now, the small courtyard was packed with rebel soldiers, mostly with minor injuries: the more serious cases had presumably been carried inside, out of the rain. She left her cousin and his horse standing by the archway, reminding him not to impede the people coming and going, and by dint of apology, explanation and her most charming smile, managed to squeeze her way into the stable.

It was fortunate that the light within was so bad: as it was, the stench of blood and sweat, and more unpleasant odours, caught her unawares, and made her retch. By force of will, she managed not to vomit: she swallowed fiercely, and accosted the first uninjured person she saw, a young man wearing a bloodstained leather apron, with some surgeon's implement in his hand. 'Please, sir, is my cousin here? Sir Alexander St Barbe?'

He stared at her impatiently. 'There are a score of men here, madam, and all of them in desperate case. I have no idea if your cousin is amongst them, and no time to look.'

'A very tall man, with black hair, a little older than yourself?' she persisted, though he was already turning away to kneel beside a groaning man writhing on a pile of straw.

'No,' said the surgeon curtly, already busy with his patient. Helpless, Louise gazed frantically around her, trying to see through the fetid gloom. It was plain that if she inspected every man, she would get in the way of those trying to help them. But then she saw Harry Prescott, a bucket of water in each hand, darkening the doorway, and ran to him in relief. 'Master Prescott! Thank God! Have you see Sir Alexander?'

He stared at her, bewildered. 'No, Mistress Chevalier, I haven't seen him in some while – not since he went out to find some news. Why do you ask?'

'Because he was apparently caught up in the fighting,' Louise told him, dropping her voice to a breathless whisper. 'And neither I nor my other cousins can find him – I thought he might be in here –'

'I haven't seen him,' Harry repeated. 'I'll tell you plain, though, he isn't amongst these here – thank God, for they're all sorely hurt. But I'll ask around, discreetly, see if anyone else has clapped eyes on him. You'd best go back to Moll, Mistress – this is no place for a lady, you can see that.'

She could, indeed. A man in agony was blubbering and blaspheming in a corner, another, more quietly but no less appallingly, was choking his life away almost under her feet. She thanked him and escaped, gasping, from that terrible place to the relative peace and fresh air of the courtyard.

Once there, she had to cling to one of the posts supporting the gallery as she fought her sudden weakness. Pain, unpleasantness, the everyday small sufferings of life, were not strange to her, and she had not thought herself so squeamish, but that ghastly, concentrated agony, the indignity and torment and her complete powerlessness to help, had shaken her to the heart.

'Louey! Louey! All right, Louey?'

She turned shakily in response to Ben's gentle touch on her shoulder. He looked horrified: unaware of her drastically altered face, she said hastily, 'It's all right, Ben – he's not there – there are a lot of men badly hurt, but not Alex, and Master Prescott hasn't seen him.'

'Alex safe?' he said anxiously. She managed a smile. 'I don't know, Ben, but we'll find him, don't worry. Go back to Bram and tell him that he isn't in the George.'

It took a while to persuade him that this was the best course, and in the end she almost had to push him back into the saddle. But when he had gone clattering away down North Street, out of her sight, a black weight of despair settled on her soul. She could not believe that Alex, so vivid and alive only two or three hours ago, could be dead – he must be with the rebels, or tippling in the Fleur-de-Lys, or even back at Wintercombe, unscathed and careless as ever, while his cousins wore themselves to frantic shadows looking for him . . .

There was no reason for dread, and yet she felt it so strongly that the thought of returning to Moll Prescott, and more interminable hours of caged and frustrated ignorance, was unbearable. She knew the village well, and the fighting, it seemed, had dwindled into a desultory bombardment, a stalemate that was no longer threatening to any but those immediately involved. And any slight danger to herself was paltry indeed, compared with the urgency of finding Alex.

Ignoring the rain still dripping relentlessly from a gloomy sky, she walked out of the George, towards North Street, and the barricade where the fighting had been thickest.

It was much worse than the stable, because she could see them quite clearly, dead men heaped around the barrier that had kept the King's men out of Philip's Norton. She was not the only woman there: several villagers, taking advantage of the lull in the fighting, were busy amongst the debris of battle, offering comfort to the wounded. Many of the dead wore red coats, and seemed to belong to the Royal army, and their congealing wounds and slack, empty faces made Louise, to her shame, avert her gaze. All her life she had been unthinkingly strong, forceful and determined: and now, the aftermath of this small but bloody skirmish had completely destroyed her composure.

For several moments she stood in a doorway, trying to calm herself. At last, propelled by the urgency of her search, she stepped resolutely back into the street, and made herself study each corpse, each wounded man, looking for grey cloth, black hair, even, horribly, the lifeless stare of eyes as blue as sapphires or the sky . . .

He was not there. The women and those rebel soldiers collecting discarded weapons or wounded men stared at her curiously, but she could not bring herself to speak to them, for if she did, she knew that her hard-won control would shatter. One of the men said something to her, but she only shook her head mutely, and made her way to the barricade. It was ridiculous, she told herself with unconvincing fervour. She would spend all afternoon looking, she would be soaked to the skin and likely to catch a chill on the lungs, and she would go back to the George and find him sitting warm and dry in the taproom, swilling Master Prescott's beer . . .

'Don't ee go through there, Mistress!' One of the rebels, a kindly-looking man old enough to be her father, was trying to detain her. 'Tisn't safe, Mistress, not with they guns a-roaring – do ee go back to your hearth, Mistress, till all be over and done with.'

She had barely noticed the pounding of the cannon – the loud deep thunder of the King's artillery, more distant, mixed with sharper, lighter explosions much closer at hand that must belong to Monmouth's little two-pounders. She said urgently, 'I'm looking for my cousin – he was seen fighting here, a tall black-haired man in a grey suit – not a soldier – have you seen him?'

The puzzled whiskery face looked at her with concern. 'No, I haven't,' said the rebel. 'Do ee go home, Mistress, *please*!'

He was standing stalwartly in front of the gap forced in the barricade. Louise, with sudden desperation, ducked past his hands and dived through, into the carnage beyond.

The familiar Bath road, stretching ahead of her along the hillside, was strewn with bodies, both of men and horses, some moving, others still. With a whimper of revulsion and fear, she turned away and ran down the sloping lane that led to Lyde Green, until her feet shot from under her in the sleek treacherous mud, and she fell painfully on to her back.

There was no one else in the lane. The guns continued their futile bombardment: she had seen no sign of any cannon balls landing anywhere remotely near. The man in North Street had presumably gone back to his own duties, ignoring the antics of a woman he probably considered to be crazed in her wits. And perhaps I am, Louise thought ruefully, struggling to her feet. Her Brandenburg dripped liquid mud, one of her shoes appeared to have lost a heel, her soaked, torn skirts clung to her legs, and she was chilled to the bone. And the rain, coinciding with the arrival overhead of an even blacker cloud, was falling still more heavily.

This would not find Alex. She could walk on, down to Lyde Green, turn right along the Wellow Lane, and come within half a mile to the warmth and comfort of Wintercombe. Or she could continue a search that was probably fruitless for a man quite likely to be safe and who would be the first to laugh at her frantic concern for his welfare.

She was not afraid of seeming a fool. Setting her teeth, she turned and hobbled back up the lane.

In her earlier panic, she had not noticed the bodies lying in the hedgerow, further up from the place where she had fallen, and there was a sword, glittering and rain-washed, flung down in the grass. She made herself look. A young soldier in a red coat, much cut about the chest, his broken, uneven teeth bared in a last grimace of defiance. A heavy man in blue homespun, face down beside him. And beyond them, a patch of grey, rain-darkened but distinctive.

Her heart turned over and began to thud sickeningly. She walked past the two dead men, and stared down at her cousin huddled lifeless amongst the rough nettles and seeding cow parsley that lined the ditch along the roadside. She could not see his face, and was glad of it, but his

305

plain grey coat and breeches, wet and stained with mud and water, were nonetheless as familiar, as unmistakable as the black hair and long, sprawling height.

'*Mon Dieu*,' Louise whispered, on a sob, and dropped to her knees beside him. It took all her courage to put out a hand to his shoulder to try to turn him over, for she dreaded what she might see.

There was blood on his face, and that was all: his eyes were closed, and he looked almost asleep. Unable to believe that he was dead, she stared dazedly down at the man who had possessed such power to arouse her, and would never do so again.

But he did not look dead: not like the other two men lying next to him. And then she realised that under her fingers his body was warm, and that his chest was moving, and that the long sword-gash across the side of his head was still leaking blood. And the relief, after such utter despair, was so intense that she buried her face in her hands, and burst into tears.

Close by, something moved. She realised that she was alone with a wounded, unconscious man, and that they were both desperately vulnerable. She took a ragged breath, fighting for calm, and removed her hands.

He was looking up at her, but it was not Alex: the blue eyes were unfocused and bewildered. She glanced round, but there was no other living being in sight. The rebel gun fired, and Alex winced; then the enemy's piece spoke in answer, there was an eerie howl, and something thumped into the field on the other side of the hedge. They could not stay here in the pouring rain: she must find shelter, and quickly. Urgently, she bent her face down to his. 'Alex! Alex, can you hear me?'

His eyes wandered to hers, his expression more vacant than Ben's. Louise knew that a blow to the head commonly resulted in some temporary disruption of the wits, but this was deeply disturbing. She tried again. 'Alex! Can you sit up? Let me help you . . .'

She pushed her hands under his shoulder, but he rolled over, away from her, and was abruptly and violently sick into the ditch. She waited until the retching had stopped, and then touched him gently. 'Do you want my kerchief?'

He said something that she could not catch; he repeated it, and she realised that he was asking for water. The absurdity of it struck her with force: enough had fallen from the sky today to fill a hundred thousand drinking vessels, but there was nothing except red liquid mud all around them. Then she remembered the ditch, and, heedless of stings, she pushed the nettles aside and saw a swift-running stream. She cupped her hands in the flow and lifted them. It was cloudy, but quite drinkable compared with the muddy rivulets and puddles in the lane. It had run between her fingers, so she wrapped her kerchief over her hands to make some sort of cup, and tried again. 'Alex! Here's some water.'

With difficulty, he drank from her hands. She scooped up more, several times, and he sucked the water thirstily. At last, he shook his head, the black wet hair tangled across his face. 'Enough. Give me the kerchief.'

She unwrapped it, dripping and smeared with mud, and watched him wipe his face. He looked ghastly, like a drowned man come back to haunt his enemies, but at least his eyes no longer held that dreadful, witless vacancy. Blood still washed sluggishly into his hair: his fingers explored the injury tentatively, and he frowned.

'Does it hurt?' she asked, and was rewarded by a growl more reminiscent of the old Alex. 'Of course it bloody hurts. Help me up, will you?'

She was almost as tall as he was, and years of vigorous riding and exercise had made her strong and wiry, but supporting his weight was almost beyond her. Somehow, gasping, she pulled and pushed and helped him until, eventually, he was on his feet, an arm about her shoulders, swaying with the effort. She braced herself, feeling the sweat soaking her bodice with exertion, and said breathlessly, 'I think there's a barn or cowshed – just down there in the field on the corner – can you walk that far?'

'I don't intend to stand here all day,' Alex muttered.

Louise gave a sob of laughter and relief, and tightened her arm about his waist. 'Are you ready? Take it slowly . . .'

It was impossible to proceed in any haste, even if he had not been as stumbling and unsteady as a drunken man. Carefully, she guided him down the slippery, rutted lane, with the guns firing at irregular intervals behind them. but nothing came as close again as the missile that had landed in the nearby field.

She had barely noticed the barn earlier, but it was the nearest shelter from the driving rain. And now that the initial panic and urgency had receded, now that she had found him, her mind had begun to work again in its usual practical fashion. He had been fighting, God alone knew why, after all he had said, for the rebels. There was a good chance that no one in Monmouth's army, drawn mostly from the southern part of Somerset, would have recognised the stranger in their midst, especially in the heat of battle. And the fewer people in Norton who knew that he had taken part in the fray, the better. For if Charles found out . . .

She shied away from that possibility and all it implied. Only she herself, Bram and Ben, and Harry Prescott, knew the truth for certain. With luck, perhaps Alex's role in the rebellion might remain a secret.

'In here,' she said. It was more of a cowshed than a barn, with a partly open front, the roof supported on posts. Two wooden mangers stood at one end, and at the other, a partition and an ancient gate divided the animal shelter from the pile of hay intended for their fodder. There were a dozen curious young heifers and bullocks, their dark red coats sleek with rain, clustered round the further manger, and they turned and stared as she and Alex slipped and stumbled through the mud at the gateway to the small field in which the shelter had been built, fortunately close to the lane. Then they were under the rough thatched roof, and there was no more rain driving into their faces. She pulled the rough barrier aside, and saw with relief that there was still a quantity of hay and straw within, protected from the rain by the stone wall on three sides, and the wooden partition and gate on the fourth. It was dry, sheltered and secret, ideal for her purpose. If the fighting flared up again, with luck they would be safe here until dark. If it did not, then as soon as Alex had recovered some of his strength, they could perhaps return to Wintercombe, just down the Wellow Lane, without molestation.

Alex walked two steps unaided, and sank down on his knees in the straw. She pulled the gate shut behind her, seeing the cattle already following with wide, long-lashed eyes to investigate these strange intruders. She hoped they would soon return to their manger, for the crowd of interested bovine faces peering into the hay store was a clear indication that someone was inside.

She piled up the soft, sweet hay into a thick comfortable heap, right in the corner and out of sight of all but the most inquisitive cow. 'Alex – over here.'

He raised his head and looked at her, and in the dim light she saw the pale shadow of a smile. 'It's six feet away – and it might just as well be six miles.'

'I'll help you,' Louise said. She clambered across and took his arm. The sleeve of his coat was soaked, and she realised that he was shivering. Somehow, she managed to help him over to the pile of hay, and pulled off the saturated coat. By this time, he was shaking uncontrollably, his eyes closed, and she knew that her first priority must be to get him warm. She removed her wet Brandenburg, guided him gently down into the soft tickling hay, and pulled her thick coat over the two of them. Then she wrapped her arms around him, pressing her body close to his to give him warmth.

For a while, she did not think that she would succeed. She was cold herself, though mostly dry thanks to the thick Brandenburg, and even the cosy hay surrounding them did not seem to help. She dragged some of it over her, as best she could, reflecting that it would conceal them better if anyone did chance to peer inside. But that seemed very unlikely: with the rain and the fighting, most of the village was probably huddled safe round their firesides, and would not venture out all day.

Her mind turned to the problem of getting Alex, hurt as he was, back to Wintercombe without anyone suspecting the truth. It would be difficult, but surely not insoluble: he was so much a law unto himself that even his most outrageous behaviour occasioned little comment amongst his household. Perhaps, she thought mischievously, we can pretend that he spent all day in the George, drinking, and did not sober up until dark – that would explain his appearance, so long as no one noticed the wound to his head . . .

She became aware that he had stopped shivering, and that a new, welcome warmth had begun to glow between them. She raised her head a little, and saw his eyes closed, his face relaxed in sleep, his breathing quiet and even. With a sudden rush of grateful relief, she very carefully snuggled closer, her head on his shoulder, enjoying this strange, unarousing intimacy. He was safe, and did not seem to be seriously injured, and after her more dreadful and lurid imaginings, the joy of finding him alive filled her to the exclusion of all else.

They would doubtless return to their usual relationship tomorrow: the barbed comments, the lustful glances, the temptation, and the fear she had almost managed to deny to herself that her feelings for him might have the power to engulf her and bring her to ruin. For now, it was enough that they were unharmed, and together, and that her foolish wild despair had been the means of saving him.

She must have slept, too, for she came awake quite suddenly. It was a little darker in the hay store, and still, monotonously, she could hear the hiss of the rain, interspersed with the dull thunder of the guns further up the hill. She wondered what had disturbed her, and then saw his eyes open, watching her.

It was unquestionably Alex, back with a vengeance. She had seen that look on his face before, and inexorably, despite her earlier resolution, the answer began to beat a pulse through her own blood. She gave him a rather shaky smile, and said very softly, 'How are you feeling?'

'I have a sore head,' Alex told her. Her arms still encircled him, and she had pins and needles in her hand. She tried to extract herself, and sit up, but he pulled her back towards him, his face so close to hers that she could hardly focus on it. 'Sweet Louise, I am well aware of how much I owe you for today – so will you not accept at least one token of my gratitude?'

She drew back her head a little, staring down at him, and knew suddenly that she was lost. Resistance was futile, she had known it in her heart all along: the attraction between them was so powerful and compelling that delay had only served to heighten their desires, rather than to quell them. And in the aftermath of danger and battle, and the uncertainty of the future, with no one to know or to see, what did her reputation matter, concealed in a cowshed with the man who had filled her thoughts for the last four months?

Her eyes suddenly sparkling with joyful mischief, she bent her head and pressed her lips to his. He responded instantly, with a forcefulness and urgency that roused a similar passion in herself. As they kissed, his hands caressed her shoulders and then swept lower, pulling the lacings of her bodice undone. The narrow belt followed with experienced speed, and then he was fondling her breasts. She moaned softly with pleasure, her own hands, slightly less practised, struggling with the innumerable buttons on his waistcoat, and unexpectedly he gave a grunt of laughter. 'Shouldn't have worn this,' he whispered, in between kisses sliding deliciously lower – neck, shoulders, breasts, nipples. 'My Puritan suit – takes half an hour to get it off!'

With rather breathless, interrupted laughter, she managed to pull the garment off him, ripping the last few buttons in her haste. Then he was kneeling astride her, his face alight with desire, his hands exploring, touching, rousing her, while she, no less bold, unbuttoned his breeches with rather more ease than the waistcoat, and pulled them down.

'Puritan coat – but a gallant's breeches!' Alex said with a gasp, as her fingers roved freely down his body, and then there was no more waiting, he was inside her, and she forgot everything – the tickling hay, the guns, the fear and the fighting in the glorious and passionate sensations filling her mind and body, bringing her swiftly to a wild explosion of pleasure that made her cry out in delight, and brought him to his own climax almost simultaneously.

It was worth it, she thought, lying buried in the hay, wondering if she was going to sneeze, with a wonderful sensuous afterglow settling in her loins. Worth all the waiting, the temptation, and the risk. She opened her eyes and saw him looking down at her, his face still very pale and thoughtful. For a long, silent moment, their gazes held, and for the first time she saw him as he truly was, without deception or malice or mockery, a man who had made love to her with passion and laughter, and treated her as his equal in desire. And in that moment, irrevocably, her feelings for him altered and became something much deeper, and stronger, and more binding than the brief fierce physical attraction that had brought them together.

It was a discovery at once terrifying and utterly glorious, and she gave him a smile that, unknowing, revealed far more than she would have wished.

'There's no doubt of it, a hay heap is not the perfect site for a tumble that it's supposed to be,' Alex observed. He propped himself on his elbows and grinned. 'I tremble to think where stray seeds and stalks have lodged themselves, and I'll swear there's a thistle in here somewhere.'

'There is – I'm lying on it,' Louise said. 'But at least we did not perform for an audience of bullocks.'

He glanced round, but there was, thankfully, no sign of them. 'I'm surprised – we were not precisely quiet.' Slowly, his fingers coiled a lock of her dark hair, and then traced the sharp, slender lines of her face. 'How ridiculous all these garments are – they take an age to put on and a century to remove, and the greater the urgency, the more time it seems to take . . . In that respect at least, heathen savages have an enormous advantage over us, who are supposedly more civilised.'

'But hardly practical, in this weather,' Louise reminded him. She was acutely conscious of his warmth, around and inside her, and the unfamiliar traces of tenderness on his face made her blood sing. In this moment, their minds seemed as close as their bodies, totally absorbed in each other, without pretence or artifice. He stroked her breasts with a gentle finger, and at once the passion, unslaked after all, flared into brilliant life. She gave a whimper of desire, and moved involuntarily under him. Slowly, his eyes holding hers, he bent his head to kiss her, and his body began a slow, luxurious rhythm against hers.

This time, it was lingering, teasing, bringing each other to the edge of ecstasy and then pausing there, savouring the moment, knowing that the final, shattering, glorious fall would engulf them both, whenever they wished. And when neither of them could hold back any longer, the fantastic rush of pleasure overwhelmed them together and then slowly ebbed, leaving them stranded, gasping, amazed.

She saw his face, so close to hers, flushed in delight and wonder, and her heart turned over with something that, at this moment, she did not want to acknowledge. She gave him a rather bemused smile, and saw the answer leap in his eyes, and knew her power over him.

'*Oh, Louise, ma chère Louise, tu es merveilleuse,*' he said, very softly, and kissed her. 'And I warn you, I don't think I can stop, now that we've begun – I shall want you tonight, and the next night, and the next, like a drug . . . and keeping it secret will not be easy.'

At that moment, she would happily have proclaimed from the rooftops the fact that they were now lovers, but she knew that to do so would be unwise, to say the least. And she knew also that, like him, their lovemaking had only served to increase her desire. The thought of it, of going to his chamber to enjoy him in the warmth and comfort and hay-free privacy of his bed, was deliciously exciting. She said, 'We'll manage, somehow – as long as we can keep our hands from each other in company.'

'The most difficult task of all,' Alex said. His eyes considered her, lazily amused, some of the usual irony restored. 'Now I know why your mama packed you off to England – you must have set the Loire aflame from end to end.'

Louise grinned. 'It was a very small blaze – but there was some scandal.' She paused, wondering if she should tell him the truth: he was not, after all, going to give her a list of his previous lovers. But of course, she reminded herself, his were probably too numerous to count or to remember: whereas she had had only the one.

'He was married, and twice my age,' she added reminiscently. 'And I regret to say that he did not seduce me – rather, it was the other way about.'

Alex did not seem shocked or horrified: he grinned. 'I can well imagine it, sweet Louise. Did you love him?'

Louise opened her chestnut eyes very wide. 'Love? That did not come into it. Lust, rather. He was handsome, accomplished and amusing, and I wanted him. So I set out to attract him . . . and succeeded.'

'You must have learned well,' Alex commented. 'And when you put your skills into practice, you are breathtaking . . . Does my beloved Aunt Silence know that she is responsible for such a dangerous grenado?'

'I fear,' Louise said demurely, 'that Maman was less than honest with her, or with Uncle Nat. Gran'mère knows that there was a scandal, but she was not told the whole truth – although she might have guessed some of it. She has been very concerned to keep me away from you.'

'I am delighted that she did not succeed in the end,' Alex said. He paused, looking down at her thoughtfully, and then added, 'Did you think that I would care that you were no virgin?'

'No virgin would have done what I did just now,' Louise reminded him. Alex snorted. 'True enough – but no answer. Did you think that I would mind?'

Louise looked at him. 'No,' she said briefly. 'You're not the kind who collects maidenheads to notch up the tally on his bedpost.'

Alex grinned. 'How right you are. That has never been my desire – my only wish is to find a woman who is not afraid, or inhibited, or suffering from coyness or false modesty, who can recognise that love is a game played between adults, and that the only rules are honesty, and fairness, and consideration. Have I found her?'

'I don't know,' Louise said, her eyes searching his face. 'I'm no paragon of any kind of virtue – and neither are you. But I don't think that either of us are prey to very many illusions, do you?'

'I doubt it, somehow,' said Alex. 'And I think that we have both been hurt in the past, and will do our best to avoid it in the future. And so, sweet Louise, is my memory of you to remain forever wreathed in hay and headache and gunfire, or are you willing to continue what we have begun so unconventionally and delightfully?'

Louise smiled. 'Do you doubt your own powers so much? Of course I will, but on one condition only – that we keep it a secret, with as much care and discretion as possible. Even in Wintercombe it should not be too difficult.' She saw something in his face, and added, 'There are too many people who would be hurt, perhaps grievously so, if we flaunted it openly. And besides, although with your reputation no one would be surprised, my good name is a slightly more fragile affair.'

'Charles, and Amy,' said Alex. 'I had of course noticed the sheep's eyes that Charles has been making at you – almost as conspicuously as his sister's rolling in my direction.'

The careless contempt in his voice stung her and shattered the mood of intimacy. She said, 'He has been a good friend to me, and I intend that he remain so – but no more than that. And you cannot deny that you have treated him abominably, despite that house in Bath – if he ever takes up residence in it.' She saw his eyes narrow, and added, 'And Lukas too, of course – he must be considered.'

If he realised her deliberate attempt to avert a quarrel, he gave no sign, but his face softened suddenly, and he smiled. 'Lukas would be pleased. He has a great liking for you.'

'And I for him,' Louise said. 'But he is devoted to you, and I do not want to come between you.'

'You won't,' Alex told her, and touched her cheek. 'You occupy quite different compartments of my life . . .' He rolled away from her and sat up, chewing rustically on a hay stalk. 'And I suppose that we must give some thought to the immediate future. It might be wise if it were not generally known what I have been doing today.'

'Before the cowshed? Or inside it?' Louise enquired tartly. She stretched luxuriously, cat-like and unashamed of her lean, small-breasted body, and saw him looking at her. 'Cover yourself, woman, or I'll succumb to my baser instincts once more,' Alex said, grinning, and tossed her the discarded belt, lying almost buried beside him. As she pulled up her laces and adjusted the concealing folds of her chemise, he pulled on breeches and waistcoat, with a grimace. 'Damp clothes are the very devil. In answer to your question – both before and inside it: as you say, your good name should be protected, although I've long since ceased to care about mine. But my evil reputation is one thing – taking part in rebellion is quite another.'

'Why?' Louise asked him curiously. She hauled her stockings back to their usual level, and fumbled in the hay for her shoes. 'After all your talk – why did you join them?'

Alex sat on his heels, a distinctly rueful expression on his face. 'Would you believe that I don't know? I don't honestly know – and my memory of it is a little vague, anyway, that blow on the head dislocated my wits a trifle.'

'More than a trifle,' Louise told him. 'When I found you, I don't think you knew where you were, or what had happened.'

'I didn't – but I can recall some of it, now that I have the space to think about it without your alluring distractions. I went to find out what was happening – I saw Bram, and spoke to him, and there was, I think, some remark made by one of his comrades – and then we were caught up in a rebel charge, and somehow, I can't quite remember how, there was a sword in my hand and I was fighting alongside them.'

Louise sensed that he was not telling her the entire truth, and that perhaps he recalled it rather more clearly than he had indicated. She said, 'There were two dead men where I found you, a rebel and a King's soldier.'

Alex shook his head. 'No, I can't remember anything except charging with the rest – perhaps it's just as well.' He picked up his coat, which was sadly muddied and still wet, and looked at it with distaste. 'I shall have to give some account of myself at Wintercombe, I suppose – fortunately, the only person there who would certainly not be deceived is Phoebe, and she would never betray me.'

'I had thought,' Louise said, glancing at him mischievously, 'that I could put the tale about that you had spent the day in the George, prevented from returning by the fighting, and attempting to drink one of Master Prescott's barrels dry.'

Alex laughed. 'In view of my headache, I rather wish that I had – but then the delightful events of the past couple of hours would never have happened, and I would not have foregone this for anyone, not even the King himself.' He got to his feet, and stretched out a hand to her. 'May I assist you to rise, Mistress Chevalier?'

Smiling, she took it, and was hauled to her feet, and into his arms. For a moment they stayed locked close together, balancing rather precariously on the heaped hay, and she saw again in his face that unaccustomed, unlooked-for tenderness, and her heart melted. 'I have not thanked you,' Alex said very softly. 'Perhaps you saved my life – and you certainly rescued me from probable denunciation and imprisonment, at the least. And I shall be for ever in your debt, sweet Louise, both for that, and for allowing me to take advantage of your wonderfully delightful attractions.' He kissed her mouth, very gently, and pulled her closer. She laid her head against his shoulder, feeling the damp prickly cloth of the grey coat that had led her to him, and the warmth and strength hidden beneath, and, deeper within, the powerful, steady beat of his heart. And she wondered, with excitement and also with apprehension, what the future would bring to them.

Outside the cowshed, one of the bullocks lowed suddenly, making her jump. She nearly lost her balance, but Alex held her, laughing. 'I think it's time we went, before some astonished yokel discovers us. And we must agree first, on our story.'

Louise had her suggestions ready. 'We spent the day sheltering from the fighting in the George. I was there for some hours anyway, in the company of Mistress Prescott – so it is almost the truth. But you will have to speak to her, and to Harry, for he knows that I was looking for you, and that you had been seen in the thick of the fighting.'

'He's a good sort, Harry – we've sunk many a pot of beer or cider together,' Alex said. 'He will certainly agree to lie on my behalf, if it ever becomes necessary. So – it seems that I had best return to the George, while you go on to Wintercombe – where they will all certainly be frantic with worry. And since I doubt very much if Mistress Prescott has hay on her floor or her chairs, I shall have to brush you down.'

She stood, her hands braced against the stone wall, as he picked strands and seeds from her hair, her gown and her laces, and then shook out her maltreated Brandenburg in a cloud of dust and stalks. Inside it once more, she felt almost respectable.

'That's better,' Alex said, surveying her critically. 'You hardly look as if you had spent an hour or two rolling in the hay with your lover. But I hope your maid is discreet – there's bound to be a great deal of evidence in places that I cannot reach at present, much as I'd like to.'

'You're not exactly hay-free yourself,' Louise told him, performing a similar service. Her hand unwarily brushed the crusted gash on the side of his head, and he winced involuntarily. 'Christ, that hurts!'

'I'm not surprised,' Louise said. She could not see the wound in this gloomy light, but was certain that, despite the thickness of his dark hair, it would be quite conspicuous to anyone who gave him even a casual glance. 'It feels quite deep, and it's bled considerably. You'll have to find some way of cleaning it, making it less noticeable, or your story will be suspect.'

'I'll do it at the George,' Alex said. He looked at her, and his hands caressed her face again, as if he could not keep from touching her. 'Have you noticed something? Listen!'

There was no sound but the soft relentless hiss of rain on thatch and grass. Louise stared at him, puzzled, and and then realised what he meant. 'The guns – the guns have stopped!'

'Yes – and what that means, I have no idea. It could be the signal for a withdrawal, or an attack, or even just because they've run out of powder or shot. So you, alas, had better go home now, and quickly, before anything further happens.'

'I will,' Louise said, and found, to her surprise, that at this vital moment she did not want to be parted from him. But she must, or their secret would be revealed; so she reached up and kissed him on the lips, both a reminder and a promise, feeling his response to her flare up again. She was confident of her power of attraction, the sensual allure of a face and body that were not conventionally beautiful, but could awaken desire whenever she wished. He would not easily forget her or discard her, for the passion burned between them like a flame.

She slipped away from the cowshed, an unlikely and humble setting for such overwhelming emotion, and made her way down the muddy, empty lane towards Wintercombe, in steady rain. Yes, she had ensnared him, already he was hungry for her body again, and the thought of the coming nights, the slaking of desire, over and over, made her weak with anticipation.

But now, she wanted more than lust: she wanted him to feel more for her than affection, tenderness, more even than that engulfing desire that had consumed them both that afternoon.

For the first time in her unthinking, wild, essentially selfish life, she had fallen deeply in love.

# 18

## 'The careful Devil'

The two armies, miserable and frustrated, had stared at each other for six long hours across an expanse of muddy field, while the guns on either side thumped pointlessly at intervals, sending cannon balls flying with very little effect, save those lucky shots which landed close enough to scatter earth, mud and stones over the enemy. One man of Monmouth's was killed by a lump of flying rock, the only serious casualty of the bombardment on either side. At last, with darkness no more than two hours away, the more forceful counsels prevailed amongst the Duke's senior officers, and despite the protests of Colonel Venner, who had advised a retreat, it was decided to cut a way through the hedges and launch a full-scale attack upon the Royal army. They were not, so far as they could see, outnumbered, and despite the weather, their foot soldiers had given a very good account of themselves. They had won the engagement thus far, and now it was time to press home their advantage.

The King's general, Lord Feversham, was a French Huguenot whose preferment by the King had caused some ill-feeling amongst his other officers, notably Lieutenant-General Churchill, who thought that the overall command should by rights have been his. He surveyed his drenched army and the appalling conditions, and decided against a night in the open in such weather. The comfortable little town of Bradford was only four miles distant: there, his men could be billeted and fed, morale restored, and the soldiers refreshed in readiness for the fray. The rebels had fought surprisingly well for ill-equipped peasants, but there was little chance of them now making a desperate dash for London. They would not go far: tomorrow, or the day after, he could deliver the *coup de grâce*.

Monmouth, watching the enemy's withdrawal with disbelieving eyes, knew that he had been cheated of victory. Now that the urgency of action was past, he felt as drained and despondent as he had the previous evening. What was the point in all this? No one had come to his help. Captain Adlam's promised five hundred horse had proved to be illusion. He had also entertained high hopes of the defection of his erstwhile comrades in the Royal army, men who had no love for King James, officers with whom he had trained and fought and drunk over the years,

317

and who had expressed their sympathy and friendship. But none of them had come to join him, none. And the man who had led that furious charge of horse grenadiers and musketeers along the lethal hedge-lined Bath road, and nearly paid for his daring with his life, had been, so a captured soldier had told him, his own half-brother, the Duke of Grafton.

He had agreed to the urgings of Wade and Holmes, who had been wounded in the fighting, that they stake all on an attack. But now Feversham was leaving: to beat of drum and blare of trumpet, the Royal army was abandoning the battlefield. And with their horse, well trained and armed, to cover their retreat, he did not dare to throw his own cavalry in pursuit. The men were not cowards, but their mounts, who until a few days ago had been quiet country nags, could not be brought to fight.

The Protestant Duke watched with hopeless eyes as his enemy tramped away into the rainy dusk to dry beds and a hot supper, and with them his chance of a sudden and glorious victory.

Afraid that Feversham might launch another attack under cover of darkness, he did not order a withdrawal to the previous night's quarters in Philip's Norton. The foot huddled round smoking fires, too exhausted and miserable even to grumble, while discussion raged in Monmouth's chamber at the George, whence he had retreated for a hasty meal. Wade and his friends argued that their hard-won advantage must not be discarded; Colonel Venner, who had already come privately to the decision that the rebellion was doomed, counselled a retreat to Frome. Monmouth, who was likewise beginning to admit defeat to himself, did not take much persuading. To the fury of Wade, and Holmes, who had lost his son in the fighting, he agreed with Venner. Despite the still torrential rain, the men's lack of rest and food and the abysmal condition of the roads, the army would withdraw to Frome that night.

After the events of the day, despite the brief triumph of beating off the King's army, the failure to follow up their advantage had depressed the rebels' spirits, and the never-ending rain completed the process. They remembered the fiasco at Keynsham, and many wondered, either to their comrades or to themselves, whether their once-beloved King Monmouth any longer had stomach for the fight. And that night, in the rain and the dark, was the first when many men, as opposed to a faint-hearted few, took the opportunity to desert.

Despite his unhappiness, Bram was not one of those tempted. He had joined the rebellion in the first flush of enthusiasm and success, but this temporary setback did not deter him. The cavalry, true, had played a somewhat limited and ignominious part in the fighting, but the foot had given a good account of themselves, and had beaten back a trained and well-equipped force. There was still hope, and he was not going to creep off cowardly, like a thief in the night, just because of a little rain.

In actual fact, it was rather more than a little. The fields were quagmires, the roads awash with muddy water and watery mud. Everyone was soaked to the skin, weary and hungry: many had eaten nothing since the morning. Bram was aware that if he had still been in the Blue Regiment, wading through mud and puddles that were perhaps two or even three feet deep in the worst places, his attitude might be very different. There was no doubt that his elevation to the horse had made a considerable improvement in his comfort.

But at least he did not have to worry about Alex and Louise. After the tense dark hours waiting for orders, or surprise attack, he had been sent back to the George with a message for Holmes, who was having his wound dressed, and had taken the opportunity to make discreet enquiries. To his relief, the red-faced, stout young man who seemed to be the landlord had the answer immediately. 'Oh, Sir Alexander? He's in the taproom, I think you'll find.'

And there he was, large as life, sprawled comfortably in front of the fire as if he had spent all afternoon there, a tankard in his hand and a big leather blackjack on a table at his elbow. Bram felt unaccountably annoyed. He walked up to his cousin and stared down at him. 'Where have you been? Louise and I have been searching everywhere. We were worried.'

Alex looked up and gave him his laziest, most irritating smile. 'Have you? Well, there was no need for it.'

Bram swallowed an indignant retort with some difficulty, and repeated his question. 'Where were you? One of my men said he'd seen you in the fighting, but you certainly don't *look* as if you were involved.'

Alex appeared, in fact, to have been imbibing for some time, and had the gently flushed, deliberate but dishevelled look that Bram had seen before in men half drunk. He said, his words slightly slurred, 'Your man was mistaken. I've been here for hours, as Harry Prescott will tell you. Have a drink? You look as if you need it.'

'I do not – and you've had quite enough,' Bram said, still annoyed. 'Where's Louise? I left her searching for you – she was frantic with worry.'

'Was she? How touching. I shall have to take advantage of her concern for me, one of these days,' Alex said reflectively. 'She's gone back to Wintercombe, apparently – as soon as the bombardment stopped.'

His young cousin's relief emerged as a gusty sigh. 'Thank God for that,' Bram said. 'I was anxious for her, too.'

'Why? Afraid she'd be ravished? Our sweet wilful little cousin can more than look after herself.' Alex drained his tankard, refilled it from the last of the blackjack, and held it out to Bram. 'Here – for Christ's sake climb down off your righteous perch and drink it. You'll need it for that march tonight.'

His cousin stared at him. 'How do you know about that?'

Alex grinned, and laid a finger beside his nose. 'I have my methods. Chief amongst them, a sharp pair of ears, a seat in the taproom, and the ability to make two and two add up to four. Come on, man, it must be all over Philip's Norton by now. Are you going to drink that beer and say goodbye, or not?'

For a few seconds longer, Bram stared down at this vivid, unprincipled and exasperating cousin, who always seemed to raise his hackles, yet who was stil somehow likable. A slow, friendly smile on the other man's face proved infectious, and suddenly he found himself responding whole-heartedly. 'Of course I will,' he said, and raised the pewter mug. 'To King Monmouth, and the Protestant religion!'

Alex did not say anything, but watched Bram quizzically as he drained the warm, thick, nourishing beer. Its comforting presence in his belly would stand him in good stead during the long dark rainy march to Frome. He set it down, wiping his lips, and said briefly, 'I'm sorry for my rudeness – although it does rankle somewhat to realise that you were snug and safe in here all the time we were searching for you – we needn't have bothered.'

For some reason, Alex's face was alight with unholy amusement. 'It probably kept you all out of mischief,' he said, and pulled himself to his feet, a little unsteadily, his hand outstretched. 'Goodbye, Bram – I'm glad we met, even if not under the best of circumstances. And good luck go with you, until we meet again.'

'And with you,' his cousin said, and they gripped hands in friendship, a brief but warm clasp. Then Bram turned, and with a last smile and a wave left the taproom in search of his horse, and his men, to prepare them for the miserable night that lay ahead.

Alone, Alex stared for a long time into the fire, a forgotten smile on his face. Harry Prescott, entering with a fresh blackjack, had to cough twice before he was heard. 'Excuse me, Sir Alexander – would you care for more beer?'

'What?' His distinguished guest looked round, frowning. 'Oh, Harry. No, thank you – I've had more than enough. I'll go home now.'

To Prescott's shrewd gaze, he looked unwell, and he seemed to have some difficulty focusing. When he recalled that ugly wound that his wife had washed and salved and stitched, he was not surprised. He said with some concern, 'Shall I come with you, sir? It's a treacherous road in the dark, and you never know what might happen.'

'There's no need, Harry – Moll's ointment and your beer have almost restored me, between them.' Alex paused, and then said softly, glancing at the closed door, 'Thank you. I am much in your debt. Are you certain that no one else knows?'

'Positive,' Prescott told him confidently. 'And Moll and I will keep your secret for you, Sir Alexander, never fear. God give you a safe journey home, on this terrible night!'

'You sound as if I was about to venture into foreign parts, instead of walking half a mile through my own village,' Alex said, with a weary smile. 'Don't worry – I can look after myself. Goodbye, Harry – and once more, my grateful thanks!'

Outside in the road amidst the steady, ceaseless fall of the rain, Monmouth's army was leaving Philip's Norton and those of their comrades who had been slain, or who were too hurt to be moved. He stood unregarded in the shelter of the inn's great bulk, watching the foot, bedraggled and stumbling, straggling through the patches of light thrown from the George's windows and into the impenetrable darkness beyond, as if their doom awaited them there. For a long while he gazed at them, the men who had refused to desert a leader who had, perhaps, already betrayed them in his heart. After a while, the sight of that endless, tragic procession, plodding like beasts before his eyes, became unbearable. With a muttered curse, he turned abruptly, and made his way down West Street to the manor, and through the farmyard mud, with stones laid in it at irregular and unguessable intervals, to Lyde Green.

There, on the right behind the hedge, was the cowshed where he and Louise, only hours previously, had come to that astonishing and splendid consummation. He had promised her tonight . . . any night, any moment, so long as they were discreet. Despite his swimming, aching head, and the combination of exhaustion and inebriation that made his feet wander, he quickened his stride. She would be concerned – the only one at Wintercombe who cared for him.

A second's reflection was enough to remind him of the injustice of that thought. Lukas loved him; and so, in their different and difficult ways, did his sister, Phoebe, and his taciturn, reserved Dutch servant, Gerrit.

It was Phoebe who was waiting for him. He had asked Gerrit to ensure that the front door was unlocked, but watched, until he came home, and although he had never imagined that he would be as late as this, he was nevertheless surprised to find, not Gerrit's broad snub face in the screens passage, but its exact opposite, the narrow white countenance of his sister.

She came forward, limping, to take his heavy coat, laying it dripping over a chair. 'Thank God! Louise said you were in the George – why didn't you come home sooner?'

'Monmouth is marching out tonight,' he aid.

Her eyes narrowed. '*Tonight?* But the men can't have had any rest, they must be soaked through, they've fought a battle – how can he force them to march *now*? It's almost midnight!'

Later indeed than he had thought. Alex felt a sudden wave of faintness and nausea assail him. At the time, the beer had seemed a necessary cover for his activities, but now he was not so sure. He leaned his head against the solid panelling of the screen that separated the passage from the Hall proper, and wondered how long he could stay vertical.

He must not collapse: if he did, someone would be certain to discover the head wound that Mistress Moll had cleaned and anointed and stitched up close, as delicately and invisibly as if the skin of his scalp were a piece of fine silk.

Phoebe was saying something, from a very remote distance, and at last her sharp, low voice penetrated his disordered senses. 'Alex! Are you all right? Shall I fetch Gerrit?'

He managed a shake of his head. It had seemed like a furnace when he had first walked into Wintercombe, but now, suddenly, he was cold. An icy touch assaulted his brow, and he flinched. Phoebe hissed in his ear, 'What have you been *doing*? You're burning as if you have a fever!'

'Then I probably have,' Alex said. Suddenly infinitely weary, he turned, still leaning on the partition for support, and looked at her. 'Is your chamber empty? I need to talk to you.'

'Mattie's sleeping in Amy's chamber tonight – the poor child was somewhat overwrought by today's events,' Phoebe said drily. 'I can't help you – you'll have to get there on your own, or ring for assistance.'

He said something under his breath, and pushed himself away from the wall. 'There's nothing wrong with me that won't be cured by a good night's sleep in a warm dry bed – which is more than those poor devils out there will have. It's all right, little sister, I won't need your stick.'

She walked behind him, with her usual painful, halting gait, determined not to make a fuss although his haggard appearance had shocked her. Unbidden, he made his way to her bedchamber, the central room of the three in the east wing below his own chamber, and the only one with a chimney. There was a small, glowing fire in the hearth, of warm Mendip coal, and the bed had been turned down ready for its mistress's occupation. Alex stood looking at it, visibly swaying on his feet, and gave her a pale smile. 'If I sit there, I shall make it all wet. Will this chair do?'

She nodded, and closed the door firmly behind her, checking that the other, leading to her study beyond, was also shut. Alex fell, rather than sat, in the comfortable upholstered chair by the fire, and closed his eyes. His black hair was wet and sleek with rainwater, or sweat, and the bones of his face stood stark and prominent under a skin that was grey-white, save for an unhealthy flush on each cheek, and beaded heavily with perspiration. Phoebe said, in sudden alarm, 'You're ill!'

'No, I'm not,' Alex said, opening his eyes. 'Suffering from the effects of a blow on the head, followed by too much rain and an excess of beer, that's all.'

'All?' Phoebe stared down at him. 'A blow on the head? How in God's name did you come by that? And then too much *beer*? You mean you compounded it all by getting drunk?'

'For the best of reasons – and the walk from the George has sobered me up,' Alex told her drily. 'Sit down, sister, and listen – and I am sure that you realise that what I am about to tell you is for your ears, and yours alone.'

She sat with a mixture of anxiety, astonishment and annoyance, as he gave her a short account of the day's events: the meeting with Bram and Ben, the arrival of Louise, and the attack of the Royal army on the barricade at the end of North Street. He told her how he had taken refuge in the George with Louise, as Monmouth's men returned from their march to the defence of their rearguard. His description of his next meeting with Bram was distinctly brief, and he gave her no explanation of how he had come to be fighting alongside the rebels. But he did not omit Louise's search for him, and her rescue, although this version had her leading him straight back to the comfort of the George, rather than revealing a very pleasurable interlude in a certain cowshed on the way.

'Did she return here safely?' he asked, rather belatedly.

Phoebe looked at him. 'Yes, she did – small thanks to you! She was exhausted, poor girl – she wanted to stay up until you returned, but she couldn't keep eyes open after supper. She didn't give us the whole story, of course, but at least she was able to tell us where you were – and once we knew you were safe in your usual haunt, we were a little less worried – or at least, some of us were.' She smiled reluctantly. 'You should have heard poor Amy – or rather, you should not.'

'If I avoided her lamentations, I'm profoundly glad I spent the evening in the George,' Alex said. He touched the left side of his head with cautious fingers. 'Does it show?'

Phoebe peered at him. 'No, but in this light that doesn't signify much. For God's sake, Alex, what possessed you? You could so easily have been killed!'

323

'I don't know,' Alex said, with a trace of his usual carelessness. 'A moment of madness, perhaps – a lapse of reason? I can't really remember.'

'I think it's as well that you don't – I doubt any excuse would sound convincing,' Phoebe told him roundly. 'And if you're so eager to fight for Monmouth, why are you here now, and not marching off with them through the night?'

Alex looked up at her, and his eyes were not friendly. 'You know why not.'

'And so you have the worst of both worlds,' his sister said, with some disgust. 'You risk your inheritance, and worse, you risk your life, for the sake of a momentary whim, and yet you take no part in the glory – instead, you're left for dead in a muddy ditch, for Louise to rescue you! If anything, *she's* the hero.'

'I put in no claims for heroism,' Alex said, and his long mouth twisted suddenly in self-mockery. 'I never have done, Phoebe. You know, none better, that I am hardly an admirable character.'

'Well, at least you have the grace to admit it,' Phoebe said. 'And I'd rather have my only brother an honest rogue than a hypocrite, any day.' She paused, knowing that she should not mention Charles, who throughout that long, weary, nerve-racking day had lost no chance to proclaim his loyalty to the King and his utter contempt for all rebels, most especially his cousins Bram Loveridge and Ben Wickham. Instead, she said quietly, 'Lukas was very anxious for you – and for Louise. He was so glad to see her, and to know that you were safe.'

'And I expect that he is now sound asleep in bed?'

'Along with the rest of the household. It has not been the best of days – we were able to watch some of the battle, on the ridge around White Cross, but we could discern very little of what was happening. And there was no news until Louise returned – we had no idea of how widespread or how fierce the fighting was.' A ghost of his own self-deprecating smile curved her lips. 'We were all quite distracted with terror.'

'Well, I expect some of you were,' Alex said. He braced his fingers against the arms of the chair, and pushed himself to his feet. 'I'm sorry, Phoebe – I must go, or I shall fall asleep where I sit, and that would be most inconvenient, for you as well as for me. I promise you, I shall be quite restored to my usual self, come the morning.'

'That's what I most feared,' Phoebe said drily. 'And, before you ask me, yes, I shall be exceeding discreet.' She smiled rather bleakly. 'Goodnight, brother – have a sound rest, and sweet dreams!'

She listened to his footsteps, uncharacteristically slow and uncertain, on the stone steps that wound up inside the stair turret leading to the large, light, beautiful chamber occupying all of the east wing, above her own. The distant door closed softly, and she could hear no more: the ceiling between them was vaulted stone, and sound did not travel down from above, a fact for which she had been thankful ever since her brother's return to Wintercombe.

The rain battered the windows with renewed frenzy. She shivered, closed her own door, and began, with her usual ungainly care, to undress. The bed was comfortable, the fire still warm: outside, the night was wet, and dark, and inhospitable to marching rebel soldiers. She blew out her beside candle and snuggled down under the blankets, listening to the wind and weather. Bram and Ben were somewhere out there, but she would not feel much sympathy for their plight, for they had, after all, brought it upon their own heads by following Monmouth's bright and falling star.

But despite her resolutely practical thoughts, a bitter tendril of pity, and regret, and sadness crept unbidden into her heart, and lodged unwelcome. For no one who had any grasp of reality, and who possessed the ability to take a detached view, could fail to see that unless a miracle, the unbelievable, the impossible happened, Monmouth and his rebel, rabble army were doomed.

They began to straggle into Frome at eight in the morning, after a march that had taken on the quality of a nightmare. The rain had not ceased, but grown heavier, if anything, and the foot had waded through mud to their knees in places. It had taken nearly nine hours to travel perhaps six or seven miles. The town, prosperous and full of Dissenters, cheered the rebels who had given so much for the Protestant cause and their beloved Duke: and the exhausted men, both horse and foot, were given a hero's welcome, dry beds, and hot food.

It was astonishing how quickly such apparently defeated soldiers, once they had been given a chance to rebuild their strength, could recover their spirits. Monmouth, well aware of his men's needs, announced that, as this was Sunday, they could rest themselves and their horses here, at least until the following day. And that evening, the inns and houses and tenements where they had been quartered, on the bounty of the good people of Frome, echoed with debate and description and argument as Norton Fight was waged again, with a variety of aids and an excess of exaggeration. Listening to them, their hosts might have been forgiven for thinking that the skirmish had ended in a crushing victory for Monmouth's men.

But the Protestant Duke did not share his troops' sudden surge in morale. On the day after their arrival in Frome, he received the unhappy news that the Duke of Argyll, who had launched rebellion in Scotland just before his own, had ignominiously failed. There was no indication of any other rising in his support, and still no sign at all of Captain Adlam's five hundred horse. All day, while the men rested and dried their garments and cleaned their weapons in every nook and cranny that the town could offer, Monmouth's council of war debated their future strategy amidst furious argument.

At first, a strike eastwards, into Wiltshire, seemed the most attractive. There, at last, they would surely encounter those elusive five hundred horsemen; and the men of Warminster were said to be eager to join him. To this end, outposts had been placed on the eastern side of the town, towards Roddenbury, and the horse, who were less weary than their footsore comrades, sent to occupy them.

But all this activity had chiefly been set in motion by the more vigorous and determined of Monmouth's officers. Their leader himself sat at the head of his council table and bemoaned his fate: the lack of support, the failure of Argyll's invasion, the weather, the disloyalty of those in the regular army who had failed to change sides . . . everything and everyone was to blame, in fact, save himself. His complaints found a ready audience in Colonel Venner, who had once been a captain in Cromwell's horse, and who had come with Monmouth from exile in Amsterdam. The Colonel's initial enthusiasm had evaporated very rapidly as the paucity of gentry support and the diminishing prospects of success alike became clear, and he had counselled caution at every crisis until Nat Wade, in particular, had conceived a virulent dislike for his faint-heartedness. Now, listening to Venner applauding Monmouth's appalling suggestion that they all run back to Holland, leaving their loyal army to shift for themselves, Wade could barely contain his disgust. Rather to his surprise, he discovered that the effete Lord Grey, whose nominal command of the cavalry had been notable only for its stunning incompetence, was also repelled by such spineless counsel. Forcefully, Grey, Monmouth's closest friend, pointed out that to desert their followers, who had risked everything for the Protestant cause, was the action of a base and despicable coward, and that if the Duke and his officers fled, they would deservedly forfeit the love and devotion of the people, and Monmouth's name would never be trusted again.

To the relief of Wade and Holmes, and the dismay of Venner, their vacillating leader was eventually persuaded to take the nobler course. They would not abandon the men of the West Country who had served them so loyally. Instead, they would march the next day to Warminster, where an advance party had already bespoken quarters and warned the bakers to prepare extra bread.

Venner, who had had more than enough of this ramshackle army and its unhappy leader, so painfully unlike his hero Oliver Cromwell, took the opportunity to slip away, and Holmes's major, Parsons, went with him. To cover the defection, it was given out that the two men had returned to Holland to buy arms for an Irish revolt, but since it was now common knowledge amongst the army that their money had almost run out, very few believed it. The prevailing comment amongst the rebel ranks was, good riddance.

It had been planned to march to Warminster on the Tuesday, but at the last minute, Monmouth's mind was changed by two pieces of news. Feversham and the Royal army were moving south from Bradford to intercept any strike he might make to the east. And then a plausible Quaker, Tom Plaice, arrived with a convincing tale of thousands of clubmen, natives of the Somerset marshes, ready to rise up as they had forty years ago in time of civil war, and smite the Papist enemy with their rustic weapons. It was, like Captain Adlam's promised and illusory five hundred horse, another straw in the wind, but Monmouth clutched at it frantically. He could not go east, as he had planned: why not turn in the opposite direction and aim for the country where his support seemed still to be strongest? There, with his loyal people at his back, he could turn and rend the Royal army at last.

Rested, refreshed, their bellies full, the rebel army marched out of Frome singing, that Tuesday morning: and if their stalwart voices disguised an emptiness, a hopelessness lying in their future, they hid it well. Besides, the sun was shining, after so many days of grey lowering skies and torrential rain, and the warmth, the birdsong, and the rich wet smell of the fertile earth and lush green vegetation all around them put heart into their voices and their step.

Behind the rebel army, the people of Philip's Norton, amazed and horrified by the battle that had taken place under their windows, began with typically practical stoicism to restore order to their village. The dead – of whom there were many fewer, on either side, than rumour had stated – were buried in a large common grave under the field where some of them had fallen, and Parson Pigott, his quavering old voice barely audible in the quiet, said a prayer over them. Most of the wounded had been removed by their comrades, but there were a few, both Royalist and rebel, fished out of hedgerows or from outbuildings, who had been left behind,

327

and they were tended by kind-hearted village women. The debris of battle – weapons, bullets, cannon balls, barricades, clothing, abandoned baggage – was collected with enthusiasm by anyone who could walk, and many cottages now possessed some treasured souvenir of the day when the Protestant Duke had defied the might of the King's army on their own doorstep, and won.

The tales spread round the village, much embroidered and exaggerated in the telling, but retaining still an essential core of truth that would, with each generation, become embalmed in tradition. The man who had held open the gate for the rebels, and was shot for his pains; the old grammer whose tiny tenement was ransacked by rebels seeking supplies, but who sat firmly on the bread crock in which she had hidden her hoarded coin; mistress Coombe, the miller's wife, who had thought herself safe from the battle raging on the hillside above her, until a cannon ball landed with a splat in the yard, as she was feeding the hens, causing a panic of poultry, but no actual harm. Colonel Holmes, wounded in the arm, was stated to have walked back to the George and hacked off the ragged remains of his limb with the cook's cleaver, thus occasioning several dark remarks about the precise ingredients of the pies subsequently served up to Master Prescott's guests. And the sudden, unexplained solvency of two members of the notoriously impoverished Grindland family was interpreted, with much whispering and winking, as the result of their fortunate capture, on the morning after the fight, of a wandering and unattended sumpter mule, said to be laden with coin. Being Grindlands, they naturally did not use their windfall to make the lives of their struggling families any easier, or to set themselves up in a trade which would keep them from being a burden on the parish. Instead, the only real beneficiary of the luck of the 'sumptuous muleteers', as some wit dubbed them, was Harry Prescott at the George, and his counterpart at the Fleur-de-Lys, the rather less reputable establishment on the other side of the marketplace.

All these tales, some more fanciful than others, came to Wintercombe on its low hill outside the village, brought by the servants and their friends and kin. Now that the danger was gone, fear had vanished, and an eager, gossipy excitement had taken its place. Maids who had trembled with each cannon shot in the servants' hall on that rainy Saturday now exchanged tall tales whenever they were out of earshot of the chief housemaid, Abigail, made sentimental comments on Monmouth's good looks and dashing gallantry, and hoped, in whispers, that he would soon topple the long-faced Papist King from his throne.

Louise had wanted to wait up for Alex, the night of the battle, but her weary body had betrayed her, and she was forced at last to admit defeat and retire to bed. She was woken by Christian at dawn, as usual, and was vastly relieved to be told that Sir Alexander had apparently returned very late last night, and was still asleep in his chamber.

'Since he spent all day in the George, I'm not surprised,' said Louise. She took a deep breath as Christian pulled the laces of her stays tighter, and watched the consequent improvement of her figure, displayed in the mirror, with satisfaction. Fortunately, her injured shoulder was now almost completely recovered, and could withstand such constriction. Alex had seen her dirty and dishevelled and soaking, and had wanted her even so: how much more desirable was she now, with her lean body enhanced by graceful curves, and the slithery cool silk of her best, peacock-blue gown adding its own allure.

She surveyed her finished reflection with delight, and a glow of anticipation began deep within her, lending a flush to her face, and making her eyes brilliant. This was how he would see her later, the exotic elegance, the low-cut mantua, her skin clean and scented and ready for his touch, and all her skill and charms and accomplishments to enslave his senses, and her own.

'The fur tippet, madam, or the double lace?' Christian asked.

She debated, and glanced out at the still unpromising sky. 'The fur – I do not think that it will be very warm today.'

It was not. Fires burned in the hearths of Wintercombe, from necessity. Outside, the torrential rain of the previous day and night had given way to a gloomy and dispiriting drizzle. Alex did not appear to break his fast, and Lukas drooped fretfully. 'Where can Papa be? I thought he was home!'

'He is,' Phoebe said, from the end of the table. 'But he probably decided to sleep late, after yesterday.'

'Why?' the child persisted. 'He wasn't in the fighting!'

'Of course he wasn't,' Phoebe said calmly, without a glance at Charles, eating silently at her right hand. 'But when I saw him last night, he was very tired.'

'Drunk, you mean,' Charles muttered under his breath. He pushed his chair back, and stood up. 'Well, since he hasn't deigned to appear, there is some urgent business I must deal with. I shall be in the library for the next hour or so.'

Although it was a Sunday, Phoebe bore Lukas off to her chamber, where her books and papers were kept, and Louise was left alone with Amy. For too long, Charles's sister plied her with questions, until her slender patience had all but expired. Eventually, Amy retired, defeated, to sit with her mother, and Louise, at last, took refuge in the winter parlour,

329

overlooking the damp garden, where she could have the peace and leisure to think, until it was time to go to church.

No one, it seemed, doubted the story she had told late yesterday afternoon, on her return, muddy and soaked, to Wintercombe. The inclement weather meant that her bedraggled appearance was entirely to be expected, and indeed everyone had been most sympathetic, insisting that she change her clothes, indulge in the rare and blessed luxury of a hot bath in her chamber, and ward off the threat of chills and colds with a succession of warming and delicious possets. No one had expressed surprise that Alex was still in the village, at the George, and no one seemed in the least suspicious.

So far, so good. Of course, if Alex was still suffering from the aftereffects of that blow on the head, then it might not be so easy to continue to allay suspicions. But if Charles chose to assume that he had returned home last night drunk, and was still sleeping it off, so much the better. And with luck, Alex would be quite recovered by tonight.

With a slow, reminiscent, cat-like smile, she curled up in the window seat, and tried to lose her undisciplined, lascivious thoughts in the pages of Amy's latest French romance.

Charles St Barbe stared down at the sheaf of papers, all dealing with the lease, the transfer and orders for repair of the house in Abbey Green in Bath. He had never really wanted the place, it was a pathetic substitute for the glories of Wintercombe, and yet now that his family's move there had been delayed yet again, he felt increasing impatience and frustration. The tenant had proved obstreperous and had been persuaded to leave without further ado only after the payment of a substantial sum. Charles, who had been given a free hand with the arrangements, had not told Alex about that, nor about the mounting cost of the repairs which were proving necessary, nor of the increasingly wild extravagance of his mother's suggestions. He pressed a hand to his brow, and tried to marshal his figures again. Under the terms of his uncle's will, he and Amy alike received goods and land worth about four hundred pounds a year, and his mother was provided with a pension. It sounded a great deal, but to decorate and furnish the Bath house from nothing would eat a large hole in those sums, and to do it in the style which Bab desired would take all they had, and more. It was impossible . . . impossible.

He thought with irritation of his mother, her fluttering eyelashes and imploring looks as she twittered on about how splendid gold leaf would look on the panelling in the parlour, and how nothing would do for the hangings but watered silk, in, naturally, the most expensive colour known to the dyer. And his mind progressed, trailing a track of venom, to the baleful figure of his cousin Alex. If he had not returned . . . if only he had died in exile . . . then Charles would have inherited Wintercombe and all the abundant wealth that surrounded it, and, with the new King a Catholic, preferment, perhaps even a place at Court, would have been his, and a glittering marriage for his sweet and lovely sister.

The dream was too vivid, too real, too wonderful to be borne. He got to his feet and paced urgently round the table. Money . . . it all came down to money. Unfairly, his uncle had given him enough on which to live in moderate ease, but nowhere near sufficient to fuel his sense of his own worth and position. His paltry inheritance would not buy more land, and without land, an estate of his own, he was of no account. And the blocks of houses and tenements in Bath and Brisol, the scattered parcels of tenanted farmland and the interests in the Bristol shipyards and his Uncle Orchard's business, could not by any stretch of the imagination be described as an estate.

Well, he had already tried one desperate means of obtaining wealth, and it had ended in humiliating failure, fortunately without anyone realising his part in it. The next time such an opportunity came his way, he would not hesitate to grasp it with both hands.

And, of course, there was Louise. If he had an estate, lands, a home, he could marry her, and she would not refuse him, for she was his friend, and he had seen the affection on her face when they spoke. He loved her so much, that captivating combination of the earthly and the exotic, the active and the decorative, the practical and the lively, that he knew she could not resist him. No woman could withstand such adoration.

He came to a halt, thinking of her, his eyes glazing unseeing at the ranks of books. The shelf directly in front of him held an assortment of theological works, sermons and so on, that he doubted very much were the choice either of Alex or of his late father. They were much more likely to have belonged to the redoubtable grandfather of all of them, Sir George St Barbe, Silence's first husband, who had been one of Cromwell's colonels. Such heretical writings held no interest for Charles, but as he moved away, his eye was caught by an anomaly. There seemed to be other books, concealed behind those he had just seen. Curious, Charles pulled two or three volumes out, put them on the floor, and reached to the back of the shelf.

The first book he drew out was anonymously bound in worn, buff-coloured leather. He opened it, expecting another treatise on divinity, and found himself staring at the unmistakable title page of Hobbes's

*Leviathan*, a pernicious, corrupting and atheistical work. Shocked, he slammed it shut as if the wickedness could thereby be contained inside, and pushed it back. But there were others, and with horrified curiosity he pulled them out one by one, books on republicanism, on mechanical philosophy, three respectable-looking volumes that proved to be disgusting collections of bawdry, and last, but by no means least, several disgraceful pamphlets, undoubtedly seditious, lampooning and libelling the present King and his Queen.

As if they had the power to burn him, he thrust them all back into their hiding place, and replaced the more innocuous books at the front of the shelf. He had no doubt at all that these repellent volumes belonged to Alex, and their presence in the library was yet one more reason for his loathing of the man. The *Leviathan* alone had infected a whole generation with the idea that all religion was no more than foolish superstition.

Charles turned away and sat down, wondering what he should do. Was this the opportunity he sought? Should he confront Alex with his discovery? His imagination shied away at once from the thought of his cousin's mockery, and his careless contempt for Charles's scruples. Nor could he contemplate laying this information before a Justice. Possession of such books might well be unwise, or lead to justified suspicion, but he did not think that, in itself, it was a crime. Even those scurrilous pamphlets could be easily explained away by someone as clever and plausible as Alex.

No, the only course was to do nothing, little as he liked it. To do nothing, and say nothing, while those books festered in their hiding place, waiting to infect all at Wintercombe with the corruption of atheism, treason and Dissent.

Charles swore silently, fervently, that if Alex gave him just one more chance, he would do everything in his power, he would move heaven and earth to bring his cousin to the justice which he had so far undeservedly evaded.

# 19
## *'Wild desires'*

When Louise and Phoebe returned from church, late on the morning after the battle, Alex still had not made an appearance, and both were becoming concerned. As soon as she had changed out of her riding clothes, Louise hurried down to the other girl's chamber, and found her cousin sitting thoughtfully by the window. She shut the door, and asked softly, 'How much do you know about what happened yesterday?'

Phoebe raised an eyebrow in a way that was uncomfortably like her brother. 'I know the truth, if that's what you mean – and I can't imagine what possessed him.'

'I can't, either,' Louise said. She paused, choosing her words carefully, and then added, 'How was he when he came home last night?'

'Ill,' Phoebe said concisely. 'The beer he'd drunk hadn't helped, but he was feverish and exhausted. It was a lucky thing you found him, wasn't it?'

'Very,' said Louise. 'And I hope I don't regret it. Do you think he's all right?'

'I don't know.' Phoebe stared out at the garden. 'But perhaps we should go and investigate. That Dutch servant is admirably loyal, but I doubt he's competent to tend a sick man.'

The two cousins, not without certain feelings of apprehension, ascended the stone steps to Alex's chamber. No sounds emerged from within. Phoebe, breathing quickly from the exertion of the climb, grimaced expressively, and knocked with firm resolution on the door.

After quite a delay, footsteps sounded on the other side, and the latch lifted. Gerrit, bulky and somehow intimidating, occupied the opening. He bowed, and looked with mild enquiry at the two girls waiting outside. 'Yes, madam?'

'I would like to see my brother,' Phoebe said briskly. 'I'm a little concerned about him – he was not well last night.'

'I know, madam,' said Gerrit, in his slow, painstaking voice: his command of English had not been much improved by his months at Wintercombe. 'He is much better – resting now. Please, not to disturb.'

'Is he asleep?' Louise asked.

The man glanced at her, with those large, doleful blue eyes, and nodded. 'Yes, madam.'

'Then perhaps we will come back this afternoon,' said Phoebe. 'In the mean time, is there anything that he may need? Medicines, or ointments?'

'I have all I need, thank you, madam.'

In the face of such a gently immovable obstacle, they could do nothing but retreat. The conversation at dinner, when not discussing the battle and the likely destination of Monmouth's army, seemed to return, again and again, to Alex's absence. Lukas, evidently worried and disappointed, picked at his food and said very little, a lack for which Charles amply compensated by seizing the opportunity to inveigh against drunkenness and vice with more than his usual fervour. At length even Amy, flushed and distressed, was moved to ask him to stop, and to the relief of everyone else at the table, he did. Louise, disturbed by his increasingly strange and bitter mood, found it horrifyingly easy, now, to imagine what he would do, should he ever learn the truth about Alex's activities during the battle.

She put it from her mind, and began to think about what the afternoon might bring, laying her plans carefully. It had at last stopped raining, but she pleaded a stiff shoulder, and persuaded Lukas to ride round the paddock under Henry Renolds's indulgent eye, ignoring the child's worries about his father. Phoebe, who was now suffering considerable pain, aggravated by the weather and the journey to church, had retired to rest on her bed, and Amy had been summoned to read romances to Bab, ensconced in her stiflingly scented chamber above the library. The Hall was empty, and Louise, knowing that with luck no one would question her whereabouts for an hour or so, slipped quickly and quietly up the stairs to Alex's chamber, thankful for the unusual geography of Wintercombe, which allowed her to approach the door quite unseen.

She knocked, rather more softly than had Phoebe that morning, and once more heard the deliberate, heavy footsteps. Gerrit stood solidly barring her way, and bowed. 'Yes, madam?'

'I wish to see Sir Alexander. Unless he's asleep, I'm sure he will not object.' Louise had drawn herself up to her full and considerable height, and looked down her aquiline nose at him, in her haughtiest manner. 'Ask him, please.'

Gerrit, some inches shorter and very much broader, did not move for a moment, and she wondered angrily if he would forbid her entry. Then he turned, and said something in Dutch over his shoulder. Alex's voice responded, in the same language, and then abruptly the door opened wider, and Gerrit was standing aside, bowing once more, and ushering her in.

Alex was sitting at a table by the middle of the three tall east windows, quill in hand. She had not entered this chamber since his occupation of it, and glanced about her curiously. There were some books and a great many papers, and the wide bed was untidy and crumpled, as if he had only recently risen f om it. A fire glowed in the hearth, and the air was rather too warm for comfort.

'Louise. To what do I owe the pleasure of this visit?' Alex asked, laying down his quill. He looked pale, but not ill, and there was a look of amused enquiry on his face that lifted her hackles a fraction.

'I came to see how you were,' she said, wondering suddenly if that strange, wonderful episode in the cowshed had really happened, or if it had been a figment of her overheated imagination.

'I am quite restored, thank you,' Alex said, and smiled, and she knew that it had not, after all, been illusion. He looked past her at the servant. 'Gerrit – can you find something to do downstairs, for an hour or so?'

No flicker of expression enlivened the doughy face. 'Yes, sir,' said the Dutchman, and bowed, and went out. Louise, all her senses suddenly awash with desire, heard his retreating steps with delight. Mischievously, she crossed over to the door, and turned the key in the lock.

'A lady after my own heart,' Alex said. 'Gerrit is as discreet as the grave – we will not be disturbed or discovered.'

Louise turned to face him, her fingers swiftly untying the fur tippet that had tickled and warmed her skin for most of the day. It slid over her naked shoulders to the floor, and she saw his eyes respond. With an intoxicating sense of her own power over him, she walked languorously towards him, and smiled. 'Are my garments more to your liking today?'

'Very much more,' Alex said, and pulled her into his arms. 'But I prefer them off you.'

With all the afternoon to while away, and a comfortable bed on which to explore each other further, their lovemaking was slow, exquisite, utterly sensuous and pleasurable. They removed each other's clothes, with rather more expertise than before, although Alex, his laughter soft in her ear, pointed out that it was strange indeed that her peacock-blue mantua took so long to remove, since it had seemed to need only the merest touch to send it slithering to the ground.

Time meant nothing: the world had diminished to the confines of their bodies, and the delights to be enjoyed therein. And when she could hold back no longer, and the pleasure crashed through her like a storm, she knew, triumphantly, that for him, too, this rush of glory was the culmination of their lovemaking.

Slowly, she became aware of reality seeping back into her mind. His

335

weight on top of her, warm and slippery with their mingled perspiration; the stir of a draught on a patch of exposed skin; the very distant sounds of the house, and the birds outside. She opened her eyes, and saw him looking down at her. So close, she could discern every tangled strand of his sweat-soaked hair, the faint indelible lines on his face, the long dark lashes that he had bestowed on Lukas, and the eyes that they fringed, that intense and extraordinary blue. He surveyed her, his chin propped on his linked hands, with a slightly bemused expression on his face. 'Why did I not discover you earlier, *ma chère Louise?*'

'I could say the same about you,' she told him, and let her eyes slide away from his face, afraid that the emotion which almost threatened to choke her would be revealed if they looked at each other too long. Let him think that she wanted only his body, as he did hers, and the delights that lovemaking could bring them: then they would continue to come together like this, for as long as their passion lasted, for she was certain now that she had enthralled him. But if he once suspected that her feelings went beyond mere lust, that she was in love with him, then such an experienced libertine would undoubtedly cast her aside before she trapped him.

Or, worse, he might respond to her vulnerability with that callous cruelty that she had seen in him already. Her previous lover had kept her at bay in such a manner, and she had learned, with no small hurt and bitterness, to hide from him what she knew that he would not wish to see. As she fully intended to do with Alex: for already this man, and the overwhelming passions which he aroused in her, meant far more to her than that distant, nebulous vicomte whose face, nearly a year later, she could no longer remember with any clarity.

'Who would have thought that I would find such a pearl, under my own roof and amongst my own kin?' Alex said. He rolled over on to his side, taking her with him, clasped tightly in his arms. 'Although I must say I had my hopes, from the moment we met. A mistress so conveniently placed . . .'

'Am I your mistress, then?' Louise enquired, lifting her head to look at him more clearly.

He grinned, and kissed her. 'What else would you be? But in secret, as you said – only Gerrit knows, and as I said, Gerrit keeps as close as the grave, even if he was able to speak English well enough to gossip in the servants' hall. Besides, he is quite accustomed to my amours, and takes them in his stride.'

'So, I am no more than another knot in your string of women?' Louise said, her voice light and teasing. 'On the same level as the ladies of the Cock at Walcot, I suppose.'

'I don't imagine you'd thought of taking up employment there? With your talents, you'd make your fortune inside a year. Ow, sweet Louise, that hurts!'

'It's meant to,' she told him. In one swift, powerful movement she had extracted herself from his grasp, and now sat astride him, her fingers tangled purposefully in his hair. 'I will not stand for such insults from anyone. Apologise, sir, or you'll regret it!'

Alex stared up at her, his eyes glowing with laughter, and she had a sudden, rather alarming sensation of the power of his body, temporarily quiescent beneath her. 'Never!'

'You know as well as I do that it'd only take a week,' Louise said, tightening her grip. A long lock of her hair fell across her shoulders and into his face: he brushed it away and suddenly, without warning, exploded into action. Laughing, wrestling, they rolled over and over, each trying to contain the other, but with little success: Louise was strong and agile, and she had been taught to fight by unscrupulous playmates. At last, however, Alex succeeded in capturing her clutching hands, only inches before they both fell off the bed. She twisted and wriggled, almost helpless with laughter, but could not win free: he had been playing with her, it was obvious, and she had already appreciated the sleek, efficient muscles shaping his arms and body. Still, it was not in her nature to give in so easily, and sometimes the old ruses were the best. 'Oh, look!' she cried in apparent astonishment. 'What on earth is that on the bed behind you?'

Alex did not move. 'Whenever I was born, it wasn't yesterday,' he observed drily. 'Anyway, I don't intend to let you go just yet – at least, not unless I've had the chance to do this.'

The kiss was long, and increasingly urgent with passion. Once more, they made love, and already the rhythm of their bodies was so closely in tune that each seemed to know the other's desires without need of words. At last, sated and dazed, they lay tangled together, too exhausted to do anything more than smile.

She must have slept, for Alex's voice intruded on her suddenly. 'My own sweet Louise, wake up. I think it is time you emerged, or people will become quite justly suspicious.'

She had never felt quite like this before, this lazy, almost remote heaviness and languor that slowed all her movements, and made her long, even as she dressed, for the warm intimacy of his body. He helped her lace her stays, and arranged the stomacher and petticoats and mantua with all the practised aplomb of an experienced lady's maid. Finally, he used his fingers to return her thick, curling hair to something approximating its original style. That done, he stood back and surveyed her, an appreciative smile on his face. 'You look as if butter wouldn't melt in your mouth – and certainly no one would guess what you have been doing for the past hour or two.'

Louise, from sheer joy, gave him her dazzling three-cornered smile. 'Just as well – although I can't quite believe that no one could know. I *feel* so different – as if all my bones had turned to warm honey.'

'A most apt and excellent description. It's a shame that you must go now, but if we are to keep this a secret, it's only for the best. Perhaps another time, we can indulge ourselves with a night of love – for the more I taste of your delights, sweet Louise, the more I crave them.' He was standing very close, clad only in black breeches and a fine loose holland shirt, rather creased, and again she found herself acutely aware of the power of his presence. She put her arms around his neck, smiling. 'So this is not the end of our encounters?'

'Do you want it to be the end? If you do, then I have been wasting my time.'

'You know as well as I do that I can hardly keep my hands from you,' she told him, laughing, and kissed him lightly and with mischief. 'And I am happy to take whatever opportunity offers to us next . . . always excepting a cowshed, of course. I'm still finding hayseeds in my hair!'

'It won't be on straw, I promise you. Ah, that must be Gerrit.'

A subdued double tap had sounded on the other side of the door. Alex pulled her into a last swift embrace, heavy with the memory of passions past, and yet to come. 'Goodbye for the present, sweet Louise – and I don't somehow think that we will have to wait very long for another stolen hour of delight.'

'I don't think so either,' she told him, and smiled brilliantly. 'Where something is so pleasurable, I see no reason to stop, do you? And if we are discreet . . . then no one will guess, just as no one seems to have suspected the truth about yesterday.'

'Phoebe knows, and Harry Prescott and his wife, and Bram, that I took some small part in the fighting, but only you know the complete story, cowshed and all. I take it that you can keep the secret, sweet Louise?'

'You shouldn't need to ask,' she said, with mock severity. 'And your head is mending very well, I can hardly see the mark and I know where to look. Does it hurt?'

'Only when you pull the hair attached to it – for which, one day soon, be sure I shall take my just revenge. Goodbye, sweetest Louise – and my thanks.'

She felt, walking across the Hall, as if she were floating an inch or so above the ground. She knew that she should try to behave as normal, but suspected that, after an hour such as the one she had just spent, her glowing fulfilment must be shiningly obvious. How long such an affair could in truth be kept a secret, she did not know. Realistically, she could not expect it to remain hidden for long. But such was the force of her emotions, and the wonder and delight and love she felt whenever she thought of making love with him, that despite all the hurt and scandal that revelation would bring, at this moment she did not really care.

On Friday, the third of July, six days following the fight at Philip's Norton, the rebel army marched into Bridgwater, not two weeks after they had left the town in warm sunshine and high hopes. Since their departure from Frome, they had tramped through Shepton Mallet and Wells, making much of the successful capture of some Royal waggons, and ignoring the steadily increasing flow of desertions. Men who had been happy to join Monmouth when success had seemed certain now found themselves almost back where they had begun, and with nothing achieved. They had not taken Bristol, they had failed to follow up their advantage at Philip's Norton, and now here they were once more outside Bridgwater, with Feversham and the full strength of the Royal army only a few miles away, ready to pounce.

A mood of despondency had filtered down from the rebel command, and even those who had no intention of deserting the cause found themselves infected. Bram kept his weapons in order, ensured that the men under his command were comfortably quartered, and that the horses were sound and fed and in good condition. More than that, he did not dare to think, for he knew that if he were once to cast his mind ahead to the grim future, his resolution would fail him. He had been proud to follow Monmouth when his fortunes seemed bright; now that doom probably awaited them, perhaps in the next few days, that same pride would not allow him to run away, tail ignominiously between his legs, to home and shameful safety.

It was obvious, from the very muted reception that the good people of Bridgwater gave to Monmouth and his followers, that they would soon outstay their welcome. It was one matter to cheer the handsome Protestant Duke on his way to success and glory, quite another to see him return in failure less than a fortnight later, his army ragged, hungry and footsore, and lacking the money to pay for their food and beds. And with growing dismay, Bridgwater heard the orders that Monmouth sent out as soon as he entered the town. They were to prepare for a siege, and to that end townspeople and villagers were required to help with the fortifications.

The men and women of Bridgwater had long memories. Forty years ago, during the civil war, they had suffered much, and a large part of the town had been burned to the ground. As Monmouth's four feeble cannon were placed strategically to guard the approaches to the town, and rough earthworks thrown up, the people watched with sullen and resentful faces. Not only were they menaced with siege, battle and destruction, but the rebels had abandoned any pretence of paying for their food and lodgings, and many houses, here and in the surrounding villages, had been ransacked for food, drink, money and, above all, arms and horses.

The preparations for a siege were, in fact, a deliberate deception. Monmouth, whatever his deficiencies as an inspiring leader, had been a professional soldier for many years, and was well aware that to allow his dwindling and depressed forces to become cornered behind the inadequate defences of Bridgwater was tantamount to committing suicide. The plan, as decided by his council, was to break out to the north-west, relying in particular on the speed of his cavalry, and march overnight to Axbridge, continuing through Keynsham into Gloucestershire, and thence to Shropshire and Cheshire, where, surely, their rebellion would attract strong support.

With some difficulty, those who had urged this very course at Keynsham, a week previously, refrained from saying, 'We told you so'. But the time, energy and resources that their fruitless march round north Somerset had wasted were at the back of everyone's mind, an ever-present but unspoken reproach.

Two troops of horse were sent off to Minehead to collect the six guns that guarded the harbour there, and others made themselves unpopular for some miles around the town, collecting horses and saddlery. Bram and Ben, however, much to the former's relief, were not amongst these, for the soldiers of the rebel army who lived in Taunton had been given leave to go home to see their families, so long as they returned the next day, a Sunday.

It was a calculated risk, for the news had just reached Monmouth that the King offered a free pardon to all those rebels who would lay down their arms and show due repentance for their transgressions. But Bram was determined not to be tempted. He would gladly ride over to Taunton, but no blandishments from any member of his family, not even his mother, would sway him from his purpose.

And so, on that overcast Saturday afternoon, Bram and his cousin rode the ten miles or so to Taunton, in company with several hundred of their comrades, both in the horse and those in the Blue Regiment, to visit their families and friends. There was much talk on all sides of the pardon that

340

the King had offered, for despite the efforts of Monmouth's officers to suppress this news, which had been spread amongst the army by a deputation from Taunton, everyone seemed to have heard of it, and it was plain, from the heated discussions to be heard wherever two or more rebels were gathered together, that some at least were planning to take advantage of the opportunity. Bram would not, but much of his mind, during the pleasant ride to his home, was given over to devising some stratagem whereby Ben could somehow be persuaded to sue for pardon.

The tall spire of St Mary's, spearing the horizon, soon announced that he had nearly reached his destination, and Bram wondered, with some apprehension, what his reception would be, particularly from his parents. Would his father argue with him, or reproach him for his defection, or would his delight at seeing his only son restored to him, albeit temporarily, overcome his doubts and fears? Bram suspected that it would not.

Taunton was in the throes of market day, and the sight of such normal activity bustling about him seemed unexpectedly strange to Bram. The presence of two armies in the neighbourhood, the prospect of battle and the possibility of a long struggle all over the West Country, had not seemed to make the slightest difference to the lives of the ordinary men and women of Taunton, who must still make a living and feed their families. As he guided his horse through the curious crowds, Bram felt humbled and suddenly alien. What did the aspirations and ideals of King Monmouth have to do with the everyday needs and desires of the people for whom he claimed to speak? Proud words and rebellion did not put bread into a child's mouth, and however fervent a man's beliefs, there must come a time when his earthly concerns overwhelmed his urge to fight for the right to worship as he pleased.

But he himself had no one dependent on him, no wife or children who would be left destitute if the worst happened. There were only his parents, and he did not know if he could face their grief without succumbing to his own sense of guilt.

He left the horses at the Red Lion, pausing to exchange news with the eager and curious stable lad, and then led Ben across the street to his father's bookshop. It was hardly more than a fortnight since he had run out of this door in his best tawny suit, to join the rebel army before Jonah could stop him; and so much had happened since then that those fifteen days seemed to have had the impact of as many months, if not years. The boy who had escaped his father's well-meaning imprisonment seemed somehow very young, naïve and hopeful, compared with the war-seasoned cornet who knocked on the familiar door as if he were a stranger.

It was opened by Jonah. To Bram's shocked eyes, he seemed to have aged considerably during the past weeks. Surely he had not been so short, or so stooped, or so plainly ridden with anxiety?

'Bram?' His father peered through his round spectacles at the imposing, hatted man on the doorstep. 'Is that really you, Bram?'

'It certainly is – and Cousin Ben, too,' said his son. 'Hullo, Father.'

'You've come back!' Jonah cried, and flung the door open. 'You've come back to us, safe!'

Obeying an impulse he had not felt for years, Bram swept his father into a loving embrace. I must tell him, and now, he thought unhappily. It must be now, or he will assume that I'm staying, and it will be so much more difficult to tell him the truth later.

Reluctantly, he disengaged himself, and said quietly, 'It's not for long, Father. We have leave only until tomorrow, and I must go back then.'

The realisation crept very slowly into Jonah's face. He stared at his son in bewilderment. 'You have to *return*? Tomorrow? But why, in God's name?'

'Because I am obliged to,' Bram said. 'I am a loyal officer in Monmouth's army, and I cannot desert him. Surely you can understand that, Father?'

Jonah was saved from a reply by the precipitate arrival of his daughters, running down the stairs to greet their brother. In the space of a few minutes, Bram was drawn, amid tears and laughter, up to the parlour, pushed into a chair, and plied with food and wine that was very welcome after the irregular supplies of recent days. Nor was Ben forgotten, and he sat beside his cousin, clutching a plate heaped with collops of cold mutton and beef, a beaming grin on his face, muttering incoherent words of gratitude.

Questions poured from Sue, Hannah and Libby in a torrent as unstoppable as the River Tone in spate, and Bram made no attempt to answer them all. He devoted his attention to the meat and drink, feeling curiously aloof from these chattering schoolgirls with their naïve enthusiasm. He had seen death and bloodshed and suffering at first hand: how could he hope to convey any of that terrible reality to these innocent children?

'Jonah tells me that you are not staying.'

His mother's voice, low and calm, cut through the girls' enquiries, and they fell immediately silent. Bram put down his glass and plate, rose to his feet, and bowed with unusual formality. Ben, eager to follow suit, spilt his meat on the floor in his haste. Tabitha Loveridge stood in the doorway, her face severe and unwelcoming. She nodded courteously to Ben, who was trying to pick up the scattered collops in an agony of embarrassment, and addressed herself to her son as if she and he were the only people in the room. 'Is it true, that you must go back to Monmouth tomorrow? What of this pardon that everyone has been talking about? Surely there is still time for you to surrender yourself to a magistrate.'

Hannah's hazel eyes were fixed on him imploringly. Bram remained standing, all his attention given to his answer. 'There is, yes – if I wanted to. But I have committed myself to Monmouth, and to the hope he brings of a better world for people like us, and I will not desert him now. I owe him my loyalty, and my service.'

'That's what I thought you would say,' his mother told him. She came over to him, and her sudden, flashing smile, so like his own, told him that he was forgiven. 'Welcome back, Bram, even if it is only for a few hours. I'm so glad to see you safe – and Ben too, of course.'

'Don't you mind?' he said in surprise.

She smiled rather bleakly. 'Of course I mind – I want to see you home, and safe. But I understand why you must return – and glad though I would be to keep you here, and see you betray your loyalties and your leader, I could not be proud of you for it. I would not like to think of my son as a fair-weather friend or a deserter.'

She put her hands on his shoulders and drew him close for a maternal kiss, and he felt as if a huge weight of guilt had suddenly flown from his shoulders. She understood: she would not reproach him for his lack of loyalty to his family, for she saw that, for the moment, his ideals claimed first place.

For the rest of that day, he and Ben were the centre of attention. With enthusiastic but limited assistance from his cousin, he gave his family some account of almost everything that had happened over the past two weeks. Some instinctive reticence prompted him to leave out any mention of Alex's possible involvement in the fighting at Norton, and the horses which Bram had pretended to steal from Wintercombe at gunpoint. But no one noticed any omission, and Ben, whose memory was at best confused, made no inconvenient comment. Bram was relieved: he knew that he could trust his parents, but the three girls, garrulous and probably bursting to relate every detail of his experiences to their schoolfriends, could not be relied upon to keep Alex's involvement secret. And such juicy titbits of gossip had a dangerous way of spreading exactly where they were least wanted. Bram could not pretend to understand his cousin, but he liked him, and had no intention of bringing harm to him.

He finished, just before supper time, with a description of Monmouth's position in Bridgwater, the superficial preparations for a siege, and the alternative plan, suspected amongst the horse, that involved a dash for the north. 'But no one knows for certain what we will do, and Feversham and the Royal army must be close at hand. Perhaps Monmouth will seize the opportunity of a surprise attack – I don't know. But the King's pardon means that if he does decide to lead the horse into Gloucester and Cheshire, the foot that are left behind can go back free and unmolested to their homes.'

There was a small silence. Tabby said quietly, 'Even so, it does not seem a very honourable course to take, after those men have followed him so loyally.'

'It certainly does not,' Jonah commented pointedly. 'Such a stratagem would surely render your Duke quite unworthy of any further trust or faith.'

'He may have no choice,' Bram pointed out, well aware of the trend of his father's thoughts. 'If you were in his place, what would you do? Would you give battle, against overwhelming odds, with the certainty of death for many of your followers, or would you flee to fight another day, leaving them to seek the King's pardon, unharmed and free to return safe to their homes?'

Jonah was silent. Libby, whose sharp, clever mind was almost entirely disguised by her plump, unremarkable face, said into the pause, 'Is the Duke in desperate straits, then?'

'Not yet,' Bram told her, with a confidence he did not feel at all. 'But he is sorely brought down by the lack of support – if only some of the gentry would join him, he feels that he would have a much greater chance of success. Money, horses, arms – those are his needs. But we fought well, at Philip's Norton, and I think we have a good chance, even against the King's army, if we don't throw away our opportunity.'

'I wish I could join you!' Hannah cried with longing. 'Oh, *why* was I ever born a girl?'

'Even if you were a boy, you'd be too young,' Sue reminded her. 'You're only eleven, after all. We played our part, remember, when we presented the colours to Monmouth.'

Hannah evidently did not consider that moment of glory to be an adequate substitute for military exploits, and sulked. Bram, who was very fond of his younger sister, reached over and touched her gently on one cheek. 'Those colours are splendid, you know. I carry one of them myself – not the one that you three embroidered, but another, not quite so fine as yours. Even if you can't ride to battle yourselves, at least you have made a considerable contribution to the cause.'

Hannah permitted herself a small smile of gratification. 'What colours

344

do you carry?' she asked. 'If you tell us, we'll know who made them.'

The ensuing discussion, or rather argument, established eventually that Grace and Moll Herring had embroidered that particular banner, and that his sisters' effort now adorned Captain Hewling's troop. Then supper was ready, and despite their earlier light meal, he and Ben fell ravenously upon the food laid out before them. The feeling of pampered luxury was enhanced by the provision of hot water for a bath, and one of the maids took away the blue suit which Bram had worn all through the wind and rain and weather and mud of the rebel army's march through Somerset. He emerged clean, warm, and wearing fresh clothes: Ben, after similar treatment, and the loan of one of Bram's suits, glowed with contented satisfaction, like a well-groomed and tended horse. Whatever fate awaited them with the rebel army at Bridgwater, at least they would be able to face it decently clad.

In the rather cramped house, he would have to share his bed with his cousin. It was a good opportunity to bring all his powers of persuasion to bear upon Ben's obstinate skull, and he intended to do everything possible to make the boy stay behind in Taunton tomorrow.

As before, his arguments fell upon exceedingly stony soil. Ben was adamant – he would not be parted from Bram, and could not understand why his cousin no longer seemed to want his company. He was obviously deeply hurt at the thought, and with tears in his eyes begged Bram, over and over again, not to leave him behind. And nothing could alter his resolve.

It was no good. Bram lay long awake, wrestling with his conscience. Whatever happened, he would be burdened with guilt. If in some way – perhaps by locking him in this chamber, just as Jonah had done – he forced Ben to remain safe in Taunton, he would have betrayed all the boundless trust and devotion which the boy had lavished on him over the past two weeks. Like a dog, or a horse, Ben understood nothing save for his need to be with Bram, and he would see only the rejection, not the concern for his safety.

But if he rode back to Bridgwater tomorrow, with Ben joyfully at his side, then sooner or later, the reckoning would come, battle, capture, or flight: and he could not protect Ben from everything. If anything happened to his cousin, he knew that he would never be able to forgive himself.

He slept at last, to the snuffling sound of Ben's snores, and dreamed, quite incongruously, that he was riding with Louise, delivering books to the villages round Taunton, as if warfare had never disrupted their peaceful, harmonious lives. And looking at Ben's beseeching blue eyes fixed on him when he woke the next morning, he knew that he could no more spurn that adoration than he could kick a devoted dog from his side.

Jonah said very little at their parting, and Bram was heartily grateful. He did not think that he could very well have borne a last-minute attempt to persuade him to stay. It would not have succeeded, and he did not want to leave in a cloud of acrimony and bitter words. But into the intensity of their final embrace, his father poured all the hope and fear and love that he had not dared to put into words.

His mother was almost as reticent, but at least she had a smile ready. And as she kissed him goodbye, her soft voice was for him alone. 'May God go with you, Bram – and please, take care.'

'I will, don't worry,' he promised her. 'And – thank you, Mother, for respecting my choice.'

His sisters were much more fulsome, and, much to his embarrassment, Hannah had even made a rather ragged garland of marigolds and late roses, tied together with twine, which she insisted on placing round his neck. Ben looked crestfallen as it became apparent that there was not one for him, and Bram, with a cunning appearance of reluctance, removed the flowers and placed them over his cousin's head. Ben's dazzling smile was reward enough, and quite sufficient to dissolve Hannah's look of pique.

At last, in watery sunshine, they rode away from Fore Street, towards Bridgwater. Behind them, Bram's parents watched, united in love and fear, as their only son rode back into danger, while Sue and Hannah jumped up and down and waved their kerchiefs in farewell.

But Libby, a curiously forlorn and lonely figure, stood to one side. She had not shared any of her cousins' exuberance, and Bram had had the impression that she was very close to tears. With sympathy, for he rather liked Libby, he had given her a cousinly kiss, and smiled encouragingly. 'Don't worry, we'll soon be back.'

'Will you?' Libby had said, with a bleak pessimism that contrasted very strongly with the other girls' unthinking enthusiasm. 'How can you possibly know?'

And there was really no answer to that.

## 20

# *'Round beset by foes'*

The commander of the King's forces, the Earl of Feversham, was well satisfied with the turn of events. After ten days spent shadowing the rebel army up and down Somerset, he now had Monmouth and his men cornered in Bridgwater. The end of this wretched affair could not now be long delayed. The announcement of the King's pardon to those who would lay down their arms seemed to have had considerable effect, and his informants reported that many rebels had deserted. But there were still several thousand of the most obstinate within the town, and these must be defeated, by any means possible.

Feversham consulted with his senior officers. Churchill, who had received many reports of the rebels gathering horses and arms, was of the opinion that Monmouth would try to break out to the north with his horse, leaving the foot behind. This was just what Feversham wanted. The Royal cavalry, well trained and armed to the teeth, was far superior to the makeshift rabble that had tried, and failed so dismally, to engage his soldiers in the past. Other officers, more dismissive still of the Duke's capabilities, considered it most likely that he would prepare Bridgwater for a siege and hide behind its inadequate defences until starved into ignominious submission.

In either case, Monmouth's attempt to seize the crown of England had come to a pathetic and contemptible end. Feversham ordered his men to pitch camp two or three miles from Bridgwater, at the village of Weston Zoyland, which lay slightly higher than the surrounding marshes and levels. A wide drainage ditch guarded the western side of his chosen site, affording some protection in the most unlikely event of attack from Bridgwater. Monmouth was beaten: they had only to wait, and he would fall ripely into their hands.

It was perhaps fortunate that Feversham was not blessed with the ability to read his adversary's mind. Ever since entering Bridgwater, Monmouth had been sunk in gloom, and his plans to march north again had had, even to his most loyal officers, an air of desperation about them. But he was well aware of the dangers of allowing himself to be besieged, and knew that escape, with or without his foot, and probably pursued by the full and awesome might of the Royal cavalry, represented his only hope, albeit a very slender one.

Until, at three o'clock on the Sunday afternoon, when many rebels were still straggling back from their visit to Taunton, and when the forty or more waggons were being loaded in readiness for the long march north, a labourer who lived in Chedzoy arrived in Bridgwater and asked urgently to see the Duke, for he had information that might be of great use to him.

Monmouth was doubtful at first: but as the man spoke, his almost impenetrable accent translated where necessary by the Somerset officers, his mercurial spirits began to rise. Here, quite possibly, was a God-given opportunity to strike, and achieve the sudden and overwhelming success which had so far eluded him.

Feversham had camped near the village of Weston Zoyland, and he did not seem to be taking any precautions against a surprise attack. It would be possible, following a roundabout route, to fall upon the Royal encampment without approaching their cannon too close. It seemed too good to be true. Spyglass clutched in his hand, Monmouth raced up the church tower to see for himself. The view was not especially enlightening, so he sent the labourer, Godfrey, back to Chedzoy to spy out the land, with instructions to make especial note of any earthworks or entrenchments which the enemy might be digging to secure their position.

It was five o'clock, some four hours before sunset, when the man returned, breathless but eager. There was no sign of any defensive works, and the Royal army seemed quite unprepared for an attack. Their cannon were stationed apart from the main encampment, guarding the road which ran from Bridgwater to Weston Zoyland, and the horse, with the exception of those on patrol, had been billeted in the village. It would be possible to attack from the north by marching right round Chedzoy, where the rector was staunchly Royalist, and avoiding the cannon altogether.

There was a hasty council of war, and for once, all were in agreement. This represented their greatest chance to reverse the decline in their fortunes. A night onslaught, when the enemy was asleep and off guard, was decided upon, and the details worked out in a mood of greater optimism than had infected the rebels for some time. Tonight would see an end to it, one way or the other, and a promise of glory, whatever happened.

An hour before midnight, the streets of Bridgwater were full of rebel soldiers, drawn up in regimental order, and impatient and eager to join battle at last. No one had relished the thought of another aimless and dispiriting march, to no good purpose, back across Somerset yet again. The prospect of a fight, with a good chance of beating the King's men, had strengthened the hearts of many waverers, who might otherwise have been tempted to slink away to seek the King's pardon.

It seemed that most of Bridgwater had turned out to see them go. Many of the townspeople were there to express their good wishes, but others, obviously, had come in a less generous spirit of 'good riddance'. The foot were to lead, for the first few miles, so that the cavalry would not be able to go too fast and lose touch. And the orders were exceedingly strict: the march must, at all costs, take place in complete silence.

Bram hoped that he had managed to impress the paramount importance of this upon Ben. His cousin sat beside him, as usual slumped in the saddle, his slanting eyes gleaming with excitement, and every so often a little whimper of anticipation escaped him. Bram had given up shushing him every time this happened, since Ben seemed to take absolutely no notice. It was not a very loud noise, and perhaps it would not matter.

The Red Regiment in the van, they left Bridgwater along the Bristol road. It was quite dark, the moon hidden by an overcast sky, and a low mist wreathing eerily along the hedgerows and ditches. The rebels, well aware of the need for quiet, obeyed their orders to the utmost. No one talked, or coughed, or spat, and many of the troopers had muffled their horses' tack with strips of cloth. All knew that success, and their lives, depended on the total surprise of the attack.

A mile or so along the road, hoofbeats were heard, and the column halted in a breathless, strained hush. A Royalist patrol was crossing their path, several hundred yards in front of them, but the dark and the mist rendered them invisible to the rebels, and likewise protected Monmouth's army from discovery. At last, the noise died away into the distance, and slowly, cautiously and with much relief, they could continue their march.

The ammunition, waggons and a gun whose carriage had suddenly developed a disastrously squeaky wheel were left behind at a farmhouse, and the army turned south along the lanes that led into Sedgemoor. So far, all had gone well. Somewhere ahead of them, the King's army lay in peaceful slumber, the perfect target. Godfrey, the peasant who had brought the information from Chedzoy, was in the van, guiding Colonel Wade and the Red Regiment along the lanes which he had known all his life. To succeed, they only had to keep their advantage of surprise.

Bram had more leisure than he would have wished, on that long slow ride, to contemplate the coming battle. The horse were to take the initiative, swing round the enemy encampment, and attack from the rear, while the foot engaged them along the front. He hoped that their skills would be equal to the task: it was obvious that only intensive training would improve the standards of Monmouth's horse, and they had had scant time for such things in the course of their marches. It seemed foolhardy for the Duke to rely so much on his ramshackle cavalry, but Bram suspected that he had had little choice. And Lord Grey, an able man but emphatically no soldier, was still in command.

He glanced uneasily at Ben. He had tried to persuade his cousin to stay behind with the baggage waggons, but all the previous attempts to prise him from Bram's side had had their effect, and Ben now refused to let him out of his sight. There had been no time to argue, nor had it been the place, so now he was encumbered with the duty of looking after his cousin, who was unarmed and certain to panic at the first shots. Bleakly, Bram thought of the likely outcome of any fighting, and prayed silently for Ben's safety.

The column of foot in front of them had halted. Belatedly, he hauled on his chestnut's reins before the gelding bumped into the animal in front, just visible as a dim blur. The mist seemed thicker here, and the silence almost absolute, disturbed only by the distant shriek of an owl, and the nearer, virtually inaudible sound of thousands of men, breathing softly and eerily in unison, as if the night itself were alive. Then the cavalry began to move forward, past the foot soldiers, to take their place at the head of the army. With no shouts of command, it was very difficult to discern what was happening, but when the horse in front of him moved on, he urged his own to follow suit. They passed the foot, crowded into the hedges to give them room, and he thought he could make out the smiles and nods and lifted hands that meant 'Good luck!' With a suddenly thumping heart, he tightened his grip on the reins, and checked by touch that his sword and pistols were ready. In an hour's time, all might be resolved, and he would be victorious, or a fugitive – or dead.

He uttered up a brief prayer, for his own safety and for Ben's, and for the success of their attack, and then concentrated his mind fiercely upon the task in hand, negotiating the first of the drainage ditches, or rhines, that lay between them and the enemy's camp. Despite the rain that had fallen so torrentially in the past week, this one was not particularly full, and their guide had brought them to the right crossing point. They splashed over it, and regrouped on the opposite bank. Behind them, the foot soldiers followed, through mist rising from the water so thickly that they could see hardly a yard's length in front.

Another mile, across the soft damp peat, muffling the horses' hooves and making walking difficult. Godfrey, the guide, moved with confidence, certain of the position of the next obstacle, the Langmoor Rhine, which he knew to be considerably fuller than the previous ditch. There was only one suitable crossing, marked by a stone, and he made for it unerringly in the darkness.

The water-filled drain, some eight feet wide, appeared suddenly in front of him, much sooner than he had expected. With a sudden and rising sense of alarm, Godfrey realised that, somehow, he had gone astray. There was no sign of the stone that marked the crossing, and for a moment, panicking, he could not work out where he was. Behind him, the column of cavalry came to an unscheduled halt. Horses jostled and bumped into each other, men cursed, and tack jingled. Godfrey in desperation ran along the course of the rhine, failed to find the crossing, ran back. Someone said something angrily, and a horse whinnied with the ear-shattering force of a trumpet.

Abruptly, terrifyingly loud and close, came the sound of a shot. At once, several horses squealed in fear. Although the Royal camp was still a mile away, all hope of surprise was lost, and Grey, well aware of it, urged the unfortunate Godfrey to find the crossing without delay.

They had missed it by only fifty yards. Sobbing with exertion, the labourer ran up to Grey's stirrup, gasping that he had found it, pointing into the darkness. Now, speed was of the essence. At a fast trot, the undisciplined horses infected with hectic excitement, they poured across the Langmoor Rhine and charged for the enemy camp.

Bram, his sword in his hand, was dimly aware of Ben, still riding leech-like at his side. He had no idea of the state of the ground over which they were travelling: his horse, like all the rest, was moving virtually blind. Suddenly, ahead of them, there was shouting, a confusion of activity, the sound of shots, and then rapidly diminishing hoofbeats. No one seemed to know what had happened, but Bram guessed that they had encountered a Royalist patrol, now galloping back to the enemy camp. As to who had fired the fatal shot that had announced their arrival, he had no idea: it might have been that same Royalist patrol, guarding the Langmoor crossing, or one of the rebel horse, either by accident or treachery. Recriminations would undoubtedly follow, but for now, their immediate task was to undo, somehow, the damage that the premature alarm had done.

More shouting: the horses in front of him had come to a milling, confused halt. Beyond, drumbeats and yells proclaimed that the Royal army was alerted, and awake.

'It's another bloody ditch!' someone wailed, not far away. Godfrey, on foot, had been left behind in the charge for the camp, and there had been no warning of this unexpected obstacle. Bram, peering into the gloom, could see very little beyond his horse's flattened ears, although his eyes had long since become fully accustomed to the darkness.

'What happening?' Ben cried, still miraculously beside him, his voice quivering with distress. 'What happening, Bram?'

'I've no idea,' he said, trying not to let his anxiety and fear colour his voice. 'Stay with me, Ben – as close as you can.'

Ahead, there was movement, shots, more shouting. His horse flung up its head in fright, almost hitting him on the nose. Someone jostled him, and he swore furiously. Then the unmistakable voice of Captain Jones, an old Ironside, yelled through the darkness. 'First two troops, follow me!'

It was total confusion. Bram had no idea how many men were before him, or behind him, where Lord Grey was, what orders he was supposed to obey. The horse in front of him plunged off to the left, and his own, with a snort, snatched the bit and cantered in pursuit. Behind him, he heard others following suit.

The Royalist camp was astir now, and frantic yells and alarms punctuated the darkness. Riding blind, Bram could not tell what was happening, although he was dimly aware that alongside, to his right, ran the unsuspected ditch that protected the enemy's tents. Somewhere, there must be a crossing point. Even if only a few of their cavalry managed to ford the rhine, they could create havoc amongst the sleepy, bewildered Royalist soldiers.

And then suddenly the flash and crash of pistol shots ahead, shouts, the terrified neighing of horses. Figures loomed up in the darkness, enemy troopers, riding to the attack. Bram found himself beating off a man on a horse with a white face, and the ghostly, almost disembodied marking was the only part of his adversary which he could see clearly. It might have been a friend, rather than foe, but there was no arguing with the sword slashing towards him. Somehow, desperately, he parried the blade, but his own horse, mad with terror, was struggling to escape the mêlée, and he could barely control it. No chance to draw or fire his pistols, all his energies were taken up with fighting his horse, and his opponent. He lunged, parried, slashed, and then abruptly his mount crashed sideways to the ground, pitching him on to the soft torn earth. Everywhere there were stamping hooves, shots, screams. His chestnut struggled wildly to its feet and crashed away through the confused tangle of horsemen. Bram, gasping, winded, knew that he stood no chance without it, and there was every danger that he would be trampled underfoot. The line of the ditch was not far away: he dived towards it, rolled clear of a rearing horse, and flung himself down the bank.

The bottom was filled with mud, or water, but at least here he was, for the moment, safe from stray bullets or flying hooves. Above him, the fighting went on, hot and fierce in the darkness, and, more distantly, he could hear the clatter of musket fire as battle was joined in earnest.

For what seemed like hours, but was probably only a few minutes, he lay half in, half out of the water, listening to the sounds of death and hurt all about him. He had lost his sword, so there was no point in returning to the fray. Perhaps, if the fighting moved away, he would be able to find a weapon, even a horse, and try to rejoin his comrades. But somehow, God alone knew how, he must also try to find Ben.

At last, one of the groups of horse, probably the rebels, had had enough. Their remnant turned and fled, pursued by the Royalist cavalry. Bram judged it safe to crawl out of his ditch. Very cautiously, he peered through the thick rough grass fringing the edge, and saw the inevitable detritus of battle: the dim, heaped shapes of dead men and horses, several loose animals wandering aimlessly about, a wounded man staggering desperately towards one of them. There were groans, and cries for help, and then, piercing his heart, a muffled, horrible, blubbering wail that could only come from one person.

He scrambled to his feet and ran towards the sound, heedless of any lingering danger. 'Ben! Ben, where are you?' He tripped and fell over the outstretched limbs of a dead horse, picked himself up, called again. The cry came from somewhere ahead of him, quite close, and then suddenly he was almost on top of a writhing, agonised heap on the ground, that sobbed his name over and over. 'Bram! Bram, where Bram?'

'I'm here – I'm here,' he said, and Ben's short powerful arms clamped around him like a vice, his whole body shuddering with terror, and his incoherent sobs spluttering against his neck. 'Oh, Ben, hush, hush now – you must be quiet, or they'll hear us!'

As the firing away to their right was increasing in intensity, joined by the sharp familiar crack of Monmouth's light cannon, this was not particularly likely, but he felt hideously exposed and vulnerable, here on the open moor, with only darkness and mist to hide them from discovery and death. Ben, however, was too deeply in the throes of panic and terror to take notice. He went on wailing and sobbing until Bram, hating himself, slapped him soundly across the face. 'Ben! For God's sake, shut up!'

His cousin, astonished, snuffled once or twice, and began to whimper softly. With difficulty, Bram disengaged himself from the boy's leech-like grasp, and knelt beside him, holding his hands. 'Ben! Listen to me! Are you hurt?'

Another whimper was the only reply. Suddenly, a party of horse galloped out of the mist, almost straight at them. Bram pushed Ben to the ground and lay beside him, holding his breath, until the tramping hooves had safely gone. Very quietly but forcefully, he repeated the question. 'Ben! Are you hurt?'

'Leg,' said his cousin, on a rising wail of fear and pain. 'Leg hurts, Bram, *hurts*!'

His worst fears confirmed, Bram examined him by touch. The left leg was sound enough, but the boy's right ankle was twisted out of shape, already swollen and hot, and obviously agonisingly painful. If they were able to escape from this battlefield, he would not be able to walk: somehow, they would have to capture a horse, put Ben on it, and lead him to safety – where?

Of course, Bram reminded himself staunchly, the fight was not yet lost, and from the incessant noise and flashes of gunfire further along the rhine, the rest of the rebel forces were pressing the attack. But he had done his duty to Monmouth, for the present. Now, his chief concern was Ben.

Surely there must be a horse nearby. He tried to get to his feet, but Ben wailed, clutching at his leg, and brought him painfully down on to his knees. 'No, Bram, don't go!'

'I won't leave you,' Bram promised him urgently. 'Don't worry, *please* – I'm going to find you a horse!'

But Ben would not listen. He sobbed and clung on to Bram like a terrified child, and nothing that his cousin could say would comfort him. At last, when he judged that the boy had calmed down a little, he said very clearly, 'Ben, please – *listen*! We must find a horse for you to ride away from here – you can't walk on that ankle, can you? Ben, let go of me – let me find a horse for you.'

'Come too!' Ben sobbed. 'Don't leave!'

There was no alternative: he must take Ben with him. But in the darkness, the thick soft earth underfoot, with the fear of discovery ever present, and the pain in the boy's injured ankle, it was almost impossible. Swearing, slipping, struggling, he tried to get Ben to stand, even on one leg, and failed countless times until at last, somehow, all his muscles straining with effort, he managed to support his cousin's solid weight. And then, gasping and sweating, they took all of two steps upright before Ben lost his balance and fell heavily, with a cry of pain that dwindled into a pitiful, exhausted sobbing.

He could not leave the boy for the enemy to find. Perhaps, if they stayed there until first light, he could see better what was happening, whether they had any chance of escape.

But of course, this darkness was their best opportunity. If they waited for dawn, the enemy would see them, finish them off . . .

'Oh, Ben,' he said, almost sobbing himself with desperation. 'We *must* go! For God's sake, get *up!*'

Something of his frantic urgency must have penetrated the boy's consciousness at last, for he stopped weeping, and began to scramble up again. This time, Bram had a better idea of the weight he must support, and of his cousin's clumsiness. With Ben's arm across his shoulders, his own gripping the other's coat, they struggled upright and stood, breathless but solidly together. Bram spoke very clearly. 'Ben – let me take your weight. Don't put your foot on the ground. Use me as a crutch, and we'll walk, very slowly, one step at a time – don't try to go too fast, it doesn't matter.'

For a miracle, this time they did not fall, although they came very close to it several times. There were so many obstacles – bodies, dropped weapons, grass tussocks, even minor alterations in terrain, unseen in the dark, were a major hazard. Behind them, the light sound of Monmouth's three little guns was almost extinguished, now, by the vaster thud of the King's artillery, brought at last to bear on the ranks of rebel foot, and the screams of dying men and horses provided a terrible counterpoint. Almost imperceptibly, it was beginning to grow light: the short summer night was almost at an end.

Suddenly, Bram became aware of the presence of many horses, gathered just to the other side of the rhine along which they were struggling. In that position, they must be the enemy. And even as he realised the danger, someone shouted, there was a shot, and Ben wailed and fell, dragging him down into the mud. Then there were horses moving, splashing, trampling all around, and as he tried to get to his feet something fetched him a great blow across the head, and plunged him down into darkness.

The daylight hurt his eyes. Someone was talking somewhere above him. A foot prodded him painfully in the ribs, and he groaned and tried to move away. A voice he did not at first recognise was babbling something in panic. Then he realised that it was Ben, and struggled to sit up.

'Get up, you Monmouth dog!'

There was a sword, sharp and shiny, pointed at his chest. Bram stared blankly at the Royalist soldier behind it. His head hurt, and for a moment he could not remember what had happened, or why he was here. The blade prodded his coat. 'Up, or I'll spit you now!'

His arms and legs seemed to move of their own accord. He got to his feet, holding his head, which seemed to have enlarged, throbbing, to several times its usual size. He looked around him, dazed, seeing the battlefield properly for the first time. The ditch that had seemed such a fearsome obstacle in the dark was in reality hardly more than that, a ditch, with a sullen ribbon of muddy water at the bottom. A dead horse lay half in, half out of it, and further along, the bare green expanse of moor was disfigured with heaped corpses, both human and equine. Groups of Royalist soldiers, red-coated, moved amongst the bodies with grim purpose, loading them on to tumbril carts. Nearer, a small disconsolate group of rebels, for the most part stripped to shirt and breeches, muddy, bloodstained and exhausted, huddled together. The soldier with the sword gestured viciously. 'Over there, Monmouth rogue, or die now.'

He began to move, but a sob stopped him. Ben sat on the ground, his leg stretched out uselessly in front of him, his ugly face swollen and streaked with tears. 'Bram, help!'

'Move!' the soldier yelled, and waved his sword. Another redcoat came over to Ben, his face gloating. 'Having trouble, Ned? Want some help? This one looks as though he'll give us some fun.'

'He can't walk!' Bram shouted. 'For God's sake, let me help him!'

'Not if you value your life, pretty boy,' said the man called Ned. 'He your lover, eh?' The sword jabbed threateningly at his chest, and Bram took an involuntary step back, and then another. Behind the soldier, he saw the other Royalist kick Ben viciously, again and again, until the boy began to crawl in terror away from him. He gave a roar of anger, and tried to dodge the sword, but the man Ned, his eyes slitted with cruel amusement, kept him at bay, retreating helplessly, for to do anything else would be to impale himself on that gleaming, wicked blade.

'For God's sake, lad,' said a Somerset voice just behind him, and he was grabbed and pinioned by several solid arms, belonging to some of the rebel prisoners. 'You can't do anything, you'll only get yourself killed as well as him – don't struggle, lad, this is for your own good!'

'Sensible,' said the soldier, grinning wickedly, his sword still pointing at Bram's chest. 'You can't help him, his sort are no better than beasts anyway – now, all of you, move!'

He could do nothing, nothing at all, but watch as four or five Royalist soldiers, calling and whooping as if they chased a wild animal, herded Ben towards the ditch with vicious blows from feet and swords. The boy's terrified screams grew hoarse with pain, blood soaked his filthy shirt, as he fell, crawled, tried to run away from his tormenters, and all the while he called his cousin's name over and over, like an incantation. Then, as Bram cried in anguish and made another vain attempt to win free of the well-meaning people who held him, Ben was brought to the edge of the rhine. He tried to get to his feet, but his damaged ankle gave way, and he fell backwards into the ditch with a splash. With laughter, and whoops of triumph, the soldiers leaped down the bank, slashing and stabbing with their weapons. 'Bram!' Ben screamed, and then his voice changed to one last dreadful wail of agony and despair, bubbling into silence as he was pushed beneath the muddy water of the rhine.

For some minutes more, the soldiers stayed on the bank, prodding and poking at what lay under the water, with much merriment. Bram, frozen with horror and pity, could not tear his eyes away from the sight, as if to watch was, in some way, not to fail Ben in these last terrible moments, although he must already be dead, the final choking agony ended beneath the turbid, muddy waters of the rhine.

The men turned away, still, dreadfully, laughing, as if they had done some unwanted animal to death. Then the man called Ned shouted at the rebel prisoners, and his comrades waved their stained swords, the blood-lust still leering from their faces, and slowly, shamblingly, the little group began to move.

Bram moved with them, like a sleepwalker, stunned by the ghastly horror of his cousin's end, flooded with agonising guilt. He had promised to take care of Ben, and he had failed him. He had allowed himself to be held back, he had watched while the boy was hunted down and murdered in cold blood, with a casual cruelty that had been the more appalling because, God forgive them, they had laughed as they tortured him, and then drowned him . . .

His mind recoiled from what he had seen, and yet he could not forget, would never forget, until the day he died – which might also be today – the simpleton boy screaming for the help which Bram had promised him, and which he had failed to deliver.

Someone, beside him, was supporting him as he stumbled along; someone else was praying, in a low fierce mutter. He hardly heard them, or the raucous shouts of the victorious King's soldiers, and the hot morning sunshine did not touch him. Driven like animals, with kicks and blows, those captives who could walk were brought to the church at Weston Zoyland, with its soaring tower a landmark for miles around in this flat, open country.

A militia man sat by the entrance to the churchyard, making a note of the prisoners as they were led past him, many tied together, many wounded. Some of his comrades had already plundered those rebel soldiers who still had garments and possessions worth the taking. Bram's

357

coat and waistcoat had been unceremoniously torn from his back, and his pockets rifled. Despite the rough handling, he had barely noticed it, even when they took his little watch, a gift from his father, that he had treasured for years. Nor had their crude, leering comments on his looks, the fumbling attempts to ensure that he was not a girl in disguise, penetrated the awful feeling of numb remoteness that had filled him, ever since Ben's death, as if his cousin's last despairing screams had separated him from the brutal horror of the reality all around him.

The church was cool and dark after the bright heat outside. He sat where he was pushed, against a wall, and stared unseeing at the men filling the space within, hearing again that voice begging for the help that his cowardice had denied him . . .

He did not look up, although many did, to see the angels that soared across the wondrously carved roof high above them, their hands spread in blessing but their ethereal faces blind, eternally oblivious to the misery and suffering of the prisoners below.

# PART 3

*'A deep and dangerous consequence'*

# 'Repenting folly'

The news of the bloody end of King Monmouth's rebel army and the brutal termination of all his hopes spread swiftly through Somerset, and further through the West Country. In hundreds of towns and villages, men, women and children wept as they heard of the disaster, and mourned the fate of their husbands, fathers, brothers, sons. In many parishes, stalwartly Royalist clergy ordered the bells to be rung in celebration of this God- given deliverance from war and rebellion, and the harsh, triumphant clamour overhead seemed a desperately cruel mockery of the hope and idealism with which so many honest men had marched away to join Monmouth's army.

The news reached King James, anxiously waiting in Whitehall, and the bells rang out in London too, expressive of joy and relief. The rebel force had been shattered, Monmouth and his senior officers were hunted fugitives with prices on their heads, and the rebellious West Country, home of obdurate Dissenters and traitors, lay quiet under the heel of the King's army. Never again must these seditious people be tempted to take up arms against their lawful King: and to force home the lesson, the captured rebels should be subjected to the full might and severity of justice. They had committed treason, the foulest of crimes, and they would pay the full penalty, without benefit of mercy.

Taunton, barely ten miles away, heard of the battle in the cheerful morning sunshine. At first, the inhabitants could scarcely believe that such a catastrophe had overtaken their beloved King Monmouth; but as the day wore on, and more witnesses arrived, eager to relate what they had seen or heard, the terrible truth seeped into their reluctant minds. Knots of subdued people, many weeping, gathered in the streets to exchange news or bring comfort to those who had friends or relatives amongst the rebels. Some of the more stout-hearted took horse, and rode off to Bridgwater to see what they could discover for themselves. The rest of the town waited, despairing and sorrowful, for the worst.

Jonah Loveridge heard of the battle from a customer, almost too eager with tidings of disaster, two hours before noon. Politely, he listened to the story of night attatck, confusion, defeat, and slaughter or flight, as if his beloved and wilful son was safe upstairs, as if he had no direct interest in the outcome of the fight. He thanked his informant, who left the shop rather disappointed at the bookseller's unemotional reaction to such dreadful news. But as the door closed, Jonah put his head in his hands and wept bitterly for Bram, his bright brave son, who was quite possibly dead, and at best a fugitive in fear of his life.

His wife found him, a few minutes later, and knew at once what must be wrong. She bent over him, touching his shoulder. 'Jonah! What's happened? Is it Bram?'

In silence, she heard the story of Sedgemoor, her still-beautiful face pale with shock and grief. As her husband faltered to a close, unable to bear the thought of what might have happened, she marshalled all her strength to deal with this terrible, but not unexpected, blow. As before in a crisis, her mind coolly assessed probabilities and stratagems, while her emotions were held ruthlessly in check. The tearing grief that threatened to overwhelm her must not be allowed to break her yet, as it had already broken Jonah.

'Don't give up hope,' she said urgently. 'There are three possibilities, after all. Yes, he might be dead – but he has a horse, he would have found it easy to escape. So, he may well be a fugitive, and he's not stupid – he has a good chance of evading capture. And, thirdly, he may be a prisoner – but that's not the most likely alternative, in the circumstances. Jonah, please, listen – there is a good chance that he has escaped.'

'But how can we know?' Her husband lifted his face to stare at her. Tear-stained and grief-stricken, he was a tragic and somehow pathetic sight. 'How can we know what has happened to him? He may have escaped, but he hasn't come back here, has he?'

'He'd be a fool if he did,' Tabby pointed out. 'They will not be merciful, Jonah – Monmouth frightened them so much, they will want revenge and retribution. Everyone in Taunton knows who joined the rebels, there will be lists, enquiries, searches. They even noted the names of all the girls in Mistress Musgrave's school, remember? Pray God they will not be so heartless as to punish the children, too.'

Some life was returning, a little, to Jonah's eyes. He said, 'Libby – perhaps we ought to send Libby home to Bristol. If even the girls will not be safe, she might escape their notice then. I could not face Deb and Henry with the news that their only child had been cast into prison.'

Tabby was thinking, a frown between her level brows. 'She cannot be sent on her own. Nor, I think, would it be safe to go by land, with Somerset probably swarming with fleeing rebels and marauding soldiers. Perhaps we could find a ship plying between Bridgwater and Bristol that would take her? That would seem to be most sensible.'

'A good idea,' Jonah said. He took her hand, and pressed it against his heart. 'But, my dear love – I cannot escort her. You must understand that – I can't leave Taunton, not when we might – we might have some news . . .'

'Some reliable friend can surely be found,' Tabby said. She kneeled beside him, and laid her head in his lap. 'Don't – don't despair. We do not *know* that he is dead. And, hard as it may be, we must not try to find him, or seek him out – that might lead the soldiers to him. We must be patient, Jonah, we *must* be, and wait. And meanwhile, sending Libby back to Bristol will give us something positive to do, and to think about.'

Jonah smiled rather wanly and kissed her hand. 'What would I do without you, my love? You are so wise, so calm . . .'

'I have a history of plotting behind me,' Tabby reminded him. 'Although it's a skill I haven't had occasion to use for years . . . We must tell the girls what has happened – though, if possible, without frightening or distressing them too much. And we must write to Mother in Chard – she is so fond of Bram, she must be beside herself with worry.'

'If news of the battle has reached Mistress Musgrave's establishment,' Jonah said, 'I expect the girls will be sent home forthwith. Even if the children are safe from punishment, I doubt very much whether their teachers will be – they'd be well advised to leave Taunton now, before the authorities catch up with them.'

His assessment proved accurate. Only a few minutes later, Sue, Hannah and Libby, tearful and distraught, arrived at the door with a confused account of the battle, gleaned both from a sorrowful address to the whole school by Mistress Musgrave, and from what they had learned in the street on the way home. Like Jonah, the girls were all convinced that Bram and Den must be dead, and Tabby spent most of the day persuading them that they were, quite possibly, still alive, and escaped from the battle. Hannah, who was after all only eleven, proved the easiest to comfort, but Sue, more realistic, announced between sobs that she preferred to believe that her adored brother had been killed. 'Because if it's true, I can't possibly be more unhappy than I am now – and if he proves to be alive, then it will be such a wonderful surprise.'

Tabby left her to weep, and with considerable reluctance went to her niece's chamber. As she had suspected, the suggestion that Libby return home to Bristol at first met with tearful refusal. The plain, plump, bookish girl undoubtedly harboured a fondness for her brilliant cousin Bram, six years her senior. It was a calf-love that was certainly doomed, even if Monmouth had never landed at Lyme. Bram, despite his startling looks, had not, to his mother's knowledge, shown a great deal of interest in the

363

various languishing young ladies who had looked longingly at him over the years, let alone paid much attention to poor Libby, who was probably lumped together with his sisters in his mind. But she could not say this to the girl, or reveal how much she had guessed. Libby would be mortified if she realised that her aunt was well aware of her feelings.

So she pointed out that her parents in Bristol would be very worried about her, and that Taunton would probably be unsafe for a while, if soldiers from the King's army were billeted in the town, as seemed to be likely. There was even the chance that she and all the other pupils of Mistress Musgrave and her assistants would be punished for making those colours, and presenting them to Monmouth.

'I don't want to go home until we know what's happened to Bram!' the girl said despairingly, and began to cry. Tabby held her, giving comfort, knowing that the battle had been won. At heart, Libby was reasonable and intelligent, and she loved her parents: she would not want to bring them grief. Tonight, or tomorrow, she would agree, even with tears, to return to the comparative safety of Bristol.

If only Sue and Hannah could be sent with her. But Tabby, selfishly, could not face losing them as well, not even to temporary safety. Bram might be dead, or in terrible danger. Her daughters were all that was left to her, and she would keep them by her side unless absolute disaster threatened.

And in her heart, she could not seriously believe that it would. Times had changed since the wars of her childhood, when ghastly atrocities had been commonplace and she herself, at nine years old, had experienced the savage reality of war at first hand. In these civilised, enlightened days, she could not believe that retribution would descend upon innocent children.

During the latter part of the day, more details of the night's battle had been brought to Taunton, and over supper, a strained and joyless meal, Jonah, who had been out gathering news, told his family of what he had learned. It seemed that the rebel cavalry had for the most part managed to flee the battlefield unscathed, but that many of the foot soldiers had been slain or captured. The Duke himself was a fugitive, with a price of five thousand pounds for his capture, but there was every chance that he would escape abroad, to the safety of Holland.

There was still no news of Bram or Ben, but if they had fled with the horse, none could be expected. Even Jonah seemed to be more hopeful, although the news did not appear to bring much comfort to Sue, who had hardly touched her food.

That evening, Tabby wrote to her mother and stepfather in Chard, telling them of the battle – although the news must surely have reached them already – and that there seemed to be a good chance that Bram and Ben had escaped. More than that, she dared not put, for even though Jonah would ask one of his friends to ride over with it the next morning, there was no telling what might happen, even in the brief miles that separated the two towns. For the same reason, it did not seem wise to send Libby away just yet, with Bridgwater occupied by the King's army, and soldiers everywhere.

The next morning, they came to Taunton.

The populace gathered to watch the Royal regiment march into the town. After the rather ramshackle, informal appearance of Monmouth's men, these well-dressed, well-drilled soldiers looked chillingly efficient. They wore the almost ubiquitous scarlet coats, with green facings and breeches, and their weapons – swords, muskets and pikes – were burnished and gleaming. The whisper went round that this was Kirke's regiment, that had until recently been stationed in Tangier. Their grim, unfriendly faces gave no hope of mercy, and the people watched them in a sullen, unhappy silence. Already, word had come to Taunton of the five hundred prisoners held in the church at Weston Zoyland, in apparently terrible conditions, without food or water. And everyone knew of the gruesome gibbets that lined the road between the battlefield and Bridgwater, each bearing the body of a captured rebel, several in chains like criminals. Some score of men had been hanged there yesterday, without benefit of trial, as an example to anyone still convinced of the merits of rebellion. With fear, the people of Taunton wondered if this brutal and summary justice would be extended to those prisoners still held at Weston Zoyland, who must include many of their friends.

The men of Kirke's regiment pitched their tents in a field just outside the town, to the west of the castle, and made it clear that they considered themselves to be the victorious overlords of a subject and defeated populace. Those unfortunates who happened to live nearest to the camp found groups of soldiers standing menacingly on the doorstep, demanding supplies of food, drink and fuel. Anyone foolish enough to suggest that these should be paid for was abused, threatened and in some cases manhandled. Several women were assaulted, and one or two raped. As the lurid stories spread through Taunton, and the soldiers could be seen on every corner, armed and brutal and unmistakably dangerous, the female half of the population kept within doors, and only went out if absolutely necessary. Jonah forbade any of his womenfolk to venture abroad at all, and told the three maids that they could stay at their homes until the danger was past. The house was well supplied, for the moment, and he or the boy, Elias, could easily slip out to buy whatever might be necessary.

From all over Somerset, the tales came in to Taunton, of fugitives from the battle hunted down, betrayed, imprisoned. And, worst news of all, the bells were rung on the Thursday morning, two days after Kirke's men had marched into the town, to celebrate the capture in Dorset of Monmouth, their beloved Duke, whom the people of Taunton, not three weeks previously, had joyfully proclaimed to be their lawful King.

There would be no reprieve for him: the handsome young man, darling of the people and of the late King, his father, was assuredly doomed. And as if that were not calamity enough, later that morning Colonel Kirke's men brought into Taunton the prisoners taken at Sedgemoor and immediately after, who had been kept in Weston Zoyland church. They were to be lodged in the castle prison, until such time as they could be brought to trial for their rebellion.

Word that they were coming had passed round Taunton like a hurricane, and the streets were packed with silent, grieving crowds. No one was sure if they would be glad or sorry to see neighbours or loved ones amongst the prisoners; but all were determined to obtain the best possible view. The press was thickest at Eastreach and around the East Gate, where the convoy would enter the town, but all along East Street, up Fore Street and as far as the entrance to the precincts of the castle, people lined the way.

Jonah and his family found themselves a place just opposite the Three Cups, not far from the shop. Their faces, pale and shadow-eyed, showed all too clearly the strains of the past few days. Even the ebullient Hannah was silent and tear-streaked, and held her mother's hand with the strength of a much younger child. Beside her, Sue stood miserably, certain that they would not see Bram because he was already dead. It was now common knowledge in Taunton that many men of the town, who had formed the Blue Regiment, had died in the battle: they had bravely withstood the Royalist cavalry charges until cut to pieces, and casualties amongst them had been heavy. Bram had not been amongst them, but that did not shake her belief. Libby, pale and somehow fierce, had taken up the opposite view, and was convinced that he was alive, and free.

And the pity of it was, thought Tabby, looking sadly at the three girls, that only the sight of her son's face amongst the captives would make his fate certain. If he was a fugitive, they might not find out for weeks, or even months, whether he was safe. And if he was dead, whether heaped into the common pits that had been dug on the rich flat field of Sedgemoor, or, much worse, swinging on a gibbet outside Bridgwater, they might never learn what had befallen him.

Something was happening: a buzz ran all along the street, people peered past each other and craned their necks, sobbed in apprehension or pity. Tabby heard the tramp of marching feet, and felt Hannah's small cold hand tighten convulsively in hers. Here came Kirke's men, nicknamed Lambs from the badge on their uniforms, and also with ironical reference to their demeanour and behaviour. Marching to the beat of the drum, swaggering, arrogant and brutal, the first company presented a poignant contrast to the huddle of men who followed them. Most had been roughly bound or roped together, they were ragged and filthy, and many wore only breeches and shirts: even their shoes had been plundered from them. A low murmur of horror and anger swelled as the prisoners stumbled past. A woman who had obviously recognised someone rushed forward, weeping, and one of the escorting soldiers shoved her back so roughly that she fell with a flurry of skirts into the gutter.

There were so many of them, Tabby saw in despair: so many, so thickly crowded together, that she did not have a hope of glimpsing every face. He had been wearing his good new russet suit, but that would surely have been plundered from him, like the rest. And if he were not here, where was he? Hiding in a ditch? Incarcerated in another prison, at Wells or Bridgwater? Or lying scantily covered with the black peat of Sedgemoor, his golden hair and empty hazel eyes filled and dulled with earth?

She was being morbid. She must not, must *not* despair. She fixed her gaze on the captive faces, brown-skinned farmers and labourers, pale craftsmen and weavers, all with a hopelessness and misery staring from their eyes, mute, like cattle being driven to the shambles. She could hardly bear to look, but she must, for Bram's sake, and Ben's.

'There he is!' Libby cried, and jumped up and down, waving frantically. 'Bram! Bram, Bram, we're here!'

For a moment, Tabby did not recognise him, her own son. His hair hung lank and matted, his face was almost unrecognisable under the dirt and stubble and streaks of what seemed to be dried blood, he had lost his coat, and his shirt and breeches were torn and filthy. But worst of all was the dead, hopeless expression on his face, as if horror had driven all feeling and all humanity from him. He must have been able to hear Libby's calls, but he paid no attention to her, or to anything else: his legs, like a sleepwalker's, carried him past them until other prisoners obscured their view, and they could no longer see him.

Sue was crying softly, her apron over her face. Hannah seemed bewildered. 'Was that really Bram?' she asked in distress, turning her hazel eyes up to her mother. 'It looked like him, but it was as if he wasn't *there . . .*'

'It *was* him,' Libby said, fiercely and inappropriately exultant. 'It was, it was – I saw him, and he's alive!'

'Aye, but for how long?' said an anonymous masculine voice somewhere in the crowd around them.

The wounded came after, piled groaning in two waggons. No attempt had been made to cover them, or to dress their wounds, some of which were appalling. Hannah gave a sob and buried her face in her mother's chest, and Tabby, suddenly sickened and angry, put her arms tightly round her. Yes, these pitiful rags of men were rebels and traitors, taken in arms against their legitimate King: but they were also human beings, and Christian compassion demanded that they be treated as such. And she silently thanked God that, whatever else had happened to Bram, at least he seemed to be more or less unhurt. Judging by the sweet, sickly stench that wafted from those terrible waggons, few of the men within them would survive very long, either in or out of prison.

Jonah's face was grey and bleak. He said quietly, 'At least he's alive, and unharmed as yet. Let's go home. We can do nothing for him at present.'

There was certainly little sense in joining the huge crush of people following behind the procession of prisoners. Tabby, gathering her family around her, was suddenly smitten by conscience. She said urgently, 'Did anyone see Ben?'

No one had. 'I forgot about him,' Libby confessed, rather shamefacedly. 'I was so glad to see Bram.'

'Glad?' Sue cried angrily. '*Glad* to see him a prisoner?'

'Of course not,' Libby said indignantly. 'I was just pleased to see that he's still alive – or would you rather he was dead?'

'Oh, *please* stop it!' Hannah wailed, distraught, and burst into inconsolable tears. Tabby was tempted to echo her words, and follow them up with a sound scolding, but she could understand the reaction of the two older girls only too well.

'Come on,' she said softly, her arm around Hannah's shaking shoulders. 'Let's go home.'

Mercy was not a word that had ever been prominent in Colonel Percy Kirke's vocabulary. He had served twenty years in the army, and his experiences, culminating in governorship of the garrison of Tangier, had hardened him to the point of brutality. He had no knowledge of Somerset, and no feelings whatsoever for the inhabitants of Taunton. They were a factious, unruly and rebellious people, and needed to be taught a severe lesson. Living amongst them on free quarter, terrorising the women and threatening the men, was not enough. Treason was a most foul and unnatural crime, and only a comprehensive illustration of the just penalities would deter these seditious peasants from future revolt.

That afternoon, a gallows tree was erected in the marketplace, in front of the White Hart Inn, and the inhabitants of Taunton, in a grim, appalled silence, watched as several cartloads of prisoners, apparently selected at random, drew up beneath it. Kirke and his officers watched from the White Hart as the men were turned off, one by one, and drank a health in claret to each jerking contorted body, while the drums and fifes of the regiment sounded below to drown the cries of the remaining prisoners and the prayers and lamentations of the people filling the marketplace.

Tabby had been afraid, so afraid, that Bram would be amongst those chosen for summary execution, but none of these faces, bewildered, frightened or defiant, belonged to her son. Indeed, only one or two, out of nearly a score, were Taunton men, although all the deaths were greeted alike with loud sobs and cries. She forced herself to watch the end of each one, feeling the grief and hatred rising from the crowd pressed thick about her and Jonah, like a real and living thing.

But Colonel Kirke, the focus of their disgust and loathing, lounged at the window of the White Hart, glass in hand, his heavy face flushed with triumph and relish, oblivious. And Tabby prayed, but without very much hope, that these nineteen men, summarily despatched today to teach Taunton the consequences of rebellion, would be the last victims of his savage brand of justice.

'Loveridge? Any here called Loveridge?'

Tabby had never had occasion to visit the castle prison before, and the reality of it, the stench, the squalor, the desperate overcrowding in the cells that normally held at most a couple of dozen, and now contained close on five hundred, shocked and appalled her. With other hopefuls, she and Jonah had waited hours for admittance, and paid a fat bribe to the gaoler for the privilege. She had been prepared to be horrified, but this was beyond all her worst imaginings: she would not have considered keeping rats confined in such conditions as these. A kerchief to her nose to muffle the worst of the stink, she stood close by her husband, peering into the dim fetid cell beyond, as the gaoler shouted her son's name again.

'Moi name be Loveridge.'

The undersized, pockmarked man who shuffled forward was not Bram. The gaoler looked at Jonah impatiently as he shut the door. 'Be ee sure he be here, sir? He bain't in any of the cells so far.'

'Try them all,' said Tabby firmly. 'I saw him brought here, I'm certain of it.'

The last room was even more crowded than the rest, if that were possible, and the reek that flowed out of it almost overwhelmed her. Her eyes watered, and she nearly retched. 'This is disgusting – they'll all die of gaol fever in conditions like this!'

'And cheat the hangman,' said the turnkey, without sympathy. 'Can't do aught without coin, Mistress. If your lad d'want comfort, he'll have to pay for en.' He peered – Tabby noticed that even he, presumably inured to it, did not care to venture too far inside – and shouted again, 'Loveridge! Abraham Loveridge!'

And after a shuffling, muttering pause, her son's voice said, 'I'm here.'

He had been chained to two other prisoners, and the gaoler refused to unshackle him. So she and Jonah had perforce to pick their way between the men lying, sitting or sprawling in the soiled straw that seemed, along with the reeking tub in one corner, to be the only concession to the rebels' comfort.

Bram sat against the far wall, his face still streaked and smudged with dirt and blood. The terrifying blank look that had so appalled her, that morning, was no longer present, to her profound relief. But there was a haunted, despairing expression in his eyes that was almost as disturbing, and he did not smile at their approach.

There was, suddenly, nothing that she could say, no adequate words of sorrow or sympathy, no realistic promise of help. She knelt in the filthy straw, and said quietly, 'Hullo, Bram.'

His eyes avoided hers. 'Hullo,' he said, so softly that she could barely hear him. 'Thank you, for coming here.'

'Are you hurt?' Jonah demanded. 'Is that your blood?'

Bram glanced briefly at him, and his hand wandered up to touch his head, as if it did not really belong to him. 'I suppose so,' he said, without much interest. 'I think I was knocked down – I can't really remember.'

'It's disgraceful!' Jonah said, his voice shaking with rage. 'These conditions aren't fit for a dog – I'll complain in the strongest terms. Gaoler!' He got abruptly to his feet, and rounded on the unfortunate turnkey, who was standing impassively in the doorway.

Tabby, well aware that this outburst was his way of disguising his distress and grief, remained by her son. She said, 'Are you getting enough food?'

'Bread – in some quantity,' Bram told her. 'And water – which is more than we had in the church.' He closed his eyes briefly. She noticed that he still had not looked directly at her, or at Jonah. It was as if he wanted to keep his distance from them – or as if, she thought, with sudden perception, what had happened to him had been so appalling that it had left a barrier between him and the safe, ordinary world he had left behind, nearly three weeks ago.

'I'm sure we can make you more comfortable,' she said. 'We're not poor – we can surely pay the gaoler, buy you a cell to yourself, perhaps –'

'No!' Bram cried, so loudly that several of the other prisoners turned their heads. He repeated it, more quietly but no less vehemently. 'No. It wouldn't be right.' As his mother stared at him, he went on, low and forceful. 'We've suffered – we've all suffered together. Why should I buy any more privilege than any of these? If anything, I deserve even harsher punishment.'

A warning pulse had begun to beat, deep within her. She said, keeping her voice level and calm, 'Why? What have you done?'

And he looked fully at her for the first time, his eyes stark with the memory of something that was too horrible to be borne. Afterwards, she thought that his words would be burned on her soul for ever. 'I let Ben die,' he said.

Their eyes met, and locked. Tabby's hand crept out, almost of its own accord, to touch him. Trying to keep the shock and disbelief out of her voice, she said, 'Can – can you tell me about it?'

For a moment, she thought that he was going to retreat into silence. Jonah's diatribe formed a furious background, upbraiding the gaoler. One of the other prisoners began to cough, with a note that intimated a consumption, and she almost missed Bram's brief, agonised description of Ben's terrible death at the hands of Kirke's soldiers.

'Oh, poor Ben,' Tabby whispered, appalled. 'He never hurt anyone . . . why? Why did they kill him?'

'They did it for sport,' Bram said, after a long and dreadful pause. 'Like hunting an animal – and I let them do it, I could have saved him, but I didn't – I let them force me back, I let them keep me away from him, and then it was too late . . . and all the time, he was calling for me, crying my name, begging me to help him, and I failed him, I didn't save him, they drove him into the ditch and drowned him there.'

Tabby saw the horror on his face, the self-loathing, and her own eyes filled with tears. She said, very softly, 'You couldn't have done anything, or you would have been killed yourself, I expect – you mustn't blame yourself.'

'But I do,' said Bram, with bitter intensity. 'I promised that I would take care of him – and I didn't. In the end, when it mattered most, I failed him.' He swallowed, and stared down at the filthy straw. 'I don't regret any of this for myself – I joined the rebellion gladly, and I accept the consequences. But before God, I wish I had never laid eyes on Monmouth, for then poor Ben would still be alive.'

There were so many things she could say, and all of them were pointless, for she understood his feelings. She found she was holding his hand, as tightly as Hannah had grasped hers that morning. 'Do you want me to tell Rachael?'

He nodded. 'She should know as soon as possible – but, please, don't tell her what happened – how horribly he died – just say that . . . that he died in the battle.' And then his desperate control broke at last, and he put his hands over his face. 'Oh, God, poor, poor Ben . . . he was so terrified, in agony, bewildered, he couldn't understand – and he kept calling to me, over and over again, and I didn't save him!'

'Time's up,' said the gaoler's voice, thickly Somerset. 'There are others wanting their turn too, you know, Mistress.'

She fumbled in the pocket of her gown, and surreptitiously drew out a little leather purse, heavy with coin. He might spurn it, but even if he gave the money, in some quixotic gesture of renunciation, to those he considered to be more deserving, it would do some good. She pushed it into his lap, and whispered, 'Goodbye for now, Bram. We'll come back often, I promise.'

Even the unsavoury air of Taunton – offal, ordure, the reek of the tannery – seemed as fragrant as a June hedgerow after the prison. Tabby walked home with her husband, her arm in his, lending comfort but also, more unobtrusively, receiving it. They had much to be thankful for. Bram was alive, and so far in good health, even if the dreadful nature of Ben's death tormented him with grief and remorse.

She glanced at Jonah's face with love and compassion. He had done his best to prevent Bram joining the rebels, and now that the inevitable consequences of his failure had befallen his last, most beloved son, his regret must be agonisingly sharp. But he had refrained from righteously pointing out Bram's errors, and she knew that he would do all in his power to help him, even if his assistance was rejected. He had his faults, and she saw them with the clarity of love: he was inconsistent, indecisive, he tended to use words to cover for his lack of action, and he could be startlingly obstinate. And she knew that she herself drew upon an inner force, a fierce certainty of purpose that Bram shared, and Jonah sadly lacked. But he was her husband, for good or ill, and she loved him dearly.

She smiled at him, and leaned her head against his shoulder as they walked, as they had in their sweethearting days: and Jonah, acknowledging her support and her strength, smiled sadly in return.

The letters, sorrowful and sparing in detail, went out from Taunton the next day. To Rachael Wickham, Tabby wrote with sorrow and sympathy, telling her of the death of her beloved youngest son, slain at Sedgemoor Fight, four days previously. She made no more than the briefest mention of Bram's survival, albeit as a captive. Rachael in grief was apt to be unreasonable, and would undoubtedly place all the blame for Ben's death on his cousin's shoulders. And even though Bram himself was acutely conscious of his own guilt, she did not relish the thought of Rachael's reaction to the news that Tabby's son was still undeservedly alive, while her own had perished.

To Silence, she could be more open. Her mother had always had a special fondness for Bram, who of all Tabby's children most resembled her daughter, and although she would undoubtedly grieve for Ben, her sorrow would be tempered by the news that Bram was alive. She advised her not to come to Taunton just yet, for the journey was not safe at present, and neither was the town, still full of the menacing presence of Kirke's soldiers. In any case, there was nothing that Silence could do, nothing any of them could do save to wait, and hope that when Bram and the other captured rebels were eventually brought to trial, their judge would be disposed to mercy.

In the mean time, she and Jonah had another, more immediate fear. The conditions in the castle prison were dreadful, and the place was rife with disease. Even Bram, young, strong and healthy, would not be immune to an outbreak of gaol fever or smallpox. And if he succumbed, who would care for him, or nurse him? He would have survived the slaughter of Sedgemoor, only to die in that squalid, stinking and desperately overcrowded prison. And although they visited their son every day, bringing money and food and clothing, he refused everything they offered him, insisting that the gifts be distributed amongst the other prisoners. It was an undeniably generous, unselfish attitude, which Jonah at least would much have admired in another, but he knew that such obstinacy was endangering his son's health, if not his life, and Bram's stand drove him to impotent, frustrated fury. As some relief from his pent-up feelings, he threw himself with fervour into organising Libby's return to her parents.

A ship was found that plied regularly between Bridgwater and Bristol, and the captain expressed himself willing to take the young lady and her uncle as passengers. Tearfully, Libby bade farewell to her aunt and her cousins, and left Taunton under Jonah's wing. There was only one reason to stay, and since he was immured in prison, and she had no hope

373

whatsoever of being allowed to see him, she was able to contemplate the excitement of her first voyage, and the prospect of Bristol and home, with something like acceptance.

And Tabby, left behind with her daughters, found that she missed Jonah more than seemed possible, even though her younger half-brother, Richard, had ridden over from Chard, at her husband's suggestion, to stay for their safety until Jonah's return. He told her that Silence had been much distressed by Ben's death, and was deeply concerned for Bram. And there was talk that the Lord Chief Justice, George Jeffreys, would be sent down for the assizes to try the rebels, and he was well known to loathe all Dissenters and Presbyterians, and to be a loyal servant to the King.

If this was true, then the prisoners in the castle could expect no mercy, for Jeffreys would have no truck with those who had rebelled against his master the King. But Tabby hid her fears from Sue and Hannah, and tried to keep them busy and cheerful. At least Bram was still alive: for poor simple Ben, brutally drowned in the Bussex Rhine that had defeated Monmouth's attack, life and hope alike had ended.

# 22

## 'Promiscuous use of concubine'

Most of the inhabitants of Wintercombe had heard the news of Monmouth's catastrophic defeat with sorrow, if without much surprise. No one had realistically expected him to succeed, and their first-hand experience of the fighting in the village had not vastly increased their respect for the rebels' military prowess. But the Duke had represented Protestantism and Dissent, and opposition to the mistrusted Papist King, and besides, he was handsome and charming and popular. When the tidings followed swiftly of his capture and almost immediate execution, more than one of the maids could be found surreptitiously wiping her eyes in a corner.

In the days following the fight at Philip's Norton, Louise and Alex had regularly found opportunities to indulge in their growing passion. Greedily, they explored each other, with a hunger that seemed to be enhanced, not slaked, at every encounter, and left them both urgent for the next occasion, whether for a few minutes or an hour or two, when they could once again allow their desires free rein.

To all the possible consequences of her recklessness, Louise had closed her eyes. She loved Alex, and could not have enough of his body, of the lovemaking that was powerful and skilled and yet, surprisingly, shot through with sudden gentleness, consideration and affection, and, most endearingly of all, unexpected moments of laughter. She knew that she could not expect love in return: but it was enough, more than enough, that he was hungry for her, that whenever they were alone together his hands strayed over her body as if he could not keep away, and that with all her forbidden arts she had enthralled his senses, if not his heart or his soul. Of the future, she refused to think: of the possible risks of discovery, she was becoming increasingly careless. The change in her must have been quite obvious to anyone with the perception to see the spring in her step, the brightness of her eyes, the dreamy abstracted look when she thought back to the last time their bodies had touched, and forward to imagine the next. Christian, her maid, must surely have guessed, but with well-trained discretion said nothing to her mistress. Nor, Louise was certain, did she gossip to the other servants. And sharp-eyed Phoebe, detached and clever, might well have noticed something. But she said nothing to Louise, who took some care to ensure that the two were never alone together in a situation that encouraged confidences.

Such was her mood of blissful ecstasy that even the news of Ben's death and Bram's imprisonment, related in letters both from Tabby and from Silence, seemed to affect her only remotely. Yes, she was sad, yes, she grieved for them both. But they were people who no longer appeared to have much relevance to her life, who belonged to the flat, uninteresting, colourless time before Alex.

More alarming was her grandmother's note addressed to her, enclosed within her more general letter. Now that the rebellion was over, and the countryside returning to normality, Silence wrote, it seemed a good opportunity for Louise to return to Chard, assuming that her injured shoulder was now fully recovered. And Richard, although at present with the Loveridges in Taunton, was very willing to ride to Wintercombe and bring her back.

But she could not leave, not now. Her whole body revolted at the thought of it: of the house at Chard, so pleasant and quiet and stifling, of the small, ordinary lives led by her grandparents and her uncle and aunt. No long, breathless rides across the valleys and hills, racing Alex and Blaze; no brisk arguments with Phoebe; no more lessons with Lukas in the paddock, watching the child's face shining with triumph and excitement at his growing skill; and above all, far above all of this, no Alex.

He was like the drugs she had heard of that encouraged addiction. They had only been lovers for two weeks, yet already her senses, insatiable, depended on him completely. She could not imagine life without him – and she knew, too, with the practical part of her mind, that had never quite been consumed by the fires of passion, that in any case this situation could not last. Sooner or later, they would be discovered, or Silence would insist, despite any excuse she might offer, that she must return to Chard; or, inevitably, he would tire of her. In her experience, such men, dissolute and unprincipled and utterly lacking in scruple, invariably passed from mistress to mistress with all the faithfulness and predictability of a weathercock. The only man she had ever known different was her stepfather: and he was, in any case, not in the least like Alex.

If she returned to Chard without a murmur, her grandmother's anxieties would be assuaged, and her suspicions lulled, but Alex would undoubtedly assume that she had tired of him. No: if the span of their time as lovers was to be brief, she must wring all the happiness and passion from their liaison while she could.

So, without a blush, she wrote to Silence, a letter full of sorrow and sympathy for her cousins, combined with a detailed and quite untrue description of her injured shoulder, so slow to mend, and the hope, not too fulsomely expressed, that it would be well within a month or so. She signed it and sealed it and sent it off, and hoped that the catalogue of falsehoods it contained would keep her at Wintercombe for some weeks more.

There was only one thing that really troubled her during this heady, blissful time, and that was Charles. She was sure that he had no idea of Alex's brief and almost fatal flirtation with the rebel cause, but the weight and importance of her twin secrets stilted her tongue whenever they spoke together, and the easy, affectionate relationship they had shared had vanished completely. She tried to ignore it, but she knew that she had in a sense betrayed his trust. He was still infatuated with her, that was certain, but his eyes, as they followed her in the garden, or stared hungrily at her across the supper table, had a bewildered, angry look. And to make matters worse, Alex, well aware of Charles's unrequited feelings, often took the opportunity to taunt him, so subtly that poor Charles had no idea of the reason for it.

This casual enjoyment of his cousin's discomfiture was an unpleasant facet of Alex's character, and one which perturbed Louise. She knew that, in the privacy of the bedchamber, the true nature of most men was displayed as nakedly as their bodies. And when he made love to her, Alex had never shown her anything other than affection, generosity, and uninhibited enjoyment of her pleasure and his own.

Unwisely, she had broached the subject of Charles, one quiet evening, very late, and had seen the change come across his face like the closing of a curtain. 'Charles? What interest have you in him?'

'He was my friend,' Louise pointed out. 'Indeed, he still is. It just . . . makes me unhappy, that you dislike each other so much.'

'Why does it? Unless you have a *tendresse* for him?' Alex's face was very near hers, and the blue eyes, so close and intense, were almost overpowering. 'Sweet Louise, I have no intention of sharing you with anyone else, least of all that Papist milksop.'

Stung by the contempt in his voice, she said sharply, 'He's no milksop – you can never be fair to poor Charles, can you?'

'So? He doesn't deserve it, believe me. He did his best to steal my inheritance and worm his way into my father's affections before I returned from Holland, and if another opportunity presented itself, he'd leap at the chance.'

'Of course he wouldn't!'

'Oh, so you know him better than I do? Charles has been a thorn in my side for most of my life, and I refuse to treat him like a long-lost brother. He can't even handle the move to the Abbey Green house with any competence – it'll be months before it's ready for his precious mama, and by that time she'll have beggared him with her outrageous extravagance. From what I've heard, the end result of all her decorating ideas will look like something from a French whore's boudoir. But of course,' he added, with a sudden, wickedly teasing smile that completely obliterated all the previous malice, 'you'd know all about that, sweet Louise.'

'How dare you!' she cried, glad of the excuse to abandon the argument, and attacked him with some spirit. It was easy to mend such quarrels, for their anger turned so readily to desire and then everything was forgotten as their passions rose. But although she did not again tax him about his attitude to Charles, she made a point, every time tempers flared between the two men in her presence, of soothing and mediating as best she could. Such scenes still almost invariably ended with Charles, high-coloured and infuriated, flinging himself from the room, leaving Alex, cool and sardonic, completely in command of the situation, and Amy, if present, snivelling into a kerchief.

'It's no good,' Phoebe said to her, after the latest such episode, which in fact she herself had begun. 'Chalk and cheese, those two are, and will never agree. Unless actual violence is threatened, I'd be inclined to leave well alone.'

'I don't feel I can,' Louise said unhappily. Amy had already gone to bed, and she and her cousin were alone in the winter parlour. It was hot and humid outside, thunder threatening grumblingly in the distance, and the air, even with all the windows open, and the door leading on to the terrace, was heavy and uncomfortably sticky. Charles was sulking somewhere, and Alex, who had been more than usually offensive, was working his way through a bottle of brandy over the remains of the supper. 'I like Charles, and I don't want to see him unhappy.'

'Charles is one of those people who will never be happy,' Phoebe pointed out. 'He's always yearning after the unattainable, never satisfied with what he already has . . . like the old woman who lived in a bottle, do you know that story? It's one of Lukas's favourites.'

'Is that the one where her husband is a fisherman, and catches a magic fish who will give him anything he asks for?'

'Yes, that's the one – and his wife nags him to ask for more, and more, and more, and each time she swears it will bring her perfect happiness, and each time she's greedy for more and more and more – until the fish loses patience and sends her back to the bottle.' Phoebe grimaced. 'What

Charles wants is you, and Wintercombe. And even if he had you both, he still wouldn't be satisfied.'

Louise went to the door leading to the garden, and stared out. There was a dark, threatening cloud hanging low overhead, and as she watched, a fat raindrop splashed on the first of the stone steps leading down to the gravelled terrace. Far off, ominously, the thunder grumbled. She said quietly, 'All I have ever offered Charles is friendship. He *knows* that – he *knows* that anything more will be impossible.'

'Ah, but does he? You are not wealthy, are you? Aunt Silence is not looking for a splendid match for you.'

'But she is looking for a Protestant,' Louise pointed out. The rain was falling more heavily, and it was fast growing dark. She closed the door on the gathering storm, and turned to the mantelpiece, where there was a box of flint and tinder, and a bundle of wax tapers. Aware that Phoebe, sitting in a chair by the south window, was studying her closely, she fired the tinder at her second attempt, blew carefully on the spark, and lit a taper. There was no breath of air from the wide open windows, but she shielded the small, clear flame with her cupped left hand, and walked about the room, lighting the candles on the mantelshelf, in the wall sconces, and on the table in the corner. The soft amber light gave a deceptive gentleness and beauty to the clean, rather severe lines of her face. Her task done, she blew out the taper, and turned to Phoebe. No amount of flattering candlelight could make her cousin's pinched, drawn features anything other than plain. But her eyes, the pupils very wide and dark, were as remarkable as her brother's. She said, her voice very matter-of-fact, 'How long have you and Alex been lovers?'

Louise dropped the taper. She cursed under her breath, and bent to pick it up. It had rolled under a chair, and there were splashes of hot wax on the polished wooden floor, as well as on her hand. She straightened, the taper securely in her grasp, and turned an innocent face on her cousin. 'Whatever do you mean?'

'Exactly what I said.' Phoebe's gaze was penetrating, and undeceived. 'Not very long, I would guess – say, two weeks? I know you, and I know my brother even better. The only surprise is that it's taken you so long to succumb to temptation.'

There was, obviously, absolutely no point in denying it further. Louise put the taper back with the rest, and sat down rather abruptly in her chair. She said, 'Does anyone else know?'

'Well, I haven't mentioned it to a soul, if that's what you mean. But anyone with a modicum of perception, and eyes in their head, must surely have guessed.' She surveyed Louise with interest. 'I do hope you know what you're doing.'

'I'm not without some experience in such things,' Louise told her.

Phoebe smiled, mirthlessly. 'And I, I freely admit, am not . . . nor ever likely to be, thank God. But I do know Alex. And I ought to warn you that since he was fifteen, with the single exception of Lukas's mother, he has never kept a woman for longer than a few months.'

'As far as you know,' Louise said. She did not wish to quarrel with Phoebe, for despite their considerable dissimilarities, they had become very good friends over the past year. 'But, yes, I know, it's an affair that's doomed from the start. But . . . can you understand that, even so, I have no intention of stopping?'

'Even though there may be a great deal of grief in store for you?' Phoebe asked.

'Even though . . . I have always tended to act rather recklessly, without thought for the consequences,' Louise told her, ruefully. 'Phoebe, I know all the arguments, *le bon Dieu* knows that I have employed them all to myself over the past few months, and in the end nothing mattered except him, and what he brings to life in me . . . and if it ends in tears, my tears, well, *c'est la vie*, but in the meantime I will have been so happy.'

'And so will he,' said Alex's sister. She looked up at Louise, and smiled suddenly. 'Happiness is not an emotion which I'd easily associate with him – it's too simple, somehow, and he is so much more complicated than that. My brother has all his faults and vices in abundance, but when all's said and done, he is my brother, and I suppose I must love him . . . and I have never seen him so besotted with any woman.'

Louise swallowed. She almost never cried, but now, suddenly and alarmingly, there were tears blocking her throat. She coughed, and said in wonderment, 'Really? Are you *sure?*'

'I told you, I know him,' said Phoebe. She added drily, 'Of course, that woman in Amsterdam must have had some hold on his affections, once – but I do not think he found her to be worth it.'

A sudden, vivid memory assailed Louise, of Wintercombe at night, months ago, and Alex's soft, drunken voice singing into the dark of a faithless woman when he had thought that no one could hear him. She said, shaken, 'I promise you, whatever happens, whatever hurt is done to either of us, I shall not betray him.'

Phobe looked at her long and hard. She said at last, 'Do you love him?'

And Louise, knowing that no other answer was possible, or indeed truthful, said, 'Yes.'

'Don't worry,' her cousin told her, as the thunder muttered, a little closer, and the raindrops fell more thickly on to the gravel and knots outside. 'I won't tell him – or anyone else. But, Louise, have you thought what might happen if Aunt Silence finds some husband for you? And that's why you were sent to England, after all – not to embark on a wild and passionate affair with a debauched rakehell nearly ten years your senior.' Her face was suddenly rather grim. 'You're not harbouring the secret hope that he will marry you, are you?'

'It hadn't occurred to me,' said Louise, with perfect truth. The man who would one day be her husband had never loomed very large in her mind, but she had always pictured him kind, pleasant, unassuming, tolerant, ordinary – everything, in fact, that the flamboyant and ruthless Alex was not.

'Just as well,' said Phoebe drily. 'Because I'd be prepared to wager a considerable sum that it hasn't entered his head either. When Alex looks for a wife, it will be some sweet, long-suffering and biddable girl with a large dowry and, probably, a father who has political influence and is of the Whig persuasion. I'm glad you have few illusions, Louise. If it had been Amy in your position, God forbid, I would have been very concerned for her. But you . . .'

'I can look after myself,' said Louise, and laughed as if she did not have a care in the world.

Phoebe went to bed soon afterwards, and the two girls said goodnight with considerable affection and understanding. For a while after she had gone, Louise remained in the winter parlour, staring out at the garden. The thunderstorm was drawing close now, and lightning flickered through the dusk, with eerie and sinister effect.

Above her, around her, Wintercombe was quiet. With a lingering, reminiscent smile, she blew out the candles, one by one. Her maid, Christian, would be waiting for her, but she could wait a little longer. She left the parlour in darkness behind her, finding her way by memory and touch and the sudden darts of lightning, through the study and so to the passage beyond and the door to the dining parlour.

It was closed, but a light still showed underneath. The wisest course, perhaps, would have been to turn her back, climb the stairs, and surprise her long-suffering maid. But wisdom had never been Louise's strongest suit, especially where her feelings for Alex were concerned. She lifted the latch, and opened the door.

Alex was sitting where they had left him an hour or more earlier. The bottle in front of him was nearly empty, and his hand lay idly around the stem of a wine glass half full, presumably, of brandy. His smile, as she shut the door behind her, was unguardedly brilliant. Besotted, Phoebe had said, and looking at him, and the sudden, raw desire that had inflamed his face as she entered, she knew that it was true.

'Come in,' Alex said, waving the other hand. 'Sit down and have a drink with me.'

She walked past the empty chairs to a place beside him. The table had been cleared, so presumably they were safe from interruption by servants eager to finish their duties and go to bed. Alex reached out to pull her on to his knee. His kiss was brandy-flavoured, long and passionate, and she felt, amidst her own rising desire, his hand slide beneath her tippet and stomacher to fondle her breast.

'Brandy?' he said a little later, into her ear. She nodded, and found the glass abruptly pushed towards her hand. It was not a taste she particularly liked, but she had inured herself to the fiery way it blasted her throat, and the warming, uninhibiting effect it had on her was most enjoyable. With soft laughter, they shared the glass until it was empty.

'Damn bottle's finished,' Alex said, slurring his words. 'Suppose we'll just have to find something else to do, won't we?' His hand, wandering more boldly, had almost unlaced her bodice, exposing her breasts beneath the lace tippet. 'You'll have to lead me – I doubt I can walk very straight.' He bent his head to nuzzle her neck, and she felt her own excitement surge to new heights. Suddenly impatient, she slid from his lap and stood, teasingly, a few paces away, her hand outstretched. 'Come on, then – let's go to bed.'

Together, their arms about each other, and their bodies pressed close, they made their uneven way out of the dining parlour. There was still a bottle half full of wine, which Alex plucked from the table as they passed. 'In case we're thirsty,' he explained, as Louise opened the door. There had been candles lit still in the Hall when she had left the winter parlour, but now all but two or three had gone out. The house was quite silent, but some belated sense of caution made them move with exaggerated care. Louise fought down the wild impulse to laugh: anyone watching them would surely find their erratic progress exceedingly amusing.

One of the chairs that normally stood against the end wall had been left pulled forward, and Alex walked into it. With a muffled curse, he pushed it out of the way, stumbled and grabbed at Louise for support. They bumped backwards into the wall. Giggling, she saw him loom close above her, his eyes gleaming. 'Want some?' he said, offering her the bottle of wine.

There was no one to see, and she was enjoying this sense of decadence. She took several generous gulps, and handed it back. The lightning was still luridly flashing at intervals outside, and a sudden loud crash of thunder startled them both. Alex almost dropped the bottle, by now

382

virtually empty, and then placed it, with drunken care, on the floor. 'Come here,' he said, and pulled her with sudden urgency into his embrace.

Louise, her mind swimming with desire, had no other thought in her head but his kiss, and his hands further disarraying her bodice, and the exquisite, burning pleasure from the touch of his fingers on her breast. She did not see the sudden movement on the gallery at the other end of the Hall: and Alex, his back to it, and all his senses concentrated on Louise, was in any case in no condition to notice.

Charles, the bile thick in his throat, stared down into the gloom, and the thunder, crashing again overhead, seemed to mock all his cherished, shattered dreams. After coming upon them together in the stable, weeks ago, he should not have been surprised, or shocked. But the man and woman below, utterly absorbed in each other, had obviously, even to his eyes, been lovers for some while, their hands moving with boldness and experience. Nor had his eyes missed, even in the dim light, the bottle they had shared, nor the extensive and indecent disarray of her gown. There was only one conclusion possible. His detested cousin, not content with taking Wintercombe and behaving with odious and drunken offensiveness, had seduced Louise, enticed her into his bed, and corrupted her innocence. That lewd, half-naked woman giggling and murmuring in the shadows was no longer the sweet, lively girl whom he had loved with hope and adoration. Alex had debauched her, and she was now no better than any drunken whore off the streets of Bristol . . .

Unable to bear the sight any longer, he turned abruptly away from the gallery, and stumbled to his chamber, his hands pressed against his mouth, and the contents of his stomach rebelling. Only after he had voided everything into a pot, and taken several gulps of stale water, could he begin to face what he had seen.

He lay, still fully clothed, face down on the bed, while the thunder diminished eastwards into the night, and the rain fell, soft and steady, outside. Louise and Alex, lovers, blatantly fornicating while the other inhabitants of the house remained in, as yet, blissful ignorance . . . It could not be tolerated. Over and over again, the vivid picture of those two shadowy, entwined figures rose behind his eyelids to taunt him.

And the worst of it was that the sight had not merely disgusted and horrified him. It had also aroused his own desires, so that a part of him, the part of which he was most ashamed, longed to do to Louise, the wanton who had deceived and mocked him, the same as Alex was doubtless doing to her at this moment: longed to take her, to possess her, to force her again and again until she cried for mercy and forgiveness . . .

Shivering with self-loathing, he pushed these dark fantasies to the recesses of his mind. He must go to Bath as soon as possible, confess his sinful and lustful thoughts, do penance, receive absolution . . . and then he would see her again every day, the quicksilver, laughing, exotic, friendly girl who had entranced him, and who was rotten, rotten at the heart, and he would never be able to look at her again without thinking of what she had done, of the lust she shared with the evil Alex . . .

I will avenge her, Charles promised, to the oblivious dark. Whatever the cost, however long it takes, I will destroy Alex. I will make sure that he does not long enjoy the fruits of his wickedness . . . Louise, Wintercombe, wealth, power, he has obtained all these by evil means, and he has no right to any of them. All I need is the opportunity, and then I will bring him crashing down, in all his vicious arrogance, before he can ruin some other poor innocent . . . even Amy, only, thank God, he did not succeed in seducing her . . .

He slept eventually, his mind filled with savage and disturbing dreams in which opportunities aplenty presented themselves, and in which, always, Alex was driven to destruction. And he woke unrefreshed, but with his heart irrevocably set upon revenge. All he needed was the opportunity . . .

At Longleaze, Rachael Wickham had received the tidings of her beloved youngest son's death with rage and inconsolable grief. She ranted against Bram, who had enticed him to war and then failed to take sufficient care of him, against the King's soldiers, who had so cruelly slaughtered her defenceless, innocent, simple son, and against Monmouth, who had brought rebellion and death to Somerset; and her sorrowful family could do nothing to comfort her.

Jan missed poor Ben, of course: the boy's skills had been invaluable, and already there were a couple of sick mares who would have benefited from his care and special knowledge. And he felt great pity for his mother, whose naked, agonised grief was at once heart-rending and deeply disturbing. But in his heart, he could not help but feel that, in a way, Ben's death was a blessing in disguise. What future would he have had? Who would have cared for him when both Jan and his mother were dead? The world was too harsh a place for simpletons, and Ben's death proved it.

His mother's anguish made the house thoroughly uncomfortable, and he was guiltily grateful for the upsurge in business which called him far and wide, buying and selling. Like a whirlpool, Monmouth's progression through Somerset had sucked large numbers of horses into the ranks of his army, and farmers and gentlemen whose mounts had been bought, stolen or commandeered were urgently in need of replacements. He himself had been questioned on suspicion of supplying horses to the rebels, but his stable lads had spoken up for him, confirming his tale that the animals had been legitimately sold to strangers, and the Glastonbury constables, who liked and respected Master Wickham, did not pursue the matter further. Hearing some of the tales and rumours from friends and acquaintances, Jan felt profoundly relieved. Some magistrates, notably Sir Edward Phelips of Montacute, had offered a bounty of five shillings a head to mancatchers who apprehended rebels, or even those suspected of being sympathetic to Monmouth's cause. It was fortunate for Jan that he was well liked and had no enemies. There were plenty of malicious people who were only too eager to denounce their neighbours out of spite, or to settle old scores.

He had lost on the deal when Bram had taken those surplus animals, but the weeks after Sedgemoor saw his shortfall amply compensated: he could have sold each horse several times over, and was able to command substantial prices for poor-quality nags that normally would have been difficult to dispose of, even at a pittance. He would have died rather than admit as much to his mother, but the rebellion had proved to be a classic example of a wind that was not so ill, despite Ben's tragic end.

He returned from a journey to Street, where he had bought three promising young saddle horses on behalf of a local gentleman, to find four strange animals being led away towards the stables. One, a very handsome bright bay stallion, caught his appreciative eye, and he wondered curiously who the visitors might be.

He hurried inside, without first removing his boots, and heard low voices from the parlour. There was a trail of mud in the hall behind him, and doubtless he would feel the sharp edge of his mother's tongue later – these days, the least transgression inflamed her temper – not to mention his wife Bathsheba's silent reproach. But it was too late now. He opened the door of the parlour expectantly.

'Hullo, Jan,' said his Cousin Alex cheerfully. 'I hear that you too have been robbed by Monmouth. We have come over to beg, borrow or steal horses from you – that is, if you still have any.'

Jan gave him a weary, rather doubtful smile. Alex, even in the plain dark suit with the silver buttons, was altogether too vivid and dangerous a person to earn his absolute trust, despite the fact that Jan had never seen him anything other than sober, pleasant and capable. The man had a dreadful reputation, both within the family and outside it, and Jan, hardworking, reliable and essentially ordinary, would always be wary of him. Charles, on the other hand, was much more to his liking. He did not have that sharp, ruthless edge that Alex possessed, and although horses were to him no more than a convenient method of transport, Jan usually felt far more at ease with him.

Not this evening, however. Something was seriously wrong, and whatever it was, it hung around Charles like a poisonous cloud. Jan, perplexed, hoped that there would be no unpleasantness. His mother had created more than enough disturbance in the house for the moment, and if his cousins were to come to blows during their visit, his poor wife would be terribly distressed. Bathsheba hated even the mildest argument, and Rachael's recent outbursts had frequently reduced her to tears.

But Charles said very little, although the way he looked at Alex made Jan, not usually given to flights of fancy, wonder why his cousin was not instantly burned to a cinder. Alex, though, paid Charles no attention whatsoever, and Jan did not know why he had brought him.

Supper was a rather constrained meal, with Rachael stiff and severe at one end of the table, and Jan, trying hard to pretend ease and normality, at the other. All the sympathy and sorrow concerning Ben had already been expressed, but his unspoken, invisible presence was a further deterrent to comfort. With some relief, Jan led his two cousins out to the stables once the meal was finished, to view the few horses which he had for sale.

'How many did you lose?' Alex asked, as the first, a long-legged brown gelding of suspect soundness, was led out by one of the stable lads.

Jan eyed the horse dubiously. It was one of his maxims never to sell to a friend or a relative any animal that was less than satisfactory, even if accompanied by a detailed catalogue of its faults. He said, 'I'd avoid that one, if I were you. I doubt it'd stand more than the lightest weight on its back. How many did I lose? Seven, Cousin Bram had from me, although he did at least pay me something for them. Do I understand that you lost some to him as well?'

'I did – although no money changed hands,' said Alex. He watched as the gelding was trotted round the yard. 'You're right – that beast favours its off-fore. Sell it to someone you dislike.'

'You know I wouldn't do that,' Jan said. 'This may sound strange, from a horse-dealer, but I do try to be honest in my business transactions.'

'Really? Then you must be unique in England, if not the world,' Alex said, grinning. 'Rest assured, Jan, I shall not deprive you of such a superlative animal. What else have you got?'

'You may mock,' said his cousin rather stiffly, as the brown was led away, 'but my honesty has served me well, this past week or so. Your position probably protects you from suspicion, but hereabouts, anyone who so much as fluttered their eyelashes at Monmouth is liable to be accused of treason. All the old grudges and feuds have been brought into the open, and spite rules: anyone who has slighted or cheated or wronged their neighbour runs the risk of denunciation, even on the most flimsy excuse – or, sometimes, so I've heard, on the basis of barefaced lies.'

A much more likely animal had been led out, a fiery young chestnut filly, barely backed or broken as yet, still very lightly built, but with the promise of speed in the long legs and a spirited intelligence in the fine-boned, noble head.

'Now that's a much better prospect,' said Alex. He turned to Charles, standing several feet away from him, as if to be any closer was to be tainted. 'What do you think of her?'

His cousin's voice was stiff, and devoid of any warmth. 'She seems fine enough.'

'She'll need a great deal of schooling, of course,' Jan pointed out. 'But she'll make a fine saddle horse in a year or so, though I doubt she'll ever be up to your weight. A ride for a competent lady, perhaps? Would Cousin Louise like her?'

'She still has that yellow dun mare – at least Bram did not take her, with all the rest,' Alex said. He smiled, and Charles could guess what he was thinking, even if Jan had no idea. 'But I'm sure I can find some use for this one, and if nothing else, she'll make an excellent brood mare. What do you want for her, Jan?'

The two men haggled over a price with good-natured chaffing, and Charles marvelled silently that Jan, who admittedly, despite his St Barbe blood, was hardly more than a simple farmer, seemed to have no perception at all of Alex's true nature. Could he not discern that the affable manner, the smile and the friendly face concealed a heart as black and evil and immoral as any Judas?

The next horse, an older, stouter gelding of distinctly somnolent demeanour, seemed to exercise Alex's interest. He walked forward to examine the animal's teeth, and then lifted each hoof in turn for inspection. Charles found himself hoping that one of the large, hairy feet would strike out, perhaps with fatal consequences, but was disappointed.

'A sound, solid sort of beast,' Jan was saying. 'It won't win any races, but it'll keep up a steady pace all day without tiring – a good ride for servants or messengers.'

'Exactly the kind I'm looking for,' Alex said, running a hand down the gelding's thick neck. 'Young Bram took all of that sort I had, and I doubt they were much use to him. From all accounts, Monmouth's cavalry was the main reason for his failure – although to blame them is a little unfair, you must know well enough how difficult it is to train horses for war, in such circumstances, and with so little time at your disposal. When I

387

saw them in action at Norton Fight, they couldn't even bring their mounts to face pistol shot, let alone cannonfire.'

Charles, standing still and forgotten in the shadows, stiffened. He had assumed that Alex had spent the day of the battle, as he had stated, drinking in the George, and so likely was this tale that he had never thought to question it. But if he had indeed been at the inn, how could he have seen the defects of Monmouth's cavalry for himself?

A wild idea came to him then, words jostling in his head, treason, the hidden pamphlets, the commandeered horses, and above all the fact that his cousin had undoubtedly been much closer to the action, that day in the village several weeks ago, than he had claimed – a fact acutely suspicious in itself.

Alex's voice had dropped very low, but, straining his ears, he could still make out most of his words. 'So, they had half a dozen of my less valuable horses – my groom, Pardice, made sure they didn't take any quality animals, that would be carrying devotion to the cause altogether too far. Nor did he make any offer of payment.'

Jan, his voice rather more distinct, sucked in his breath sharply. 'I trust you did not appear to give them willingly?'

Alex laughed. 'Hardly. I had some exceedingly villainous-looking rogue pointing a loaded pistol straight at me, and there's no arguing with such a forceful means of persuasion. Moreover, nine-tenths of my household were eager witnesses. No, they may be keen to pin a charge of treason on me, for all my past sins, but since returning from Holland my life has been – almost – blameless. And that particular charge has not a hope of success.'

'I sincerely hope not,' said Jan. 'In these times, even the innocent or the unlucky are in danger, as much as the guilty. I should be careful, Cousin – you never know who might bear a grudge.'

Alex laughed, a carefree, reckless sound. 'No, indeed – but since in this matter I am as guilt-free as a new-born babe, why should I waste my life worrying?'

It was as well that he did not see Charles's face in the dusk, for the triumph written on it would have told him, with wordless eloquence, that one person's grudge, at least, could not be dismissed so lightly.

That night, Charles lay exultant in his narrow bed under the eaves of Longleaze, his mind a ferment of activity. Only yesterday, at this time, he had been cast into the depths of despair and loathing, and his impotent longing for revenge, the more complete and destructive the better, had almost bereft him of any sleep. And now God, through the unwitting agency of Cousin Jan, had put the instrument of vengeance into his hands.

He had no doubt that a magistrate, eager to root out rebellion and sedition, would listen to him, and to the tale he would tell. Taken by themselves, the separate facts seemed trivial, easily explained away. The proscribed, hidden pamphlets; Bram's seizure of the horses (had any others in the village been taken? He would have to find out); Alex's past, his association years ago with that rogue Shaftesbury, and the republicans, and the Green Ribbon Club, dedicated to the overthrow of popery and the exclusion of the Duke of York from the throne; and, most mysteriously and possibly most damning of all, the extent of his involvement in the fighting at Philip's Norton. Alex's words seemed to imply that he had seen some of the battle at close quarters: and if his actions that day had been innocent, why lie about it, and put around the tale that he had spent the day getting drunk at the George?

Faced with that list, Charles had no doubt that any loyal Justice would conclude that Sir Alexander St Barbe was ripe for further investigation, at the very least. An enticing prospect opened up in his mind: Alex accused of treason, his guilt proved beyond all doubt (a few well-chosen interviews with villagers and captured rebels should confirm the facts), and the inevitable but well-deserved consequence of his sins. And then . . . what else could King James do but reward his fellow-Catholic, who had so loyally brought the activities of this vicious traitor to the attention of the authorities, with the title and estate that were rightfully his?

For a moment longer, he was intoxicated with the thought that in a few months' time he might be Sir Charles St Barbe, fifth baronet, owner of Wintercombe, heritor of wealth, power, position and influence . . . all he had ever wanted from life. There would be no need to leave his beloved Wintercombe, to live in that poky little house in Bath. Amy, his lovely sister, would have the jewels and gowns her beauty deserved, and a splendid marriage, and his mother would be provided with lavish comfort for the rest of her life.

And Louise . . . surely, when the dreadful truth about Alex was revealed, she would realise how terribly she had been deceived and corrupted. Surely she would repent of her wanton, reckless behaviour. She would come to look upon Charles once more as her friend, and perhaps, in time, for he still loved her, still desired her, despite the loss of her innocence, he would take her for his wife, and found his own dynasty at Wintercombe . . .

But his conscience, the voice of God or of reason, pointed out, quietly, the true reason why he wished to denounce Alex. His motive was not pure and altruistic. He was a Papist, and loyal to his religion and to the King, but that was almost irrelevant. He wanted vengeance, nothing more nor less; and, after his cousin's destruction, to enjoy everything that Alex had possessed, and which his own sense of justice, not to mention his mother's revelations concerning his cousin's birth, had encouraged him to consider his by right.

The edict of the last Commandment rose in his mind: 'Thou shalt not covet thy neighbour's house, thou shalt not covet thy neighbour's wife . . . nor anything that is thy neighbour's.' Undeniably, he coveted Alex's house, his wealth, his position, his lover, and everything that was his: and his secret envy had grown and festered, over the past few months, fuelled by his cousin's contemptuous attitude and despicable behaviour, until it had become the poisonous mainspring of his life.

But was such jealousy, however justified, a valid reason for the betrayal of his own cousin, who had treated him abominably, but who had also, he had to acknowledge, shown some generosity in the matter of the Abbey Green house? To many, it would seem at best ungrateful, at worst, a terrible betrayal of a man who was, after all, his own kin.

But of course, he was not. If Bab had told him the truth, then Alex could not be the legitimate son and heir of Sir Nathaniel, but the nameless bastard of his mother's lover. And if Alex was not a true St Barbe, then he was not, either, the rightful owner of Wintercombe.

He lay in the darkness, his mind at war, his conscience protesting that what he was considering was wrong, prompted by malice and envy, his heart urging action, the irrevocable deed that would end Alex's ruthless domination of his life, once and for all and for ever.

And when sleep finally claimed him, late into the night, he still had not resolved what he would do, one way or the other.

# 23

## *'Teach rebels to obey'*

At the end of August, 1685, six weeks after the battle at Sedgemoor, and almost as long after the gruesomely botched execution of James Scott, once called Duke of Monmouth, who had aspired to the throne of England, retribution, in the person of the Lord Chief Justice, George Jeffreys, descended upon the rebellious counties of the West Country.

It was a burden that Jeffreys had, initially, been minded to refuse. He had spent the summer taking the waters at Tunbridge Wells, in a vain attempt to cure his agonising kidney stones, and had asked for the less arduous home circuit, around London. But despite the extra work involved on the western circuit – for the Summer Assizes had been cancelled because of the rebellion – the Lord Chief Justice agreed to go. He was already high in the King's favour, and to prosecute these rebels with his customary zeal and despatch would undoubtedly raise him still higher, perhaps even as far as the position of Lord Chancellor, which he had long coveted.

The Grand Juries and constables of Somerset, Dorset and Wiltshire had been busy, and over two thousand people had either been named as rebels, or were languishing in prison, awaiting their fate. To deal adequately with this vast number of accused, five judges had been appointed to assist Jeffreys in his task. And a swarm of agents, pardonmongers and parasites descended upon the gaols, to interrogate the unfortunates held within. Obviously, with so many to be tried, some way of speeding up the proceedings must be found. If large numbers pleaded not guilty, the trials could take months, even years. So in each prison, agents and clerks took the necessary details, and used all their powers to persuade the recalcitrant to plead guilty, and so save the courts' time.

Since many of the prisoners, especially those held immediately after the battle, had actually been taken in arms, most had already elected to acknowledge their guilt, and throw themselves on the mercy of the judges. But the reputation of the Lord Chief Justice was not, as yet, widely known in the West Country: and besides, despite the swift execution of their leader, many of the rank and file rebels were confident that the authorities would deal with them comparatively leniently.

Late in August, Jeffreys, with his assistants, left London to travel the western circuit. He stopped first at Winchester, where amongst the routine cases of murder, felony and rape, was scheduled his first treason trial, that of Dame Alice Lisle.

Dame Alice was an elderly lady of good family, a republican past (her late husband had sat in judgement on Charles I), and waning faculties. She had harboured two of Monmouth's chief adherents after the battle, and claimed that they were old friends and she had not known of their part in the rebellion. Her defence was of no avail: her status and history had already marked her out for retribution, for the King was determined that the very few gentry who had dared to support Monmouth should be singled out for exemplary punishment. Dame Alice was sentenced to be burnt at the stake, and only the horrified pleas of her friends and the local clergy persuaded the King to commute the sentence. The old lady, so deaf and failing that she seemed at times not to understand what was happening to her, was beheaded at Winchester, on the second of September.

Suddenly, as the news spread, mercy seemed to be a commodity in very short supply. The judges continued to Salisbury, and then to Dorchester. Here, thirty rebels unwise enough to plead not guilty were convicted despite their denials, and sentenced to hang two days later. As the executions outside progressed, slowly and gruesomely, and the air of Dorchester filled with the stench of burning bowels and boiled meat and the cries of the men who waited their turn, those prisoners still to be tried, who had intended to plead their innocence, rapidly changed their minds. More than a hundred and seventy were brought before the court in the space of two days, tried in batches of a dozen or more, and almost invariably sentenced to death. Only the rebels who had especially distinguished themselves, however, were singled out for execution. The King had already told Jeffreys that those who had come with Monmouth from Holland, those who had known of the invasion beforehand, and those who had accepted commissions in his army, were to be shown no mercy.

Dorchester was already festooned with the heads and quartered bodies of the first men to be executed. Accordingly, the further seventy selected for death were despatched to the principal towns around the county, to Lyme and Sherborne, Weymouth, Poole and others, to meet their ends and to exhibit to the cowed populace the full force and dreadful might of the King's justice. Then their mutilated remains were distributed among the surrounding villages, a ghastly warning against rebellion.

*

'Your name?'

The question was said briskly, but received no answer. The assize clerk, quill poised over the paper, looked up irritably. 'Are you deaf? Or have you forgotten it? Your name!'

'Abraham Loveridge,' said the prisoner, after a pause. Like all the other rebels who had been brought for interrogation, he was filthy, gaunt and louse-ridden, his face grey and grimy after the weeks of sunless confinement, and his clothes hung on him in ragged folds. The clerk wrote briefly, and snapped his next question. 'Age?'

'Twenty-one.'

'Place of residence?'

'Taunton.'

'Your trade?'

'Bookseller.'

After the procession of weavers, combers, husbandmen, yeomen and serge-makers, this was something different. The clerk, interested, studied the young man in front of him. A handsome boy, or had been once, before privation, dirt and illness robbed him of his looks. The shirt and breeches, though now only fit for burning, were of good cloth, and the hands bound before him had never known manual labour. 'A bookseller, eh?' he said, tapping the end of the quill against his nose. 'What sort of books?'

'All sorts. Divine works, histories, poems, songs, essays, romances . . .' Bram stopped himself before his tongue could run too free, and added, 'I help my father. He has a shop in Fore Street.'

'And do you also sell seditious pamphlets?'

He had been expecting that question, and a look of pained surprise crossed his face. 'No, of course not.'

'Taunton and these parts are full of them – they must come from somewhere,' said the clerk suspiciously. 'So – your father sent you off to join the rebels, did he?'

'No,' said Bram, with some vehemence. 'No – he didn't want me to go. In fact, he locked me in my chamber so that I couldn't, but my sister found the key and let me out.'

'A misguided action, which she probably now bitterly regrets,' the clerk commented. 'So – you joined the rebels, where? In Taunton?'

'Yes.'

'The foot, or the horse?'

'The foot at first. Later, they gave me a horse because I could ride.'

The quill scratched its way to the end of the line. The clerk looked up, and his face became more grave. 'You have been told, I take it, of His Majesty's graciousness and mercy, even to such as you?'

393

'I have.'

'And you understand that if you are honest in this enquiry, and confess truthfully all that you know, without falsehood or omission, then you may be confident of the King's forgiveness and favour?'

'I do.' Bram stared at him, his mind already wandering again. Since an attack of fever, almost three weeks ago, he had found it difficult to concentrate on reality. It was so much easier to turn away from the stinking, overcrowded prison, the groans and cries of his suffering fellows, and the hideous future that awaited them all, and to return to the love and laughter of his family, and the sweet, calm, golden days before Monmouth landed at Lyme.

And in those daydreams, Ben was still alive, and his terrible death, that Bram had failed to prevent, had never happened.

He had no great faith in the King's mercy or justice. It was already common knowledge, amongst the prisoners, that those who had been officers in the rebel army could not expect reprieve. Since everyone had been encouraged, at these interviews, to confess everything concerning their own part in the rebellion, and the involvement of their fellow-prisoners, it must already be known that he had been a cornet in Captain Hucker's troop. And since he was therefore marked for death, he would not abandon what remained of his self-respect, and betray his comrades.

'And in what capacity did you serve in the rebel army?'

'In the horse, after Glastonbury,' Bram said. His fatal commission might already be known to this repellent man, but he had no intention of incriminating himself unnecessarily.

'Our information is that you carried a colour. Is this true?'

There was little point in denying it. 'Yes.'

'So, you accepted a commission from James Scott, late Duke of Monmouth?'

'Not formally. There was nothing written down. Somebody gave me a colour, and I carried it.'

'Who? Who was your captain?'

Bram looked at him guilelessly. 'I can't remember.'

'Your lapse could have very serious consequences for you,' said the clerk, his tone suddenly sharp and much more hostile. 'Make no mistake, you have admitted to being an officer in the rebel army, and His Majesty will have no hesitation in recommending that you suffer the ultimate penalty. But he has also stated that even those who might otherwise expect to die may still be saved if they make a full and repentant confession of all that they know.'

Bram stared down at the desk in distress. He thought of his parents, their visits, the money he would not accept, their grief and fear that filled him with such guilt, the anguish they would suffer if he were executed, their bewilderment if they realised that he could have saved himself, even by betraying his friends. And then, hard on the heels of these thoughts, the vivid image, all too explicit, of the death he would die: the hanging, the butchery, the agony, the stench, watching his comrades suffer while waiting his turn . . .

He thought he knew himself, but who could predict how they might behave in such a ghastly situation? Could he face such a dreadful end? More, could he subject his parents, and his sisters, and perhaps others of his kin, to the ghastly privilege of watching him die in such a manner, his body dismembered and his head and limbs hung on poles or gallows in Taunton, or distributed in the villages around?

But was his life worth such tainted coin? Sick at heart, the choice impossible, he closed his eyes. Nausea rose in his throat, and he felt his balance going. From a very great distance, he heard someone saying something, and then there was nothing.

'All right, lad?'

It was one of the other rebels, a kindly, middle-aged man called Jacob Powell. Bram opened his eyes and saw the man's concerned face bending over him, and behind him, the cobwebbed ceiling of the cell where they, along with several score others, had been imprisoned for the past four weeks.

'I – I think so,' he said. He felt light-headed and a little strange, but this was not unusual: that bout of fever had left him seriously weakened, and such moments of faintness were quite frequent.

'I'll tell you something, lad,' Powell said quietly, putting his face closer. 'You may think you're doing us all a favour by keeping your mouth shut – oh, yes, I know, so do we all, you can't keep anything secret in here – but it makes no odds in the end, you know. If we all kept silent, perhaps it might make a difference, but since all the rest of us have told all we know, in exchange for a reprieve, what does it profit anyone if it's just you who is obstinate?' He gave a bleak smile. 'I followed King Monmouth too, but I've learned my lesson – I wouldn't do it again, not if he went down on his knees to me. Would you?'

Bram looked into his soul, and knew the truth. 'No', he said at last. 'No, I don't think I would.'

'Then don't throw your life away, lad. I've seen your mother, and a lovely lady she is too – I've seen her care for you. Do you want to put her through the agony of watching you die *that* death?'

Bram closed his eyes. The spectre of the gallows, the knife, the fires and the cauldrons and pitch, rose up again to haunt him. He said, very softly, 'No.'

'Then for God's sake tell 'em,' said Powell, with brisk common sense. 'Don't make a martyr of yourself. It's not worth it.'

He was summoned again that afternoon, to the same small room, to face the same clerk. Whatever he did, his conscience would torment him, but in the end, Powell's arguments had won. What was the point in holding out and keeping faith, when almost every other man in the gaol had made his confession without compunction? And, if the choice must be made, he would rather betray the men who had been his comrades for a scant three weeks, than the parents and sisters who had given him a lifetime of love and happiness.

Anyway, Captain Hucker was already in another cell in the castle, and so were many of the other men with whom he had served. His obstinate silence would not protect them, for other tongues had already been busy. He himself had evidently been the subject of talk. Why hold out any longer, for conscience's sake?

So when he was asked about the other men in his troop, he gave names – those of men he knew to be dead, or already imprisoned in Taunton. He knew that he was only doing what almost all of his comrades had done, and that he was following the wisest course. But it did not make him feel any less like a traitor when he saw the clerk's neat old-fashioned hand making a careful note of every detail. And when he was returned to the squalid, packed room – though not so packed as it had been four weeks ago, before the fever epidemic – and chained again to the wall between Powell and a young carter called William Leigh, he sat for a long time, lost in thought, trying to accept what he had done.

On the seventeenth day of September, the Lord Chief Justice and his train entered Taunton, and the two months of waiting that the rebel prisoners and their families had endured was at an end, for better or for worse.

For Bram, unwell, demoralised, still haunted by Ben's death and his own understandable but reprehensible betrayal of his friends, the arrival of Jeffreys was a blessed relief. Whether he lived or died – and after these months of privation and misery, he had almost ceased to care very much either way – at least, in a few days, his punishment would be known, and he could prepare himself for his fate.

Talk, of course, was rife within the prison, and rumours circulated and flowered to monstrous proportions as those whose friends had passed on various items of news from outside told the less fortunate what was likely to befall them.

Jeffreys had possessed an evil reputation before this circuit, and the recent carnage which he had perpetrated in Dorset only served to increase his menace. Bram knew that, realistically, he could not hope for a reprieve: his transgression had been too great. He only hoped, for his parents' and his sisters' sake, that the ghastly penalty for treason would be commuted, as it often was, to transportation. True, slave labour in Barbados or Jamaica was very often equivalent to a sentence of death, and there would, even in the best case, be small chance of ever seeing England again. But at least he would be alive, for a while, and they would not have to watch him die.

For the Loveridge family, the probable end to their son's suffering was also a relief. But they knew, too, that while he remained in Taunton Castle, even in those miserable conditions, he was still alive, and they could, after a little bribery, see him, and speak with him, and try to bring him comfort, both material and spiritual.

As the date for the assize drew close, Tabby wrote to Wintercombe. It was a slender chance, but perhaps, if Bram were sentenced to die, the money and influence of his cousin might effect a reprieve. Although she had not seen Alex for several years, she remembered him as a clever, subtle and competent man of the world. She and Jonah were small fry, their wealth comfortable but limited, and they were well known to favour the Dissenting faction. According to her mother, Alex had taken up his inheritance with capable efficiency, and it seemed, improbably, as if he might indeed have left his wild and irresponsible days behind him. The intercession of a man of such significantly high standing might well impress the petty officials and pardonmongers who infested Taunton, eager to wring what they could from the anxious and desperate relatives of the prisoners, now gathering in the town.

There was no reply to her letter, and she wondered, bleakly, if it had gone astray, or if Alex had chosen to ignore it. And then, late on the Wednesday afternoon, the day before Jeffreys and his entourage were expected, there was the sound of a coach drawing up outside, and a knock on the door.

She opened it, and saw a very tall man standing on the step in travel-stained clothes, his hat in his hands and a very attractive smile on his face.

There was no mistaking him, for her dear dead half-brother Nat had possessed those eyes, and the splendid smile was inherited from Patience, who had been like an older sister to her. Tabby gave him her own smile of delight, and held out her hands. 'Welcome, Alex – and thank you so much, for coming.'

'I could do no other,' he said, his face suddenly serious. 'Although whether I can actually be of use to you I don't know. And since Bram is dear to all of us, I have taken the liberty of bringing a coachload of assorted St Barbes with me – I hope you don't mind? Charles has gone to bespeak chambers for us at the Three Cups, so we will not be imposing on you.'

'The town is very full – I hope that there is room,' said Tabby. The coach, plainly painted and probably hired, was disgorging its passengers. She saw the familiar, stylish figure of Louise, and the dowdy black of Alex's sister Phoebe, being helped, stick in hand, from the coach by a maid. Sue and Hannah appeared, with cries of delight, to welcome them, and there was the usual flurry of greetings. Then Charles arrived, to inform them that the landlord of the Three Cups, after a little persuasion, had agreed to provide them with two chambers, and a parlour between, on the first floor.

Tabby remembered Charles very well, as a rather quiet but pleasant young man who had made himself extremely useful at Wintercombe as her brother Nat's health declined. She was profoundly shocked by the change in him. Once stockily built, he had lost a great deal of weight, so that his good dark green suit no longer fitted him, and he looked ill, his face pale and drawn, his eyes creased and shadowed, and new deep lines running between his brows, and from mouth to nose. Nor did he join in the general talk and welcome of the rest of the family, but stood to one side in the upstairs parlour, hat in hand, looking as if all the burden of the world's cares lay on his shoulders. Concerned, she seized the opportunity to speak briefly to Phoebe, who also sat a little apart, obviously very tired from the journey. 'Whatever is the matter with Charles?'

Her niece glanced up and shrugged in characteristic fashion. 'I don't know. He's been moody and uncommunicative for months now, but much worse during these past few weeks. He and Alex don't get on, and there's been much ill feeling, but nothing to explain this.'

And she could hardly ask him directly, as she would her own son. She had not laid eyes on Charles for well over a year, and although he was her nephew, he seemed now like a stranger. Perhaps, she thought charitably, Bram's plight is preying on his mind.

It was dark before all the news had been exchanged. Once the initial pleasure of meeting had worn off, the real purpose of this visit rose once more to the forefront of everyone's mind, and the company became more serious. Sue and Hannah sat together on the window seat, and watched gravely as the six adults pulled up their chairs and began to discuss what might lie in store for Bram. The cat, Jezebel, spoilt for choice of laps, decided on the most familiar, and settled sleek and purring on Tabby's knee. Her furry, affectionate warmth was a source of considerable comfort, and Tabby stroked her, feeling her fears soothed a little as her hand settled into the gentle rhythm.

'All of the prisoners have been assured of the King's mercy if they will assist the officers of the law in their enquiries,' Jonah was saying. 'Bram has said very little to us, but we understand from the friends and relatives of other prisoners that they have been told this.'

'Does this mean that he has confessed to treason?' Louise asked.

Phoebe gave a dry laugh. 'Taken in rebellion, he could hardly plead other than guilty.'

'Which is just as well,' Alex said. He had stretched out his long legs to the fire – it promised to be a clear and rather chilly night for mid-September – and was sipping a glassful of Jonah's best claret with remarkable restraint for one of his reputation. Tabby glanced idly at Louise, and saw the look, secret, longing, unmistakable, that passed at that moment between her and Alex.

So Mother's fears were justified, she thought, with resignation and some misgivings. If Louise has succumbed to his advances, it will hardly be so easy, now, to find her a suitable husband.

But that, at the moment, was the least of her worries. She returned her attention to what her nephew was saying.

'From what I've heard about the proceedings at Dorchester, if a rebel pleads innocence, he's as good as dead. All the prisoners have been encouraged to admit their guilt, as you said, Uncle, under the promise of mercy. After all, there are more than a thousand prisoners, all over the West Country, and the King surely cannot be so thirsty for vengeance as to hang every one of them. Besides, I've recently heard it said, with what truth I do not yet know, that His Majesty has now resolved to recoup a little of his expense in crushing the rebellion by selling the prisoners to his courtiers for transportation to Barbados.'

There was a pause. Oh, no, thought Tabby, suddenly struck with fear. The death of a traitor is dreadful enough, but at least they do die comparatively quickly. In the Indies, it can take years . . . and even if he survives, he will be as good as dead to us, thousands of miles away.

But none of this showed on her face, or in her voice. 'If it is money that the King requires, then surely it will be possible to procure a pardon for Bram?'

'Perhaps,' Alex said. He gave her a rather grim smile, very different from that dazzling earlier one. 'I may be able to exert some influence, and the length of my pockets may count for more. But remember, I am not exactly regarded as His Majesty's most loyal subject, and if anyone remembers the rather lurid details of my past – which are, of course, common knowledge – then my present, more respectable position will count for nothing. But I will do the best that I can, I promise you that. If you like, I'll go to the castle tomorrow and make discreet enquiries. But please, Aunt, Uncle, do not raise your hopes too high. I'm no worker of miracles.'

And the sour, ominous smile on the face of his Cousin Charles gave additional point to his words.

There was no room in the Loveridges' cramped house to entertain such a number of unexpected guests, so Alex invited them back to the Three Cups for supper. By tacit agreement, the conversation, although hardly light-hearted, avoided all mention of the imminent trials, or of the rebellion. Instead, they exchanged innocuous family news, discussed the poor condition of the roads around Taunton, and amongst the younger, female members of the company, the latest fashions as described, with wit and enthusiasm, by Louise. But no one was deceived: the meal ended quietly, and several of the company slept very little that night, for a variety of reasons.

Louise, sharing a bed with Phoebe, the maid Christian tucked up in a truckle at the foot, was thinking of Bram, who was her friend, and who might, if Alex had never existed, have been rather more. True, there was a good chance that he might escape death, but there was no certainty of it. And she could not bear the possibility that her cousin, boyish, exuberant, idealistic, might meet such a dreadful end. Ben was dead, and that was bad enough: they had stopped at Longleaze on the journey from Wintercombe, and she had been deeply shocked by the change in her Aunt Rachael. Her face harshened with sorrow, her hair almost white, she seemed to have aged twenty years in the space of a few weeks. The thought of Aunt Tabby, whom she liked so much, similarly tormented, was appalling. And her grandmother, too, loved Bram dearly. If he were executed, Louise doubted that Silence would recover from such a blow.

She was not in the habit of praying, but she prayed now, soundlessly, lying in the bed beside the sleeping Phoebe. Let Bram live, she cried silently into the dark. Please let him live, even if he is sent to Barbados – he doesn't deserve to die.

And such was her concern for Bram that even her longing for Alex, who of necessity had not made love to her since they left Wintercombe, seemed a pale and feeble wraith of complaint by comparison.

In the other bedchamber, Charles also lay wakeful, his mind churning round and round, over and over, the choice he must make, within the next few days. To do nothing, to accept his diminished destiny, to stand back and let Alex enjoy the girl he loved, and the house which should belong to him, to install his mother and sister in the Abbey Green house and live a life of genteel poverty, limited horizons, a post perhaps as secretary to some gentleman who would not mind the taint of a Papist in the house, to marry Amy, if at all, to a humble younger son with no property, for want of anyone better, and he himself similarly restricted in his choice of wife . . . that was the safe course, the one which Alex, with callous ruthlessness, had allotted to him.

And the other?

The other would bring him wealth, respect, and Wintercombe, possibly even Louise, although he had realised, after watching her very carefully over the past few weeks, that at present her feelings for Alex ruled her life. And it would also, probably, lead to his estrangement from the rest of the family. His mother would understand, he knew, for she had always encouraged him to think that Wintercombe should be his, and it was she who had told him that Alex might not, in fact, be Nat's son. And if he explained to Amy the true nature of Alex's crimes, the evil which had threatened her, the fate which had so nearly befallen her, then she would surely take her brother's part. And Louise, too . . . she liked him, he knew, although relations between them had become somewhat strained of late. She too must surely, once apprised of all the facts, see that his action was entirely justified.

He stared into the dark, while Alex slept deep and quiet beside him, untroubled by conscience. It made Charles's skin creep to share such intimacy with the man he hated above all others, and whom he wished to betray. But he had no choice, in that at least. And he hoped that Alex's mind was so taken up with the fate of Bram – who was, after all, a traitor and thoroughly deserved whatever punishment was meted out to him – that his suspicions would not be aroused. The man, in his arrogance, obviously believed that Charles would meekly accept his appointed fate. Well, he was due to receive a very unpleasant surprise.

But Charles, even as he vowed vengeance, his choice made, was aware of niggling doubt. It was easy enough to lie here in the dark, planning his betrayal. But would he, at the sticking point, have the courage and the boldness and ruthlessness to put his plan into action?

He could not know. All he knew for certain was that he could not for ever continue like this, in limbo, tortured on the rack of his own indecision, seeing the right strategy but lacking the resolution to carry it out. Much more of this, and he would surely be driven to madness.

The Lord Chief Justice, George Jeffreys, rode within his splendid coach into Taunton on Thursday, the seventeenth day of September. His business in Exeter had only taken a day to complete, but in this town, hotbed of Dissent and rebellion, a rather different situation awaited the assize judges. The castle gaol and the Bridewell were alike packed with prisoners, more than five hundred of them, and in order to deal with them all, they would have to be brought to trial in groups of several dozen at a time. But the assize clerks and officials had done their work well, and it was reported that only a handful of rebels had proved resistant to all persuasion and were determined to proclaim their innocence. With luck, the assizes could be finished in two days, as planned, and then, after a day's rest on the Sunday, Jeffreys would continue to Bristol, another nest of sedition, even if it had taken no active part in the rising, and after that to Wells. Then, a triumphant return to London, his report to the King, his duty executed with speed and efficiency, and the western counties shown, most emphatically, that rebellion did not pay.

He and his companions were fêted by the mayor, fervently loyal to the King, and housed in splendid quarters in the castle, not very far from the cramped cells where the men over whom he had the powers of life and death were chained in reeking squalor.

His circuit more than half completed, the Lord Chief Justice accepted the fawning flattery which was his due, relaxed in his temporary freedom from the agonies of the stone which had plagued him intermittently over the past weeks, and looked forward to his meeting with the King. The post of Lord Chancellor had just become vacant. Surely, if His Majesty were pleased with his activities in the west, then that coveted and prestigious position would be his reward.

It was an enticing prospect: and if the five hundred rebel prisoners, incarcerated within the red stone walls of the castle failed to share his enthusiasm for the trials of the next two days, neither did Jeffreys waste any sympathy or concern for their fate.

# 24

## 'Imagin'd crimes'

Nick and Silence Hellier, united in their sorrow and fear, rode the ten miles from Chard to Taunton to attend her grandson's trial. On the journey, they talked of trivial things, neither wishing to contemplate, yet, the dreadful fate that might befall Bram and the other rebels. But his image, vivid, doomed, unseen, lay clear in both their minds.

Their son, Richard, had not wanted his mother to attend the trials. In vain, he had protested that the experience would distress her, that she could do no good, that the strain would make her ill. Rather to his surprise, his father took his wife's part. 'She's no frail old lady, you know – she's seen a great deal in her time, much of it far more unpleasant than a treason trial, and she's probably far stronger and tougher than either of us.'

Richard, rather disconcerted, eventually accepted their argument, but insisted on coming with them. Even in this, however, he was thwarted by the sudden fever that attacked little Nicholas. The child did not seem to be in danger, but Richard's wife Sarah was very anxious about him, and wnted her husband to stay with her.

Because of the imminent assizes, there was very little room left in the town's inns. But there were, at least, a couple of stalls and a tiny chamber available at the Red Lion, where Mistress Savage, well-nigh distracted with worry about her husband, who had been in hiding ever since Sedgemoor, and her son John, a prisoner in the castle, recognised the Helliers and was able to make special provision. They thanked her, and after installing their baggage and Silence's maid, Fan Howard, walked across the cobbled marketplace to the Loveridges' bookshop.

They were greeted with surprise and delight by Sue and Hannah, who, apart from the servants, were alone in the house. Everyone else, Sue explained as the maid brought in beer and wine, was at the castle prison. 'Cousin Alex is here, and Mother thinks that he may be able to use his influence to help Bram.'

Nick raised his eyebrows. 'Alex here? What influence could an old republican possibly hope to command over the King's officials?'

'He doesn't think there is much hope,' Sue said, glancing at Hannah, who was sitting in the window seat, ostensibly playing with Jezebel. 'But he wanted to try, even so. And Cousin Charles is here too, *and* Cousin Phoebe, and Cousin Louise as well.'

'Louise? But I understood that her shoulder was still too badly injured to ride,' Silence said.

'I don't know about that,' Sue told her. 'She doesn't seem hurt at all, that I could see. But anyway, they came in a coach.'

'A coach!' Nick said. He caught his wife's eye and grinned. 'What decadent luxury. Nat always used to say that he'd far rather ride comfortably and wet in a rainstorm than be drily jolted to death in a coach.'

'Phoebe can't ride for long distances, because of her leg,' Silence pointed out. 'Now, what have you and Hannah been up to recently? Are these the gowns that Louise helped you to make?'

There was soon an animated conversation in progress, and Nick, excluded by its feminine content, sat and watched his wife, and was not deceived, for he had known and loved her so long. Her smiling interest did not disguise the tension that whitened her knuckles and stiffened her shoulders. What mattered to her most of all, at this moment, was her beloved grandson, and his fate.

Louise and Phoebe had brooked no denial in their wish to see Bram. Charles had objected that such sights were inappropriate for two gently reared females, and the gently reared females had rounded on him with alarming disgust. With bad grace, he gave in, and followed behind the St Barbes and Loveridges as they walked to the prison, still secretly tortured by his own private and dreadful dilemma.

Here, if anywhere, was the time and the place for denunciation. The Lord Chief Justice and all the panoply of the assizes expected hourly; the trials due to take place tomorrow; the prison conveniently to hand. He was repelled by the conditions within, but could not muster any sympathy for the rebels – after all, what else could traitors expect? They hardly deserved feather beds and generous meals.

Although Louise and Phoebe were both pale and obviously horrified, neither of them betrayed any feminine weakness. Charles realised suddenly that he had never seen Louise weep, even from the agonising pain of her dislocated shoulder.

Bram, whom he did not know very well in any case, was barely recognisable. The filthy scarecrow with lank hair and chained wrists bore no resemblance to the assured young officer he had last seen demanding horses at Wintercombe, only a few months ago. Charles watched from the doorway with Jonah and Tabby, as the two girls and Alex kneeled beside their cousin, heedless of the filthy soiled straw, and talked in soft voices. It required only a small leap of the imagination to put Alex there in the boy's place, amidst the fetid morass of captive humanity, anonymous, reviled, condemned. So tempting was this vision that he almost enquired of the gaoler where the governor of the prison could be found, or someone else in authority to whom he could pour out his accusations.

But once more, his habitual caution – or was it cowardice? – asserted itself. This was the place, but not the time, not now, with his enemy here, and the clear eyes of Phoebe and Louise to witness his act of betrayal. The best course, the wisest and most discreet, would be to return later when the Lord Chief Justice had arrived, and request an interview with Jeffreys himself. It would be far better to lay his information before the most powerful judge in the land. He did not want his accusation to be lost or muddled by some minor, self-seeking petty official. Jeffreys was the King's servant through and through, and he would never ignore such damning evidence against a man of wealth and status.

Alex was coming towards him, picking his way between the bodies of the prisoners, sitting or prone. Phoebe, looking even more pale than usual, held his arm, while Louise, also thoroughly distressed, followed just behind. It was a relief to breathe the slightly fresher air outside the cell. As the gaoler shut the heavy oaken door behind them with a gloating rattle of keys, Alex said quietly to Jonah, 'So he has refused *all* your offers of help?'

'All of them,' said Bram's father, with a resignation that had long since progressed beyond despair. 'Food, money, blankets, we've passed everything to him, and he distributes it to the other prisoners. He doesn't want any special treatment. The only time he didn't argue was when he was sick of the fever, a month or so back, and his mother managed to persuade him to take some medicines and an egg posset – but as soon as he'd regained the strength to refuse them, he did.'

'I admire his stand,' said Alex drily. 'Although I somehow doubt I'd have the force of character to continue it so long . . . Jonah, I'll do my best for him, but I can't promise anything – you know that.'

'I know,' said his uncle, with a tired smile. 'But thank you, all the same.'

They left Alex at the castle to make enquiries about pardons, or reprieves, and, as he put it caustically, to jingle his pockets, and walked back to the house. Louise, who had tried not to notice Charles's brooding, miserable demeanour, for the best part of a month now, was pricked by her conscience. She let Phoebe take Jonah's arm, and matched her pace to her cousin's with a bright, rather false smile. 'Oh, Charles, please cheer up! You look sad, you have for weeks – what's wrong?'

The hand that grasped his arm so confidently was small, narrow, with long sinewy fingers and a single gold ring, stamped with the crest of her long-dead father, on the first. It looked so innocent, untouched, and yet it had clasped Alex in passion, had doubtless done obscene and unmentionable things . . .

Charles shuddered involuntarily. He would rather have no friendship at all than this lying, deceitful counterfeit. He shook her off, without gentleness, and said curtly, 'It's no business of yours, Louise. I would be grateful if you would leave me alone.'

To his secret gratification, the brief look of hurt and surprise on her face was genuine. Then she withdrew her arm with a snap, her brows raised acidly. 'I'm very sorry to have intruded, Charles,' she said, with the haughty, foreign intonation that had always fascinated him. 'Pray forgive me.'

He looked at her trim, expressive back as she marched briskly in front of him, with hopeless love and unrequited longing, and knew, unhappily, that he had already pardoned her.

The arrival of Silence and Nick, although not unexpected, was a rather unwelcome surprise for Charles. Although he had a deep respect for his grandmother, he nevertheless felt like a small boy again, every misdeed and transgression laid bare before her shrewd, perceptive gaze. She would know, none better, that something was disturbing him deeply, and he shied away in horror from the thought of the gentle, but implacable inquisition that would surely follow, the humiliating revelations which he might be tempted to make . . . and her horror and revulsion if she ever discovered the truth. His best hope was to let her think that he suffered from the pangs of unrequited love, for she would undoubtedly notice the blistering force of feeling that now linked Alex and Louise, as if they were joined by an invisible skein of lightning. Then, perhaps, he would be able to slip away unsuspected, this afternoon or tomorrow, and lay the evidence of Alex's treachery before the Lord Chief Justice. And once the wheels of the law had been set inexorably in motion, his vengeance upon the man who had treated him so despicably would be at last complete.

The Lord Chief Justice had supped well. The agony from his kidney stone had diminished to a dull, almost dismissable ache, and he was looking forward to relaxing with his fellow-judges and a bottle or two of brandy to banish the pain altogether. He was not best pleased, therefore, to learn that a gentleman wished to speak to him privately, on a matter of great urgency and importance.

'Can't the fellow wait until tomorrow?' he demanded irritably. 'No business can surely be so great at this hour of the evening.'

But no, the gentleman was most insistent: and it was a matter of treason, so he said. Despite his longing for the brandy, Jeffreys pricked up his ears at once. 'Treason, eh? Well, perhaps I can spare him a few minutes. Show him into the closet.'

Charles's nerve had begun to fail him during the wait to see the judge. It had been difficult enough to find an excuse to slip away after supper, while the others were settling down for an evening of quiet talk, reflection and, probably, prayer for Bram, who faced trial tomorrow. He knew that if he were gone for long, his absence might well arouse suspicion, particularly from Alex. And if his cousin were to be arrested as a result of his interview with Jeffreys, he did not wish to make him aware of the fate in store for him until it was too late to flee.

But he had been kept in this dingy little room for what seemed like hours, while the sun sank further and further outside, and he had begun to regret having come. It was ridiculous – they would laugh at him – and he would have risked the odium and contempt of his family for nothing.

But then the lackey came back, still with that supercilious face, and told him that the Lord Chief Justice was graciously prepared, in these unusual circumstances, and as a mark of great favour, to grant him a few minutes of his time. And Charles, sweating and apprehensive, was ushered into Jeffreys's presence.

The great man was surprisingly young, no more than forty or so, and possessed of a very handsome face, with sensitive features and large eyes. Charles, making his bow respectfully low, was not too nervous to notice the broken veins and flushed cheeks of the habitual drinker: Jeffreys, like the man he was about to accuse, was said to be more than fond of the brandy bottle. But the quick, hectoring voice which asked him to state his business as speedily as possible was sober enough.

It was, in any case, too late now: no possibility of admitting that he had made a mistake, of melting away again into decent obscurity. Charles took a deep breath, and said, rather too forcefully, 'I am here, my lord, to lay accusation of treason and rebellion against Sir Alexander St Barbe.'

The other man stared at him. Charles realised abruptly that Jeffreys was rather more than the brutal buffoon of popular and hostile repute. A horrible feeling crept into his mind, that it was he, and not Alex, who was on trial.

'And your name, I am told, is Charles St Barbe. What relationship have you to this man?'

'I am his cousin, my lord. My father and his were half-brothers.'

'I see. I know the name of Sir Alexander . . . he's lived in the Low Countries for some years, I believe? And recently returned after his father's death? He was once a notorious Whig, I seem to remember, a crony of Shaftesbury and Monmouth. But the Justices here do not seem to have thought him a danger, or he would already be in custody.'

'He is surpassing devious and cunning, my lord.'

'I see.' Jeffreys leaned forward, his hands spread on the table between them. 'Well, he has obviously not been sufficiently crafty to escape your notice. May I ask for details of his misdeeds?'

Charles had spent night after night rehearsing everything in his mind, expunging anything that might reveal his more personal motives, emphasising his loyalty to the King and his loathing of rebellion. In a clear, almost unemotional voice, he detailed his suspicions. Alex had lied about the day of Norton Fight, and had obviously been a witness to the action, if not an actual participant. He had given horses to his cousin, a member of Monmouth's army. There were seditious pamphlets hidden in his library, along with books concerning republicanism. 'I know that each can be explained away, my lord, or might seem trivial. But taken together, to my mind they make up a damning indictment.'

'And what is your interest in this, sir?'

Charles stressed his devotion to King James, and his abhorrence of treason and rebellion. Jeffreys studied him as he spoke, and when he had finished, stabbed a sudden finger at him. 'Your interest, sir. Any fool can prate of loyalty. What do you gain, by informing on your cousin?'

'I – I do not know, my lord.'

'Who is his heir? Has he brothers? Sons?'

'A bastard son – and a sister who is a cripple and unlikely to marry.'

'So you are his next heir? I see. I have no objection to venal motives,' said Jeffreys, showing his teeth. 'But it were wise, perhaps, not to admit to them in court. Jurymen can be over-scrupulous, on occasion. So – you hope to gain your cousin's inheritance, and doubtless you will be more loyal than he seems to have been. Do you yourself believe that he is a traitor?'

Charles, from somewhere, acquired the courage to look this formidable man directly in the eye. 'Yes, my lord,' he said, with absolute certainty.

'Then we had better discuss,' said the Lord Chief Justice, with considerable relish, 'the way in which this rogue of a cousin of yours can be most speedily brought to face his just deserts.'

The trials of the rebel prisoners were set to take place in the Great Hall of Taunton Castle. To accommodate the large numbers of friends and relatives of the accused, not to mention loyal townspeople intent on seeing

408

justice done, and those who were simply curious or who loved spectacle, makeshift scaffolding and boards had been erected at the keep end of the hall, and it was full long before the allotted time. At the other end sat the five judges, Justices, local gentry, the sheriff and his deputy, clerks and all the other court officials, and partitioned boxes for the jury, and the prisoners.

The usual proceedings at an assize were somewhat tedious, full of ceremonial, long speeches and the roll-call of officials and the swearing-in of the jury. But with five hundred men to try in two days, time was exceptionally short, and if those who had no concern for the captives had expected a day of spectacle, they were to be sadly disappointed.

The St Barbes and Loveridges had found places on the lowest part of the stand, quite close to the prisoners. It was not usual for women to attend the assize, but the large numbers of wives, daughters and sisters of rebels had ensured some relaxation of custom. Sue and Hannah, by virtue of their youth, had been left behind to spin out the hours of waiting in desultory activity. Louise sat between Silence and Phoebe, with Tabby by her mother, Jonah and Charles beyond them, and Alex next to his sister. Amongst the pressed, anxious people all around them, muttering or sobbing in apprehension, there was an atmosphere of dread so tangible that it seemed as if a headsman's axe could sever it.

The judges entered, resplendent in their robes, but the speeches were brief, and Jeffreys, who spoke on the heinousness of rebellion and the inevitability and severity of the King's justice, roused no hope. Four men were brought in, manacled together, named and charged. These were the obdurate, who despite all persuasion, and the dreadful examples already set in Dorset and Devon, were determined to plead innocence.

They received very short shrift indeed, their excuses and explanations briskly interrupted with ridicule and mockery by Jeffreys, and the jury obediently found them guilty. A moan of horror went up from the crowd, as if this had not been expected, and the four men, three dazed, one shouting in protest, were hustled from the hall.

In view of their probable sentence, it was hardly surprising that the other prisoners had elected to admit their guilt, and now, to the Lord Chief Justice's evident satisfaction, matters proceeded much more quickly. The rebels were brought in from their cells chained together, in batches of twenty or more at a time. Their ragged, pitiable state aroused compassionate murmurs from many of the onlookers, some of whom pressed kerchiefs to their eyes. Other, more prosaically, covered their noses as the stench of two months' close confinement wafted through the hall. There were some prisoners who stood upright, looking boldly around for familiar faces, but more seemed bewildered and cowed by the overbearing ceremonial of the court, and in every batch, at least three or four were so ill that they had to be supported by their comrades. Their names were read out, their pleas recorded by the busy scratching quills of the clerks, and then they were hustled, with much clanking of iron, back to gaol to await sentence at the end of the trials, while their friends called to them from the stands.

Louise began to feel that there was little point in sitting here. The bench was hard, the reek increasing, and the danger of infection considerable. Bram had not been amongst those unwise four who had pleaded not guilty, and as the morning wore on and group after group of rebels was brought to the bar, her head began to ache savagely. Despite its size, the Great Hall was hot, and the air thick and close. She felt sweat seeping into her gown, and prickling her skin, and she restlessly dried her face and hands with her kerchief. The endless procession of misery before her was almost more than she could bear: these humble, abused, defeated men were hardly deserving of the ghastly punishment which might well befall them.

Yesterday, she had been horrified at the change in Bram: he had lost so much flesh, and looked as frail as a wind-blown leaf. Even so, he was still quite substantial compared to some of the skeletal figures before her. And when he did appear, in the last batch before the adjournment for dinner, she did not recognise him: only Tabby's sharp gasp alerted her to his presence, and she was still seeking him amongst the shaggy, ill-kempt heads when his name was called.

'Abraham Loveridge of Taunton, bookseller, how do you plead?'

'Guilty,' said Bram, his voice firm and clear, in contrast to the mumbled replies of most of those who had preceded him. And then she saw him standing at the bar, still proud despite the rags and the dirt, and found that she did not in the least regret the discomforts of the morning. For what was a little stiffness and inconvenience compared with what he and his comrades had already suffered, and would continue to endure until their fate was settled, one way or the other?

He turned, and she saw his eyes searching the massed ranks of spectators, and waved. But already he was being pushed back into the group, and another man was taking his place, to admit guilt in his turn. A few minutes more, and it was over. The prisoners were being led out by the gaoler, and the court was rising for dinner. Sentence would not be passed until the end of the proceedings, which would probably, if they continued at this rate, come at some time tomorrow. No one, however, was in any doubt about what that sentence would be. The only lawful

410

penalty for treason was death, and only the mercy of judge or King could commute it.

There was no point in returning to the assize after dinner, and in any case, they had all had more than their fill of the pathetic parade of rebel prisoners. They went back to the Loveridge house, and over a rather subdued meal, told Sue and Hannah what had happened at the trial.

Alex decided to visit the castle again that afternoon, to further his enquiries about obtaining a reprieve for Bram. He had been given little hope yesterday, but, as he pointed out, it was usually merely a question of finding the right official, and everyone in such positions had their price.

The crowds were thick in the castle precincts, as they had been that morning. He did not make any attempt to visit his cousin, for the gaol was in some confusion, with prisoners being herded to and from the Great Hall for trial. Of course, all the most important officials were busy in the court, but he greased several palms, and learned the identities of those who might be most favourable to his request. Tonight, or tomorrow, after the court's business was ended, would be the best time to return.

He was just about to leave the castle when a man stepped into his path, two soldiers behind him. Alex stared down at him, for he was of very insignificant stature. 'Are you looking for me?'

'Are you Sir Alexander St Barbe, of Wintercombe in the parish of Philip's Norton in this county?' The little man's voice was almost as high as a woman's, and Alex was tempted to smile. He said briskly, 'I am.'

'Then I must ask you to accompany me, sir, to answer certain questions.'

Something had gone wrong. Some error had been made, for there was no mistaking the air of menace around those two soldiers, nor the stern gaze of the undersized official. But it could not, surely, concern his efforts to free Bram?

But if it were not, if this were in some way connected with his past, either years ago or more recently, then he might indeed have cause for apprehension. Whatever the reason for this, though, there was only one course to follow, that of the innocent man.

So he stared in surprise at the official, and inclined his head in courteous agreement. 'Of course I will, although I cannot imagine why any information which I possess may be of interest.'

He was led to a small chamber on the upper floor of the castle. It contained two tables: at one, a clerk sat with pen and ink and paper, evidently ready to record whatever he said. At another, a stout man whom he did not recognise, but who seemed to be a Justice, sat with his arms folded, and a sheaf of papers in front of him. He did not rise, but glared up at Alex with an ominously hostile expression. 'Sir Alexander St Barbe?'

'Yes,' Alex said pleasantly. This was not, he reflected wryly, a novel situation for him. He had faced various similar inquisitions since his wild schooldays, and had become adept at evading retribution. There were few offences so great, in his experience, that he could not use a plausible tongue and affable manner to escape punishment. And this, surely, was no more than an unfortunate misunderstanding.

But there was always the chance that it was not, and already his quick mind was mustering defence and explanation and excuse.

A chair was brought, and his interrogator leaned forward. 'You may sit, Sir Alexander. No doubt you are wondering what this is about?'

'I am indeed,' Alex said. He had adopted a relaxed posture, one leg crossed over the other, indicating a man untroubled by guilt. 'I can only assume that it concerns my efforts to help my unfortunate and misguided cousin?'

The Justice stared at him in some surprise. 'Your cousin? You have a cousin amongst the rebel prisoners?'

'I have – a foolish boy, easily led, who was seduced by Monmouth's lies,' Alex told him, wondering what Bram would say if he could hear this unflattering description. 'I cannot condone his despicable action, of course, but for the sake of our kinship, and at his mother's pleading, I feel honour bound to do what I can to help him.'

'No doubt,' said the other man drily. 'However, that is not the matter which concerns me here and now. There has been information laid against you, Sir Alexander, and of a very serious nature – in brief, an accusation of treason.'

It was suddenly very quiet in the little room, and even the clerk's quill had ceased to scratch. With the confidence of long practice, Alex stared in well-simulated surprise at the Justice. 'Of *treason*? That is a ridiculous slander, sir.'

'What is writ down before me here, Sir Alexander, is not in the least ridiculous. It is alleged that on the twenty-sixth day of June in this year, you rendered unlawful assistance to the traitor and rebel James Scott, late Duke of Monmouth, by freely supplying an officer of his forces with horses and money. It is further stated that on the following day, the twenty-seventh of June, you took part in the fight at Philip's Norton, as a member of the said forces of the late Duke. In addition, you are also stated to have in your possession, at your house known as Wintercombe, an unknown number of proscribed and seditious pamphlets, and to be concerned in spreading the same. And finally, and perhaps most seriously of all, you are said to have had prior knowledge of the invasion of James Scott, late Duke of Monmouth, and to have returned to this country from Holland in order to prepare the way for him. What say you to these charges?'

'First,' Alex said forcefully, 'that all of them are without exception malicious lies, and I can prove them to be so. And secondly, I would dearly like to know the identity of the person who has laid these accusations against me.'

The other man regarded him coldly. 'At the present, I am not at liberty to divulge that information. I would, however, be delighted to hear your defence against the charges.'

The quill scratched busily. Alex leaned back in his chair, and marshalled his thoughts with the swift clarity that always seemed to come to his rescue in moments of crisis. He waited until the clerk had finished writing, and then said calmly, 'For the first – supplying horses and coin to Monmouth, was it? Well, I did not give him any money, freely or otherwise, and there are many witnesses amongst my household who will doubtless tell you so. Horses, yes, I do admit that the rebels took those, but I did not give my permission – indeed, I had little choice in the matter, as a rebel trooper was pointing a pistol at me, and I had every reason to think that he would fire it if I refused. Again, a large part of my household witnessed these events, and you are quite free to ask them.'

'I expect we will. Do you know the identity of the rebel officer who took your horses?'

Something in the Justice's face warned Alex that this was, in fact, known. He said, 'I do. Unfortunately, it was my cousin, Abraham Loveridge. He was apparently under the impression that our kinship would incline me to give him what he asked without question.'

'And he was mistaken, was he? So much so that he had to threaten you with a pistol?'

'One of his men did. I am a reasonable man,' Alex said drily. 'Argument with a loaded and cocked weapon is, to say the least of it, somewhat reckless, especially as shots had already been fired. They took six horses, but none of any great value. I suppose young Loveridge was afflicted with some pangs of conscience, after all.'

'And you say that this episode was witnessed by members of your household?'

'By at least three-quarters of them,' Alex told him. 'Some fifteen or sixteen people, I should say.'

The Justice looked at him assessingly, but did not pursue the matter. He said, 'How do you answer the allegation that you joined the rebel forces at Philip's Norton?'

'The simple truth should suffice,' Alex said. 'I went into the village early that morning, in an attempt to persuade my cousin to leave the rebels and seek the King's pardon before it was too late. Unfortunately, he would not be persuaded – he's a proud and stubborn lad, and he refused to leave what he considered to be his duty. Then the fighting began, and as the field of battle lay between the village and my house, I judged it safest to take refuge in the George – which is the principal inn – and I spent the day there.' He gave the Justice a dry smile. 'The landlord's son, Harry Prescott, will vouch for me. His beer, by the way, is excellent.'

'And what are your answers to the other accusations?'

'To the pamphlets? Yes, I do have one or two in my possession. But as items of curiosity, no more. Half the gentlemen of Somerset could say the same, from what I've heard. As for the other, that surely must be no more than malicious gossip, pure and simple. I served with one of the English regiments in the Dutch army, but when I heard of my father's death, I left the Prince of Orange's service and came home to take up my inheritance last February. I don't think that Monmouth himself knew at that time that he was to lead a rebellion.'

'How do you know that, if you had no contact with him?'

'Holland is not a large country, and there are many English people living there – merchants and soldiers, as well as rabid republicans and political exiles. Of course there is gossip, talk, rumour – everyone seeks to know everyone else's business, and Monmouth was a very frequent topic of conversation.' He smiled again. 'And not usually to his credit, amongst the people with whom I consorted.'

'I see.' The Justice linked his hands and stared consideringly at Alex, who gazed benignly back. 'You have a very plausible tongue, Sir Alexander, and I am almost inclined to believe you. However, my task is merely to examine you, and make a note of your answers to these accusations. I cannot recommend that you be set free immediately. In view of the seriousness of the allegations, the Lord Chief Justice is of the opinion that you be conveyed as soon as possible to London, where all these matters can be fully investigated, to everyone's satisfaction. Do not be alarmed, Sir Alexander – if you are innocent of the charges, then there is no need for you to fear the process of the law.'

'Then I am to submit meekly to this dislocation of my life, to the extreme inconvenience of leaving my estates and all my business here, because some anonymous person seems to have laid this ridiculous tarradiddle against me out of malice and spite?' Alex demanded, and for the first time a spark of real anger infused his voice. 'I can only assume that someone has remembered that I got into bad company in my wild youth –

not an unusual situation, and if everyone were prosecuted for such misdeeds, there'd be hardly a man left free in England. But I am now a man of property and substance, and I wish only to enjoy and enhance my inheritance. I would hardly put everything left to me by my father in jeopardy for the sake of such as Monmouth.'

The clerk scribbled urgently on into the silence. The two men, interrogator and accused, twenty years between them, stared at each other intently. Then the Justice sighed, and sat back. 'I admit, Sir Alexander, that you have my sympathy in this. If, as you think, malice is the motive for these accusations, then no man can consider himself safe. But, as I said, you claim innocence, and state your case convincingly. Of course, full investigation will be made into all the charges. We will be thorough and fair, and if you are not guilty, then you have nothing to fear.'

Alex doubted very much whether fairness would even figure in the plans of such as Jeffreys. If he had already been considered a danger to the government because of his standing and his unruly and politically dubious past, or even if the King or his ministers decided to make an example of him to discourage other gentry from giving full rein to their Whig or radical inclinations, then no amount of proof, no plausible speeches, no denials of guilt, could save him from their revenge. And if that were indeed the case, then he was condemned already, months before any possible trial, and he might as well be dragged out to the gallows immediately to suffer the penalty that faced all convicted traitors.

But it would do his case no good to protest too strongly now. He said at last, 'It seems that there is nothing I can do – I am in your power, for the moment, and you must send me where you are bid. But I would ask one favour of you. I would be most grateful if a message could be conveyed to my sister, and that I be allowed to speak with her and other members of my family, before I leave. As you can appreciate, I have affairs that must be settled, and she will also be most concerned for me.'

'Of course, Sir Alexander,' said the other man. 'You may have pen and paper now, and a boy will be sent round with your message directly.'

A little later, it lay in Phoebe's palm, a folded, sealed rectangle of thick paper, bearing her name in Alex's bold, uncompromisingly individual hand. He had not been gone very long, and no one had expressed any concern: and yet, as she looked down at that unrevealing piece of paper, its contents hidden, a premonition of disaster came over her so strongly that she almost succumbed to the impulse to throw it into the fire.

I am not a fanciful person, she reminded herself sternly. I deal with words, and facts, and figures, things that can be measured and counted, heard and seen. This is ridiculous: why should I feel so powerfully that it is bad news?

There was only one way to prove her foolishness. She opened it, and read, and found that all her worst fears were confirmed.

It must have shown in her face, for Tabby said abruptly, 'What is it?' And Louise, warned by some wild intuition, got to her feet, her eyes suddenly wide with alarm. 'Is it Alex?'

'It's Alex,' Phoebe said starkly. 'He's been held at the castle. For questioning. A misunderstanding, he says – but he wants me to go now, to see him.'

She looked up, seeing all her kin, aghast, horrified, disbelieving. Except for one. There was no surprise on Charles's face, and no matter how he controlled his expression, the sudden, triumphant excitement shone through like the sun behind thin cloud. And suddenly Phoebe knew, with total certainty, what had happened to cause that 'misunderstanding', and the terrible danger in which her brother now stood.

# 25
## 'Close designs, and crooked counsels'

'You are an admitted rebel, and death is the prescribed penalty for your crimes.' The assize clerk, Andrew Loder, stretched his rather cadaverous face into something vaguely resembling a smile. 'You have been convicted, and you will soon be sentenced. However, as I am sure you know full well, the King is disposed to be merciful to those whose repentance of their crimes takes, shall we say, a more practical course?'

Bram knew already what he would be asked to do, and his conscience quailed within him. He had given them information weeks ago, everything that they had asked for, also in the expectation of mercy. Which of his unfortunate comrades was marked out for special punishment, that they wanted still more evidence from him?

He closed his eyes briefly, thinking of the court that morning, the face of Judge Jeffreys, beautiful but cruel as he had always imagined Judas to be, the inevitable sentence to be pronounced tomorrow, and Louise's face suddenly familiar and vivid amongst the crowded anonymous ranks along the benches, her smile of encouragement, her raised hand, and his parents and cousins sitting with her . . .

That life was gone. Whatever happened, death or transportation, he would never again ride the green lanes around Taunton, or smell the dusty, musty, evocative aroma of his father's shop, or tease and laugh with his sisters and Libby, or talk to Louise of things that no longer seemed to matter. He had been an officer in Monmouth's army, and mercy was unlikely. Why should he further betray his friends for a fragile hope that was probably cruel illusion?

He looked at Loder's expectantly greedy face, and said flatly, 'What do you want?'

'Information,' said the clerk. 'We have evidence laid against a most dangerous and devious traitor, and we require corroboration. Help us to convict him, and you can be assured that the Lord Chief Justice himself will look upon your case with favour. Deny us your assistance, and the full rigour of the law will descend upon you. Is that clear, Loveridge?'

'Yes,' Bram said, his heart cold within him. So this was to be the test of his loyalty, his readiness to betray some unfortunate and thereby save his own skin. He added, 'Who is this man?'

Loder smiled, showing an array of unevenly rotted teeth. 'Your kinsman, I believe – Sir Alexander St Barbe.'

In complete astonishment, Bram stared at him, open-mouthed. '*Alex?* You suspect my cousin *Alex?* In God's name, why? What reasons have you?'

'We were hoping that you could tell us that, Loveridge.'

'Well, I can't,' Bram said despairingly. He stepped forward to put his manacled hands on the table between them, and as his unwashed stench assaulted Loder's nostrils, he had the satisfaction of seeing the man recoil. 'To my knowledge, Sir Alexander is a loyal subject of His Majesty, and had nothing whatever to do with the rebellion.'

'What of the horses he supplied to you?'

'You have that wrong,' Bram said. 'I forced him to hand them over. I asked him to give us as many horses as he could spare, and he refused. So one of my men held him at pistol point, and we took what we needed. He didn't give us permission, nor was any payment made. We were desperate, so we stole them.'

Loder did not seem particularly convinced, despite the passionate sincerity in Bram's voice. 'You expect us to believe that?'

'Why not? There were plenty of witnesses – ask them. It's nothing but the truth, may God help me!'

'You may be in sore need of his assistance, should you continue to be intransigent,' Loder observed maliciously. 'However, we will return to that matter later. Did your cousin take any part in the fighting at Philip's Norton?'

Someone had talked, and Bram wished desperately that he could discover who it was. But his course lay clear and terrible before him, for of all people, he could not betray Alex and buy his own life and freedom with such squalid and tainted coin. He would rather die, and put an impossible burden of grief on his family, than have that despicable treachery on his conscience.

He said emphatically, 'No, he did not. He came to persuade me and another cousin, who is now dead, to desert our places with the army, but that is all. Hardly an act of treason, surely.'

'Our information is different. I repeat – did he take part in the battle?'

'No!' Bram cried, and slammed his fist down on the table. The rusty chains clanked and rattled, and Loder jumped. 'No, no, *no*, he did not. For God's sake, who has told you all this nonsense? It's nothing but malicious lies.'

'You are proving most obdurate, Loveridge,' Loder said, softly and with menace. 'I repeat – the consequences for you will be exceedingly severe, unless you help us as we wish.'

'But I *can't*!' Bram shouted frantically. 'Do you want me to *lie*? I have told you the truth, I have told you all I know – do you want to accuse an innocent man?'

'But he is not innocent,' Loder said sharply. 'The Lord Chief Justice is convinced of his guilt, and he can sniff out a rebel a hundred paces off. There is no doubt that Sir Alexander is a traitor, and deserves punishment. Now, I suggest you abandon your misguided loyalty to your cousin, and tell us the truth. It will make matters so much easier for you.'

'I told you – what I said is the *truth*!' Bram stared at him, caught in the coils of nightmare. They seemed to have made up their minds already that Alex was guilty, and nothing he could say seemed to make any impression. And yet, despite his passionate denials, he knew that they were right. It had been fortunate that Trooper Taylor's aggressive manner had given Alex the perfect excuse to hand over the horses: their original stratagem, hastily conceived at Midford, would not have been nearly so convincing. There had been plenty of witnesses, but no one, he had been certain, had suspected any collusion.

But the fighting . . . He had known that no good would come of that lunatic and quixotic episode. What in the name of God had possessed his devious, ruthless, amoral cousin to throw away all his careful subterfuges and engage openly on the rebel side? He remembered some taunting remark, made by Trooper Taylor – pray God no one thought to question *him* – that might perhaps have stung Alex into action, to prove himself . . .

It seemed unlikely, to say the least. And his cousin had denied it all to his face afterwards, and sworn that he had spent the afternoon drinking in the George. He had not been convinced at the time, and now he was certain that Alex had lied to him. Again, he wondered who had made these accusations against his cousin. It must be either a man who had fought in Bram's own troop – Taylor was the most likely candidate – and witnessed both episodes, or, much worse, far more disturbing, someone in the Wintercombe household. And if the latter, how had they come to Taunton to lay evidence?

Loder was barking his questions again, with increasing anger and frustration. He had no choice: if someone else had betrayed Alex, he would not compound that evil deed. Through the interrogation that followed, abused, bullied, shouted at, he clung desperately to his answers, and would not be shaken off them. Alex had been forced under threat of death to hand over the horses to him; and he had taken no part in the fighting.

419

It was almost dark when they let him go at last, and he was exhausted to the point of collapse. But he walked proudly from the room, a small bleak core of satisfaction burning at his heart. This time, he had not betrayed anyone, and although his own life might be forfeit because of his obstinacy, he had kept his self-respect. They would have to look elsewhere for the second hostile witness that a successful treason trial would require.

'I know who has done this,' Phoebe said softly to her brother.

He had not, of course, been herded into the fetid cells with the other prisoners, but had been given a small but pleasant chamber, overlooking the Castle Green. It had a bed, chairs, table, and every comfort and convenience save one: the liberty to walk freely out of the room. A guard stood on the other side of the door, his ears doubtless alert. When her half-hour of time had expired, he would unlock the door and usher her out.

It had been surprisingly easy to gain access to him – apparently the mayor of Taunton, who had interrogated him, had agreed that she could visit. After seeing the ghastly conditions which Bram and the other prisoners were suffering in the same building, she had been dreading what she would find. It seemed almost an anti-climax to be sitting here, sipping surprisingly good wine, as if this were a chamber in some inn, and to see Alex sprawled on the bed, his hands behind his head and his legs negligently crossed, looking as if he had not a care in the world.

'Do you, indeed?' he said, and abruptly sat up, dispelling the casual air. 'Don't tell me – I think I can guess. Charles.'

Phoebe looked at him unhappily. 'I'm not sure. But his face, when your message arrived . . . he couldn't hide his glee. And above all others, he has the motive to betray you.'

'Even if it's a pack of lies,' Alex observed. He glanced significantly at the door, and added, 'He's taken a few very slender threads of the truth, quite innocent, and woven them up with some very thick strands of conjecture to make a fine web of falsehood, all done out of greed and malice.' His mouth twisted suddenly. 'I must share part of the blame, for underestimating him so drastically. I thought he was nothing but a feeble milksop, always complaining, but lacking the courage of his convictions. It seems there's some spirit in him after all.'

'If it was him,' Phoebe said, with a vehemence that surprised her, 'I shall take him to task for it, and I don't care who hears me – the very thought of it makes me retch.'

She stopped, shaken, and Alex smiled suddenly. 'Oh, my little sister, could it be that you really do care what happens to me?'

'Of course I do – you're my brother, after all. And besides,' she added, briskly retreating to her usual sharply practical manner, 'it will do the St Barbe name no good at all if you are accused of treason. We do have a certain position and standing to maintain, after all.'

'Of course,' Alex said, and their eyes met, identically blue, and both revealing an unaccustomed affection. He glanced down at his hands for a moment, as if unwilling to acknowledge the depth of his feeling, and then continued. 'I don't at present know exactly what is to happen. Mayor Smith seemed to think that I am to be sent to London, perhaps in the next few days, for enquiries to be made. Don't look so alarmed – it's the usual procedure to be followed with their more important catches.' He grinned suddenly. 'And I've never seen the inside of the Tower – it'll be a novel experience. Meanwhile, I should imagine they'll do their best to turn up more evidence against me here – from some of you, perhaps, or, much more likely, from Bram.' His voice hardened suddenly. 'If he is made to suffer for this as well, I shall claim my due from dear Charles when it's all over – you have my word.'

'And if you do not have the opportunity,' Phoebe told him, with uncharacteristic savagery, 'then that's a duty I shall gladly undertake on your behalf.'

Alex smiled at her. 'You have my blessing, and my thanks – although I have every intention of surviving this. Now, time is limited, and there is much to say. Can you be my agent in all I ask?'

'Of course, as best I can.'

'Excellent – I know that I can rely upon you, absolutely. Has sentence been passed on the prisoners yet?'

'No – that will come tomorrow, I think, when all the pleas have been entered.'

'It's quite likely that I will be taken to London within the next few days. If that's the case, don't follow for the present. Nothing will happen to me for a while – the wheels of justice grind exceedingly slowly. At the moment, the Loveridges must be our chief concern. I don't know if Bram can be saved, but one of the assize clerks, Loder, is said to be a greedy man, open to persuasion. You have my full permission to try any means at your disposal to secure a reprieve. Give this letter to Philip Cousins in Bath – he knows all about my affairs, and he will help you in any way he can.'

Phoebe took the paper reluctantly, as if it were the final proof that they were trapped in a nightmare from which there might be no waking. She said slowly, 'What shall I do when Bram's fate is decided?'

'Return to Wintercombe. Doubtless various officials will be visiting, to interview the servants and ask questions in the village. Unless someone else has a grudge against me, they won't discover anything, but they're probably quite capable of manufacturing evidence if necessary. I'd like you to stay there until that unsavoury business is done. Then, if you can face the journey, come to London . . . and bring Lukas with you.'

'I will, and gladly,' Phoebe said. 'You'll have to tell me where all the best booksellers are . . .' She looked at him, her eyes suddenly brilliant with hatred. 'What of Charles? If we are both right, he will try to assume the management of Wintercombe, just as he did after Father died. I didn't mind it very much then, although it did irritate me, the way he seemed to think it was his right, rather than his duty. But now, after this . . . quite frankly, I don't think I could bear to see him take your place.'

'You won't have to,' Alex said grimly. 'That letter to Philip authorises him to make out a power of attorney, putting my affairs entirely in your hands. You will have the authority at Wintercombe, and I'd like to see Charles gainsay you. In any case, he will probably be summoned to London as a witness, so you won't have to share your roof with him for long.'

'Thank you,' Phoebe said, with profound gratitude. 'I'll do my best to manage everything, although I can't promise – as you know, my health is not perfect.'

'Ever since I planted you in the knot on the lowest terrace at Wintercombe, and watered you to make you grow,' Alex said, and his smile was suddenly brilliant. 'Have you forgiven me for that, little sister?'

'Yes, without reservation,' Phoebe said, and held out her hand. Alex got to his feet to take it. 'I'm glad. That has been weighing much on my conscience.'

Phoebe snorted. 'A likely tale. Alex . . . before I go, I must ask if there will be any other visitors allowed you. Louise, in particular, would very much like to see you.'

'Louise . . .' Alex said, and his voice told her all she needed to know, of longing and desire. 'She is a very remarkable young woman . . . Have no fear, little sister, she will survive this.'

'Will she?' Phoebe rose with her usual lack of grace. 'Will she? I don't think she's as tough and invulnerable as you seem to believe. And I'll add now, so that there's no misunderstanding, that I know that the two of you are lovers. It wasn't exactly difficult to deduce – the air positively crackles between you.'

'And you aren't going to pass judgement? I'm surprised.'

'It isn't my place – what do I know of lust or passion? But I wouldn't be surprised if Charles also knows – and if that were the reason, or one of them, for his treachery. He genuinely loves her, I'm sure of it – and don't sneer, he's as capable of sincere feeling as anyone else. I don't think, though, that he loves the real Louise, but some cherished phantom that he's created in his mind. And for him to realise that you and she are lovers must have been the most bitter disillusion.' She saw his face, and added quickly, 'I am not attempting to excuse or justify his behaviour, just to offer some small explanation. He may still cherish some hope of attracting her, once you are out of the way – they used to be good friends, after all. But I think he is deluding himself.'

'I trust that he is,' Alex said, and the sudden vicious savagery in his voice startled her. 'For if he tries to snare her as well, I swear that I shall take the first opportunity that offers to kill him.'

It was almost dusk when she returned to Jonah's house, with Louise's maid Christian a faithful and silently sympathetic escort. Every halting step of the way back, she rehearsed in her mind what she would say to Charles as soon as she encountered him, and the vast depths of her fury astonished and disturbed her. Surely her natural but limited affection for her brother was not strong enough to spark this terrible anger?

It was the deceit and the treachery that really disgusted her, she supposed, as she approached the Loveridges' door. And the hypocrisy of a man who never lost the opportunity for righteous condemnation of Alex's licentious ways, while plotting to betray him, possibly to a hideous death.

Elias opened the door, and she hobbled past him on Christian's supporting arm. 'Is Master St Barbe still here?'

Elias was still not quite certain of the relationships and names of all his master's cousins by marriage, but he knew Charles. 'Yes, Mistress, and all the ladies as well – upstairs in the parlour.'

They were waiting expectantly when she arrived, breathless and aching, at the parlour door. Hannah and Sue sewing in desultory fashion; Louise trying to read; Jonah and his wife side by side next to the warmth of the fire, and Silence and Nick opposite. Significantly, Charles sat on his own, a book on his knee, but somehow isolated from everyone else by more than just his position. Phoebe, looking round at the crowded parlour, wondered if anyone else had suspected him. Had Silence, or Louise?

She said bluntly, to the familiar, apprehensive faces, 'I have some unpleasant news.'

'About Bram?' Tabby's expression was suddenly anxious. Phoebe hastened to reassure her. 'No – not about Bram. This concerns Alex.' She looked round at all her kin, and let her eyes rest last and longest upon

Charles. Under her condemning gaze, he shifted in his seat, and a faint flush rose under his skin, despite his defiant face. 'He is in custody, under threat of trial for treason, and all the hideous consequences of that, because someone went to the Lord Chief Justice and laid false information against him.'

There was sick, appalled horror on every face before her, save for one. Phoebe directed her implacable gaze on that exception, and spoke almost sadly. 'Oh, Charles – why did you do it?'

'*Charles?*' Silence cried, with disbelief stark in her voice. 'No – no, that can't be true!'

'It is,' Phoebe said bleakly. 'I had my suspicions, and I made certain enquiries at the castle before I returned here. Charles saw the Lord Chief Justice himself last night. I don't know exactly what accusations he made, but they were obviously serious enough to lead to Alex's arrest.'

'They were the truth,' Charles said, between stiff lips. He had risen to his feet, the book falling forgotten to the floor, and his face was closed and hostile. 'He is a traitor, and I was able to give Jeffreys clear evidence of it.'

'You *betrayed* him? You're no better than a traitor yourself!' Louise cried. She leaped from her chair and strode over to confront him, her hands clenched into fists at her sides, pale with fury. '*Mon Dieu*, Charles, I thought you were my friend!'

'I am,' Charles said. 'That was why – partly why.' His voice roughened suddenly. 'The man's a traitor, a low and despicable rogue – he helped the rebels, why should he not suffer for it, like all the rest? Why should he escape scot-free? He doesn't deserve it – and least of all after what he did to you!'

'To me?' Louise stared at him in astonishment.

Her grandmother interrupted suddenly. 'Explain yourself, Charles. What exactly did Alex do to her?'

'He seduced her,' Charles said baldly, the horror of the night when he had witnessed them together suddenly and appallingly plain in his voice. 'He took her, he exploited her innocence, he dragged her down to his own hideous debauched level –'

'Stop!' Louise said sharply. 'Charles, what are you talking about? It's nonsense – Alex didn't debauch me!'

'Did he seduce you?' Silence asked, and her face seemed to have crumpled suddenly, so that all her years showed plain upon it. 'Louise, please tell me the truth – did he seduce you?'

'No,' she said, her anger making her less tactful than was perhaps wise. 'He did not seduce me. We became lovers by mutual consent, and are still. If you're looking to apportion any blame, then I must share it equally with

Alex. And if you thought that I was innocent until I climbed into his bed, Charles, well then you must be blind, or stupid, or both.' She stared at him, breathing hard, urgent with the desire to do hurt. 'He is not my first lover, nor is he likely to be the last, whatever foolish illusions you might have cherished. This is the *real* world, Charles, not some cloud-cuckoo-land from the pages of a romance!'

'You're lying!' said her cousin. He had gone very pale, save for a spot of scarlet on each cheek, and his voice was hoarse. 'You must be – Louise, tell me it isn't true!'

'I'm sorry if it hurts you,' she told him, in tones that indicated the opposite. 'But I have spoken the plain and unvarnished truth. Alex is my lover, and I was no virgin when I came to Wintercombe. Is that blunt enough for you? Do you wish me to spell it out again?'

'No – *no!*' Charles cried, and put up his hands as if to ward her off. 'I thought – I thought –'

'You regarded me as your rightful property, just like Wintercombe,' Louise said, on a note of discovery. 'And when you realised that Alex possessed me, as well as the house – did your jealousy grow so great that you could not bear it, and betrayed him?'

'No', Charles said desperately. 'No – I did not *betray* him – he's a rebel, he helped them, for God's sake, he gave horses to Monmouth, he even fought for him – *he's* the traitor, not me! I was only doing my duty!'

'Your *duty*? Your idea of duty stinks,' Phoebe said suddenly. 'Would you have done the same if Louise had helped Monmouth? Or me, or Aunt Silence, or Uncle Nick? Of course you wouldn't. You betrayed Alex because you hate him, and you're jealous of him.'

'No, that's not true! It was my duty, I tell you – my duty as a loyal subject of the King.'

'Loyal? You make me sick,' said Phoebe savagely. 'For twenty years you and your mother and sister have had every comfort at Wintercombe – you've been sheltered and clothed and fed and provided for, and still you cannot accept it gracefully, *still* you want more, you want everything – and loyalty to your family means nothing to you when your own profit is at stake! What did Jeffreys promise you? Wintercombe as a reward, and Louise's hand in marriage?'

'I wouldn't have him if he were the last man in England,' said Louise vehemently.

Phoebe stared with loathing at the cousin with whom she had played as a child, with whom she had grown up. 'Alex has his vices, I grant you, but not so very much more than most men – and there is a great deal of good in him, as I have discovered, and no doubt Louise too – and Lukas. He is your *cousin*, Charles, your kin, your flesh and blood –'

'*Is* he?' Charles's wild pale-blue eyes swept round the other people in the parlour, their expressions frozen, appalled. '*Is* he my cousin? Or is he, more likely, some nameless bastard that my uncle's wife foisted on him?'

'You forget yourself.' Silence was on her feet, her face suddenly harsh. 'That is a despicable slur upon my poor sister, who cannot defend herself, and there is not a syllable of truth in it, as you well know –'

'Then why was it whispered all over Somerset, eh?' Charles stared defiantly at his grandmother, whom he had always respected, and who now seemed to be ranged against him with the rest. 'Why did everyone talk about it if it wasn't true? Everyone knew about the dance she led him, how flighty and faithless –'

'That's enough!' Silence was shouting, something she had not done for many, many years. 'Charles, that lie is more revolting than anything else you have said today. My sister Patience was lively, she flirted, she wore fashionable clothes, and if the truth be told she was vain and rather spoilt – but she was also kind, and generous, and she loved Nat very, very dearly. They had ten years of happiness together, marred only by her difficulty in bearing children – she had four miscarriages before Alex was born, then several more afterwards – but she desperately wanted another child, even though Nat tried to dissuade her. He professed himself happy with one, but she insisted, and so Phoebe was born – and in the bearing of her, Patience died.' Silence stared at her grandson, apparently unaware of the tears streaming down her face. 'How dare you – how *dare* you say such things about a woman who died before you were born – repeat such slanders – blacken her name because you want to justify your own heinous deeds. Nat was not stupid – he was a generous man who cared for his family, he knew that Patience had never been unfaithful to him, and although he heard the rumours, and they hurt him, for her sake he never for a moment believed them. Alex is his son, as Phoebe is his daughter, he was kind and good to your mother and you and your sister, beyond all duty – and this, *this* is how you repay him, by vilifying the wife he loved so much?'

Charles stared at her, his mouth working. He made a sound in his throat, and backed away. Silence stood ramrod straight before him, her whole body shaking with emotion. Nick came up to her, and took her very gently in his arms, and abruptly she collapsed, sobbing, against his shoulder.

'I hope you're sorry,' Phoebe said to Charles. 'I hope you regret all the grief and woe you've caused today – I hope you regret it most bitterly. I hope you suffer as much as you've made all of us suffer with your lies and your self-righteousness and hypocrisy. Have you *really* thought of the consequences of this? Have you? You probably didn't look further than getting rid of Alex. What about Bram?'

'What about him?' Charles had found his voice, and it was plain that he had no intention of backing down, even in the face of such an attack. 'He's a traitor too – taken in arms against the King. He deserves whatever he gets, just as Alex does.'

Tabby cried out then, and Jonah exclaimed in horror. Phoebe said furiously, 'Have you thought of what they might do – might have already done? Will they offer him his life, at the cost of betraying Alex?'

'He'd be stupid not to tell them everything,' Charles said.

Louise drew in her breath with a hiss. 'You – you are loathsome –*un salaud, une espèce de merde*! You disgust me, and I feel ashamed that I was ever deceived into thinking that you were my friend – the worst gutter rat has more honour than you! Get out, Charles, go – I don't ever want to speak to you again, and I don't suppose anyone else in this room does either, after what you've done.'

'Louise –' Charles stared at her, stricken, his dream vanished as if it had never existed. 'But Louise, I love you!'

'Love? That's a worthless coin, from you,' she said viciously. 'Here's what I think of your love.'

She spat in his face, and turned away. Charles gave an inarticulate cry, his hand outstretched, and then abruptly, pushing Phoebe aside, ran from the parlour. They heard his feet crash down the stairs, the slam of the door to the street, and he was gone.

'Good riddance,' said Louise, and flung herself down in her chair, her face white with rage. But she knew, as did they all, that although Charles himself might be banished from their lives, the consequences of what he had done would have a direct and terrible impact upon them all.

George Jeffreys, the Lord Chief Justice of England, pronounced sentence upon the Taunton rebels the following afternoon. All five hundred were condemned to death, but only those who had dared to protest their innocence were ordered to be executed on the following Monday. The gallows and fires were being prepared as the assize judges left Taunton for Bristol. For the rest, although under sentence of death, no date was set for their hanging. It seemed as if the promise of mercy, held out to all those who pleaded guilty, might after all be fulfilled.

On the day after the procession of judges, clerks and officials left for Bristol, another coach, under armed escort, rattled away from the castle, bound for London. And inside it, treated with courtesy and respect, but undeniably a prisoner, was Sir Alexander St Barbe, suspected traitor:

although anyone seeing his relaxed, casual demeanour would never have suspected it.

After all, there was nothing he could do. His fate lay in the hands of others now, the cousin who had accused him, the sister whom he trusted to save him, and Bram, who must surely be faced with a ghastly choice, betrayal or death, and could not be blamed if he decided on the first.

He had said goodbye to Louise, although not in the way he would have wished. She had spoken of Charles with such deep disgust that he had no fears that his cousin would ever succeed in resuming friendship with her, let alone make her his wife. She had not wept, nor bemoaned his fate, but given him her dazzling, gallant, fly-away smile, and recklessly kissed him in a way that woke all the familiar, overwhelming passion in them both, to no purpose. But Louise, his sweet Louise, had never been wise, or cautious: she had taken what she wanted from life, with both hands and a carefree heart, and it was that wild quality in her that had first drawn his attention, then aroused his desire.

As she left him, he saw in her eyes the true nature of the feelings that had been awoken in her, and felt a sharp regret that surprised him. His future was clouded and uncertain, his past reprehensible, and she was too young, despite her worldliness and confidence and experience, to waste any unnecessary emotion on a suspected traitor and avowed libertine, nearly ten years her senior. And he realised, now, why Phoebe had warned him that she might be vulnerable.

He wanted her, for her body and her skilled, delightful lovemaking, for her wild laughter and her reckless riding and the way her clothes always seemed ready to slide seductively from her shoulders, and the deeply sensual look in her eyes when she desired him. And the longing and the regret stayed with him, like a shadow, all along the dusty, jolting roads that led to London, and the Tower.

On the twenty-sixth of September, Jeffreys sent to the High Sheriff of Somerset, Edward Hobbes, the list of those tried and condemned at Taunton and at Wells, whom he judged to be deserving of the ultimate penalty for their crimes, two hundred and thirty-nine men in all. The other prisoners, those who had not already died in gaol, were to be transported. Some of the considerable expense involved in suppressing the rebellion could be recouped by selling able-bodied rebels to the owners of plantations and property in the islands of the West Indies, such as Barbados or Jamaica. At a price of ten or fifteen pounds for each man, the eight hundred or so selected were valuable assets.

Bram knew that he must be marked for death. His refusal to inform against Alex, and his commission in Monmouth's army, surely admitted no reprieve. And yet, when the list of those who were to die was announced, the name of Abraham Loveridge was not amongst them.

He could not believe it, but there was no doubt. There were nineteen men ordered to be hung, drawn and quartered at Taunton on the last day of the month, including Captain Hucker, and young John Savage, son of the Red Lion's landlord. The rest of those condemned were to be executed in towns all over Somerset, at Ilminster, Chard, Keynsham, Porlock, Philip's Norton, Yeovil, Dunster and many other places, and their heads and quarters set up on poles there and in the surrounding villages, so that all might see and understand the inevitable result of rebellion. But Bram would not be one of them.

He had escaped death, and yet somehow, strangely enough, he felt almost cheated. It had seemed so certain, and he had prepared himself for it: to be reprieved, and sent to the plantations, seemed an anti-climax by comparison. But, faced with the blessed relief of his parents, he began to accept this different, though perhaps no less lethal fate. He did not know why he had been spared, but after the first hours of astonishment and shock, he was profoundly grateful for this unexpected mercy.

The revelation of Charles's betrayal of Alex had horrified all who had witnessed that furious, illusion-shattering confrontation, and they wished never to speak to him again. He had informed on his cousin for motives of jealousy and greed, and he had spoken of Bram in the most callous terms. He was an outcast, who did not deserve to bear the honourable name of St Barbe.

In his blackest moments, Charles would have been tempted to agree with them. Rejected and despised, he had returned to the Three Cups, removing his belongings from the chamber he had briefly shared with Alex, and taken a room at the George, round the corner in the High Street. There he had spent a miserable evening, going over, again and again, the events of the past few days. He was right – he *knew* he was, as surely as the sun rose in the east. Alex was guilty of the most obnoxious crime of all: he had rebelled against his rightful sovereign, and he would have got away with it, had it not been for Charles's vigilance. Louise, and Wintercombe, had nothing to do with it – nothing at all. He deserved it – he was an unprincipled, lecherous rogue, and hanging was too good for him.

So his thoughts had revolved, round and round, justifying what he had done, denying, because the alternative was too painful to bear, the loathing and the repelled disgust on the faces of the people whom he had known all his life, his cousins, his family, his friends. They were wrong, terribly misguided, deluded by Alex's wayward and deceptive charm. He and he alone saw the truth, the evil behind the easy smile. He was right, he was right, he was *right* . . .

But later, much later, when he was lying on the bed, staring into the darkness, he remembered what Phoebe had said about Bram. At first, he ignored the insistent pricklings of conscience. The boy was a rebel, and must suffer with the rest of them. Why should he escape justice?

But his Aunt Tabby's face, stricken with anguish, rose up to haunt him. She did not share his quarrel; and nor did her son, rebel or no. In vain, his sterner self protested that Bram must be left to his fate, whatever it might be: he could not forget the grief of the boy's family, who might be forced, in a few days' time, to watch their beloved son hanged until he was not quite dead, cut down, disembowelled still living, quartered, his severed head and limbs boiled in pitch to preserve them, and set up within sight of his house, for his mother and sisters to pass by every day . . .

He slept fitfully, and dreamed of it, and woke sweating and shaking, knowing what he must do. He pulled on his clothes, jammed his periwig unceremoniously on his head, and ran down to the street without bothering to shave or to order his breakfast, as if all the devils in hell were after him.

As, in a sense, they were.

But, much later, when he had been passed from guard to official to clerk to Justice and, finally, briefly and blisteringly, to Jeffreys himself, and explained his purpose, he found that the demons of his conscience were quieted. He could not say why it had become so important to him to ensure that Bram did not die. To the Lord Chief Justice, he spun some tale about his cousin perhaps being useful as a witness, and Jeffreys, clearly preoccupied with other matters, seemed to be convinced by the argument. Charles hinted, too, that if Bram were executed, he might not feel obliged to give evidence against Alex. Since the latter was a much bigger fish, he thought that the judge would listen. At any event, whatever happened to Bram now would not be his fault, and he would not be the means of bringing another member of his family to the gallows.

But still the unhappiness persisted, even as he sat in his little chamber at the George. He had assumed that the taste of vengeance would be sweet. At long last, he had obtained some recompense for the years of contempt, of being the poor relation, living on the charity of his uncle, always the object of covert pity. He had done his duty as a loyal subject, and, far from praising his honesty, even those whom he loved best had recoiled in disgust.

Louise . . . was she so hopelessly infatuated that she was lost to him for ever? The memory of her revulsion, the loathing on her face, the way she had spat her contempt, returned again and again to his mind with dreadful clarity, no matter how sternly he tried to suppress it. He did not dare to make any attempt to seek her out, to explain that he had betrayed Alex for her sake as well as his own. But in a few weeks, perhaps, he might try to see her, when she had had the opportunity to think matters over, when some sense, some acknowledgement of the essential rightness of his action would have had the chance to dilute her obstinacy.

For there lay the nub of it. He had betrayed Alex because he hated him, and the cause which he had secretly assisted. But the fruits of that denunciation were as ashes and aloes in his mouth if he no longer possessed the affection and friendship of his Cousin Louise.

They had been marched over the same roads as those they had tramped behind Monmouth's banner, in weather almost as wet, and very much colder: it was now the middle of October. A hundred of the rebels tried at Taunton and languishing in the castle gaol, long after their less fortunate fellows had been executed, had been sold by the King to Sir William Booth, who had business interests in the West Indies. At Bristol, they were to be shipped aboard a converted frigate called the *John*, and transported to the island of Barbados to serve out their ten years as bondservants to whoever would buy them.

It was a dismal fate, but better than that suffered by so many others. Everywhere in Somerset, the pickled and blackened remains of their less fortunate comrades decorated poles, bridges, gates and gibbets, so that it was impossible to travel more than a few miles without seeing the anonymous, mutilated quarter or head of a man with whom they had fought.

The sentence of transportation had fallen upon some prisoners like a death blow. To leave wives and families to probable destitution, and be shipped an unimaginable distance across the seas to slave in some sugar plantation for ten years, alongside black men, under a hostile sun and in a climate which killed large numbers, was for many only a lingeringly cruel method of execution.

But although Bram's parents and sisters were grief-stricken at the prospect of losing him to such a fate, they knew that it could have been very much worse. And Bram himself felt surprisingly optimistic. The tumultuous events of the past three months had changed him, he knew, in ways which his family could not even guess. They wanted their son and brother back, and life to continue as if Monmouth had never existed, but that was impossible. After what he had seen and experienced, he could never return in comfort to that cosy, quiet, limited little existence. And even if he died in Barbados, he would have seen a little more of the world than many.

He had tried to explain to them, but only Louise, perhaps, had understood, for she shared that restlessness, that thirst for things new and different, that had afflicted him over the past months. It was she who suggested to Jonah and Tabby that money be found to ensure that their son arrived in Barbados a free man, even if he could not leave the island for ten years. Booth's agent in the West Country proved amenable to bribery, and Jonah, who had never been particularly wealthy, scraped together as much as he could. The sum of sixty pounds would buy Bram's liberty: and as his father handed it over, he saw the agent's greedy, venal smile, and prayed desperately that the heavy bag of coin would in fact do all that he had been promised.

They said goodbye to him in Taunton Castle, with tears and many wishes of good luck, but Bram, in surprising contrast to the lamentations of his family, was cheerful and philosophical. He was clever, resourceful, and educated. Surely, in the exciting new world of Barbados, he could use his gifts and skills, his strength and youth, to rise to a position of wealth and power that would be impossible in Taunton.

So, almost alone amongst the dreary, demoralised men around him, he sniffed the salt-laden air of Bristol with eagerness, and stepped gladly aboard the *John*, his scant belongings in a box on his shoulder, and a secret store of coin sewn into his belt by Sue's careful, loving hand. Even the sight of his Aunt and Uncle Orchard, with Libby, stricken and weeping, watching from the quayside, could not temper his enthusiasm. His voyage to Barbados was no longer a punishment: it represented a challenge, the chance to prove himself, a new life dazzling in its possibilities, and perhaps, who knew, a fortune at the end of it.

He had a smile and a wave for Libby, but no more; and as the *John* turned her bows to the west and the open sea, he did not look back to England, and home, and family, but forward, to the unknown and enticing future.

# 26

## 'Hireling witnesses'

The fate of one prisoner was settled, but that of the other still hung in the balance. Phoebe had told Louise not to worry, that nothing would be moved against Alex for some time, but the month that elapsed between his arrest and Bram's departure from Taunton seemed to pass agonisingly slowly, even though there was much to distract her, for the business of arranging Bram's freedom in Barbados took a great deal of time and much discussion.

Although the voyage would be arduous and his life hard, even if the sixty-pound bribe was effective, he was so confident, and so endearingly enthusiastic about the unknown hazards that lay before him, that she could set aside most of her worries. Bram would survive; and after the dark days of prison and idleness, when Ben's death had weighed so heavily on his mind, the change in him was very welcome.

And then Jonah was summoned to the castle, and told that his daughters, Susan and Hannah, having committed an act of sedition by working the colours and presenting them to Monmouth, must face punishment like all the other rebels. To his heartfelt relief, it was not proposed that any of the girls be incarcerated in Taunton Gaol, which was still desperately overcrowded, despite the removal of so many men for execution. But in order to qualify them for a pardon, their parents some wealthy, the rest comfortably well-off, and of Whig or Dissenting persuasion – must pay a ransom to the Queen's Maids of Honour. The sum of two hundred pounds for each daughter was mentioned, to Jonah's absolute horror: to raise twice that sum, to pay the fine for both Sue and Hannah, he would need to sell his shop and his livelihood.

Fortunately, he was not the only father in such a position, and the mayor told him, with a meaningful smile, that the sum was in any case open to negotiation. 'It is not our intention to beggar you, Master Loveridge, merely to remind you of the necessity of rearing your daughters to a proper respect for the King's authority.'

But the threat of such a large fine nevertheless hung over the Loveridge family, yet another twist to the rope of agony binding them all together: Bram's sentence, Alex's arrest, and now this: no wonder, Louise thought

433

with pity, that Jonah seemed to have aged ten years in the past few weeks, bent by the cares that his children had unwittingly inflicted on him. Even Tabby, a much stronger and more forceful character, had lost much of her usual resilience, and her attempts to maintain calm, order and routine in her fraught household had an air of desperation.

Once it became certain that Bram would not be executed, Phoebe consulted with Silence, Nick and Louise, and decided to return as soon as possible to Wintercombe, where poor Lukas, who had not wanted to be left behind in the care of his nurse, would have to be told about the arrest of his beloved father. There was also her urgent need to discover what inquisitions, if any, had been conducted amongst the servants and the people of the village. And if any money were needed to save Alex, she would need the help of Philip Cousins, the St Barbes' lawyer, to collect as much as she could.

Besides, Charles had disappeared. He had spent only two nights at the George, and by the time Nick managed to trace him, he had left. He was nowhere in Taunton, so far as they could discover. Either he had gone to London, to further his accusations against Alex, or to Wintercombe, to take possession in his cousin's absence. And if the latter, Phoebe wanted to follow him there as quickly as possible, to assert her own authority and to try to undo any damage which he might already have done.

Louise was tempted to go with her, but knew that she should stay with her grandparents. The revelation that she had become Alex's lover had, obviously, struck Silence very deep. Louise could not be ashamed of what she had done, but she did feel more than a twinge of guilt. Her grandmother had been entrusted with her care, and charged with the task of finding her a husband. And she, Louise, had betrayed the faith that she had asked Silence to put in her, and entered into a passionate and hopeless affair with, probably, the most unsuitable man in all Somerset. Small wonder that her grandmother's expression, when she looked at her, was full of hurt disappointment.

But that did not assuage the desperate longing she felt, in the first days without Alex. Her body, bereft and lonely, craved his warmth, and the inflammable touch of his hands, and the feverish desire to which even his presence in the same room seemed to arouse her. She could not sleep, and she was not hungry, for food and drink had no savour. She lost weight, and her mirror, implacably honest, showed her the dark rings under her eyes, the hollows in her cheeks, the sallowness of her complexion, and the starkly hopeless look in her eyes, in painful contrast to her previously lively manner. Even if that mythical, suitable husband did appear from the woodwork, he would not give her a second glance.

Worst of all was the feeling of helplessness, the bitter knowledge that, whatever she did, Alex would still languish in prison, that she was over a hundred miles away, unable to see or to speak with him, as if he were already dead.

And Charles, who had, appallingly, done this dreadful thing for her sake, had also vanished. So she could not, as she had first imagined, seek him out and beg him to reconsider, to abandon his evidence, to do whatever was necessary to ensure Alex's safety.

When Phoebe had left, Louise agreed to Silence's suggestion that she return with them to Chard. It was not far away, and it was plain that Jonah and Tabby, while grateful for their help and support, would appreciate some little time to devote to themselves and their daughters, without having to think always of their guests.

But of course, going to Chard meant that, sooner or later, she would be faced with something that, so far, she had managed to avoid: a confidential talk with her grandmother.

It came in the lovely walled garden lying on the southern side of the house, that over the past thirty years had been Silence's joy and creation. Now, in the second week in October, it was already beginning to look bare and dead with the coming winter, and recent rain had not improved things. But the brown-edged foliage and damp, earthy, melancholy smell had suited Louise's unhappy mood, and she had taken to walking along the gravelled paths, thinking of Alex, and Bram, and all the extraordinary events of the past three months. Sometimes her little cousin, Nicholas, who was now two and a half, accompanied her, chatting happily of childish matters, but more often she was alone, save for her memories.

So far, in the week she had spent at Chard, she had managed to avoid encountering Silence alone. But now, when she turned a corner by the far wall, she saw her grandmother, pruning knife in hand and a basket by her side, kneeling by a rather bedraggled knot full of rose bushes.

For an instant, she checked, and then walked briskly forward. This confrontation was inevitable, and the longer she postponed it, the more she would dread it. And, after all, she was the transgressor, and it was her guilty conscience that shied away from an intimate discussion. Nor was Silence an ogre, although somehow that only made her granddaughter's misdeeds worse.

I am not ashamed, Louise reminded herself. I am an adult, not a child, and prey to adult passions and emotions. My affair with Alex was no sordid seduction, and I walked into it with my eyes open. And although I am sorry for the distress I have caused her, if I had the chance, I would do it all over again, and gladly.

'Hullo, Gran'mère,' she said, stopping by the basket.

Silence laid a prickly branch down on the heap, and looked up with a smile. 'Ah, Louise. Could you help me up, do you think? Once I kneel for more than a few minutes, my joints seem to lock into that position.'

Louise bent, took the outstretched arm, and lent her support as Silence rose. 'I can almost hear everything creaking. The worst thing about growing old is that I don't *feel* ancient – I feel no more than thirty-five or so.' She surveyed her granddaughter, her eyes narrowed against the sun, and the girl returned the scrutiny calmly. 'You don't look well, Louise. Are you sleeping properly?'

'Yes,' she lied, with the memory of the lonely, miserable nights spent tossing in her comfortable bed treacherously fresh in her mind.

'I don't believe you,' Silence commented. She paused, and then added gently, 'I do know what it is like, to pine for someone. Do you love him?'

'Alex?'

'Well, I don't mean the King of England,' said her grandmother tartly. 'Of course I mean Alex. Do you love him?'

'Yes, Gran'mère, I do,' Louise told her quietly. Honesty compelled her to add, 'But I don't think that his feelings are as . . . strong as mine.'

'That's not the point, at present. Was what you told Charles the truth? That Alex is not your first lover?'

Louise took a deep breath, and slowly shook her head. 'No, Gran'mère, he is not. My mother sent me here to avoid scandal in France.'

'And did you love that man, too?'

Only the truth was possible, whatever Silence might think of her. She said, 'No. Not as I love Alex. I desired him, and he desired me, and . . . I wanted to learn.'

'I see,' Silence said. She brushed a stray leaf from the sleeve of her old black gown, and added reflectively, 'I wish that Kate had told me more of this. I might have been . . . better prepared.' She glanced at her granddaughter, and smiled suddenly. 'Protecting a shy young virgin is a very different matter from guarding an experienced woman of the world. How many people know that you and Alex are lovers?'

'Before I admitted it to you all . . . only Charles, and Phoebe, and Alex's manservant, who is very discreet, and speaks very little English. We were very careful, Gran'mère – I didn't want Charles to know, and I still can't understand how he found out. Phoebe guessed, though – she's very perceptive.'

'Then your reputation, if it still matters to you, remains intact?'

'As far as I am aware, yes,' Louise told her. She hesitated, and then added, 'To be honest, I don't really care about my reputation any more. If I can't have Alex . . .'

'You don't want anyone else? No husband, home, children? Or is an uncertain future as his mistress, always supposing that he survives, enough for you?'

Louise shut her eyes. She said, very softly, 'It doesn't matter – can you understand, nothing matters except the hours we are together, because there may not be a future?' To her horror, she felt tears pricking her eyes. She must not, must *not* break down: she never cried, this was ridiculous.

'As it happens,' Silence said, 'I understand very well. I'm sure you know what happened forty years ago . . . Love may strike where we least expect it, and come to rule our lives in a way we could never dream of. Alex is not the man I would have chosen for you, but if you truly love him, I cannot condemn you, for that would be hypocritical in the extreme. What distresses me is that perhaps he has taken advantage of your feelings to indulge his lust.'

'No!' Louise said vehemently. She smacked her fist into the palm of her hand. 'No, that's not what happened. If – if you want the plain, shocking truth, Gran'mère, the lust was not on his side alone, not at all. And it was only afterwards that I realised I was in love with him . . . He is not so wicked as you all seem to think.'

'Oh, dear,' Silence said, after a pause. 'You do have it badly . . . I know that too, Louise. Oh, Alex can be exceedingly difficult, and there are times when I positively detest him, and I suspect that he virtually pushed poor Charles into acting as he did. He is far too clever for his own good, he can't resist meddling and manipulating – and in that, he's exactly like his mother – and as a boy he indulged in all sorts of bad habits which he hasn't been able to break – not that it seems he's tried very hard, mind you. But he loves Lukas, and Wintercombe, and he will manage his inheritance very capably, if he is allowed to.' She looked compassionately at Louise, who had succeeded in beating back the shaming tears. 'But don't, please, nourish any thoughts of trying to change him or reform him. Part of Alex will always be a drunken wencher, I suspect.'

Louise managed a smile. 'I know. I don't want to change him, don't worry.' She might have added that nothing would matter, so long as she could hold his heart: but she had no wish to appear foolish.

'Just as well – it would be a thankless task,' Silence said drily. 'We seem to understand each other tolerably well, I think, don't you? And I feel that you realise that there is very little prospect of him making an honest woman of you – unless . . .'

437

Her voice trailed away, and Louise looked at her curiously. 'Unless what?'

'Unless you are expecting his child,' her grandmother said bluntly. 'Are you?'

Louise sustained her scrutiny calmly. 'Not so far as I am aware. It may be possible that I am barren, Gran'mère – I have had two lovers without conceiving, after all. But even if I were – I don't – I *don't* want him to offer me marriage because of that. I'd rather die a spinster.' She smiled rather bleakly. 'I think he would feel that I had trapped him.'

'Well, in that case, let us hope that you do not become pregnant, for then your reputation will be tattered beyond all redemption,' Silence observed. 'But if it ever does happen, then you may yet change your mind, rather than lose him for ever. It surely can't have escaped your notice, or his, that if he were to acquire a legitimate heir, Charles's plans and pretensions would be destroyed for good.'

Louise stared at her in surprise. 'Do you *want* me to marry him?'

'I want what is best for you, and Alex – and Charles, despite what he has done. But of course, we are talking as if Alex were still a free agent. I doubt very much that he will be allowed to marry anyone while in prison, let alone produce an heir to rob Charles of his reward.' She gave Louise an encouraging smile. 'But there is much that we can do to help him, and Phoebe has already begun. As soon as she has gathered sufficient resources, she will go to London to try and negotiate his release. I know that the King's officers have been ferocious in their vengeance – Chard looks like a charnel-house, it's disgusting and barbaric and inhuman – but by now passions in Whitehall may have cooled. And I think that anyone's freedom will be available – at the right price. Kings are always short of money, and His Majesty must have incurred considerable expense putting down the rebellion. Moreover, I can't imagine that the evidence against Alex is very strong. The one who might have testified most damningly is Bram, and he has said nothing, although they questioned him very closely. He has been lucky, very lucky, to be transported, terrible though such a sentence is – but, thank God, someone seems to have been merciful. Perhaps Charles had some influence.'

Louise made a scornful noise. 'Charles! That viper doesn't know what mercy is!'

Silence looked at her sadly. 'Perhaps not. But it is Alex whom he hates. It's possible that he could not face the thought that another cousin might die because of him.'

'I doubt it – you heard what he said. To him, Bram is just a traitor who deserves any punishment, however brutal. To think that I once looked on

438

him as a friend – ugh, he sickens me! I hope I never see him again.'

'I received a letter from Phoebe, this morning,' Silence said. 'She says that he did indeed go to Wintercombe, but has now left, she does not know where – London, perhaps. Apparently, the sheriff's men were making enquiries among the servants, and in Philip's Norton, but failed to find anyone who would testify against Alex. They may have discovered someone among the rebel prisoners, of course, but at least no one else who knows him is prepared to betray him. The house was searched, though, and they took away many books and papers – let us hope that Alex has been careful enough not to leave anything that will incriminate him.' She looked at Louise's anxious face, and added, 'I think that we should go to London, too. Phoebe said that she would leave this week, and she will need all our support and assistance – and I suspect that Alex, however self-sufficient and careless he may appear, will appreciate it too.' She smiled at her granddaughter. 'So, with luck, you will see him soon. Will that restore your sleep?'

And to her own distress, Louise, overwrought and exhausted, embraced Silence and burst into thankful tears.

She had never been to London, although she was familiar with Paris. In ordinary circumstances, she would have longed to see Whitehall and Westminster, the great houses, the fashionable, teeming shops, the gallants, the theatres and pleasure-grounds and all the entertainments to divert her, the luxuries and adornments to be purchased. But there was only one reason why the weeks until their departure from Chard dragged so slowly, why the journey in the hired coach along the hills and valleys of Dorset and Wiltshire, Hampshire and Surrey, seemed to take an eternity, although in fact it was only ten days. Every delay – the weather was wet, the roads bad, the horses unreliable – only served to increase her impatience, until by the time they drove past the enclosure of Hyde Park, full of elegant ladies and gentlemen taking the air, in coaches, on foot or on horseback, she could hardly believe that they had almost, at long last, reached their destination, and Alex.

Phoebe, accompanied by Lukas, her maid Mattie, and Philip Cousins, had already been in London for a fortnight. In that time, news had travelled back and forth over the long miles between Chard and the capital, keeping everyone informed. Phoebe would know that Bram had now embarked for Barbados, apparently a free man, and full of hope for his future. Her own letters had described her journey to London, the lodgings in Westminster, close to the Court at Whitehall, which she had managed to obtain after some difficulty, and her efforts to discover exactly

439

what was to happen to Alex. He was held in the Tower, where several other important men connected with the rebellion had also been imprisoned while the parts they had played were investigated. His rooms were pleasant, he was allowed liberty to walk along the Tower walls every day, and his servant, Gerrit, had ridden from Wintercombe to attend him. Phoebe reported that he had been allowed books and other comforts, and seemed in good spirits, and infuriatingly unconcerned about his fate.

Phoebe, of course, had been far more anxious, and had made strenuous efforts on his behalf. In this, she had apparently been very fortunate, for the gentleman who owned the house in which she had found lodgings was one of the King's courtiers, and had proved to be surprisingly sympathetic, and helpful. However, he had not yet been able to obtain for her an audience with His Majesty, nor had Jeffreys, now made Lord Chancellor in recognition for his loyal and zealous support of his royal master, agreed to see her. As for Charles, she had no idea where he might be.

There was, in short, very little hope of a speedy resolution to Alex's plight, and his sister had been told that, if matters progressed at the usual pace, he would not be brought to trial before the spring. But at least he was in no immediate danger, and the time could be spent in trying to obtain his release or pardon by any possible means.

The streets of Westminster were crowded, and their hired coach could hardly force a way through the press. Several times the coachman had to ask for directions to Bell Court, where Phoebe's lodgings were situated. At last, however, he found it, just before the Palace of Whitehall. It was a rather narrow alley off King Street, and not nearly wide enough to admit the coach. Nick got out to investigate, while the traffic, hackneys, coaches, sedans, horsemen, waggons, carts, ebbed and flowed and cursed all around them.

The journey had been exhausting, but both women peered curiously through the mud-splashed glass. Silence had been born and reared in London, but she had left at nineteen, and had returned only a few times since, to visit her brother and sister who had stayed. Her life was in Somerset, and the packed streets, the noise and bustle and rush that had once been her environment, as natural and appropriate as a fish in the sea, now seemed alien, almost threatening. As for Louise, London, once, had represented everything she wanted from life: excitement, adventure, clothes, dancing, shops, society, all the empty, giddy whirl she had enjoyed so much in France. Now she realised with surprise that she could enter Whitehall tonight, resplendent in silk and jewels, and it would mean nothing to her if she could not dance with Alex, see the promise and desire and need in his eyes . . .

A vast longing filled her suddenly, to feel his touch again, and his voice in her hair, rough with passion. Tomorrow, she told herself fiercely, clenching her fists. Tomorrow, we will go to the Tower, Phoebe can arrange it – and I will see him again.

'Found it,' said Nick, putting his head in through the window. 'It's only two doors down the court. There's an inn over the way that will take the coach – if you would care to disembark, if that is the right word, Phoebe is waiting for you.'

The lodgings proved to be a suite of rooms on the first floor of quite a substantial building, fairly new and brick-built, in contrast to the crooked, low, half-timbered and elderly houses which comprised much of Bell Court. The main parlour, with tall windows looking out on to the alley, was comfortably but plainly furnished, with yellow silk hangings, and an air of cheerfulness.

London had made little difference to Phoebe's style, or lack of it. Her only concession to fashion, and perhaps the chill weather outside, was a fur tippet, apparently new, hiding her thin shoulders. Underneath, she wore, as ever, a simple dark grey gown. She stood at the door of the parlour, smiling, as her aunt, uncle and cousin climbed the stairs to meet her. 'Did you have a terrible journey? Come in and warm yourselves, and Mattie will find refreshments for you. And there are two people I would like you to meet.'

Louise saw the small, familiar figure of Lukas, sitting in one corner with another boy, a little older, with very fair hair. As soon as he saw her, he leaped to his feet, and ran across to greet her. Halfway, he remembered his manners, stopped, and bowed very low, while the other child, also mindful of etiquette, rose more decorously and did likewise. Lukas gave her a smile that was a dazzling, heartbreaking replica of his father's. 'Hullo, Cousin Louise. I'm glad you're here.'

'So am I,' she said, and held out her arms, and with an abrupt return to childhood, he ran into her embrace.

Phoebe made the necessary introductions. 'My aunt and uncle, Master Nicholas Hellier, Mistress Silence Hellier. My cousin, Mistress Louise Chevalier. The gentleman of the King's, whose house this is – I told you of him in my letter. Sir Hugh Trevelyan.'

The courtier who had proved so helpful and sympathetic to Phoebe was a tall man, well built and exceedingly richly dressed, with a preposterous yellow periwig in the latest style, golden ringlets hanging down his back. Louise could not guess his age, save that he was probably not as young as he appeared. But his smile was warm, and friendly, and she knew Phoebe for an excellent judge of character. This elegant and exotic peacock had obviously won her confidence.

A maid brought chocolate, steaming and fragrant and very welcome, and sundry cakes and sweetmeats, and the travellers took their seats in comfort by the roaring fire. At first, the conversation turned on trivial matters: the difficulties of the journey from Somerset, the weather, the crowded Westminster streets, and the happy coincidence that had brought together Phoebe and Lukas, in need of lodgings near Whitehall and access to the Court, with Sir Hugh, who could offer both of these, and friendly support besides. The fair-haired boy was his son, nearly eight years old, called James, and very like his father, with the same long, amused grey-green eyes. Silence, complimenting the courtier on the child's looks and manners, asked if he had more.

An expression of sadness and regret entered Sir Hugh's easy-going face. 'Alas, no, Mistress Hellier. My dear wife Susannah died three years ago, bearing his brother, who also died, and since then James and I have been alone. Usually, he lives with my niece in the country, in Suffolk, but every so often they send him up to London to plague me.' He glanced at James, and his fondness for the boy was plain. 'In fact, it was he who brought your niece and Lukas to my attention – the two boys struck up a friendship by the pond in the park, and James suggested to me that Mistress St Barbe could lodge with us, instead of the inn where she was staying. So not only do I now have someone to fill these echoing rooms, but James has a companion.'

'It's a situation of great benefit to them both,' Phoebe said. She too glanced at the two boys, who had a set of crudely carved wooden soldiers, and had lined them up on the floor in something approaching battle order. They were utterly absorbed in the game, and she turned back to the others. 'Poor Lukas is very distressed about his father. He can't understand the situation at all, and he often cries himself to sleep. James's company can distract him during the day, but at night . . .' She shrugged. 'To make matters worse, they hanged twelve men in Philip's Norton, in the field behind the Fleur-de-Lys, and hung their remains up on poles everywhere, in all the villages – only a blind person could avoid seeing them. It affected him very deeply – you know how thoughtful and sensitive he is. Now he thinks that Alex will suffer the same fate, and no amount of reasoning can persuade him otherwise.'

'Poor Lukas,' said Louise, sadly. The child was only six years old, but already he had seen far too much of life's cruelties and injustice. 'For his sake, if nothing else, we must obtain Alex's freedom.'

'Is it likely?' Silence asked, looking at Sir Hugh. 'You obviously know my nephew's situation, and you must also be close to the King and to the Lord Chancellor. What chance of freedom does he have?'

The courtier spread his hands. 'At present, Mistress Hellier, I cannot say. As you must be aware, His Majesty is very hot against all rebels, and my suspicion is that it was he, and not Chancellor Jeffreys, who was determined to enforce the full rigour of the law against all who joined Monmouth. And in particular, any one of them who held a position of power, or wealth, or authority. Your nephew is a baronet, of an ancient and well-respected family, and possessed of a considerable estate. In His Majesty's eyes, such men are the more dangerous because they can command the loyalty of many lesser men, and are therefore more deserving of severe punishment. At the moment, from what I can discover, there is little firm evidence against Sir Alexander, although a great deal of suspicion, largely because of his past activities. And, unfortunately, the history of the St Barbes has also played a part – they have a reputation for favouring Dissenters, and Sir Alexander's grand-father was a Roundhead colonel, I understand. Unjust though it may seem, such matters do influence and colour people's prejudices.'

It was plain, from his tone of voice, that he did not necessarily agree with, or even support, his royal master. Her curiosity getting the better of her, Louise said, 'Please tell me, Sir Hugh – why are you willing to help us?'

The older man looked at her, and his long eyes crinkled suddenly with amusement. 'It would not, perhaps, be altogether wise, or discreet, to tell you. Indeed, sometimes I am not completely sure myself. But suffice it to say that although I have served His Majesty loyally for many years, while he was Duke of York, I dislike injustice. And when a charming lady begs me for help, how can I possibly refuse?'

'In that case,' said Phoebe tartly, 'I can't imagine why you agreed. But I'm exceedingly grateful for your assistance, even though it seems at present as if we are both battering our hopes against a wall. Alex is in the Tower still, but perfectly well, and apparently quite unworried by his situation. He has been frequently questioned, of course, but so far his interrogators seem to be losing the battle.' She grinned suddenly. 'Alex could always argue the hind legs from a donkey. He has staunchly maintained his complete innocence, and very convincingly, so Sir Hugh has heard. If that alone could obtain his freedom, he would walk from the Tower tomorrow.'

'But it can't,' Nick said thoughtfully. 'There is Charles to consider. Is he here, in London?'

'I don't know,' Phoebe told him. 'We have tried to find him, but without success. It's possible he may still be in the West Country, but unlikely, I think. Of course, he will be the most important witness for the King. Even if all his accusations are pure conjecture, without any solid evidence to

443

back them, he loathes Alex so much that he will be eager to testify against him.'

'I thought that a second witness was needed, in cases of treason,' Nick said.

'Yes, so Philip Cousins assures me. But it's not absolutely necessary if there is other evidence. Algernon Sidney was convicted because of what he had written, as much as by the testimony of witnesses. They searched Wintercombe, as I told you, before I returned from Taunton, and apparently they took books and papers from Alex's chamber, and from the library. Even if those are trivial pamphlets and the like that wouldn't normally rouse suspicion, they may assume considerable importance when used as evidence against him, together with everything else. It's like building a house of cards – using fragile, flimsy things to construct something elaborate and out of all proportion to their real worth.'

'And like a house of cards, one puff of truth and common sense may bring the whole edifice crashing to the floor,' Sir Hugh remarked. 'And, so far, the case against your brother seems to be exceedingly insubstantial. If, as you say, his cousin's greed and malice have provided the motive for these accusations, then all the more reason to expose them for what they are. It is a great pity that we haven't managed to track down Master Charles St Barbe.'

'I'm sure he's here,' Louise said. 'Unless he's trying to find some rebel who hasn't yet been transported, to bear witness against Alex. Thank God Bram is out of his reach!'

'If he succeeds in finding a second witness, then, I warn you, the situation will become much more serious,' Sir Hugh pointed out. 'But it might be possible, even so, for Sir Alexander to be freed without trial. Once the King's anger has had time to settle, he will be more amenable to pleas for mercy or reprieve. And . . .' he coughed drily, and glanced round at the company '. . . the late rebellion cost His Majesty dear, and many did him loyal service who have not yet been adequately rewarded. If some recompense were to be offered . . .'

'You mean a bribe,' said Phoebe bluntly, and roused his smile. 'Yes, Mistress St Barbe, although my courtier's sensibility forbids me to mention so indelicate a matter so plainly. But certainly there are many of influence in Whitehall who would be willing to put your brother's case to the King, in the hope of monetary gain.' He saw Silence's disapproving face, and added quickly, 'It is not a pretty practice, Mistress Hellier, and I do not condone it – I am merely acknowledging its existence. And let me make it quite clear that I will seek no reward for myself in this. If His Majesty should prove obdurate, you will need all the coin you can lay your hands on.'

444

'It's as well that I have made some provision,' said Phoebe grimly. 'Don't worry, Aunt, I did not bring the family wealth clinking in a treasure chest in the coach for the first highwayman to appropriate. Master Cousins has arranged for funds to be made available through a goldsmith and banker in Cheapside – in fact, that is where he is now, drawing some money for our expenses.' She glanced at Sir Hugh. 'If all you say is true, we shall need a great deal more in due course. But to free Alex, I shall do all that is necessary.'

For someone who had always, in the past, professed to dislike her brother, her voice was remarkably sincere. But Louise, whose opinions had also been transformed – and lust was very different from liking – knew that she meant what she said. If nothing else, the terrible events that had overtaken them all had brought Alex and Phoebe to acknowledge their mutual affection, even if they had also sundered all civilised connection between Alex and Charles.

Somehow, she must find Charles, and speak to him. Phoebe had already done her utmost to help her brother, and would continue to do so until he was free. But she, Louise, had other methods which she could employ. Despite her loathing and contempt for Charles, she suspected that he was still in love with her. Such an obsession, as she had good cause to know, was not easily abandoned or forgotten. And if that was so, then she must still possess some power over him, be able to influence him, perhaps to persuade him . . .

But there was something that she must do first. She wanted to visit Alex, because the longing and the hunger had grown almost too great to bear, and she had missed him more than she had ever suspected that she would. And she wanted, too, to see the expression in his eyes when she walked into his presence, for only then, perhaps, would she know how great his own need for her had been.

She knew, realistically, that he would never love her. But desire, longing, affection, tenderness, were almost as good. Almost, but not quite. And it was her mistake, for she had fallen in love with a man whose nature did not admit of such feelings. So far, she had persuaded herself that what they already shared was sufficient for her needs. But soon, she suspected unhappily, it would no longer be enough. And in demanding of him something that he could not give her, she would probably drive him away for ever.

But still, like Phoebe, she would do whatever lay in her power to free him from the threat of death.

She looked up at Alex's sister, and said quietly, 'Is it possible for us to visit him?'

'I should think so,' Phoebe told her. 'Sir Hugh obtained permission for me and Lukas and Master Cousins to see him whenever we wished, and I expect he could do the same for anyone.'

'Within reason,' the courtier pointed out. 'But the Earl of Sunderland, who is the principal secretary of state, deals with such matters on the King's behalf. I regret to say that, like most, he and his officials will require some payment for the privilege, but I see no reason why it should not be granted. It will, however, take a day or two to arrange. In the mean time, I suggest that you take the opportunity to explore London, and all it has to offer.'

The city was a very poor substitute for Alex, but it would be pointless to complain about something that could not be altered, or hurried. And, Louise thought, with sudden eagerness, perhaps the time could be usefully employed in trying to find Charles. For, it was plain, he was the basis of that tottering house of cards. Remove his testimony, and the case against Alex would collapse into nothing.

As it happened, Charles St Barbe rode into London the next day. He had spent much time in Wells, where exhaustive enquiries and interrogations had eventually produced a man who had been in Bram Loveridge's troop, and who was prepared to state on oath that he had seen Sir Alexander St Barbe fighting with the rebels at Philip's Norton. That man, one Taylor, had been promised the King's pardon for his information, and had been despatched to London under escort, for further examination. And Charles, the other witness, went with him, jubilant.

He left behind, at Wintercombe, his mother and sister, in a state of considerable distress. He had hoped to spare them many of the more sordid details of his activities, but that had proved impossible. The search of Wintercombe, courteous but thorough, had alarmed and angered Bab, whose own chamber had not been sacrosanct, and Amy had been very distressed by the news that Alex was in prison, and still more so when she learned that her brother's evidence had put him there. Phoebe, returning to Wintercombe a few days after Charles, had made sure that everyone knew of his betrayal, and to his anger and dismay he found his attempts to assume the management of the house and estate thwarted by the crippled, intellectual cousin whom he had always tended to dismiss from his calculations. She was clever, damnably so, for she had a paper, signed by Alex and verified by the family's lawyer, making Wintercombe temporarily over to her. Faced with that, and the hostility and resentment of the servants, all of whom, incredibly, seemed to have taken Alex's part, and had refused to incriminate him, he had no choice for the moment but to leave.

The discovery of Jem Taylor had been some small recompense for the frustration of his hopes at Wintercombe. Taylor, already doomed to transportation, had no wish to go to Barbados, and talked eagerly and volubly. He knew Sir Alexander by sight: he had seen him first on the march between Bath and Philip's Norton, speaking most earnestly to Cornet Loveridge, who had shortly afterwards led a group of men, including Taylor, to Wintercombe, to seize horses. The conclusion, reached by Taylor as well as Charles, was obvious: there had been a plot between the two men to make it appear that Sir Alexander was being forced to surrender the horses, whereas in fact he was quite willing to do so.

Not for the first time, Charles cursed the officials at Taunton, who had sent Bram for transportation. It would undoubtedly have been better if he had been left to languish in gaol, as he had suggested, with plenty of time to contemplate his gloomy future, and the promise of a free pardon to tempt him into submission. But while Charles had been scouring the West Country for another witness, in case Bram still proved obstinate, his young cousin's name had been put down for transportation. By the time that Charles had discovered the mistake, it was too late – the boy was already at sea aboard the *John*, out of reach, and they would have to construct their case without his testimony.

But at least he did have his second witness, and Taylor would be invaluable. Most damningly of all, he had actually seen Alex in the thick of the fighting, in front of the barricade at the end of North Street. It was the opinion of the Justice who examined him that he would make a convincing witness. He had already seen Sir Alexander twice, after all, and his identification was absolutely certain. Charles, exultant, could have hugged the rebel, filthy and unsavoury and stinking though he was. Taylor had provided the proof that he needed, and although hardly impressive in manner or appearance, there was no doubt that he was telling the truth.

With a joyful heart, Charles left Wells with his precious witness, and headed for London, and, at last, his longed-for, long-planned vengeance against the cousin who had so often humiliated him.

447

# 27

# 'A pardon might be won'

The Tower of London had a sinister past and a bloodstained present. It was only three months since James Scott, late Duke of Monmouth, and a prisoner within its walls, had been messily executed on Tower Hill. Despite the cheerful November sunlight, the place seemed full of menace, and Louise knew that it still contained many men of quality, imprisoned, like Alex, on suspicion of treason.

The order allowing her and her grandparents access to him had been signed the day after their arrival in London, through the good offices of Sir Hugh Trevelyan. His reasons for such apparently altruistic assistance still puzzled Louise. Had it been anyone other than Phoebe, she would immediately have suspected that he intended to worm his way into her affections. But Phoebe, plain, acerbic, intellectual and crippled, was no languishing lady ripe for romance, and besides, Sir Hugh was probably fifteen years her senior. But there must, surely, be some hidden motive for his kindness and generosity. Men of his sort, she knew full well, did not concern themselves with such affairs unless they perceived some advantage to themselves in so doing.

But she did like Sir Hugh: he was an engaging man, lazy, good-natured, but with a cynical sense of humour that made her laugh. He did not take himself in the least seriously, and his dry, deprecating wit had the effect of deflating any exalted illusions she might have harboured concerning life at Court. His son, James, was a kind child – not normally an attribute of small boys – who seemed quite happy to play with Lukas and thereby distract his thoughts from the perilous situation in which Alex stood.

They went to the Tower by river, hiring a boat at Westminster Stairs. It was, explained Phoebe, who after nearly three weeks in London seemed to have become very well acquainted with city life, much quicker, more convenient and pleasant than the same journey in a hackney through the crowded streets – so long as it did not rain. In common with most prudent passengers, they disembarked at the Old Swan stairs, just before London Bridge, for the river, forcing its way between the huge piers, was so fast and turbulent that 'shooting the bridge' when the tide was flowing could be extremely dangerous.

Public hackneys were everywhere, shabby but convenient, and they hired one for the rest of the way to the Tower, although it was only half a mile or so. Normally, this encounter with London at close quarters would have exulted Louise, but even the river journey, with splendid views of the new, brick-built city that had risen phoenix-like from the ashes of the Fire nearly twenty years previously, had failed to rouse her from her preoccupied mood.

She had not seen Alex for seven weeks, but time and distance had failed to diminish the power of his image in her mind, or the strength of her feelings for him. She wanted to see him, yes, most desperately, but in private, not under the interested gaze of her grandparents and his sister, all of whom were doubtless intensely curious about the exact nature of their liaison. Nor could she rid herself of the fear that nearly two months of separation might have cooled his ardour. And if that proved to be the case, she must hide her distress – if she could.

Phoebe had told her that he did not yet know that she was in London. In the first, unguarded moment when she walked in through the door of his chamber, she might glean some clue to his real feelings for her. But she had no doubt that, in the presence of Phoebe and the Helliers, he would treat her exactly as if there were nothing between them but friendship.

The Lieutenant of the Tower, Thomas Cheek, had told his deputies to permit their visit, but, even so, there were frustrating delays. The sun disappeared behind a lowering cloud, as they were passed from guard to warder to official. Louise had not realised that wild beasts were kept in the Tower, just by the entrance, for the curious to gape at on payment of a penny. The enraged roars of one of the lions, obviously suffering from his captivity, followed them as they proceeded inside the Tower.

The warder led them to a tower at the far corner of the walls. Louise looked about her with surprised interest: she had not expected the precincts to be so crowded, both with buildings and with people. When they reached their destination, there were more guards to pass, stairs to climb, and an oaken, iron-studded door. The warder turned a key, knocked on it, and went in. 'Visitors for you, Sir Alexander.'

Louise had a brief impression of stone walls, hangings, a deep window embrasure with several cushions, books, a guitar, a bed, table and chairs. And then there was Alex, rising to his feet by the window, his eyes instantly on hers, and she saw them widen, and the desire and delight undisguised on his face before he could control it, and knew with unutterable relief that her fears were groundless. If anything, he wanted her even more now than he had at Wintercombe, and her blood sang and tingled in exultant answer.

But she had to behave, even in front of the other three who knew everything, as if he were no more than a friend. She watched as he embraced Phoebe with brisk brotherly affection, and his aunt and uncle likewise, and then turned to her. 'I thought you would not be able to deny a good excuse to enjoy all the facilities that London has to offer. But I seem to recognise that gown.'

'I haven't had the opportunity to find a mantua-maker yet,' Louise told him, as he put his hands on her shoulders for a decorous, cousinly kiss. But his eyes, blazing and sapphire blue, told another story entirely, and the subtle pressure of his fingers was as eloquent as any declaration of passion. Almost sick with longing, she felt his lips on her cheek, and then he released her, smiling. 'I thank you all, for coming so far. I only hope you won't have to kick your heels too long in London, before we can all go home again.'

'There is nothing to draw us back immediately,' Nick pointed out. 'Richard is perfectly capable of managing affairs at Chard without my interference, and indeed he and Sarah will probably relish the opportunity to be alone for once. As for Louise . . .'

'As for me, I'm at your beck and call,' she said, smiling at her grandfather with a dazzling mixture of sudden happiness and mischief. Alex's need for her had not diminished, and that was all that seemed to matter to her at this moment. He still wanted her, and he was delighted to see her. With that knowledge hugged secretly to her heart, she felt suddenly exuberant.

The warder had withdrawn, with one of Phoebe's silver crowns hidden in his palm, and they could talk quite freely. But somehow, the conversation never rose above the trivial or the harmless, although Louise wondered who could possibly hear anything of what they said, behind three inches of solid oak. But she could see, looking about the pleasant chamber, that Alex was being kept in comfort, with his servant to attend him – Gerrit had already appeared, incongruously familiar in these alien surroundings, to bring wine for them – and a plentiful supply of books, provided by Phoebe.

'I did not know that you played the guitar,' she said, as the talk diminished a little. It lay propped against the wall, plain and sturdy, not at all like her mother's beribboned and frivolous-looking instrument.

'I learned when I was young, but I've forgotten most of it from lack of practice,' Alex said. He leaned across and picked it up, running a gentle finger down the strings. Louise's musical accomplishment consisted of a limited and reluctant acquaintance with the spinet, but her ear was acute. 'The fifth is flat.'

Alex glanced up in surprise. 'You're right – but I didn't know you were interested in music.'

'I love to listen, but I haven't the patience to practise,' she told him. 'Much to Grandfather's disgust, I think – he's the one with ability in that field.'

'You flatter me,' said Nick, who could handle spinet and fiddle with equal facility and accomplishment, and who had tried to encourage Louise, in vain, to play a little during the last few weeks at Chard. 'But I would like to hear a piece or two, if you don't mind sharing it with us.'

'If you don't mind missed notes,' Alex said. 'I have been practising assiduously, but poor Gerrit has suffered much over the past weeks, I fear. And I certainly won't do you the disfavour of singing – that would be altogether too much.'

'But you have a good voice,' Louise said, without thinking.

Alex looked at her over the top of the guitar, which he was tuning. 'Do I? I wasn't aware that you'd ever suffered my singing. I don't actually indulge in it.'

'I – I must have overheard you at some time,' Louise said, unable to stop the betraying flush which suffused her face. One day, perhaps, she would be close enough to him to reveal that she had heard him singing once, at Wintercombe, a song that betrayed far more of his innermost feelings than he had ever admitted. She did not know, even now, who was the woman who had been false, although it was most probably Lukas's mother. But she wished that she could tell him, somehow, that he would never have to fear such treachery from her.

The tuning completed, he bent over the guitar, rippled a hand across the strings, and launched into a complicated and fiery piece that was admirably suited to his flamboyant style. There were plenty of missed and mistaken notes, as he had warned, but they passed almost unnoticed amongst the wild flood of sound. And Louise gazed at him as he played, entranced and enchanted for ever, and did not know how strongly her feelings shone from her face.

They stayed for two hours and more, talking and listening, and as they said their goodbyes, Louise felt suddenly and utterly bereft. To her horror, she found tears beginning to fill her eyes, and it took all her determination, and fierce control, to blink them back, and smile, and kiss him like the others. She must never, ever allow herself to weaken, for if he once suspected that she was not so light-hearted as she pretended to be, he would surely discard her at once.

But Phoebe noticed, for she drew Louise aside as they walked back through the Tower precincts, and said softly, 'Nothing has changed, has it?'

She had mastery over her treacherous emotions by now, and was able to give her cousin a swift smile. 'No, nothing has.' She paused, took a deep breath, and said in a hasty undertone, 'Would it be possible to – to see him alone?'

Phoebe raised her brows pointedly. 'I don't see why not – although a palm full of silver should make it certain. I thought you might wish for that – and I don't think Alex would object, either, from the way he was looking at you today.' She grinned suddenly. 'I don't suppose it escaped your notice that he is still besotted with you.'

'It didn't,' Louise said. Silence and Nick had drawn a little ahead, and she stared at their respectable, elderly backs with a small frown between her brows. 'But how can I return here alone? I can hardly cross London unaccompanied without rousing comment.'

'You won't have to,' Phoebe said. 'I promised Lukas that I would bring him here tomorrow, to see his father – and the lions. We can hire a hackney, grease a few palms, and while I look at lions with Lukas, you can have an undisturbed hour with my brother.' She glanced sideways at her cousin. 'I have no experience of such things, myself, but I can see your need for each other, plain enough. And although he seems to have adapted well to life in such comfortable captivity, I can tell that it has not been very easy for him, these past weeks.' Her expression became more serious. 'I think that he has been forced to examine aspects of his past life which, perhaps, he now regrets. Of course, being Alex, he would die rather than admit as much to me, but I know him as well as anyone, if not better, and there are some thoughts which he can't hide from me.' She gave Louise a sudden vivid smile, very like her brother's. 'If we can get these ridiculous accusations dropped, somehow, then I think this incarceration, in a curious way, will have been very good for him. And perhaps – who knows? – your affair could possibly become more permanent.'

'There's small hope of that,' Louise said, unable to eliminate the bleakness from her voice. 'I've known from the beginning that it is purely a matter of lust – on his side, anyway. Our liaison will last only until his eye lights on someone who attracts him more than I do.'

'Will it?' Phoebe said, her face thoughtful. 'I wonder . . . Well, you have far more knowledge of these things than I do. But whatever the outcome, whatever happens in the next few weeks, remember this and hold to it – you have the power to make him extraordinarily happy, and that is something greatly to be cherished.'

Louise had feared that Nick and Silence would divine her intention when she announced casually that she planned to visit Alex again the following day. But since Phoebe and Lukas were going too, they did not seem to suspect anything untoward, despite the inner excitement that she feared must blaze from her face. Dressed in the peacock-blue silk mantua that was her best, her hair covered by a soft dark hood and with a fur tippet to warm her shoulders, she stepped into the hackney behind Phoebe's familiar plain grey, and folded her hands in her lap as the vehicle jolted its slow way up King Street, hoping that Lukas would not notice their trembling.

There was much traffic in the streets that morning, adding to her impatience, and considerable delay, quite usual, Phoebe told her, around the new cathedral of St Paul's, already ten years in the building and surrounded by scaffolding, piles of stone, waggons and workmen. It took more than an hour to reach the Tower, and by that time she was sweating with anticipation, despite the chilly, overcast day. The usual pettifogging procedures held them up at the entrance to the Tower, but at long last, nearly two hours after leaving Westminster, they were climbing the stairs to Alex's quarters, Lukas holding tightly to her hand as he towed her eagerly upwards, while Phoebe, encumbered with her stick, limped doggedly after them.

A word to the warder, the discreet clink of coins, and they were once more admitted. Lukas rushed in, shouting joyous welcome, and Alex swept him into his arms and up off the ground, his own delight glowing unguarded in his face.

Her time would come presently, and she did not grudge Lukas his father's undivided attention. She sat with Phoebe, watching, as Alex and his son, two almost identical dark heads, bent over the paper on which Lukas, with happy pride, was demonstrating his skill in penmanship. This was another side of Alex, and one that was completely different from the one which most people saw. The big man, smiling with unconcealed affection at the small boy kneeling on the stool by his side, concentrating all his efforts on writing his name, was also the man who desired her so passionately, who loved horses and books, and who despite the façade of casual, callous cynicism, was as vulnerable to emotion as she was. And realising that, suddenly, gave her hope.

She glanced round at the little chamber. There was, she was glad to see, a closet off to one side, to which, presumably, Gerrit could retreat to give them privacy. How long would they be allowed? By now, the waiting and the longing had heightened desire to such an intensity that she felt that she would burst into flame at his first touch. And if she shut her eyes, she was aware of him, only a few feet away, as strongly as she could tell the direction of the sun at midsummer.

Phoebe touched her arm, gently, and she could not help starting in surprise. Her cousin glanced at her meaningfully, and smiled. Louise, suddenly tense, smiled stiffly back. Then the older girl rose, and limped over to the table. 'I'm glad you have remembered so much of my lessons, Lukas. Your hand is very neat and careful now.'

'More than mine is,' Alex said. He took the pen from the boy's hand, and wrote a few words. 'What does that say?'

Lukas looked at it, and then peered closer. 'It doesn't say anything. Is it French?'

'No, it's English.'

'No, it's not!' The child twisted round, laughing. 'It's not anything at all – it doesn't make sense!'

'Yes, it does. Look at it harder.'

'I *am* looking!' Lukas sat back on his heels, scratching his head. 'They aren't words, they're just scribbles.'

Phoebe bent down and whispered something in his ear. Lukas's face broke into a wide, delighted smile. He picked up the paper, scrambled off the stool, and ran to the closet door. '*Gerrit, Gerrit! Hebt U een spiegel, als het U belieft?*'

The servant emerged, smiling, with a small wooden-framed mirror. He held it steady as Lukas stared intently at the paper's reflection. 'It's backwards writing! It says . . . "How many lions in the Tower?"'

'You'll have the chance to find out,' Phoebe said. 'And you can tell your father, the next time you come. They will be fed soon, so if you want to watch that, you'll have to hurry.'

'Oh, yes, please,' Lukas said. He put the paper back on the table, and flung his arms around Alex with childish abandon. 'You will still be here tomorrow, won't you, Papa?'

'I think so,' his father assured him. 'I can't imagine that I will go anywhere different, for a while at least.'

Lukas withdrew his embrace and stood still, looking up at him, his face suddenly serious. 'When *are* we all going home to Wintercombe?'

'I don't know,' Alex told him. 'I don't know, Luikje. But they can't keep me here for ever. Sooner or later, they will have to let me go.'

'I hope it's sooner,' Lukas said, suddenly fierce. 'I wish they could let you go now, and then we could all go home.'

'So do I,' Alex said, with a wry smile for Phoebe, standing by the child. 'Believe me, so do I.'

'But at least the Tower does have its compensations,' his sister pointed out. 'Lions, for example . . . if we don't go now, we shall miss their dinner. Say goodbye to your father, and then we must leave.'

There was another embrace, and then Lukas, as was his habit, gave his aunt a supporting arm. Louise remained sitting by the fire, wondering if the child would notice that she was not going with them. He did: he stopped by her chair, and said earnestly, 'Don't you want to see the lions, Cousin Louise?'

'I saw them yesterday,' she lied, smiling. 'And once is quite enough for me . . . I will catch you up in a little while.' And she watched as he led Phoebe from the chamber with a gravity and sense of responsibility far in advance of his years. The door closed behind them, and for the first time in two months, she was alone with her lover – save of course for Gerrit, who had discreetly withdrawn to his closet and shut the door.

'How long have you planned this?' Alex asked. He came to stand in front of her, and although his face was calm, even dispassionate, his eyes were not.

'Since yesterday,' Louise told him. 'You have Phoebe to thank – it was her idea.' Now that the moment had come, her mouth was dry, and she seemed to have lost the power of movement.

He stretched out his hand to her. 'Well, since she has been kind enough to give us the opportunity, we must not waste it. And Gerrit will not disturb us, do not worry.'

She was pulled into his arms, and the kiss that followed confirmed, overwhelmingly, that separation had not diminished need or passion in either. Their lips still melded together, they crossed the few feet to the bed. Alex took his mouth away to say softly in her ear, 'In case the guards take it into their heads to enter – shall I draw the curtains?'

The world within them was dim, and green, and totally private. Clothes were an impediment, to be feverishly cast aside, and their bodies a familiar landscape that yet held pleasures and secrets and undreamed-of delights. She gazed up at him, her soul, unknowing, in her eyes, filling her vision, and her mind on his face, his body, lean and hard and muscular, possessed of a power and strength that he always, with her, held in check. He smiled back, and the look in his eyes, dark with ungovernable passion, took her breath away. 'Oh, sweet Louise, I have waited so very long for this,' he said softly, and lowered his body on to hers.

It did not last long, but the intensity of pleasure, and the final cataclysmic explosion of joy, made her dizzy and faint. She lay beneath his warm weight, her mind dazed and wondering, wanting this moment of utter peace, and fulfilment, and love, to continue for ever.

'Are you all right?' he asked her quietly.

Slowly, she became aware of her surroundings once more, the closed curtains shutting out all but a trickle of light, the comforting feel of his skin next to hers, and the overwhelming, sensual languor that had invaded all her limbs. She opened her eyes, and saw him smiling. One lock of black hair dropped forward, tickling her face: she smiled lazily, and brushed it aside. 'No,' she said, teasing. 'I think I must be ill.'

'You don't look ill,' Alex observed. His hand caressed her cheek and her hair, with tenderness. 'Your face has a very healthy glow, and your eyes look as if you have just beheld some wondrous marvel.'

She grinned at the mischief in his voice. 'You flatter yourself, surely.'

'Not unduly. For the wonder is also of your making, my sweet Louise, and after nearly two months without even a sight of you, let alone the chance to enjoy each other once more, I was beginning to pine and waste away.'

'So was I.' Louise lifted her hand and traced the sharp line of his jaw, feeling the dark, shaven hairs of his beard beginning to grow through the skin and rasp against her fingers. 'And I hope that we will have the chance to be alone together again.'

'If Phoebe is willing to bribe enough people, it should not be too difficult. Discretion is everything – even if the guards are prepared to condone it, they will find it very difficult to ignore if I flaunt my mistress openly. I am supposed to be held in comfort, but not *that* much comfort.' He kissed her, with affection. 'Which is why, delightful as it is to lie here and dream the day away in love and idleness, we must up, and dress, and pretend that nothing more has passed between us than friendly conversation.'

As so often before, they helped each other to put on their clothes, discovering in the process that to make love but once, after so long an abstinence, was not nearly enough. But she tried, with some success, to ignore the feelings that his touch roused once more in her, and knew that he would do the same. Her mantua, only a little creased, was decorously arranged, her hair just slightly disordered, and she hoped that Lukas, at least, would notice nothing unusual.

Alex tied the tippet about her shoulders, his hands drifting, teasingly, over the swell of her breasts above the embroidered stomacher. 'There – you look almost respectable, save that your eyes tell a different story. Now I think you should go, and join Lukas and Phoebe – if they have to come back for you, it will only draw attention to the fact that you have been here with me alone.' He kissed her, in a way that left her in no doubt of his feelings, and led her to the door.

The guard was on duty at the bottom of the stairs. He was a surly, venal-looking man, but such was her happiness that she gave him her most brilliant smile, and slipped a coin into his hand as she went past.

There was no harm, no harm at all, in ensuring that the fellow was suitably rewarded for his co-operation.

The Tower precincts were, as usual, crowded with people: there were soldiers garrisoned here, as well as the Mint, the Ordnance with its stores of arms and gunpowder, and, of course, all the state prisoners, not to mention the parties of sightseers, come to marvel at the Crown Jewels, gape at the lions, and revel in the bloodstained and sinister past of this grim fortress. Hoping that she could remember the way back to the menagerie through the maze of buildings and throngs of visitors, Louise pulled on her hood and walked quickly, threading her way through a group of stout country folk being shown the more notable sights by a warder.

There was a man coming towards her, not tall, but broad-shouldered, and strangely familiar. She stared at him for a moment, bewildered by the lack of shock or recognition in his face, and then realised that her black velvet hood, a fashionable accessory for any lady abroad in London, effectively shadowed her face. He was about to pass her; hastily, she put out a hand to detain him. 'Charles! What are you doing here?'

He looked as amazed as if the ground had opened up to reveal an abyss at his feet. For a moment, she thought that he would ignore her, but, evidently, his wish to speak to her defeated the anger also prominent in his face. He said abruptly, 'I might say the same to you. Have you been visiting him?'

There was no point in denying it. She said candidly, 'Yes, I came with Phoebe and Lukas – they've gone to watch the lions being fed. Have you seen them?'

Charles's face was an extraordinary mixture of guilt, and revulsion, and yearning. He said curtly, 'No, I haven't. Good day, Louise.'

'Wait!' She gripped his sleeve urgently. 'Charles, don't go – I must talk with you, in private.'

'Here is as good a place as any,' he said. 'But you told me that you never wished to speak to me again.'

'I was very angry at the time – but since then, I've had the chance to think.' Louise drew him to one side, out of the way of an advancing party of visitors. 'Charles, it is no use any more in giving full rein to rage, or spite, or hatred. It has only brought misery to everyone.'

Charles stared at her, his face closed. 'I have only done what I know to be right. He is a traitor, and fully deserves his punishment.'

'No, he *isn't*!' Louise cried urgently. Several people glanced at them curiously, and she lowered her voice. 'Charles, he is no traitor, and no rebel. You have misunderstood certain things, jumped to conclusions –'

457

'Have I? Well, let me tell you that there is a man called Jem Taylor in Newgate Prison, who saw your precious lover colluding with Bram over that episode with the horses, *and* also saw him fighting for the rebels. He is telling the truth, no doubt of it, and he will make a very damning witness. Add to that the books and pamphlets found at Wintercombe, and I doubt very much whether even you, infatuated as you are, would still think him innocent if you heard all the evidence.'

'What did you promise this witness? A pardon, if he betrayed Alex? He'd doubtless swear black was white for such a reward, with his comrades hung and quartered and stuck up on poles all over Somerset.' Louise drew a deep breath, aware of her trembling. 'Please, Charles – think not of vengeance or righteousness for once, but of all of us – the family. Have you realised how terribly unhappy you have made poor Gran'mère? She feels you have betrayed not just Alex, but everyone, all her grandchildren. And from what Phoebe says, even your mother and sister are horrified at what you've done.'

'But I haven't had the chance to explain it to them properly,' Charles said. His eyes had taken on a hunted, desperate look. 'They'll understand when I tell them the truth – I know they will!'

'What truth? About me and Alex?' She saw his face, and put out a hand, but he flinched away from her touch, as if she repelled him. 'Charles, we were *friends*. I never intended that we should ever be more – if you jumped to conclusions, I am very sorry for it, but I did nothing to encourage you to think so, did I?'

Charles stared at her, mute and desperate, and despite everything, she felt a sudden stab of pity for him. She added softly, 'Your hatred for Alex has blinded you to so much else . . . I enjoyed your company, I *valued* our friendship, and now you have destroyed it . . . But I *love* Alex, Charles, and nothing will ever alter that.'

'You can't love him – not you – not a man like that!' Charles cried, almost on a sob. 'Louise, he is not worthy of you, he seduced you, he's a drunkard and a lecher . . . can't you *see* what he is?'

'I see what he is,' Louise said. 'But the Alex I see is very different from your picture of him.'

'You say you love him. Does he love you?'

She would have given anything, anything in the world, to say 'yes' with honesty. The memory of his expression that morning, the passion and affection and tenderness plain in his eyes, rose up to haunt her. Yes, he was fond of her, he desired her, needed her, but love . . .

'He has not yet said so,' she told Charles, and knew as soon as the triumph inflamed his face that it had been a mistake to admit it.

458

'Love?' said her cousin exultantly. 'He doesn't know the meaning of the word. Louise, are you blind? Can't you *see* that he is using you, he'll drag you down to the gutter with him, and then he'll grow tired of you, and you'll be no better than a whore in most men's eyes –'

'Including yours?'

'No, because I know the truth about him. I don't blame you – I just wish that you could see him for what he really is, his viciousness – *please*, Lou, leave him before it is too late!'

'And if he dies because of your accusations? What then?'

'He doesn't have to die.' Charles clasped her hands in his, his face flushed with passionate urgency. 'It's not too late – the charges can be dropped, for the right price.'

'A pardon?' she said, thinking of Phoebe and the money that she had gathered to buy her brother's freedom. 'Why should you want him pardoned when you've spent all this time and effort constructing a charge of treason against him?'

And Charles, her cold fingers gripped in his hot, clammy hands, said desperately, 'None of that matters – none! He can walk free today for all I care – so long as I can have you.'

She did not believe it. For a moment, looking at him, she wondered if his thirst for vengeance and his desire for her and for Wintercombe had unhinged his mind. Certainly, his eyes, wild and staring, were deeply disturbing. She said, trying to be calm and rational, 'What do you mean – if you can have me?'

'If you marry me, I won't testify against him,' Charles said, his voice low and intense. 'Louise – I love you! I love you so much! Why should you waste your life and your looks and your reputation on that evil man? He doesn't love you – he never did, and he never will – and I adore you, I'd do anything for you. Leave him, and marry me, and we can live quietly somewhere and you'll grow to love me as much as I love you.'

She felt sick and faint. Her instinct told her to tear her hands free and run, run from this deranged, desperate travesty of the Charles who had once been her friend. But his grip was too tight. She said urgently, 'Have you thought that I might be carrying his child?'

The possibility evidently had not occurred to him, for he stared at her in blank amazement. She went on, praying that she would convince him, 'We have been lovers since June – would you really want to marry me if I were to bear Alex's son or daughter?'

'Are you pregnant?' Charles asked fiercely. 'Are you? You must know, one way or the other. And anyway, it wouldn't matter – the child could be fostered out. Are you really with child?'

It was extraordinarily difficult to lie, in the face of that devouring gaze. 'No,' she said at last. 'No, I am not.'

Of course, that morning's lovemaking might bear fruit, but she could not possibly know yet: nor did she want Charles to be aware that she had managed to snatch an hour alone with Alex, for he would undoubtedly try to put a stop to any further assignations. And there was also the unhappy suspicion, already voiced to her grandmother, that she might be barren. Her first lover had had a wife and children: Alex had sired Lukas. And yet she had failed to conceive with either of them.

'I'm glad,' Charles said. 'Louise – will you marry me, if I have him pardoned? Will you?'

A terrible feeling of sadness descended over her. She stared unhappily at his beseeching face, the misplaced, unmerited adoration shining from his eyes, and found that she wanted to weep. She could not, she could *not* – she loved Alex, heart and soul and body, and to take Charles instead seemed the most appalling betrayal of her feelings. Nor would it be fair to Charles, for such a union, begun in poisoned and distorted love on the one hand, forced acceptance on the other, could only end in bitterness, resentment and misery for both of them.

And besides, there was Phoebe, and her accumulated coin, and the help and advice of Sir Hugh Trevelyan to consider. There were other ways of freeing Alex, there must be, but instinct told her not to refuse Charles outright, as she was tempted to do. Let him think that there was a chance she might accept, and meanwhile, Phoebe and Sir Hugh and Philip Cousins would try to negotiate a pardon.

And if not, if the worst came to the worst . . . could she really, for Alex's sake, marry Charles to ensure that he did not suffer execution?

She did not know. But time was valuable, and a soft answer now would commit her to nothing, save the burden of seeing him again and enduring further appeals. To respond with ridicule and contempt to this deluded, desperate proposal would only arouse his anger, and quite possibly seal Alex's fate. So she gave him the best smile that she could muster, in the circumstances, and said gently, 'Charles – I can't possibly tell you now – not here – I must have time to think. Will you grant me that? I'm not saying no, but I'm not agreeing either, not yet. I need time, time to think everything over, all the things you've said.'

'Of course,' he said, although his disappointment was written plain on his face. 'Can I see you – in a week's time, perhaps? Will you have an answer for me then?'

'I hope so,' she told him. 'But I can't guarantee it – this is all so sudden – please be patient, Charles. If you force me into a hasty reply, we may both come to regret it.'

Despite everything that he had done, she still felt sorry for him, for such massive self-delusion could only end in disaster. She looked at his face, and saw that, despite his disappointment, he was already putting the best possible interpretation on her words. And she wondered, with unhappiness and foreboding, how strong was his grip on reality.

'Where are you living?' he asked.

Reluctantly, she gave him the direction of the house in Bell Court, adding that his grandparents were also in residence. His present state of mind greatly alarmed her, and she could easily imagine him haunting the doorstep, pestering her for an answer, the victim of a growing and insatiable obsession. It was a horrible and disturbing thought.

'Next week, then,' Charles said. 'I will come and see you in a week.'

'I can't promise an answer for you, even then,' she told him gently. 'But, yes, in seven days I will see you again.'

And with the memory of Alex, whom she loved but who did not love her, still warm inside her, she withdrew her hands at last from his, kissed him lightly, cousin-fashion, on the cheek, and left him to find Phoebe and Lukas, her body trembling and her mind feverishly busy. But the sadness still stayed with her: for who was she to mock or deny the agonies and despair of unrequited love?

# 28

## *'Resolv'd to ruin'*

When Louise, Phoebe and Lukas returned from the Tower, just in time for dinner, Sir Hugh Trevelyan was waiting for them, his face grave. Evidently he had news to impart, and it would probably not be welcome. With apprehension, the people concerned with Alex's fate gathered in the dining parlour, where steaming plates were already sitting ready and fragrant on the table, and took their places. This meal, it was plain, would be more of a family conference.

Sir Hugh, resplendent in golden periwig and a magnificent suit in a rich blue silk lavishly adorned with gold braid and frothing lace, made everyone else seem like country bumpkins, although Louise still wore her peacock mantua, graced now with a tippet of fine Bruges lace, and Silence's amber gown was her best. Nick was in plain silver-grey, very much the country gentleman, and Philip Cousins in lawyer's black. Phoebe, even more careless of her appearance than her brother, wore her finest gown, but it was fully five years behind the times and had a mended tear conspicuous on one sleeve, where she had caught it on a nail. Louise, looking at her cousin, thought, not for the first time, that Phoebe, with a little enhancement, might share in some of Alex's extreme good looks. Her hair was good, when washed and curled, being deep black and as glossy as the proverbial rook's wing, and those sapphire eyes quite remarkable. A few pounds of extra flesh to round out her thin face and meagre figure, and the right choice of clothes, and no one would notice the dragging leg . . .

But Phoebe was Phoebe, and to think of her tricked out in the highest mode of fashion was ludicrous – as well try to transform chalk into cheese. And she would laugh any such suggestion into well-deserved oblivion. Louise, however, could not help speculating anew about Sir Hugh's precise reasons for helping them to free Alex. What, apart from Phoebe, and that seemed ridiculously unlikely, could he possibly hope to gain?

He did not keep them waiting very long for his news, and preceded it with apologies. 'I am afraid that this will not be pleasant . . . but Lord Sunderland, who is the King's chief secretary of state, has given me to understand that, at present, there is no chance of granting Sir Alexander a pardon or a reprieve, no matter how great the price for it. Apparently there are two good witnesses against him, and the King is most concerned to make an example of him. To see such a man walk free would, according to Sunderland, make a mockery of justice. There is every chance that the trial will take place quite soon, after Christmas perhaps, and given the testimony of two witnesses, and his past, I do not think it very likely that he will be acquitted.'

After the hopes they had allowed themselves to entertain, this was a crushing blow. Silence put her hands to her mouth, and Philip Cousins, his face very serious, said quietly, 'Is this, do you think, the final decision? Or do they still intend to pardon him, but think to force more money from us by painting such a black picture?'

'It's possible,' Sir Hugh said, looking round at them. 'I would certainly not give up all hope yet. But we have only two months left, perhaps, in which to try and save him. And the appearance of this second witness is something that I had not expected. It would help us if we could know who he, or she, is, and then it might be possible to influence them in some way, or at least to have an idea of the testimony they are likely to give. But of course Sunderland would not tell me.'

'I know,' Louise said.

They stared at her in astonishment. She had said nothing of her encounter with Charles, either to Phoebe or to anyone else, for reasons which she could not adequately explain to herself. Most likely, she decided eventually, it was because the more she thought over his words and his manner, the more she became convinced that he was in serious danger of . . . of madness? It sounded so unlikely, when she remembered the old Charles, reserved, cautious, self-effacing to a fault. But that deceptive calm had evidently concealed a torment of desire, jealousy and hatred, until Alex's wanton behaviour, and her own, had brought it all boiling to the surface. And now, his emotions out of control, he did not seem able to think rationally about what he had done, or what he intended to do.

'*You* know?' Nick said bluntly. 'How?'

Louise took a deep breath. 'I – I met Charles this morning. In the Tower. I think he was there to see Alex. And he told me, with great satisfaction, that he had found his second witness, and his name was Jem Taylor, and he was in Newgate Prison.'

Sir Hugh whistled, a surprisingly uncourtly sound. 'Well, well! I spend all morning trying to twist Sunderland's arm, and the information drops unasked into Mistress Chevalier's lap. So this Charles, I take it, is the one who has made all the accusations against Sir Alexander? Well, at least we know he is here in London. And if the second witness is in Newgate, it should not be too difficult to gain access to him. Who knows, perhaps *he* might be amenable to bribery.'

'But who is he?' Phoebe asked. 'Did Charles say anything about that? He's certainly not one of the Wintercombe servants, or anyone from Philip's Norton – I've never heard the name before.'

'I think he's a rebel prisoner from Bram's troop,' Louise told her. 'And he seems to have been promised a pardon, in return for his testimony.'

'In which case, bribery may not be of any use,' Cousins remarked thoughtfully. 'But it's certainly worth trying it.'

'There is something else which Charles said.' Louise glanced round the table, knowing that this, too, must be disclosed, for it might help Alex, much as the prospect appalled her. 'He told me that – that he still loved me, and wanted to marry me. And – and if I agreed to it, he would arrange to have the charges against Alex dropped.'

Phoebe made an exclamation of disgust. 'My God, he has the devil's own effrontery! As if you'd even consider doing such a thing.'

'Have you given him any answer?' Silence asked her granddaughter sharply.

'I knew that we would need time . . . and so I told him to come here next week. I tried to make it clear to him that he might not receive an answer, even then – I wanted to keep him in uncertainty for as long as possible – but I don't think he was in any state to understand me. He's convinced himself that marriage to me is all he wants, and that I will come to love him – I think he is obsessed beyond all reason.'

'He's certainly deluding himself about the pardon,' Sir Hugh said briskly. 'I can't begin to understand what cloud-cuckoo-land your Cousin Charles inhabits at present, Mistress Chevalier, but if he thinks that he can influence the mills of justice, not to mention His Majesty's officers of state, with a few pleading words, he is sadly mistaken. He has no importance in this matter now, beyond his role as a witness against Sir Alexander. And even that is open to doubt, since he hasn't actually *witnessed* very much, has he? All he has really done is to air his suspicions in the right quarters, and because of that, he believes that he can have the charges dropped at a moment's notice, if he so chooses.'

'He may think that he has special influence, because of his religion,' Phoebe pointed out. She glanced meaningfully at Sir Hugh. 'The King is widely thought to favour Papists, after all.'

'Well, you see in me the proof that you don't have to hear Mass to rise at Court,' Trevelyan said. 'Not to mention General Feversham, John Churchill, and of course Lord Chancellor Jeffreys himself, amongst many others, good Protestants all. But I digress. Are you seriously considering marriage to this man, Mistress Chevalier? Because I really don't think that he can have any influence, one way or the other. I agree, it is a good idea to keep him dangling as long as possible – and if you have interpreted his feelings for your charming self accurately, then I think it will take some time before he realises that you have no intention of marrying him. It certainly doesn't seem as if you *want* to.'

'I don't,' Louise said. 'Not if he were the last man on earth. Perhaps, if he really could influence Alex's fate, I might be desperate enough to consider it. But if what you say is true, than I think I'd rather marry Judas.'

'That may be so,' Phoebe told her. 'But you still feel sorry for him, don't you? Don't deny it, you do, I can see it in your face. *Why*, in God's name?'

The real reason, Louise knew, had to do with her sympathy for Charles's hopeless love. If Alex had spurned her, refused to take her into his bed, she knew that she would feel the same anguish and torment as Charles. And even though she had Alex's need and desire in thrall, she knew that she did not have his love, heart and soul, as he had hers. But she could not admit this, in front of comparative strangers, so she said sadly, 'We were good friends, until this happened. And . . . and he was in such a pitiable state this morning – if you had seen him, you would surely have felt the same.'

'I doubt it,' Phoebe said drily. 'As far as I'm concerned, it's no more than he deserves – he has forfeited any claim of friendship or kinship that we might once have shared.'

'I can understand Louise's feelings,' Silence said, with sadness. 'Oh, I am appalled and disgusted by Charles's behaviour. But he is still my grandchild, still William's son, whatever he may have become, and I cannot forget that entirely. And you have to admit that Alex is not completely blameless, either. If Charles has fallen off the edge of rational thought, then it was Alex who pushed him. But we are not here to discuss my nephew's actions or morals. After all, it is hardly seemly to drag all our family's past and present indiscretions into the open, even before good friends such as these.'

'I am not cast in a judgemental mould,' Sir Hugh remarked. 'And certainly you will find, in the history of my own family, episodes quite as lurid, if not more so. Not to mention what I could tell you about life at Court . . . But, since I can be surprisingly discreet on occasion, I assure you that our conversations here will go no further. Mistress Chevalier need have no fear that her cousin's unusual offer will ever become the subject of gossip through my agency.'

'I'm glad to hear of it,' Silence said. 'The name of St Barbe is not usually notorious, although my nephew has done his best to make it so in the past, and will, if I know him, continue to do so in the future, if allowed. But we have strayed somewhat from the subject in hand. If a pardon at present is out of the question, Sir Hugh, and my grandson's promises are worthless, then how may we best help Alex?'

'The man in Newgate may represent our best chance,' said the courtier. 'If he were to be persuaded not to give evidence, then Sir Alexander's position becomes much less precarious. And with only one witness remaining, His Majesty and Sunderland might well become much more ready to sell his freedom to us. I cannot promise anything, Mistress Hellier, but there is no reason yet for despair.'

They had given Jem Taylor special treatment at Newgate, as a potential witness for the Crown: a cell to himself, a bed, and blankets. It was hardly comfortable, for he was not rich enough to buy himself further privileges, but at least he did not have to share a cell with many other men in conditions of stinking and infected squalor. And in return for this, and for the pardon which he had been assured would follow, all he had to do was to provide information about Sir Alexander St Barbe.

This he had done, with enthusiasm. He remembered the man clearly, and had taken a dislike to him at the time – an arrogant aristocrat too proud or too cowardly to lend his wholehearted support to the cause, his sort had been the undoing of the Protestant Duke, and Taylor had no compunction in telling all he knew. His copious evidence had been taken down in Wells, and again in Newgate, and when the door of his cell swung open on yet another man in sober, legal black, he thought at first that a third deposition was required of him.

Not so, apparently. For the lawyer had a companion, a foppishly dressed courtier wearing clothes that had cost more money than most men saw in a lifetime, and which immediately aroused Taylor's resentment. They introduced themselves as Master Cousins, the lawyer, and Sir Hugh Trevelyan, and from the way in which the turnkey left the tiny room, with much obsequious bowing and scraping, they had paid handsomely for the privilege of a private talk with him.

'You are Jem Taylor?' said the lawyer. As the prisoner nodded, he gave him a tight smile. 'Excellent. We do not have much time, so I will come straight to the point. You are, I believe, prepared to give evidence against Sir Alexander St Barbe at his forthcoming trial?'

'Yes,' Taylor said, looking at the two men in bewilderment.

'And, so I understand, you will receive a full and free pardon if you do so?'

466

'That's what they told me,' Taylor said suspiciously. 'What's it to you? Why are you here?'

'We are here,' said the courtier pleasantly, 'to persuade you, Master Taylor, that it might well be to your advantage to change your mind about giving evidence.'

'To my advantage? It won't be if I don't get my pardon,' Taylor said indignantly. 'What can you offer me that's better than that, eh? I don't want to spend the rest of my days slaving on some hot-as-hell plantation in Barbados – and that's where I'll be sent if I don't oblige them.'

'You might not be,' said Trevelyan smoothly. 'I have considerable influence at Court, you know, and certain resources. Every man has his price, and I am sure that you are no different. Have you a wife? Children?'

'None.'

'Then perhaps the chance to start a new life, in another country, with a substantial amount of money to help you set up in business, is attractive to you?'

'How much are you offering me?' asked Taylor suspiciously.

'The sum of five hundred pounds seems fair,' said the lawyer, with a smile. 'We are prepared to offer you that, if you in return undertake to withdraw all your testimony against Sir Alexander.'

'How? They've already written down all I told them, and I signed it. That's evidence in itself, is it not?'

'It would not be if you were to stand up in court and state that you had given the information under duress, and that you had lied to protect yourself.'

'Yes, and then what'd happen? I'd be back in here, in the common gaol, and left to rot, or hanged for my pains – and your precious five hundred wouldn't be much good to me then, would it?' Taylor glared belligerently at the two men. 'No – I won't do it – not for five hundred pounds, nor a thousand. The man's a rebel, and all I did was tell the truth.'

They argued until the turnkey came back, jingling his bunch of keys to warn of his arrival, but could not dent his obstinacy. If Taylor had had doubts about giving evidence before their attempts to dissuade him, he was utterly determined now, and said so, over and over again, with increasing aggression. As Sir Hugh had feared, the promise of a free pardon far outweighed any bribe, for if Taylor denied the truth of his testimony in such dramatic fashion in open court, the pardon would undoubtedly be withdrawn.

It was no good. In a mood of gloomy resignation, Trevelyan and Cousins left Taylor's cell, and returned to Westminster to give the news to the people waiting in Bell Court. They had failed to bribe the second witness. The first, Charles, might believe that he could influence the decision to bring Alex to trial, but he was deluding himself. And no one wanted Louise to submit to her cousin's offer of marriage: the idea was repugnant to them all. The only chance left was, somehow, to persuade the King, or his secretary of state, that it would be worth granting Alex a pardon. And to change their minds, a very large sum of money indeed might have to be offered: perhaps as much as ten thousand pounds, or more.

'But that's a vast amount,' Phoebe said, horrified. 'I haven't managed to raise a quarter of that!'

'It would severely deplete the estate,' Philip Cousins said. 'I have already made a detailed study of Sir Alexander's affairs, and I can tell you with some confidence that a considerable amount of land would have to be sold in order to produce such a sum. Perhaps all the Bristol and Bath properties would fetch what is required – they are valuable assets, and bring in a handsome revenue yearly. For that reason they would be worth a great deal.'

'But also for that reason, disposing of them would be unfortunate,' Nick pointed out. 'And to whom would this bribe be paid? To the King, directly, or to one of his courtiers? Or, God forbid, to Charles?'

'That at least is not likely,' Sir Hugh told him. 'His Majesty has many loyal servants whom he might wish to reward – Lord Sunderland himself, perhaps, or John Churchill. But, I repeat, I was told that at present they do not intend to grant Sir Alexander a pardon, at any price. I will not give up, don't worry – I will continue to press for his release. But if his estate is capable of producing a very substantial inducement, then perhaps it might be wise to mention the fact. For if the worst happens, and Sir Alexander is tried and condemned, I take it that his cousin Charles St Barbe will inherit?'

'That is correct,' said Cousins. 'Certainly, Wintercombe and the very substantial lands around it are under an entail, which cannot be broken. Perhaps if you could make that fact clear to Lord Sunderland, it might help. If Sir Alexander is executed, the bulk of his wealth will pass to Charles, and the King will be able to lay his hands on very little. But if he is pardoned on payment of a large bribe, then of course the King will gain substantially. So it might well be in His Majesty's best interests to show mercy, at the right price.'

'Excellent,' Sir Hugh said, looking relieved. 'I hope – I hope very much that you are right. Now that the rebellion is over, the country quiet and passions cooled, vengeance may no longer seem so attractive. It is a shame that we could not persuade that man Taylor, but he was very stubborn, and I must say that I could not blame him. A pardon in the hand, after all, must seem much more valuable than the vague promise of money in the future. But rest assured, ladies, gentlemen,' he added, looking round at the worried faces, 'I shall do my very best to bring this matter to a satisfactory conclusion, even if it costs Sir Alexander dear. But it may take some considerable time, I warn you – negotiations such as these always do. And in the meanwhile, of course, poor Mistress Chevalier must keep her cousin dangling for an answer. Do you think that you can do that?'

'I don't know,' Louise said honestly. Her heart quailed at the thought even of seeing Charles again, let alone soothing him with fair words and half-promises, but for Alex's sake, she must, every day for a year if necessary, until her lover was pardoned, or until her cousin realised that he was being gulled. And when that happened, she dreaded to think what his reaction might be.

He came to see her, a week after their chance meeting at the Tower. Those seven days had been busy, yet seemed to pass desperately slowly. She had seen three plays, had gone shopping with Silence and Phoebe in the fashionable streets, had walked in the pleasure-grounds and parks that surrounded the city, and had played with Lukas and James Trevelyan. And on three separate occasions, she had managed to snatch an illicit hour with Alex in his Tower prison, and enjoyed the time, and his lovemaking, to the full. So far, the guards seemed more than willing to turn a blind eye, although they must have realised what was happening: a quantity of silver had proved most effective. And Louise, reckless as ever, eager to snatch all she could while it was still possible, took every opportunity that offered.

She had tried not to think of Charles, but the night before his visit, she lay awake, deciding what to say to him. There was always, despite what Sir Hugh had said, the remote chance that her cousin did in fact wield some influence, that somehow he could decide whether or not his cousin came to trial. And the same love that made her so desperate to enjoy Alex while she could also urged her to take any chance that might conceivably lead to his release.

Even at the cost of marrying another man, one whom she despised? At the cost of driving Alex for ever from her side? She did not know, for she was not yet sufficiently desperate. There was still hope of a pardon, even though it might cost Wintercombe dear. And while that hope remained, she must keep Charles hopeful in his turn.

Besides, the man who had confronted her at the Tower, deluded, passionate, irrational, had frightened her more than she would admit.

He arrived in the middle of the morning, neatly dressed as usual, which was somehow reassuring: were not mad people supposed to take no pride in their appearance? Although of course Alex was undoubtedly sane, yet habitually affected a careless and informal, not to say slovenly, style of dress. The housemaid showed him into the smaller of the two parlours, where they could be private, but she was glad that Phoebe, Lukas and James were within calling distance. Philip Cousins had temporarily returned to Bath, to begin the long and complicated business of raising money for a possible pardon; Sir Hugh was on duty at Whitehall; and her grandparents had gone out to visit Silence's nephew – her brother's son and his family.

'Hullo,' she said to Charles, with a smile that she could not make sincere. Deliberately, she had worn her plainest and least enticing gown, unfashionable and devoid of allure, but his eyes still glowed at the sight of her. Not for the first time, she wondered why. Alex had seen her as a kindred spirit, a woman as reckless and uninhibited in love as he himself, but Charles, no sophisticate, would surely fail to recognise such alien and exotic characteristics. And she could not believe that her lean body and unfashionably olive-skinned and aquiline face could attract him so strongly, when she did not wish it. As with so much in his present behaviour, it mystified and disturbed her.

'Hullo, Lou,' Charles said. He looked at her expectantly, and she realised, with a sinking heart, that during the past week he had convinced himself that today she would give him a favourable answer. And the thought rose again, why did he want to force her into marrying him, if he truly loved her?

'Sit down,' she said, indicating a comfortable, upholstered chair by the fire. 'I have asked for refreshments . . . there is chocolate, or coffee, or even tea if you would prefer it.'

Charles ignored her suggestions. He took a step forward, and said eagerly, 'You promised me an answer, Lou – will you marry me? Please say you will!'

'I didn't promise an answer today,' she said, resisting the urge to back away from him. 'I only said that I would *think* about it – and I have been thinking, a great deal.'

'And?'

'And . . . I haven't come to any decision as yet.'

Charles stared at her in disbelief. 'But . . . but you said you'd been thinking!'

'I have – but please understand, Charles, this is very difficult for me . . . I never wanted to have to make such a choice, and I need more time. Charles, please don't push me, don't force me –'

'I'm not forcing you! But I can't understand – it seems so obvious –'

'Not to me, Charles.' Something occurred to her suddenly, and she snatched upon it, the perfect excuse. 'My mother brought me up to follow the Protestant religion that was my father's too, and she sent me to England to find a Protestant husband. In all conscience, I'm most unhappy at the thought of marrying a Catholic.'

'I wouldn't try to convert you – I'd let you follow your own worship, you know I would!'

'But what if we had children? Doesn't your faith ordain that they be brought up as Catholics too?'

Charles looked bewildered and distressed. He said, 'Yes, but . . . but I did not think that it mattered so much to you. Hasn't your mother herself embraced the faith?'

'To please my stepfather,' Louise said. 'And, as you know, life in France is not easy for Protestants – as it may not be here, in a few years' time.'

'All the more reason to rear our children as Catholics,' Charles said urgently. 'Louise, why did you not mention this before? I thought you cared little for religion.'

'You thought wrongly,' she said, praying that he would accept her reasons for further delay. Certainly, for most women, his religion would be sufficient pretext. But she had never made any secret of her boredom during sermons, her lack of interest in matters theological, and her pleasure-seeking, godless life. Surely he must be suspicious?

He was certainly staring at her very narrowly. He said slowly, 'Is that the true reason, Lou? Or are you seeking some convenient excuse?'

'It *is* the true reason,' she told him quickly. 'I know I have not given the impression of being religious – indeed, I am not, as a rule. But I love and respect my mother, and I would not want to go against her wishes, or those of my dead father. And it *does* matter to me – I was reared a Protestant, and I still hold allegiance to that worship. Despite what you may think, it is no easy matter for me to decide to bring up my children in another faith.' She swallowed, and stared at him imploringly. 'Charles – please, I beg of you, give me more time to decide.'

'But how much more do you want? A day? a week? A month? At least give me some idea!'

'I don't know!' Louise cried. 'I can't decide, Charles – I *can't*! But if you will tell me where your lodgings are, I promise you that I'll send word to you as soon as I have an answer for you, one way or the other.'

Charles stared at her in dismay. He said, 'I would rather come to you here. On Thursday, perhaps?'

471

'But I may not have reached a decision by Thursday. If I send word to you, you'll know for certain that I have my answer ready.'

He still looked doubtful, but finally gave her his direction, in a street off Long Acre that was, she guessed, in a far from wealthy area. Firmly, she told him that he must wait patiently for her reply.

'I can't be patient for ever,' Charles said, and then added, in desperation, 'I love you, Louise – please decide soon. And if you say yes, I'll gladly make sure that Alex is set free, if only I can have you for my wife.'

Sincerity shone from his face. To be able to attract two men so very different, so strongly, gave her a strange, not altogether welcome feeling of power. She said, 'Alex's freedom is the most important thing. But please, Charles, don't put pressure on me . . . I need more time to think.'

To her relief, he accepted her argument at last, and left her. When he had gone, she found that her knees were weak, and an overwhelming feeling of revulsion caused the bile to rise in her throat. She longed to fling the door open, and shout her defiance down the stairs after him. Did he really think that he could coerce her into marriage by such means? Was he so adrift from the real world that he imagined a happy future could be built on such foundations? Did he seriously expect her simply to forget Alex, once he had been freed, and go joyfully to wed a man who had betrayed his cousin for reasons of personal gain and vengeance, and was now forcing her into this intolerable situation?

But she realised that he thought her blinded by love, and believed that, once sundered from Alex, she would be bound to realise the truth about him, and would turn with gratitude to Charles, her husband and saviour. And that assumption, that she was a deluded ninny with no mind of her own, was the most insulting and infuriating of all.

Well, if Sir Hugh Trevelyan spoke the truth, Charles was also deluding himself, and Alex could not be freed through his agency alone. And Louise, recalling, act by damning act, all the grief and harm that he had caused over the past three months, prayed desperately that the courtier's efforts would prove fruitful, and Charles's schemes brought to an ignominious end.

In Newgate Prison, the condition of Jem Taylor was giving his gaolers cause for concern. Despite his separate cell, the man had contracted a severe fever, which rapidly rose to threaten his life. A physician was summoned, prescribed a variety of remedies, but held out little hope of recovery. It seemed as if the King would, after all this time and trouble and expense, be cheated of his witness.

Charles heard the news with alarm. True, he had promised Louise that he would obtain Alex's freedom if she agreed to marry him, but he had no idea whether this would in fact be possible. And if he could not have Louise, he was determined that the other part of his plan, the destruction of Alex, must be carried to its final conclusion, or he would have nothing to show for all the agony and effort of the past few months. His hatred for his cousin, he had realised, was still almost as strong as his obsessive love for Louise, and the thought of vengeance was a powerful lure.

In desperation, he paid for a second doctor to attend the sick prisoner, only to have him make the same diagnosis as the first. Charles was too afraid of infection to venture into Taylor's cell, but a quick glance from the open door, a vinegar-soaked kerchief to his nose as a protection, was enough to tell him that, alas, both physicians had spoken the truth. And indeed, when he returned to Newgate the following morning, he was told by an apologetic turnkey that Taylor had died in the night, and, because of the risk of infection, had already been interred.

Bitterly, Charles cursed the fact that Bram, who might have proved an even better witness, was out of reach and halfway to Barbados. And it was surely too late to find another: by now, most of the rebel prisoners in the West Country had been executed, or transported, and his chances of discovering someone prepared to testify against Alex were very remote. Despairingly, he sought an interview with the Lord Chancellor to discuss the case, and to his delight found that Jeffreys was prepared to receive him. With the great man's help, the death of Taylor need not be the disaster it had at first appeared. In the present climate of opinion, with feelings running so high at Court against all Whigs, Dissenters and Monmouth men, and juries hand-picked for their loyalty, a conviction would be easy to secure, however nebulous the evidence. And they still had Taylor's signed depositions.

It was, alas, not one of Jeffreys's good days. A bottle of brandy, the only substance that could dull the pain of his kidney stone, stood at his elbow, and his expression was belligerent and unwelcoming. With a dreadful feeling of foreboding, Charles faced the man whom he had considered to be his ally, and whose support now seemed, suddenly, to be flimsy indeed. 'Good afternoon . . . St Barbe,' said the Lord Chancellor, after a swift glance at the paper in front of him to check the name. 'I've news for you – may not be welcome, but that's your misfortune. For various reasons, not the least of which is the unhappy death of the witness Taylor, His Majesty, in his infinite mercy and wisdom, has decided to grant Sir Alexander St Barbe a pardon, for all crimes that he may have committed before, during and after the late rebellion, and restores to him all the lands and privileges that are rightfully his.'

473

Horrified and incredulous, Charles stared at Jeffreys. 'A *pardon*? But you can't – he can't – he's as guilty as Monmouth himself – haven't you read those depositions? There's no doubt of it, my lord, he's a proven traitor – and you're going to let him walk away *scot-free*?'

'Not quite free,' said the Chancellor. 'The pardon has been granted upon the promise of payment of a very substantial consideration. His Majesty doubtless feels that Sir Alexander, who is a man of wealth and influence in north Somerset, is of more use to him alive and at liberty than imprisoned or swinging on a gibbet. He is satisfied that your cousin has learned his lesson, and will prove to be a devoted and loyal subject in the future.'

For several moments, Charles could only splutter his rage. Finally, he found his voice, and said, with bitter venom, 'How much did he pay you? That's all that matters, isn't it – the amount of the bribe! And rogues walk free and prosper, while honest men discover that justice is nothing but an empty mockery.'

'I should be careful, if I were you, St Barbe,' said Jeffreys, his eyes narrowed. 'Such wild accusations are false and malicious, and I would be within my rights to see you punished for them. However, I am persuaded that your natural disappointment with the result of all your loyal endeavours has temporarily overruled your better judgement, and so I shall forget your hasty words. My advice to you, sir, is to return to your home, and make your peace with your cousin.'

With disbelief, Charles glared at the Chancellor's bored, hostile face. 'You can't drop the proceedings just like that – you *can't*!'

'Are you setting yourself up as a lawyer now? You forget yourself, St Barbe. I suggest that you remove yourself from my presence forthwith, before you say something that you will come to regret.'

His usual dignity and caution deserted him then. He shouted, he argued, he railed at Jeffreys, until two burly manservants came in and hauled him bodily away. His last sight of the most powerful lawyer in England was of the Lord Chancellor swigging brandy, his fine–featured face drawn with sudden pain.

They pushed him out in the street, and he stood, shaking with rage and humiliation, while the citizens of London brushed past him, oblivious. He was helpless, for what could one man, honest and loyal but poor in money and influence, do against the corrupt and vicious wealth of such as Alex, and the greed of the Lord Chancellor?

Alex would be pardoned, and freed. The money paid for his liberty would mean nothing to a man with all the wealth of Wintercombe and the St Barbe estates at his disposal. He would be restored to his position, and

Charles would have nothing. Even the house in Bath, legally leased to his mother, could no longer provide a refuge. For how could he possibly live within seven miles of the man who had so contemptuously defeated him?

His world in ruins, he walked back to his lodgings in Covent Garden, sick and angry, his mind in turmoil. There was still the hope, the very distant hope, that Louise would make the right decision: but with Alex's freedom apparently assured, why should she prefer Charles, penniless and landless, to Alex with all his riches? To a girl who loved amusement, fine clothes and the delights of wealthy leisure, even a precarious and immoral existence as his cousin's mistress must seem better than the humdrum, narrow life of poverty as Charles's wife. True, he would adore her, cherish her, protect her, but what was love when set beside the lavish gifts and sensual pleasures that Alex could offer her?

He could delude himself no longer. She would never have him, not until the moon fell from the sky, not while Alex lived in freedom. There was no hope, none at all: he had lost everything, and his cousin had won.

Then a voice whispered something at the back of his mind as he walked, a suggestion so daring, so appalling that he rejected it immediately. But in vain: again and again, no matter how fiercely he tried to suppress it, the solution to all his problems grew to monstrous proportions in his head, no matter what the dangers, and would not be denied. One stroke, one bold stroke, and then, if he were fortunate, and careful, his troubles would be over for ever.

One deed, reprehensible, but necessary. And then he would have Louise, and Wintercombe, and all his heart had ever desired.

After the terrible uncertainties of the past few weeks, the news of Taylor's death, swiftly followed by the offer of a pardon for Alex, at first seemed almost too good to be true. But Louise knew that despite her worst fears, despite the horrible dreams that sometimes assailed her sleep, Alex would be freed.

It was not, of course, quite so simple as that. Yes, the King was prepared to grant a pardon, but at a very extortionate rate. The sum of ten thousand pounds was required, to be paid in several instalments. Once the first two thousand had been handed over, Alex would be freed, on condition that the rest would be produced within six months.

It seemed an enormous amount. Louise, hearing it, wondered with dread whether the St Barbe property could in fact bear such a depletion. But Phoebe, who seemed to know a great deal about her brother's financial affairs, seemed to think that such a fine – for that, in essence, was what it was – would not be impossible to raise. There was a good chance that Alex's uncle, Henry Orchard, would be prepared to buy the Bristol properties, so that at least they would be kept in the family. Other lands would also have to be sold, but at least the bulk of the estate was safe, and it was so productive that, within a few years, the loss could probably be made good. Alex could have his freedom, and still remain a wealthy man.

Nick took it upon himself to travel back to Somerset, to tell Philip Cousins the good news, and help him raise the money for the first payment that would set Alex free. There seemed, so Sir Hugh said, a good chance that he might be released before Christmas if the two thousand pounds could be gathered quickly.

Of course, Alex himself could not be kept in ignorance of the good news, and Silence decided to visit her nephew, to tell him of his imminent freedom, bought on his behalf with the proceeds of his inheritance. Despite Louise's entreaties, she insisted on going alone. It was high time, she thought, climbing into the hackney and listening to the relentless, dreary battering of the rain on its roof, that she had a serious talk with Alex.

She might be old, almost in her dotage in the probable view of all the young people who surrounded her, but she was not stupid, nor unobservant. She was well aware of several things that Phoebe and Louise, for instance, fondly imagined to be a secret. And although it was quite possible that Alex would treat her opinions with the cynical mockery that was part of his outer shell, she had seen some change in him during the months of his captivity that led her to be hopeful. And for Nat's sake, and her sister's, she wanted to help their son, even if her assistance was spurned.

The guards knew her by now, and waved her by with smiles. Really, she thought, looking about her at the familiar jumble of buildings old and new, and the jostling people crowding the paths and walks despite the inclemency of the weather, this is hardly a prison at all. Alex has every comfort, visitors may come and go virtually as they please, his servant attends him, he is allowed to take the air on the walls . . . Compared with that poor wretch who died in Newgate, he can hardly be said to be suffering. And if this period of enforced inactivity has forced him to confront certain unwelcome truths, then it may even have done him some good . . .

It was plain that he had not expected her. In shirtsleeves beside the blazing fire, he was softly strumming his guitar. Silence, who had never learned to play or sing, but who loved to hear other people do so, stood and watched him for a moment. He was well aware of her presence, but evidently wished to finish the piece, which was intricate and difficult.

476

Looking at him, the black head bent over the instrument, the long fingers deft on the strings, she had a sudden sense of the power and strength that usually lay concealed behind the lazy, careless manner, and the irresistible attraction that had drawn Louise to him. Her granddaughter's conduct might be reckless, irresponsible and immoral, but she, with her past, could hardly condemn or blame her. If she were fifty years younger, she herself would probably have been tempted to succumb.

He finished with a delicate ripple of notes and laid the instrument down, away from the damaging heat of the fire. 'Hullo, Aunt. This is a pleasant surprise. I hope you don't mind that I didn't greet you at once?'

This was accompanied by his most charming smile. Silence was not a short woman, but he was considerably taller than she was. His mother, too, had been higher than the average, and her father nearly six foot. She thought suddenly of Charles's belief that Alex was not Nat's son, and for the first time could understand how it had seemed plausible to someone who had never known Patience, only the gossip about her. Alex had towered over Nat, his father, and his face strongly resembled his mother's. To the malicious and gullible, it might indeed have been likely that he was the child of adultery.

But she would never mention Charles's slander to Alex. She smiled up at him in return. 'Of course not – it was delightful to hear. I didn't know you could play so well.'

'You haven't heard me play badly yet,' he pointed out. He kissed her cheek, and led her to the comfortable chair, nearest the fire. 'But those times are becoming less usual . . . If nothing else, being mured up in this benighted place gives me time to practise – the one element which my tutor always said I lacked.' He grinned disarmingly. 'I always seemed to have better things to do – or worse.'

'Usually worse,' Silence said drily. She watched as he sprawled down in the other chair, stretching his long legs to the fire. His hair was untidy, his shirt creased and rather grubby, but at least he was, or appeared to be, quite sober. She added briskly, 'I have news for you – excellent news, on the whole.'

'Oh!' Alex glanced up, his expression suddenly and intently alert. 'What is it, Aunt? Don't keep me in any more suspense.'

'The King has been pleased to grant you a pardon,' she told him, and saw the sudden delight flooding his face. If he looks like that at Louise, she thought, no wonder the girl's in love with him.

She told him as much as she had gleaned from Sir Hugh's talk earlier that day, and did not bother to hide her disapproval of the corruption and venality of the Court. When Alex heard of the price demanded for his freedom, he whistled softly. 'Well, I suppose I should be flattered that they think me worth so much. It could be worse – at least I won't be beggared. Is Philip raising the money?'

'Yes, he is in Somerset at this moment, and Nick will be travelling down tomorrow, to tell him how much is required, and to help in the arrangements. Sir Hugh thinks that if all goes well, you may well be free before Christmas.' She smiled at him. 'I hope you're not averse to paying such a vast amount as a fine for crimes of which you say you are innocent?'

'Ah,' said Alex. 'Do I detect a note of disbelief in your voice, dear Aunt? Innocence is a variable commodity, according to the view of the beholder. If it will purchase my freedom and my pardon, and permit me to return to Wintercombe unscathed, if somewhat poorer, then in my view it is money well spent. Besides, there is Charles to consider. He wishes me dead, or at least indefinitely incarcerated, so that he can enjoy my property for himself. And it will be an unmitigated delight to see the expression on his face when I walk free.'

'Have you ever wondered,' Silence said carefully, 'just *why* Charles should hate you so much?'

Alex stared at her, his brows drawn together. He said casually, 'A severe case of envy run riot, I suspect. He covets his cousin's house, lands, wealth, even his mistress.'

'It's rather more than that,' his aunt said. 'As you well know.'

His eyes, Nat's eyes, intelligent and intense, rested on hers. 'Oh?' said Alex, at his coolest and most impenetrable. 'Do I?'

'Did you know that he has asked Louise to marry him?'

There was no mistaking his reaction. With one of the sudden, explosive movements that were characteristic of him, he leaped to his feet and flung away to the window, barred and looking down on to the green, turbid moat. 'Has he, by God! And I trust Louise has sent him packing?'

'No. She has as yet given him no firm answer, although he first asked her nearly three weeks ago.'

Alex swore, long and fluently, while she tried not to listen. He turned away from the window and came to stand in front of her, his eyes blazing blue. 'In God's name, why not? She's surely not thinking of *accepting* him, for Christ's sake?'

The sudden pain and disbelief in his voice told her a great deal, but she took care not to reveal it. 'I don't know,' she said mildly. 'But he has told her that if she agrees to marry him, he will ensure that the charges against you are dropped.'

Alex stared at her, and then laughed. 'Now I know he must be mad. Once the likes of Jeffreys get their hooks into you, only the payment of large sums – ten thousand pounds, for instance – wil induce them to let you go. And Charles, as you and I know, can no more command such a price than he can order the sun to rise in the west. Does Louise *know* that he is deluding himself, and her?'

'Yes, she does,' Silence said, still watching him closely.

Some of the tension seemed to go out of him: he sat down in the chair, and ran his hands through his hair, leaving it in some disorder. 'So – what is she doing? Playing for time? You realise, she's told me nothing of this – it's all come as a complete surprise.'

'I can see that,' said his aunt. 'Yes, she is playing for time. She knows that his threats and promises are all empty – Sir Hugh Trevelyan has confirmed that.'

'A sood man, Sir Hugh, for a courtier. He's been here several times – seems to have taken a liking to Phoebe.'

'To *Phoebe?*' Silence said, astonished. 'But . . .'

'My sister is plain, crippled, bluntly spoken and undoubtedly has designed herself as a confirmed old maid. She also has a brilliant mind, a reluctantly generous heart, and a handsome dowry, even if it was not meant as such. Why not? And Sir Hugh has told me himself that he admires independent women. His niece, for example, is an artist, and he is very fond of her. So why should he not favour Phoebe?'

'And what are her thoughts in the matter?' Silence asked, diverted. Not by the remotest stretch of her imagination could she envisage her intellectual, prickly niece enslaved by passion.

'I haven't dared ask her,' Alex said, with a candid grin. 'She'd give me exceedingly short shrift, I don't doubt. Anyway, I'm not my sister's keeper, and she knows she doesn't need my permission for anything she may intend to do. And I'm hardly in a position to dictate to her how she should behave, am I?'

Silence heard the note of self-mockery in his voice. She said quietly, 'No, you are not. You must have broken every rule of decent behaviour in existence.'

'Not all,' Alex said. 'Not all. I have not, for example, betrayed my kin for venal reasons. Nor have I tried to coerce a girl into marriage on the basis of empty promises. You need not preach my vices to me, Aunt, for I know them only too well, and I have had an excess of leisure, recently, to contemplate my sins. If they can be called sins, of course.'

'You wouldn't persuade a churchman to give them any other name.'

'Perhaps not. But I have not killed in cold blood. I have taken no woman who was unwilling. Louise and I came together in mutual desire, and I have not seduced her, or exploited her, or hurt her.'

'You have not hurt her yet,' Silence told him softly. 'But you will.'

'Will I?' Alex's gaze was suddenly very uncomfortable. 'What do you mean?'

'If you, with all your worldly wisdom, have not yet noticed what she feels for you, then you are blind indeed,' Silence said sharply. 'And where such emotions are not equally shared, hurt is bound to follow.'

'Yes,' Alex said. 'Yes, I know . . . did you think I hadn't seen that she is in love with me? She's hardly the first, after all. And did you also think that I have never been hurt by love? Well, you are wrong, Aunt – I do know what it means to love a woman, and be rejected. I made the mistake, once, of falling for a face, a voice, an outer shell of perfection, and I will never be so gullible again.'

'Lukas's mother,' she said, seeing his eyes darken with remembered pain. 'Alex . . . have you thought what you will do if Louise should be with child?' As he stared at her, she went on. 'As I said, I am not stupid. I can guess that she has been able to visit you here alone, and has been doing so regularly since she arrived in London. Nor am I naïve. So – what if she is carrying your child?'

'Is she?' Alex countered. For all her skill and perception, she could not tell what he was thinking. 'Do you know anything for certain?'

'I know nothing for certain, and she has not confided in me. But you must surely allow the possibility of it, given your regular meetings here.'

'There is always the possibility of it, yes,' Alex said drily. 'So far, it does not seem to have happened – call it luck, or good fortune, or what you will.'

'If she were – a hypothesis pure and simple – *if* she were with child, what would you do?'

Alex looked at her for a long, long moment. Then, suddenly, he laughed. 'I know what you'd *want* me to do, Aunt. But would Louise want that? Would she want me to consider marriage only for the sake of a possible heir? Perhaps she would wish to be worth more to me than that.' He smiled with sudden, gleeful mischief. 'On the other hand, if I did marry her, for the sake of a child, it would certainly squash Charles's pretensions, once and for all.'

It was hardly the response that Silence had wanted, although she knew that her idea of wringing an admission of love from him was unrealistic, to say the least. She said, 'I asked you this earlier, and you made me only a superficial answer. Have you never thought about *why* Charles should hate you so much? You must know that you are not entirely blameless in the matter.'

'Of course I know,' Alex said, with sudden vehemence. 'Like you,

480

Aunt, I am not entirely stupid. I despised him, I goaded him, and I misjudged him. I did not think he had the . . . spirit, and the strength, to react as he did.'

'Oh? So you would not have abused and browbeaten him if you had thought him capable of responding in kind?'

Alex looked at her for a long time. He said at last, 'Do not mistake me, Aunt – when I think of how I treated him, I am not especially proud of my behaviour. And he has amply had his revenge, has he not? Ten thousand pounds' worth of it, although he will not see a penny.'

'I'm not condoning what he did,' Silence told him. 'But you made him suffer, from malice pure and simple, and he is still in torment. Louise, Wintercombe, perhaps even the affection of his mother and sister, all will be lost to him. What will he do, when he discovers that you will be set free?'

'I don't know,' Alex said, and his voice was reflective, even thoughtful. 'But I know what *I'm* going to do.'

'Which is?' Silence asked, not without misgivings.

Alex grinned at her, suddenly and ominously wicked. 'I shall go to a certain tavern I know in the Strand, and there get exceedingly drunk.'

And to that, she had no adequate answer.

# 29

## 'The fury of a patient man'

For several days, following his confrontation with Jeffreys, Charles had kept to his lodgings, almost ill with rage and frustration, unable to believe that after all his effort and expense, he had been cheated of his vengeance. But unless he acted, and swiftly, his last hopes would vanish like the rest: and eventually, after sleepless nights and tormented days, he had gathered his courage, and gone to Bell Court to see Louise.

As so often that November, it was raining heavily, and he arrived wet, muddy and dishevelled: his money was running out, and he could not afford a hackney. Louise was in, so the maid informed him, with a sweeping, supercilious glance that, obviously, consigned him to the lowest rank of supplicant, and shortly afterwards returned with the news that Mistress Chevalier was prepared to grant him a few moments of her time.

His suppressed anger still festering inside him, he climbed the stairs to the small parlour where he had seen her before. She looked glorious, in a mantua of emerald velvet that enhanced her skin and hair, and made her chestnut eyes glow. Acutely conscious of his lowly status, his poverty, his dripping, well-worn clothes, he stood ashamed, and stared at her as if she represented all that he had ever desired.

'Hullo, Charles,' Louise said. She was in high spirits, her eyes sparkling, and her face kept breaking into smiles which, resentfully, he attributed to her amusement at his appearance. 'Have you come for your answer?'

'I have, since I have heard nothing from you for weeks,' he said, unable to keep the indignation from his voice. 'Surely it doesn't take so long for you to make up your mind?'

'I told you then, it is no light matter for me, to consider wedding a Papist,' Louise said. She came across to stand in front of him, perfumed intriguingly with orange water, her hair glossy and intricately dressed, and the smooth curve of her face adorned, he saw in growing dismay, with a neat, dark, heart-shaped patch. 'But I have reached a decision, Charles, and it was not an easy one to make.' She smiled, and despite the levity of her manner, there was sadness, surely false, in her voice. 'I am very sorry, Charles, but I cannot possibly marry you.'

'But I love you!' he cried, as if that were all that mattered. 'I *love* you – why can't you marry me?'

A little of the sparkle had vanished from her face. 'Why can I not? Because you may well love me, in your fashion, but I love someone else.'

'Alex,' he said, with profound disgust. 'That's not love, not as I understand it, that's –'

'It is, as *I* see it,' she said quickly. 'Charles, can't you understand that such a one-sided marriage as you suggest is bound to fail, and sooner rather than later? You would always be demanding of me what I could not give, and wondering if I were unfaithful – and I would resent you, because you are not Alex. It's impossible, Charles, quite impossible, and it always has been – can't you see that?'

'No,' he cried wildly. 'No – I can make you love me, I can make you happy – for God's sake, Lou, *trust* me, please, *trust* me – marry me and I'll adore you for ever, I swear it!'

'Oh, Charles,' Louise said, and the sadness, now, was transparently genuine. 'I can't agree, I can't – it would be fair to neither of us, and we would only end by hating each other. If you think we would be happy then you're deluding yourself. We were friends once, but that can never be so again, you know that –'

'Why not? Because I laid charges against him?'

'You betrayed him,' Louise said. 'For whatever reason, I can't forgive that, or forget it.'

'I was doing my duty, as you should have done, as a loyal subject of the King.'

'Duty? To betray your own flesh and blood? Duty wasn't the reason, and you know it!' Louise turned away from him and strode to the fireplace, her emerald skirts swishing vehemently with every step. She swung round, her eyes burning, and faced him. 'I have tried to be sympathetic – I have tried to link the Charles who was my friend with the Charles who would do such a despicable thing – and it's as if you've changed into a monster! What can I say that will convince you? I have never had any intention of marrying you. I played for time because I believed that you might have the power to influence Alex's fate. Now I know that you lied to me, you never intended to have him freed, you were determined to have me by whatever means you could, however many falsehoods you told. And Alex will soon be free, the King has pardoned him, and there is nothing you can do about it, Charles, nothing at all . . . you have lost, and in all honesty I think you deserve to.'

He stared at her, sweating, aghast, hardly able to believe the contempt and revulsion in her voice, and plain on her face. He said hoarsely, 'So – so you would rather be his whore than my wife?'

'I would rather be *any* man's whore than your wife!' Louise cried, in sudden rage. 'But Alex, yes, I am proud to be his mistress – he is far from perfect, but neither is he a Judas. You make me sick, I want to vomit when I hear your sanctimonious self-righteous preaching, you think yourself so pure and good, because you haven't the courage to go drinking or wenching, and then like a true hypocrite you condemn your own cousin for sins you'd joyfully commit if only you had half the spirit of a field-mouse – oh, get out,' Louise said, her voice shaking. 'I never ever want to see you again – I've been as patient as I can, and now it's all run out – please, Charles, just go, leave our lives – it's better for everyone that you do.'

Helpless once more, gripped by his rage and impotence, he had no choice. He stumbled down the stairs and out into the rain, the brutal words of her last tirade ringing in his ears and reverberating hideously in his mind. He walked back to Long Acre, oblivious to the curious stares of the people jostling past, while the dark voice in his soul reminded him that there was still a chance of vengeance, both upon Alex, and upon Louise, who had scorned and slighted him. And before he had reached his mean, uncomfortable lodgings, the plan that would ensure his triumph had sprung into his mind.

On the first day of December, in a season noted for its unusual mildness and the excess of rain, Philip Cousins returned from Somerset, with Nick Hellier, and the first instalment of money for Alex's freedom. It was paid; a warrant obtained for his release from the Tower, conditional upon the rest of the fine, or bribe, being handed over within six months; and four days later, on a wet and blustery morning, after nearly three months in captivity, the door of his comfortable prison swung open, and Sir Alexander St Barbe was at liberty.

Accompanied by his servant, Gerrit, who had shared his incarceration, and by his lawyer, Cousins, and the solid, spectacular figure of Sir Hugh Trevelyan, he walked through the Tower precincts, feeling the rain on his face, and the free air around his skin, and an intoxicating delight swept over him. The long nightmare was over. What did ten thousand pounds matter, beside his freedom, freedom to walk the wet, filthy streets of London, to visit old friends, to drink and sing and laugh in smoky taverns and coffee-houses, to dine with his family, to see Lukas without the shadow of the future tainting their meeting, and above all, to consort with Louise . . .

Ironically, he realised, as Sir Hugh's handsome coach began its jolting, obstructed journey to Westminster, he would now have much less chance to make love to her in freedom than he had had in captivity in the Tower. But there was an answer to that, an answer so obvious that he could curse himself for not having considered it before. Silence, in her quiet wisdom, had shown him the error of his ways, and in the weeks since that revelatory conversation he had had plenty of time to ponder his future. He knew himself too well, after nearly thirty years, to suppose that he would change a great deal. He would always drink too much, take too many risks, trample rough-shod over feelings and sensibilities. Life was to be lived, for he had no faith in the hereafter, and death, as he had discovered, lurked menacingly around the most unlikely corner. So, he intended to enjoy the rest of his days to the full. But not alone: no longer alone.

The coach passed through the city, and he wondered how many of his old friends, from his wild and bawdy past, were still to be found in the haunts he had once frequented. There would be no harm in discovering if anyone had been left behind after the searches, purges and arrests of the past few years. And besides, a wild mood was on him, a desire to break free of these two apparently staid, conventional men, and celebrate his release with people more akin to himself.

They were progressing, very slowly, down Fleet Street. He made his excuses: an old friend whom he had not seen for years, who had once rendered him valuable service, and to whom he owed much gratitude. He thanked Cousins and Trevelyan, with charm and sincerity, for all their help and their efforts on his behalf, and added that he was unlikely to be at Bell Court in time for dinner, but that Phoebe could be told to plan a celebratory supper.

The two men accepted his explanations with good grace; the coach was stopped, just by Chancery Lane; and Sir Alexander St Barbe, with coin in his pocket and liberty pulling joyously at the skirts of his coat, stepped down into the packed anonymity of London.

Just here was the King's Head, a large and prosperous tavern that had achieved notoriety a few years ago as the headquarters of the Green Ribbon Club, devoted to the Protestant cause and the exclusion of the Papist Duke of York from the succession to the throne. With the exile and death of the Earl of Shaftesbury, its founder and guiding light, and the triumph of the Duke of York, now King James, the Green Ribbon Club had been swiftly disbanded, its members dispersed overseas, or in prison, or safe anonymity. But the tavern's wines were excellent, and there was still a good chance that he would encounter a familiar face with whom he could let his tongue run loose at long last.

Smiling, he threaded his way through the streaming crowds, and walked with pleasurable anticipation into the thick wine-scented warmth of the place that had once been almost a second home to him.

By dint of bribery and repeated enquiries, Charles had managed to ascertain the day that would mark Alex's release. Until then, he had eked out his uncomfortable existence in his lodgings, scrimping on fuel, dining in the cheapest ordinaries and chophouses, conserving his meagre and dwindling store of coin, and his hatred, for the final confrontation with the man who had taken everything from him, and left him with nothing save an overwhelming hunger for revenge. If the King's justice could not accomplish that, then he had no choice, whatever the cost, but to carry it out himself. If he succeeded, and escaped, then he would snatch the ultimate victory. And if not, well, what did the consequences matter, when his own life had been so utterly destroyed?

So he had spent the day in a ferment of waiting for the moment when he could strike. He had gone first to the Tower, and discovered that his quarry had already left. Then he had hurried through the crowded streets back to Westminster, arriving sweating and exhausted, only to discover, as the resplendent coach disgorged its passengers some time later, that Alex was not amongst them. From a discreet distance, he had watched the three men go into Bell Court. Philip Cousins he knew well, of course, and the lumpen Dutch servant, but the overdressed and magnificent man of fashion was presumably the unknown courtier whose influence he had come up against at every turn, and who had done so much to free his cousin. Alex must have left the coach at some point on its journey, for what debauched purpose Charles could well guess, but the presence of Gerrit, not to mention the quantity of bags and boxes now being unloaded, surely indicated that he intended to return to the house in the near future. That did not worry Charles: indeed, it might suit his plan very well. And besides, he was quite prepared to wait as long as necessary for his vengeance.

There was a tavern, one of the many lining King Street, which had several rooms with a good view of Bell Court, over the way. Charles paid for one, and a cheap dinner, with a much-begrudged half-crown, and settled down to wait out the rainy afternoon. If his cousin returned before dark, he would surely see him; and if not, the narrow alley provided plenty of places in which to linger unseen.

The short afternoon melted into winter dusk, and he swallowed the last of his beer and walked across the street. At least the rain had stopped, for the present, and it was not cold. Keeping to the edge of the alley, avoiding various piles of strewn rubbish, he walked hastily past the St Barbe lodgings, and found a convenient place to watch, in the shadowy doorway of a house a few yards further into the court.

There had been several familiar faces in the King's Head tavern in Chancery Lane, and Alex dined with some of them, well and up-roariously. The afternoon passed most congenially, lingering over the remains of the meal, bottles of wine and brandy, catching up on three or four years of missed news. By the time he emerged, his head swimming pleasantly, the street outside was almost lost in the early dusk. It had stopped raining, and the weather was mild, as it had been for months. He hailed a link-boy, who was hovering outside the tavern, and with the light from the torch illuminating their path and warning hackneys and other wheeled traffic of their presence, he set out to walk the rest of the way to Westminster. It was more than a mile, but the air, even laden with the smells of London, filth, river mud, coal smoke and less palatable aromas, would clear his head. And after the months cooped up in the Tower, his exercise limited to decorous strolls along the ramparts, he wanted to stretch his limbs, and to use the time to think about the past, and the future.

He had a long stride, and the link-boy, a scrawny child of ten or so, was forced to keep breaking into a trot to keep up. As they progressed westwards, the crowds thinned, for most people were keen to retreat indoors on such an evening. King Street, normally thronged with traffic and people, was all but deserted. He had never been to the house in Bell Court, but Sir Hugh had given him directions, and one of the few passers-by told him the exact location. He dismissed the link-boy with thanks and a generous coin, and turned into the dark mouth of the alley that had been pointed out to him. A house on the right, two doors down, Sir Hugh had said: and there it was, and above, lighted windows spoke of his family, and Louise, awaiting his arrival.

Invisible in the shadows, his Cousin Charles had been waiting for almost an hour. Several groups of people had come into the court, and passed him, but none was the man he sought, nor did any appear to notice him, for he was well hidden in the doorway, and the house to which it belonged seemed, fortunately, to be empty. Muted noises – talk, laughter, the fragile sounds of a harpsichord – came from the houses and lodgings crowded around him. Someone emptied a chamber-pot into the street, luckily nowhere near him, and a dog, small and yappy, set up a ridiculous barking that reminded him of his mother's Floss, and set his teeth on edge.

A man turned into the alley. By now, Charles's eyes were used to the dark, and two or three public-spirited citizens had lit lanterns by their doors, so he could see comparatively clearly. A man very tall, broad-shouldered, walking slowly, looking at the doors on the northern side of the alley. Charles stiffened, and his heart began to pound heavily. Although no light shone nearby, he knew, without any sliver of doubt, that this was his quarry.

He would have to act quickly, before Alex had any chance to knock on the door. With a rasping sound that seemed terrifyingly loud in the quiet court, he drew his sword. It was old, but serviceable, and above all sharp and clean: he had spent many hours, over the past few days, caring for it with sand and polish and whetstone.

Alex turned sharply towards the sound. He had been a soldier in the Low Countries, Charles remembered, and he was taller and stronger than his cousin. But Charles had the advantage of surprise, and hatred, and an overpowering urge to finish this matter, once and for all, whatever the consequences.

He did not know if Alex was armed, but it seemed unlikely, since he had just been set free from the Tower. Anyway, he was past caring. Savagely, he ran forward and lunged with furious force at the dark figure in front of him.

Alex dodged, and the blade plunged past him, through the air. Charles, carried forward by his own momentum, turned and slashed wildly at the object of his hatred, not caring where his blows landed, so long as he hit the target. One connected, with a wrist-jarring impact, and his enemy grunted and stumbled back. Suddenly jubilant, Charles pressed forward, still jabbing and slashing, and at every step Alex retreated, a shadowy shape against the yellow lights further down the alley. He was breathing hard, and must surely be hurt: but although Charles lunged again and again, still his cousin managed to evade the lethal sword, with an agility unexpected in such a tall man.

In desperation, Charles changed his tactics, and thrust his weapon low and fast. This time, there was no escape: again, the unmistakable impact, the plunge of steel into flesh. With a crow of triumph, he wrenched the blade free. He did not know what part of Alex he had hit, nor if the blow was a mortal one, or merely disabling, but the dim figure in front of him seemed to have fallen to his knees. He stepped forward, exultant, peering down, ready to deliver the *coup de grâce*.

He never did know what happened next. One moment he was standing over his wounded enemy, sword lax in his hand, the joy surging so fiercely that he could have shouted his triumph to the rooftops: and the next,

488

something hard, perhaps one of the pieces of wood that had been stacked to one side of the alley, crashed agonisingly against his legs, knocking him off balance. He fell backwards, and lost hold of the sword, which rolled away with a metallic clatter into the shadows.

Gasping with pain, clutching his shins, he forgot everything save the desperate need to finish what he had begun. He struggled to get up, and head someone shouting, some way behind him. And then there was more light, flickering from a link or torch, and in the dim erratic glow he saw Alex, on hands and knees in the filth of the alley, blood black on his coat and breeches, his face smeared with it, devilish in the evil glare of the torch as it came closer, and then he lurched to his feet, and Charles saw, with sudden fear and horror, the wildness of his eyes, and the sword in his grasp.

He could not move: frozen with terror, he watched aghast as his enemy staggered across the few yards that separated them. 'Shall I kill you?' Alex said, his voice almost unrecognisable, taut with pain. 'Before God, you deserve it . . . don't move, or I'll spit you.'

The sword-point that Charles had so lovingly sharpened only a few hours ago did not waver: it came nearer, and nearer, unerringly aimed at his throat. He tried not to quail as the cold metal slid through the folds of his cravat, to rest against the soft, vulnerable place beneath, and he knew that one twitch of Alex's hand, just a little more pressure, and his life would end.

There was more shouting. 'Put up your weapon, sir! Put up your sword!' And then, suddenly, a woman's voice, surely Louise, screaming, 'Alex! *Alex!*'

His cousin did not move. For what seemed an eternity, he stood above Charles, his eyes dark with pain and loathing, the blood welling thickly from the wounds in his thigh and chest, keeping the sword steady by an almost inhuman effort of will. Charles swallowed, and felt the sharp edge fretting menacingly against his skin. He said hoarsely, 'Please . . .'

'You deserve it,' Alex said, on a gasp. 'God's bones, I should carve you in pieces – and be hanged for it.' He managed, suddenly and appallingly, a smile that chilled Charles to the soul. 'But I've escaped one execution, no thanks to you, and I'll not risk another on your worthless account. Live in your own hell, Cousin, and remember to the end of your days that you owe your life to me.'

For an instant, the pressure increased, and Charles, in a paroxysm of terror, thought that he was about to die after all. Then his cousin, in one abrupt movement, pulled his arm back and sent the sword spinning and crashing along the wet muddy stones of the court. As Charles's eyes followed it, Alex dropped to his knees in front of him, his breath coming in huge, agonised gasps.

'Alex!' It was Louise, and beside her, horrified, the Helliers and the overdressed courtier, followed by Philip Cousins and a crowd of other people, residents of the houses in Bell Court, summoned by the sounds of conflict. As Charles, seized suddenly by the urge to escape, tried to struggle to his feet, he was grabbed by several burly arms, and hauled upright.

This, then, was the consequence. But despite his fear, and the final humiliation to which Alex had subjected him, he looked down at his cousin with an expression of savage defiance. His vengeance might yet come, for wounds such as those could well prove mortal.

'It's Charles!' Louise's voice held only utter horror and revulsion. 'Oh, Charles, what have you done?' She dropped down on to the filthy cobbles beside her lover, heedless of the damage to her new emerald gown, worn in honour of his freedom. And with a sound that was disconcertingly akin to a laugh, Alex fell forward into her arms.

'He has lost a great deal of blood, but I don't think he will die.' Silence finished tying the last bandage, and pulled the bedclothes up over her nephew's unconscious body. 'The wounds are as clean as I can make them. With time, and God's help, I think he will recover.'

Louise shut her eyes, flooded with relief. She had not prayed so urgently since childhood, and now it seemed as if the miracle had, after all, been granted. 'Grâce au bon Dieu,' she whispered. 'And to you, Gran'mère.'

In the frantic moments that had followed Alex's collapse, she had thought that he was dead: and she had never felt so bereft, or helpless, or alone, kneeling in the muddy court with his warm weight, sticky with too much blood, sagging so heavy against her that she could hardly support him. But others had taken charge, with swift efficiency. Charles had been bustled away, his face still ghastly with shock and, far worse, that appalling triumph; the Watch had arrived, late and unwanted, and were soothed with coins and explanations and sent away again; and then Philip Cousins, Nick, Sir Hugh and Gerrit, with gentle care, had prised Alex from her grasp, and carried him into the house.

'He's not dead,' Phoebe had whispered to her, as she stared in numb horror at the slack, lifeless body of her lover, trailing blood, as he was borne away from her. 'Louise, he isn't dead – come on, come inside, there must be something we can do.'

In fact, there was little enough. Silence had the reputation, in her

490

family, of being uncommonly skilled in the healing arts, and she took charge with her usual competence. Phoebe prepared bandages, Louise fetched salves and lotions and hot water, and waited, her stomach churning squeamishly, as her grandmother, and her maid Fan Howard, swift but gentle, stripped the ruined clothes away, revealing the long, lean, powerful body that she knew as well as her own. There was a wide, leaking gash across the upper part of his chest and left shoulder, that looked dreadful enough, but the thigh wound, bleeding copiously, was far more serious. She watched, for as long as she could, Silence's desperate efforts to staunch the flow, and then, overwhelmed by a sudden and relentless wave of nausea, she fled.

Phoebe found her retching into a basin in their chamber. With her usual cool, capable support, she held her until the spasm passed, gave her a kerchief dipped in the ewer to wipe her face, and a cup of wine to remove the sour taste left in her mouth. She said nothing, but Louise, drained and gasping, knew what she must be thinking. The wine made her feel much better, and improved her courage. She glanced at the dispassionate blue eyes, and said quietly, 'Aren't you going to ask me?'

'What is there to ask?' Phoebe smiled suddenly, and touched her cousin lightly on the cheek, a gesture so affectionate and so unlike her that Louise wondered afterwards if she had imagined it. 'Are you recovered? Can you face going back? Aunt Silence will surely be in need of our presence, at the least.'

But to Louise's profound relief, her grandmother had almost finished her task, and although the chamber still stank of blood, the reeking bowls and soaked cloths had thankfully been removed. And he would not die: with God's help, he would live.

'He is not safe yet,' Silence said, standing by the bed, her face thoughtful as she gazed down at his still figure. 'But I have some skill and knowledge of such matters – I nursed your grandfather back to health twice, after wounds as serious as this, or more so. He's young, and strong, and healthy, and this is an excellent start.' She smiled at Louise, and her face, suddenly, betrayed her exhaustion. 'Forgive me, but I think I have done enough for a while. Would you sit with him for an hour or two, in case he wakes? Fan will bring you your supper, if you would like some.'

'I – I'm not sure,' Louise said. She still felt queasy, but the thought of food was strangely attractive. 'Perhaps – I'll see.' She walked to the bed, and looked down at Alex. The uncompromising blackness of his hair and brows contrasted sharply with his extreme pallor, but even like this, temporarily devoid of the vivid, individual personality behind it, his face had a stark, arresting and entirely masculine beauty that wrung her heart.

*I hope*, she thought, the tears she so rarely shed suddenly flooding into her eyes, *that our child looks like him.*

For long, dreary hours, Charles had been locked in a small, chilly room that was normally used for storing food. The floor was made of cold, damp flagstones that offered no comfort, and the cheeses and pots and crocks and baskets of produce ranged on the shelves around the whitewashed walls did not tempt him. In his bleak mood, utterly drained of all emotion, he could not imagine ever savouring food and drink again.

He had failed in every aspect of his plotting. Alex had walked free from the Tower, after paying a fine which he, with all his wealth, probably would not even notice. Louise was as far beyond his reach as the moon, and he could not even command the friendship on which his love for her had been based: instead, her affection had turned to a deep and bitter loathing. And his attempt to murder his cousin had gone dreadfully wrong. Alex was still alive, and seemed to have some chance of remaining so, while he, Charles, had not even managed to escape. Instead, he had been hustled inside the house, and flung unceremoniously into this dank, dark store-cupboard, without even a candle, to meditate upon the error of his ways.

The key turned, and the door opened. He turned his head, and blinked as the light from the three-branched candlestick hurt his eyes. It was his grandmother, with the hostile face of Philip Cousins behind her. 'Get up,' she said, her voice curt.

Slowly and stiffly, Charles rose to his feet. Whatever Alex had used to hit him across the shins, it had certainly been effective: the bruised bones ached and throbbed. He said, his voice sounding strained and hoarse, 'What – what are you going to do?'

'Talk,' Silence said. She gestured at the open door. 'There is a little parlour empty. We shall not be disturbed – but Philip will be present, for safety's sake.'

'I wouldn't hurt you!' Charles cried, aghast at the implication of her words.

Silence smiled grimly. 'Perhaps not. On the other hand, I might very well be tempted to hurt *you*. Come on – out you come.'

He hobbled up two flights of stairs, past curious servants, to the little wainscotted parlour where he had begged Louise to marry him, not long ago. The lawyer, his expression still hostile, drew up a seat by the fire for Silence, and took another for himself. Charles, left standing, stared at them in bewilderment.

'Perhaps you are wondering why you are not at this moment in the

492

hands of the Watch,' Silence said coldly. 'Well, I agree that that would have been no more than you deserve. But after everything you have done, I find that blood is after all thicker than water. You are my grandson still, much though it grieves me to acknowledge it, and your father was very dear to me. It is for his sake, and for your sister, who is quite innocent in all this, that I am going to offer you a final chance. Do you understand?'

Charles's face was still dazed. 'A chance? What chance?'

'A chance to begin again, to forget these last months. A chance which you did not give to Alex, or to Louise – although I think that perhaps you granted it to Bram. And for that reason, there may still be some hope for you. At all events, I am prepared to let you go tonight, on one condition, and one condition only.'

Amazed, he stared at her. 'Let me *go*? Why? What condition?'

'I have told you why. Because you are William's son, although you seem, alas, to have inherited nothing of his generosity, or honesty, or good nature. Because I feel that a little of this has been your foolish mother's fault – she has been dripping a subtle poison into your mind for a long time, I fear. Because your sister is not to blame for anything, and deserves more than the ignominious poverty that she will otherwise face. And because, also, Alex himself must share some of the guilt – though he, at least, has had the grace to admit his fault. Do you, now, accept that you have acted wrongly? Would you do differently, if you had another chance?'

There was a long, long pause. The candles flickered gently, and the flames in the hearth copied them. At least, Charles raised his head. 'I think so,' he said, in a voice so low that it was barely audible.

'Good,' Silence said, studying him. 'That is why I am prepared to give you that chance, instead of handing you over to the nearest Justice for the crime of attempted murder – but, as I said, on one strict condition, which is this. When I have finished with you, you will return to your lodgings – near Covent Garden, I understand. Tomorrow at dawn, Master Cousins will meet you there, and he will escort you back to Somerset on the public coach. There, you will make, with his help, all the necessary arrangements to enable you, and your mother and sister if they so desire, to take ship at Bristol for the New World.'

His face, so deceptively similar to her beloved, long-dead William, was a picture of blank disbelief. 'What?'

'The New World. Where you can make a fresh start, where there is land for the taking, and all that is required, I understand, is a sum of money to start you off, and the capacity for hard work, and patience. Within a few years, you could be master of far more wealth than you could ever hope for in England. If Amy wishes to go with you, and I think that

493

she will, she will undoubtedly find that pretty girls, even those with modest dowries, are much in demand. The point I am making, Charles, is that in Virginia, or some other place, you can have the opportunity to make the best of yourself, and acquire all the riches you could want. All you need is the strength of will to take full advantage of it.'

'But the New World . . .' He stared at her helplessly. 'It's too far – I would never see any of you again – or Wintercombe – or Louise.'

'Don't you think that you have forfeited the right to do so? I doubt very much that she would wish to meet you again, after what you have tried to do. I suggest the New World because there you can begin again, and forget all that has happened, let the wounds and scars heal over – ours, even more than yours. Do you think that, if you lived in that nice little house in Bath, you would be able to resist the temptation to visit Wintercombe? Even if you did not pester her, your presence would be deeply disturbing, and not only to Louise.'

'She wouldn't be at Wintercombe,' Charles began, and then saw his grandmother's face.

'I think, I very much hope, that she will be,' Silence said. 'And she at least deserves your consideration, does she not? You claim to love her to distraction. You know that she can never, ever be yours, and all your dangerous, foolish, selfish scheming has collapsed around your ears. Very well. If you love her, remove yourself from her life for ever. In Virginia, you will be so busy that you will have no time to brood on your misfortunes – and in time, unlikely as it may seem, the agony will grow less. It may not cease altogether, but it will become more bearable, I promise.'

He had one last, desperate objection. 'But I'm poor. I have virtually nothing left. How can I even pay for my passage, let alone establish myself in a new country?'

'You have property worth four hundred a year. It can be sold, and your sister's inheritance, and your mother's, if they wish to go with you. It should not take long to raise the money, and Philip has many contacts – he will help you, and so will I. I have talked with my husband, and we are prepared to give you the further sum of two hundred pounds. It may not seem over-generous, but I understand that land and labour are very cheap there. Well? Will you go? Will you agree? Or must I summon the Watch?'

He had no choice. His heart sick and defeated, he knew it. Her anger, her vengeance, he could have defied. But to this generosity, unlooked-for, unwanted, he had no answer. And the sting of it was that his grandmother was offering him the chance to redeem himself for Louise's sake, for his father, for Amy, even perhaps for his fat, foolish mother – but not for his own sake. He was to be cast out, denied, parted from the house and the

494

woman he loved, for all time. And yet, cruel though this punishment seemed, it was gentle and forgiving and impossible to refuse.

He said, his eyes filling with tears of self-pity, 'Can I see her? Can I say goodbye?'

'Oh, Charles,' Silence said, and a note of honest exasperation entered her voice. 'Can't you let her go, and accept defeat, even after this? She is with Alex now. She loves him with a passion that far exceeds what you feel for her, and I strongly suspect that she is carrying his child. Her future lies with him, at Wintercombe. You *must* accept that, or you will never be free of her, and your life hereafter will be warped and distorted into eternal misery.'

'She may be infatuated with him,' Charles said. 'But he doesn't love her ... he's only using her for his own lusts, just like all the others, and sooner or later he'll tire of her.'

'Will he?' Silence said. 'I wonder. In any case, do not delude yourself with hopes that she will be discarded and turn to you for solace. She may once have harboured friendly feelings towards you, but I fear no longer. Can you not understand that your actions have put you utterly outside the bounds of all decent, civilised behaviour? Even if your betrayal of Alex could be forgotten, your attempt at murder cannot, nor will it ever be, in this family. I'll remind you exactly what you did. If our neighbours had not come into the court at the right time and raised the alarm, Alex probably would have died. And they tell me that, by some miracle, he managed to get the sword away from you, and then, although he had every chance to do it, he refused to kill you. That, that is the man whom you condemn as evil and depraved beyond all measure. Do you still think yourself so righteous? Or has a little sense of reality crept into your heart? If so, there may be hope for you yet.'

It was a question he shrank from answering. He said, avoiding her eyes, 'I will accept your offer. I will go to the New World. I swear it.'

'Good,' Silence said, and her voice softened suddenly. 'I'm glad you have seen sense at last. I wish you good fortune in your new life, little though you deserve it, and I will pray for you always.' She rose to her feet, and Cousins followed. 'We will not meet again, I think, and so I will say goodbye, and Godspeed.'

The light kiss on his cheek was cold, but her face, as she looked at him, was suddenly sad. 'Farewell, Charles,' she said. 'God give you a safe voyage, and a happy future.'

And as he left the parlour, shepherded by Philip Cousins's firm, uncompromising hand, he did not see the tears beginning, uncontrollably, to pour down her face.

*

'Louise?'

She had almost fallen asleep. She sat up in her chair with a jerk, and the sewing with which she had been attempting to while away the hours, and calm her fears, fell to the floor. She ignored it, and stared at the man in the bed. He was looking at her, his eyes open and alert, and a faint smile on his face. 'You look as if you'd been tapped on the shoulder by a ghost.'

'Alex!' Her joy spilled over, and a smile, huge and delighted, cracked across his face. 'You're awake!'

'Well, I'm not asleep,' he said, and grinned suddenly. 'My leg hurts like the devil, and my chest too – who patched me up? Aunt Silence?'

'Of course.' Louise stood by the bed, looking down, the vastness of her relief and happiness like an aura glowing all around her. 'But at least you're alive, and well.'

'Hardly that – I've barely the strength to speak, let alone move.' He belied his words by bringing his hand out from under the blankets. She sat on the edge of the bed to take it, and smiled. 'Your fingers are cold.'

'It means a warm heart, so they say.' Too late, Louise remembered all her efforts to seem light-hearted, uninvolved, still a stranger to the agonies of love. She tried to withdraw her hand, only to find it gripped with surprising strength. 'You can't gull me,' Alex said softly, his blue eyes brilliant in his ashen face, compelling a response. 'How long have you been in love with me?'

'I – don't know what you mean,' Louise said, with a brittle laugh.

His hand still gripped hers; slowly, his head moved from side to side on the pillow. 'Oh, yes, you do. Since the cowshed, I suspect – and have fought against it, and tried to hide it, ever after. Am I right?'

To her horror, her eyes were filling with tears. Helpless, and hating it, she nodded at last.

'Good,' Alex said. His grasp slackened abruptly, and he closed his eyes. Free, not wanting to be, she stared at him in sudden anxiety. 'You see,' he added, in a voice hardly above a whisper, 'I was determined to ask you something this evening, if that thrice-damned Charles had not intervened, and nearly put an end to me. And I too have an admission to make.'

She waited, holding her breath, hardly daring to move. His eyes opened, creased with reflective amusement, and found hers. 'Sweet Louise . . . you do not have the monopoly of love, you know. Like you, I ignored it, saw it as an inconvenient complication in an affair based on honest, unashamed desire . . . and I was wrong. I will make no promises, for I know myself too well. I do not know if my love for you will last a month, or a year, or a lifetime. I sincerely hope that the last is most

496

accurate, for if it isn't, I will have done you a terrible wrong . . . but I want, very much, to marry you.'

She could not believe it. Her breath released at last, she said in amazement, '*You* – want to marry *me*? Why? *Why?*'

'Why not? Let us be practical for a moment. Your mother sent you to England to find a Protestant husband of wealth and birth. I could be said to fulfil all those qualifications quite adequately, even the first – at least I'm no Papist, and I'm as willing as any man to snore my way through Parson Pigott's sermons every Sunday. I have to admit that in seeking a wife, I thought that a nice meek, biddable virgin would be the most suitable, but somehow you have caused me to abandon that idea altogether. And since the very sight of you inspires my lust, even at this moment, and I cannot imagine that life in your company will ever be tedious, or quiet, or devoid of passion, I have decided, to coin a phrase, to make an honest woman of you.' He smiled. 'And in addition, Lukas likes you, and so does Phoebe, and I value their judgement above anyone's . . . Well? Are you really quite lost for words? That in itself is something of a miracle.'

'Are you sure?' Louise asked him urgently. She found that the tears had begun to flow copiously, and swept them impatiently away with the back of her hand. 'I don't – I don't want you to feel *obliged* to marry me – I'd rather you had me willingly for your mistress than reluctantly for your wife . . . Please, Alex, tell me the truth. Do you *really* love me?'

His eyes met hers, and they gazed at each other for a long, wordless moment, and she saw the answer in his face, before he spoke. 'Oh, yes, I love you,' he said. 'With all my selfish, debauched and reckless heart, I love you, sweet Louise. So – will you marry me, as soon as I am fit to stand before a parson?'

She took a deep breath. 'Before I answer – there is something I must tell you. I didn't think it would ever happen – I thought I was barren – Alex, I am expecting your child.'

He did not move, but an expression of such love and tenderness crept into his face that she nearly wept again. 'Are you sure?' he whispered.

'Yes,' she said, and added, trying to return to her usual down-to-earth manner, 'I think it will be born some time next August, if all goes well.'

'You must have known for a little while . . . why did you not tell me before?'

Louise shrugged. 'Because . . . because I knew that, if I did, you would feel that you *had* to offer me marriage, whereas now, you have asked me freely, and you love me – and the baby is not the reason.'

'Not the reason – but very glad news, all the same. And you still haven't answered me. For the third time, will you marry me?'

She looked down at him, and her expression was suddenly mischievous. 'Well . . . I shall insist on certain conditions before I agree.'

'I'm trembling with apprehension – come on, woman, for God's sake put me out of my misery. What conditions?'

'That you come to my bed sober at least two nights in a week . . . that you do not dally with my maidservants under my nose, although I do recognise that the attractions of the ladies of the Cock at Walcot may sometimes prove irresistible . . . and that you never, ever complain about my riding, or about the amount of time and money I spend at the mantua-maker's,' Louise said, grinning. 'Well? Do you accept?'

'You know damn well I'm in no state to resist – and in no state either, alas, to make love to you, much though I want you . . . You have defeated me, sweet Louise, you see before you a helpless slave – ah, don't make that very unladylike noise – and I accept all your conditions, but for God's sake answer me. I won't ask again – will you marry me? For I love you immoderately, and I don't think I could bear it if you reject me now.'

She looked down at him, and the mischief drained slowly from her face. He lay there, uncharacteristically defenceless, all the strength and vigour and energy that had so attracted her vanished, although she had no doubt at all that within a few weeks he would be fully recovered. And she saw love, and need, and desire in his face, and knew that at last she had won him, heart and body and soul.

'Did you ever think that I would?' she said softly, and bent her head to kiss him. 'Of course I'll marry you – I love you so much.' And at last, overcome, she bowed her head on to his shoulder and wept, for joy for the future and sorrow for the past, and his warm arm held her close with the tenderness that had once seemed so alien to him, and his voice whispered comfort and endearments into her hair.

Phoebe knocked, gained no answer, and peered cautiously round the door. With sudden alarm, she saw Louise, sobbing, her arms around her brother. Then, his hand moved, soothing and stroking her back, and she relaxed, with relief. He had innumerable faults and vices, but he was her brother, and she supposed that she must love him.

He must have sensed someone's presence, for he moved his head to see who it was. At once a smile, gloriously and hugely joyful, spread across his face, and she understood. Very softly, she withdrew, and closed the door on their happiness.

# Historical Note

Paradoxically, Monmouth's rebellion is extremely well documented, with several eye-witness accounts on both sides, and yet is still the subject of considerable controversy, particularly concerning the roles of the protagonists, and its gruesome aftermath. How many rebels were actually executed? Was Judge Jeffreys really the infamous monster of legend? And did the Duke of Monmouth's personality contribute to the rebellion's failure, or was he a misunderstood and maligned hero?

Of necessity, I have had to steer my own path through these quicksands, using the available evidence as my guide. I have tried to depict the course of the rebellion as it actually happened, despite, at times, being forced to choose between conflicting accounts. The St Barbe family, in all their ramifications, are fiction, but many of the situations in which they find themselves are not. Alex's plight, for instance, is similar to that of Edmund Prideaux of Ford Abbey, who was accused of supplying money and horses to Monmouth, imprisoned and threatened with trial for treason (for which a second hostile witness proved hard to find), and eventually freed on payment of nearly £15,000 – which went straight into Jeffreys's pocket. And the Maids of Taunton were eventually pardoned, at considerable cost to their parents, although one of their teachers died in prison.

I am indebted to the many people who have helped me in various ways with this book, and who are in no way responsible for those errors which may remain. The staff of the Somerset Record Office, and the London Library; Mrs Pat Lawless, of Norton St Philip, who took the time to discuss the course of the skirmish in the village, and supplied several rare books, and local legends; Dave Ryan, of the English Civil War Society, for his advice, and sundry useful volumes; my sister, Vicki Hunt, who corrected my schoolgirl French, and Mrs Katie Mitchell, who helped me with the snippets of Dutch; Mr and Mrs Robert Floyd, of Great Chalfield Manor, the original of Wintercombe, for their continued interest and kindness; and last, but never least, my mother, and Steve, whose unfailing help, faith and support over the years have been beyond price, and without whom much less would have been possible.

PDAB
2nd March, 1990

All the quotations heading the chapters and parts are taken from Dryden's political poem, *Absalom and Achitophel*, published in 1681, which tells the story of Monmouth, the Earl of Shaftesbury, and the Popish Plot.